Di Morrissey is one of Australia's most successful writers. She began writing as a young woman, training and working as a journalist for Australian Consolidated Press in Sydney and Northcliffe Newspapers in London. She has worked in television in Australia and in the USA as a presenter, reporter, producer and actress. After her marriage to a US diplomat, Peter Morrissey, she lived in Singapore, Japan, Thailand, South America and Washington. Returning to Australia, Di continued to work in television before publishing her first novel in 1991.

Di has a daughter, Dr Gabrielle Morrissey Hansen, a human sexuality and relationship expert and academic. Di's son, Dr Nicolas Morrissey, is a lecturer in South East Asian Art History and Buddhist Studies at the University of Georgia, USA. Di has three grandchildren: Sonoma Grace and Everton Peter Hansen and William James Bodhi Morrissey.

Di and her partner, Boris Janjic, live in the Manning Valley in New South Wales when not travelling to research her novels, which are all inspired by a particular landscape.

www.dimorrissey.com

Di Morrissey
Blaze

PAN
Pan Macmillan Australia

First published 2000 by Pan Macmillan Australia Pty Limited
1 Market Street, Sydney

978-1-250-05345-9

Blaze is a work of fiction. The characters in this book are ficti-
tious and any resemblance to real persons,
living or dead, is purely coincidental.

With love and thanks to . . .

Boris Janjic . . . after too many years!

Opa and Nina Bubica

Jim and Rosemary Revitt

My mother Kay Warbrook, and my children Gabrielle and Nick, for their constant love, support, and stimulation

Ian Robertson for his wise counsel and friendship

Everyone at Pan Macmillan Publishers

All my friends and colleagues during my years in newspapers, magazines, television, radio, and film

Thank You . . .

Carolyn Beaumont, James Black QC, Mike Bloomberg, Susan Bradley, Jane Cadzow, Delin Cormeny, Ken Cowley, Barry Crocker, Jenny Cullen, Consul to Croatia Mirko Dolarevic, George Epaminondas, Louise di Francesco, Dr Merle Friedman PhD, Shelley Gare, E. Thomasine Griggs, Fran Hernon, Linda Jaivin, Phillip Knightley, Jenny Main, Jillian McFarlane, Maxine McKew, Sue Neales, Max Oldfield, Leonard Osborne, Roland Rocchiccioli, Sheila Scotter, Diana Simmonds, Kate Stead, Brian Stonier AO, Dawn Swain, Deborah Thomas, Dr Mckenzie Wark, Julia Zaetta, Carla Zampatti . . . and to those who preferred not to be named!

Author's Note

The poem at the end of this book was written by the English poet Adelaide Anne Procter and published in her anthology *Lyrics and Legends* in 1858. Her talent as a poet had been recognised and encouraged by Charles Dickens. My thanks to Rosemary Revitt for introducing me to Miss Procter's timeless work.

Di Morrissey

TAKE ONE...

New York, 2000

Friday, 6 p.m.

The Division 7 fire chief was panting as he raced up the flight of steps to the entrance of the Triton building and into the elevator, stabbing the button marked 35. Running up steps wasn't his strong suit these days – he spent most of his time behind a desk and had a paunch to prove it. Keeping up with the fitter, younger guys was getting harder and harder. He knew where he'd rather be – with a Bud watching the Lakers–Bulls game, not responding to a fire call. But when one of the guys wants to be there for the birth of his first kid, what can you do but haul your ass back on the road?

'Looks like only the sprinkler system has been triggered, chief. Don't smell any smoke, do you?' The lieutenant, aide to the fire chief, trotted ahead.

'These high-tech outfits can go off with anything – overheating, or a computer glitch. Gotta be sure.'

The lieutenant knew what his boss meant. You didn't take chances anywhere, but when the building was home

1

to one of the biggest media empires in the world, you were doubly cautious.

Walking along the corridor of level thirty-five, their flashlights shone on soaked floor and walls. The problem was certainly sourced near here. The chief's walkie-talkie, clipped to his shoulder, crackled to life.

'Chief, it's Joe in Fire Communications. From the board it appears to be an office in the right corridor, round about one fifty-nine.'

The private offices were spacious. Tall windows held views to Central Park, floors were softly carpeted and the touch of the interior designer reflected an expansive budget. The executive offices of *Blaze* magazine ringed the building on this floor, the editor-in-chief's leading to a private terrace. The inner area was open plan – ergonomic chairs tucked into desks, rental palms the only dividers. 'The worker colonies surrounded by the queen bees,' thought the chief.

His lieutenant rattled the doorknob of Suite 159 with one hand, pushing his mask over his face with the other.

'Can smell smoke now.'

'Seems contained. The door's locked,' the chief replied.

Their voices were muffled behind the breathing apparatus.

The lieutenant shrugged and, at the nod from the chief, banged his boot into the lock, followed by a hefty shove with his shoulder. The fire chief's hand rested on the small axe hooked to his belt, which bristled with a coiled rope, hoses, a knife, a small fire extinguisher and several tools. But the door gave way with a short sharp crunch.

The two men paused, staring across the room through the smoke from a bonfire of *Blaze* magazines burning on the carpet.

A woman was seated at a desk, her stockinged feet resting on a scramble of papers and photographs. Beside a framed picture of her with Jacqueline Onassis stood an empty bottle of vodka and a decanter of Scotch going the same way. She waved a Waterford tumbler at them, slopping its contents. Her Armani suit was drenched from the spray still bursting from the sprinklers in the ceiling.

'Good evening, gentlemen. You two certainly look the part. What can I do for you? Care for a drink?' Despite the effort at politeness, her voice was slurred. She chortled at the sight of the blue fireproof suits, the helmets, the ropes and gear attached to their bodies. She gave a cough, waving away the smoke from her face with a glossy poster and, putting down her glass, screwed up the picture and tossed it into the smoking pile.

Seeing the furious expression begin to darken the chief's face, the lieutenant rushed forward using his portable extinguisher to douse the burning pages.

'Dear heart, where are the hoses? Where's the backdraft action? Not good enough, man. More bells and whistles.'

Beneath her practised flippancy, the chief recognised the edge of hysteria in her voice. He removed his mask and gazed at the woman. She was a bit above fifty, he guessed. His age. She had been well groomed before her drenching, and must hold an important position if this was her office. In seconds he'd taken in the expensive decor, the view to the park, the framed photographs of this same woman with a cast of celebrities.

'Ma'am, I have to ask you to come with me. You can explain this scenario outside. Have you started any other fires in this building?' He strode towards her.

But she was quickly on her feet, hurling the heavy glass at him. The chief ducked, his lieutenant too stunned to make a move as the crystal shattered against a wall. 'Have

I started fires in this building! You bet your blue ass. And thank God for *Blaze* that I have. I've put more fires under those lazy sons of bitches than you've ever seen.'

The chief's shoulders slumped. Christ, a vindictive nutter of a broad who was going to dump a heap of emotional baggage on them. He could still make it home to watch the second half of the game if they could hurry up the cops. This was out of his territory now. The lieutenant was on his walkie-talkie explaining to Dispatcher 332 what was happening.

The fire chief wiped his brow. 'Lady, whatever your problem is, this isn't helping matters. Come downstairs and you'll be taken home. I'm afraid the police will want to ask you a few questions. You've caused considerable damage on this floor.'

The chief was losing patience. He reached for the woman's hand, which she wrenched away from him, then she staggered sideways to a closed door.

'Stay away from me. Don't you harass me.' Her fierce anger caused the fire chief to lower his arm. The woman was out of control.

'Calm down, ma'am. We want to help you.' He spoke in a placating tone, cautious now of her reactions.

'Help me! You're a bit damned late. Unless you can turn back the clock. Come on,' she taunted him, waving her manicured hands, inviting him forward. 'Come on, make me thirty, sexy and beautiful. Why don't you try, eh?'

The involuntary flicker in the chief's expression said it all for her. This dame was never going to be any of those things again.

She briefly closed her eyes, bitterness and sadness etched in the smudged mascara on her face. She spun around, opened the door into the next suite and closed it behind her.

4

The chief leapt forward as he heard the lock click. 'Harry, bust open that door.'

The lieutenant was already rushing to throw his weight against the polished oak while the chief prepared to add his own broad shoulder.

As the chief moved back to try again, he froze. Now she was on the terrace. Through the plate glass, he could see her clearly outside the adjoining office, stumbling between several potted topiary trees.

The door lock smashed under the force of the lieutenant's axe and the chief rushed through the French doors to the terrace.

'Hey, lady . . .' But she was climbing over a box hedge that lined the rim of the editor-in-chief's al fresco entertaining area. He stopped, breathless.

Two metres back, the lieutenant, still in the suite, was on his walkie-talkie telling his colleagues in the truck outside to hurry-up the police.

'Ma'am. Please don't move. I'd like to talk to you. You're upset.' He held his arms towards her.

Without looking back or pausing, the woman leapt.

'Oh Christ, no . . .' The chief lunged forward in a futile grab at empty air.

Lloyd Frencham, fire chief of Division 7, Manhattan, was the last person to see Lorraine Bannister, editor of the world-famous magazine *Blaze*, alive.

Friday, 7 p.m.

Alisson Gruber stood before the mirror slicking back her hair with gel. She studied the reflection, satisfied she looked as stunning as she felt. She was going to make this her big night. She'd waited for her chance since she was sixteen, when she'd taken her first step inside the revolving doors of the Triton Communications Tower. She'd decided before her first shift was over that she would one day be editor of the world's most feted magazine. Well, she hadn't waited. She'd worked and hassled her way towards this goal, even without a college degree. Her dream now seemed possible – that she would be the editor to carry *Blaze* forward in the new millennium.

She had hoped Nina, the editor-in-chief, and the Baron would tell her this was the case before Nina's party tonight. Instead, Baron Triton had stipulated that the formal birthday dinner to mark the sixtieth birthday of Nina Jansous was to be a social occasion. Ali knew that making an announcement of a new editor would shift the limelight from Nina. It made her seethe. How typical that the Baron would not allow anyone to nudge Nina from centre stage. Editor-in-chief or not, Nina's revered position with Triton would soon be immaterial. Alisson had plans. Big plans. She was twenty-eight and deputy editor of the New York edition of the world's most successful magazine. She had spectacularly worked her way up the ladder in Triton Communications. And, if the gossip was hot, it was Nina's retirement that would be announced tonight. And tomorrow? Ali was convinced she would be named the new editor of *Blaze USA*.

Times had changed. The days of mature, sophisticated doyennes sitting in the editor or editor-in-chief's office, was over. It was a new age of young, dynamic, powerhouse achievers who ran a hard race. They were not afraid to stick out a foot – Manolo shod or pumped-up pink Nike – to trip up a rival in order to win. Nice ladies came last now. Stuff the sisterhood. The new motto was 'make it to the top as fast as you can, any way you can'.

Talent and ability still counted. A talent to out-manoeuvre others, an ability to sell yourself as being better than you were. The rules had changed and, as the army of Alis surged through the publishing ranks, the ageing trailblazers who hung on were being pushed into smaller offices, their names appearing further down the masthead, their collective morale in shreds.

Alisson's black Versace dress, with its dramatic back drape lined in scarlet silk, looked as if it had been spray-painted onto her angular, stick-thin body. Her only jewellery was a set of earrings made from strands of tiny red and black Victorian beads and rhinestones. With her ivory skin looking even more translucent against the scarlet and black, with her dark-brown eyes and jet, slicked-back hair, she had the look of a mean, underfed whippet. One that might snap a hand if approached. She exuded a rather dangerous sexuality that appealed to men and women. She narrowed her eyes, assessing her face in detail. She'd never forgotten the time a student in high school had called her 'ferret-face'.

Ali had used expensive cosmetics to highlight her sharp features, emphasising the peak of her eyebrows. She had pulled her hair back from her forehead to show a widow's peak, defined the curves of her mouth with plum pencil and, as a last touch, had extended the eyeliner to give her round, slightly pop eyes more of an oriental slant. Perhaps it was time for plastic surgery to sculpt her face. After all, she would be in the public eye a lot more now. And she could easily afford it. She had fought and argued over her salary package. She'd started out with nothing but a hunger and drive and was making up for those times she'd gone without. Now she was avaricious and wanted only the best. Yet she was as mean with a nickel as she'd been when poor and hungry. Ali didn't give generously now she could afford it. She'd arrived in

New York as a sixteen-year-old, and had been virtually on her own ever since. She'd worked hard to make it to here. Let everyone else do the same.

The phone rang. Glancing at her watch, she clicked the switch on the portable by the bed.

'Ali, it's Bud Stein. I have a piece of news. You sitting down?' The editor of the Triton-owned tabloid, the *New York Gazette*, had a tense pitch to his voice.

'What is it? I'm about to leave for the big bash for Nina.'

'Yeah. I figured you'd be there. But you should know this. There will be an extra dimension to the announcement of the new editor's appointment tomorrow.'

'And what makes you think there's an announcement tomorrow?' Ali was querulous that her big news, yet to be confirmed by Nina, might be common knowledge.

'There's a rumour you might be next in line for the top job. Especially now.' He paused and dropped the bombshell. 'Your current editor has just offed herself.'

'What! Lorraine Bannister? For God's sake, how?'

'She made very sure. Leapt off the terrace of the lovely Nina's office. She's very dead. Didn't go quietly either. Tried to start a fire. Nina won't be able to keep this one discreet.'

'I was with Lorraine this afternoon!' Ali was shocked and she couldn't help the rush of guilt that washed over her. Had Lorraine known Ali was expecting to be named as the new editor? It was said the person to be replaced was always the last to know.

'You there, Ali? What do you say to that? Any theories?'

Ali thought quickly. 'Strictly off the record, right? She's been unstable for a while, drinking and using, er, addictive substances even more in the past month or so. Totally lost her grip a couple of times and I had to cover for her. She'd believed she was in line for promotion to editor-in-chief to take over from Nina.'

'Nina going somewhere?'

'Well, there's a rumour . . .'

'You wish,' Stein thought. The newspaper editor was well aware that the new breed of hot women executives was tough, but this young woman was too much, certainly for the conservative attitude of this hardened newsman. He'd admired the thoughtful and balanced opinions of Nina and her loyal lieutenant, the now deceased Lorraine Bannister.

'Anyway, Lorraine has been losing it. Was finding it hard to deal with life for a whole lot of reasons, one assumes. I know she was also upset about her daughter.' Alisson was keeping the subject off Nina. 'I think it was mainly because she couldn't come to terms with my generation doing things differently. I frequently told her to get her head into third-millennium thinking but she seemed stuck in the twentieth century. I mean, she was really past her use-by date,' she quickly added with an effort at trying to sound genuinely sad.

That line irritated Bud Stein. He was due to retire in four years. Lorraine Bannister, at fifty-one, was his junior by ten years. This was scarcely an old dame in his book.

He took a deep breath, trying to control his annoyance. 'Well, I'll be happy enough to keep my head where it is. Anyway, thought you'd like to know. We'll need a comment from you as her 2IC, Ali, naturally. We've already got someone chasing Nina and the Baron over who will be the next editor.' In the same media empire or not, news was news.

'I'll fax you a sentence or two. I'm shocked. I'll have to think of the appropriate words. Thanks for the call, Bud.'

As the *Gazette* editor hung up, Ali held on to her

portable wondering how she should play her next moves. The news of Lorraine Bannister's demise would dull the sparkle at Nina's party. But Ali couldn't repress a ripple of excitement that her dream of becoming editor of *Blaze* had, if tragically, moved forward. It was still difficult to come to terms with what had happened though. Ali closed her eyes, thinking back to the scene she'd had to endure with Lorraine that afternoon.

Friday, 4.30 p.m.

When Ali walked over to the editor's office the door was shut and Lorraine's editorial coordinator, Pat, had shook her head, running her hand across her throat in a slicing motion as if to say, 'She's cut herself off from the office for a while, forget it'.

Pat had been Lorraine's editorial coordinator for several years. A veteran of more than twenty years in publishing, Pat had started as a secretary and gladly adopted the more stylish title of editorial coordinator that secretaries in New York publishing wore these days. She knew the magazine business from boardroom to basement, understood the nuances of corporate power play, and held strongly to the belief that protection of her immediate boss was the prime requisite of her job.

Over time, such dedication had made her very protective of Lorraine's professional image. In recent months, this commitment had become far more complex. She was aware of the aggressive machinations of the ambitious young woman, Alisson, and knew it had badly shaken Lorraine. Pat had watched with alarm as Lorraine slipped into an often poorly concealed decline in the sanctuary of the editor's office. Thanks to Pat's support, Lorraine generally had been able to keep a bold and composed front when dealing with advertisers. However, her guard was slipping more and more and Pat wondered just how much the other staff members had noticed.

There was something about the slight stiffening of Ali's posture and the questioning twist of the head that immediately told her Ali had the picture in focus.

'I'm sorry Ali, but Lorraine asked not to be disturbed for a while. She's working on an important presentation. Not even taking phone calls.' Pat had fussed with a bunch of papers beside her computer keyboard, giving Ali a half-smile as if inviting understanding and a decision to try again another time.

'I can wait,' said Ali aggressively. 'Just let her know I'm waiting.'

Pat sighed and flopped back in her chair, looking utterly exhausted. 'She's just told me to go home, that she would be working late . . .' Pat didn't complete her effort at subterfuge and, in capitulation, took Ali into her confidence. 'She's not well, Ali, I can feel it,' she whispered. 'She's sick.'

Ali leaned across the desk towards Pat and answered gently in return, as if she were sharing a huge secret and the responsibility that went with it. 'I know . . . now why don't you just take your bag and go home. I'll have a little talk with her. She needs help. We both know that. Now, off you go.' She straightened up and waited until Pat had gathered her bag and coat and was on her way to the elevator. Then she went to the office door and, after a single knock and without waiting for a reply, she swung it open and marched in.

Lorraine was lying on the sofa, which was part of the lounge setting on one side of the spacious room, well removed from the huge executive desk littered with magazines and files, proofs and art work. One hand was over her closed eyes, the other resting on the coffee table and holding a near empty glass. She hadn't moved at the sound of the door opening, hadn't opened her eyes. 'Pat, I told you I wasn't to be disturbed,' she said firmly, a tension in her voice as she struggled to maintain control. 'Please don't say a word, darling. Just make a lovely exit stage left.' She let go of the glass to gesture weakly with a dismissive wave of the hand, which then dangled beside the sofa.

'It's not Pat,' said Ali quietly.

Lorraine stiffened, flicked her hand from her forehead and twisted on the sofa to face Ali across the room. She slowly sat up and arranged her skirt and touched her hair in a tidying gesture. It gave her a few seconds to muster her composure. 'Oh, Ali, you'll have to excuse me. I was just taking five on the horizontal to get the brain in gear for tackling the desktop,' she said with forced brightness. 'But I don't remember having an appointment with you. I'm sorry, but Pat must have slipped up somehow.'

Ali walked over and sat in one of the lounge chairs. 'No, she didn't slip up, Lorraine. There's no appointment. I just felt it was time we had a talk.' Ali had abandoned her planned agenda of talking about the future of the magazine in broad terms, hoping to discover a clue of just how much Lorraine knew, or suspected, about the executive changes that were being contemplated.

'Oh, about what exactly?'

Ali eyed the bottle of vodka on the table near the glass. It was half empty. 'That, for starters,' she said with a nod towards the bottle. 'It's showing rather badly. Your long lunches are starting to look like something else altogether, Lorraine. Nobody does long lunches in this town any more. What's happening?'

Lorraine struggled to maintain control, but her hands

were shaking and she felt nauseous. 'It's the workload, I guess. The pressure's on, you know. Circulation time coming up again.' She rummaged in her handbag, took out a Christian Dior compact and looked briefly in the mirror. She was shocked at her image of bloodshot eyes and smeared mascara.

Ali wondered if Lorraine would admit to her whether she'd been informed that morning that she was being moved sideways to make room for a younger editor. 'The lunches are being talked about in the corridors, Lorraine. And drinking in the office like this . . . How much, how often?'

'Enough, Ali,' snapped Lorraine as she rose to her feet and angrily slammed the mirror shut. 'This is not something that concerns you, nor would you have any comprehension of what it's about. You're not much older than my daughter and, like you, she can't understand either. She does a number on me and thinks it's no big deal.'

'Your daughter? What's she done?'

'Only announced she's leaving me.'

Ali had a hazy recollection of staff gossip about Lorraine's daughter. 'She's grown up, isn't she? I mean, where's she going?'

'Australia. For chrissake. Wants to find her long-lost father.'

Ali jerked in surprise. 'Why there?'

'Her father was Australian. He left us here in New York when she was a baby. God knows where he is now. He's never done anything for Miche. And now, right when I need her, she decides she's going to look for him in a godforsaken place where she knows no one, and has no relatives that I know of, and if they did exist they probably wouldn't care. I thought I'd cut Australia and her father out of our lives.' Lorraine looked teary. 'Why would she do that, Ali? Especially now, when I need her with me? I've protected her. There's nothing in that place for her.'

Lorraine had no idea of the javelin she'd just thrown at Ali's composed demeanour. Ali's memories of the Australia she'd been sent away from at the age of ten were vastly different from the Australia Lorraine's daughter would be going to.

Lorraine explained to Alisson that Nina had tried to reassure her that every young woman needed to spread her wings.

Ali could only agree. 'She'll find that out by going down there. There's not a lot you can do about it.'

'So I've been told,' said Lorraine with a tinge of bitterness, her face draining of colour to a translucent grey.

Ali watched as the older woman pulled herself up from the sofa. Lorraine was trying to regain her composure, but her eyes held a new panic.

'Now, if you'll excuse me, I'll go to the bathroom for a moment. You can leave.'

Ali stood up. 'Pat has gone. Can I organise a cab for you?' She tried to sound sympathetic.

'Don't bother, thanks. I'm going to do a bit of work, as I told you. See you tomorrow.' She walked a little shakily to the en suite and closed the door.

Ali hadn't mentioned Nina's party. Lorraine was in no shape to go anyway. Surely she wouldn't go in this condition? Moving over to the desk, Ali ran her hand along the edge of the ornate woodwork, a gesture that matched the possessive gleam in her eyes. Yes, she would be moving into this very office one day soon. Nina had virtually indicated that to her earlier in the day.

Ali stood deep in thought, her hand still resting on Lorraine's desktop, replaying her confrontation with Nina that morning.

*

Friday, 11 a.m.

Ali had picked her moment. With Nina celebrating her sixtieth birthday amid a retrospective of her years as founding editor of the world-famous *Blaze*, it seemed the ideal time for Ali to discuss her future and that of *Blaze*, forever linked as they were in Ali's mind.

'If possible, I'd like to know what my chances for advancement are, Nina?' Ali had decided to put the question directly to the older woman. 'In a realistic, immediate time frame, not a year or two down the track.'

Nina had studied Ali before answering. 'I'm not in a position to give you a definite answer just at the moment, Ali. There are certain matters to be taken care of before I can let you know what, as you put it, your chances of advancement are.'

'I think it only fair that I know where I stand when there are other opportunities out there,' said Ali, tempering the remark with a small smile.

'Ali, you are talented and, I know, ambitious. Nothing wrong with that. But you're not thirty. You have enormous potential and I urge you not to rush into anything on a short-term basis when there could be a stepping stone to a much bigger career move.'

'Can you give me a little more information?' probed Ali.

Nina drew a deep breath. 'Let me just say that the Baron and I have watched your progress with a great deal of interest. And we may have a challenge and an opportunity for you in the very near future. As I said, I can't say anything more than that at this stage, and please keep this conversation between us for the present.'

Ali had left Nina's office buoyed and confident that, despite the vagueness of her remarks, Nina was saying she would be the new young editor to replace the ageing Lorraine Bannister.

Nina had always been protective of Lorraine, until faced by a series of younger staff representations, cleverly engineered by Ali, over replacing the old brigade. Nina had listened to the strenuous arguments from the younger staff about reflecting the issues and interests of their generation, that the look of the layouts was no longer appropriate, that *Blaze* wasn't adequately addressing the people and lifestyles of the big-spending twenty and thirtysomethings. Nina had finally agreed the magazine needed an injection of energy and attitude and had said she'd raise the matter with the board, bearing in mind the allegiance they owed their loyal staff.

'. . . and buddies,' thought Ali. Lorraine and Nina had been close friends and Nina was godmother to Lorraine's daughter, Michelle. That was typical of Nina. Always the gracious and caring matriarch. Well, her old-style thinking was out of date as well. In this new millennium, *Blaze* deserved a fresh look. It was tired, stale, and getting old like Nina. Why couldn't she just admit she was past it, hand the baton over and move on? Ali had spent months developing ideas that could eclipse even the innovative Nina Jansous. How could a woman turning sixty, who had devoted so much of her life to just one institution, be on top of where young women were at today? Nina might have been raised as a 'little Aussie battler', as she was constantly telling everyone, but Ali had decided she would be the one to win the new battles.

It was ironic that she and Nina shared an Australian background, each had been an only child, and each was self-taught without the advantages of a tertiary education. But whereas Nina had been hands-on and had promoted herself as a woman of style, Ali knew she had to be streetwise. She had vowed never to be deflected

16

from her goal. She had put her own history of setbacks behind her and, if she could overcome a childhood she no longer allowed herself to think about, she could achieve any challenge she set herself.

Since she was sixteen, when she'd joined *Blaze* in New York as an editorial trainee, Ali had chosen to hide behind a carefully contrived facade. Her past was her past and would never be known to anyone. It had made her the person she was today – a survivor, a fighter, cynical and determined. Reaching executive heights and having the trappings that went with them was tangible. That counted. Nothing else mattered. Ali wasn't a giver. But she didn't think of herself as a taker either. She was a doer. And nothing would stand in her way. What she wanted, what she intended, was to be editor of *Blaze* in New York.

Friday, 5 p.m.

Ali walked to the big window of Lorraine's office, resenting the time the older woman was spending in the bathroom. Another five minutes and she'd have to check on her and God knows what mess the old drunk would be in. Ali knew she'd need to leave soon to dress for Nina's dinner. But she hadn't finished with her rival yet. She wanted Lorraine to confirm that she'd been sacked as editor of *Blaze*. Then she might be able to find out if Lorraine knew who her replacement would be.

Ali was looking at the sun setting over the Manhattan skyline, the rays highlighting the blanket of smog that most New Yorkers ignored, as Lorraine came out of the bathroom. She turned and saw a transformed woman walk firmly to her desk, ignoring the fact that Ali was still in her office after being so pointedly dismissed.

'Now where were we?' Lorraine had said, sounding very sober and alert.

'We were talking about your drinking . . . and other things,' said Ali.

'Help yourself if you'd like one,' sallied Lorraine brusquely, waving a finger towards the little refrigerator set discretely in a wall of packed bookshelves.

'No thanks, too early for me.'

Lorraine looked up from the papers scattered across the desk and caught the severe look that went with Ali's curt rejection of the offer. Their eyes locked, Lorraine's gleaming with bitterness, Ali's glistening with calculated coolness.

'You have that disapproving look my daughter gives me,' said Lorraine with a sharp edge to her voice.

'Sorry, but it's time you faced up to what's happening to you and took a grip on life.'

Lorraine exploded. 'You too! Christ, that's what Miche said this morning. Among other goddamned bits of rubbish. Well, I have a damned firm grip on life around here, Ali, and you'd better believe it.' Her shouting contradicted her words, but she was unaware of her raised voice as she continued to stare down her rival.

And then, with a shock that had sent shivers down her spine, Ali realised that she was looking into the eyes of a drug addict. Lorraine Bannister was stoned. That was the real purpose of the trip to the bathroom. A quick hit. She broke eye contact and took a couple of steps to the door, then turned back and coldly fired the shot that denied her better judgement. 'Well, now I understand better just what sort of grip you have, Lorraine. And it's not firm. It amounts to nothing. You're finished. It's over.'

'Over? Over?' shouted Lorraine in uncontrolled

anger. 'Who the hell do you think you are to talk like that? What's over?'

'Your job,' replied Ali in an icy tone.

'You're crazy. Get out.'

'Crazy. Hardly an appropriate word for you to invoke at this point,' said Ali, with irony that again hit the target and caused the fevered eyes to flash alarmingly. 'Nina and the Baron have something big in store for me, Lorraine. I've been given the nod, if you take my meaning. Only a few hours ago. And when I'm in charge around here, there'll be no accommodation of junkies.'

'Get out!' screamed Lorraine. 'Get out.'

Ali had left without looking back, slamming the door with such force that the noise had echoed up the corridor and caused the last of the staff waiting for the elevator to look over their shoulders in surprise.

Friday, 8 p.m.

Nina still found it hard to grasp. The call had come from the building's head of security just over an hour ago.

Her hands started to shake as she dressed for the dinner that the Baron had insisted must go ahead, despite the tragic circumstances.

It was only now, when it was too late, and she was struggling to come to terms with the terrible events of that day that Nina realised she hadn't tried hard enough. She hadn't paid enough attention to Lorraine's hurt and personal pain. She had been too focused on her own life events and this evening's formal recognition of her sixtieth birthday.

Her mind went back to her breakfast meeting with

Lorraine when she'd broken the news to her that she wasn't being reappointed editor of *Blaze*.

The possibility of losing her beloved job, and with it her place in New York society – for Lorraine had no doubts about the consequences – had been Lorraine's worst-case scenario for months now, a situation she had too often contemplated after a drink or three.

'Lorraine, I'd give anything to change this, but I can't. You are not being reappointed as editor of *Blaze*. It's a board decision with the Baron, as chairman, in agreement. They want an editor with a different, fresh approach to attract a younger audience. You'll be taking over a new position as special projects editor. Your appointment will be announced with due ceremony and you'll be able to carve a niche for yourself there.'

'Appointment! You mean, dis-appointment . . . dismissal is what I call it, being shoved aside is as good as being out,' Lorraine had said bitterly.

Try as she did, Nina had found it impossible to convince Lorraine that she was not obsolete, that there could be a role for her in the reorganisation of the staff. She could still hear her own attempt to rationalise the situation. 'Lorraine, we are both in the same boat. A new generation of journalists want to take over the oars . . . and the helm. Remember what it was like to be young, impatient and ambitious. Remember how we came by our breaks.'

'We waited our turn! We learned from the bottom up. An inexperienced editor! Never, never in our day.'

'Our day has gone, Lorraine. Today is for girls like your daughter, and our bright girls on the staff like Ali.' Nina was trying to be gentle. Or was she also trying to convince herself?

'Not so!' cried Lorraine. 'My days aren't over. I still have so much to do and give and teach. Yet, goddamn it, here I am being pushed aside professionally and even my own daughter wants to take off and leave me.'

'Lorraine, Miche is not leaving you. She has to sort out her own dreams.'

'Listen, Nina, I'm going to need her now more than ever. At least do this for me. At least try one more time to talk Miche out of this mad idea of going to Australia. Suddenly the most important thing to her seems to be a part of her life that was so brief that she doesn't even remember it.'

'Lorraine, her links to Australia are tenuous, a father she never knew, and possibly won't like if she does meet him. He did abandon her, after all. But there is still a connection with a country that she knows nothing about. It's only natural that she's curious. Let her work it out of her system,' said Nina.

As she uttered the cliché, a deep illumination flashed through Nina's mind. Suddenly Nina saw the need behind her god-daughter's drive to find her roots. It was an insight into her own need, which shook her soul, but she pushed it to one side as she sought to calm her distressed, now ex-editor.

'I worry about Miche. Nina, I don't want her to be like Ali.'

Nina had fumbled for the right words to say. She didn't want to be disloyal to a senior member of staff, but Lorraine was a personal friend, Miche was her god-daughter. 'Lorraine, Ali doesn't always handle situations as sensitively as she could, she's so ambitious, but she has a right to chase her own dreams.'

'I know Miche has to find her own way, but she doesn't understand my needs, especially right now.' Lorraine gulped her drink. 'What's going to become of me, Nina?'

'You have to pull yourself through this, Lorraine. You

don't have a lot of choice and you have to stop holding on to Miche and let her go.'

Lorraine was terse. 'You may be the boss, Nina, and I can't fight the board, but none of you really knows what I'm dealing with.' Her voice was strained and it seemed to Nina she sounded irrational. It was the whisky talking again.

Nina rose. 'Lorraine, sleep on it. Let's talk again.' There was no criticism, no judgement in her voice. Just the concerned tones of a friend, who also had other issues to deal with.

Lorraine had waved an arm. 'Forget it, pal. I'll pull my act together.' She attempted a wan smile. 'If you can't dump on friends, who can you . . . ?'

Nina fumbled with the clasp on her necklace. She couldn't stop imagining what Lorraine must have felt in those moments of stepping off the balcony and through the dark door of death.

There had been frantic phone calls to try to control the media coverage so the details would be confined as much as possible to Triton's morning paper, the *New York Gazette*. At least that way it would cause the least damage.

Bud Stein, after catching the lift upstairs to Nina's private apartments, arrived exasperated. 'Nina, how do we downplay this? The other papers and radio and TV are going to beat it up once they know it was suicide.' He'd listened to Nina's rapid suggestion of how she wanted the *New York Gazette* to report the incident and sighed, 'Okay, Nina, we'll try. Yes, we'll talk about how successful she was. Yes, we'll use a nice photo. No, we won't mention she might have been drinking. No, we won't mention the daughter. So, can you give us a brief statement, at least?'

The Baron had called her as soon as he'd heard. 'Nina, dearest, this is terrible. So very sad. Please, I know you're probably blaming yourself, but . . .'

'I do blame myself, Oscar. I knew she was unhappy, and obviously removing her from the editor's position was the final straw. Oh, that poor child. Poor Miche.'

'Nina, I don't wish to seem insensitive, but . . . this evening . . . you must be there. It is for you, and people have come from around the globe to share it. It's too late to cancel. The guests will already be on their way here. Be strong, my dear. We must go through with the dinner.'

Nina had taken a deep breath. 'I understand. I've asked that the news be kept as quiet as possible until the morning. The police are cooperating and not releasing any but the most basic details until the morning media call.'

'Nina, we will mark your birthday tonight but we will not refer to any celebration. I think it best we make no reference to this unfortunate incident.'

A shiver went through Nina. A woman's most desperate act, driven by a sense of inadequacy, loss and anger, fuelled by booze and pills, was reduced to 'an unfortunate incident'. She ached for Lorraine. If only she had been more aware of the extent of her friend's desperation – but what could she have done? Now, there was Miche, Lorraine's daughter and Nina's god-daughter to think about. What lay in store for her?

TAKE TWO …

The metal grille clicked. A cold, hard sound that for a moment sent a shiver through the woman whose hand still curled around the forged iron. A picture, a fragment of memory, a sensation, flashed into her consciousness. A light that blinked on, then off. The flashes – subliminal pictures from her past – had been coming more regularly. Ever since her mother, Clara, had died. The images were blurry, unrecognisable. Yet there was the nagging knowledge she knew where and what they meant. Then, like a film speeding up, the still-life flashes changed from out-of-focus black and white to a faint sepia, then to full colour. A tantalising glimpse, and they were gone.

Nina Jansous knew she couldn't share this. She was perceived as always being so sure, so in control. And deep down was the notion people might think it a sign of advancing years. While it was impossible to hide her age, she had always taken pride in acting and looking as youthful as she felt.

What was pulling her back to this time and place of

unresolved questions? She wished she could switch off this mysterious projector in her mind. Or that a clue to these visions would appear.

Taking a deep breath, Nina lifted her head, pressed the brass button marked Private and stepped back in the small elevator, inhaling the rich smell of oiled wood that also permeated the two eyrie penthouse apartments on the sixtieth floor of the Triton skyscraper. In the softly lit interior of the gilded baroque birdcage, she glanced at the rosewood inlaid mirror.

The laughing face of her mother rippled into focus. Clara, wearing a frivolous and extravagantly decorated hat, was posing as if for the cover of a magazine.

Nina was back in that moment – a teenager, home from the beach smelling of sea, salt dry on her skin, the pinkness of too much sun already showing on her cheeks and nose, sharing her mother's delight in the finished hat.

Nina closed her eyes, feeling the senses of the girl she'd been. How she loved the surf and the sun. Australia. It was always connected in her mind with the ocean. How long ago it was.

Nina opened her eyes as the lift stopped. She turned as the outside door of the elevator was pulled open and Baron Triton extended his hand.

'Nina, *ma chérie*. How beautiful you look. As always.' He bent his head, his silver moustache brushing her hand.

'Oscar. *Tu es très charmant. Comme toujours.*' Nina gave a wan smile.

The distinguished and celebrated Baron tucked her arm in his and patted her hand abstractedly. 'I understand how you are feeling. We must help the daughter. I'm told she doesn't have any close relatives.'

'That's kind of you. I've made a statement for the

press. I will have to speak to the staff. Maybe I should change my plans . . .'

'Nina. You can't go back now. You have taken this step, it is not like you to back away from a commitment.' He squeezed her hand. 'Unless you have changed your mind . . . about me?'

Nina shook her head, but returned the pressure of his hand as he led her along the Aubusson carpet to his fifty-ninth floor reception rooms where the murmur of voices mingled with Mozart played by a string quartet.

To Nina, the corridor suddenly seemed to telescope, the doors at the far end receding, the walls leaning in towards her on either side. Their steps were silent. If it hadn't been for the Baron's arm, his hand resting on hers, her knees might have buckled. It wasn't nerves, it wasn't even the shock of Lorraine's death, it was the pushing inside her chest, her heart, her head, longing to be free, to be young and challenged. To live with wonderment, to feel as she had when she'd first started *Blaze* in Australia as a young widow.

She felt like there was a miniature volcano inside her chest, ready to explode. Soon she would have to heed the pressure of her long-buried emotions. Like Miche, her childhood was calling her. For Nina, it was her early childhood in a strange country, for she barely remembered Croatia, before her mother had fled with her to Australia.

For Miche, it was the unknown part of her life – her Australian father who had disappeared from New York, leaving no imprint on her heart or in her memory. Miche wanted to find answers in Australia.

Nina had discussed Miche's plans with her and was convinced the young woman was mature enough to face whatever the searching for her father would bring.

Breaking the news of Lorraine's tragic death to Miche

was, Nina thought, the hardest task she'd ever performed. Over the telephone first, she'd organised Miche's best friend to be there when she'd made the dreadful call. Miche had first refused to believe that her mother could intentionally take her life, that she would desert her, and she'd tried to insist it must have been an accident. Then, after the initial shock had passed, Miche had impulsively and bitterly reiterated her determination to leave America.

'Are you sure in your heart that this isn't a matter of taking flight, Miche, dearest? You know you take the same fears and tears with you when you run,' Nina had said gently.

Miche was adamant. 'I'm going. I don't know where to start, but there's nothing to keep me here in New York.'

It had touched Nina's heart to hear the bitter twist to the young girl's grief. At twenty-two, Miche should be carefree and reckless, shaking coconut trees and tilting at windmills. Nina became practical. 'Very well. I'm going to be in Europe in a few months. Why don't we meet in Paris? That will give you time to wrap up things here. I'll treat you to a little holiday, a rest, and then we'll organise your travel to Sydney from there.'

Finally, Nina had been able to talk Miche round. Miche had agreed to stay the night with her friend's parents who, Nina knew, would comfort and care for the distraught child until she could join her in the morning.

Pulling herself back to the here-and-now, Nina turned her head to one side to confront the pictures hanging along the corridor. They were elaborately framed covers of *Blaze* magazines from all the fashion capitals of the globe – Paris, Rome, London, Tokyo, New York – many of them announcing groundbreaking issues from the seventies to the present. The stylish, sometimes startling cover designs and images were now classics. On the other wall were photographs featured in the magazines – celebrity interviews, news exclusives, exotic fashion spreads, magnificent gardens, elegant homes – each with the stamp of famed photographers noted for their innovative approach and visual impact. Class and glamour were the hallmark of *Blaze* magazine as created by Nina. In recent years, the magazine had evolved to include current affairs as *Blaze* strode the world stage.

It had been an interesting journey from the first edition started by Nina in Australia more than two decades before. Within two years, *Blaze* had become Australia's top magazine. A year after that she had agreed to move the magazine to New York in partnership with Baron Triton and start *Blaze USA*.

The tall, polished timber doors were opened by the butler as Baron Oscar Von Triton loosened her arm from his, stepped back and Nina made her entrance.

There was warm applause as hushed murmurs sprang to lips.

'She's beautiful. How does she do it?'

'Money, darling. And good genes.'

The invitations had described it as an occasion to celebrate Nina Jansous' birthday and it was no secret she'd reached sixty. She'd been profiled in the media for too many years to keep secrets. It was also to be the occasion for an important announcement. In the gentle hum of office gossip had been speculation that Nina and the Baron might take this opportunity to announce a personal liaison. With their adjoining penthouses on the sixtieth floor, many thought Nina had been his mistress for years. But no one ever whispered she'd held the reins of *Blaze* solely because of this. Her talent and acumen were unchallenged. She had created *Blaze* and she had come to epitomise all the magazine stood for – beauty, strength, intelligence and daring.

After the war, Oscar Triton had been made a Baron in his homeland of Belgium for services to his country by financing the underground resistance fighters against the Nazis. His fortune had been accumulated by his grandfather who'd started tobacco plantations and factories in Haiti and the Belgian Congo. During World War II, the Baron had regularly, and very discreetly, alerted the underground when a truck filled with tradeable commodities would take a certain route. The goods would be hijacked by friendly forces and sold on the black market to raise money for the resistance.

After the war, Oscar had opened emerald and ruby mines in the Belgian Congo and diversified into industrial plants and printing companies. Printing and publishing had been a means of spreading his business interests outside Europe until, by the 1970s, he had quietly bought into or taken over enough small media enterprises through Europe and Asia to form one of the largest newspaper, magazine and associated printing companies in the world.

He had chosen to remain in the background, an unknown, until a clash between warring super moguls in America and Britain had given him an opportunity to slip between them, steal the prize and seal the deal. The price he'd paid for these US and British media outlets meant he could no longer slide back into obscurity. Once outed as a major media player, he had managed his public persona through a screen of protecting attendants, keeping his private life above scrutiny, to become *un homme mystérieux*. Triton was a high-profile company. The man behind it was low key and discreet.

*

Nina wore a deep violet velvet gown that was almost as black as her eyes, and on her shoulder perched her trademark, an art nouveau diamond dragonfly pin – the motif that alighted daintily on the masthead of every issue of *Blaze*. She moved amongst the guests, a peck on the cheek, a gentle embrace, a warm handshake, a kissing of champagne glasses. Her throaty laugh, her voice with its strange mixture of European cadence and a hint of sun-toughened Australian vowels, charmed everyone who spoke with her. Her beauty, her intelligence and grace, fascinated anyone within her orbit.

Women surreptitiously studied Nina, trying to analyse her elegance and magnetism so that they might emulate her. Few had her slim, willowy height, wide, high cheekbones, dark eyes, full lips and a smile that stunned with its joyous delight in a face that could have belonged to a high-fashion model. Her thick, dark hair had, over the years, become a lustrous silver subtly rinsed with gold. The colour was dramatic set against her olive skin that still remained taut and smooth. She liked the small lines of life about her eyes, although she had been fortunate that the years of harsh Australian sun had not damaged her complexion. 'Wog blood,' she'd cheerfully commented in her Australian way to a shocked make-up artist and hair-stylist one day during a photo shoot. And explained, 'In the fifties in Australia all immigrants were called wogs, unless they were from England. My mother and I came from Eastern Europe.'

To any observer of the ebb and flow of seriously influential powerbrokers and policy makers, shapers of trends and manipulators of opinion and financial markets, this group was the elite. They were placed like pieces of an expensive chess set against the backdrop of antique European furniture, master artworks and collector objects in the elegant, beautifully lit room that made the simple statement – excellent taste bred from old money.

The party setting subtly combined restrained festivity with a hint of the commercial. In the centre of each table was a bouquet of Nina's favourite Princess of Wales rosebuds arranged delicately in maidenhair fern. Perched atop each flower arrangement was a tiny translucent dragonfly with glittering glass eyes. At each guest's place was a souvenir of the evening, a small glossy book titled, simply, *Nina*. On its cover was an Erté illustration for a 1920s *Vogue* cover. Nina had revived the brilliant art deco style for *Blaze USA*'s early covers. Inside was a potted life story of *Blaze* with photographs of Nina, the magazine's staff, its famous models, controversial stories and interviews, along with a selection of the most famous *Blaze* covers.

The guests had been carefully chosen – kings of the business world, academics from the sciences, arts and humanities, titled aristocracy, a royal head or two from Europe and Asia, diplomats. The A-list celebrities mingled with the chosen handful of key *Blaze* personnel. Among them, and never taking her eyes off Nina, was the magazine's dynamic features editor, Larissa Kelly.

Larissa admired Nina and had learned more about magazines since working for *Blaze* than in all her previous years in publishing. It wasn't just the flair Nina had for recognising a trend before everyone else, or the way she explored stories by never taking the obvious route, it was how she sought out the opinions of her staff. She listened, she encouraged, she managed to gently push everyone beyond what they thought they could do. She wanted you to be prepared to take risks, to take a step further than you might, experiment, stand your ground for your beliefs and accept the verdict if you didn't always win. There was always the safety net of Nina's attention and her respect for your ideas. The close-working editorial team had learned to respect each other and use humour to defuse potential explosions. Ambition was accepted and expected, but not at the cost of personal feelings or destabilising manoeuvres.

Larissa had started at *Blaze* as assistant to Ivor Dennison, the former chief-of-staff, but it had been Larissa who was the hands-on, day-to-day keeper of the keys, holder of the reins, organiser of staff and assignments. Ivor was mostly out to lunch or in meetings with his contacts and had been happy to leave the actual work to his capable assistant.

He was not alone. The coterie of male hierarchy in the print media had a consistent modus operandi – positions of administrative power were filled from what had developed over the years as an old boys' network and they came with a fat and padded salary package, based on years of mediocre experience. They hired smart female assistants who made them look good by working hard, and who were cleverly led to believe they'd eventually move up the ladder and assume the title. But the members of the club of male senior management protected each other and by the time the women assistants discovered advancement opportunities were limited, they had invested too much time, energy and talent to make effective waves.

Larissa's experience at *Blaze* was rare. On Ivor's retirement, Nina had formally promoted Larissa to the job she was already doing. For most of the female assistants on New York magazines, the only way up was to move on to other publications, working for similar men or for the few powerful women who were wildly protective of the breakthroughs they'd made and weren't about to help pull younger women through their crack in the glass ceiling.

Manny Golan, the financial vice-president, glanced around the party. The atmosphere was friendly and intimate. Despite the endless circling waiters carrying trays of crystal flutes filled with the best wine and champagne, guests were consciously on their best behaviour. Manny, squat, balding and apple-cheeked, turned to the head of the legal department, Roberto Iano, who'd just delivered, in confidential whispers, the details of Lorraine's death. He'd been contacted by the Baron to immediately investigate any legal implications or liability.

'In the light of that little glitch, I wonder what Nina will announce tonight,' said Manny.

The financial VP didn't keep close tabs on the internal machinations or the face *Blaze* showed the world. Lorraine Bannister had been just another hefty contract package for him to oversee. His world was spreadsheets, fiscal reports and projections. It was all numbers in columns to him. He didn't want to know about staff problems in the editorial side of the company, or what cover stories were being mooted, provided they sold the magazine. Circulation figures were what it was all about. Sales, subscriptions, advertising.

Roberto was a study in contrasts to the pudgy Manny. Taller, beaky thin, hair a tad too long, and funereal expression the norm, he did try to take more of a personal interest in the staff. He knew the major contractual arrangements and the minefield of legal difficulties the magazine tiptoed around with each issue.

He sipped his Cristal champagne as he watched Ali making her way past Larissa who, at thirty-five, was seven years older than Ali. Roberto knew Larissa was more hands-on and therefore a more efficient worker. 'Look at those two – Alisson and Larissa. I predict a showdown between them one day. That Larissa is very nice. Thoughtful kind of gal. Like dear old Lorraine.' He shook his head and lowered his voice. 'What the hell do you suppose happened?'

'She jumped,' said Manny.

'Sure. But why?'

Manny shrugged and glanced back as Ali circled around a high-flyer Texan rancher–businessman, who turned and greeted her self-introduction with a throaty joke. 'She knows a vulnerable target, that Ali. Ole Charlie has just lost wife number four. Gotta be worth a billion. For a farmer, he has a shrewd handle on where the next international futures market will take off. But he's a lost cause with attractive young women.'

'Attractive? That young woman? Not in my book,' declared Manny, thinking of his plump, acquiescent wife and happy mother of his two sons. 'That's a girl with balls. I prefer boobs. But I'll admit that Ali can work a room like no one else.'

While being careful not to upstage Nina, Ali had cut a smooth swathe through the crowd, welcoming the powerful on behalf of *Blaze*, barely pausing to acknowledge members of staff. There was always speculation among them about the levels of self-confidence attained by Alisson Gruber, who never hid her ambition and was not shy about pointing out her strengths. When her ideas were taken up, she was always quick to claim credit. No one suspected how much it rankled Ali that she was forever conforming to Nina's imprint, though many of the old hands could sense a tension in Ali, and they wondered which way it would take her . . . up or down? Clearly, for now, it was up.

This party was no mere social function. There was an undercurrent of expectancy when diplomat met banker, the head of the IMF met the heads of international aid agencies or bumped mildly against a senator and congressman. The head of the Department of Defense chatted to the chairman of the largest construction company in the US. And feeling their way gingerly onto the corporate stage came smaller players, such as a major movie star whose outspoken pacifist political views would have little in common with her soon-to-be table partner, the flamboyant Texas rancher.

Everyone had come at the invitation of Baron Triton, whose favour they sought to keep and encourage, and with respect and fascination for a powerful and beautiful woman. Each knew they were included for a reason and that somewhere along the line a price would be extracted. A price each would willingly pay if it meant staying within this charmed circle of power and influence.

Larissa joined Ali and introduced herself to the Texan. She managed to ignore the faint tightening of Ali's smile as the man changed the subject from himself.

'So you two young ladies work together. What do you do? I'm Texan, so I know oil wells and cattle. I'm not up on the magazine business.' The words rolled out at a lazy pace.

'That's right, we are colleagues,' said Ali brightly. 'Larissa has worked for me for what . . . two years now? She is the features editor, sort of the general in charge of field troops.' Ali beamed her professional smile at Larissa who could have passed for twenty-five with her fresh, scrubbed face touched with minimalist make-up, and naturally curled blonde bob.

'And you?' asked Charlie.

'I'm the next rung up the ladder from Larissa.' Ali waited for the penny to drop and when he still looked at her expectantly, she added, 'Nina is the commander, while I'm sort of the major-general. The deputy editor.'

Larissa smiled inwardly. Ali couldn't help herself, she had to stress her dominance, even over a colleague.

Before the Texan could throw them any more

questions and flirt with them, he was claimed by a Swiss banker and wheeled off to another introduction.

'Full on, isn't it?' observed Larissa blandly.

'It's supposed to be,' retorted Ali, and gave a slight lift of her shoulders as she turned away to work another part of the room.

The delicate announcement from the butler to be seated for dinner heightened the air of expectation as the guests were ushered into the formal dining room where three long tables of twelve places formed a U shape.

Nina was seated in the centre of the middle table.

The Baron rose to make a toast. He glanced around the faces, highlighted by the candelabra and soft, recessed lighting, as he lifted his flute of champagne. 'It is an honour to be here to pay homage to this very beautiful and talented lady,' he paused for the murmur of agreement, then continued, 'who has been so instrumental in not only the success of *Blaze* worldwide, but in everything that Triton has achieved these past years.' He turned to Nina and gave a slight bow of his head, which those present knew referred to Nina's seat on the small, tight-knit board of Triton.

But his gesture went unacknowledged by Nina. She sat with lowered eyes, her expression soft, but inscrutable.

'Nina's achievements are known to you, her journey to this place this evening has not been without challenges. And, as you know, our Nina likes a challenge.' He gave a wry, fond smile.

Here Nina lifted her head, looking at the candles burning in the candelabra. Their reflection in her dark pupils made her eyes flame eerily.

The Baron continued speaking in the quiet intimate style the occasion dictated. 'And tonight is no exception as Nina is ready to take on another challenge in her life. As you know, Nina tends to do the unexpected.' He waited for the anticipated buzz of reaction, which he silenced with a lifted finger. 'Nina will tell you of the decision she has made at the conclusion of dinner. But for the moment, please join me in toasting the occasion of her birthday. *Nina, ma chérie. Nina, bonne anniversaire.*'

There was a scraping of chairs as the guests rose and chorused, 'To Nina. Happy birthday,' then sat down.

Nina felt herself smile in automatic response, but her mind remained mesmerised by the candlelight as she felt the sound of her name resonating through her until it touched that deep, inner part of her. Her very soul.

'Nina! Nina child. Such a dreamer! Come.'

Her mother, Clara, was calling her.

Clara looked like a Christmas tree. Festooned with ribbons, scraps of lace, a velvet wristband stuck with pearl-headed pins, a spray of colourful, long hatpins decorated with jewelled knobs pinned to her lapel, clusters of silk flowers arranged around a soft brimmed hat that flopped over one eye.

Nina closed her book and hurried from the tiny garden at her mother's call.

Clara struck a pose, chin lifted, snooty pained expression, one hand on her hip, the other out in the air with artfully poised fingers. Her mouth twitched and she began to laugh. 'So what do you think, darling? How does it look? The rose or the gardenia?'

'Not both? I rather like the cluttered garden look, Mama.'

Clara held up a length of ribbon. 'The cream or the lemon?'

'You're the milliner. You decide. Who's the hat for? Is it to go with a special dress?'

Clara pulled the hat from her head revealing a mass of dark hair sprinkled with silver, loose strands springing free, mussed from the hat. 'You're no help. Lady Benson wants something "frothy" for the races. What is such a word? Frothy?'

Nina kissed her mother's cheek. 'Like a milkshake.'

'Ah! Thank you, precious. I know exactly what you mean now. Vanilla and banana. With sprinkles on top . . . pretty beads on a bow. Yes, that's it. You are so clever, darling.' Satisfied, she turned back to her work-room, humming an old tune from Europe.

Nina trailed behind. 'Mama, don't you think you should tidy up, comb your hair? Mrs Morgan will be here soon.'

'Oh, my. Oh, that's right. Is her hat finished? Is it in the box yet? It's the red cloche on the black velvet band.' Clara fussed among the rows of bald and faceless wooden heads until she found the smart hat destined to adorn the coiffured head of Mrs Cedric Morgan, wife of the publishing magnate who owned the most popular news-papers and ladies' magazines in Australia. As she packed it in the hatbox with tissue paper, Clara glanced at her daughter. 'I see you are prepared to meet Mrs Morgan.'

Nina smoothed the skirt Clara had made and fiddled with her simple blouse. 'She said she would talk to me about a job when she came for her hat.'

Clara stood back and regarded her striking teenage daughter. 'You look very nice, Nina. I've taught you to dress well. But I think it needs a little something . . .' She squinted and tilted her head.

'No, Mama. Please, no frills. No bows. No flowers. No beads. I like things simple.'

'Ah, simple. Like a peasant woman,' clucked Clara. Then beamed. 'That's it.' She rummaged in a large box and pulled out a wondrous scarf of shot silk in muted

lavender and blue. She slung it around Nina's waist, knotting it low over her slim hips on the soft grey skirt. 'There. Perfect.' Clara tilted the mirror stand so she could see.

Nina nodded, looking pleased. 'You're right. It's just the finishing touch that my outfit needs.'

'You can always add a little something to finish an outfit, Nina. And also, you can take away something. When you think you're dressed and ready, stop and look again. Ask yourself: Add on? Or take away?'

A rap on the door of their cottage in a quiet back street in Sydney's Double Bay made Nina jump and she hurried to answer. 'Good afternoon, Mrs Morgan. Please come in, Mama is just packing your hat.'

'Oh, no, I must try it on. Just to check it's as lovely as I imagine it's going to be.' She swept in and greeted Clara while Nina went to prepare the good cups for afternoon tea.

When she carried in the tray and made space on Clara's cluttered work table, the two women were admiring the hat now hugging Mrs Morgan's head.

'It's perfect, Clara. I'm so glad we decided on the black velvet band. I've bought a new black bag, with velvet trim. I think I can get away with it in daytime. It is the big race day, after all. My husband has a horse or two running. All very exciting when one can cheer on one's own, don't you think?'

'Tea, Mrs Morgan?' asked Nina, the teapot poised.

'Lovely idea. Do you mind if I sit down? Been such a day at the art gallery, on my feet for hours.'

Clara caught the worried expression on Nina's face as Mrs Morgan turned her attention to the hat designs Clara had painted on a stack of white cards. She wished Nina hadn't taken to heart a tossed-away remark made by Mrs Morgan about helping her find a job. 'Please excuse me *for a moment.' As she left the room, Clara prayed that this woman, the wife of such an influential man, would indeed take an interest in her daughter. Nina was beautiful, talented and worked hard to better herself. She always had her nose in a book 'to learn something'.*

Clara had brought Nina to Australia from postwar Yugoslavia. Just one of many families hoping for a better life who'd plunged their meagre savings into one of the immigration schemes offered by Australia. The country needed workers and for men there were many job opportunities in the postwar boom years. But for a widow with a small girl, little money and no relatives, it was a brave move. Especially as they had been forced to escape from Zagreb. Clara was not one to look backwards and felt her options in Europe were limited.

She had been the only child of an upper-class family in Croatia, her father a doctor, her mother's family the owners of a large country estate and city home. Clara, against her parents' wishes, had married a struggling musician with little money or, they felt, prospects. He had been killed in the war, leaving Clara with their only child, Nina. Despite her entreaties, Clara's elderly parents had refused to abandon their home. They had hung on during the war and, difficult as times were, would not consider leaving. However, hard though it was, they had convinced Clara she had to move to a safe and distant country with their beloved grand-daughter. The escape was planned and paid for and they farewelled Clara with what American dollars they had and jewellery to sell. But her mother gave Clara one piece of jewellery to keep, and one day to pass on to Nina. It was a goldsmith's work of art, a magnificent brooch in the shape of a dragonfly.

Australia had been good to them. Clara had been taught sewing and millinery under a migrant training scheme and, remembering the beautiful gowns owned by her mother, she had started altering clothes for dress shops and friends. After being asked to restyle one lady's hat, Clara saw an opening and concentrated on making hats. She soon had a thriving millinery business in Sydney. She had saved every penny to send Nina to a private girls' school near their home, but she worried how she could manage the extra cost of putting Nina through university. Taking money from her parents back in Croatia was impossible.

'Don't worry, Mama. I will make my own way in the world. I can't sew like you, but one day I will work with beautiful clothes too and buy you a Paris-designed dress.'

'Where do you get your big dreams from, girl?' Clara wondered what had given Nina such ambitions and she fretted they would never be fulfilled.

Nina handed Mrs Morgan a cup and passed the milk jug.

'Sugar?' She watched Mrs Morgan add the milk and cubes to the strong brew. How could she remind Mrs Morgan of the promise she had made on her last visit? Had it just been idle chatter? Nina burned inside. What could she say to jog her memory yet not appear pushy or rude?

'I love the way you've wrapped that scarf on the skirt, Nina, very nice touch.'

'I love clothes and fashion ideas – and, of course, hats,' said Nina, adding with a smile, 'How could I not? I live in the middle of it all.'

41

'Your mother is an inspiration,' declared Mrs Morgan. 'Coming here after all that sadness in your homeland, making a new life for herself when she had never worked. If I fell on hard times – heaven forbid! – I don't know what I could turn my hand to doing.' She sipped her tea.

Nina leapt in. 'I would love to go to university, but Mama can't afford that. And I do know what I'd like to do,' she said quite firmly. 'Writing and working with clothes is what I love. If there was a way I could combine them . . .' she looked at Mrs Morgan with a slight questioning air.

'My goodness, Nina. I nearly forgot! After our last talk and the folder you gave me with your ideas and articles – I passed them on to the editor of In Home and Garden. It's one of my husband's little magazines. There is an opening there for a young girl willing to start at the bottom. Write little bits, help the staff ladies, that sort of thing. It would be a start if you're interested. I'm afraid In Home and Garden isn't where we look for fabulous fashion ideas – have to go abroad for that – but they're lovely ladies and they do nice homey stories in the magazine.'

'I'd love it! Just to work in that world! I'll do anything, Mrs Morgan,' said Nina, her excitement tinged with relief. 'Who do I see?'

Nina lifted her eyes. She saw the main course before her and picked at it, forcing herself to make small talk with the Baron and other guests at the table.

'You're not entirely with us, my dear,' he whispered eventually and touched her hand softly.

She nodded and smiled. The dessert was served. Nina's choice of birthday cake, a *pièce montée*, had been wheeled out, the chef igniting a trickle of brandy at its peak, lifting a single flaming profiterole onto the scoop of sorbet on Nina's plate. The guests applauded as she gently blew the brandy flame out. A delicious botrytis dessert wine was poured and the guests settled into their chairs, eyes fixed on Nina as if a curtain were about to rise and a diva to perform.

The Baron stood, lifted his glass towards Nina and said, 'Nina, we wish you happiness and joy on this special occasion. If you could share a few of your thoughts it would bring us much pleasure.'

He saluted her with his glass as Nina placed her napkin on the Wedgwood plate, slowly smoothed her skirt then rose to her feet. She looked around the tables at the candlelit faces, every eye on her beautiful, serene face. A master of timing, she paused enough for each guest to feel she had looked directly at them, and them alone, with an intimate, private message.

'My dear, dear friends and colleagues.' A warm smile, a slight embracing gesture of her hand. 'How can I thank you for sharing this special evening with me, and especially . . .' and here a brilliant smile at the Baron '. . . *mon cher ami*, Baron Triton, for making it possible.'

There was a swift acknowledgement between them and Nina lowered her eyes, took a small breath and continued. 'What I have to say may surprise a number of you. As I approached this tidemark, I began to think more deeply about my life and the future these past weeks, particularly outside the world of *Blaze*. I have been thinking back to the start of my journey to create this magazine. How I started working in magazines in Australia and was bold enough – and naive enough – to think that I could create a magazine of my own. One that I would like to read and so, hopefully, would others. And so *Blaze* was born and grew to become *Blaze USA*, which has now expanded to include many international editions.

'But rather than sitting back and basking in *Blaze*'s wonderful success – due to so many of you – I have become nostalgic, a little sad that perhaps my usefulness here is limited.'

She gave a slight smile at the ripple of disagreement in the atmosphere of the room. 'And I feel a little angry – well, frustrated – that I have crossed a kind of mythical border in society's mind. I find myself assessing my reactions and actions. As a result, questions present themselves to me. Have I performed well as a human being? Have I properly used my gifts and talents? Have I fulfilled my responsibilities and obligations? Are there still contributions that I can make?'

Her gaze swept the still and silent room. 'Yes, perhaps these are the expected reflections of a woman passing yet another milestone, but I realise I have asked myself these questions before this, and rarely answered them satisfactorily. It seems that when one enters one's seventh decade, one should bow out gracefully and settle into a luxurious retreat and enjoy life. My friends, let me tell you what I enjoy.' She paused for effect, noting every face was riveted to hers. 'I enjoy a challenge, the cut and thrust of daily jousting, internally and in the wide world that comes with running a magazine. In this age of electronic, digital and satellite communications, I still believe the printed word and images on paper will never become obsolete.'

There was a hearty outbreak of applause. Nina's voice was steady as she continued, 'There is still a huge need for independent publications to be read and digested at leisure, publications that can provide pleasure, entertainment, in-depth analysis and varying points of view. The magazine market has changed somewhat since I began my career as a seventeen-year-old on a small magazine called *In Home and Garden* in Sydney.' She smiled in acknowledgement of the understatement and the mood she had created among her audience.

Nina continued, 'Today, women from their forties to their nineties have much to offer. And, as such women come into their power, they should embrace it, and *use it*.' Her voice rose on the emphasis. 'We are the role models to adolescents, to younger women in and out of the workforce, to other older women. I don't like to pigeonhole anyone as old. I prefer to think of reaching a specific point in one's trajectory through life. Each point should be considered an opportunity to learn, to grow, to enjoy life. I don't want to be an adolescent again. Life was challenging enough then, but how much harder it is for them today. And how they see themselves is a result of how they see us.'

She looked down briefly, thinking of Lorraine, then continued, 'Therefore it is our responsibility as mature women, or as wise women elders, to show our young people that life is rich and that we can each bring about changes in the world. We must take control of our lives for everyone's benefit.' She paused and there was a ripple of polite applause, with most of the audience of older men and younger women wondering where Nina was heading with this speech, while the women of fifty and over clapped the loudest. Nina gave a broad smile, 'So . . . I am not retiring.'

Here Ali's head jerked up and she glanced around, seeing others were also surprised.

Nina lifted her glass of champagne as if to salute them. 'Yes, I intend to take an extended break to enjoy myself. I know I leave *Blaze* in very competent hands.'

Ali lifted her head expectantly, waiting for Nina to announce who would be taking over as editor. Instead Nina dropped her bombshell.

'I am moving back to Australia. We at Triton

Communications,' and here she beamed a smile down at the Baron, 'have decided to launch *Blaze Australia*, to resurrect the original magazine that I started all those years ago, perhaps a little too ahead of its time, before merging with Triton and moving it to New York. Sydney is ready now to become the latest international city of style and taste, to join New York, London, Paris, Rome, Tokyo . . . to have its own edition of *Blaze*. Yes, I'm going to do it all again!'

There was a united gasp, a tinkle of laughter and wild applause as the audience rose to its feet, muffling Nina's final, 'Thank you for coming.' She raised her champagne glass in a salute.

'Dear God, she's amazing!'

'She's mad! Who'd want the headache of starting from scratch at her age?'

'She loves the power.'

'Australia's too small. They'll blow their money in two years.'

The reactions buzzed around the candlelit tables as the Baron leaned over, kissed Nina on the cheek and clinked champagne glasses with her.

'As always, my dear, you stun, stimulate and cause a sensation. You never give up, do you?' he said. Then added softly, 'And nor will I, until you agree to marry me.'

Roberto Iano raised an eyebrow to Manny Golan beside him. 'Australia? That sounds like going backwards to me. Even if she grew up there, why on earth . . . ?'

'Australia produces and sells more magazines per capita than just about any other Western country,' said Ian Marcello, Nina's Australian lawyer who looked after her international affairs and had timed one of his frequent trips from Sydney to celebrate Nina's birthday. 'It's very competitive. Don't forget Rupert Murdoch cut his teeth there and he's moved production of some of the Fox movies down there. I hear more than a few actors are buying up real estate in Sydney.'

'It's supposed to be a combination of New York and LA, pretty sophisticated yet laid-back,' said Larissa. 'Ali, you'd know, you come from there too. How is it really?'

The others at the table stared at Ali in surprise. She looked and sounded like a total New Yorker. Only those at *Blaze*, or within the small world of publishing, knew of her Australian roots. While many successful Australians in New York trumpeted their origins, Ali didn't broadcast the fact.

'How would I know . . . *really?*' she said, looking slightly put out. 'I've been here eighteen years without any contact with Australia. I have no relatives there to speak of. I don't keep up with anything Australian. Ask me about Milan, London, Cannes.'

No one took up the offer.

Larissa changed the subject. 'Nina is very hands-on. I wonder how long a break she's taking.'

'She's earned a long one. I can't recall her ever taking much time off,' said Manny.

'With her money I'd gladly rest on my laurels and live it up in Europe,' declared Roberto. 'Trust Nina not to retire quietly with a large share portfolio and drift into the sunset,' he added, concealing his irritation at not knowing of this intriguing development before now.

'Days of the big golden parachute will soon be gone, Roberto,' Manny reminded him. A job for life was becoming a forgotten concept, even for pampered executives.

'Nina has guided *Blaze* for so long, that she and the magazine seem inseparable,' commented Roberto, glancing at Ian Marcello, hoping for a bit of inside information.

The dark-haired, twinkle-eyed lawyer merely smiled.

Nina was more than another client on his impressive list. They were friends who trusted, liked and respected each other. If she ever had a doubt about a decision, she dined with Ian who loved fine food and wine. At the end of an enjoyable meal, Nina came away satisfied in every sense. Ian's advice, questioning and analysis, sandwiched between courses, always proved invaluable.

Larissa looked at Ali and wondered what was going through her mind. With Lorraine sadly out of the picture, the path was clear for Ali to intensify her campaign for the editorship, a position Larissa suspected Ali had been quietly lobbying for in recent months. Larissa didn't have the ruthless dedication to a career that drove Ali. Probably because she had a stable personal life with a man she loved, whereas Ali – as far as anyone knew – was very single. And very single-minded. Ali was thinking rapidly. If Nina stayed out of New York long enough, she could entrench herself with senior management and implement her ideas. Already Ali was assuming her appointment as the next editor of *Blaze USA*.

She glanced at Manny and the three other vice-presidents of the Triton company who were sitting at the same table. That was where the power was concentrated. She hadn't worked her butt off as deputy editor to impress Lorraine Bannister or Nina Jansous. Ali had slaved hard and made sure she'd been noticed by the male hierarchy . . . Even if it sometimes meant resorting to sexual innuendo and low-cut tops that showed her bra-less, small, pointed breasts. They controlled the money. And whoever controlled the money had the power. They ran the company. While Nina had powerful input, it was always the dollar that underscored the big decisions.

Nina was certainly no figurehead, but since Triton had recently gone public, and although she held substantial A-list shares, she had less say in running the corporate flagship. Now the company had to answer to shareholders, meet the responsibilities and obligations of a public company, be even more disciplined over profit margins, and watch out for possible takeovers.

Manny reached into his pocket for a cigar, but it was then he remembered his wife had removed the temptation as the invitation had politely requested they refrain from smoking. He picked up his brandy and spun the goblet between his pudgy hands. 'So what do you make of this, Roberto? She's not doing it for money. In fact, they could blow a helluva pile. The Baron must have agreed to the idea. Is he indulging Nina or does he want to make money? If Triton is backing this, he must think she can pull it off.'

Roberto agreed. 'Though why would a woman at her stage in life, with so much achieved, want to start over again? A helluva risk. People remember the failures, not the successes. Why is she bothering?'

'The challenge,' chimed in Larissa. 'It's fantastic to think that when you turn sixty you could be starting a whole new life.' She gave the two executives a wide-eyed look. 'What are you both going to do when you turn sixty?'

Neither man wanted to answer. Manny changed the subject. 'There's always politics, eh Roberto? In fact, I wondered whether Nina may be considering running for something, or working on someone's campaign in the near future.'

'Nina has always been a political animal,' agreed Roberto. 'Though she's never let her views interfere with her job as far as I can tell. Tempting when she wields so much power.'

'Yeah, it always amazes me that a magazine has such political influence. I mean *Blaze* isn't the *Washington Post*.'

'Do you read it?' asked Roberto with a grin.

'*Blaze*? Yeah. But then it's part of the job,' confessed Manny. He quickly turned to Ali and Larissa, 'Not that I don't enjoy it, of course.'

The girls rolled their eyes.

'I bet you don't read everything Triton publishes,' said Roberto.

'You mean other than the financial reports?' Manny downed his brandy. 'Yeah, I find the mag interesting. Gives me a few controversies to debate with my sons who think they know everything now they're costing me private college fees. Mind you, I don't need to know about women's circumcision in Eritrea.'

Larissa was about to argue the point, but Ali kicked her under the table indicating there was no need to antagonise the executives.

TAKE THREE...

The call Ali was waiting for came two days later.

She smoothed her hair, added another coat of lip gloss, waved the atomiser of Georgio around her head and went to the bathroom.

Then she walked calmly down the hall to Nina's office.

Nina was relaxed, cool and somewhat preoccupied with a field of paper, which unnerved Ali. Nina waved at the sofa and Ali sat down feeling slightly nervous, but she managed to rearrange her face into what she hoped was an expression of studied nonchalance.

Nina closed the folder then moved to the sofa opposite Ali. She gave a half-smile. 'You might remember our last conversation.' Ali nodded slightly. 'We were not to know the tragic events that would unfold. Fate has a strange way of stepping in at times. However, that is not changing any of my plans.'

Ali said nothing, but her stomach began twisting. Surely, without Lorraine, she had to be appointed the new editor.

'I have been reassessing my life and, as I said at the dinner, I have been thinking about how I want to spend the next few years,' began Nina.

It sounded so calm, so reasoned, belying Nina's sleepless nights, the anguish of losing her mother, her fear of being alone in old age. In the few months since Clara had peacefully died, Nina had begun to seriously rethink her life. No ripple showed on the outside to indicate her inner turmoil. Most people would have been shocked to think that the celebrated, exquisite Nina Jansous was suffering insecurities, confusion and melancholy. She had decided to plunge ahead with the resurrecting of the Australian edition of *Blaze*. And to try to bring a level of coherence to the mental flashbacks that plagued her. She knew they were linked to her growing up in Croatia. Secretly she had made a tentative plan. But first she needed time in Australia, not just to settle in the staff and infrastructure for the first edition, but also to be clear in her mind why she was feeling the way she was. Ali was tempted to fidget, but kept motionless. What had Nina's life plan to do with her, here, now? Get on with it, Nina, she urged silently.

'As you now know, I am temporarily easing out of *Blaze* here in the US – though it's been a wonderful and fruitful relationship. Since the company went public, my role has not been so hands-on and, I have to say I miss it. So, after discussions with Baron Triton and the other members of the board, we have agreed to start a new *Blaze* – in Australia.'

'So you mentioned the other night,' said Ali, trying to calm her impatience.

'It may seem a strange move in some people's eyes, but it's what I want to do. After all, it was where *Blaze* started and, now that the magazine is so highly regarded internationally, it is not as if we're faced with launching an unknown name into a competitive field.'

Ali shifted and recrossed her legs. She really was not interested in Nina's plans. What about her future? Sensing her impatience, Nina leaned forward slightly.

'It will have to be an excellent magazine to live up to the *Blaze* standard. Like the other international editions, *Blaze Australia* will carry a number of features from *Blaze USA*, which will always remain the flagship magazine, but it will also have an identity of its own, purely Australian. It will have the opportunity to be very contemporary – technologically and creatively – so I want the best people in there. There will be a lot of reorganising to create the slick and classy magazine I envision will reflect the character of this young yet sophisticated country.'

'Are you starting from scratch or taking over an existing magazine?' asked Ali, feeling that she needed to show at least a bit of interest.

'I have bought out an independent Australian magazine started by a woman who was backed by a financier, apparently with very deep pockets. She tried to do what I had done with *Blaze* decades ago. Unfortunately for her, it didn't work.'

'I imagine it's difficult to survive without being part of an . . . empire,' finished Ali, after searching momentarily for the right word.

'That's right. Most Australian magazines have traditionally been run by Packer or Murdoch. News Corp dominates the newspaper industry, but they have also started to move into the magazine market. With Triton's backing, I intend *Blaze* to target a unique quality market in Australia, as it has in other countries.'

Ali recalled Nina telling her when she first started working for *Blaze* that she'd used her own money inherited from her late husband to start her magazine. It was one of the early lessons Ali had learned and filed away – money equals power.

Nina continued, 'So, my best people must be right up there. Ali, I'm asking you to be the founding editor of *Blaze Australia*. You are ready to take on what will be a formidable job . . .'

'Australia! An editor in Australia!' Ali couldn't stop the exclamation that exploded from her.

Nina interpreted her stunned response as surprise and didn't appear to hear the negative shock that registered in Ali's voice. 'The Triton board has moved quickly to accept the recommendation of Irene da Costa as editor of *Blaze* here in the US following Lorraine's tragic death. This is one of the cream jobs in publishing. Naturally, Irene has accepted.'

It took a minute for the fact to register that someone else had already been appointed editor of *Blaze* in New York. Ali fumbled to make a sensible comment while her mind was spinning. 'Irene's leaving *Bazaar*?' Ali knew the glamorous da Costa. 'She must be nearing forty. Is she up on today's issues and tastes?' asked Ali with a hard edge to her voice.

'If she isn't, she'll hire the right people who are. I should tell you that she has made it clear who she intends to appoint as her deputy, although that information is confidential at this stage.'

Ali was shocked. Not only had her long-craved ambition to become editor of *Blaze USA* been thwarted, she had also been supplanted in her role as deputy editor of *Blaze*. And what was just as frightening to her, as a woman who prided herself on being on top of what was happening in the executive suites above, she had known nothing of these manoeuvres that now threatened her entire career.

Nina continued. 'Ali, being an editor is more than keeping up with trends. With *Blaze* you inherit the mantle of a successful institution with profit expectations.

The administrative role is as powerful as the editorial. This will apply equally with the new Australian *Blaze*. I believe you are up to this – that is, if you want to take it on?'

'I was hoping to make my mark in New York,' said Ali tensely.

'And you have. Which is why you have been chosen. Your Australian background will be useful too.'

'I'm totally out of touch with what's happening there!' said Ali vehemently, wondering if by some miracle she could at least hold on to the deputy editor's job in New York, if da Costa hadn't yet signed on someone else.

'I would imagine you'll be on top of things in Australia very quickly,' said Nina smoothly. 'Starting up *Blaze* in Sydney will certainly put you on the map.'

'Big fish in a small pond, eh?' Ali managed a weak smile. 'Of course I'm very flattered, Nina. It's just not what I expected . . .'

'Ali, I am hoping to announce your promotion as soon as possible, before the announcement of Irene and her deputy on Friday. But if you want to think this over, please do. Keep in mind that *Blaze* is the jewel of one of the biggest media empires in the world. Not many people as young as you have the opportunity to be part of something new and exciting within such an organisation. Make it work in Australia and you'll write your ticket to the world.'

'And how long would that be?' Ali was still in shock. And furious, Nina was so out of touch. Most of the new magazine editors nowadays were barely thirty. Nina was still acting as if you had to wait for the old birds to drop off the perch before you could move up a notch. It didn't work that way any more. The strongest of the young birds pushed the mother and siblings out of the nest these days. Cuckoo-land ruled Nina, she thought. When was Nina going to recognise she couldn't keep hanging on to her position? Maybe she was feeling insecure and going back to Australia for someone in her position was a pretty safe option. God, Australia. What a nightmare.

Nina smiled. 'Twelve-month contract, renewable for another twelve months. You can thrash out the details with Roberto. However, once in Australia you will be answerable to me as editor-in-chief.'

'Nina, no offence, but just how much say would I have?' asked Ali. 'If I am to grow into the company and write my own ticket, I would need to make my own decisions for the magazine. And the move would be expensive for me.' A sinking feeling of resignation that she had no option began to surface in Ali. Therefore she'd better make the most of it.

'I agree. You know I don't like to interfere with my editors. I understand editors need to establish their own authority. I'm going out next week to finalise details of the new offices and to talk to existing staff. Part of the deal was retaining the main core of workers. However, in addition to yourself, I will be taking Manny Golan to train a new financial vice-president. I also want a deputy editor that we know is capable and creative. I haven't raised it yet, but I would like that person to be Larissa. I know there are terrific people in Australia, but *Blaze* has a certain ethos and a look that you both understand. Once you are installed as editor, and once the first edition is ready to go to press, I'm off to Europe for three months or so and you'll be on your own. You know I've always believed an editor should edit a magazine, not the editor-in-chief. Those three months will be your baptism.'

Ali looked out the window, past the round table Nina used as a desk. A whirlwind of feelings and thoughts were rushing through her. But her face showed no emotion.

'Think about it, Ali. If there is a problem, money . . . your personal life . . .'

Nina let the sentence hang. As far as she was aware, Ali was very unattached. But perhaps this was not the case. She was frankly surprised Ali had not leapt at the job offer. 'Should you accept, I will leave it up to you to persuade Larissa to come on board as your deputy. Offer her a twelve-month contract to start. She probably won't agree to leave her life in New York longer than that. I think it will be an exciting adventure for everyone.'

Nina and the Baron, arms linked, walked slowly around Central Park across from Fifth Avenue.

'I will miss you, dearest Nina.'

'I'll be back here regularly. Thank you for allowing me to keep the company penthouse. I hope you will come to Australia and see me, as well as keep a paternal eye on our new *Blaze*.'

'You know I love Sydney. But I was thinking you might enjoy sharing your holiday in Europe?' He gave her an affectionate look with the question.

Nina removed her arm and ran her fingers through her hair, adjusting her sunglasses. 'Oscar, we've been through this, so many times . . .' She couldn't explain to him how she really felt. That this time in Europe wasn't just a . . . vacation.

'The situation is different now.' The Baron was referring to the recent death of his wife, who had long been confined to a private hospital with a lingering illness.

'No it's not,' she said with gentle insistence. 'We've never been lovers. Just because we won't have such a close working relationship doesn't change anything. I value and treasure our friendship. I worry that would change. I am so fond of you. And I know you are of me. Please, let's leave things as they are.' Then, seeing his crushed expression, she added, 'For the moment.'

Nina stood in her now empty office at *Blaze*. She looked out at the New York landscape that had been familiar for so many years. The view across the park to the buildings on the East Side, the rumble of the traffic below on Fifth Avenue, the gleam of the Hudson where boats churned its sludgy surface. Her office looked so bare, just a few cartons left from the packers. A painting she'd chosen – an Aboriginal painting from the Yolngu of north-east Arnhem Land – and a favourite camphorwood chair, also from Australia, were all that remained. They would be moved to her apartment to vacate what would now be Irene da Costa's office, with her deputy moving into the former editor's office.

This building had accommodated Nina's growth from a nervous young publisher to what the press had called 'the dynamic doyenne of US magazine media'. In an interview with a columnist of the *New York Gazette*, she had spoken positively and bravely of the new challenge facing her. But was it what she really wanted? Or was it just a frightened grasp for something to fill the yawning gap in her life? No husband, no children. And, with her mother dying recently, no family. What counted more in life as one entered these golden years . . . the joy of family or career success? And what of the clamour of those faraway memories? They were becoming more insistent.

Memories of her late husband, Doctor Paul Jansous, touched her at this moment. His death more than a quarter of a century ago had turned her life upside down. Yet it was thanks to him she had been able to push through her grief by being utterly focused on her work and plunging into a big challenge.

Her quiet husband, dedicated to his medical work, had totally shocked her when his will revealed a huge amount of money that she hadn't known existed. Shrewd investments and the sale to a pharmaceutical company of the interest in his fertility treatment had bolstered his already immense family wealth. And so Nina had found herself in a bewildering situation. She was beautiful, in her thirties and richly single, and suddenly at the top of the list of the most eligible women in Australia.

Against the advice of her bank manager – he'd wanted her to keep her fortune invested and be given the right to manage it – she'd decided to plunge the money into her own magazine. She'd moved carefully and thoroughly, seeking sound advice from business people she trusted with solid track records of their own. While it was a gamble – 'an indulgence' in a number of people's eyes – she'd never wavered in her belief that she knew what she was doing. The timing was right, she'd picked the ideal people to help her and she'd simply refused to entertain the thought she would not be successful. The aspects that had attracted and interested her drew her to the conclusion that she should run her own magazine.

Clara had been utterly supportive. 'Darling, we came here with nothing but a beautiful piece of jewellery from your grandmother. I never had to sell it, though I came close. But we managed. If you lose everything, you have had the satisfaction of trying to snatch a star, so here, I give you now the pin. I think of it as our good fortune, a lucky pin. As your Grandmother Bubacic wished. You might never need it, but if you do, it is yours to sell.' And, despite Nina's protests, Clara had retrieved from the safe the exquisite ruby, sapphire and diamond brooch, in the shape of a delicate dragonfly, and given it to a teary Nina with a hug.

But Clara had refused to answer Nina's questions, as she always had, about the details of their life in Zagreb. 'One day, darling, one day when the time is right you will go back there and then I will tell you why.'

Within two years Nina's magazine, which she'd titled *Blaze*, had been embraced by readers and advertisers and had become so successful it was the target of several buy-out offers. She'd chosen a tiny dragonfly as the logo for the magazine and it perched atop the masthead, a reminder of her grandmother and mother. Nina always wore the diamond dragonfly pin on special occasions and it had become her trademark. It was a happy marketing accident as well. Research surveys had shown that the picture of a dragonfly was instantly associated with *Blaze* and Nina. Despite the lucrative offers, Nina had kept control and she'd driven the magazine forward to undreamed success. Then she'd sat down to reassess her life.

She was alone. She had her mother and a small circle of close friends, but there was no constant lover. A few cautious and discreet affairs, yes, but the only passion in her life was her work. She had scarcely had a break from the office since the launch of *Blaze* – except for one weekend with her sales manager and a client on the Great Barrier Reef.

And it was while she was on the small up-market island off the tip of the Australian coast that she'd received a message to phone her office. Fearing a problem with Clara, she'd called in and was quickly reassured her mother was fine. But Baron Oscar Von Triton was trying to reach her. 'He's in Brussels,' her secretary, sounding impressed, told her. 'He's the head of Triton Communications and he's very insistent you talk to him.'

'It can't be urgent enough to interrupt my weekend.

I will be back in Sydney on Monday, ask him to call me then.'

The Baron hadn't phoned. He'd walked into her office instead, charming, handsome and all business.

'Congratulations on what you've done with *Blaze*, Madame Jansous. It is an outstanding publication.'

'I'm glad you like it.' Nina was trying not to be swayed by either the man or what he represented.

'I like it so much, I'd like to buy it.'

Nina had burst out laughing. 'Thank you. But *Blaze* is not for sale.'

The Baron had been unfazed and laid before her a plan where *Blaze* could become part of his international media empire, pointing out, 'A company like yours could, after time, find shares spread in many hands and the company becomes vulnerable to a takeover or being split up due to unfriendly attacks.'

Nina nodded. 'I'm aware of that. It's one reason I've never wanted to go public. I'm flattered, of course, though there is a streak of self-preservation in me which asks – are you planning on moving into this part of the world and what better way to dispense with any opposition than buying it and burying it?'

'I would prefer to own *Blaze* than attempt to try to challenge, recreate or kill it,' he replied.

Nina was frank. 'You have caught me unawares. I am still deeply involved in the magazine. I'm not a figurehead, what would I do with myself? Thank you for the offer. But *Blaze* and I are welded together, I'm afraid.'

'There would always be an essential role for you,' said the Baron quickly. 'Think it over at least. I am staying here two days. You were my main reason for this trip, but while I'm here I plan to investigate the media scene more closely.'

'Shopping?' asked Nina with a smile.

'My shopping list, as you put it, has only one title on it.'

Nina had not dismissed the offer. If there was one publishing conglomerate she had respect for, it was the low-key Baron's group of media concerns. She had followed his trail of acquisitions over the years, just as she had taken an interest in the activities of all the major players. Watching Rupert Murdoch's onslaught into the northern hemisphere, she had been pleased to see a European also tackling the American market. She'd run a check on the full extent of Triton, gathering every scrap of information that was publicly available, and realised Triton's American mastheads lacked a quality magazine like *Blaze*. Why would he want to break into such a small market as Australia with one magazine?

Nina had rung Ian Marcello, the brilliant young lawyer who advised her on financial as well as legal matters.

'Ian, how quickly can we run a check and find out the fiscals on Triton Communications?'

'Are we talking due diligence or responding to a take-over offer? Are you thinking of taking a bite out of one of the big guys? You're not bored by any chance?'

'Very shrewd of you. I am heading towards forty. *Blaze* is well established. I hadn't any thoughts of moving on or making any dramatic changes, but seeing as a serious and considerable opportunity has presented itself, I feel I should at least investigate the ramifications. Perhaps it's time I moved to the next level.'

Ian surmised immediately what had transpired. 'I heard the Baron was here, the top end of town players are interested. There's talk he might look at a few of the new broadcasting licences. And there are rumours of another TV licence, which couldn't go to a foreigner, though he could inject a lot of capital. I haven't heard he's looking for print media.'

'That's because the only publication worth buying, that isn't locked into a large network, is *Blaze*. And I've always made it clear I would never sell.'

'With just reason,' Ian had reminded her. 'Though there's a time to reassess, move forward or make changes in the direction of every company. In a few years you should be in a very different position from where you are now.'

'You know what I'm thinking?'

'Nina, I wouldn't try to second-guess you. You've surprised me often enough over the years. I'm here to advise you, lend an ear, be a friend. I know you always listen to my advice, but you still do what you want.'

'You wouldn't let me do anything foolish, Ian. We always seem to come to the same decisions. What I'm thinking is a partnership with Triton.'

The lawyer smiled to himself. God, she was bright. It was one of the reasons he so enjoyed representing Nina. He also liked and respected her as a good friend. 'Could be costly. You could become lost, rolled over. It's a big outfit.'

'Not with you looking after my interests. I said I'd call him back.'

The lawyer sighed. 'Gawd, Nina. I'll start digging around. I'll call your accountant. Come over for a working lunch in my boardroom tomorrow.'

That was the beauty of being a private company. Nina could make these decisions quickly without facing a board or shareholders. She had paid off her bank loan and was well ahead financially. Sinking her money into the magazine and buying an old building in the inner city had paid off. She'd sold the building a year ago for a large profit and now leased office space. Instinct, as well as Ian and the accountant's advice, told her not to commit herself to buying another building.

When the Baron had phoned and asked if she'd thought about his offer, Nina countered with, 'Indeed. In fact, I have a proposition to put to you!'

Baron Oscar Von Triton had done his homework on Nina Jansous – she was as smart and shrewd as she was charming and beautiful. But what attracted him most was Nina's flair and style. She did everything in a manner that set her apart. It was more than taste and class, it was a gift you were born with for seeing things differently, inventive thinking, a creative yet pragmatic mind. Given scope and backing, she could conquer the world.

With Ian at her side, Nina laid out what she saw as a way forward, considering she would not sell *Blaze* outright. She suggested a partnership with the Baron in taking *Blaze* to the biggest marketplace, the US. She would run the magazine and they would co-own it, splitting costs and profit. Each brought to the table their own assets. Triton had the infrastructure and a solid power base. Nina would make *Blaze* into the flagship magazine of the Triton empire, marketing it worldwide, until they were ready for the world's major cities of style – Paris, Rome, London – to each have its own edition.

She would edit the magazine as well as be the figurehead who created it. She would close the Australian *Blaze*, and pay out her staff generously, doing all she could to help find new positions for them. It was time for her little dragonfly to dance on the world stage. And one day, she knew, the new *Blaze* would come home to launch its own Australian edition.

Alone in the New York office, Nina glanced again at the pile of correspondence on her table. Handwritten notes, email printouts, the cards – from well-wishers outside the company and, the most special, from her *Blaze* staff around the world. This was her family. Soon she would have the joys, the pain, the problems, the laughter and tears of rearing a new child, a new magazine with new staff in Australia. It would link her to the wonderful years of her own childhood, to the country that had sheltered her mother and given them both security and happiness in those critical and difficult postwar years. She owed Australia. Her mother may have been born and raised in Eastern Europe, but it was Australia that had given mother and child their belonging and a future.

Ali had decided to 'sleep on' Nina's offer, though sleep was elusive. She tossed and kicked the tangled sheets, a few tears of anger and disappointment slipping onto the pillow. She knew Nina was right, that she should stay in the Triton stable, but she'd wanted the New York editorship so badly. New York was the peak of publishing. Australia, in comparison, was a backwater. Once she'd established herself in New York, Ali figured she'd left Australia behind. No matter how Nina dressed up the offer, to Ali's mind it was an agonising choice – the editor's chair in the small pond of Australia, a title with no real power in *Blaze USA*, or find another job in American publishing.

Forcing herself to be practical, Ali knew that being editor of a major publication, even in Australia, was the right way to go. Nina's words came back to her about writing her ticket to the world. Being part of a major corporation, being appointed editor with the responsibility of starting up a new magazine while not yet thirty years old, was a challenge and a compliment. If she made it work, who knew what opportunities might present themselves? These factors made up the plus side.

But in Ali's heart there lurked an unspoken fear. No one, not even Nina, could imagine what she would have to confront by returning to Australia. She'd believed the past was behind her; the nightmares stifled, her secret safe. But for how long would it remain so if she returned to the country of her childhood as a high-profile achiever? This was supposed to be a big career move. If only Nina realised, sending Ali back to Australia could crumple the tightly locked mask she showed the world.

TAKE FOUR...

Sydney, 2000

Manny Golan sniffed the red wine appreciatively as his lunch was put before him. 'Promising,' he conceded. 'And the food is beautifully presented, but what is it?' He raised an eyebrow at the waitress.

'Roast emu fillet, wild pear wrapped in a crispy crepe with munthari berry and apple,' said the waitress with a smile.

Steve Vickers, managing director of Trends Advertising Agency explained to the bemused New Yorker, 'Edna's Table is one of Sydney's top restaurants that's made a name for itself with Australian native cuisine. It used to be known as bush tucker, but this is a far cry from witchetty grubs and a goanna thrown on the hot coals.' He lifted his glass, '*Bon appétit*, welcome to Sydney.'

'Thanks. I really do feel I'm on the other side of the world.' Manny gingerly tasted his meal, then nodded in satisfaction. The two men talked food and dining experiences until the main course was cleared and their wine glasses refilled. Manny glanced around, 'I suppose a cigar is out of the question?' But he knew the answer to that one, so he broke off a piece of bread and chewed it instead of his cigar. 'Let's talk business. Nina's brought me out for a couple of months to set up the financial structure, break in the new financial controller and drum up business. That's where you come in. We want the big boys to advertise with us. We have a head start as Nina is pals with most of the multinationals. We intend *Blaze Australia* to be as successful as the others. To do that, in a small country like this, we have to dominate the readership – male and female. We're printing one million for Australia, New Zealand and the South Pacific islands to start. And we'll be injecting enough resources into the marketing of *Blaze* to make every one of those one million copies sell. As Nina has said, this is not just a new magazine. It's a revolution in publishing standards for Australia.'

Steve let out a low whistle in an expulsion of breath. 'That's more than a sizeable chunk in this crowded marketplace. Nina might be able to pull in favours to start with, but you'll have to deliver those circulation figures to keep attracting the cream of the big accounts.'

'Chicken or the egg, eh?' grinned Manny. 'Listen, you tell your account executives they are buying into Triton, one of the slickest, biggest media organisations in the world. Now, instead of having to buy the New York edition in Sydney, they'll have their own baby, the sophisticated sister of the biggest magazine in the world. This baby'll be carrying enough material from the New York edition to keep the old readers happy, but she'll also be tackling the top local stories.'

'I take your point. There's an established readership already buying the US edition of *Blaze*. If your research is right, this new one should have a lot of appeal.'

'Cost less too. The infrastructure is in place,' added Manny.

'So let's go over your profile of the readers,' said Steve making notes in a small notebook.

'Smart women, clever men . . . women who want to be on top of more intelligent information than fitness and fashion, though they will have that too, and men whose interests stretch past sport,' said Manny quickly.

'It's not going to evolve into yet another classy version of a women's magazine?'

'No way. This country is full of women's magazines that you and I wouldn't pick up. Nor would our wives. To quote the august David Ogilvy, the consumer ain't a moron, she's your wife.'

'I'm gay,' smiled Steve.

'So what. Partner then. Who decides who buys what at your house?'

'He does.'

'So he'll buy *Blaze*. Look at *Vanity Fair*, they do a cover story on Armani, his lifestyle, his clothes, his house, then go to the Balkans with the UN ambassador and explore the conflicts there. Both subjects are tackled in depth. Moving on, here is the list of the top companies, and their products, we want to advertise with us. Exclusively in *Blaze*. In return, we're going to offer them one helluva international deal.'

Steve took a deep gulp of his wine. 'This could create a storm. You're essentially asking us as an agency to take the cream of advertising revenue available out of the other magazines, and TV too, and plonk it all in *Blaze*.'

'You got it.' Manny was unperturbed. 'We'll be briefing you on the deal before we make the presentation to your clients next week, then we'll go on to the other agencies. Let's just say, for now, the benefits to your clients will be dynamite internationally.'

'Define intelligent women, smart men for me.'

'Hard to find,' grinned Manny. 'Nah, just joking.'

'I meant demographically . . . age?'

'You'll find Ali Gruber, the editor, will go for the big-spending thirties.'

'Ah, the VAs, SAs and YOs,' said Steve. Then seeing Manny's blank expression explained, 'Visible Achievers, Socially Aware and Young Optimists.'

'Yeah. Nina has been saying for a while that women over fifty are the big market, but *Blaze*'s demographics are spread across the board, so we're happy with thirties as the median target. Male, female, gay, whatever, so long as they have smarts and money.'

'They're the advertisers' top targets,' said Steve.

'So tell your account execs to go get 'em.' Manny leaned back eyeing the menu, then asked the waitress, 'You got decaf coffee? Real beans, not berries from some Aborigine tree?'

'Certainly, sir. Would you like to try one of our fine ports or liqueurs?'

'Normally, yes. But I like this red, I'll take another glass of that.'

'It's Penfolds Grange, sir, our most famous wine.'

Steve ordered another bottle of the expensive classic, knowing this lunch would be taken out of the huge account the agency had just landed. As well as the pleasing prospect of selling advertising space in the new *Blaze* to its top clients, Trends had only yesterday signed with Manny Golan to become the agency behind the multi-million dollar campaign to launch *Blaze* in Sydney. The offices of *Blaze Australia* were close to the city in a stylish development at east Darling Harbour. Overlooking the sparkling waters, they were near the Cockle Bay wharf development and a favoured waterfront pub in Sussex Street, as well as being close to Chinatown and its restaurants.

Nina spent hours with Manny Golan poring over the budgets. She loved his approach to the numbers game.

'Money makes the world go round, Nina. Without money to spend, you ain't got no magazine. Money is the power. You gotta spend big to make big.'

Nina was used to his 'big' talk. She knew he could also quibble over where twenty dollars might have been wasted. 'We have to deliver a perfect product, Manny.'

'Hell, Nina, you've done it often enough. You started out here and built an amazing magazine, which you moved to New York and bowled 'em over. Then you spread it round the world. You got the formula and the magic touch, honey.'

Nina smiled inwardly at Manny treating a sixty-year-old woman, who was his boss, like a junior girl. 'Times change, Manny. What worked yesterday mightn't work in this new millennium. That's why I want you here to make sure we start off with a solid base financially, but also to keep an eye on everyone. I'm betting my whole reputation on Ali Gruber injecting young ideas into this edition, to reflect the precocious attitude of this country. I'll act as deputy until Larissa arrives. As soon as we have the first edition ready for press, I'm giving her complete editorial freedom and I'm off to Europe.' It was a light remark that meant little to Manny, but a small fissure of steam from Nina's inner volcano carried her words into the world.

'So you're not letting Ali do the first issue on her own? Wise move.'

'She will be the editor and make the decisions. I can't relinquish total control straight off the bat,' admitted Nina with a slight smile. 'Besides, I know what pitfalls there can be in setting up a new publication. After that, she's on her own. And I'm not going away forever . . . three, maybe four months. I've told Ali she will handle the media launch. It's important that she is the focus of this new magazine. And the Baron will be there to introduce her. I'll hardly be missed.'

'I doubt that.' Manny turned his attention to the spreadsheets in front of him. 'Okay, let's look at what we're spending where.'

Nina was welcomed back into the media fray in Australia with mixed reactions – speculation, suspicion, scepticism and sarcasm.

Nina shrugged it off and followed up on her plans that had been quietly moving along. Triton had bought out an independent magazine called *Carina*, started by Carina Brett-Moir, a multimedia identity who saw herself as a latter-day Nina Jansous. The magazine had been launched three years ago with a lot of publicity, branding itself as the alternative working woman's magazine with the latest hip styles and trends. Carina was identified with the magazine, but the cult of personality was to become more of a handicap than an asset. Despite her media appearances and work for charities, her first night attendances, her radio show, and the fact she was written about flatteringly in friendly publications, women still didn't buy the magazine. Advertisers, who had been initially responsive to her apparently healthy financial backing, soon withdrew their support and, with dwindling advertising revenue, the magazine was in trouble. Carina Brett-Moir had quietly searched the international market for more backers. When none was prepared to put money into a sinking enterprise, she'd accepted Triton's offer of a buy-out.

The staff at *Carina* magazine had not been told of the 'new arrangements' until the deal with Nina and Triton had been signed. When informed the magazine would resurface in a new guise and that the bulk of the staff would stay on the payroll for a minimum of six months as part of the sale, there was relief. Knowing that Triton was the buyer also meant they could feel relatively secure as part of an internationally successful corporation.

Nina had ordered modest but stylish changes to the interior design of the now defunct *Carina's* offices, but she'd put her main effort into technology. The computer systems she'd installed were the best available and sleek new PCs hummed on the soft blue desktops. TV monitors, tuned to CNN and Bloomberg News, as well as the local channels, were strategically placed for monitoring the 'happening' stories. In the new Syndications Centre, computer screens revealed the latest purchases of top international stories from the *Blaze* dealers around the globe. *Blaze* was a monthly magazine, but Nina had always held the news pages open until the last minute. Similarly, if someone died and was featured in a story, it would have to be pulled overnight. Like most magazine editors, Nina would make sure they had stories in reserve that wouldn't date and could be dropped in at a moment's notice. And the obituary file on famous people was always ready to go to press when the inevitable occurred.

Wanting technology that would give her the shortest print time, Nina had signed a contract with Pacific Magazine Publications to print the magazine from electronically transmitted page layouts. Once received by Pacific, the pages would be converted directly to plates for the printing presses. She appointed a new production manager and instructed him that where possible *Blaze* was to be environmentally friendly, even down to using soya inks on paper produced from plantation loppings and recycled paper. She'd negotiated a three-year fixed price for paper. PMP had acquired the nation's largest distributor, and they would freight her magazines into sales outlets around the country.

Nina's first 'social' function gathered together the existing staff of the new *Blaze* for drinks and hors d'oeuvres after work.

The staff eyed the lavish spread of finger food, quality wines and fresh juices, wondering if this were a softening up 'last supper' before the axe fell. There had been rumours in the gossipy media world that Nina would bring in staff from the US. The long-time editor of *Carina*, Dorothy Power, who had worked under Carina Brett-Moir – a demanding editor-in-chief and publisher – had already announced her retirement. This was interpreted in Sydney's gossip columns as having been gently pushed.

However Dorothy, at fifty-nine, was only too happy to retire with a substantial package and avoid the upheaval associated with yet another magazine launch. Nina had called Dorothy to make sure she was going to be at this 'little function' so they could wish her well in her new life.

'New life?' Dorothy had exclaimed to her long-serving secretary, Belinda Gordon. 'I'm not going anywhere. I plan to potter in the garden, go to lunch, spend time with my grandkids, drag Charlie around the wine country. All the things I haven't been able to do with a full-time job.'

'So that's a new life,' said Belinda. 'Carina doesn't have a family like you do. That's why she headed to London the minute the cheque was in the bank. She's not ready to step out of magazines. Or the limelight.'

'I think Nina Jansous sees a new life as taking on a gung-ho career again. That's for the birds. Especially at sixty,' replied Dorothy, wondering how Nina managed to look the way she did. Money and America she supposed. Not that Nina appeared to have had cosmetic surgery – she just radiated youthful energy. Her health and looks must be in her genes, Dorothy decided.

74

Nina approached the microphone and a hush fell over the restaurant.

'Good evening, everyone. I'm Nina Jansous. I'm so happy to be here and I thank you for coming.'

'Royal decree, wasn't it?' whispered Fran Hirshcombe, the promotions director, to no one in particular. 'It'd be like being late for your own execution.'

'I'm sure each of you has been speculating about what I'm going to say this evening. I imagine there is no small amount of tension in the ranks, and that there's been a lot of speculation over the past few days with appropriate bitter-sweet jokes and smart satire.' She spoke with a lightness in her voice and the hint of a smile that immediately lowered the emotional temperature. Then she added with a grin, 'I would dearly like to hear a few of the more clever jokes that the changeover fertilised, and perhaps they will filter through over the next few days.'

Surely she couldn't smile like that and then tell them they were out on their ears? Everyone was nervous. Who might be buried along with the *Carina* masthead?

'With the acquisition of *Carina* there will be changes. And that is not to demean the achievements of this magazine, which has been superbly led by Dorothy Power. Dorothy, as you know, has decided to retire after a very successful career in journalism, both here and in the UK, to pursue other interests. Dorothy, we wish you much happiness and success in your new life.' Nina gestured to Dorothy who, with a slight bow of her head, acknowledged another burst of clapping from her staff. Suddenly the retiring editor felt close to tears and hoped Nina wouldn't ask her to speak. While she hadn't made radical changes to *Carina* in its brief life, she had hoped the magazine would take off in a big way. But sales had never reached Carina's levels of hype. And Dorothy was pragmatic enough to know there would not be a place for her at the helm of a magazine like *Blaze*. Nina was bringing in her own top people. Dorothy was satisfied that she could retire with a respectable track record.

Nina continued, 'Our magazine will aim at a broader and younger demographic. The details will be made public at a media event in a few weeks. It will be the duty of the new editor to introduce herself to Australia as well as to introduce the Australian edition of *Blaze*. I have appointed an editor who will come from *Blaze USA*, but . . .' she held up a finger at the murmur from the audience, 'she is Australian and is looking forward to coming home to begin this exciting new venture of which you will all be a part. Once the first issue is put to bed, I will be taking a temporary leave of absence. I'm due for a long holiday and I would like your new editor to settle in without me looking over her shoulder. Finally, I'd just like to say to those of you I don't know well, I'm looking forward to getting to know you and hearing your ideas and comments.'

By now the atmosphere was relaxed, a communal sigh of relief running round the room. Their jobs were safe – for the moment – and thankfully the new editor was Australian. She'd be on their wavelength.

Nina gave a slight smile. 'I hope you feel as I do, that this is an exciting challenge and that we have the opportunity to start afresh, to build a new era and make a significant contribution to the rich heritage of magazine publishing in this country. I look forward to your support and enthusiasm. Thank you.'

'I haven't heard the dramas of producing a magazine described as a rich heritage before,' murmured Bob Monroe, the features editor.

'Maybe she was just referring to rich and heritage in the sense of proprietor's pockets,' said Fran. 'It's hard to survive like she has in the magazine business these days,' she added.

'*Carina* must have eaten up a whack of cash,' said Bob. 'Anyway, with Triton behind her, Nina can't really lose. We're part of a big group now.'

Fran was wistful. 'Paris, Rome, London, New York, Tokyo . . . do you suppose any of us might get a guernsey to the other offices?'

Nina followed the staff function with a series of intimate luncheons in the boardroom to network with the movers and shakers across the spectrum of social, political, marketing and corporate worlds. Manny sat in on these, outlining details, where needed, about the backing of Triton and the fact they were sparing no expense in setting up a major publication to 'smother the market', as Manny put it bluntly.

Nina spoke about her reasons for returning and what she hoped to achieve with her new magazine. 'Thanks to its success in the States and Europe, *Blaze* is a respected and internationally known name. As you are aware, *Blaze Australia* must sell a lot of magazines in order to make it financially viable. To do that, we plan to appeal to a broad-based popular readership in Australasia. Given a choice of *Blaze*'s classy, ethical entertainment or down-market exploitative superficiality, I trust Australian readers will choose the former. The dramatically falling circulations of the women's magazines in this country is proof that the readers are fed up with the diet dished out to them in past years. And while we are a general interest magazine, women are the largest buyers of magazines.'

'Most of those women's magazines are still making money, Nina,' an advertising agency executive reminded her.

'Thanks to clever people like you, James. Hype and

large promotional budgets still feed that particular market. But for how long? At the rate the circulations are falling, my guess is not for long. What we're doing is putting hype and larger promotional budgets, on a scale never envisioned in this country, into a product that will be thought-provoking, glamorous and creative. *Blaze* has never been an elite magazine, marketed to a few readers who know and care about quality and are prepared to pay for it. It has always been, and will always be, a magazine of the highest quality in its content and production standards, offering something for every reader, male and female, in the particular country it serves. *Blaze* has proved this worldwide. *Blaze Australia* will be no exception.'

'Is that why we're here today, Nina?' asked Bevan Lean, Australian CEO of one of the largest international hotel chains. 'To help you bridge the gap between consumerism and culture by providing the advertising support? In other words, our dollars are to support your idea of some sort of consciousness raising of popular culture in Australia.'

'And what's wrong with that?' asked Nina with a disarming smile. 'I do want *Blaze* to provide news features, information, entertainment and, yes, meet that voyeuristic streak of looking at how other people live, think, behave, as well as discovering new ideas on a wide range of subjects. I see this magazine as having a tangible link to the readers' lives. Television is transient, and being cyber-savvy doesn't give the same satisfaction as holding a beautifully designed magazine that is also stimulating to read. There are such rifts in society and families today. I would like to think our magazine, reflecting the standards of a civilised society, could help close that gap.'

'Pretty ambitious concept,' remarked another of the businessmen at the table. 'How can – dare I use the expression – a mere magazine do that where government, the media and society itself have failed?'

'For all its misdemeanours, the tabloid press is still considered to echo the voice of the people. *Blaze* will not lecture or impose, but it will try to reflect current issues, interests and concerns . . . and celebrate the joy of life. To give positive messages, while not ignoring the problems. Yes, we need to address the bleak side of society and ask the hard questions – such as why are our children killing themselves, how can we reduce teen drug use and pregnancy, and why is there so much poverty in such a rich society? What can we as individuals do to improve our world in this new century?' Her voice softened as she spoke, and the men and women around the table fell silent.

Finally it was a woman banker who spoke. 'If you can produce a magazine that answers those questions, I'll buy it.'

'All I'm asking is that you consider what we plan to do in light of this discourse. We are about glamour, yes, but we're not backing away from the serious either.'

'*New Yorker* and *Vanity Fair* also manage to tackle the meaty stuff and they've managed to succeed in the most difficult market in the world,' said Bevan Lean. 'And look at the new mags that try to copy that success. Along with the buzz, they slap in a lot of solid meat. Australia's history of quality magazines hasn't had a healthy run lately. Advertisers here are used to putting their money into what they call the fast-food mags, the read-it-on-the run popular rags, even though the circulations have dropped.'

'That's because they've had no alternative, no promise of better returns. A few years ago, if someone had asked you to invest money in selling bottles of water to Australian consumers, would you have done it?' asked Nina.

The group burst out laughing. 'So *Blaze* is going to be a gourmet hamburger with spring water on the side?' declared Bevan Lean. 'Healthy, filling and tasty with a sparkle.'

'And an affordable meal, don't forget,' responded Nina.

'Can't we cut to the chase, Nina? We're anxious to know more about who's actually going to head up the hunt,' said Campbell Gordon, chief of one of the biggest electronic companies in Australia.

Nina looked at the five men and two women representing a cache of international companies at the table. 'I don't want to steal the new editor's thunder. She is very capable, exceedingly clever and has a terrific track record. I will tell you this much, she's young. This generation doesn't want to hang around and wait to move up the line, they find their target and make things happen. At Triton, we have had to sit up and take notice. I think it's time others did, wouldn't you agree?'

Nina had accepted the shift in ageism in magazines. Young, bright and pushy versus over-forty, experienced and baby-boomer idealistic. She enjoyed seeing young women make their mark, but not at the expense of a generation of women who still had much to offer. It was difficult to make them cooperate as a team because each threatened the other. She tried to set an example, but when something like the death of Lorraine happened, the generational split shifted once again. Sometimes Nina felt overseeing the staff of a magazine – men and women – was like peering down a microscope at amoebae that divided and doubled, clinging to one another and then breaking apart on the glassy slide of magazine media.

'I have a thirty-year-old woman on our board. Wouldn't have happened even a few years back,' said Bevan Lean, interrupting her thoughts. 'Some of the old codgers find her difficult. By that, I mean the fact she is where she is, and that she has opinions that she defends quite spiritedly. Others assume she's there because the government has made an issue of gender representation.'

'A woman on the board can be a token,' said Nina. 'Not that our two lady guests here today are that by any means. But I think you have to agree that most major boards still do not include women, especially young women. I also wonder about a few of the women who are on boards. Is it because of their ability or because it puts the board in a positive light?'

While the two women nodded in agreement, none of the five men present answered, so Nina deftly turned the questioning over to her guests, inviting them to update her on their own fields of interest, and the present and future problems and directions of the community and the country. In the course of the conversation, they shared information in a loose, off-the-record chat that none of them would construe as gossip. Nina found this helpful in filling in the background of local personalities, politicians and their agendas.

In the following days, Nina paid official visits to the Prime Minister, leaders of the other major political parties, CEOs of the country's key corporations, bankers and lobby groups. She talked to women's lobby groups, Greens Party MPs, conservation people, mining bosses, heritage minders, the Reconciliation Committee and an adolescence foundation.

With news that the world's most famous magazine, founded in Australia, was being re-launched in Sydney, Nina found community and corporate groups knocking on her door. The fact that she was keen to meet people and listen to their ideas created a sense of excitement and expectation. Among those hoping the magazine would support their cause were women's preventative health organisations, arts bodies, children's rights movements, women's affirmative action groups, and animals' rights activists who made appointments with the former editor's secretary, Belinda, to meet Nina Jansous.

Belinda had never had to deal with such a string of luminaries and was somewhat awestruck. Always first in line were the advertising agencies sussing out the page and position rates, along with value-added incentive deals. They were also curious on behalf of their clients who'd heard of the fabulous returns to be made from the various *Blaze* publications abroad.

Nina included representatives of these groups in her round of lunches, then politely and firmly advised the agencies that briefings with the advertising manager and the finance controller would be taking place with the new editor on her arrival in Sydney.

Privately, Nina found it frustrating not to dive in and immediately involve herself with the nitty-gritty, but as publisher and editor-in-chief that was not her role. When Ali was in place and the first issue off to the printers, Nina would temporarily step out of the picture.

Many assumed she was tired and needed to recharge her batteries. Nina had never taken more than two weeks break before. No one knew something was troubling Nina – something that even Nina had only recently identified as her 'little volcano'.

The increasing flashbacks and powerful dreams had concerned Nina so much that, once back in Sydney, she had sought the advice of Doctor Richard Leitch, a retired psychologist friend of her late husband, Paul Jansous.

After several quiet dinners at his home, they'd sat in

his study and talked about her thoughts and emotions. Gradually she had come to realise it was a combination of circumstances that were contributing to her feeling so unsettled.

Living back in Australia was one. Based in New York, apart from making fleeting trips to Australia to visit her mother, Nina's focus was devoted to work issues. Now, on a regular basis, she was confronting places, people and memories of her life growing up in Sydney before *Blaze*. It occurred to her that her life was divided into compartments – her early childhood in Croatia, growing up in Australia, a career and marriage, and then *Blaze*. And *Blaze* had been the major and most demanding chunk of her life. It *was* her life. Now her mother had died and she had turned sixty. The combination was unsettling.

Then had come the death of Lorraine, and Miche's need to come to Australia and find her father. In a talk together before Nina left New York, Miche had confided that it was more than a desire to meet and find out what her father was like.

'Nina, since losing Mom, I've felt so adrift. I have no family here and we've never kept in touch. You're my family, as are all Mom's friends on *Blaze* here in New York. This is the only place I've ever lived. I'm half-Australian and I still want to know what that means. I'm not a whole person till I explore that. It's just a need to come to terms with what and who makes me the person I am . . . or want to be.'

Nina had agreed with Miche. And then she'd begun to think along similar lines. She also had lost her mother. But she hadn't wanted to burden the young woman with her sorrow. For Nina, there was a lifetime of loving memory. For Miche, only bitterness. Time was all that could mend Miche's pain, time would recall the sweet times she'd spent growing up with her adoring mother.

Maybe it was because of Miche's words, or maybe it was something to do with age, but Nina found herself thinking more and more about her roots, her heritage, her childhood. Her mother, Clara, had always refused to talk about Croatia.

'Nina darling, it's gone, it's over. There is nothing there any more for us. This is our home. Australia. This is a good place. Good for you. Forget everything from before.'

Nina had little to forget. Her knowledge of her mother and father's country was sketchy.

But when Clara fell ill and knew she was not going to recover, she had begun to talk to Nina about her homeland, her parents. She never mentioned Nina's father. He'd died so young, Nina had so little time with him, he didn't seem to come to the foreground of Clara's memories. But in her sedated state in the hospital bed, she was back in Croatia with her parents and little Nina.

During Nina's final weekend visit to her in Sydney, Clara had grasped Nina's hand, mumbling a disjointed story that made little sense to Nina.

'The tree in the garden at Papa's house. You remember the tree, Nina? Seven big steps left when you look at the house. That's where it is, darling.'

'Where what is? What are you talking about, Mama?' Nina stroked her hand, paying little attention.

'Important papers . . . many things. Find them, Nina. Before it is too late. I was too afraid to go back . . . you must . . .' Clara's eyes closed and her breath came in shallow, short bursts.

Nina tightened her grip on the still elegant, white hand with the pink oval nails and lace of blue veins. 'Mama?'

Clara opened her eyes and gave Nina a penetrating look, a fierceness with such a depth that it startled her. Then Clara's face softened, her eyes filled with love for the beautiful woman who was her daughter and had been her closest friend for most of her life. A sweet smile that hovered for a moment and then she closed her eyes, her hand fell slack in Nina's and she slipped quietly into peace.

Months had passed since Clara's death and the questions that still haunted Nina could not be answered.

Doctor Leitch had listened as Nina talked through these thoughts. 'So Nina, do you want to find answers? Or leave the past to rest? You have a choice.'

It hadn't hit Nina that she could resolve the dilemma of her feelings by simply making a decision to return to Yugoslavia. What would she find? What was she looking for? The fragments of her own memories didn't match the wars, the refugees, the harsh weather and the deprivation she saw in the media. As she allowed herself to think back, certain incidents, oblique comments from Clara, and the knowledge they had fled postwar Yugoslavia to come to Australia leaving the rest of the family behind, made her realise what a time of danger and sacrifice it had been. But her memories were mostly those of an adored child, cosseted in the wealth of doting grandparents.

The memories, the vague questions, Clara's enigmatic last words could not be ignored. It was time for her, like young Miche, to visit the country of her past. While there was no question in Nina's heart where she belonged, it was time to bridge the parts of her life she'd kept separate from each other.

She made arrangements to go to Europe for her holiday with Miche in Paris, with the deliberate plan of visiting Croatia next . . . To go back to her mother's home that had sheltered Clara from birth to motherhood and so swiftly through widowhood. Nina's soldier father was an enigma, a shadow, a cypher. Clara had dominated Nina's life and yet here she was at sixty wondering where had she come from, and what or who, remained?

Manny Golan and Fran Hirshcombe met Ali at Sydney Airport and whisked her by limousine to the Observatory Hotel and into a penthouse suite that looked over the city. Despite her growing apprehension at coming back to the land of her birth after so many years, Ali was impressed. She felt secure in this aviary of luxury. There were dark red roses from Nina and a handwritten note suggesting lunch the following day.

When her colleagues left, Ali looked around the luxurious suite with the trappings of welcoming flowers, complimentary fruit, chocolates and champagne from the management, the million-dollar view. Would she be so feted if they knew who she really was? How vastly different this setting was from that of her Australian childhood. And, for the first time in a long time, the horror of the night when her life had changed swept over her. It was a memory she thought she had buried. The fear of being back in Australia, for the first time since she'd left to go to America as a young girl, made her stomach twist and she felt she might gag. But a swift look around the luxury of her surroundings reassured her. Ali gave a hollow laugh and reached for the bottle of champagne in the ice bucket. Well, no one was going to know. She had been deliberate and thorough in obscuring her past. Tomorrow the business pages of the morning newspapers would carry the announcement of her appointment, with background details of the latest financial success of *Blaze* magazines worldwide but, at her request, there would be very little about herself. The media handout included a posed portrait with Manhattan's skyline in the background taken by one of *Blaze USA*'s top photographers.

The past, she was confident, was behind her. The future was within her grasp. She would not be seeking answers to old questions that had plagued her as a young woman. She had buried, ignored and overcome the events that had changed her life when she was ten. There was only going forward and upwards, as she'd always planned.

Ice settling in a champagne bucket, the muted sound of traffic below the elegant rooms, the soft music from the CD player, the valet exiting quietly with murmured wishes to enjoy her stay. These were sounds that mattered. The hidden cries of a bewildered young girl had been silenced long ago.

Nina had carefully considered where to take Ali – plush, up-market dining at Banc or Forty-One? Machiavelli's or Otto? She decided on superb seafood at Catalina's on the water at Rose Bay. The day was so sparkling, so Sydney.

The fish was freshly caught, the waiters young, charming and attentive and the old pelican with the damaged foot flew down, as it did every day, to the restaurant balcony, limping with exaggeration until fed fish by the maître d.

Ali raised her glass of fine Hunter Valley verdelho. 'You chose well. It's not New York, but it's pretty sensational.'

Nina agreed, but added, 'Ali, may I suggest you stop comparing. There are positive and negative sides to both cities. You've chosen Sydney, so enjoy it. You have a big job ahead of you, and I know you will rise to it. I've brought along briefing notes on the staff, the contacts I have made, the business plan. Manny and I have begun the advertising structure and completed the set-up of the editorial environment. We're primed for you to put the first edition into shape and we're ready to work with you. Now let me fill you in on how I see your role while I'm away.'

'Shoot.' Ali produced a small leather notebook and pen.

'First up, what is happening with Larissa?'

'Still unsure. She wants to come, but the boyfriend is a problem. I've asked her to decide quickly,' answered Ali.

'I hope it's yes. You'll need a deputy you can talk shorthand with. And Larissa is such a lovely person, as well as being excellent at what she does.' When Ali didn't come back with even a platitude, Nina moved on. 'We're going to have to do a bit of shuffling of the staff in order to accommodate new people. We need more young guns to cater to the eighteen to thirty-year-olds. We've targeted advertisers for that age group and they are expecting to be briefed by you tomorrow on *Blaze Australia*'s profile. They know we're about current affairs, high fashion, lifestyle, fascinating hip places, provocative articles – as in thought provoking, not shock tactics. So how you approach the potential advertisers will be important. I've left you a brief on the deal we are offering the Australian-based multinationals like Qantas, and one of the newly merged Australasian/US IT companies to name two. It's an international deal promising them space in the US and European editions for the first twelve months. That's an offer no other magazine in this country can match.' Nina tapped the folder beside her plate. 'There are other equally attractive deals for foreign-based big boys.'

'I've also had a few thoughts,' said Ali, quickly establishing her ground. She was not going to merely follow a list set down by Nina.

'Excellent. Let's hear them.'

'I want cross-promotion with the top-rating TV network and their website, and to establish product placement for us and our advertisers in the major international films being produced here now. I want to set up a radical, interactive website for the magazine that will offer subscription sales, access to previous articles, reader feedback and input and so on.'

Nina nodded thoughtfully. 'The Internet is a massive promotional tool. Making money from it is another question, but as a means of reaching and selling to an audience, let's go ahead. Combining with a TV network is harder. Those marriages between magazines and TV stations have already happened here with the major players owning both.'

'Pay TV is making big inroads, I understand,' said Ali, who had done her homework. 'Why don't we look at having our own show and make it interactive. Talkback radio is still big.'

Nina chuckled. 'Talkback TV. Not a bad idea. But first let's establish the magazine and put issue one to bed. I've kept everything under wraps. I thought it would be a way of introducing you to the media by letting you handle the launch of the magazine. I'm talked out anyway. I'm really looking forward to tooling around Europe with no set itinerary.'

'I'd like to splash on the launch. What's the budget?' asked Ali, reaching for Nina's folder of notes.

'I haven't been so specific, Ali. You have a budget and you are scheduled to meet with Manny to discuss the administration of that in two days time. As in New York, he will oversee it, but it's up to you how you meet it, what you do with it. Naturally the board has to agree to any major decisions, but I believe an editor should have the freedom to edit the magazine without hand-holding, but by following the guidelines and recommendations I've spelled out in the big picture.' Before Ali could speak, Nina shifted in her seat. 'However, there is one staff decision I've taken which I hope you will agree with, and that concerns Lorraine Bannister's daughter.'

At the mention of the late Lorraine, a shadow passed over Ali's face. Ali pushed aside the thoughts trying to re-emerge in her mind. She wasn't going to carry any guilt for Lorraine's death. It was Lorraine's instability that had caused her to end her life. 'Lorraine's daughter? Isn't she at college?'

'She's just graduated. With a journalism degree.'

Ali's heart sank. She saw what was coming. A sassy, know-it-all graduate with a piece of paper that said she knew everything about the newspaper and magazine business. Like hell. Ali had come through the ranks the hard way. She was a rare species. An ambitious, clever, articulate young woman who'd made it without a college degree. By sheer luck. Not that she admitted this publicly.

At sixteen, Ali had been desperate for any kind of work to give her the independence she craved. Unskilled, she had registered with a domestic agency that had sent her to Nina's apartment as a house cleaner, dog walker, and plant waterer while Nina was touring the overseas *Blaze* offices. As soon as Ali had realised she was working for the famous Nina Jansous, she'd been quick to detail her desire to work in magazines and make something of herself. Discovering the girl also had an Australian background, though Ali was shy about going into details, Nina had decided to help the bright youngster and she'd taken her on at *Blaze*.

Even Nina had been surprised at the speed with which Ali had taken off. A sixteen-year-old running messages for the staff, Ali would also submit small but well-polished articles. But it was mostly as office trouble-shooter that Ali had made herself indispensable. She had leapt upwards at a rapid rate. Just as Nina had done.

Ali managed a tight smile. 'Not like you and I learned the business, Nina – hands on, from the bottom up, eh? Graduates from the hard school.'

'Right. They didn't have journalism degrees in Sydney in my day. I know you would have liked to go to university also. Ali, I've never pried into your family background . . . Maybe one day you'd like to share it with me.'

But Ali had no intention of prising open the tightly locked box that held her past. 'I knew what I wanted,' she said quietly. 'Are you saying you've offered Lorraine's daughter a job?' continued Ali, adding to herself, 'whether she can write or not.'

'Miche also happens to be my god-daughter, so I suppose I can be accused of nepotism,' smiled Nina, adding without rancour but reminding Ali, 'I gave you your start when you were still a teenager.' Then she continued, 'Miche is finding it hard to handle her mother's death, and . . . before Lorraine died, Miche had already made the decision to come out to Australia.'

'Yes, Lorraine told me. She wasn't thrilled about it. Something about Miche looking for her long-lost father. I didn't know Lorraine had been married to an Aussie,' said Ali, suddenly slipping back into the vernacular she knew she'd have to adopt for her new role.

'She was very bitter. He seems to have been a larrikin charmer who talked big but couldn't match the silver tongues of the slick city. I know very little. Lorraine had put him out of her life once they split. Miche is, was, her life.' Nina brought the conversation back to the present. 'Miche is willing to start at the bottom. I can objectively say I think she has talent as a writer – I've been reading her college pieces for years – and I think it best she be away from New York and its memories,' added Nina quietly.

'You mean you're giving her a job, here? With me?' God, not only an uppity graduate who knew zilch about the real world of journalism, but a girl who would be a constant reminder of a very unpleasant situation.

'That's right. I think it will be excellent for her. You can teach her a lot, Ali. I'm sure you remember the days when you had a lot to learn,' added Nina pointedly.

Nina was well aware of Ali's machinations behind the scenes to undermine Lorraine as editor of *Blaze* in New York. It had been a board decision to bring in a new and younger woman to be editor and Nina could not disagree with the board's decision. Nina only wished she had been more aware of Lorraine's personal instability. Then she would have fought harder to find a balance between Lorraine and Ali's roles at *Blaze*.

'Miche has grown up with the magazine business. She understands the situation,' said Nina diplomatically, remembering Miche after her mother's funeral breaking into a tearful tirade over the unfairness and bitchiness Lorraine had railed about at home. 'What is important for Miche now is that she moves on with her life. Like you, she knows what she wants. There's only one way to find out if she can achieve it.'

'Coming to Australia to start out seems a big step for someone straight out of college,' said Ali, thinking Nina could have arranged a job on any magazine in the US for the girl.

'She's determined to continue in her mother's footsteps. There's also the issue of finding her Australian father. It's understandable she wants at least to meet him after all these years.' Nina paused. 'She is my god-daughter, Ali, so I want to help. She holds dual citizenship, so it's no problem for her to work here. I did suggest she might like to write a piece or two about her impressions of Australia for *Blaze USA*. But where you use her, I leave up to you.'

Ali saw it was a fait accompli. Whatever Nina said about editor's independence, Ali knew the older woman still held the power. Such decisions would never be hers alone. Ali longed for the day she could rise above Nina Jansous, not here, but in New York. She'd be the person to lay down the rules, and no one would argue.

In Greenwich Village it was evening. A time of movement and light – flashing neon, warmly lit interiors, a river of car headlights, doors opening, people hurrying, grabs of music, laughter, calls and car horns. Everyone on the sidewalks moved with purpose.

In the rear of the speed-then-slow cab, Larissa yawned. Her day was done – at last. She glanced at her watch in the reflection of the street lights and the glow from busy shops and restaurants. Ten-thirty. She was tired. This was madness. Since Nina and Ali had left, her workload had trebled.

She paid the cabbie and hurried into her building, glancing to each side, checking she wasn't being followed – a habit acquired since moving to New York from California fifteen years ago.

The building was a warehouse makeover that had become a desirable address after years as a riverside slum. Sections of the block were still a little scummy, but this building had been renovated in recent years and attracted a yuppie vanguard, though the boom expected by the developer had not occurred. The few tenants loved their spacious floors and wide windows that glimpsed the

Hudson and shared a sense of community, born of attraction for the riverfront neighbourhood.

The world's slowest elevator creaked to the fourth floor, one floor short of the sprawling penthouse rented by a photographer who always seemed to be away in Europe doing architectural photography. Only occasionally did the sculptor below them make his presence known with the tapping of hammer and chisel.

Larissa stepped out of the elevator into white space that normally smelled of turpentine and oil paint from Gerard's work, but tonight these were buried under the rich wine and garlic flavours of boeuf bourguignon.

'Gerry . . . it's me,' she called, dropping her bag and kicking off her shoes as she threw her coat on the sofa. Gerard appeared from the kitchen through an ornate wrought-iron archway. He had a teacloth over one shoulder and carried two glasses of red wine.

'Say nothing. Sit. Drink. Take a deep breath. And then regale me with the drama of the day.' Gerard's theory was that if she unwound slightly, the recounting of the machinations at *Blaze* might be edited slightly and they could move on with their evening, or what was left of it.

'Gerry, it's a nightmare. Why am I always expected to have all the answers? Da Costa is leaning heavily on me until her deputy starts. I know coming into an organisation, even at the top, you need a period of adjustment. But *hell* . . .' She sipped the wine and eased into her favourite chair. 'Even Ali in Sydney is on at me about what I'm doing, wanting to know every detail of what's going on back here and, of course, what I'm going to do. I have to give her a decision by the end of the week.'

'The cut and thrust of Ali's rapier, all the way from Australia,' drawled Gerard, sitting opposite her.

'For a few days there I almost forgot what a rapacious bitch she can be. She was always champing at the bit with ambition, ideas, conniving schemes – you name it. It's just so damned shocking the way everything has fallen into place for her. It's like she waved a wand and made it happen, and I include poor Lorraine in that.'

Gerry tilted his head with a quizzical look on his face. 'That's a bit harsh, isn't it, darling? Things fall into place for you from time to time.'

'We're not in her league. The rest of us slog away doing the female foxtrot – one step forward, two steps backward – but Ali has the magical capacity to achieve her needs and dreams.'

'That could be construed as envy, my dear, when, in fact, Nina has made you an offer and Ali obviously wants you there as an ally.'

'Yeah, the devil you know. What she doesn't understand is how hard a decision this is for me.'

Gerry heaved his shoulders and looked into the glass of wine as if seeking answers, but instead came up with a question. 'What *do* you want, Riss?'

An answer didn't automatically spring to Larissa's lips. Christ, what did she want? She used to be so sure. It was always the job. The drive to charge through the ranks, to be a success, to make her mark, to work for the best. And then along came Gerard and she'd fallen in love. 'Since Lorraine's death and Nina dropping her bombshell, Ali going . . . nothing seems sure and stable and reliable and predictable any more. My life has been turned upside down. Where the hell are we going?'

Gerry took a sip of his wine. 'Where are you going, you mean. That's the big question you have to answer. And was your life ever stable and predictable?' He paused, thinking how she used to enjoy the upheaval of life on a top magazine. 'You know, in light of your offer to go to Australia, I've been thinking about my life too. I'm about to turn forty. I hadn't thought anything of it till a day or so ago when my mother rang and wondered when I was going to have a proper life. Marriage, kids, a job in the country where I could spend time on my art. The things I always talked to her about wanting.' He ran his fingers through his hair. 'I'm a big deal stockbroker, I make a lot of money, yet I suddenly feel life has passed me by.' He finished the glass of wine. 'She also wanted to know what we were doing to celebrate.'

Larissa had forgotten his birthday. At least it was two weeks away. 'What would you like to do?'

'Are you going to be here? Or in Australia? Bit hard to make plans.'

'Gerry, I just don't know. Ali is nagging now. Why don't you toss in your job and come to Australia? Take a year off.'

'I can't do that, Larissa. I'm responsible for a couple of very big clients. Look, we've been over this. Would twelve months apart be impossible? We could fly to see each other a couple of times in the year.'

'Gerry, it's not the same. Oh God, why is life so unfair!'

Gerry stood, took their glasses and went back into the kitchen to refill them. 'After my mother's phone call, I did think of another option.'

Larissa rubbed her eyes. They'd had this conversation several times since Nina had offered her the job as Ali's deputy in Australia. She loved him, they'd been living together for seven years. He had a demanding job at the stock exchange, but he was able to unwind in the section of the apartment he had turned into a studio. Here he splashed paint on large canvases and occasionally exhibited and sold a few of them. She knew she was lucky to come home to a loving companion but, like tonight, he was often resentful of her dedication to her job.

Gerard sat on the arm of her chair, handing her the wineglass. 'I did think I'd like to mark my fortieth in a special way. In fact I have given it a little thought.' He gave a sheepish grin. 'I was thinking we should go to Greece, hang out, drink ouzo, eat octopus or whatever. Make love in the afternoon, indulge myself into believing I'm still virile and sexy.'

'You are.'

'Yeah. How often do we make mad love in the day in funny positions, spread whipped cream and crushed strawberries on the belly and nether regions, eh?'

Larissa's mouth twitched. She was always so tired these days, sleep had become an obsession. 'It's been a while, I guess.'

'Yeah. Thanks to *Blaze*. So, let's go to Greece. Make it a honeymoon, eh?'

'Oh, Gerry, please. Let's not go through this again.' Larissa stood up. 'Why am I the one who has to choose? Why don't you toss in your job for a year? You say you hate it, that what you really want to do is paint. Well, prove it! Come out with me and paint for a year. See if you can make it.'

'While you're working till ten at night, totally wrapped up in the job. And I'm in a strange city. Sounds wonderful,' he said bitterly.

'Well, if I married you and stayed here, I'd end up being resentful, wondering if it was the right choice. It's hard enough to be in a position choosing between staying here with you, or loping off to the other side of the world to be with Ali, of all people.'

'I wouldn't have thought it too hard a choice,' he said with a wry smile.

'You know what I mean. I've worked so hard to reach where I am. This would give me a big plus on the résumé and I'm one step away from an editorship. You think you're feeling old. I'm feeling the heat on my heels from girls ten years my junior.'

Gerard snorted. 'Hell's bells, if you're being stood over and feel like you're being pushed aside at thirty-five, you're in the wrong job, babe. COME TO GREECE!' he shouted at her as Larissa headed for the bedroom – a suspended loft with huge windows that also overlooked the river.

'YOU COME TO AUSTRALIA!' she shouted back.

'Go then. I can tell you're going to hold it against me if you don't. You'll blame me for holding back your career. Anyway, it wouldn't work.'

'What wouldn't?'

'A holiday in Greece. We'd have a wonderful time and that would make it so much harder to say goodbye.'

Larissa peered over the balcony from the loft to see Gerard standing forlornly in the sitting room. 'Goodbye? So I'm going, am I?' she asked quietly.

'I know you are, even if you haven't realised it yet.' He turned to the kitchen. 'Have a shower. Dinner's almost ready.'

Larissa let the hot spikes of water stab into her skin. She was tired and confused. She felt an irrational annoyance at Gerry. She wanted him to make the decision. Marriage just seemed a way of tying her down. Only those in the magazine business really understood the pressures, the competitiveness, the drive to be innovative, the juggling of personalities and egos, the circulation and advertising figures that ruled their existence, the constant threats of budget restraints or financial crises. With several magazines and two newspapers in the Triton American stable, one of them was always haemorrhaging cash. Nina was brilliant at running the ship, protective of her staff and the whole ethos of *Blaze* and what it represented, yet she could be firm and initiate effective cost-cutting when necessary. The employees, unless they were not performing, were the last to be slashed.

With Ali at the helm of *Blaze Australia* . . . could she work with her? There was something about Ali that Larissa could never trust, and if she was honest, couldn't like. Was it the competitive threat? While Larissa accepted it was every woman for herself striving for the top positions, was it jealousy that Ali may succeed where Larissa may not? Ali was superficially pleasant and efficient, and occasionally very clever, but it was her ruthless streak and frightening ambition that disturbed Larissa. And what about Gerard? Would he still be waiting for her, could their relationship survive such distance?

Larissa turned off the shower knowing the real question was how much did she value Gerard? It rattled Larissa when she realised she was leaving Gerard – even temporarily – to throw her lot in with Ali. No matter how reassuring Nina had been, Ali holding power over her gave Larissa the jitters.

They got through dinner sharing stories of the day, and no more mention was made of Larissa taking up the job in Sydney. But later, wrapped in Gerard's arms, with his familiar smell of aftershave and linseed oil where he'd run his paint-streaked hands through his hair, she wondered how could she be apart from him.

At breakfast, Gerard was affectionate and attentive. The memory of their lovemaking glowed in his smile. They sat across from each other at the small table. Gerard had his tie around his neck, his blue shirt unbuttoned as he spread jelly on his croissant. As he lifted it to his mouth, a speck of jelly dropped onto his shirt.

Larissa leaned over and dabbed at it with her napkin.

'How are you going to look after yourself while I'm gone?' she said softly.

Pain clouded his eyes for a moment, then a resigned expression settled on his face.

'I'll manage,' he whispered.

TAKE FIVE...

Larissa and Gerard skirted around any confrontation. Oblique references or awkward silences became the pattern as Larissa sorted and packed, cancelled regular hair, manicure and gym appointments. Gerard left the room when she talked to friends on the phone about her new assignment. At one point, Larissa wished he'd just blow up and yell at her not to go. The less they said about the forthcoming separation the more strained the silences became and the more Gerard retreated into his own world. He spent hours at his easel, late into the night, slipping into bed in the dark so as to not wake Larissa.

But Larissa was aware of him settling on the far side of the bed. It had always been her habit to reach out and curl herself around him – now she hugged her side of the bed, each aching to reach across the chasm between them.

Slowly her anxiety turned to guilt and then to resentment.

Gerard was experiencing the same feelings, yet neither

showed these to the other. Instead a false brightness, a cheerful industriousness covered the hollow words, the pang in their hearts that neither knew how to overcome. Even Gerard's birthday, a formal cocktail party Larissa had organised at Alain Ducasse on Central Park South, with old college friends Gerard had not seen for years, had done little to relax them. The impasse, forced by their imminent separation, and each one's defiant refusal to give in to the other, was relieved only after Gerard had pecked Larissa formally on the cheek and waved her through the gate at JFK.

Nina had agreed that after six months Larissa could review her situation. This irritated Ali, and she'd pointed out the inconvenience of making her deputy established and known, a task made harder because she hadn't worked in Australia before. Nina had appealed to Ali to be understanding, explaining the sensitivities involved in Larissa's long-term relationship, reminding her an editor had to be aware of the senior staff's personal lives as well as their professional capabilities. Neither raised the subject, but the spectre of Lorraine hovered in their minds.

Ali surprised Nina by changing her mind and agreeing to Larissa's review of her position after six months. It occurred to Ali that by then she would want a deputy who answered to her and not to Nina. A deputy who would do her bidding and add to her power base. For Ali had no doubts about assuming as much power as she could while being editor of *Blaze Australia*. It wasn't just for the power, the money or the position. In Ali's view, Australia owed her. And she intended to take as much as she could.

*

Gerard wasn't happy about Larissa's move, but he knew better than to try to stop her. They had agreed at the start of their partnership and living together that their careers had equal merit. When one was under particular pressure, the other tried to be the supportive one on the domestic and emotional front. The arrangement had worked fairly well because Gerry held his peace. He never passed on his mother's barbed questions about when they were going to settle down and marry, have children and Larissa give up work? It occasionally irked him that he was the one to hold his tongue, but he had come to realise how much *Blaze* meant to Larissa. His job was a means of making money. His painting was his passion. It seemed to him that for Larissa the daily machinations at *Blaze* consumed her energy, her interest and her devotion. Maybe this time apart, while she was in Australia, would put their relationship in its true perspective.

He never spoke these thoughts, but a question about what books and CDs she planned to take with her brought anguished cries from Larissa.

'I'm not moving there, Gerry. I can live without those trappings for a while. They'll make me homesick. I can't play our favourite music when I'm on the other side of the world from you. I'll cry. I'm going to live a minimalist lifestyle. Besides, I can buy new albums there. I like quite a few of those Aussie music groups.'

Ali had planned her foray into the Australian media scene carefully. She stayed at the hotel for the first few weeks while she looked for an apartment, settling on 'The Toaster', the building that had caused so much controversy a few years earlier for being a blot on Bennelong Point, the most sacred site of Sydney Harbour, next door to the famed Opera House. She'd hired an interior designer who chose a stark black and white theme with futuristic metallic furniture and fittings. Wide windows without drapes had transitional glass to dim subtly or clear with a faint tint, according to the strength of the sunshine so the main room was always bathed in a fluid, balanced light. Abstract paintings and a large sandblasted sculpture were by avant-garde Australian artists. Several dramatic dracaena trees fanned spiky fronds towards the vaulted ceiling. The effect was contemporary and stylised, if sterile. Ali had no personal photographs, favourite pictures, knick-knacks or anything that gave a clue to the person who inhabited this space.

She combed the city and its eastern suburbs' neighbours of Double Bay, Woollahra and Paddington, all the while looking at shops and fashions. She watched the men and women in the streets and restaurants, trying to grab a handle on the style of her Australian contemporaries. On weekends, she felt they revealed their true taste – casual, sporty, yet a more healthy and softer style than New Yorkers. Maybe the climate was more like California, but here there was a far more natural look. The girls didn't have a weekly manicure and pedicure, they did their own hair and appeared to relish individuality. Fashion must-have fads were identifiable in certain looks or accessories, but Ali came to the conclusion these women were not slaves to fashion labels. And from what she'd read of the salary scales here, few could afford to wear expensive brands.

However, she soon discovered the 'ladies who lunch' groups. Successful career women or wives with rich husbands held court at their favourite restaurants in outfits Ali could put a name and a price tag to with ease. While fashion was only a portion of *Blaze*'s content, Ali had been schooled by Nina who'd said readers – men as well as women – were always interested in fabulous-looking fashion with a story, not just way-out photos of clothes no one you knew would wear.

The first issue of *Blaze Australia* had been put to bed under tight wraps so that no clue to its cover or contents would leak. It would hit the streets in two weeks with the media launch a few days before.

Nina hadn't moved anything personal into her new Australian office other than her favourite Aboriginal painting she'd brought from New York, her cedar chair and several framed photographs of Clara's millinery creations as seen in *Vogue* in the late fifties and early sixties. She'd wait till she was back in harness, after her trip to Europe, to settle into her new office. That was the plan. Nina was unsure about her true future. She'd wait and see what happened. For the first time in her life, she had no definite goal – just an unsettled feeling she couldn't pin down.

Ali would take over a large area where a partition had been ripped out to make an editor's suite, which included her private rooms, then another area with a custom-made round table where the staff could attend editorial meetings in comfort. The office belonging to former editor Dorothy Power had been refurbished for Larissa.

Nina dropped an arm lightly across the newly arrived deputy editor's shoulders. 'Welcome, and how do you find Australia so far?'

Larissa laughed, glancing at her watch. 'I've heard that's the classic question. Judging from the past few hours – not bad.'

'Seriously, Larissa . . . I do hope you enjoy it here. I know you'll give creative leadership to the staff. You understand how Ali can be . . . well, prickly. Clever, but she doesn't have your people skills.' Nina glanced at her, trying to read behind Larissa's cheerful smile. 'How did your nice guy take this, er, break?'

'It wasn't easy. Why is it when anything positive comes along it's the female who has to make the hard choice?' Larissa looked out the window at the harbour and said softly, 'At least he was happy with his fortieth birthday celebrations. Thank you so much, Nina, for understanding how important it was for me to organise that evening for him, even though it meant me not being here to help with the first edition of *Blaze*.'

Nina squeezed Larissa's hand. 'As important as *Blaze* is to me, your happiness, and therefore Gerard's, is important to me too.'

Larissa sighed. 'He'd love this. It would be such an inspiration. All his life he's wanted to paint. Here he'd have the chance to prove it to himself. Maybe he didn't have the guts. All that male ego about being a house husband, me supporting him, not knowing anyone . . . it was too hard. He let me go.'

'Could he have stopped you?' asked Nina quietly. And when Larissa didn't answer, she continued, 'It's always the women who take matters into their hands. But, Larissa, I promise this will be rewarding for you. The launch of a new magazine – one that is successful – will jump you up the ladder very quickly. This is an enormous responsibility and the fact I will be away for a couple of months means I can relax knowing you're here.' Nina gave her a pointed look and, without saying any more, both women understood the subliminal message – keep an eye on Ali. Nina squeezed Larissa's shoulders then broke away. 'You have a lot of ability, and different skills from Ali's, which is why I wanted you both with me to set *Blaze* on the right road. You have the talent to go where you want, it's up to you to make your own choices in life. And whatever you choose, I'll support you and wish you well.'

Larissa turned her back on the magnificent Darling Harbour view and opened her arms to embrace the office space. 'I've made my choice. I'm here, aren't I? Where do I start?'

Nina gave a *c'est la vie* shrug and became businesslike. 'I decided to sit in for you for the first issue as Ali's deputy and I've been very impressed with her ideas and her achievements, as I knew I would be. I felt it best that I let her be on the front foot, seen to be making the decisions. I stepped in once or twice, quietly and privately, but she is certainly a quick learner. Now it's up to you to work with Ali. I'm leaving in two days. I know I'm handing you a double-edged sword. Guard my dreams and keep your cutlass sheathed.' Nina gave a slight humorous bow. 'Larissa, I charge you with protecting my creation, keeping an eye on *Blaze*, on Miche when she arrives and, most of all . . . love what you're doing.'

Larissa returned Nina's embrace. 'Nina, it's not going to be easy without you here, but I want you to enjoy this break. Don't worry, I'll be your backstop.'

Ali had quickly unearthed the hottest new hair and beauty salon in Sydney – the Yellow Brick Road. It still had the industrial high-tech trimmings, but the decor was technicolour *Wizard of Oz* – flamingo pink, tangerine and lime. It was run by Brian Standish from Revesby, except that he now called himself Dane. Sometimes he was known to fling on a large black satin cape studded with stars, 'for wizardly inspiration'. Dane ruled his salon with imperial autocracy. He was over six feet, with a shaved shining head and a wispy four-inch goatee on the tip of his chin.

His two stylists were also bald, though Miles sported a scalp tattoo while Rex wore earrings. Dane was the cutter, Miles the colour expert, Rex did make-up and manicures. Dane required them to work their lean muscular bodies at the gym with him before dawn and by 7 a.m. the coffee was brewing and they opened the doors to their elite clientele – businessmen and women like Ali.

In their black ballet tights and soft ballet slippers, each wearing a big black artist smock with a distinguishing coloured bow at the throat, the men moved silently between the clients. In contrast was the young girl trainee, who did the shampooing and carried the breakfast orders. They called her Tottie – after Dorothy's dog, Toto, in *The Wizard of Oz*.

Ali and Dane had hit it off straight away. As part of her contract, Ali had access to a car to travel to and from *Blaze* and to appointments. Her personal assistant, Belinda, had set up an account for her with Sydney's main taxi company, which Ali instantly changed to a limousine service. Tom, the chauffeur, collected her at seven each morning and took her to the Yellow Brick Road for hair and make-up. Despite a full early clientele, Dane had quietly discouraged one of his lesser clients and moved Ali in, smelling publicity for himself in *Blaze*. He would also trade subtly on the fact they 'did' the new editor. Not that he would ever dream of passing on this news publicly. He had his own pet news leaks who would spread the word.

Ali had instructed Dane to keep her informed of the latest looks. He had executed a perfect pirouette and dropped his hands on her shoulders as she sat in a lemon suede chair before the silver and gold mirror.

'Mademoiselle Ali . . . it's not just about having the latest, but much more about how it comes together,' he ventured politely but firmly.

'Then put me together,' growled Ali, opening the *Financial Review*.

'Grouchy, grouchy. Where's our little ray of sunshine? Tottie, bring Missy Ali her morning coffee. Very strong. Very black. Very thick. Like we like our men!' He roared and signalled to Rex to start her make-up.

Rex tilted her head onto the headrest. 'So who's starring on the first cover?'

'I haven't actually decided yet,' Ali lied. Rex was not to know that the cover of the magazine, which was already being printed, had been a major decision discussed by all members of the editorial board. It was a decision that could have taken days. Instead, including Nina, they had unanimously applauded Ali's idea for the first cover of *Blaze Australia*, and Ali had received a personally written note from the Baron in New York complimenting her choice.

Ali hoped Rex wasn't going to keep questioning her, or she'd have to speak to Dane about it, or choose another salon. She had never agreed with Nina's policy that one never knew where the next good idea was coming from. Ali's policy was to rely on herself, with a strong staff back-up, and to always give the impression everything was her own idea. Nina had always listened to what others had to say. If a copygirl or secretary had an idea, they were encouraged to present it to their immediate superior. That was the *Blaze* way, Nina would say.

A young journalist had once ventured a suggestion while working for Ali, who'd been a senior editorial assistant in New York at the time. Ali had seized the idea, put it up to Lorraine Bannister and earned brownie points all round. The cadet had made one stab at telling the features editor it had been her idea, and had been quickly warned off.

'Too late, kiddo. Even if it was your idea, don't take

on Alisson Gruber and make her look bad. She'll have you transferred to the midnight shift on the Sunday rag in this organisation before you can say hello. Then it's goodbye. A tip – the first lesson in magazine publishing is to try to figure out who's the most dangerous and who's the least. Deciding you can't trust anyone is the safest. If you want to move up the ladder, be as treacherous as they are.'

The girl had resigned and gone to university to do her MA in gender studies – 'Male and female strategies for survival in the workplace'.

Ali never asked why she'd left. If she'd even noticed. Ali had learned to keep moving forward and not become sidetracked by other people. They were in your path to help or hinder and you dealt with them accordingly.

'I have an idea,' said Rex bringing her back from her reverie as he plucked a stray hair from the thin arc of her brows.

'Umm. What's that?'

'You! Put yourself on the cover. You'd look outstanding in that new Hugo gear.'

Ali was only momentarily entranced with the idea, then put him down. 'It's not *Lear* magazine.' Even Nina had never gone on the cover of *Blaze*.

'People love reading about the people who set the trends and move with the jet set. And what's *Lear* anyway?'

'Mag from the dark ages,' said Ali. 'Came out in the eighties. A leader for its genre, but it was too early. A woman called Francis Lear started it in New York "for the woman who wasn't born yesterday". The forty-, fifty-plus set. Good idea for a while. Copied in other countries, but disappeared. Hard to keep it going when it identified so much with one woman. And one who was growing older all the time.'

'Who wants to read about old ladies? You should put more music people and friends of Dorothy's in your magazine.'

'Pretty boys, and wild music, eh?' mused Ali.

The cloaked wizard stepped in quickly. 'Rex, it's not your job to criticise, sweetie.'

'Just trying to be helpful.' He began packing away his make-up box.

'Don't be sulky, sexy Rexy.' Dane leaned closer and inspected Ali's make-up. 'Russet. Super choice for the lippie.'

Rex held up Ali's hand. 'Nice on the nails too.'

Once Rex had moved away, Dane set to work with lots of flourishes and twirling of scissors. Ali's short hair was swiftly styled into a smooth, sharply angled crop.

'Maybe a change of colour next week, Ms Ali? A bit of plum in this would make it so much richer, darling heart.'

He cocked his head and studied her. Despite his flamboyance, Dane was a shrewd character who analysed his clients carefully. While this style wasn't what a lot of his lady customers wanted, the look suited Ali – slick, contemporary, androgynous. The opposite to Nina Jansous, whose look he'd been following for years. As he continued to look at Ali's reflection in the mirror, he decided that Nina would look as stylish as hell with such a hairdo. But then Nina was one of those chameleon women who would look fabulous no matter how she was styled. The inner woman always shone through. But this Ali was harder to read. She was a collection of mirrored surfaces. She gave nothing away. She was strong. And tough. Armour-plated. Dane wondered what secrets were buried beneath her steely exterior.

Dane knew about temperament – his tantrums were legendary – but they were always over swiftly. His staff went with the flow. He doubted the *Blaze* staff would flow along with the same nonchalance when Ali was in full flood. She was not a woman to be crossed. He gave a professional smile. 'So, until tomorrow, eh? Tottie, bring the little red shoes. Good luck with your day.' He waved an imaginary wand over her.

Ali signed the red book – the account would be sent to the office. She didn't feel the need for luck. She put down the pen, picked up her Prada bag and strode out of the Yellow Brick Road to her car, which was pulling into the kerb. She never left tips. She'd arrange for copies of *Blaze* to be sent to the salon to entertain its clientele, which included more than one potential advertiser.

Walking into the *Blaze* offices that morning, her first day as editor since Nina had left, Ali wondered whether she'd keep Belinda, the personal assistant to former editor Dorothy Power. Belinda had looked after Nina until Ali took over and wasn't looking forward to working for Ali after the gracious and competent editor-in-chief. Belinda had instantly recognised the hunger in Ali. An appetite for power, success and recognition.

Neither was Ali thrilled with the idea of inheriting Belinda. She wanted someone more stylish to arrange her personal affairs, to be answerable just to her. Someone she could rely on, yet hold in check. And unlike Belinda, it would have to be someone who understood punctuality.

In Ali's opinion, Nina had been too accommodating and easygoing with the staff as they'd made the transition into *Blaze*. It was all right for Nina, as she had been there only a short time before making her quiet exit on extended leave to Europe. Ali believed it was now up to her as editor to mould the staff into a slick machine that operated under her instructions. Everything was in place from an administrative point of view. Nina had handed over the business and creative reins to Ali. And Ali intended to exercise this power.

Ali nodded at the front office receptionist and walked down the hallway to her suite, remembering the morning not so long ago when she'd arrived at work for the first time as editor of her own magazine. Nina had taken Ali on a tour of the *Blaze* offices and introduced her to the staff at an informal gathering in the boardroom the evening before Ali had started work as editor of *Blaze Australia*.

On that first day as editor, Ali had sent herself a huge bouquet of flowers and two smaller ones with cards from corporate high-flyers she figured would never know the difference. Ali had always been an assiduous reader of the business section of the New York newspapers. Now she looked forward to Australia's *Financial Review* and *Business Review Weekly* so she could tap into the manoeuvres of the corporate leaders and top entrepreneurs. She knew Belinda would read the cards on the flowers and word would filter out to the staff.

Now Nina had left for Europe, it was time for change. To Ali's annoyance, Belinda had not arrived. Ali glanced at her watch, it was twenty to nine. Not good enough. She'd been late on Ali's first day in the office and after a clumsy excuse about family problems, to which Nina had clucked-clucked in sympathy, she'd been making a habit of it. That would stop today.

Ali walked slowly round the office deciding what had to go from the newly decorated editor's suite, and what style she would prefer in its place. Nina's democratic idea of using a round table instead of a desk had always irritated her. That would be the first piece of furniture to go. Ali started making a list of what she wanted, including what she expected of Belinda – to arrive early, to turn Ali's computer on, to make a note of all emails, and to have her espresso coffee ready to pour. Flower arrangements were to be replaced twice a week.

Belinda appeared at her door, pulling off her coat as she described the traffic chaos that had delayed her. Ali cut her off mid-sentence.

'Belinda, I'm sure it won't happen again, as I'd like you in here early. I've left a list of tasks on your desk that I expect to be done before I arrive.'

Belinda paused, clutching her jacket. 'Oh, I'm sorry, Alisson. I'm normally very punctual. Just tell me what you want and . . .'

'My name is Ms Gruber. And please keep the door between my office and your area closed unless I choose to leave it open.' Ali made her displeasure known despite Belinda's stuttering explanation that she'd had a problem taking her two young children to school.

Belinda's lips tightened. 'I apologise. Buzz me when you need anything.' She closed the door behind her. Dorothy had never kept it shut.

With Nina safely in Europe, Ali had scheduled her first editorial meeting to start at 9 a.m. The editor checked her papers at 8.55 a.m. She had spent the weekend clarifying the changes and strategies she intended to implement. No sense in sliding into position and creeping in her new regime. She wanted to be regarded as incisive and authoritative from the beginning.

Ali and Larissa had lunched and talked about the magazine only in general terms. Ali believed in not telling anyone anything that wasn't absolutely necessary. Simply good tactics.

Larissa knew this, so didn't probe too deeply into her plans as Ali repeated several times, 'I'll go over everything in detail at the first editorial meeting.'

Ali wanted to make a stand right off, so everyone would understand she was now in control, and she was prepared to make unpopular decisions if she considered them necessary. She would show them her authority was not to be questioned. Nina was gone. Ali had the baton in her hand and was ready to run.

Ali kept busy until she heard the murmur of voices outside. Peering through the glass panel in one wall, she could see most of the senior editorial staff clustered around Belinda's desk.

Smoothing her hair, she ran her tongue over her lip gloss, picked up a folder and opened the door. 'Good morning. Shall we?'

Ignoring the round table in her suite, where the first edition of *Blaze* had been planned with Nina, Ali headed for the boardroom, and added, without glancing at Belinda, 'Tea, coffee and mineral water please, Belinda. No food.'

Tiki Henderson, the fashion editor, and Barbara Jamieson, the beauty editor, exchanged a glance and mouthed at each other, 'No food?'

'No biscuits?'

'No donuts?'

The weekly editorial meeting had always been a time of bagels, Danish and croissants. Following Ali's bony body through the door, the two older women who wouldn't see a size twelve again, sighed.

'Shall we boo?' whispered Tiki.

'You mean as in boohoo or hiss and . . . ?'

'No. Bring Our Own.'

'I don't like your chances.'

The staff who would make the decisions about the

content and direction of each issue of *Blaze* settled themselves along one side of the boardroom table where neat folders of documents had been placed, each named to mark where the men and women on the senior staff should sit. The new boardroom table was glass and steel. Nina had agreed that Ali replace the old teak veneer, but the staff were instantly uncomfortable as they seated themselves at the apparent floating sheet of glass.

'Can't pass notes or scratch your balls under this table,' commented Bob Monroe, the features editor, to contributions editor and senior writer, Jonathan Gibb.

Ali surprised them by taking the single chair opposite, putting the long table between them and herself. Dorothy had always sat amongst them, flanked by Fran, the promotions director, and Tiki. Their editorial meetings had always had the feeling of an intimate tea party where conversation, ideas and differing opinions were exchanged.

The atmosphere was chilly. Even the new decor ordered by Ali seemed intimidating – cool beige, icy white, gleaming metal, lots of glass and sleek, clean lines. No trims, no falderals. Ali had removed Nina's touches – flowers, pot plants, paintings and comfortable, elegant chairs. The room was now coldly businesslike, avant-garde steel chairs drawn around the bare table. Stylish contemporary slatted blinds had been installed to screen the stunning – and potentially distracting – harbour view.

Larissa caught the tense mood in the room and thought back to how Nina had conducted these meetings at her egalitarian round table in New York. There was always an agenda but under Nina's gentle guidance everyone felt free to voice their opinions, even if they conflicted with other views. If there was a visitor included in the conference – perhaps the art director or advertising director or a specialist in a field who'd been invited to address the section editors and then leave them to business matters after the coffee break – that person would sit at Nina's right. If they were contemplating covering a sensitive or difficult topic, a specialist in that area would come in to address them and answer questions.

Ali had no intention of continuing this pattern. Instead, she would privately seek out such people and produce their advice, statistics or knowledge as a fait accompli. She did not intend to run meetings like a girl guides' show-and-tell. She'd already, she reminded herself, had to carry most of them to make the right decisions for the first edition. They really had no idea what quality was about.

To the men and women seated opposite her along the table, it seemed as though electricity crackled around Ali, a threatening energy. They each felt it and each was on guard, defensive and apprehensive. While Ali had been editor since the start of *Blaze Australia*, Nina's quiet presence had kept her in check. The staff knew this. But there had been enough prickly one-on-one confrontations with Ali that had sent a clear message to the staff – Ali was tough and uncompromising and they wondered what she'd unleash the minute Nina was out the door. For once the editorial team felt united. Them against Her. Bickering and competitiveness between the staff were commonplace. They worked in a supercharged atmosphere of pressure and creative energy that each person handled in their own way. Occasional frictions were inevitable. But here they sat silently waiting, wondering who would first feel the sting of Ali's tongue.

Ali moved straight to business. 'Before we start on long-term strategies, there are more immediate matters I'd like to address. First off, as you know, Larissa Kelly is my deputy editor. We have a working relationship from *Blaze* in New York, which means we understand the *Blaze*

117

ethos. However,' Ali threw a polite smile at Larissa, 'this magazine will act completely independently of the New York edition. *Blaze Australia* will have its own identity. It is up to us to make *Blaze* a success.'

Larissa nodded, but Ali had no intention of allowing Larissa to say anything and moved quickly on to her agenda. 'Housekeeping first. I intend to make a number of significant changes. I realise they will not all be welcome, but they are in the best interests of the magazine. I have been given a charter for a fresh start. Before I explain what that is, however, would anyone like to say anything?' Ali sat back expecting a little speech of welcome, at the very least an expression of goodwill. There was stony silence.

Fran Hirshcombe leapt into the lengthening abyss. 'I think I speak for all of us when I say, while we are excited about this new challenge, big changes are always destabilising. Most of us have worked here since *Carina* began – and all of that with Dorothy and, er . . . Carina Brett-Moir. So, while we were never complacent, there was a certain familiarity about the magazine which . . .'

Ali held up her hand and cut in. 'Precisely what I intend to change. The cliché that familiarity breeds contempt doesn't quite apply, but familiarity gives readers predictability and that's tedious. I intend that *Blaze* will shake Australia's magazine readers, and gain us new ones who have had plenty of reasons lately to be contemptuous of magazines in this country.'

The group around the table stared at Ali, each silently absorbing the insult. Larissa decided to maintain her silence. This was Ali's scene.

Ali returned their gaze. 'In your folders, you will find briefing notes of the market we are aiming at and the initiatives expected from the senior staff of *Blaze*. So what stories have you come up with?'

The group examined the notes in front of them, suddenly unsure about their ideas.

Jonathan Gibb, employed by Nina on her arrival in Sydney, spoke first. 'There's a new study out showing the alarming rise of alcoholism among young and middle-aged women. There are also aspects of the study about ageing women that I thought worth exploring.'

'I read that report too. I was surprised at the large numbers of middle-class women . . . women who are our readers,' broke in Barbara. 'Why do these women, who are financially comfortable, in apparently happy homes, with achieving kids, take to the bottle?'

'So is that the story angle we look at?' asked Jonathan. 'What makes a woman start drinking? Why are there so many women in their middling years out there who are not coping well with growing older? They can't cope with changing lifestyles, or keeping up with their careers? Why are there so many husbands that leave to look for younger women, or have no sense of identity or achievement?'

Bob Monroe warmed to the topic. 'So let's look at the reasons why a typical middle-class woman, who works, looks after a husband and family, who seems to be balancing her life and having it all, suddenly starts to lose her grip. Is it sudden, or had it been coming and no one saw it?'

'Sounds like it's worth exploring in depth,' said Tiki. 'I suppose there are always relationship problems – abusive, alcoholic spouses, or no partner at all, lack of love and companionship.' Tiki paused, wondering if she should raise the issue of ageism, then decided to go for it. 'If we did a feature, whoever wrote it could spell out the smouldering conflict of "maturity and experience" being pushed aside for "fresh and innovative".' She continued. 'And we should talk to women who've survived ageism.' Nina Jansous was sixty and she'd managed to keep a contemporary slant on life. 'I suppose a lot of our readers are experiencing the life-changing thing,' she finished carefully.

Ali was dismissive. 'Old hat, matronly stuff. And if you're talking change-of-life readers, that is about to go,' said Ali briskly, annoyed Nina's senior writer had brought up this subject. He should have known ageism was not a subject that would interest Ali. 'Those people will enjoy reading *Blaze*, yes, but we're targeting where the money and action is – the achievers, the twenty-five to forty group. Men and women who are confident, cluey, tuned into technology and not afraid to aim high, whatever the cost.' Ali spoke softly, but matter-of-factly, reeling off a description that seemed to everyone present to describe Ali. 'This is not a women's magazine, even though we may sometimes address subjects that might be of particular interest to women. The *Blaze* approach is to make these articles – fashion, beauty, style, health – of interest to go-get-'em men and women. I am also not about giving advice to readers on self-improvement or solving life's problems.' At this, the former *Carina* staff who'd been briefed by Nina blinked. They understood that had been very much the credo of responsibility, as well as entertainment, that *Blaze* strived for.

'What are we on about then?' asked Bob Monroe.

Ali came back swiftly. 'We don't treat our readers, men or women, as losers with problems. They want to be promoted, exploit opportunities, make the most of life because they have the income to do so. They want to start achieving before thirty. By forty, it's too late.'

'Oh, it's all over at forty, is it?' said Fran Hirshcombe who'd just turned forty and now felt fragile.

'Well, if you haven't made it by then, yes,' said Ali, a hint of patronising surprise in her voice as if to say, don't you understand yet?

'Yes, what do you mean by . . . made it?' asked Barbara. 'I'm over forty and like to think I still have goals to achieve.'

'What do you think of when you say "have it all", Ali?' asked Fran quietly.

'Name it. Silver Porsche, smart condo in the best part of town, designer gear, skiing at the top resorts, always being given the best table at the hottest new restaurant in whatever town they happen to be working or playing in. And independence. No ties.'

'No responsibilities, you mean. No kids, no husband, no elderly parents to care for?' added Barbara in a neutral voice.

'You bet. Unless it's on your terms – a partner who can look after him or herself, a nanny and a housekeeper. That's getting there, today.'

Ali's interpretation of achievement jarred with the older women. They were baby boomers, they were still idealistic, still believed one had to care about others and a woman could still do it all – thanks to the women of an earlier generation who'd made big changes possible. Ali came from a more selfish generation. The old hands felt her definition made the magazine sound too elitist and that it would alienate readers who didn't fall into Ali's category.

Reg Craven, the advertising director, secretly shared Ali's definition of their ideal reader. He was a consumer and lived to encourage conspicuous consumption. Advertising was the key to increasing the desire for goods and a materialistic way of life. It was his own philosophy and the way he'd earned his income since first joining the heady world of advertising. But he knew pushing unwanted and unnecessary products on a gullible public didn't sit well with these middle-aged, baby-boomer women. He kept quiet.

Tiki spoke up. 'Some people don't have any choice about how their lives are run, Ali. You fall in love, babies come along, your folks grow old and ill and depend on you.' Tiki was thinking of her own situation with ageing parents.

'They should plan their lives better. There are lots of plush retirement places around.' Ali was dismissive. 'Can we move on? I have a number of important staff movements to announce.' Ali leaned forward speaking calmly. 'I am making some major changes.' Without flinching she began reassigning positions. 'Within the next month, I am appointing a new fashion editor and a beauty editor from outside the publishing industry. Tiki and Barbara, you will continue in the positions until they are ready to start, then you will be offered a number of options. Barbara, you will be fifty-three this year, so you are eligible to cash in your retirement package, if you so choose.'

Barbara flushed, she had kept her age deadly quiet and no one believed she was over forty-five.

Ali sailed on, speaking in a friendly tone. 'Both of you have the option of staying on in a different capacity, either administrative, assisting the new editors who have the inside run on the fashion and cosmetic companies – or freelancing, doing reader surveys and writing the occasional piece. Fiona, you will stay on as stylist and fashion coordinator.' Ali looked up for the first time, throwing a swift look at the young stylist. She did not glance at anyone else.

The staff members were in shock. It was so callous, so calculated, so surprising. Everyone across the table from Ali felt immediately vulnerable.

Tiki was first to speak. 'Strike me off that list. I'm out of here, thank you very much,' she growled and started gathering up her papers, leaving Ali's unopened market research notes on the table.

Barbara hadn't moved. The job of beauty editor was her lifeblood. She'd been in magazines since she was twenty-four. Fiona Black touched Tiki's arm as Tiki, red-faced, crammed the papers into her folder, then turned on Ali. 'This is pretty shocking news to dump on us, especially those involved. I think Nina Jansous should have a say in this. Does she know what you're doing? And what do you mean when you talked about appointing people from outside publishing? Just what kind of experience could they have that can replace the talents of myself and Barbara?'

Ali didn't answer, just stared icily at Tiki.

Fiona turned to Larissa, who had remained tight-lipped. 'I'm afraid this is news to me,' Fiona said. It sounded a lame excuse and no one believed Fiona wasn't aware of Ali's plans. Most of the women figured Fiona was angling to move in to Tiki's seat as fashion editor, even though she was years younger. She already had a reputation as a fierce terrier in the way she had relentlessly moved her way up from copy girl to fashion coordinator and stylist. She was very pretty and had used her looks wherever it helped her.

'Nice try, don't worry about it, Fiona,' murmured Tiki. 'Good luck to you. As I said, I don't want to be here any more.' She stood up and pushed back her chair. 'It's been nice, guys. A nice three years working with you. I wish you well with the next three months. If any of you lasts that long.'

There was silence as she strode towards the door, almost bowling over Belinda with the tray of cups and a coffee pot.

'For God's sake, send in some strong nourishment, Belinda. They're going to need it.' Tiki swept from the room.

Attention swivelled to Barbara, who was close to tears.

'If you want the pages done differently, Ali, I mean, I had no idea my stories were . . . dated? I know you rewrote them for the first issue, Ali, but what . . . what was wrong with them?' It was a plaintive desperate cry that sent shudders of sympathy through everyone in the room, each now feeling utterly vulnerable. Barbara, always beautifully dressed and groomed, who'd faint rather than be seen with a chip in her nail varnish, was crumbling before their eyes. It was painful and embarrassing.

Ali was relentless. To the others around the table it was staggering that in her assuredness was the assumption she was absolutely right. Just as staggering was the fact that she seemed to feel no discomfort at humiliating the older women. Or indeed, even considered the blow she was delivering. She was so sure, and somehow naively unmoved. It would be easier if Ali had been old and bitter, a hardened cold bitch like some they'd worked for over the years. But Ali was still a young woman, not much older than some of their daughters.

Patiently Ali explained. 'What we need requires a whole new rethink. It's not just about the eye make-up colour for this season, or which of our advertisers' products gets a rave plug this month. We have to look at the science of cosmetics and do well-researched stories. One of the girls I'm looking at trained in a pharmaceutical company and then moved onto a big cosmetic company. Our readers will storm the make-up counters when we tell them what goes into some of these new cellulite and anti-ageing creams.'

'That'll thrill our advertisers, if you take on the beauty industry. They pay for half the magazine ads, Ali,' said Fran cautiously.

'It depends how it's done. And there's a huge market in alternative beauty and health products and programs out there. Look at the anti-ageing clinics. Even the old cosmetic queens are looking at the new millennium research to change how they position their products. We're not knocking them individually. We'll handle the sponsors. As I said, it needs a fresh approach.' Ali looked pointedly at the shell-shocked Barbara.

Barbara took a deep breath and tried to restore her pride. 'Well, I suppose I'll have to move elsewhere. It's not as though I haven't had offers over the years.'

Ali smiled sympathetically. 'You could have a very nice redundancy package, Barbara, but frankly finding a job as a beauty editor might be difficult. It's a generational thing. People of your era just aren't being hired any more.'

Reacting to the shocked intake of breath from a few of the women, Ali shrugged and tried to soften her style. 'Sorry, but that's how it is. This generation is ready to move up, the entrenched and the old guard have to give way to the new wave. You've had your turn.' It was said without animosity but as a statement beyond argument and it sent a chill through those around the table. So much for Nina's assurances of job security.

Business again occupied Ali's attention. 'I'll talk to each of you individually in the coming week to discuss where we are heading. In the meantime, could we run through ideas for the winter issue, Fiona? Fashion-wise, what have you been working on that you can put up to the new fashion editor?'

Fiona realised this was her big opportunity. She had been feeding clever ideas and research to Tiki this past year, trying to make her look at fashion from a more holistic viewpoint. It wasn't just clothes, it was people, marketing, gimmicks, showmanship. She was quick on her feet and plunged in with energy, trying desperately to overcome everyone's shock at what had just happened. 'What's new again? Never throw anything away.' Fiona opened her notes, glad to be distracted and to not have to look at the stunned and hurt faces around her. Everyone was rattled but nobody dared show it. 'It's fur. Made a comeback recently, but now it's back, big time.'

'God, those animal rights people will hurl ice-creams and stick gum on fur coats if they can. We're asking for trouble if we promote fur fashions,' said Fran. 'Remember that anti-fur ad the conservationists did with top models draped in bleeding, dead animals? Horrible.'

'But effective,' Larissa reminded her. 'In New York and Europe they've made faux mink so realistic that a mink mother wouldn't know the difference.'

'Exactly. I thought we could maybe arrange the real and the fake together and play spot the difference,' said Fiona still trying to sell her story. Ali's face gave no clue to her reaction. 'But shoot it in a particular outdoor setting, make it a whole spread.'

Ali raised an eyebrow. 'What do you mean . . . models standing in the snow among bashed seal pups?' It was an attempt at humour that failed dismally.

'Not quite. But, yes, do a fashion spread somewhere really different and not well known to Australian readers. I was thinking of the Inuit in northern Canada.'

'Eskimos, the wild Arctic et cetera?' said Ali as she made notes.

Fiona ticked off a few more points on the notes she'd been gathering. 'They achieved independence a year or so back. I thought the people might be a terrific story and heck, how many spreads have been done in the tundra round Nunavut? How many Australians have ever heard of the place?'

'So what's there? I mean, is this a husky-drawn sled, snowmobile-type trip? Or fur-lined carriages à la *Doctor Zhivago*?' asked Bob, smelling more than a fashion feature.

'Pulled by caribou. Stunning idea,' enthused Fran.

'It is a kind of modern-day fairytale,' said Fiona, looking at her research notes again. 'They're a people who were virtually deliberately wiped out – stolen children, vicious Mounties, government policies to break their cultural ties – but they're true survivors. There are a lot of parallels with Aborigines. What interests me is one of their beliefs that once upon a time,' she glanced up, worried she was losing Ali's attention, 'the Inuit believed they were the same race as the creatures they hunted. Humans and animals were controlled by the spirits of earth and sea.'

'How does this fit in with your spread idea?' asked Ali wondering where this was leading. 'We're not *National Geographic*.'

'I thought it would be sensational to have the models dressed as creatures, real and Arctic mythical beings, in the furs with wild animal make-up and body paint.'

'I like it,' smiled Larissa.

'Stunning. We could organise a music video clip at the same time, shame to waste all that effort. Can we hook up with one of the record companies?' asked Fran, who saw a promotional angle straight away.

Ali made more notes. 'Okay, but it could cost a bomb. See if we can find a record label willing to foot part of the bill. Throw in a celeb singer who wants a different backdrop for an appropriate song. Of course, it will have to be good enough to reach number one. Come back to me with figures and logistics and how we can reduce our end of the costs. See if they have a tourist commission that can come to the party and pay travel and accommodation. It's time the rules were bent. Cost-cutting is the bottom line.'

There was silence, until Larissa spoke quietly. 'Ali, that's contrary to Triton Communication's policy where free travel or promotional goods are banned,' she said mildly. To consider changing this was revolutionary.

Bob backed up Larissa. 'I'm sure you know that arranging for someone involved with the story to subsidise part or all of the expenses puts constraints on the journalist. Travel is the worst; they fly you to a resort, fete and spoil you and there's no way you can be objective if you want to be critical.'

When it was announced Triton was incorporating the *Carina* staff in *Blaze*, copies of Triton's editorial policy on expenses and contra deals had been issued to the journalists and section editors. There was a very clear ethical mandate for Triton publications about dealing with 'freebies' – simply, they were not tolerated.

Ali knew what they were thinking. 'We can find a way to maintain integrity by disguising any outside financial support. If we have to, we'll put a disclaimer at the end of the story. It's all based on the story angle. And saving dollars for other areas of the publication.'

Fiona noted Ali's instructions, but she didn't want to see the Inuit exploited. Her aim was to make a visual statement, and background the photos with references to the political and cultural struggle of these people she found so fascinating.

Reg cleared his voice and adjusted his bow tie. 'From an advertising point of view it could be profitable, bring a lot of different, new clients on board.'

The two other men at the table glanced at him, thinking it was typical of Reg to hold his tongue until he was sure of the lay of the land. Ali ignored him. 'Fran, you and Reg brief the agency to come back to me with a TV ad concept, tell them to include the song, and we want footage of real igloos and natives.' Ali warmed to the idea. 'Get a caribou coat, or an Eskimo woman to knit a fabulous cape or something that we could give away to a reader.'

'Giveaways!' shuddered Bob. 'Next we'll have shrink-wrapped hair-conditioner packets on the cover. I thought we were above value-added and gift promotions.'

'Even rich people like something for nothing,' said Ali.

Fran, as director of promotions, spoke up. 'My understanding of Triton policy from Nina is that *Blaze* was to be a high-quality magazine. Which makes my job more challenging. Promotions are a way to increase circulation and subscriptions as well as promote awareness of the magazine. If *Blaze* is to be competitive, yet still maintain its quality image, our promotions must be above the run of what the others are doing.'

'Fran, I agree with you, we don't want to damage a classy image by resorting to anything too . . . supermarket tabloid,' said Bob.

The staff had embraced the idea that *Blaze Australia* would set the highest standards under Nina's classic hand.

'Well, it's going to be up to you to create innovative ideas then,' said Ali. Fran backed down.

'What's Nina think of this idea?' asked Larissa, voicing the question all the others were thinking, knowing very well Nina probably had no idea of Ali's slash-and-burn plans.

'Nina is out of the loop. In fact, she has already left the country.'

There was a brief pause. They knew that a new editor had the power to exercise control of staff and content. With Nina as publisher and editor-in-chief out of the picture, it would be up to the proprietor to argue with the new editor. That presumably was Baron Triton and they couldn't see him interfering, even though he was due to arrive any day for the magazine's first edition launch. Ali was his new star. He was about to introduce her formally to Australia as the founding editor of what would be the corporation's latest success story.

'How is your wife's new job going?' Fran whispered to Bob, while they waited for the conference to resume.

Without lifting her head, Ali cut in, 'This is a business meeting, not coffee klutch. Can we get on with the meeting?' Ali scanned her agenda, made a few more announcements of changes she intended for the offices, and they all sat numbly making notes, wishing Nina were there. Larissa was an unknown quantity and she was under Ali's authority, so she was a doubtful ally for them. Privately, everyone was working out ways to entrench and consolidate their positions, even at the cost of office friendships. With Ali at the helm, no one on board was safe.

Ali reached the end of her list. 'And, finally, arrival and departure times, including lunch hours, will be monitored. Time clocks are being installed to keep track of hours spent away from desks.'

Jaws dropped and Jonathan laughed out loud. 'What! Ali, this is a magazine, remember, not the public service. That's how we work – out of the office. Stories don't walk in the door.'

'Belinda will be keeping a check on all staff, just what they are doing, where they are going and how long it takes.'

'Ali, is that fair, to make her the policeman?' asked Larissa. 'Is it really necessary?' She looked about the table. 'Have hours worked been a problem?'

There was a faint shaking of heads. No one had ever considered the situation. They had just put in long hours to get the first edition under way and Nina had approved overtime payments, making it clear this was an exception for the first edition only. Normally they were used to working whatever hours were needed. If that meant working late then an occasional long lunch or late arrival compensated.

Ali was unmoved. 'And that includes the senior staff.'

She looked quickly at her notes and snapped her Filofax shut. It had been a productive first morning. 'That's it. Email me if you have a query.' She rose from her chair. 'I'll have the human resources people deal with the new arrangements.' She gave a brief nod at Tiki's empty chair, her glance sliding over Barbara as she left the room.

The others gathered their bags and papers and left without the usual chatter and laughter. Each person felt they were on their own now, engaged in a personal battle for survival. And no one was looking forward to the rest of the day, let alone the longer term. Each of them was composing what he or she would say to Nina the minute the opportunity arose. But then, where was she? The staff had been so thrilled to be working for Nina Jansous. How could she deliver them into the nightmare clutches of Ali the Ambitious and then disappear?

TAKE SIX...

It was past eleven o'clock that evening when Tom, the chauffeur, opened the door of the limousine outside Ali's apartment. He handed her a bundle of folded newspapers and her briefcase.

'See you at seven, Tom.'

'Righto,' he responded brightly. 'Not planning to sleep-in then?' he ventured with a big smile.

'No, Tom. Not at all.' Ali was still trying to adjust to the casualness of Australians, who seemed to have remarkable resilience. A chauffeur in New York City would never dare to be so familiar.

Despite her cool response, the driver looked admiringly at her slim figure, a cape draped from one shoulder as she swept into the lobby. He wondered who or what waited for her upstairs. For the past three weeks he had been driving her to the beauty parlour each morning, to work and then home each evening, and from the few snatches of conversation he'd managed to draw from her, she didn't seem to have a life outside *Blaze*. The only calls she made on her mobile phone were business related.

In her apartment, Ali ignored the big window display of glittering lights on the harbour foreshores and the giant coat-hanger of a bridge that was one of the city's icons. She made a cup of green tea, kicked off her shoes and turned on the cable TV news in case there was a story worth following up, but then ignored the images on the screen. Her attention was mainly on the newspapers, a selection of dailies from around the country.

She turned to the financial and business sections, quickly scanning the stories, circling several paragraphs with a gold pen as she went, ripping out a long story on a high achiever in the corporate world. She then turned to the obituary notices. One sent her scanning eyes into freeze-frame, and with a satisfying 'Hmmm' she under-lined a name that matched the one she had marked in the business news and turned back to read it again:

> Bulmar Enterprises chairman, John O'Donnell, is tak-ing extended leave following the death of his wife, Carol May. In a brief statement issued by the company yesterday, Mr O'Donnell said he planned to spend time with his children. The funeral will be a private service for family only. Mr O'Donnell has specified no flowers and suggested instead that donations be made in his wife's memory to a cancer research facility in Sydney.

Ali sat for a moment and then picked up the small dicta-phone from the coffee table. 'Belinda, pull what bio material you can find on John O'Donnell from Bulmar

Enterprises. As much personal stuff as possible, also anything new about the company. Make an appointment for me to see him as soon as possible. Make a note to bring up a special feature on ovarian cancer at the next editorial meeting.'

Something complex had stirred in Ali's neatly ordered emotional deep-freezer. And it was due to John O'Donnell, a man she didn't know apart from what she'd read and seen in the bizoid press, which had alluded to his wife's cancer. Attractive lean face, grey hair, about sixty. This was when these men were at their most vulnerable, a window of opportunity that rarely lasted too long before another woman stepped in and slammed it shut. Ali, ever the opportunist, decided the chairman of one of the largest construction companies in the country would be a useful new friend – professionally and especially personally.

It was a prospect that made her feel excited, a nice thought to end the day on, she mused. She switched off the TV and headed towards the bedroom, pausing briefly to take in the world outside the window. A full moon hung low over the bridge and seemed to balance on the top of the arch. It was a pretty scene, but Ali felt none of the emotion an expatriate may expect to feel at the classic image of Sydney's harbour with the span of the bridge and the sails of the Opera House. Ali was here for business, nothing else, she reminded herself.

Larissa and Belinda were having a quick lunch with Tiki Henderson. Even though she hadn't set foot inside the building since being pushed aside by Ali, Tiki liked to keep up with the internal news.

'So how's the velvet steamroller, the Yank Tank, doing

upstairs? Who's been squashed today?' Tiki inquired with a grin.

Belinda gagged on her coffee as Larissa laughed.

'So how are you settling in then, Larissa?' asked Belinda, quickly changing the subject. 'Like your little pad in Paddo?'

'Love it. A terrace house in Paddington seems to be regarded as right up there in yuppie-ville. Which, I have to say, isn't me. But it is a fun area.'

'Used to be arty-farty years ago. Before the money belt took it over. Still, you're close to the CBD and surrounded by sensational shops, terrific restaurants and some interesting art galleries,' said Tiki.

'Yes, I've started exploring those. I wish my boyfriend was here with me. He paints.' Larissa's face clouded over. She wondered if she were missing Gerry more than he was her. At least his life was still a familiar routine. 'So why isn't he here?' asked Tiki in her blunt manner, propping herself on one hand on the table as if settling in for a long explanation.

'Work. He's a stockbroker. The paint splattered overalls only came out on the weekends or nights I worked late. Which was frequent, I have to say.' Larissa took out her wallet and pulled out a photo of Gerard.

'He's so handsome,' said Belinda with genuine admiration.

Tiki took the picture and examined it in silence for a while, then gave an appreciative nod and a raised eyebrow. 'Hmmm. Must have been hard leaving a hunk like that.' She handed back the photo. 'He still going to be there when you go home next year? When's he coming to visit?'

'Tiki, that's not a nice thing to say,' chided Belinda. 'Lots of people have jobs that keep them apart.' She gave Larissa a comforting smile. 'Absence makes the heart grow fonder, isn't that what they say?'

'A cliché which, like most clichés, one hopes is trite but true,' sighed Larissa.

'Do you want to tell us how you met, how long you've been together, what he likes, that kind of thing?' asked Belinda hoping that would make Larissa feel better.

'I won't bore you with that . . . at this moment. I will another time. I have to go back to the office to phone a friend's daughter who is leaving the US tomorrow to come out here. She's taking a small holiday in Paris on the way. I'm looking forward to taking her under my wing a bit.'

'Ooh, can I help? Who is this?' asked Belinda, ever curious about details of other people's lives.

Tiki chuckled. 'Always the mother hen, as you might have noticed, Larissa. How old is this girl? Need babysitters? One of my nieces is available.'

'Thanks. But Miche is twenty-two. She needs to be away from the States for a bit.' She paused, wondering whether to divulge more, then decided these two women could be helpful to Miche. 'Her mother died – well, committed suicide. She worked for *Blaze* in New York. Nina is Miche's godmother.'

'Oh, my. How sad. Where is she staying, what's she going to do? Can we help?' Belinda was all caring concern.

'Thanks. Maybe when she arrives. Nina thought a small break might help her move on with her life. They're meeting in Paris. When she turns up, she'll stay with me for a bit, till she decides what to do. She's just graduated from college . . . in journalism.'

'So she's going to work for us!' said Belinda.

'Handy to have a godmother who runs the biggest magazine in the world,' mused Tiki.

'It's actually not like that,' said Larissa, suddenly defensive. 'Miche has had a few freelance pieces published already. Nina says she has a lot of talent. She has to learn the ropes of the business now. Having a degree doesn't always mean a lot when you start out in the real world.'

'Dorothy used to say you can't beat a thorough cadetship training,' said Belinda. Then a thought hit her. 'Ali's a tough boss. Working with her will be the real world. At least Miche will be with other Americans.'

'Ali is Australian. She only wears a New Yorker's skin,' laughed Larissa. 'In the States, foreigners usually end up sounding just as American as the natives. It's something of a survival tactic and it's a catching accent, though Ali has been there since she was quite young. What her background is, no one knows. Never talks about herself,' Larissa stretched, 'which suits me fine. I've always kept our relationship on a professional level.'

Belinda leaned forward, 'I would never have guessed Ali was Australian. Surely she has family here? Yet she doesn't seem to have much of a personal life. She never has personal calls. And do you mean to say that you and she haven't talked about . . . the changes, you know, what she plans to do? She's certainly been hands-on once Nina was out of sight.'

Larissa looked into Belinda's eyes. 'Tell everyone – there's Ali, and there's me. I may be her 2IC but I am as much at Ali's mercy as they are. I'm a worker, and a newcomer. I don't want to be lumped on the other side of the table with Ali so that it's a case of us and you. I'm not going to denigrate a colleague . . .'

'But . . .' said she diplomatically,' interjected a faintly amused Tiki.

'But . . .' Larissa ignored her, 'it is in all our interests to make this magazine work. Sometimes you have to put personal feelings to one side.' She continued looking at Belinda, who nodded slowly.

'I understand, Larissa. Believe me, I really do.'

Larissa relaxed. She knew she now had an ally in Belinda. Ali, on the other hand, wouldn't need allies. She had a knack for looking after herself.

It had taken all of Belinda's persistence to line up an appointment for Ali with John O'Donnell.

'Ali, he's a high-flyer still trying to run a business while recovering from his wife's death,' said Belinda. 'His secretary says very firmly that he's unavailable.'

'Tell him it's to do with a story on ovarian cancer. That'll make him sit up. It killed his wife.'

When Belinda finally convinced John O'Donnell to come on the line, Ali was all caring and charm. 'I understand how you must be feeling. I appreciate the fact you want to be with your children, so I hope you'll forgive this intrusion.'

'Thank you. Your secretary mentioned you were writing something on cancer . . . ?'

'Specifically, ovarian cancer. It doesn't command the attention breast cancer does and there needs to be a lot more awareness of it . . .' Ali rattled off statistics knowing the man's wife was one of them. 'However, I don't want it to be a cold, statistical type of story.' Before she could go further, the man broke in sounding alarmed.

'I'm sorry I can't speak publicly about any of this. Naturally I support the idea, but if I can help in any other way . . .'

'Well, yes, you can. I have two very special projects I'd really like to talk to you about and hopefully enlist your support. One is a special ovarian cancer program, the other a foundation for young people . . .'

'I don't see how this concerns me. I'd be happy to make a donation, but . . .'

'The cancer program is as yet unnamed, I thought perhaps, as a tribute to your wife . . .'

There was a moment's silence. 'If it's connected to *Blaze*, I assume it will be appropriate. Could you send me the details, please?'

Ali gave a soft chuckle. 'I'm afraid I'm the detail at the moment. My magazine's interest in this is still in the early stages, and I would prefer that nothing is bandied about on paper. With Bulmar's experience, you can appreciate my sensitivity on this.'

Her remark hit home. Several months before, O'Donnell's corporation had been the target of a sophisticated piece of corporate bugging in which details of a construction bid had been revealed and they'd lost the contract to an Asian firm that had seriously bid below Bulmar's bottom line. 'Yes,' he said. 'I see you keep tabs on the construction industry as well as your publishing empire.' Before returning the call he'd had his secretary check why Ali was calling and not Nina Jansous.

'I find the corporate world utterly sexy. Fascinating in fact. I follow the high and lows, takeovers and mergers like my girlfriends follow the major league baseball.'

His voice thawed for the first time. 'I've never considered the business world sexy, but I'm flattered to think I'm part of such an intriguing world you describe.'

'I'd be extremely flattered if you'd give me ten minutes. I wouldn't waste your time or mine on anything trivial,' said Ali with a hint of flirtatiousness.

'You're a very persuasive lady. I look forward to hearing what you have to say. Karen will set it up with your PA. Goodbye for now.'

Ali waved the receiver in the air with a triumphant salute before calling Belinda.

'Make an appointment with O'Donnell in a week's time. I'm leaving the building for a meeting. Call me on the mobile if you need me.' Ali had taken to using the local expression rather than the American term cell phone. She didn't elaborate further to Belinda. To Ali's mind her whereabouts were of no concern to her secretary. She wasn't going to set a precedent of being answerable every time she left the building. This was despite expecting everyone else in the company to be at their desks or leave precise details of their movements.

Belinda watched Ali leave, waited ten minutes and then rang the garage security attendant. 'Has she gone?'

'Yup. The car's halfway down the block.'

'Thanks, Steve.'

Belinda had set up the Ali coastwatch. Several times Ali had left the office and then caught the elevator back upstairs to surprise anyone standing around chatting or otherwise slacking off. She unnerved staff by descending unannounced into cubicles and offices, demanding to see what they were working on. Once, on finding a small group sharing a birthday cake for one of the art department boys, she had issued an edict that personal celebrations should be observed out of office hours. Two people poring over personal photographs would jump apart feeling guilty if Ali came into view.

More and more, staff members kept to themselves, busying themselves with their individual tasks until meetings and collaborative decisions had to be made.

Ali liked it that way. *Blaze* was a business and she ran it according to her rules. If someone needed to see her they could make an appointment. Occasionally she would step out of her office and ask a particular staff member if he or she had any problems. This was her compromise to executive–staff relations. She found she quite liked to prowl the halls checking all was humming along, without a lot of time-wasting and noisy chatter. Aware of Ali's expectations, the staff sat before silent computer screens and emailed each other rather than stroll around the corner with a cup of coffee in hand to chat over an idea or problem.

Nina's innovative ideas to make the work environment a comfortable, relaxing and productive place now seemed as far away as Nina herself. The floor below the *Blaze* offices was a private club, available to the *Blaze* staff as well as other tenants in the building. It had a gym and pool, a relaxation centre with a meditation room. On call were a masseuse, reflexologist, chiropractic healer and reiki practitioner. Meals were served bistro style in an open room filled with bright, funky furniture. In one corner were lounges with a large-screen TV, magazines and newspapers. Off this were rooms with beds and showers for those who worked extra long hours or into the night.

The staff also had access to a children's creche nearby and there were plans to establish more facilities. Nina had called in a specialist in workplace environments to make *Blaze* a friendly, non-toxic, efficient, fun place to be. It encouraged people to be productive, to enjoy their work and not to feel they were choosing between a life and a career.

Under Ali, people who had taken advantage of these facilities in office hours were soon unearthed. Ali had made it clear they either changed their attitude to fit this leisure space into their own time, or they could go their own way.

Ali was rarely seen in any of the communal areas. She ate in her office or attended business lunches. No one was aware of her ever meeting friends. Indeed, she had dropped a comment, at Belinda's constant attempts to intrude into her privacy, that she wouldn't be allowing time for friendships during her twelve-month stay.

Ali slipped into her chair at the Yellow Brick Road and Dane took over, shooing Tottie away. 'I'll do Miss Ali. Head massage darling?'

Ali leaned back and felt the warm water slide through her hair. Dane's fingers worked from her temples across her head. Ali closed her eyes and slowly the tension eased in her neck and shoulder muscles.

There was no one near them and Dane leaned close to her as he worked, the running water muffling his voice from the rest of the salon. 'Been big changes at *Chic* magazine. Their style editor has been poached by *Glory* mag. She whipped in here in a brand-new baby Merc convert . . . a little inducement to leave, I believe.'

'Umm. Is she any good?' asked Ali drowsily.

'In bed or at work, dearie? Though it's now the one and same I hear. She's in bed with the owner of Boysies, that new homewares that's growing bigger than Conran ever imagined. Heard about the inside running on their new home collection. Lots of money being spent on big swishy ads. We're doing the rugs and slap.'

Ali opened an eye and looked at Dane.

'Hair and make-up sweetie,' he translated.

'What else? What about cover stories?'

'Wouldn't know about storieeees . . . but they're after our serious footy star hunk to pose in leathers on a Harley. Saying he's been offered a guest appearance in a TV police series. Seems he was caught misbehaving in an S&M bar and so his people are doing a cover-up job in the legit press in case it's leaked. Making hard core look like high fashion or something.'

'He was researching his role, right?'

Dane laughed. 'Something like that. The football fans might buy it, but nobody round the Oxford Street end of town will!'

'Wasn't he just paid zillions to front a bunch of health food products? One of those wholesome family companies?'

Dane sniggered as he wrapped a towel around Ali's head, beginning the lengthy highlights process. 'Puts a whole new meaning on lunch boxes and snack foods if you ask me.'

Larissa tapped at Ali's door, marvelling at the editor's sleekly groomed appearance. Larissa had not slept well. Gerry still couldn't work out the time difference, or didn't want to, and had rung her at 3 a.m. They'd talked for an hour and he'd listened patiently to her stories about Ali, the staff, Miche's impending arrival, the hassles of living in a new city.

Finally he'd asked: 'Riss, what about me? Do you miss me?'

'Of course I do. I hate this lonely bed. I have a lovely house and no you to share it with.'

'No one to cook you dinner, eh? Rub your back, give you a cuddle . . .'

'All of that. Do you miss me?'

'Hell, no!' He gave a low chuckle that made her tingle. 'Riss, I'm not going to tell you how much I miss you. It's not fair to lay that on you with all you have on your plate. You chose to do this.'

'Gerry . . . we agreed, this is a step up for me. I know it's hard but . . . it's the middle of the night . . . I'm really tired.'

'Yeah, yeah. Sorry I woke you. Just remember, Riss, you chose to do this . . .'

'You could be here! You'd love it! It'd be so good for you . . . This is a perfect place to explore your potential as an artist. The pressure wouldn't be on here like it is in New York. Gerry, come over, please.'

'Riss, calm down. We agreed you needed two months to settle in. I'm working on it. Listen, go back to sleep. Email me the shit and then we can just talk about the happy things. I miss you, cupcake.'

She smiled in the darkness. 'Be good. I miss you too.'

'I love you, Riss.'

'Love you.' The phone went dead. Larissa punched her pillow and settled under the covers. But she didn't go back to sleep. At 6 a.m. she rose and made coffee.

Now it was 10 a.m. and Larissa felt exhausted. Ali was looking at her expectantly. 'Ali, the LA bureau has called to say that Dixon Landers is engaged to be married. They could go for an exclusive.'

'Landers . . . What do you think?'

'Well, he was Australia's biggest soapy star, and he's made two major movies since he's been in LA. And he's tipped for an Oscar nomination. He's celeb news.' Larissa stressed the derisory word 'celeb'.

'He works for me.'

'There's a hitch – so to speak.'

'Money?'

'No. I hear he's gay.'

'That is news. So who's he marrying? His boyfriend or his manager?'

'He's marrying a lady. A female. A make-up artist.'

'You saying he wants to change?' asked Ali.

'No, he wants a green card. To stay in the US. It's a business deal.'

'And we can break this story?'

'I was thinking of the Hollywood Wedding for Aussie Star angle, not the Gay Star in Sham Marriage deal. Though it will be obvious to anyone with a few smarts. He's never been publicly outed.'

'Makes it less of a story. How would we play it?'

'Do the honeymoon. Exotic location, exclusive, intimate photos.' Larissa was making her distaste clear. 'If we want it.'

'What's it going to cost us?'

'You don't think it's too showbizzy, too tabloid? We'd be competing with the paparazzi and the supermarket sleazoids if the word leaks.'

Ali ignored Larissa's last comment. 'Where are they going for the honeymoon?'

'The Great Barrier Reef. An island. I didn't pay that much attention to the details. I'm really just letting you know about it. I didn't think you'd be interested.'

'He's big news. We can make a deal with London to share the costs on this. That Aussie TV soap of his was the top rater in the UK. Can't we set up something else at the same time to defray the costs? A fashion shoot? Travel piece? Competition to join the happy couple?'

Larissa winced. 'Ali, I thought we'd discussed freebies and promotional tie-ins. It's just not us.'

Ali flicked a hand dismissively. 'It's time to drop that stuffy thinking. We're in business like everyone else. We have a product to sell and competition is the name of the game. We just have to do it better, right?'

Larissa's head was thumping. 'Fine. Tell me how we deal with trailing after an airhead actor on his phony honeymoon with two competition winners in tow – who could be from the other side of the country, a farm outside Perth, who have never left the state before, and have probably never read *Blaze*?'

Ali grinned. 'You're saying some hick couple who love

Dixon Landers' movies only bought *Blaze* for the competition, and therefore are not our usual readership.'

'I guess so.'

'So if we do it and they win, then we ask our farmer friends why they bought *Blaze* and we use them as a promotion to show them this magazine is for all Aussies. That's how wide our market needs to be in this country. It's something for nothing, Larissa. We should be making sure a couple like these people win the chance to holiday on a tropical island with their own Hollywood heart-throb. If they win, how many of their friends and neighbours will start buying *Blaze* to see what's in it for them?'

'Ali, such competitions aren't new to magazines.'

'To us they are. We'll do it with our usual style, first class all the way. We can do a contra with the resort for a free ad in *Blaze*. Make the island *Blaze*'s "Place in the South Pacific".' Ali was warming to her idea. While it wasn't Triton policy elsewhere in the world, it seemed to her it could work in the commercial free-for-all of Australia. Piracy and entrepreneurs disguising themselves as Robin Hood, while feathering their own nests were alive and well below the equator. The rules that applied back in New York seemed unnecessary here. 'Every couple of months we could do a "Favourite Place of *Blaze*", like Fiona was suggesting for north Canada. Is this island like Mustique, or is it touristy?'

'Ali, I have no idea. I'll look into it.' Larissa hurried from the office before Ali could take off again. At her desk, she rested her head on her hands and wished she'd never passed on the message for Ali about Dixon Landers' wedding. She'd assumed it would be dismissed out of hand. This was supermarket tabloid stuff.

Oh, God, what was she doing here?

*

146

Ali buzzed Belinda. 'I want to talk to the head of advertising at the Happi Food company. The one that just signed up that football star . . . it was announced last week.'

When the advertising director of Happi Foods came on the line, Ali kept the niceties brief before plunging in. 'I'm wondering if I could send my advertising manager around to persuade you to take out a contract to advertise your products in *Blaze*. Our demographics are very suited to your market.' She listened as he waffled at the other end of the line. 'I am very aware you're planning an expensive TV campaign with your star spokesperson. That's why I thought you might be changing tack and would be open to new avenues for your advertising. Given the circumstances.'

There was a pause at the end of the line and Ali went on pleasantly. 'I understand one of those nasty TV shows is planning to do the whole sordid story about him . . . yes, it could be very unfortunate.' She visualised the man at the other end of the phone with his head in his hand. 'Of course, there are ways to stop the story . . . if one has influence. And if it's worth one's while . . .' She waited, smiling slightly. 'I thought you would see it that way. No promises, but I'm sure the network would see fit to drop the story. Shame to disillusion all those sports fans. Though it would have been a nice way for them to stick it to their competition, which has the football TV rights. Now, could Reg Craven see you in the next day or so?'

Ali called Reg. 'Happi Foods are going to take out a nice fat advertising contract with us. They're dumping or downplaying their football person's budget to go in *Blaze* instead . . . Why? Well, I did him a small favour.'

Ali hung up, pleased at Reg's stunned reaction – glad for the revenue but annoyed he hadn't landed the account. So much of this was mere wheeling and dealing in perceptions. As far as Ali knew, unless Dane had talked to someone else – and for what she was paying him privately for any information he gleaned, he'd better not be – no TV show knew about the incident in the bar. She had bluffed the food company. She needed Reg to sign them up quickly before anything did leak out.

The concierge at Georges Cinq opened the door of the limousine waiting for Miche, Nina and Claudia Harrison, the elegant Belgian-born wife of the Australian Ambassador to Paris. '*Mesdames, amusez-vous bien aux collections*! *Lesquels voyez-vous aujourd'hui?*'

'Christian Lacroix. *Merci*, Pierre.'

Miche glanced out the window of the limousine at the Parisian scenes, so familiar from movies and postcards. 'I can't believe I'm here doing this!'

Claudia leaned over and tapped her knee, 'Me too, petite. After eighteen months here, I pinch myself every day. Despite being Belgian, I adore this city.'

Nina and Miche laughed at Claudia's rich guttural and rolling 'Rs'. Even after spending many years of her life in Australia, her Belgian accent hadn't softened.

'Nina, this must be so humdrum to you,' sighed Miche. 'You go everywhere, know everyone – or rather they know you. In New York I hadn't realised how famous you were over here.'

'Only in small circles, Miche. I've been lucky with friends. And don't forget my work opens doors. Though when I started, that wasn't a consideration.'

Miche gave her an affectionate smile. 'Well, when you turn out something as spectacular as *Blaze*, it's no wonder. I so want a successful career in journalism. I love writing about life, what's happening around me. One day I would like to publish my journals.'

'Miche is a serious chronicler. And really that's what magazines are about, reflecting what's going on around us,' said Nina.

'Well, *chérie*,' said Claudia to Miche, 'are you going to write something about the collections? It's madness, wonderful, but crazy. We are having a reception at the embassy for a few Australian designers soon – two beautiful people, Collette Dinnigan and Len Osborne – and also the new little model everyone is mad about. She's Australian and she is already going to be sooo famous. And still such a baby. You must meet her.'

Nina was quietly delighted with Claudia's idea. It was a fabulous opportunity for Miche and the concept came free of any suggestion of pressure from Nina. 'It certainly does sound like a first-class story,' she added. 'What do you think, Miche?'

'A peer perspective?' mused Miche.

'Why not? You aren't qualified to comment on the fashions, but a story on how the Australian designers have made it this far sounds like interesting copy. The model angle adds a touch of spice. I'm sure you'll produce a story that's different from the fashion coverage,' suggested Nina. 'As far as I know, this new model has done a few covers and spreads and this is her first time on the catwalk. There hasn't been any personal stuff.'

'It's not Sally Shaw, is it?' said Miche, crinkling her forehead as she vaguely recalled reading about the new Australian find in the model world.

'That's her. But you know, Miche, you too are so pretty, you could be a model. You can make *such* money . . .' Claudia shook her wrists making her bracelets jangle. 'Though maybe you are too attractive. Some of these models, they look like creatures from space.'

'Not me! I'd hate it. I'm too shy. And I couldn't pose, do that stuff.' Miche dismissed the suggestion.

But the two older women appraised the lovely younger one sitting opposite them in the stretch limousine thinking she could very well be a model – if classic good looks and a wholesome body were back in vogue. Miche had high cheekbones, wonderful green cat's eyes and silky blonde hair that today was swept up – normally it fell in smooth waves to her shoulders. Her complexion tended to be light olive and tanned easily. Miche detested the way everyone in New York seemed to favour dark clothes and pale skin tones. Just like the artificial light and grimy, sunless streets so many lived in. She had always loved Nina's more Mediterranean look and choice of brilliant colours.

With Miche in Paris, Nina became her god-daughter's guide to the city of chic, leading Miche into the grand salons of the design houses, where the couture price tags made Miche gasp.

'We'll buy you one good outfit, a classic that you'll wear for years. But you must love it first,' said Nina.

Miche had been unable to fall in love with suits or dresses that could pay for her first six months in Australia. So they had compromised. Nina bought her a pair of Ferragamo shoes and a Chanel handbag, labels she loved. Both were in quality black leather that was elegant yet could be worn and carried with jeans. Then they'd gone shopping along the Right Bank. As they passed the Louvre, Miche clutched Nina, 'I must spend a day in there!'

'You must. But today – and tomorrow – is for shopping.'

'Where are we going tomorrow? I see why you said wear comfortable shoes,' laughed Miche.

'Saint Germain des Prés, the 6th Arrondissement. It's more sophisticated. But you must develop your eye for appreciating quality and style. Even a simple white T-shirt can be incredibly chic if it is cut well, the cotton the finest and the shape very now. Then you can wear it with a chiffon evening skirt and a shawl or with linen resort pants and coloured tennis shoes – without the laces.'

Miche had shaken her head. 'Just looking at the women in the street, I'm beginning to understand what the word chic really means.'

'You keep your own sense of style and what you like, Miche. It's understanding the quality of the fabric, how it's made, and how it feels. Clothes should feel like part of you, move with you, flatter you, make you feel positive about yourself when you wear them.'

Let loose in a sea of boutiques where every item had been chosen with care and a discerning eye, Miche had burrowed through shelves and racks choosing interesting fabrics, delicate prints and pastel colours. Nina found several unusual little jackets, exquisite scarves and a fifties-style, cropped pair of black and white pants that Miche adored.

In one tiny overflowing shop, Miche twirled in front of the small mirror. She was wearing a cream cashmere shrunk top, black seventies flared hipster pants, teamed with a grey chiffon print evening top that floated around her slim body. Laced ankle boots in mulberry suede with curved twenties heels were a favourite find. 'I would never have thought of putting these together! Nina, you're brilliant.'

'Inherited talent from Clara. My mother was very creative with scraps of fabric and design. She was a milliner, but would have been a clever couturier had she had the opportunity.'

Their shopping ended when they came to a small specialist jewellery store selling handmade one-off designs carefully selected from around the world. Both Miche and Nina fell in love with some beautiful beadwork from

South Africa – traditional intricate patterns, from the Ndebele people, woven into elaborate necklaces. Nina bought herself a dramatic high, beaded collar that had a cascade frill of diamonds and gold.

'These are beautiful pieces. Who makes them?' asked Miche.

'These pieces are crafted by a South African jewellery designer, Kevin Friedman, who works with the Ndebele village women. They make the beadwork under a special scheme to help them become independent and protect them from exploitation,' explained the shop owner. 'I like to find jewellery that combines contemporary ideas while still keeping the old ways alive. The Ndebele people are one of the only tribes in South Africa that have kept their heritage and traditions so strongly. I travel the world looking for such special pieces.'

'Now there's a story for *Blaze*,' smiled Miche. 'I'll add that to my list.'

Late that afternoon, Nina had taken Miche to the funky, revamped 11th Arrondissement on the Left Bank. On Rue Oberkampf they spurned the newly trendy bistros and restaurants for old-world venues that had become fun cafés with artistic menus and a partying crowd, where music, laughter and energy pumped into the street.

Two days later, as their car headed towards Rue du Faubourg Saint Honoré for the showing of Christian Lacroix's latest collection, Miche felt more attuned to the undercurrent of fashion that was a Parisian's lifeblood.

Claudia was wearing a Richard Taylor suit. 'He's from Australia, so I'm waving the flag. And for the reception, of course, I'll wear my Carla Zampatti. The cream silk skirt and top.'

Today Nina had chosen Chanel. Miche wore pale grey pants with a simple white T-shirt under a cropped black jacket and relieved the severity with a jaunty red beret trimmed with a scarlet quill. Her new Ferragamos and Chanel handbag teamed perfectly.

Nina had always been a regular at the Paris fashion house collections. As renowned for her own style and beauty as for her powerful position, she was automatically ushered to one of the fiercely fought-for small, gold front row seats. Behind the velvet ropes, fashion writers, buyers and celebrities entered into a type of warfare that sometimes erupted into shrieks and tears. The world's photographers – fashion, news and freelance – scrambled and pushed against the catwalk. Elegant or just rich women, who could pay the thousands of dollars for couture outfits, bashed at the photographers who blocked their way, hitting them with rolled programs, sunglasses, handbags or stilettos.

Nina, Claudia and Miche settled themselves on the thin-legged gilt chairs, noting the movie star, pop star and famous writer seated along the row. Nina nodded at the cream of the fashion editors and the elite heads of the international model agencies who were quick to attract her attention.

'I suppose you know everyone here,' whispered Miche.

'Most of them. It's a bit of a smorgasbord every year. But a lot of familiar faces, of course. I've always wondered whether people come for the clothes, the models, the show or the whole scene.'

'All of that. Okay, there's Bandeau.' Claudia glanced along the row to where a tall man dressed in leather, his silver hair in a ponytail, a braided band across his forehead, tinted glasses and a goatee, was kissing the women around him.

153

Nina laughed. 'You sound like a fan at a rock show. How come you know a fashion photographer?'

'Well, they did make a movie about him. He did a photo session at the Baron's estate in Liège when we were visiting. You remember how beautiful it is. It was for the Paris edition of *Blaze*. Wedding dresses. Very romantic.' Claudia gave an arch smile. 'How is the dear Baron?'

'Oscar is well. Now I'm moving to Australia we won't be in daily contact. But we will still have *Blaze Australia* as a bond, and I will see him at board meetings in New York.' Nina turned her attention to the salon, which was jammed with people. The world's fashion press were sparring and jostling for positions to see the narrow white walkway that was flanked by tubs of flowers and had suspended screens above the tiny stage at one end. A flash went off, capturing the personalities in the front row.

'Nina, the Baron adores you. Why are you bothering yourself with this new magazine? Why don't you . . .' Claudia fumbled for the right word, waving her expressive hands, 'do more of this? Enjoy yourself.'

'This is work for me. Of course, these showings and our luncheons at L'Orangerie are lots of fun. It's always necessary to keep up with the collections.'

'I meant spend more time in Europe. Surely Oscar can let Triton run itself these days. Bernard can't wait to retire. This summer we're cruising in Greece. Do come. Forty people. Bring Oscar.'

'Stop matchmaking, Claudia, but thank you for the invitation. If Oscar and I have one big thing in common, it's not a wild attraction for each other. Rather it's keeping our hands on the business. Not that we don't have excellent people, but it's a massive part of your life.'

'Too much, Nina. Make the most of this break.'

To Nina's relief, Claudia was distracted as the ceiling

lights dimmed and the floodlights on the runway blazed to life, synchronised with the live music.

Miche nudged Nina. 'It's like a rock concert.'

'Look at the stars, darling. Here they come.'

Miche fell into a trance as the models came out and *performed*. This was not as she'd imagined from the edited shots on TV . . . the laid-back somewhat haughty stroll of clothes horses. Here the models were part of the entire creation of each outfit, from their make-up to hairdo, to body movement. They *sold* each outfit, giving the clothes personality and life. No matter how wild and excessive, the girl was never overwhelmed by the fur, the feathers, the metal spikes and studs, the weight of exquisitely jewelled fabrics. They became fantasy creatures, reinvented for this moment as a fairytale image, the embodiment of a designer's imagination. They acted with their bodies, breathing life into the creations that flowed down the catwalk one after the other, the audience oblivious of the chaotic bedlam reigning backstage.

Nina knew what it was like at most of the shows. In just one room egoists, prima donnas, hysterical assistants, dressers and frazzled hair and make-up artists screamed for attention. The models smoked, many taking more than recreational drugs, and drank Dom Pérignon as if it were Perrier. A few of the girls were pushed out onto the catwalk in a state of revved hyper energy or an out-of-body stupor that all seemed part of the performance. For the younger models, it meant being thrown into a cauldron where you either survived or sank further in this sometimes murky world.

'There's Sally,' said Claudia above the chatter, the music, the occasional bursts of applause, the intrusion of video cameras, photographers jostling and popping of flashbulbs.

Miche looked up at the sylph figure of the sixteen-year-old, who looked all of twelve. Pale skin scattered with glitter, blackened eyes ringed with circles of green and mauve, black lipstick and nails, hair extensions that fell in coils to her knees. Ethereal and death-like she floated in carefully ripped and shredded silk and tulle, the tatters caught in tiny flowers. Half-tied ribbons trailed from her hair, her satin shoes were covered in seed pearls. The child bride clutching a spray of shedding overblown roses, her fragile beauty, her apparent bewilderment and virginal frailty underscoring the wispiness of the bridal dress titled '*Mademoiselle du lac*'.

Miche was fascinated. The girl seemed from another time, another world. So incredibly young, so vulnerable. Had she had been swept into a milieu beyond what she knew, or could have expected? Miche wondered how she would deal with this.

Nina had similar thoughts. Young girls like Miche and this Sally Shaw were dealing with issues and situations far removed from the secure world of Sydney in the fifties, which she had known at that age. Yet, as she'd thought about it, she'd realised she had also been ambitious and dedicated to a career as a young woman. But, how different were the pressures and values. Nina thought of the protective Clara, and resolved to keep a watchful eye on Miche.

Meanwhile, Miche was pondering how quickly circumstances could change one's life. Since the loss of her mother she had been forced to address her priorities, her career and her family situation. Now, thinking about the young model, Sally, she wondered what the girl was feeling.

Sally had been a young Aussie schoolgirl, on an exchange program in France, who'd been plucked from a café by a fashion agent. Within six months, she was on the covers of the top international fashion magazines, courted by the couture houses for the photo layouts and was now debuting on the world stage of fashion before critical, envious eyes that had seen it all before. Yes, this was a story she'd like to explore. Miche decided she would take up Nina's suggestion – and use her help – to delve behind the shimmering veil of the lighted catwalk, where the clothes and their creators were the engine in the streamlined vehicle of the couture models.

These days it was a nervous group that gathered for the *Blaze Australia* weekly ideas and editorial conference. Photo layouts were looked at and stories discussed. Knowing Ali's unpredictable reaction to editorial ideas, the senior staff members were hesitant to present any. They avoided eye contact, kept their heads down and rattled through their spiels.

'So, is that it? Not too exciting. Worthy, but dull.' Ali leaned back. 'Let's go for a bit more pizazz. Be more outward looking, more of what's happening out there.' She waved an arm towards the window.

Larissa looked in that direction, wondering again at the beauty of Sydney Harbour. 'Do you mean out there, as in Australia? Or the other side of the world?' she asked. 'I'm still intrigued with the notion of what Australia has to offer.'

'Our readers are probably longing to be in Paris or New York,' suggested Fran.

'No, I think we're still interested in our own backyard,' ventured Jonathan. 'So long as it's somewhere special. It is a big country, as has been observed.'

'We certainly have the writers,' said Bob.

Ali tapped her pen on the table. 'Hmmm. Now, about that island, Dixon's honeymoon story. I've decided we should do it . . . romance, escapism, beautiful people, maybe there's a hard edge to be found once we dig in and win his confidence. Let them think we're doing the usual . . . How'd the projected costings come out?' Ali looked around the table as Larissa suppressed a shudder.

'I made a few inquiries, just on a spec basis,' said Fran carefully. 'There's a bit of money on offer from the tourism people. A wine company is launching a new label – they're willing to throw in the champagne and do the launch on the island as part of the festivities in return for coverage.'

Ali turned to Bob Monroe with a questioning look. He gestured at Jonathan who flipped back through his notebook. 'I did look into angles, just in case. Heron Island is a national park – protected species, the turtles, birds, the reef, and so on. Maybe dear Dixon could suddenly go green – become environmentally aware and have a cause.'

'The setting and the turtles sound photogenic.' Ali glared at them. 'Let's do it. Call Dixon's agent and tell him we think it's a wonderful idea and ask whether the airhead might have something interesting to say about endangered species or the environment. Makes it more interesting than just a honeymoon. Write something for him, Jonathan. They'll thank us, I'm sure. Pretty boy looks don't last forever. And, remember, this has to be kept under wraps. Larissa, London is interested in our Dixon. See if da Costa in New York wants to use it.'

'It will depend on how hard the edge is. We'll need to find a deep angle,' said Larissa, knowing *Blaze USA* wouldn't run a fluff piece about a movie star's marriage – exotic locale or not. 'Unless, of course, we break the real reason he's marrying his make-up artist.'

'So she can give him a facial and pluck his eyebrows every day?' asked Barbara innocently.

'That. And to prove he's not gay. And, oh yes, he wins residency in the US of A as a bonus,' finished Fiona.

Ali started to put her papers together. 'I'm sure you'll find the angle we need, Jonathan. Bob, ask Tony Cox to find a writer to do a travel piece as well. That will cover the airline and accommodation costs.'

Reg Craven made notes, seeing opportunities for advertising tie-ins.

Ali pointed at Fiona. 'Find the best of the current hot designers and organise to have their new collection photographed on the island. Kasha, welcome on board. You'll enjoy working with Fiona.'

The new fashion stylist nodded quickly. She knew she'd been thrown in the deep end to assist Fiona, who'd convinced Ali to let her direct the magazine's fashion pages, after Ali's chosen editor to replace Tiki had accepted more money to stay in her old job.

What Kasha didn't realise was that Fiona had wanted a young stylist who could be trained to set up the mag's fashion shoots the way she liked them. Fiona would have the creative input, Kasha would do the work to make fashion spreads happen.

'Ali, just before we finish, I want to mention that I had a call from Miche Bannister,' said Larissa. 'She's in Paris and wants to do a story on the collections, well, the new model, Sally Shaw. She's Australian, but Miche thinks there's more to the story than local girl makes good.'

'Better be, or I'm not interested. Miche might be Nina's god-daughter, but she'll still have to prove herself to me.'

'Is Miche a *Blaze* reporter?' asked Kasha to the table in general.

'Not yet,' said Ali. 'Tell Miche if she hooks onto something really worthwhile . . . if she hangs out with the models and unearths something meaty, to call back quickly and we'll see if we can arrange for Donald Heavney to go over there from New York to do the shoot.'

'Why? There are photographers on the ground in Paris we could use,' said Larissa. 'Surely that would be less costly than flying one in?'

But Ali didn't want to stamp *Blaze Australia* as a fashion magazine. This story, if the kid could bring it off, had the promise of couture covered more as a news or profile feature. 'Donald is a fantastic portrait photographer. We used him in New York a lot if you recall, Larissa. He's creative. He made his name in fashion, then moved on. He is young, clever and quick on his feet. He's been heralded as the new Herb Ritts,' said Ali, wondering why she had to explain this to people who worked for *Blaze*.

'He's Australian too,' added Larissa. 'Do people here realise what a lot of Australian talent there is out there on the international stage?'

'I think where possible *Blaze* should feature the best of Australian talent,' decided Ali. 'Readers will appreciate that.'

'Does "where possible" mean that if there isn't an Aussie who is the best, use a foreigner?' asked Fiona with a slight smile.

'*Blaze* only runs with the best,' answered Ali curtly. 'Thank you all. I expect full proposals outlining the stories and logistics on my desk, soonest.'

Bob walked beside Larissa as they headed back down the hallway to their offices. 'Sounds like your young friend, Miche, won't be getting any special treatment.'

'She doesn't expect any. No one did her mother any favours,' said Larissa with a hint of bitterness. Back in her office she turned on her computer, opened her email address file and sent a brief message to Miche, then leaned back in her chair and swivelled it round till she had a view of the city. The scale of skyscape made it so different from New York, let alone the light, which she still marvelled at. How Gerry would love it. There was something about this sunny place and its people, their up-front attitudes and fun lifestyles that had started to intrigue her. She wondered how Miche would like it. Again her mind threw up the unanswered question that had concerned her ever since hearing Miche was coming to Australia. Despite Nina offering to open career doors in New York and Europe for her god-daughter, Miche had decided that Australia would be her future. She might forge a strong and satisfying start to her journalism career in this country. But would her search for a long-lost father give her the happiness she deserved?

TAKE SEVEN ...

The vintage cars hired to collect guests snaked down the canopied driveway to the palatial mansion on Pittwater for the unveiling of *Blaze Australia*. The grand old house, regarded as something of a mausoleum by the locals, had been transformed. It, and the defunct private zoo in the still lavish gardens, had been turned into a scene from *Arabian Nights*.

Ali had argued, cajoled and finally convinced Manny to expand the budget for the launch party, persuading him that the attendant publicity would give them the equivalent of a major outlay on advertising by gaining free exposure in the media.

She had hired Tracey Ford as *Blaze*'s public relations manager. Tracey was to be responsible for the magazine's public image, its social functions and media events and she was to act as Ali's personal publicist.

The theme for the launch party was A Thousand Nights in One, an exotic blend of oriental romance and Arabian ambience.

As guests arrived through the main gates to where the front lawn of the house was encircled by the driveway, a fountain with a goddess statue glowed under a spotlight that also highlighted foaming iridescent bubbles and floating flowers holding small, lighted candles. This was the centrepiece to a changing parade of entertainment – fire-eaters, jugglers, magicians, contortionists dressed as lions and leopards, masked dancers and singers.

Between the house and the gardens, braziers burned with musk and verbena. Fake, jewelled fruit hung from tree branches and the shrubbery bloomed with fat silk flowers that glittered from the twinkling lights in their centres.

Standing calmly on either side of the portico were two elephants, each magnificently decorated with a studded silk headband, a plume pinned by a large ruby-coloured stone in the centre. Ornate fabric cloaks hung across their broad backs.

From this greeting at the entrance, guests began to realise they were in for something never before seen in Australia in the way of magazine launches. The spectacle of the setting as a background to the lavishly costumed men and women stepping from their limousines was dazzling.

Valets dressed as young princes spirited away the cars as guests were greeted in the main foyer by Baron Oscar Von Triton and his thirty-year-old son, Jacques – one of the world's most eligible bachelors – elegantly dressed as sultan and heir. Between them stood Alisson Gruber, making her own entrance into Sydney's social and business community.

Ali's harem pants were gathered at the hips below a gold satin jacket, open just enough to glimpse the red jewel in her navel and the embroidered bra top. Her hair was buried beneath a tight-fitting gold scarf caught in the centre by another rhinestone in an antique clasp, with matching long earrings.

As she'd planned to, the editor of *Blaze* perfectly complemented the older man and his dashing son. Oscar carried off his exotic outfit with easy comfort, his silk turban held by a small plume and jewelled pin, his bisque silk pants and shirt covered by a green silk coat, delicately trimmed with what looked like black mink. Jacques' ruby brocade tunic and tight pants with the emerald silk turban more than matched his handsome face.

Ali, having memorised every name on the invitation list, introduced each guest to the Baron and his son, who congratulated her on the spectacular setting.

'There's more to come,' she promised.

The mansion's grounds, which had once housed the privately owned, but open-to-the-public, zoo, swept down to an old seawall beyond large marquees lit by candlelight and oil torches. The marquees' interiors were lined in silken swathes. Flamingos and peacocks strolled on the lawns. Swans drifted sleepily on the dark waterlily-strewn pond. Spider monkeys dressed in silk ruffs chattered in the old trees, thin silver chains keeping them a safe distance from guests.

Throughout the house and gardens, music and song were provided by strolling flautists, zither players and carolling singers. Dancers wrapped in gauzy gold and silver fabrics – the men wearing feathered turbans, the women swaying behind large elaborate feathered fans – interpreted the exotic themes. At a row of small intimate tents, mysteriously shrouded in red velvet with glowing crystal balls at the entrance, early guests began lining up to hear their fortunes.

Inside each marquee, and through the main rooms of the exotically decorated mansion, massive sheathed cages were suspended from the ornate ceilings, hinting that they held secrets yet to be revealed.

After an hour of cocktails, the official ceremony was held in the decorated main ballroom, which continued the theme of the evening. A small orchestra played. Low tables were set with heavy silver cutlery and goblets, plump velvet and brocade cushions replacing chairs. The richness of scattered Persian carpets was reflected in the subtly lit Triton art collection imported from galleries around the globe. In turn, tall gilt-framed mirrors enlarged the ballroom and multiplied its guests as they gathered to hear the speeches.

With a trumpet fanfare, the party buzz settled and the master of ceremonies stepped to the discreet microphone on the flower-smothered podium. Throwing aside his Lawrence of Arabia scarf, which had hidden his face below the eyes, he began to speak in husky tones, a voice known around the world. 'Good evening, I am Charles Vaughan, welcome to the world of *Blaze*.'

There was a gasp as the most famous and loved of America's long parade of movie stars flashed his trademark smile.

'How on earth did she manage that?' whispered Maxwell, one of the top fashion designers in Australia, who was seated next to Fiona.

'The Baron is the major financier for his new production company which has just signed up to work with Fox Studios here at Moore Park. It didn't hurt either that Larissa, Ali's American deputy, has a cousin, Julie, who is casting agent for the first production, which, naturally, is starring our MC.'

'What's this cost?' The designer was quickly plotting how he could talk to the star. Perhaps offer to make him an outfit, though there was nothing in their current line macho enough. Vaughan would probably want R.M.

Williams gear anyway. But if he could at least be photographed with him, Maxwell thought, he could do a deal.

'We're doing an interview with him and a big spread on the new film, which will be one of the biggest to be made at Fox here,' Fiona said with a wry grin, reading Maxwell's mind.

'That's a great look on him,' said Maxwell, studying the rugged, fifty-something movie star in his white jodhpurs and soft leather knee-high boots with a small sabre on his belt. The silk shirt fell carelessly open to reveal his chest. The celebrity MC flung the white parachute silk cape back over his shoulder.

'I am an actor,' Charles Vaughan began in his beautiful voice, his poised manner lightly acknowledging the tittered response to his supposed humility – he had just out-polled Rudolf Valentino and Clark Gable as the World's Sexiest Star of the Century. He continued, 'and even for me, this extraordinary set . . .' he waved his arms about the room, 'deserves a special mention. All credit . . . to the writers, photographers and designers at *Blaze* . . . and their editor, Alisson Gruber.'

'Was this Ali's idea?' asked Steve Vickers, the Trends ad man sitting next to Larissa.

'Ali was given free rein, and she bolted,' said Larissa. 'Not just the theme and cover of the first issue, but this party as well. They make an interesting contrast.'

'Whose place is this?' asked Steve, who had seen more than a few lavish homes in his years in advertising.

'The family who've just bought this are overseas, surviving Internet e-commerce zillionaires apparently,' said Larissa. 'This is going to be their little weekender. Ali rang them and talked them into letting her use the house. They'd die if they could see what she's done.'

'Who'd she find to put this together?'

Larissa smiled. 'As always, Ali went to the top, to Opera Australia and hired their people, props, costumes. I don't know the figure, but I gather they couldn't afford to say no. The opera company features in the first issue as well.'

'I've seen the ad for the new membership drive. And the design for the ticket offer for *Blaze* readers next season.'

'Ali is rather good at networking exercises,' commented Larissa.

'You scratch my back . . .' smiled Steve. 'Well, this will have everyone talking and buying the magazine. The ad campaign is a big one.' He shook his head in admiration. 'Ali was always going to be a name in this town because of her position, but after this bash, she's going to be a power figure in her own right.'

'She's certainly making the most of it while Nina is out of town,' agreed Larissa mildly.

'But I suspect, for Ali, our little backwater is just a stepping-stone to a New York editorship. Look out Tina Brown, eh?' added Steve, turning his attention back to where the Baron was thanking Charles Vaughan, then began speaking about *Blaze*.

The Baron radiated dignity, charm and warmth. His accent had softened after so many years in America. Always courteous in public, he could be a fierce business opponent, used to having his way in boardrooms and behind the scenes. Though, legend had it, never by bullying or temper. It was not becoming or necessary for him to descend from the commanding peak where he ran his affairs. His lieutenants charged middle management with firing the bullets when necessary.

In reflective mood he began, 'Once entering the milieu of publishing, I embraced it as a business. And Lord knows, a firm business hand was needed. I was not about to join the ranks of the so-called "press barons" and continue the ruthless folly of their ways. Along the way I stumbled occasionally, but it is a foolish man who does not learn from his mistakes. One of my wisest decisions was to convince an energetic and independent young woman in Sydney back in the seventies to join our organisation. She wouldn't sell me her magazine so we joined forces.

'That partnership with Nina Jansous has grown into the most successful family of magazines in the world. So it is exceedingly pleasing for me to be here tonight to see the newest star in the *Blaze* stable rise again from where *Blaze* was born. Over the years, Nina has persuaded me that newspapers and magazines are as much arbiters of public opinion, taste and knowledge as they are a business. Marrying experience with explanation and possibly influence, is the challenge that daily absorbs us.

'Nina suggested I do what the renowned British newspaperman, Cecil Harmsworth King did, and send our editors and senior writers to the emerging, as well as established, corners of the globe so that they might more fully understand what motivates and concerns people and governments. And she taught me that within the big picture there is also the pulse of daily events that involve each of us.' He paused, glancing at Ali. 'One of the strengths of *Blaze* has been the people who make it happen. And none shines more brilliantly in our firmament than the orchestrator of not only this evening's grand entertainment but also our new *Blaze Australia*. A star in her own right, and I salute her . . . dear guests, our reigning editor of the new *Blaze Australia*, Alisson Gruber.' He held out his hand to bring Ali to the podium.

She paused, smiling at him. The Baron gallantly kissed her hand and stepped back, leaving Ali alone at the microphone. There was a flurry of flashlights and she waited while the cameras snapped and whirred before speaking. 'I am delighted to be founding editor of the best magazine in Australia, playing our part in an international arena where *Blaze* is the leader – technologically as well as creatively. I hope you will share in, and be part of, the grand vision of *Blaze*. Thank you for coming, I hope to know each of you better in the near future. And now, if Monsieur Jacques Triton would like to step forward and do the honours, I will introduce you to *Blaze*. Then, please enjoy the rest of the evening.'

Obligingly Jacques leapt forward and Ali led him to where a gold-tasselled rope held midnight-blue velvet drapes closed. At Ali's direction, Jacques gave the rope a tug and the drapes swept upwards revealing three huge video screens. The lights dimmed, the music swelled and the vision began.

In a six-minute presentation, guests were surrounded with *Blaze*. It began as an introduction to Triton Communications and expanded its focus to Nina Jansous and her string of *Blaze* magazines in the leading cities of the world. Then Ali became the star . . . summing up the *Blaze* ethos, finally presenting what everyone had been waiting to see – the cover and page after page of the first issue of *Blaze Australia*.

The lights went on and fifty child models, dressed as space-age, cyber-chic cherubs, danced into the ballroom handing out copies of the first issue of *Blaze* to every guest.

Ali had talked through the concept of the first issue with Nina and the editorial board in Sydney, and Larissa had sat in on a conference call. After tossing around the idea of major celebrities to grace the inaugural cover, Nina had suggested they go 'classic' and there was none better than the deco artwork of Erté that had launched the first *Blaze* magazine in New York all those years ago.

Ali had disagreed. 'Fabulous as it is, that's looking backwards. We have to be ahead of the new millennium changes. Let's be innovative and set a new standard and concept that's right out there.'

Nina and Larissa were taken aback at Ali's enthusiasm, quickly admitting that 'out there' was no doubt more her area.

'Let's see what you come up with,' said Nina.

Ali had tracked down a young Sydney company specialising in experimental media effects. They had latched onto Ali's ideas with alacrity and had negotiated a deal where part of the cost of the inaugural cover could be absorbed as a promotional product for their company.

The first issue of *Blaze Australia* looked like a metallic silver semi-disc. Instead of the rectangular shape of magazines, it was shaped like a capital 'D', the gatefold being the straight line. The semicircle cover shone with an iridescent glow, the letters of *Blaze* embossed in deep violet against the silver. It took a moment to see that the shimmering illustration was a version of a naked Venus arising from the sea like a Botticelli nymph. But, as the magazine moved, the image changed, and a 3-D hologram revealed a surreal fashion shot of a space-age woman. Sleek in a body fabric of rubberised metal under a glittering hand-stitched lace overcoat, she'd had the front of her hairline shaved, the rest of her long hair multi-hued and threaded with jewelled lights that seemed to spark with their own power. On her head, a pure gold skullcap held golden halos suspended above by thin gold wires. Her make-up was extreme – lips and lids sparkling fantasy colours, giving her huge eyes and high cheeks an alien look.

There was no cover copy, just a delicate outline of *Blaze*'s logo – a shimmering dragonfly. On the bottom right corner was a thumbprint. When pressed, a voice from a micro-chip embedded in the cover spoke, listing the contents of this issue.

Articles raised questions of eroticism, gender, generation and style – and inspired the theme of the launch. There was also a commissioned article by Britain's latest Booker Prize author looking at Celtic characteristics in Australian heritage. An Australian Nobel Prize science laureate contributed an article hypothesising that there could be evidence to support the weird but famous 'bloodline conspiracy theory' that extra terrestrial-human hybrids had ruled Sumer, Babylon, Greece and Troy, and were today putting in place world leaders to continue the line. There was an in-depth article called 'Secrets of the Soil', showing the link between soil health and human health.

Guests eagerly spun through the limited edition preview copies. 'Do you put it into a CD-ROM, an integrated system or serve hot food on it?' wondered Charles Vaughan.

Jacques fingered the slick magazine, still reeling from the cost factor. 'You're not doing this with every issue are you? We'll be paupers in two issues.'

Ali had known she'd face this kind of comment. But criticism coming from the proprietor's son, who would step into his father's shoes one day, was unnerving. 'It's just for the preview edition, a limited edition we're selling as a collector's item. Other copies are going to target advertisers, media, and the boys and gals at the big end of town.'

'You think this will attract the advertisers? It's a gamble. They could think an ad in *Blaze* is going to be very expensive. I assume your ad manager has already done deals with the big clients – as insurance. And what about your competitors, they are likely to unite to defend their advertising turf when they see a threat like this?'

Ali's eyes narrowed slightly but she continued to smile. 'Is there anything you *like* about the magazine?' Not waiting for an answer, she continued. 'We did hefty research,' she said, omitting the word expensive. 'We will have everyone wanting to be in this magazine as well as read it. I know Reg Craven is extremely happy with the advertising support so far.' She glanced across the room where she'd last glimpsed the advertising manager, mentally planning a discussion with him. They had already clashed over the style and type of ads he wanted for *Blaze*, which Ali knew did not fit comfortably with ads the other *Blaze* magazines carried.

'It's building on and maintaining that advertising support that makes a magazine work,' said Jacques. 'Believe me, I've seen my share of publications birthed, then murdered. I hope you don't become swayed too much by the Nina mystique that seems to mesmerise my father. She has done a brilliant job over the years, but this . . .' he lifted the magazine by a corner, 'could be construed as a very indulgent last fling.'

Ali suddenly saw a chink of light. 'Jacques, I won't pull punches. While Nina is away, with the board and management behind me, I will make this magazine work. Tonight is only the . . .'

'Of course, it has to work,' interjected Jacques. 'We are financially committed. There is more than one magazine at stake. This could unravel a sizeable skein of the corporation.' Seeing his father about to rejoin them, he changed tack. 'I'd like to visit the offices as soon as I can.'

'Let me know when would suit you.' Ali gave a big smile as the Baron held out his arm.

'My dear girl, may I escort you to the terrace, the buffet is ready. Joining us, Jacques?'

'In a moment. I will just circulate a little more. *Au revoir, à bientôt.*'

Ali nodded at him and turned her attention to the Baron. 'Dare I ask for your opinion?

'Of you? Exotic, dazzling. Of this party? Superb, brilliant and clever.' He led her towards the terrace.

'I meant the magazine, the reason we're here.' Ali tried to make her voice light but her stomach was in a knot.

Baron Triton gave her arm a fatherly pat. 'Dear Miss Ali, I think I know what my son might have been discussing with you. I think this issue is sensational, revolutionary. Expensive, yes. But you have achieved what I'm sure you intended – that everyone will be talking about *Blaze*. And you. You have done brilliantly. And I know you will subsequently rein in the horses and find creative ways to maintain the standard with, shall we say, less extravagance. The second edition is always the big test. I am not worried.' He was handed a plate by a waiter and turned his attention to the food. 'This Sydney seafood, *incredible*.'

Ali was grateful for the expression of faith in her, but she knew it also carried an undercurrent of warning. Watching the bottom line, no matter how dazzling the magazine, was what Triton was about.

Later in the evening, the shrouded cages that hung in each marquee were unveiled. A tug on a cord and each coloured cloth dropped away along with the bottom of the cage, showering the guests with silver balls, confetti and tiny fun gifts tied with silver ribbon.

Later the guests were summoned by the costumed staff tinging on small silver triangles to gather on the terrace that faced the waterfront for a special fireworks display.

The oohs and ahhs of delight came to a crescendo as, from the final blazing display, emerged a giant dragonfly hovering beneath the letters *B l a z e*.

*

173

Nina rang to speak to Ali for a report on the party. Belinda was still agog at being included in such a happening and told Nina that Tracey Ford was being swamped with requests to interview Ali and the Baron.

'He won't talk to the press, but Ali is all over the radio and TV and the biggest-selling Sunday paper is doing a piece,' Belinda gushed. 'Tracey says she's lined up more media for Ali than a football star on Grand Final eve. Er, no Nina, Ali's not here. She's lunching with Baron Triton. Jacques is in the building, though. Would you like . . . ?'

'No, don't bother him, Belinda. I just wanted to know how it went. The ship is launched, good luck to all who sail in her, eh?'

'Could be stormy seas ahead,' said Belinda quietly. 'But don't you worry, you just enjoy your holiday and stop thinking about us back here. *Blaze* can carry on for a bit while you have a break.'

'You're right, Belinda. Please pass on my thanks for a brilliant job to everybody . . . absolutely everybody. I'll email you a note to that effect. Personalise it and send it to everyone please. I will periodically check email messages where and when I can.'

'I hope you don't have a computer or a mobile in your handbag. Toss it in a bin! This is a break, remember,' advised Belinda.

Nina gave a small chuckle. 'Not even a lipstick. A map and a credit card, that's all I'm carrying. I'll send you back a little gift with Miche. Take care and thanks, Belinda.'

Sally Shaw was like a rocket with a fire beneath, waiting for maximum lift-off. Without Nina's intervention with Sally's Paris agency, Piste, Miche wouldn't have been granted an exclusive interview, even with the *Blaze* connection. It was the power of Nina that had clinched it.

'You understand the ground rules for the interview, Miche,' Nina had said gently before Miche left.

'Anything I do or say reflects on you, I know.' Miche didn't add that also put constraints on her story. But Nina knew what the neophyte reporter was thinking.

'That shouldn't stop you writing the story as you see it. I merely ask that you don't abuse any privileges.'

Miche nodded and Nina read her reaction swiftly. 'Young Sally is likely to be as nervous as you. She's made a few important covers and is now the new discovery. Remember, she hasn't ever been profiled. I'm not saying that she is hiding a dark, dreadful secret, but this is a pretty heady world to sling an innocent lamb into.'

'Why would she do it?'

'Ask her. What pretty young girl wouldn't consider fame, money, glamour? Maybe, because of your background, you know more about the pitfalls of the fame game.'

'Okay. I shall do as I was taught by my mom . . . never write the story before you have it.'

Now Miche sat on a stool in the corner of Bandeau's photographic studio. She was somewhat amused at the bedlam happening around the large room, on the roof above the small penthouse Bandeau used while in Paris. It was a higgledy-piggledy building, as if disjointed shapes had been snapped together from giant toy building blocks.

A glass skylight gave the room a luminous quality. Dark drapes could be pulled across the French doors that led onto the roof where Bandeau had bright geraniums in giant urns and a small wrought-iron table with chairs. From here you were part of a rooftop community of attics, terrace gardens and sloping tiles that had seen a hundred or more years of sun, snow and rain, above the crowded narrow street that ran into a tree-framed square.

Inside the studio it was another world. Miche scribbled notes trying to pin down the atmosphere . . . *energy . . . frenetic . . . abandoned . . . sexual . . . chaotic . . . so many people spinning around Sally as if she were in the eye of the hurricane . . . hairdresser, make-up artist, stylist, dresser, two photographer's assistants and Bandeau giving orders . . . constantly peering through the camera, directing lights into position, fiddling with a gauzy curtain draped behind a small dais. A deep-blue velvet cloth unfurled behind the drifting gauze. A fan whirring to one side . . .*

During a lull, Bandeau strode towards Miche, a smaller camera and light meter hanging round his neck. He lifted the camera and snapped off several photos in quick succession as Miche stiffened, then flung her hands before her face. 'Oh no, please . . .'

'Gotcha,' he grinned, lowering the camera. 'You're the girl from *Blaze*, right?' He perched on an upturned box. 'Is this an interview or an audition?'

'I harbour no desire to be a model, thanks,' said Miche firmly. 'But tell me, what does make a model? How can you pick a "star" from those famed auditions?'

'Ah, you've heard stories of casting couches and the *affaires* between models and their photographers.' He caught Miche's quizzical expression and laughed. 'All true.'

He tapped his camera. 'No one can make a model. This does. You can't tell about a girl until you print the evidence. She works on film or she doesn't.'

'But surely there are aspects of the job that a top photographer can teach someone like Sally. She is still quite new at this,' suggested Miche.

'You can teach a few of the skills . . . but a top model

176

has an innate sense . . . they just know how to connect with the camera. They find the light, they use their body. There is this chemical reaction that happens between the girl, the camera and the photographer. Sometimes even I don't know, until I see the shots, how magical a girl can be.'

'What is beauty? Lots of the top models aren't actually beautiful in real life,' said Miche, recalling the few models she had met in New York who appeared to be plain, yet in photographs looked ravishing.

Bandeau glanced around. 'Sally is having her hair and face done.' He lit a cigarette, fitting it into a long ivory holder, the affectation looking very natural. This was a man comfortable with being the *provocateur*, thought Miche. The stories about this supermodel-making photographer had been cited in the fashion bibles and been backstage fashion-show gossip for years. His reputation for finding, creating and making a girl famous then dropping her to find a new challenge, had even become the basis of a B-grade movie.

'Being a top model is a bit like being a movie star – they have that indefinable charisma and the camera loves them. This is more intimate because they have a direct way of connecting with the beholder on the other side of my lens,' said Bandeau slowly, as if thinking this through, aloud for the first time. 'They have to have a sense of fun and abandonment. After all, they aren't following a script. They have to interpret the clothes in their own way. Actors tend to take their roles more seriously. They are playing a specific part, where models fantasise. And they're a lot more physical. They have to be aware of how their bodies move and look and express a feeling in a frozen moment. I love girls who have trained as dancers.'

'So what's more important, the look of the picture, the

clothes, or the model?' asked Miche. 'I always thought models were manipulated by the photographer, what she wears, by those kind of people.' Miche pointed her pen at the fluttering, fussing women and men around Sally in the change room.

'Models are manipulated to a degree – especially when young and starting out like Sally. Behind the lens, as well as when they're in front of a camera. Agents, editors, stylists, designers – each one has a say in the interpretation of the clothes and the girl. With girls like Sally, they will want to keep her childlike for as long as possible. Each model has her own "Look", even though they may change their hair colour, make-up and so on. They are still slotted in as a certain type and designers tend to want to use the models whose look marries with their collection.'

'Do the girls wear the clothes, or the clothes wear the girl?' asked Miche.

'Designers might think clothes create the persona, that they are the director – the dictator – but I believe the model makes the clothes look good or not. And that is the art of a top model – to make even ugly clothes look appealing.' He leaned back, satisfied that he had summed up the complex world of modelling in a few words.

Miche looked up from her notes. 'So if Sally is successful because she has that childlike quality . . . does that mean her career is over when she changes . . . matures?'

'Fashion is ephemeral and greedy. Everyone is always looking for something new, new, new. The latest, the hottest. The next big trend. If she lasts more than three years at the top she will be one of the few. And remember – for every one like her who makes it to the top, there are thousands and thousands who don't even make it onto the ladder.'

Miche shook her head. 'You'd have to want it an awful lot.'

'Yes, this modelling world can be cruel, heartless, shallow, bitchy. More than it ever was. And there are the girls who are so hungry to succeed they will do anything – and I mean anything. Others, though not many, have such beauty and knack for the camera they don't have to do anything. And don't seem to care whether they succeed or not. They are relaxed and nonchalant in front of a camera. Interestingly, they are the girls that tend to go on to success in a big way, or move into other fields like acting.' He studied Miche for a moment. 'I think you'd photograph well, but you wouldn't succeed as a model.'

'Oh?' she looked faintly amused. 'Why not?'

'Because you don't want it enough. You don't want it because it doesn't interest you. That would come through in a picture. You couldn't *sell* a dress in that way.'

He stood up as Sally entered, holding up the hem of a long red evening gown, her eyes and mouth dramatically outlined in red, her hair pulled under a tall wimple-styled head-dress set with gems, a glistening gold snake wound up her thin pale arm. She carried heavy black sandals with carved, shiny black heels and walked into the pool of light where a giant throne armchair was placed in front of the gauze drape. A smoke machine began chugging and a low mist rolled across the studio floor. An assistant stood ready by the fan.

Bandeau lifted his camera as a conductor before an orchestra. 'Your ladyship, this way, face into the light, chin down . . . oh, yes, little baby lady . . .' He began moving as he snapped the shutter, the camera held to his face as if swaying in a private trance. Without moving his eye from the camera, he gestured and the fan clicked on and began blowing the smoke and billowing curtain around Sally.

She moved slowly, arcing an arm, allowing the folds of the long single sleeve of the dress to cascade. A tiny hand weighed with large rings touched the wimple. She turned, she looked over her shoulder straight into the lens, a shy but challenging look, before folding herself into the foetal position in the chair where she seemed lost in its massive wooden embrace. A small impish smile replaced the child seductress and suddenly, to Miche, she looked like a little girl dressing up in her mother's clothes.

Bandeau finished the roll and handed the camera to his assistant who handed him a Hasselblad, which he held in front of his abdomen, framing the picture that would eventually be seen worldwide.

Miche was mesmerised. It was like watching a ballet. And she was suddenly aware there was music playing – a contemporary, wild harp piece. Everybody involved in this shoot stood in the shadowy corners of the studio watching the dance between the photographer and model.

Then it was over and Sally slipped from the chair to change clothes.

Bandeau took the glass of Scotch from his assistant. 'This is part of a series. The other outfits were shot at a house in the country, sleeping hounds and dead heads on the wall, blazing fire, fur rugs. And at dawn on the wild moors leading the giant hounds. You get the scenario.'

'Yes. Sounds . . . expensive,' said Miche.

'Who's counting when a dress costs thousands of dollars?' He shrugged, lighting another cigarette.

Miche poked her head behind the screen where bottles of champagne stood open. Sally was standing in flimsy lingerie – bloomers and a lacy corselet. Miche was shocked at the frailness of her body, her translucent skin and shadowy bones. Sally sipped champagne as her hair was raked by metal brushes, hair dryer and curling rod. The dresser handed her several pills.

'Here you go, *chérie*, they'll keep your eyes bright.'

Sally obediently swallowed and waved her glass at

Miche. 'Help yourself. French champagne by the bucket!' She emptied her glass. 'Where are we going for dinner, Bandeau?' she shouted, adding in an aside to Miche, 'It's wild, we go to these crazy places for dinner, then clubs, end up at someone's place . . . it's wild,' she repeated.

'Surely you have a few hours of sleep before you go to work?'

Sally gave a giggle as a dresser poured more champagne into her glass. 'Work, you call this work!'

Larissa and Ali sat opposite each other doing the final rundown for the next issue.

'Ali, I can't agree about this Dixon Landers story . . . it's tacky, his last movie has bombed and, frankly, my biggest problem is the contra deal on the island. When we take something for free, we're under an enormous obligation.'

'Don't be so po-faced, Larissa. Reg Craven is going all out for it. '

Larissa drank some mineral water to gather her thoughts. The advertising manager was fast becoming Ali's enemy. She didn't particularly warm to Reg, a blustering salesman who favoured bow ties and a hearty but arrogant manner – especially towards women. He had bulldozed his way through the ranks from sales, to circulation to advertising. Now as head of advertising – the revenue-making side of the magazine – he held equal power to the editor, in theory. 'And how many pages is all that contra going to take away from editorial?' Larissa finally asked.

Ali frowned. 'I've told him he can't go over our forty-five per cent advertising–editorial balance.'

'Ali, you know how it is. I bet they're no different over here. That guy will come in at the last moment having done a deal and sold off another couple of pages. Management isn't going to knock back revenue – especially when the magazine is becoming established in the media-buying world.'

'I'll speak to him,' said Ali shortly. 'So are you with me, or not? I want to do it.' Ali waited for Larissa's response out of courtesy, but as editor, if she wanted *Blaze* to cover the wedding story, it would happen.

Larissa spoke slowly, phrasing her words carefully so as not to offend Ali, who tended to take any criticism personally. 'The advertising space aside, there is the ethical dilemma of accepting paid-for expenses in return for pretty-picture coverage in the magazine. You know what a sensitive issue this is . . . look at how the "cash for comment" blew up in the faces of those radio guys. Print at least has always made it clear when something has been paid for – "advertorials" always have *Advertisement* or *Advertising Supplement* at the top of them. The papers here have had to adjust their policies, so why should we charge in and abuse the ethics?'

'So? We put a disclaimer at the bottom – *Blaze* staff working on this story were the guests of Heron Island.'

'Ali, Triton editorial policy has always been no contra deals. You know how it was in New York. You can't change the rules out here and expect them not to know. And if you declare it, that looks worse . . . *Blaze* paying for the wedding, *Blaze* going along with a sham event so this guy can have a US green card, *Blaze* doing a travel feature in return for accommodation, *Blaze* doing a fashion spread to disguise the reason we're on Heron and dressing the bridal party.'

'Listen, this has enormous potential for *Blaze*. We are doing a side deal with the record company. We allow them in on our exclusive and they can use the footage in their next video clip.'

'They won't wait till our issue comes out, and you run the risk they'll leak pictures. It's too dangerous, Ali. Besides, it's unethical for *Blaze* to be involved.' Larissa sat back, folding her arms.

'That's your final opinion?'

'Yes.'

Ali paused and leaned back in her chair. She could insist on it going ahead, but there was the niggling worry that Larissa was correct in what she said. Ali believed there was still a way to do the story, sliding past the Triton policy, and come out with the scoop she wanted. It was risky because of the time frame, and guests had been known to sneak quickie pictures and sell them to a tabloid overnight. Perhaps it wasn't worth fighting Larissa over a point of honour and losing in the end. If she gave in now, Larissa would feel vindicated and be less vigilant or aggressive in the near future. Ali didn't like anyone scoring points over her, but she had to admit, the Dixon Landers story wasn't the one she'd want to stick her neck out for, if any problems arose. Maybe Ali should cast around for a truly big fish before making a stand on the issue of contra deals. The less she paid and the bigger the name, the more credit she'd accrue. Okay, she decided. She'd let this one go and plan for bigger fish to fry. Let Larissa think she was being amenable. Then Larissa wouldn't complain about her to Nina. Or watch Ali too closely.

'If we drop it, what do we lead with instead?' challenged Ali.

'Miche's story on Sally Shaw from Paris.' Larissa mentally crossed her fingers hoping Miche had a story.

Ali didn't answer immediately, and it seemed to Larissa she was sifting through other options and couldn't come up with a suitable alternative. Finally, she shrugged. 'Okay. I'll talk to her. Call Donald Heavney, the photographer, and confirm we want him in Paris ASAP.'

Larissa nodded and began gathering up her papers. Ali gave her deputy a slight smile. 'It'd better be better than good, or young Miche won't ever work for me again. Nina or no Nina.'

Larissa was saved from answering. Reg Craven loomed in the doorway so she slipped past him and headed to her office.

'Fantastic news. I've sold a spread to the film distributors of Dixon Landers' movies. Plus tickets to the premiere of his next film.'

'Forget it. We canned the story.'

Reg choked. 'What! You can bloody well resurrect it then. We don't go back and say no deal to these kinda people. Advertising pays for this magazine, and pays your salary!' He raised his voice and pulled his red-framed glasses off, shaking them at Ali. 'Editorial is there to stick on the back of ads. Get your priorities right!'

Ali stayed calm, her voice steely. 'I have just reminded Larissa of the ethics embraced by Triton and I will now remind you. *Blaze* and Triton do not accept freebie or contra deals. This whole business has been tacky and unethical. We don't want to be seen as buying stories. Once we set a precedent for doing deals like this our credibility is shot.'

Reg Craven gaped at Ali, speechless for a moment, then managed, 'Since when?'

'Since I say so.'

'Advertising has as much say in this as editorial,' said Reg, a slow red flush creeping up his neck. A warning sign to those who knew him.

'Do you want to take it further?' Ali had her gloves off.

'Listen, you pseudo-Yankee bitch. You might think you know it all, but what works in New York doesn't necessarily work here. We've always done deals. It's how the publishing business works. Same as all the media. Advertising rules, okay? Without us, you and your magazine don't exist!'

Ali flinched but held her ground. 'Clients aren't going to buy space in a crap magazine. And that's what you seem to know best – crap. Lift your game, forget the footy pubs and lunches with topless waitresses. I know your type, Reg, and that's not what *Blaze* is about.'

'Bullshit.' The remark about the topless lunch club had hit home. He'd recently lunched too long, and he'd become drunk and loud and made a pass at one of the waitresses. Next day it had been written up by the town's raciest columnist, April Showers, causing *Blaze* some embarrassment.

They eyeballed each other for a moment before Ali lifted the phone. 'Do you want to speak to Jacques Triton and Manny Golan or shall I?'

Reg Craven leaned across Ali's desk, his club jacket falling open to reveal a paunch and red plaid braces. 'Don't cross me again. You might be able to kick around the birds and blokes on this floor, but never forget – without advertising, you're nothing.' He thrust a finger towards the ceiling where the sales representatives of *Blaze* worked from the floor above.

Ali stood. 'I have an appointment. Don't sweat, Reg. We're replacing Dixon Landers with a better story.'

Reg Craven stomped from Ali's office and she sank back into her chair. Suddenly she felt shaky.

Belinda stuck her head in the door. 'Coffee?' she asked in a sympathetic tone.

'No, haven't the time. I have an appointment.' Ali made no effort to thank Belinda, who must have heard Reg shouting. She picked up her bag and brushed past Belinda.

As the gentle ping marked the elevator doors closing

behind Ali, Belinda looked in the editor's diary. There was no appointment marked.

Ali walked fast, but with no direction. Half an hour later she was sitting on a bench in Hyde Park watching the birds peck around the Archibald Fountain. Her mobile rang and she debated for a moment, then answered it.

'Miss Gruber, it's John O'Donnell's secretary. He apologises for the short notice, but he is unexpectedly free for dinner this evening. And, as he is going overseas tomorrow, he wondered if you might like to join him?'

Ali smiled as she accepted and listened to the details of where to meet the newly widowed powerbroker.

TAKE EIGHT...

Nina's rented sedan headed through the fields of Bassigny, a bright red dot in a misty lilac landscape. She opened the sunroof and the balmy air, smelling of freshly tilled earth, reminded her how countries, places, houses, all had their own smell. She turned onto a small road that wound over a one-lane bridge into the walled village of Langres and spotting a café, parked and crossed the street.

Three old men sat in a row at the outdoor tables, heads low over folded newspapers, brows furrowed, deep in concentration like schoolboys in an examination room. A woman and a boy eating ice-cream were the café's only other customers. Nina put her head in the doorway where the smell of coffee and baking was intoxicating. The proprietor, wiping his hands on his long white apron, waved at her to be seated.

*

Refreshed from her *café au lait* and *croque monsieur*, Nina walked up the street, savouring the fact this small village appeared to be unchanged from a hundred years ago, even though it was only a few kilometres from bustling Dijon.

Pausing at a larger bistro, she read the menu fluttering outside and realised she could no doubt enjoy the finest Provençal cooking if she ate here. Too bad she'd just eaten bread and melted cheese. For the first time she wished she had someone with her. Up until now, she'd been relishing the freedom and spontaneity of travelling through France wherever the whim took her. Enjoying a superb meal was always better in company.

As she crossed the road to go back to her car, a community notice board covered with posters and handwritten announcements caught her eye. One poster had a dramatic image on it of a falcon on a woman's arm. The bird glared at the camera, its talons gripping the leather glove that emerged from a red velvet sleeve slashed with fur and gold that gave an impression of medieval grandeur. While the image was arresting, it was a name that leapt out at Nina, causing her to feel unsteady – *Lucien Artiem. Preview release of his new masterpiece*, Bridal Crown. Scanning the details in French of the screening of the first in a trilogy of films from the esteemed auteur, what shook Nina was the final line on the poster. *In person. Thursday and Friday evening. Cinema Dijon.*

Dijon was a short drive away, she could be there and make the screening. And in that short distance she would travel back forty years.

It was high summer in Sydney and twenty-year-old Nina had just graduated from *In Home and Garden* to

188

the *Australian Women's Weekly*. She had finished her cadetship and was writing feature articles, as well as the occasional fashion piece for Betty Keep, the fashion editor. Nina was popular among the female hierarchy, each taking a special interest in her career and all predicting the lovely young woman would 'go far'. Fleet Street was mentioned quietly. Occasionally Mrs Keep used Nina to model for the magazine and took her to meet the couturiers who created the clothes for the fashionable set who appeared in the *Weekly*'s social pages. To the fashion editor's initial surprise, most of the top dressmakers knew Nina through Clara.

Mrs Keep asked to meet her mother, was entranced with Clara and wrote about the wonderful milliner with photos of Nina modelling her mother's hats.

This brought Clara more work than she could manage and with her new prestige, she raised her prices and began saving a nest egg for Nina.

Nina decided to extend her writing away from the fashion world and she began taking an interest in the cinema. With girlfriends from work, she regularly visited the small movie houses on the edge of the city that showed foreign films, and she became a keen reader of a movie magazine published by the owner of the Savoy cinema. When he asked Nina if she'd like to review a film once a month, she accepted with delight, writing under the name of Emily Grace.

And so 'Emily' had met Lucien Artiem, a young French film-maker who was living in Australia for six months and studying with Franco Paquot, a European cinematographer who had fled Hungary after the war and settled in Sydney. Franco had taken on a few students and Lucien was considered a star pupil. He had made several films of his own as a learning exercise and was determined to become a director of photography.

When Nina discovered that one of Franco's films was being screened she went along to interview him. And it was there she met Lucien. He was twenty-three, she was about to turn twenty-one.

He was sitting in the small studio Franco used for students. It was set up for filming commercials for cinema and the new medium of television. Lucien worked for a newsreel company, filming in Sydney and the bush, the special events, accidents or offbeat humorous segments, which were shown in the newsreel theatrettes or the big theatres as a support to the feature films. Whenever he had free time, Lucien sat with Franco, taking movie cameras to pieces and reassembling them and learning about lighting techniques, which Franco told him was the key to being a top director of photography.

While waiting for Franco, Nina was ushered into the studio where Lucien was framing a close-up shot.

She introduced herself – 'I'm actually Nina, not Emily' – and asked what he was doing.

'An experiment. I want to film a dragonfly taking off from this daisy.'

Nina gave him an incredulous look. 'You can direct dragonflies?'

'Through a camera, you can command or create the universe,' he said flippantly.

Nina was fascinated. She watched as he went to the freezer of an old refrigerator and took out a jar containing a large dragonfly.

'Is it dead?'

'No, sleeping. Well, a sort of coma.' He looked at Nina. 'May I?' And before she could answer, he tweaked a strand of her hair. Carefully he glued one end to the leg of the dragonfly, the other end he pasted to a table. Then he placed the unconscious insect on the petal of the daisy. Looking through the camera, he made several adjustments. 'I've set the exposure to the length of your hair and framed the shot to that distance. Poor little bugger won't be able to fly out of shot. Now, a couple of clouds before it wakes up.'

Nina watched as he turned on a chugging smoke machine and a small fan that blew puffs of smoke across the blue background. Then, as he went back behind the camera, the dragonfly began to stir. Nina heard the button on the camera click and the motor begin to whirr.

The dragonfly unfolded its wings, fluttered them, looked around to orient itself and, gaining its bearings, gracefully lifted off, its wonderful wings glimmering in the studio light. It flew in a small circle, then aimed for heaven, only to find it was tethered to earth by Nina's hair. The camera rolled as the dragonfly plunged and spun and circled before landing once more on the daisy to reassess the situation.

'Oh, that's so cruel. Let it go,' cried Nina.

Lucien turned to her in surprise. 'Why? It's not in pain. Confused, maybe. It looks brilliant through the lens, it's flying against a summer sky with little clouds.'

'No it's not. Let it go,' said Nina angrily.

Lucien shrugged. 'It's an experiment.' He turned off the camera, broke the thread of hair and lifted the dragonfly, which suddenly sprang free, flew at Nina and landed on her shoulder. She looked at its large pop eyes and burst out laughing. Lucien cupped his hand around the insect.

'Come with me.' Together they went outside and he opened his hand. The dragonfly, feeling the warmth of sun, the vibration of the air, lifted lightly and then dipped and dived in a small dance before it flew away. Lucien turned to Nina. 'Happy now?'

Nina found it difficult to express how she felt about that moment when the shimmering insect had danced against the sunlight. 'I'll never feel the same about drag-onflies again. They are meant to be free spirits. Thanks for letting it go.'

Lucien was tempted to say something else but gave a smile. 'That's okay. I have my shot.'

Nina frowned. 'Is that all you think about?'

They were interrupted by Franco and she disappeared to do the interview without speaking to Lucien again.

Two days later, a card arrived at her office with an exquisite watercolour painting of a dragonfly. He'd writ-ten, *'I will never forget the dragonfly alighting on your shoulder . . . Like it, you are immortalised for me as a creature of poise and delicacy. I hope I see you again.'*

They did indeed see each other again – at the opening of Franco's film in Sydney. And so began a friendship that quickly blossomed into a deep attraction.

Lucien was Nina's first true love and Lucien loved her deeply in return. But not enough to hold him to her. After four months, his visa ran out and he had an offer to return to France and work as a camera assistant on a Truffaut film. At the same time, Nina was offered a promotion at the *Weekly*. The clash of careers was heart-breaking. But neither was prepared to walk away from the path they'd chosen. They compromised, promising to stay in touch, to visit and 'see what happened'.

Nina turned onto the Lyons Road. She'd planned to drive through Dijon anyway . . . but should she stay on this evening and see the film and Lucien? The thought of him resurrected so many memories. He'd become famous as a film-maker – an auteur, writing, directing and photo-graphing his appealing, quirky art house films. He had been labelled Europe's answer to America's Woody Allen and John Sayles, but serious cinema critics put him in a league with the masters he admired – François Truffaut, John Cassavetes, Jean-Luc Godard and Ingmar Bergman.

In the early years after they'd parted, she'd followed his career at a distance. But she'd heard little of him for ages. They had seen each other once in those early years, but even now her heart ached thinking about it, and she pushed the memory from her mind.

Instead, as her career progressed, she'd met the handsome, older, Doctor Paul Jansous at a dinner party. He was quietly humorous, gentle and caring. It was comforting to have a protector, a man who adored her, a wealthy man who could give her the best in life. He'd courted her and quite soon they'd married. It was a stable if stolid pairing, but Nina was unprepared for the shock of becoming a widow in her early thirties when her husband had collapsed with a heart attack while playing tennis.

In time her thoughts had turned to Lucien, but just as he knew little of her personal situation, so she knew little of his. In the end, she'd decided against disturbing his life by contacting him. Instead, Baron Oscar Von Triton had stepped in to fill the gap in her life with the offer to buy *Blaze*, the magazine that she'd started and made her so successful in Australia. She was ready for a new challenge so she had persuaded him instead to go into partnership and launch *Blaze* in America.

As she had so often through her life, Nina decided to let her instinct decide what she should do, what was best, when the moment arrived. She drove on along the Lyons Road through the sunny afternoon.

*

Belinda sat opposite Ali's desk in a straight-backed chair taking notes. She felt like a secretary out of a fifties B-grade movie with Ali playing Joan Crawford.

'And send a further staff memo that invitations to commercial promotional events are to be vetted by me.'

Belinda glanced up in surprise, then resumed scribbling as best she could without the knowledge of shorthand. For all Ali's high-tech leanings, her inter-office communication was outmoded. It seemed another way of keeping herself above the rest of the staff and reaffirming her authority.

Tony Cox, the young travel editor, was first to query the edict.

'Ali, I have an offer to go to Guyana – it's starting to become something of an eco-adventure holiday destination. A number of young Australians out there are setting up tourist operations. There'd be a lot of interesting stories from a part of the Americas that's written about by the freelancers whose stories we buy. I'm wondering what you think . . . with regards to this.' He fanned the air with her last memo.

'We have axed a story on Heron Island off our own shores, why would we involve ourselves in the expense of going to South America? Especially as it is company policy not to accept any free contra deals,' she answered airily.

Tony spoke patiently, not wanting to rile his editor, but finding it hard not to lose his temper. 'It's a form of advertising for the client, interesting copy for us. So long as we say this trip was paid for by so and so, readers can make their own judgement as to how biased the coverage may be.'

'Not every reader makes that leap,' said Ali blithely. 'So what's being paid for?'

'Air, accommodation, internal stuff. Travel infrastructure in Guyana is still a bit . . . loose.'

'Doesn't sound like the sort of place our readers would want to visit. They'd be more into up-market safari stuff.'

Tony decided to save the details of the delights of the former British Guiana. 'Advertising thinks it's an excellent idea.'

'Reg Craven doesn't have the say on what we cover just because he can sell a couple of ads. I don't imagine too many five-star hotels are in Guyana. We have to maintain a certain standard of quality of advertisers. If this was going to bring in a lot of money or a lot of kudos without compromising us . . .' Ali paused, then added, 'we have to be very careful about protecting our credibility.'

Tony didn't say anything at the obvious recent turn-around in Ali's attitude. He'd heard how she'd originally pushed to cover the movie star wedding on Heron Island before Larissa had convinced her of the danger of con-travening Triton policy . . . though Ali liked to give the impression it had been her idea to stick to ethics.

But as she hadn't dismissed it out of hand, he ploughed on. 'Guyana is exotic, different, has spectacu-lar scenery, a ton of natural assets – waterfalls, big rivers, fishing, hunting, Amerindian culture, diamond and gold prospectors . . .'

'Yes, yes. Would someone like me enjoy it?' asked Ali, and Tony realised she was serious.

'I'm not sure. You seem, um, very New York . . . Guy-ana's charm is, well, somewhat primitive.'

'Perhaps I should check it out.' She cocked her head.

Tony hesitated, the impact of the memo sinking in. 'Do *you* want to go out there?'

'I can't spare the time. Rio sounds more to my liking. When that kind of trip comes up, I'll take it.' She was brisk. 'I'm yet to be convinced we can afford to send you to Guyana. I'll think about it.'

'Ali, I edit a travel section. I know we commission most of our stories from freelancers, but sometimes I actually go places. It's in my contract. And someone has to pay!' he said in exasperation.

'I'll talk to Reg shortly.'

Tony left her office and went straight to the advertising manager before Ali called Reg.

Ali watched him go, knowing he'd be trotting straight down the hall to Reg. These boys stuck together. There were definite divisions in the office – the older women of experience, the young female challengers, the male management hierarchy, the editorial men who tended to side with the older women . . . and Ali. Ali was a force unto herself. It was not just the way she worked, it was the pattern of her life. Ali was a loner. And she had long ago trained herself not to analyse the reasons why.

After talking with Tony, Reg went to Ali's office armed with figures and a strong argument. He was pleased he had ammunition to fire. It annoyed him how she was able to see through his arguments and refused to be intimidated by him. Though he saw it as respect. Reg considered his power and role at *Blaze* superior to that of Ali. He kowtowed to senior male management. Women were expected to know they were below him on the executive ladder.

He spoke through stretched lips, but to Ali his tone was condescending. 'We have to attract advertisers with content that's different, special, a deal no one else has. We could pull in advertising to support a South American feature. If we have to, an advertorial. Fran in promotions can whip up a few deals.'

Ali cut in curtly. 'I've already knocked that idea sideways, Reg.'

'It's not up to you where we spend or do not spend our advertising budget. You stick to content and editorial,

I'll find the money to pay for the bloody magazine.'

His face was turning red with annoyance, his bow tie seeming to tighten round his neck where veins stood out. She knew he was itching to make one of his usual comments such as, 'Let us men run the show, you make the pretty pictures.'

Ali remained unruffled. 'I haven't said no. I've asked Tony to come back with story ideas, a list of what arrangements are being made and what it will cost us. We need to drum up something of note other than stay at such and such a lodge.' She looked thoughtful. 'Guyana, isn't that where the Reverend Jim Jones and the Jonestown suicide mess happened back in the late seventies?'

Reg shrugged. 'Maybe. Doesn't sound like a reason to go on holiday there.'

'No, but there must be a damned interesting follow-up story after all these years. Leave it with me.'

Reg Craven felt he was being dismissed and, while he left the office without a word, he grudgingly had to admit Ali's idea of a meatier story had merit. She was just so damned arrogant. When would she realise he held a parallel position in the hierarchy, but had the advantage of being closer to the money men and that they controlled the power?

Back in his office, Reg Craven called Jacques Triton.

'I have a potential problem, can we lunch?'

Jacques had little desire to lunch with the blustering Reg Craven, a man in his forties who gave off waves of constantly protecting his job and his butt. He listened as Reg explained the situation.

'I think I should talk to Tony. I'll call you back.' Jacques had his temp assistant – blonde, buxom and available – contact the travel editor on the phone.

The two men chatted briefly and Tony picked up the undercurrent in what the Baron's son was really saying.

'Lunch sounds terrific. Do I know any clubs in this town?' Tony laughed. 'Name your scene. What say we make it dinner instead?' Tony hung up the phone looking pleased. He'd get rid of Reg as soon as they'd eaten. Then . . . two rich young men on the town! That would give him a closer contact with the Triton empire heir than Ali would ever have.

Larissa was starting to get emissaries from the staff complaining about Ali.

Trudi Fanelli, the new beauty editor who'd been Australian PR for one of the top international cosmetic companies and appointed over Barbara, was first to make a stand.

'Larissa, on every magazine, the beauty editor is always buried under free products. The PRs send in everything from a full colour range of lipsticks to perfumes, night creams. If we want anything, we ring up and it's sent. Ali says we can't do this. We have to buy anything we write about. It seems crazy when the companies are dumping heaps of products on my desk.'

'Trudi, it's just not Triton policy. We can't accept anything for free – it compromises us editorially. There have been too many abuses of the system over the years and it's getting out of hand. It's not coming out of your pay,' she added with a slight smile. 'Those other magazines can be accused of taking "cash for comment" – accepting freebies and writing promotional editorial to back them up.'

'Okay. Understood. But, Larissa, the staff have pointed out that, in the good old days when the magazines received so much stuff, they used to get a share of the products. Now we buy the products, photograph them, and Ali walks in and says to send them to her office when we're finished. Even Guy, the photographer, is pissed off. He told me he's always been able to take stuff home to his wife.'

'Trudi, I'll have a word to Ali. But remember, *Blaze* is not a women's magazine like its predecessor. Gender is not an issue in magazines now. We're a news magazine too. And our credibility is paramount. Yes, we're glossy and we're Australian, but we're part of an international company that treats this matter differently.'

'Don't tell me to think globally,' moaned Trudi.

'Think smart. Clever. Different. Ali wants you to find news angles on beauty products. The cosmetics industry, like everything else, has to be able to stand up to scrutiny. Glamour still counts, but being into beauty is morally suss these days.'

'Listen, you can't tell me that any woman is ambivalent about how she looks,' said Trudi firmly.

Larissa beamed. 'Great. There's an angle. Go deconstruct Naomi Wolf and Germaine Greer. Vanity versus Sanity.'

Trudi relaxed. 'Okay, I take the point. But when you have that word with Ali, drop in one from me – selfish.'

Now Trisha Forbes, the entertainment writer, was in Larissa's office.

'It's out of control! Ali takes the best invitations. How can I do my job? I can understand Ali insisting on film and theatre critics buying tickets so they can review the shows fairly. But the PRs send me tickets for launch parties, first nights, et cetera, and Ali demands they're handed to her. I can't do my job if I don't go to these functions. And I'm embarrassed telling them my editor has taken them for herself.'

'She's trying to raise her profile, and that of the magazine, by being seen everywhere,' said Larissa. 'I'll talk to

Tracey to make sure Ali receives invitations to everything important.'

'Most editors leave the schmoozing and networking to their staff. It's really getting up my nose,' sighed Trisha.

'I'll speak to Belinda and ask her to contact the consultancies and PR firms and make sure invitations are sent directly to Ali as well as relevant staff and contributors,' said Larissa soothingly. Privately she agreed with the frustrated young woman trudging from her office. Ali was working overtime at making her presence seen and heard. She was being photographed at social functions and had become a fixture in radio and TV interviews that had anything to do with the media, current social issues or gender matters. She issued press releases about *Blaze* exclusives or innovations and Tracey, her publicist, was working on a promotional campaign with Steve Vickers at the ad agency that was going to star Ali.

Larissa poured out her current grumbles to the ever-sympathetic Belinda. 'I feel like I'm here slaving away, holding the braying staff at bay, trying to smooth over arguments hour after hour. Not to mention making sure the nitty-gritty is done in actually seeing the magazine come together. Ali isn't into production meetings. She's more into sending everyone back to the drawing board. Honestly, Belinda, sometimes I think they present the same stories again in another way because they think Ali rejects them the first time just to exercise her power.'

'In other words, you're feeling like an ashtray on a motorbike,' laughed Belinda. 'Listen, you're spending too much time moping without your fella. What do you do on weekends?'

'When I'm not doing something for *Blaze,* or at work, you mean? I've been exploring Sydney, the northern beaches.' Larissa hurried on before Belinda could probe further. 'I went up to the Blue Mountains, I browse around Double Bay and Darling Harbour, and I love the Art Gallery and Mitchell Library. I've been quietly reading up on Captain Cook's voyages . . . fascinating.'

Belinda gave her a shrewd look. 'In other words, you're lonely.'

Larissa bit her lip. 'Yes, I miss Gerry. A lot.' She was tempted to pour her heart out to the warm and sympathetic Belinda. The separation from Gerard was proving harder than she'd anticipated. The creative fulfilment and job satisfaction hadn't worked out quite the way she'd hoped. Everything was very similar to how they'd worked in New York, but different enough to be slightly irritating. The difference in the casual Australian attitude of 'she'll be right, no worries', compared to the energised dynamism in the US office, made her feel she was being too much of a taskmaster. She worked long hours because she had little social and no family life, but she didn't want to become another Ali, who was always in early and the last to leave the office. Larissa saw her role as that of a mediator between Ali and the staff. Even the most ambitious of the young women made it clear they'd never make the apparent sacrifice Ali had made for her career. She had no life outside *Blaze*. Larissa longed to share Sydney with Gerard and his long-distance disinterest made her feel even more depressed.

Belinda assessed her mood very quickly. 'I'm having a lunch for Tiki. I like to keep our *Blaze* girls in touch.'

Larissa had become friends with Tiki even though they hadn't worked together. She was sympathetic to Tiki because of her walkout over the treatment Ali had dished to her. Tiki had made it easy for Ali by walking. Larissa could imagine how tormented life would remain for Barbara, who felt she had no other option but to stay on, at Ali's discretion and beck and call.

Belinda pointed out that leaving *Blaze* had spurred

Tiki into submitting the manuscript of her novel to a leading publisher who promptly accepted it. Soon Tiki would see her real ambition come to fruition – with the books carrying her name displayed at the front of her favourite bookshops.

'It's fabulous. Every journalist swears they will write a book, few ever do it,' laughed Belinda.

'You mean finish it. We've all started a book at one stage or another. Look in any journo's top drawer,' agreed Larissa.

'Tiki told me her book starts in the outback and ends up in the midst of Sydney's magazine wars that started when all those editors were sacked. What else would she write about?' commented Belinda.

'Ali pushing her out the door no doubt gave her the impetus she needed. I have to confess I've harboured the desire to write a big fat book too,' smiled Larissa.

'This weekend, come to Sunday lunch. I'll invite Tiki too. No reason you shouldn't socialise a bit. I have several nice men up my sleeve.'

'Belinda, I'd love to come to lunch, but please. I'm attached, I don't want to . . . lead anyone on. Put myself into a position where it's . . . awkward.'

Belinda chuckled. 'Grow up, girl. And I thought you were a slick, glib, smooth-talking Yankee son-of-a-gun! You're as insecure as the rest of us!'

'And why not? Ali makes me feel that way. For the first time in my life, I'm questioning why I'm doing this job. And I've always loved my work. Well, Gerry used to challenge that when I came home full of complaints so often. But that goes with the territory.'

'So what's changed?'

Larissa spoke more to herself than Belinda. 'Maybe me, maybe I'm changing.'

*

202

Ali was wearing Armani pants and jacket – black, silk, cut to fit her lean body. A dramatic antique pin of a lion sat on her lapel, the effect oddly modern. Ali hoped everything about her was modern. Dane and his boys had shaped and coloured Ali's dark hair with a deep magenta that highlighted her brown eyes with their golden flecks. He'd personally sprinkled a dusting of gold powder on her eyelids. Her nails were polished with bronze gold, her lipstick a moist plum. The severity of the suit was lightened with the tip of a black lace hanky showing in the breast pocket, the neckline plunging to a single button at the waist. A black satin camisole top under the suit was a concession to modesty.

Her skin was still pale, she avoided the sun – even daylight, a few of the staff surmised with giggles – and kept her dark Chanel glasses on top of her head, hooked on her décolletage or wore them rain or shine. It seemed to be a defence mechanism rather than an affectation. Whenever she left her office, she immediately reached for her sunglasses. As she was meeting John O'Donnell for dinner, she slipped her glasses into her bag and abandoned her daywear, low-heeled black Ferragamo pumps for a pair of stiletto sandals in black snakeskin from Dato shoemakers in Sydney. Her long, narrow feet were bare of stockings, her nails bronze.

As she followed the maître d through the elegant restaurant, her sharp features and dramatic make-up made her a striking figure.

John O'Donnell smiled. He gave her an appreciative look and rose from his chair as she was seated. They'd had dinner and two telephone conversations. Now he'd asked her to dinner again, 'To put their discussions on a more friendly basis.' He noted the feminine touches to her outfit and was relieved. He'd initially found Ali rather intimidating.

They settled themselves with a glass of champagne each and caught up on general news.

'Congratulations again on the launch of the magazine. I'm sorry I was out of town. It sounds like it was a splendid effort. I hear sales are booming. I'll have to give our annual executive party a rethink.'

Ali had read in the business news about the impressive top-level gathering of his company execs and invited high-flyers prior to their AGM. 'I gather your functions are known to be technically very advanced. I'd like to tap more deeply into the information technology world. There must be new telecommunication resources that we can apply to magazine publishing. Even the book publishers are waking up.'

'You're so right. There aren't a lot of women embracing this new field. A shame. We have made a special effort to attract corporate women with these skills. There seems to be the perception that it requires at least a Masters Degree and that it's a field men resent women entering.'

'Women often think they're going to be ridiculed or sidelined by men if they go into a company as a computer specialist. We're supposed to opt for the nurturing, caring jobs rather than interacting with computers – let alone comprehending advanced science and information technology,' said Ali.

'Not so. It doesn't matter what your schooling. If you have an interest, you can be trained. Perhaps there's a story there for *Blaze* – to encourage women to take control and educate themselves in IT. Companies need more women managers. But first we have to create a more female-friendly environment.'

Ali nodded. 'Not a bad idea for a story. And what advice do you have for a woman wanting to succeed in a man's world?' she asked lightly, but her attention focused on the powerful CEO like a searchlight.

'Do your homework, don't be afraid to ask questions, and be a woman. So many women think they have to act like a man in a man's world.' He finished his champagne. 'Tell me how you find working with the women on your staff.'

Ali had read up on O'Donnell's company. It had a corporate culture of equality and sharing where management and staff considered themselves a team, where decisions were made by cooperative committees. It had slowed the company, made it less aggressive, sometimes to its detriment when they lost contracts because no one person could make a snap decision.

She spoke carefully. 'I respect how you approach your business. The women and the men at *Blaze* have a lot of input at editorial meetings and in the production of the magazine, but while I'm sitting in the editor's chair, I call the shots. Women are just as competitive as men, but the old boys' network doesn't have a strong counterpart amongst younger women. We pretend, but frankly it's every woman for herself.' She gave a wry grin. 'Nina, as you know, is on extended leave and the proprietor, Baron Triton, is tied up with their other publications abroad. So I'm running the ship.'

'And young Monsieur Jacques Triton?' asked John O'Donnell with a slight smile.

'He's visiting for a month or so, but he has assured me he thinks the company is being well looked after,' said Ali. 'As does his father.'

Ali had accepted the Baron's invitation to lunch following the *Blaze* launch party. But it had been a small, short-lived triumph. He had been amusing and charming company, his knowledge of the magazine and media business fascinating. Ali had flirted outrageously with him and both had enjoyed the ritual, though he had not taken her seriously. He was, after all, nearly forty years her senior. Ali, however, had been deadly serious, but realised it would take more than one lunch to lure the Baron into her web. She could tell from the way he'd spoken of Nina that he was in love with her. What a coup it would be to steal the Baron away from under Nina's nose. It was obvious he was lonely and liked the company of women. But Ali had set in place a connection with the Baron that she would now be able to renew with reasons linked to *Blaze*. She'd bide her time.

Jacques Triton was different from his father. He and Ali had sparred over the business agenda, especially where money was to be spent and budgets cut back. He hadn't liked the fact that she refused to be impressed by him. He was handsome, wealthy, scion of a famous family and, so, was usually forgiven for also being something of a classy European playboy. To Ali, he held little interest, outside her wish to impress on him how efficient she was with his family's money. Men were stepping-stones for Ali. And like her, Jacques was still treading carefully with his father. Whenever Ali could, she would arrange to see Baron Triton again. He had expressed a genuine interest in how she was running *Blaze*. In the meantime, she and the Baron had exchanged friendly emails and he'd kept her briefed on news of the company's movements internationally, now seeing himself as something of a mentor to the bright young Australian editor.

John O'Donnell was a different matter. In his fifties, he was slim and fit, attractively greying and at this vulnerable point in his life, very fragile. Ali realised this second invitation to dinner was a big step for him. She turned her attention back to what he was saying about the business world.

'We have always taken something of an altruistic approach – we give away a percentage of profits to charities decided on by the staff. We try to involve the various sectors of the company to be part of our decision-making process when it concerns their work.'

'Doesn't that create a too-many-cooks situation?'

'I take your point, and I know the company has been criticised for not acting swiftly on several occasions. But we are an industrial manufacturing company and the decisions we make affect many organisations, companies and industries. We can't afford to make a mistake.'

'Hare and the tortoise, eh?' Ali was relieved as the maître d returned to make suggestions for their meal.

Never a passionate gourmet, Ali selected swiftly and listened with feigned interest as John talked of food he loved and places he visited for their food. He chose the wine with care and knowledge and settled back to await their meal with anticipation.

Ali suddenly asked, 'What do you do about dinner each evening? I know your children are away at school. It must be hard for you now.' At the mention of his wife's recent death, he flinched and Ali regretted taking the plunge. 'Oh, I am sorry. Forgive me for bringing up such a painful subject.'

He quickly dismissed her apology. 'I'm still raw. Carol was the perfect corporate wife, loved entertaining, always had a nice dinner prepared for the family and later for the two of us. I was out such a lot, I really treasured our evenings at home. Now that I'm back in the office, I tend to eat out for lunches, and my secretary accepts the invitations to those dreaded black-tie dinners. I have to confess it's hard . . . and lonely.' He lifted his glass to taste the wine, nodded at the sommelier, and continued, 'I'm enjoying this. Talking business with interested and charming company. Carol was never that concerned with my business . . . we had the family . . . well, that's how it was.'

'I'm enjoying this too . . . there aren't many people I

can share my work with, and I can learn from experiences such as yours. I very much value your opinions.'

He gave an embarrassed but pleased shrug. 'Any time you need advice or think that I might be able to help, please call me.' He gave the food being put before them an appraising look. 'Let's enjoy our meal. We'll talk more about Carol's Foundation over coffee, eh?'

Ali had used the leverage of O'Donnell's name as a leading Australian corporate executive and the plan to set up a special fundraising program for cancer in his late wife's name as a means of reaching other influential heads of corporations. O'Donnell was well liked and respected and other CEOs had listened and agreed to support her plan – based on a similar foundation in the US. It had given the magazine a link to a national cause that showed *Blaze* as being philanthropic as well as giving Ali the reason she needed to maintain contact with a powerful man who was totally unaware of her ulterior motives.

After dinner they never did move on to discussing planning and organisational matters for the foundation. Instead, she talked him into reminiscing about his childhood and early days in business. He needed to talk and, with several glasses of wine, he chatted on about people and events he had never shared with a woman. Ali listened, stifling a yawn, thinking of other subjects that might interest him.

They finished the wine and he suddenly glanced at his watch. 'I had no idea. I'm sorry . . . I seem to have been doing all the talking . . . I can't remember going on so much about the business . . .'

She laid her hands on his, her eyes warm. 'It was lovely, really lovely. I feel I know you better now that I've caught up on the years I'd never have known about.'

His voice was husky. 'I'd like to hear your life story . . . next time, eh?'

Ali leaned back in her chair. 'Not as interesting as yours, I'm afraid.'

He gave a rueful smile. 'That's because I'm twice as old as you.'

Ali gave him a playful poke in the chest. 'Bullshit, O'Donnell. You are younger than you think. You've been too wrapped up in your job. Always doing the right thing. Live a little. Come on over to where we play, you might find it interesting.'

He was amused and surprised at not feeling the least bit offended. 'We?'

'It's a different ball game in my business. Maybe we both have something to learn from each other.' She picked up her Kelly handbag and pushed back her chair as he gave a hearty chuckle. He'd never had a young woman give him cheerful, intelligent cheek. He liked it.

'You're different all right. I look forward to our next meeting.' He steered her outside and opened the door of a waiting hire car. 'Leo will take you home. Thanks for a stimulating evening.'

Ali gave him a quick kiss on the cheek and a cheery wink. 'It's been a delightful evening. Thank you.'

As the car drew away she leaned back and closed her eyes. God, it had been a long and boring evening. But she'd made headway in breaking through the barrier John O'Donnell had built around himself.

And it was reaffirmed the next day when Belinda carried in a bunch of tulips with a note, '*I enjoyed our dinner. Hope you weren't bored with my reminiscences. We never did talk about Carol's Foundation – how about a "business" lunch. I'll call you. Best, John.*'

TAKE NINE...

The splendid medieval and renaissance buildings of Dijon complemented the indulgences of the four-teenth and fifteenth century Dukes of Burgundy, who had helped to make it one of the most famous centres of Western art. As she passed the classical Palais des Ducs, Nina drove around the public square in front of the pal-ace, where dozens of students gave the old city a modern and invigorating air.

She consulted her city map to find Rue Michelet and the Hostellerie du Chapeau Rouge, an establishment that, she was pleased to note, had been operating since 1847. She gave the keys of the car to the concierge and, after being shown to her elegant room, drew a bath.

She then went downstairs and sat over a leisurely *café au lait*, debating whether to visit one of the museums. Instead, she decided to wander through the Jardin de l'Arquebuse and its hundreds of plants. As she paused to read the botanical names, the letters appeared to melt, forming Lucien's name.

Leaving the formal garden washed in twilight, she realised the fading, beautiful day matched her sense of melancholy. She felt haunted by the passage of time, lost opportunities, the passing of youth and beauty. All that she stood for in the public domain – glamour, brilliance, style, intelligence – seemed empty and meaningless at this moment. She kept noticing plump women toting children as they did the shopping, others holding firmly to the hand or arm of a man in a manner that signalled ownership.

What did she have to show for the years of her life thus far? Certainly she was recognised as a woman of achievement in many fields, she was financially very secure, and respected and loved by many. Yet she hadn't envisioned this would be her life at age sixty. She had imagined children and grandchildren, and a deep and loving relationship with a lifetime mate to share experiences and laughter . . . What choices had she made to find herself so alone? She was not one for regrets, but as she walked, she cast her mind back over the years to those decisions that had changed her life. Could she have done things differently? Was putting her career ahead of Lucien wrong? So swiftly and easily she recalled those heady days. How in love they'd been – with each other, with their work, with life. There hadn't been a decisive moment where she made a deliberate choice between Lucien and her career. They'd just drifted in separate currents of a fast-moving stream. Then, suddenly, they were on different faraway shores.

So she had agreed to marry Paul Jansous. He'd come along at the right moment in her life. She loved him in a steady, caring way, pushing the giddy, consuming passion for Lucien into the realm of wild young experience. The first love you never forgot, that would never come again.

Her body had refused to create a child. It had taken a long time to accept that she could not conceive. Paul was a dedicated and influential physician. He had been caring, supportive and, despite his own sadness, his professional knowledge and advice had helped her deal with their situation. They discussed adoption, but somehow the right time and circumstance didn't eventuate. She put aside the notion of a family and became increasingly absorbed and involved with her work. Paul's dedication inspired her to be as good at her career as she possibly could be.

Then, suddenly one sunny morning, she was alone. A widow. With the responsibility of a mother to whom she owed everything. Nina buried herself in work. She was determined, creative and took risks. Eventually with *Blaze* she soared to heights even she hadn't imagined.

So why was she feeling so restless? She told herself it was turning sixty, the recent death of her mother and facing the fact she was virtually alone in the world.

Her relationship with her god-daughter, Miche, had been light-hearted, not taken as a binding commitment. It was lavish gifts and an occasional celebration that her mother, Lorraine, could not afford. It had been helping her in her school and career choices, in polishing her sense of style, her self-confidence and her sense of values.

Now Miche was alone and her future loomed as a seriously important factor in Nina's life. She would look out for Miche, but who was there to watch out for Nina?

These thoughts had been swirling in her head for several weeks. She hoped the stimulation of restarting *Blaze Australia* would douse the smouldering feelings, but it had not. Instead, as she'd tucked away her mother's mementoes, she'd begun to question and to wonder about Clara's life. And her grandparents' life in Croatia. Nina was seeking ties and links with the family she'd never had and the family she'd never known. She'd decided it was time to revisit her heritage.

And now, the neat package of her past had burst open, spilling memories. And the overriding ones were those of Lucien.

She dressed slowly, discarding three outfits before settling on tailored charcoal slacks and a white linen blouse with a soft cashmere shawl. She swept her hair up and took care in applying her make-up. Why did she feel so nervous? Lucien was an old friend. Their paths had crossed and their lives had taken very different directions. Everyone catches up in some way, sooner or later, with their first true love; whether by word or meeting or memory. And the further behind you creeps the past, strangely, the more important it looms. With this thought and a sense of a need to confront her ghosts, Nina headed for the Dijon Cinema.

In Paris, days blurred together for Miche. She barely noticed if it was sunny or cloudy, day or night. It felt as if she were in a whirlpool, generated by Sally, that was swirling everyone along in its whorls. Miche had been embraced as part of the entourage of hangers-on surging in the wake of the hot young Australian model.

Sally had taken to Miche as a friend – someone close to her in age, who spoke English and wasn't a threat, despite her attractiveness. Everyone seemed to have forgotten Miche was writing an article for a magazine.

Donald Heavney, the brightest of the hot photographers challenging the crowns of Annie Leibovitz, Patrick Demarchelier, Peter Lindbergh and Steve Meisel, had flown in from New York via a quick shoot in London. He was negotiating with Piste, Sally's Paris model agency over how and where to photograph Sally. Her image was still being developed and they wanted to be sure she was presented only 'in character'. Wasted punk waifs were gone, the voluptuousness of the Cindys and Elles were now considered less haute couture, ethnic diversity was no longer new and, while cyber-chic was still *au courant*, smart designers were straddling two generations – the youth market and the baby boomers who could afford lavish, one-off creations.

As soon as Sally had arrived in Paris, Piste had sent her to a top stylist to be photographed by Bandeau. They had come up with her look and how to market her. Each top model had to define her individual image. And so Sally's frail, exquisite looks were married to a fantasy, futuristic version of a renaissance heroine – Camille in cyberspace.

'Piste even wanted to change my name to Camille,' giggled Sally to Miche, as they sipped coffee in the soft Parisian sunshine. 'Not on your nelly, as my mum says. Then they wanted Vivien, but it just didn't feel like me. I'm a fun person.'

'Vivien?' wondered Miche, not making the connection. Sometimes Sally's conversation tripped like a bee from flower to flower making it hard to follow her train of thought.

'Mistress of Merlin. I was deep into Arthurian legends for a bit. Knights of the Round Table and damsels in distress. She lived in the centre of a lake.'

'Ah, the lady of the lake,' said Miche, surprised at Sally's reading interests. 'Do you study the Arthurian legends at school in Australia?'

Sally nodded and spooned potato salad into her mouth from a plastic tub she'd taken out of her carry bag.

'Do you read much?' Miche asked. 'I suppose you have to keep up with the fashion magazines.'

'No time. And I don't want to copy what other people do. I just go with the flow at the moment. Bandeau told me photographers like to work with fresh blood. I'm not trotting out pose number seven like a lot of the super-models used to do. They tell me to do my own thing, or try this or try that or what feels right for the outfit. Something sort of comes. I don't know how.' She stuck her finger in the tub, licking the last of the mayonnaise and gave a grin. 'Seems too easy. But I must be doing something right – they keep paying me.'

'What about living here? You haven't been here long. How's your French?'

'Not a word. So they think!' She winked. 'I did well in French at school, but I'm not telling them that.'

'Why not?'

'Dunno. Self-preservation. Just some kinda instinct.' She reached in her voluminous black backpack and pulled out a colourful comic book. 'Asterix . . . I'm keeping up my French with this. Don't tell anyone.'

Miche was amused. The girl was a mix of contradictions. On one hand, a down-to-earth Aussie kid from a Queensland country town, on the other, a vulnerable young girl thrust into 'a pool of piranhas' as Bandeau had described the modelling world. While she looked like a little lost kid out of her depth, Sally had remarkable sangfroid, an easygoing attitude to the extraordinary world she'd been thrust into.

Sally tucked up her legs and wrapped her arms around them, dropping her chin onto her knees. 'So. What's your story? Are you a real New Yorker?'

'Born and bred. But I'm half Australian. Which is one reason I'm off to Sydney. Bit nervous about it,' she confessed.

'Sydney is fantastic. You'll love it. Are you going to work there?'

'Yes. For *Blaze*. It's my first big job.' It suddenly hit Miche how ironic it was that she was starting her career under the hand of the woman who had so tormented her mother. She doubted Ali was aware how much Miche knew and understood of the tensions that had racked Lorraine as Ali clawed her way through the ranks at *Blaze USA*. Most nights at dinner her mother had spewed forth the minutiae of the day-to-day traumas of working with Ali.

While Miche was excited and nervous at beginning work as a first-time professional journalist in a strange country, she was also apprehensive about working with Ali. In her heart, she still felt that the thought of Ali being promoted in her mother's place had sent Lorraine literally over the edge. And while she felt enormous pity for her late mother, deep down she resented her for leaving her alone. It had intensified the need to find her father, to even up the seesaw of emotion that had weighed so heavily on her mother's side.

Sally was looking at Miche expectantly.

Miche felt a need to unburden herself to a young woman out in the world and as vulnerable as Miche was feeling. 'My mom died recently. I don't know my father. I thought . . . well, maybe it was time to find out about the other side of my heritage. My identity.'

'Oh, wow. That's so sad. Gee, I'm sorry. It sounds like something on TV. Are you going to write about it?'

'Gosh no. Besides, I don't even know where he is. If he's alive. He might be an axe murderer or something.' Miche now wanted to change the subject.

'Will you tell me what happens?' said Sally earnestly. 'I had a girlfriend whose mother left her with her dad when she was a kid and her father beat her up and abused her. She ran away and found her mother and her mother was on drugs and tried to make her work as a prostitute to bring in money for her habit. I mean, aren't some families awful? Mine are boring, but at least they're ordinary.'

Miche shrugged. 'What's ordinary?'

'What I wanted to escape from,' giggled Sally. 'Hey, gotta go. See ya at the shoot.'

Donald was laid-back and unfazed about the merry-go-round they seemed to be riding. He'd been hired for a week by *Blaze* for this shoot, so the delays at the outset didn't faze him. He didn't mind hanging out with Miche on the fringes of the entourage, understanding he was forbidden to take any candid shots of Sally. *Blaze* abided by the agency agreement, so he spent his time watching Sally – her moods, the way her body moved, assessing her personality.

To Miche, it seemed a crazy way to work. Time, schedules, organisation, whatever she understood as professionalism was abandoned in what appeared to be a pursuit of a good time above all else.

Miche lost all sense of time, order and focus as she trailed along with Sally. She thanked Nina in her mind, day after day, for setting her up to stay in the residence of the Australian Ambassador to France and his wife, Claudia.

When she did return to the elegant, quiet mansion after the raging of the modelling crowd, it resettled Miche, even if she did arrive home at all hours.

One evening, over dinner in the formal sitting room, waited on by a butler, Miche told Claudia and Bernard of the strange world of fashion, models and magazines.

'I'm sorry to be creeping in so late. I thought I knew about partying in New York, but these people are crazy. I'm certainly discovering stuff to write about. I hope it's printable,' she added with a grin.

Claudia was less amused. 'I insist you take our driver with my car to ferry you about and act as an unofficial bodyguard. Or use the embassy car and driver. Don't you think that's a sensible idea, darling?' she asked her husband.

The ambassador hesitated. Embassy cars were only to be used for official business. He decided to deal with matters on an as-need basis. 'As Nina's friends, we feel very responsible for you, Miche. It seems to me I've heard a few bad stories about this modelling business . . . something to do with girls going to wealthy Arabian countries for parties and not being able to leave.'

'Used as sex slaves,' added Claudia in a low voice.

Miche laughed. 'Claudia, surely not. Maybe back in the seventies there were stories . . .' She turned to Bernard. 'That is, unless you know something? Maybe I should accept your offer of a driver.'

'It pays to err on the side of caution. I can't remember anything specific very recently. Maybe a bit of gossip at a diplomatic reception. Certainly nothing of substance for your article.'

'We're on call. I'll give you Bernard's private number at the embassy. You phone us any hour of the day or night if you have any problems, and one of us will be there. I don't want Nina to think I'm not looking after you,' said Claudia.

'Thank you both, very much. You and Nina are very close,' remarked Miche.

'Oh yes, we were your age when we were best friends. We met in Sydney when we were fancy free and ready to set the world on fire. Nina was in magazines and I was at secretarial college. Then my parents, who were also in the diplomatic service, sent me to Switzerland to a finishing school. Nina came to Paris once back in those early years, to write a story just as you are doing now. I met up with her again and we had such a delicious time. "Our Hearts Were Young and Gay", to quote the writer and actress, Cornelia Otis Skinner. Nina was covering the collections for the first time. She and Lucien were so in love, and then I met Bernard.' She gave her husband a fond look. 'Our lives started to change after that, but it never altered the friendship between us. The friends you make in your youth seem to stay as the bright benchmarks of your life.'

'Who is . . . was . . . Lucien?' asked Miche. 'Nina has never mentioned him. My mother only told me about Paul Jansous, that marriage.'

'She never talked about him once they went their own ways. Too painful, I suspect. One day you must ask your godmama the story of her life.' Claudia reached over and touched her arm. 'We all have secrets in the corners of our hearts, *chérie*.'

Miche didn't need to call on the services of the embassy driver. Sally quickly learned to hire limos, replete with booze, drugs and rock and rollers to ferry them to clubs and parties.

'It's so cool,' she told Miche. 'I just ring up and charge it back to the agency.' If this was a new game, she was learning the rules on the run.

Miche and Donald tagged along. This was research? To Miche it was mind-blowing.

They were in a stretch limousine and it was after 10 p.m. They'd been part of a swelling entourage in a photographic studio where Sally and two other top models were shot in evening wear. It had seemed more like a party with loud music, endless liquor and champagne and one model and four guys locked in a toilet doing coke. The French fashion editor had been screaming about the clothes. An assistant kept insisting the group in the loo were doing hair and make-up. By the time the model emerged, she was wildly stoned.

Miche fidgeted on the periphery of this seeming madness. Donald chatted casually to the studio people. Sally cruised through the shoot unperturbed. Her make-up and hair had taken two hours.

Miche nudged Donald. 'Is this what you spend your time doing?'

He was vague. 'The fashion stuff is neurotic. So are major movie stars. I only do profiles now. I'm good at them. But I kinda like feature stuff where you have to shoot on the run.'

Sally was ready. She looked like a somewhat mad Alice in Wonderland, sitting cross-legged on the floor, her ballgown heaped around her, holding a sleepy white rabbit. The other two girls – one fair, one dark, in dazzling, clinging dresses that seemed to be cut from rich Indian tapestries – were draped over each other on plush cushions. One held a huge peacock fan, the other the end of a brass hookah. She looked dazed and pretended to drag on the pipe and the next instant rolled on her back, gagging.

For a moment the photographer's assistant thought she was play-acting. Then the other girl screamed, 'God, she's out of it. Do something!'

There was a rush as everybody dropped what they were doing and someone dashed to the phone. 'Call the medics!'

The fashion editor started to go crazy as the girl began to gag. 'Take the dress off her. It's a Valentino, it will be ruined . . .' The dressers leapt in, dragging the gown off the unconscious girl, pulling a baggy sweater onto her thin, convulsing body. Donald slipped outside to wait in the street, leaving Miche standing on the sidelines in the studio. Within minutes, ambulance paramedics rushed in and the girl was carried from the studio.

The fashion editor grabbed one of the male nurses, shouting in French, 'Can she work tomorrow? We need this picture!'

Sally, still holding the tranquillised rabbit, hadn't moved.

The photographer flung up his hands. '*Merde*!'

'Call the agency. See if they can find another girl. And we're not paying for that stupid bitch,' snapped the fashion editor, who worked for one of the second-rate glossies. They'd blown half the month's budget on this shoot in an effort to boost sales.

'Is she going to be all right?' Miche tentatively asked the French photographer.

'Guess so. I've seen this before. Let's wrap it and go to a club.'

'Here we go again,' Donald said quietly to Miche. He opened his jacket slightly, showing her a small pocket camera and gave a slight smile. 'There are a couple of shots in here for your story.'

'God, keep it quiet. If they find out you've sneaked shots of a top model drugged out of her mind, they'll throw us out.'

'Or worse,' said Donald, and strolled out of the studio to where the partygoers were piling into several waiting stretch limousines. They travelled in a haze from the studio to the club as they'd been doing every night. No one seemed to eat, everyone had their own supply of uppers, downers, poppers, pills and phials of white powder.

Sally seemed unconcerned, finding it all 'a bit of a hoot', telling Miche, 'A few of the girls were so wired during the last shows, I don't know how they didn't fall off the catwalk.'

'What about you?' asked Miche.

'I started using pot in school. A couple of the photographers on shoots here give me stuff to help me loosen up.

221

Course they then put the hard word on you,' she added with a world-weary shrug.

'Don't take any 'ludes,' advised Donald. 'In the old days, they'd give them to the new models who'd pass out and then they'd take porn shots. Those girls were never booked for a serious fashion shoot again.'

'The old days? You're not over thirty, are you?' asked Miche.

He grinned. 'So people tell me stories. Some of those old-fashioned guys are legends now. Not nice legends. They've been known to feel bored and horny and call the agencies to send new models – male and female – round for look-sees, make them drunk, drug them and screw them silly. Same with the hairdressers and make-up guys and girls.'

'Yeah. These guys tell you if you don't sleep with them, they won't use you. Stuff 'em, I don't care.' Sally peered out into the Paris night.

'So . . . what happened? Did you complain to your agency? You're only sixteen,' probed Miche.

'The bookers didn't seem to care. Said they're not my mother. If I had a problem, to go to Françoise – she runs the Paris office. I only met her when I was signed up. But you know, the more I don't give a shit, the more they want me.' Sally seemed unconcerned.

'If you're fucking up, you don't run to mother,' muttered Donald.

'How long do you want to do this?' asked Miche. 'What happens if you're not flavour of the moment any more?'

Sally leaned back in the limo's leather and took a drag of her joint. 'I'll piss off. Do something else. Go back home.'

Donald raised his eyebrows. 'Yeah, sure. You're sixteen, making more money in a good week than your father earns in a year. Your face is on newsstands round the world. You could give this up – the parties, hanging out with the A-list? Come on . . . now you do sound sixteen.'

'What would you do, if you were me?' she shot back.

Donald grinned. 'Go for it. Give 'em hell, babe.' He winked at Miche. 'You're on the right end of a top story. She's too cocky to keep her mouth shut.'

Sally waved her arms. 'Let's break out the bubbly.' She yanked a champagne bottle out of the small bar in the limo. 'I don't care. I escaped tonight. Avoided that PR lady, anyway. She had more coke in her bag than anyone. So, let's live it up.'

'What did you do with her?' asked Donald.

'I introduced her to this hunk model from another agency. She fell instantly in lust, and the last I saw of them they were gazing into each other's blurry eyes.'

The car headlights and streetlights flickered into the mellow interior of the plush car. Miche caught the look on Donald's face as he watched Sally with part admiration, part sadness. He'd seen it all before.

Tony Cox and Jacques Triton were gloriously drunk. They had come to rest in the depths of the Parrot Club after another of their nights on the town. From their first social outing, the travel editor and the son of Baron Triton had connected, despite the disparity in their backgrounds. Both had a strong taste for a sybaritic lifestyle and Tony was happy to introduce Jacques to the nightclubs available to rich, trendy young professional men. *Blaze*'s travel editor came from a wealthy North Shore family and, from their first exploration of the hip/yuppie/

shake-it scene in Sydney, they recognised in each other the same need for extreme indulgence that bordered on saturnalia.

It had started out as a social introduction to a city, but quickly the barriers had fallen away and Jacques attracted around him a coterie of rich, fast-living Beautiful People with well-connected names. It amused Jacques that this heavyweight, social, often profligate set came with family money acquired through sometimes unclassy means.

What started as two young men out for a fun time soon sank into the heady world of lap-dancing in Sydney's more raunchy restaurants, and experiments with new drugs and pills amid the constant availability of cocaine. They set a pattern that was whispered in media corridors, and on occasion, hinted at publicly.

They had spent lunch and the afternoon in Jacques' pet eating hole, in a risqué private room where sexy, partly clad waitresses spoon-fed them, sat in their laps and wiggled their buttocks to the music, until, teasingly, they escaped the men's growing need and desire, and sometimes spontaneous orgasms. From the inebriated, titillating lunch, a visit to a high-class brothel became a regular event.

Now, hours later, club-dazed, eyes glazed, they sank into the leafy green cushions of a booth beneath the mock jungle plants and stuffed parrots. Music blared and lights flashed across the dance floor where a few couples moved independently of each other, lost in their own headspace of light and noise.

Tony finished his drink. 'It's that time. Stay, go, night-cap, find a girl?' He resisted looking at his watch. It wouldn't be the first time he'd fallen into a cab outside a club at dawn to get home for breakfast, shower and straight into the office.

Jacques downed his champagne. 'Where're the

women? It's a desert out there. Where're the models? They're the party girls.'

Tony looked around. 'Must be having their beauty sleep.'

'No shortage of them in Europe and the States. Ring up one of the agencies and have them sent over by the truckload.' Jacques gave a short laugh. 'I should start a new business here. There are always pretty girls wanting to be models. A magazine is a good place to start.'

'And if you own the magazine, you own the girls. Hey, I like it,' chortled Tony.

They both stood and were heading through the near-deserted club when a burst of laughter caught their attention. Two attractive girls and an older man were settling themselves on the stools at the bar.

'Hey, this is more like it.' Jacques was looking at the blonde girl. Petite yet buxom, she was striking, if a little theatrical looking. Her friend was tall, dark-haired and, to Tony, the man looked vaguely familiar. He followed Jacques, who cruised into the bar and went straight to them.

'Congratulations, you have won party animals of the week award. We thought we were going to snare the trophy.' Jacques was all humorous Gallic charm.

The small blonde, who looked to be around thirty, gave him a cool, slightly arrogant look. She reminded Jacques of a chihuahua, tiny in stature yet big in self-confidence. 'And what's the award?'

'A live parrot that can sing all the songs of Simon and Garfunkel,' said Jacques off the top of his head.

'Who?' asked the dark girl.

The man laughed. 'Now you're showing your age, kiddo.'

'I'll take the prize. So long as it can sing *Sound of Silence*,' challenged the blonde.

'Give me your address and I'll have it delivered first thing in the morning.' Jacques bowed and kissed her hand.

'Would you fellows like a nightcap? We've been celebrating my daughter's graduation as a fully fledged fashion designer.'

'With her own label,' added the blonde.

'This is your father?' asked Tony, quickly clarifying the situation.

'John Bass, my daughter, Patti, and her pal, er, Tallulah.' The older man made the introductions.

'Tallulah? You don't look like a Tallulah,' said Jacques, sitting on the bar stool next to the blonde.

'I'm not,' she answered enigmatically.

Tony stood between the two girls as Mr Bass signalled to the waiter.

'Champagne.'

'The gentlemen have been drinking Moët & Chandon. The same?'

'Why not?'

The blonde Tallulah looked at Jacques. 'Supporting your country's wines, eh?'

'I'm Belgian, via the US.' He gave a charming smile. 'So who are you? Let me introduce myself.'

'You don't need to do that, Monsieur Triton.'

Tony laughed, seeing Jacques's composure wobble slightly. 'You have been in the social pages a bit lately, Jacques.' He turned to both girls. 'I'm Tony Cox.'

John Bass shook his hand. 'Should we also know you?'

'Not at all. Though you look familiar if I may so, sir.'

Tallulah leaned closer to Tony. 'He's CEO of Vortex Bank. The one that bankrolled the new telecommunications company.'

'Of course!' Tony clapped his hand to his head. 'Sorry. You were all over the business pages. I signed on. Should I buy shares? I love dot coms. It's thanks to guys like you I can dial up the newspaper, download the fruit prices in Istanbul . . .'

'Do you two work together?' Patti, the budding fashion designer, spoke up.

'Yes, you could say that. But we have more in common out of the office,' said Jacques graciously.

'What he means is, he's the boss. I'm a mere hack travel editor,' said Tony.

'Which Triton publication do you write for?' asked Tallulah with sudden interest.

'*Blaze*.'

'Oh, it's great. Do you know the editor?' jumped in Patti.

Before Tony could answer, Tallulah threw back her head. 'Ahh! Alisson Gruber. How do you find working for the Yank Tank, Tony?'

Jacques grinned. 'Is that what they call her?'

Bass topped up their glasses as Tony, very relaxed after so many drinks, confided, 'Hell, yes. She breathes fire and has scorched a few backsides. I mean,' he looked at Jacques, 'I'm not telling tales out of school.'

Jacques shrugged. 'She isn't my favourite person. Though my father thinks she's pretty hot.'

'She'd have to be good to run the place, wouldn't she?' commented Bass. 'Where's Nina Jansous? I thought it was her baby.'

'Editors run the magazine, editors-in-chief keep out of their way and read the circulation figures and balance sheets. If Ali stumbles, Nina will put someone over her and Ali will lose her power and resign,' explained Tony.

'Seems to me there have been a lot of editors resign these past few years in Sydney. A precarious profession, from what the gossip columns say,' said Bass with a smile at the two girls.

'Who would you put in if Ms Gruber stumbles?' Tallulah asked Jacques, smoothing her shoulder-length blonde hair.

He gave her a frankly flirtatious look. 'Maybe me. I'm starting to like this town.'

'So what do you do?' asked Tony. 'And I don't believe Tallulah is your real name.'

'It's not. And that's for me to keep a secret.' She pulled a tiny red mobile phone from her handbag. 'I'm calling it a night.'

'We'll come with you,' said Patti. 'Is the car still there, Dad?'

'Yes. Can we drop you lads anywhere?'

'I have a hire car on call,' said Jacques smoothly. He kissed the mysterious blonde's hand. 'I hope we meet again.'

'We may well do that.'

'Congratulations on your graduation, business, label . . .' said Tony to Patti.

'Thanks. It's called Patti Cakes. Put in a positive word with your editor.'

John Bass shook hands with both men and the trio left.

Jacques shook his head. 'Tallulah wasn't giving much away. *Très formidable.* So, do we call up the agency and ask for a couple of girls? The last ones were fun, eh?'

'I think I'll head home, Jacques. I have to face Ali tomorrow. I'm still trying to sell a story on Guyana to her.'

'For travel? Who'd want to go there?' Jacques signalled the waiter.

'The intrepid traveller. Why do the same old places that everyone else does?'

'That's a point. What's her objection?'

'Cost. Triton doesn't allow contra deals. Oh, we have a pact not to talk shop. Forget it.'

But Jacques wasn't listening. He put a few twenty dollar notes on the counter and the waiter stood on a chair and pulled down one of the large colourful parrots.

'What are you going to do with that?' asked Tony as they headed for the exit.

'Teach it Simon and Garfunkel songs,' said Jacques, grinning.

'What! How are you going to send it to her? You don't even know her name?' Tony stared at the suave Belgian.

'Bass. Vortex Bank. One phone call tomorrow should do it.'

Belinda's Balmain home had been a rundown cottage with a terraced rambling garden and a tiny jetty. Laurie, her husband, had extended the house, added a boatshed that doubled as a workshop, and transformed the garden. The place was now worth a fortune.

Laurie was big on barbecues. He kept a crab trap hanging from the front of his jetty and threw a line in just about every day to catch a fish, whether it fed them or the cats. But when they entertained, he went to the fish markets where an Italian fishmonger friend kept aside the fattest tiger prawns, the juiciest mussels and the sweetest Sydney rock oysters. These he threw onto his roaring hotplate and doused them in wine, garlic and a squeeze of lime. Laurie didn't believe in marinating when he had the freshest ingredients.

Larissa had been overwhelmed. 'Belinda, you must pay a fortune for food like this. And the setting . . .' She flung out an arm to embrace the nearby sprawl of the harbour. 'Not to mention the company.'

Belinda gave her a happy nudge. 'I'm glad to see you've made a few friends.' She turned her attention to the newly arrived guests, allowing Larissa to recover her composure, absolving her of making any comment. In the past three weeks Larissa had enjoyed careful and discreet attention from the owner of an advertising agency – Kevin McCarthy, divorced, rich and very amusing.

'You haven't lived till you've been cruising on Sydney's waterways,' Kevin had said at their first meeting. 'Come out next Saturday. A few buddies and I are taking the boat up to Palm Beach. We'll pull in somewhere along the Hawkesbury for a picnic.'

Knowing it was a group outing, Larissa had finally agreed and had enjoyed the best time she'd had since arriving in Australia. The Fjord cruiser was sleek and comfortable, the company convivial with other ad men from his agency, including the brilliant young creative director and two women clients – Julia, from a financial institution, and Sonia, a product specialist from a pharmaceutical company.

Larissa had never experienced anything so exhilarating as sailing out through Sydney Heads. They turned north to run along the coastline and eventually round Barrenjoey headland into Broken Bay. The bushland hills of Ku-ring-gai National Park rose above small sandy coves, larger bays filled with picnickers and campers, sweeping back to the residential and holiday cottages off Church Point.

Kevin anchored in Refuge Bay, a small deserted cove. They rowed ashore with iron barbecue plate and steaks, an Esky – nicknamed 'The Richard' after the *60 Minutes* reporter who travelled with an Esky of lavish food and wine supplies to Third World hot spots so he would not be without the comforts of home. Belinda had filled this cooler with bowls of salad and fresh bread. They'd swum and lazed on the tiny strip of sand then, after lunch, Kevin had taken them hiking up the hill, following a footprint-wide track made by wallabies.

Larissa had seen and heard her first kookaburra. 'They really do sound like they're laughing,' she said.

'Watch out if you picnic at a popular place,' said Sonia. 'They fly down and grab the food off your plate.'

'Buggers killed or flew off with the goldfish in my terrace pond,' added Julia.

'They're kingfishers. That's what they're programmed to do,' said Phil the creative director. 'All our behaviour patterns are programmed.'

This had started a good-natured debate over genetic and environmental influences governing behaviour and Phil had started talking about new IT developments that could also influence how humans interact.

Larissa had been fascinated. 'Tell me more, how do you know this stuff?'

'Agencies spend fortunes on market research. But my sister is doing her PhD at MIT in the States. We talk a lot. She's working on audio delivery by light source. There's a bright IT guy, Dan, that we use as well.'

Larissa wanted to know more and they trailed behind the others while Phil explained as best he could how this new technology worked.

'Why are you so interested? I thought magazine people like you were just into image.'

'We can't afford to limit ourselves like that. Everything is technology-based now. But content and the talent that creates it will always be a vital ingredient. Technology can't replace a creative and fertile mind.'

'What makes *Blaze* different from the rest of the pack out there?' asked Phil. 'A lot of the ads I create are for a generation that read screens rather than paper. They want movement, music, flashing lights, bells and whistles. Aren't magazines going the way of stone tablets?'

Larissa studied Phil, who looked every inch an ad man – hair buzz cut with a five, a discreet tattoo of a small frog on his arm, an earring, the latest gear, shades, shoes. But he wasn't cynical, slick, arrogant. He seemed a nice boy in his early twenties. Probably ten years younger than her, probably gay, yet Larissa felt a generation older.

'As *Blaze* is a new magazine, Nina, our editor-in-chief, has been quite innovative in the presentation. It's not locked into a niche market or even just mass market. Yes, it's popular culture, but there are well-written, challenging articles, exciting images, disposable information and thought-provoking stuff. Ali, our editor, is trying to be as cutting edge as possible. She sees it as sonic information – boom!'

'Ali Gruber? The Yank Tank? We know about her!' he laughed. 'Hey, sorry, she's probably a close friend.'

'We worked together with Nina in New York. She has made a bit of a name for herself here. She's sees it as part of her job to promote the magazine,' said Larissa noncommittally.

'Yeah, you've arrived when you're carved up by April Showers.' His attention was suddenly diverted. 'Hey, they've found something.' They hurried to where the others were clustered around a large rock.

Kevin pointed to the outline of a huge fish. 'Aboriginal carving. There are plenty around here. Most of the Aborigines in Sydney were wiped out by smallpox soon after the First Fleet arrived.'

Larissa was fascinated and bent down and traced her fingers in the engraving etched into the sandstone. 'How, why is this here?'

'According to Jim Macken, our local expert, it could

be a male initiation or a female birthing ceremony site. The elders drew the outline in charcoal or ochre, and then they took sharp flint stones to dig holes along the outline and joined them up to make the final engraving. It's called a pictograph. He can tell you fantastic stories of this area. We'll bring him along next trip.'

'I'd love to know more about the Aboriginal history. I love the art,' said Larissa.

'Don't get Kevin started,' said Phil. 'He's quite a collector.'

Kevin took Larissa's arm and helped her to her feet. 'You must come and see my Wandjinas and Papunyas.'

'Well, now I'm curious without even knowing what or who they are,' she laughed.

Larissa had lunched with Kevin the following week to talk about some of his advertising clients taking ads in *Blaze*. But they'd talked about a lot of other matters and enjoyed each other's company. She was glad to see he was here at Belinda's lunch party.

Belinda drifted among the guests who were dotted in bright bursts about the shady garden. The mothering attitude she showed in the office continued in her role as hostess. She had a knack for putting people at ease, showing a genuine interest and concern in their well-being. She came to light at the table where Larissa and Tiki Henderson were talking.

'Thanks for sending us a copy of your manuscript, Tiki,' said Larissa. 'Congratulations. When's it due in the shops?'

'Not sure. They tell me they're bringing it out earlier now because another book on their list fell through.'

'Ooh, you'll be on the talk-show circuit. Tell me when you're going to be on TV. I'll tape it. Unless we can sneak a look in the office,' said Belinda.

'Not in working hours. Ali will deduct half an hour

from your pay,' said Tiki with a touch of irony. Although she had walked out of the job, her demotion by Ali still rankled. 'Anyway the publisher's PR has warned me they'll have a hard time arranging any interviews. The media doesn't want to know about "sacked ex-journo writes romance novel",' she sighed.

'It's not a romance novel,' said Larissa. 'It's romantic, but it has a strong message, gutsy, provocative characters, and touches on a number of sensitive issues. Boy, the mother and daughter stuff touched my heart.'

'The publicist wants to push the angle that the book dishes the dirt on the Yank Tank. I hope they don't want to talk about just that and not the book.'

'Don't worry, interviewers never read the books anyway,' said Larissa.

'How can they ask the right questions then?' puzzled Belinda.

Larissa and Tiki burst out laughing. 'They read up a bunch of newspaper or magazine cuttings – if you've been interviewed before – so they can repeat the same inaccuracies, and write it from that and the press release. They phone you up with a series of set pet questions . . . "Where do you find your ideas? Why did you write this book?, How long did it take you?, Are you writing another book? What's it about?"' chanted Tiki. 'It's been so frustrating. And to top it off, that dreadful April Showers has had a go at me a couple of times.'

'Ooh. That's bad when the only publicity you can get is in that column,' said Belinda looking at Larissa.

Tiki sighed. 'The publishers don't think so. So long as the name of the book appears. And I've never spoken to April Showers. I don't know why I'm being called ex-hackette, or why it's being inferred I went through everyone's desks and took out every journo's half-finished manuscript and stirred them together.'

'At least you weren't escorted from the building,' added Larissa. She'd been appalled at tales of the grand Aussie magazine tradition of firing a senior journalist or editor on the spot. There had been cases where the poor unfortunate was to clean out their desk while every move was watched by a security guard who then escorted them out of the building, making them leave their company ID and cars keys at the front desk.

Belinda poured herself a glass of wine. 'I know why April Showers is having a go at you, Tiki.'

The other women's eyes swivelled to Belinda and wine glasses were refilled.

'Do tell,' said Tiki. Belinda always seemed to find out the low-down, the behind the scenes, the ridgy-didge goss as she called it.

Belinda sipped her wine. 'I have to preface my remarks by saying I have never met the dreaded April Showers. But a certain publisher told me he'd been given a manuscript by April Showers, who thought knocking off a light lady's romance would be a quick way to fortune and more fame. April wanted to buy a huge house and needed extra cash.'

'What happened? Where's the book? Don't tell me it's about to come out at the same time as mine,' wailed Tiki.

'The publisher knocked it back. Said he wouldn't give five bob for it,' said Belinda.

'Everyone thinks they can write romance or mass-market fiction. That Mills and Boon is a piece of cake that mints you money. Dead wrong. Tell 'em to try it,' said Tiki. 'So what happened, Belinda?'

'The agent representing April Showers tried to sell a manuscript to your publisher and he knocked it back – too defamatory apparently. So they publish you and not her. Work that out for yourself,' finished Belinda.

Tiki sighed. 'This media trip is such a pain, especially seeing it from the other side. The PR girl told me that being over forty – excuse me – I wouldn't generate much interest media-wise.'

'Have your boobs done and pay through the nose for a face-lift,' suggested Larissa.

'Sleep with someone famous,' giggled Belinda.

'You can't sleep with everyone in the media, Belinda. You should know that. The men are either too pissed or the women figure they could've written your book better,' said Tiki, liberally splashing the wine into her glass.

'Miaowww . . .' laughed Belinda.

Larissa leaned over and, in a stage whisper, warned, 'Look out for any write-up by April Showers.'

'These gossip columnists throw around inaccuracies and innuendo that can harm your book more than any publicity can help it.'

Tiki dropped her head in her hands. 'God, between Showers and Ali I'll be crucified. I figured the one positive part of leaving *Blaze* was I'd have the time to write another book. I'll be lucky if this one sells a hundred copies.'

'We'll all buy a few copies,' said Belinda squeezing Tiki's arm.

Kevin loomed over the table. 'This looks like a wake. Come on, there's delicious food over yonder.' He gave Larissa a questioning look.

'It's all right, Kevin. We're just figuring out how to disrobe Caesar's wife.'

He took Larissa's hand to lead her across the lawn. 'So who is always above suspicion?'

'My boss. Don't ever tangle with ambitious women in the workplace.'

'That's why I've surrounded myself with gay and nice young men. Come on, think of something to look forward to. I hear it's your birthday in a week. Can I arrange a party for you?'

'Oh. Goodness. I never celebrate birthdays.' A feeling of guilt swept over Larissa thinking how she'd initially forgotten Gerard's last birthday. At least she'd made up for it by organising the bash at Alain Ducasse at vast expense. Would Gerard remember her birthday without her around to drop hints? Their communication was relying more and more on email because phone calls were missed or mistimed.

'We always celebrate birthdays in Oz. It will be a wonderful excuse for a party,' smiled Kevin.

'Please, no cake, no candles, no silly song.'

'What about rude balloons and vintage champagne?'

Larissa laughed. 'Now you're talking. It sounds fun.' And she felt childishly pleased.

TAKE TEN ...

Miche and Donald were following the red sports car driven by Sophie, the Piste representative appointed to watch over Sally. Bags of clothes, accessories, props and Pete, Donald's English assistant, were piled in the back. Everyone had finally agreed on the *Blaze* shoot for Sally's story. The young model's repeated litany to Miche – 'none of this seems real' – had led to a fantasy theme.

They were driving to the Rhône Valley to shoot dream sequences at a vineyard attached to a chateau. It was once part of a grand estate and the family had almost died out. The unmarried and elderly heir, unable to maintain the grounds and buildings, had turned the family vineyard into a boutique winery.

Miche gasped as Donald drove through the arches in the old stone wall as she glimpsed the chateau and its gardens surrounded by terraced grapevines that produced a fine shiraz under the label Château Soleil. 'Wow. It looks like a postcard. Or a scene from a French movie!'

'Funny about that, eh?' said Donald. 'It's a cool place. I've been here before. Did shots for a classy calendar. Naked girls romping among the grapes, the vats and the old rooms of the chateau. Pretty wild time was had by all.'

'Is it going to be like that, this time?' asked Miche. She was finding the lifestyle in the modelling world less fun and more debauched and dangerous. She wondered how it was affecting Sally.

Donald reached over and casually patted her knee. 'Maybe it's time for you to live a little, Miche. For a New Yorker, you're pretty stitched up.'

It was the first time Donald had made anything like an intimate remark to her and Miche bridled. His laid-back Aussie friendliness had put her at ease. Knowing they had three days together ahead of them, she retorted, 'Remember, everything you say and do goes into my article.'

He laughed easily. 'You're one of those writers, huh? Talks about everything but the subject – all the peripheral happenings and what who said to whom. Readers are interested only in Sally.'

'Yes. But in her case, it's how others treat her, relate to her, what they think and say about her that adds to the picture. Let's face it, Sally isn't delivering a lot of heavyweight intellectual material here. Her youth, her fragility, the fact that she's awe-struck and scared one minute, acting like a princess the next is intriguing. Someone who is learning how to use coke and still sleeps with a ratty teddy could be losing their grip on reality.'

'Is that what you're writing?'

'I'm not telling.' Miche saw a butler come down the wide steps, which were flanked by stone lions at the front entrance. 'Who lives here? Is it just staff and guests?'

'Old family retainers. The vineyard workers live on the other side, in the old cottages close to the new section

239

built for the winemaking facilities. Occasionally the Count is here. If he isn't completely out of his tree.'

'Alzheimer's?'

'No, just mad as a meat-axe. Inbreeding, I suppose.'

Miche followed a silent but courteous maid to her room. It was huge with large floor-to-ceiling windows. Enormous swags of brocade drapes were swept to each side revealing a clipped green maze below. The bed was old-fashioned ornate iron with hand-painted cameos and massive pillows and bolsters. A small desk and chair with Château Soleil stationery was in one corner, a chaise longue on an antique Chinese carpet in the other. The wardrobe was old, ornate and smelled of lavender and camphor. There was a sink in a dresser holding a bowl, mirror and towels. Miche glanced at the collection of paintings and old photographs. Although it was warm outside, the room felt draughty and cool and she noted the rolled eiderdown and antiquated steam heater.

The bathroom was down a hall lined with family portraits and busts on marble pedestals. The ancient faces seemed to watch her as she walked softly along the antique Persian carpets. But her slight sense of unease disappeared in a burst of laughter as she entered the giant bathroom. A huge claw-footed enamel tub stood, throne-like, in the centre of the black and white floor tiles. A small stool that served as a step into the bath was beside a wooden bath mat, and around the walls raced paintings of thoroughbred horses. A large basin, heated brass rails that held towels embroidered with the family crest, and a chest of drawers and a shelf with basic essentials barely filled the mausoleum of a room. A tall window overlooked the stables and cobbled courtyard.

They met for pre-dinner drinks in the sitting room where a very old, very large television set mumbled in a corner. Bookcases lined one wall, a collection of impressionist paintings covered another. The heavy, faded swathes of brocade buried tall windows. Wood panelling and the sense of being behind thick walls gave the cocoon of the crowded room a feeling of invincibility. The ambience was that of being underwater; the pale light from weak bulbs in shrouded lamps, fat cushions, faded thick pile carpet and solid furniture absorbed sound. Crystal decanters were dust-coated dull. Miche sensed generations of lives spent in this room, imagining the ghosts of the past standing to one side, watching. She shivered as she sank into a deep chintz sofa.

Sally sat on the arm of a lounge chair. 'Isn't this amazing? Wow. My bedroom is bigger than half my house at home. This is unreal.'

'A bit spooky. What's your home like, Sally?' asked Miche.

'Gosh. It seems another world away now. Hmm. Ordinary. But nice. Simple. Barby in the back garden, Mum's little plants she loves. Dad's vegie patch. God. Nothing like this.' She flung out an arm. 'Unreal.'

'Can you go back to that? To home?'

'Jeez, Miche. I dunno. Heck. Once you leave home that's it, isn't it? Nothing is ever the same again. But even though I'm okay here, my parents would be so uncomfortable here, I mean even for dinner. You never forget where you came from. One of the models I met came from a really poor family and she's married this rich rock star who also grew up poor. They have everything, but she said they still feel like they're toys in someone else's doll's house. I mean, when does it feel real?'

'When it becomes utterly boring,' said Donald, entering the room. He turned to Sally. 'When nothing is fun, or interesting, or a novelty any more. That's it. That's when you've arrived.' He lifted his glass. 'Enjoy the journey, kid.'

Sally was unfazed. 'I'm doing that. Maybe I feel okay because I *can* always go home.'

'Could you really go back to your country town life after this? I don't think so,' said Miche.

'Hey, who's talking about leaving?' Sophie came breezing in, refreshed and ready for the evening, followed by Pete. 'We're going to have company for dinner.'

'Are there other guests staying here? Will we meet the Count?' asked Miche.

'A couple of the wine people are coming up for dinner. They like to socialise when they can. Doesn't sound like they find time to leave the estate much. Hope they bring a few vintage bottles with them.'

'You're a fund of news, Soph. You been checking out the kitchen?' asked Donald.

'Just lining up accessories. We need a few things for the shoot. Have you sorted out your end? Your slave here checked all the gear.'

'And it's all there,' added Pete.

'Better be . . . or I look for a new assistant. I hope you gals don't mind travelling by tractor. We have to go across the fields,' said Donald.

'Another welly boot shoot. Don't ask me to explain,' said Pete as Donald burst out laughing at Miche's questioning face.

The door was opened by the butler who stood back as the Count entered. A silence fell on the room. The gentleman was tall, slightly stooped and thin, yet gave the appearance of strength – perhaps because of the overly developed shoulders and chest. His face was pinched, his bald head, of a peculiar conical shape, fringed in sparse ginger hair tied in a small ponytail. His gaunt features reflected the same lost chin and sallow cheeks of his ancestors dotted about the chateau walls. He was dressed in a type of riding habit, part British eccentric, part Lawrence of Arabia, part Hollywood interpretation of European gentry. He carried off the bizarre ensemble with élan, the riding crop and leather boots looking entirely correct.

'*Bonsoir, mesdames. Messieurs. Je suis Comte Jules Fabian. Soyez les bienvenus!*'

'*Merci, merci.* We are so glad to meet you and thank you for allowing us to use the chateau again as a location,' said Donald rising to shake his hand.

The Count, who could have been fifty or seventy, looked around, his eyes glittering. 'Location? You mean cinema? You are making a cinema here?'

'*Non, non.* Only photographs. *Pour un magazine, la couture.*'

'Ah.' He lifted a glass and sank into a chair looking disappointed. 'So *Poirot et moi* . . . we will not be a part of your . . . *photographique extravaganza?*'

Donald gave an expansive gesture. 'Of course, we would be charmed to have you pose for us. With Poirot.'

Miche blinked and gave Donald a cross look. Sophie put her hand to her mouth and Sally smiled as she asked, 'Who's Poirot?'

The Count broke into a vague sort of smile. 'At dinner, you'll meet him at dinner. Oh, oh, oh,' he snorted in glee. 'Poirot loves parties.'

'Does this guy have all his oars in the water?' Sally hissed at Donald.

'You mean is he playing with a full deck?' whispered Donald, then grinned. 'Depends what you call normal.'

A bell rang from the courtyard. The Count settled himself. 'Ah, our vignerons approach. What delights do they bring to taste?' The butler hurried to open the door at one side of the conservatory.

Two men, one young, one old, came in holding bottles and smiling. It seemed to Miche they brought healthy sunshine and earthy smells. A living energy bounced into the fusty drawing room. The older man had a weathered face, lurking smile, greying hair beneath a quickly removed cloth cap and a smoothed moustache. He placed a bottle on the sideboard and nodded at the butler.

The second man was younger, cheerful, sandy-haired and muscular with a self-confident smile. He added the bottles he was carrying to those already on the sideboard.

The older man went straight to greet the Count while the younger man ran a hand through his hair and glanced at the guests. 'Hi, I'm Jeremy Foster. Nice to see you all.' The Australian accent surprised everyone.

'You're Australian?' Sally seemed incredulous. 'I can't believe the Aussies I've found over here.' She pointed at Donald, 'He's one, I'm from Queensland.'

She ran around the introductions.

Jeremy quickly introduced the older man. 'Monsieur Soulvier. My boss. And, yes, I'm an Aussie. Over here for six months. Studying winemaking from a French perspective.' He gave Sally an amused conspiratorial glance, but she didn't notice. Miche did, and wondered what it meant.

Monsieur Soulvier beamed at them. 'Jeremy is what we call one of your flying winemakers.' He shook hands with each of them, then sat beside the Count chattering in rapid French and pointing at the bottles with hand-written labels.

Donald shook Jeremy's hand. 'G'day. How long you been over here, where're you from?'

'Hunter Valley. I work for a vineyard there. I'm originally from Melbourne.' He lowered his voice. 'I'm over here seeing how the so-called experts do things.'

'So-called experts? Aren't the French the best winemakers?'

'They think so. I happen to think the young guns

in Australia are often better. Australia is becoming a major producer of the best wines in the world this new century.'

The Count's ears pricked up. 'Best wines? Here, try this Château-Grillet blanc.'

While the butler, the Count and Monsieur Soulvier fussed with the bottles and glasses at the sideboard, Jeremy turned to Sally. 'You must be the model.' His gaze moved to Miche. 'And you too?'

'Not me, I'm working for a magazine.'

'We all are, sweetie,' interrupted Sophie, moving closer to the handsome young winemaker.

'So what are you taking pictures of, then?'

'Essentially Sally . . . but of course Château Soleil is the other star – to complement Sally,' added Donald, giving the Count a small nod.

'I can make your photographs very, very special,' said the Count.

Sophie and Pete exchanged a look.

'Poirot?' asked Donald with a slightly world weary air.

'*Certainement*. He is still a star. Since our last little accident he has special shoes. Dancing shoes.' The Count chuckled to himself.

'Er, what about his friends from the circus? What happened to them?' asked Sophie.

'They are here, dear child. We saved them. They live here.' The Count turned his attention to the wine tasting that the butler had set out with a range of glasses, dry biscuits, water and spittoon. The Count and Monsieur Soulvier began an intense conversation in French over the merits of each wine – its qualities, its year and its potential.

Miche nudged Donald. 'Circus? Dancing Poirot? What's all that about?'

Jeremy heard her. 'I've seen them round the place, a weird bunch.'

Donald put his finger to his lips. 'Don't tell her. It'll spoil the surprise.'

'I don't like surprises. I'd like to be prepared for whatever is planned,' declared Miche.

'You must be a Virgo. Nothing is planned here. That's half the fascination of the place. But believe me, something is always going on.' Jeremy rolled his eyes.

'What did he mean, about the circus. And what or who is Poirot?'

'You ask a lot of questions.'

'I'm a reporter.'

'Ah.'

'I don't want to influence you then. What are you writing about anyway?'

'Sally. She's the hottest look-to-be, the model of the minute.'

'That's often as long as it lasts, I hear. You're American. Did you come out just to do this story? Who do you write for?'

'Actually, I'm on my way to Australia. I'm writing for *Blaze*. Do you know it?'

'Well, I've seen a copy or two.' Jeremy shifted in the chair. 'I don't seem to find the time for reading.'

'So what do you do?'

'Know anything about winemaking?'

'Zilch. I drink wine, but I don't have any knowledge about it.'

'When you have time, come over to the vineyard and I'll show you round. That is, if you're interested.'

Learning the intricacies of winemaking had never been high on Miche's list of life priorities. But looking at Jeremy, she felt a faint tingle of the special attraction to another human being that starts with a warm smile, an interest in whatever they are saying and the knowledge that a chemical reaction, something beyond her control, was beginning to stir. She'd experienced this before and it had either fizzled like a spent rocket, or run its course and been a painful or valuable experience. Here we go again. Maybe. 'Sure,' she said. 'Whenever we have a break or finish our own shenanigans. This photography business is a bit of a strange dance. I'm just trailing along,' she confided.

Jeremy gave a shrug. 'Models, fashion, whatever. Not my scene.'

They were all called to the taste testing with Monsieur Soulvier conducting. After several rounds of swirling glasses, admiring the colour, sniffing the bouquet, finally tasting, swilling in the mouth and spitting, the younger ones were glad when dinner was announced.

Miche paused to take in the dining hall. 'Is this the set for King Arthur or what?' She gazed up at the silk banners hanging around the walls below the minstrels' gallery. It was suspended above the huge open vestibule that led through wide doors to a flight of broad stone steps into a terraced garden.

The group was led to a massive antique table that seated twenty. Heavy iron candelabra hung at both ends of the hall. A supplementary glow came from subdued electric lighting installed in the fifties. Fat beeswax burned in multi-tiered silver candelabra along the table.

Jeremy sat between Sally and Miche. The Count had Sophie on his right and Donald on his left. Pete was between Sophie and Monsieur Soulvier. The remaining length of the dining table stretched into the gloomy nether reaches of the huge room. The food was served by the butler and two silent waiters. The cook, Madame Verve, was discussed but not seen.

Miche had been to a number of formal dinners in

Washington and New York, but this eclipsed anything she'd seen. What fascinated her was the omnipresent pervasiveness of the past, a mixture of musty grandeur mingling with a modern awareness of time and attitude.

The Count talked of the latest movies, of rock stars, whom he seemed to have met, and openly described a pornographic network, operating from this region, that was hot on the Net, and again, giggled at references to his party-loving Poirot.

They began with a little known sparkling wine from Clairette de Die in northern Rhône, followed by a Châteauneuf-du-Pape white and a fine Syrah blend from the Soleil estate, served with the meal, followed by a rich muscat de Beaumes de Venise. A rosewood humidor was set on the table and the Count stood to offer fine cigars. Jeremy and Monsieur Soulvier shook their heads. 'Spoils the palate.'

With expressionless faces, the waiters set a silver tray on the coffee table by two long, low sofas. On the tray were chocolates, petits fours, bowls of white powder, small snifter spoons and neatly rolled hashish.

'Help yourself, help yourself.' The Count stood and gave a slight bow. 'I will return and introduce Poirot.'

Jeremy and Miche were the only two not making themselves comfortable. Monsieur Soulvier threw the fine Swiss chocolates in his mouth, Pete and Sophie quickly lit up the hashish cigarettes. Sally reached for a spoonful of the coke and Miche shuddered. The next second she felt Jeremy's restraining hand on her arm.

He gave a slight shake of his head. 'Feel like a moon-light stroll?' He picked a bottle of Armagnac off the sideboard and Miche followed him from the great hall, the others seeming not to notice, or care.

Outside, she ran ahead of him down the steps marked by lichen-smudged stone urns filled with sweet white flowers. The moonlight was bright and Miche, feeling light-headed from the mix of wines, gulped lungfuls of the clear air. She turned to Jeremy as he joined her. 'Why did you do that? Stop me from helping Sally? She's a baby.'

'You think this is the first time she's been around drugs? Better she use it here than in a sleazy club with people she doesn't know. Besides, you're not looking after her, are you? You said at dinner you were a reporter. I thought you'd be an observer, not a keeper.' He sat on a carved stone bench and opened the bottle and took a swig. 'Hmmm, very fine brandy.' He held the bottle to her. 'Nightcap?'

'No, I've had enough. How are that lot going to work tomorrow?'

'Stop being a mother hen. You going to write about all this?'

It was a question that had already popped into Miche's fuzzy brain. 'I don't know.'

'They'll party on till dawn. The Count's party trick is quite an act.'

'Is this how you spend your evenings off?' asked Miche. 'The flying winemaker takes on a whole new meaning.' She sounded snappish. She was tired and annoyed at the turn the evening had taken.

'I'm dragged along by Monsieur as he's head vigneron, my boss so to speak. He drinks too much and passes out and I take him back to his cottage. Part of the job, I've discovered. Still, not for much longer.' He looked at Miche standing miserably on the lawn, her arms wrapped around herself, a sign of defence and protection. 'Do you want to see the vineyards?'

'Now? Where are they?'

'Nice moonlight, brandy to keep us warm if the wind fills in. Come on, we'll take the early bird tour. This way.'

He led her round the formal garden to the side driveway next to the walled kitchen garden, their feet crunching on the fine gravel. He opened the door of the old Citroen for her, bending down to lift the edge of her flimsy skirt from being caught in the door. It was a small but thoughtful gesture that registered with her.

They drove across the north-east section of the estate, past the stables and fields with jumps and bales, along a small road through a gateway to where the fields gave way to the open hillsides with neat rows of twisting vines trained along trellises.

Jeremy stopped and helped Miche from the car. He pointed to the distant buildings, 'The crusher and fermentation vats are over there. The cellars are separate.'

She followed as he began inspecting the vines, touching a leaf, pinching one of the hard green buds of baby shiraz grapes, running his hand along the thick twisted rope of the vine snaking along its trellis. 'Imagine, these grapes have been grafted from *Vitis vinifera* that were being grown before white fellas ever settled in Australia. Mind you, as soon as the first settlers arrived in Australia, they planted grapes, though many didn't survive. It's taken a while to adapt the grapes to the soil and conditions back home.' He gave her a grin. 'But we've figured it out now. I've had to bite my tongue a bit these past months.'

'Ah, now I understand. I thought there was a conspiracy between you Australians and the French. What is it?' asked Miche as they strolled between the vines.

'It's hard for an old dog to accept the young pups might be racing ahead of him. And it's hard for these guys to break old habits – like lunch,' he chuckled to himself.

'So, tell me the joke,' asked Miche.

Jeremy shrugged. 'I don't want to sound like I'm big-noting myself. But hell, a few months back the grapes had been picked – and knowing when to pick is an art,' he said, warming to a subject he obviously loved. 'So what do these characters do? They head off for lunch just as a load of grapes had been picked and brought to the winery and they leave the grapes in the bloody sun!'

'So?'

'They start oxidising right away. But the pickers and the old men headed down to the local café to celebrate for a couple of hours. Crazy.'

'What did you do?'

'Made the wine. Well, started the whole process. The crushing takes two hours for four tonnes.'

Miche laughed. 'Flying winemaker strikes again. What did they do?'

'Mumbled and muttered. They don't like brash young Aussies coming in and telling them, the experts, how to do their job. Mostly, I love being here, but sometimes I can't wait to go home,' he suddenly added. He turned into the next row and they started heading back.

'Where's home exactly?'

'My parents and sister live in St Kilda. It's a suburb of Melbourne.'

'I'm heading to Australia next. I'll be in Sydney and I can't wait to get there. I was glad for this detour, but now . . .'

'You're going to Australia?' he asked in surprise. 'I thought you worked in America.'

'My mother died recently, and I was given a chance to start work on the new *Blaze* magazine in Australia. Seemed like the best way to go,' said Miche quietly.

'Oh God, I'm sorry,' said Jeremy. 'What about your dad, do you have any brothers or sisters?'

Miche's voice was tight. 'No. It was just my mom and me. My father is Australian, but he left Mom when I was small. I don't even know if he's alive or where in the world he might be. I probably have cousins somewhere. But I have a terrific godmother and my mom's friends are like family.'

They walked in silence for a few minutes. Jeremy didn't know what to say. It seemed unfair to mention he came from a loving extended family, people who enjoyed spending time with each other and while not well-to-do, were comfortable. His life seemed uncomplicated in comparison.

They arrived back at the car and, as Miche made herself comfortable, Jeremy exclaimed, 'Oh hell, your shoes, they're covered in soil. I hope they're not ruined. I forgot it's a bit gluggy down there. Here, let me.' He bent down and pulled the soft kid shoes from her feet. 'I'll ask Hortense to clean them for you.'

The gesture made Miche feel weepy. God, I must be drunk, she thought.

As they drove back to the main château, the moon went behind clouds, throwing the vine-covered facade into deeper relief. But as they turned into the side entrance, lights were blazing in the dining hall, spilling out the open doors and down the stone steps.

'Uh oh, here he goes,' said Jeremy. 'Stay by the car for a moment.'

'What's going on?' asked Miche getting out, thinking everyone must be looking for them.

But as Jeremy came to stand next to her, she heard voices calling and the muffled sound of hooves. Before she could say anything, a large white horse came cantering across the lawn, up the driveway. Miche saw the old Count, wearing a plumed helmet, sitting comfortably on the magnificent animal which didn't pause, but took the broad stone steps in its stride and trotted into the great hall to cries of delight from those inside. Miche went to hurry forward, but Jeremy held her arm. 'There's more.'

Sure enough, a second horseman appeared. A black and white Shetland pony was being ridden by – Miche leaned forward to make sure she was seeing what she thought – yes, a very small man was standing on its bare back, holding the reins with one hand, waving a feathered cap in the other. He was a dwarf. The pony also clopped up the steps and disappeared inside. Miche broke into a run, 'I don't believe this.'

There was music, a saxophone. She could hear Sally and Sophie's voices cheering and laughing. As Miche came into the entrance to the hall, she stopped to watch the Count guide the huge white horse into the cavernous dining hall, around the table, weaving between a suit of armour and a white marble statue and past a tall black man who was playing a saxophone and wearing nothing but skimpy red satin shorts. The pony followed on the white horse's trail, but now the little man was balancing on his head on the pony's back, holding the reins between his teeth and kicking his legs. The horses seemed to know the routine and came to a halt before the enormous marble and local-stone fireplace. The Count swung from the saddle, took a bow, handed the reins to the saxophonist, who stopped playing. Waving the gold instrument, he jigged and sang as he led the horse back outside. The little man did a somersault and landed beside the Count and they both gave another bow as Pete, Monsieur Soulvier and the two girls cheered. The waiters and butler politely clapped. They had obviously witnessed the extraordinary scene before.

Miche glanced around for Donald and saw he was standing on a chair with his pocket camera jammed to his eyes, his mouth stretched in a delighted smile.

She turned to Jeremy, 'What the hell was that?'

He gave a slight grin. 'Rocked me the first time I saw them.' He handed her the brandy bottle and this time she took a swallow. The liquid was velvety smooth and warming.

'That's wild, just fantastic, Count. Brilliant,' Sally pumped his hand. Looking pleased, he swept off the antique helmet and handed it to the butler.

'That was José, our musician, who has taken my beloved Poirot back outside. And now permit me to bring in my friends.'

The small man held out his hand with a big smile. ''Ello.' he turned to the pony. 'Say 'ello.' The pony pawed the floor, scrunching the carpet.

'How come the horses don't slip on the timber floor?' asked Sophie.

The little man addressed the pony, 'Shake 'ands.' The pony lifted a hoof and the man grasped it, showing the rubber glued to its shoe.

'Old circus trick,' said the Count with glee. 'Poirot, my horse, wears them too. My friends used to travel with a circus. Now they live here.'

'Occasionally we perform, we miss the big tent, eh?'

The butler handed the dwarf a bottle of wine from the sideboard. '*Soixante six, monsieur.*'

The small man set the pony's foot on the floor and gave the label on the bottle a critical look. 'A fine year for a Bordeaux, was it not? *Merci, Monsieur le Comte. À bientôt.*' He bowed again and, leading the pony, walked from the great hall, the rubbery clops of his charge making strange noises on the wooden floors.

Miche raised an eyebrow. 'And the musician. What's his story?'

'My dear friend. He was in a band, he came to the village and . . .' the Count gave an expressive shrug and lifted his arms, 'he went no further. I need a refreshment.' He turned to the butler who leapt to the sideboard to refill the Count's glass.

Sophie hissed to Miche, 'Last dinner party I was at here, I sat next to that musician. Doesn't say much. Maybe he was too cold. He was starkers as far as I could tell. Just had a white napkin in his lap!' She burst out laughing and lit another handmade cigarette.

Donald came to Miche and, swaying slightly, tapped his pocket. 'More pictures, princess.'

'Did you take shots of that? I won't believe I saw it all by breakfast time.'

'I may be somewhat smashed, princess, but they'll be in focus. We're partying on in the library. Some good stuff. You in?'

'No, I'm going to bed.'

She followed Jeremy out into the vestibule. 'Thanks for the tour. Will you be around while we're shooting?'

'Undoubtedly. Speaking of shooting, they're going after pheasants for you guys. If you want to come . . .'

Miche shuddered. 'I couldn't face it. Right now, I just want to go to sleep. Thanks, Jeremy. It's been quite a night.'

'It's morning. Sleep well, Miche. Nice meeting you.'

As Miche went up the grand staircase, trying to remember which corridor to take to her room, the deep gongs of the grandfather clock on the landing told her it was 3 a.m.

She splashed water on her face from the basin in her room and fell into the depths of the bed. Sleep came immediately. She knew she was too tired to dream. Besides, no dream could match the evening she'd just experienced.

Sally was parading up and down the long dining room table, her audience clapping and singing to the throbbing music as she gyrated along the mini catwalk. Occasionally she stumbled, her glazed eyes barely registering the leering faces. The Count had a strange smile on his face as he peered up her long thin legs that ended in a flash of white panties.

With a sudden movement Sally snapped the velcro waistband of the silver circle of fabric that passed for a skirt encasing her small bottom. Twirling it gleefully, she flung it into the shadows as the music reached a crescendo, then she flung herself in an attempt at a swallow dive off the end of the table.

She was caught by the tall, near-naked black sax player who dropped her into the Count's lap. Grabbing his champagne glass, she drained it. The Count reached for the small table beside his chair and handed Sally a chocolate as the jazz player refilled the crystal flute.

Sally giggled as she drank, watching the dwarf undo her high silver sandals. If she noticed, it didn't concern her that she was the only guest left with the Count, the dwarf and the sax player. Before she had finished the champagne, and as the dwarf slid the sandals from her feet, the glass fell from her hand onto the floor. Her eyes rolled back in their sockets before they closed and her head lolled loosely onto her chest.

The sax player scooped her up like a broken doll in his muscular black arms and strode from the room. The Count grasped the walking stick the dwarf handed him and struggled to his feet. 'It is time,' he announced with anticipation and glee.

'The bitch! How dare she! Who talked?' Ali's screams echoed from her office. Belinda, uninvited, hurried into Ali's office, closing the door.

'What's up? Can I do something?' she asked nervously. This was the maddest she'd seen Ali.

'Do? Can you go and burn every copy of this rag this so-called columnist writes for?' She flung the Sydney CBD's favourite weekly, *Exchange*, across her desk. Belinda reached for the scattered pages.

'Oh dear. April Showers again?'

'If they write about *Blaze* it's fair game, even if it's wrong. But me! My personal life. How I run this place! How dare they!'

'Oh. Did they get it wrong? Again?' remarked Belinda blandly. 'Shall I send for coffee?'

'Call Larissa in here,' muttered Ali. 'Tell her I want a strategy meeting.'

Larissa had read the column and was waiting for a summons. Belinda delivered it in person.

'How mad is she?'

Belinda rolled her eyes. 'Steaming. What's made her most cranky is the personal dig. About the staff supposedly calling her the Yank Tank. How all the goodies and tickets and so on end up on her desk.'

'Someone has talked. Wouldn't have taken Showers long to find out that kind of information,' sighed Larissa, gathering up her notebook.

'Publishing is so gossipy. And it seems to be a growing trend.' Belinda shook her head. This would never have happened in the old days under Dorothy Power.

'The April Showers column isn't just gossip. It's shrewd and influential, but biting. And the sources must be good because no one ever sues. April Showers hones in on hot issues and people. Clever writer. Funny, too. But not when you're the target.'

Belinda followed Larissa down the hall. 'What are you going to say?'

'Laugh it off and move on.'

'Somehow I don't think that's what Ali wants to hear,' said Belinda.

Ali strode around her office. 'I wouldn't be this upset if so many people didn't read the damn thing.' She drew a deep breath. 'Lightweight. *Blaze* is accused of being lightweight.'

'April Showers' report that we considered paying for a movie star's wedding doesn't put us in a positive light,' agreed Larissa.

'What I want to know is – who talked? I've sent around a stiff message to the staff. Anyone who leaks anything about internal matters and is found out will be out the door, on their ass, in a minute.'

'It is a problem. If we let it be. This is what, the fourth attack?'

'Larissa, it's getting a bit close to the bone. I don't like being caricatured.'

In that morning's paper, the cartoonist who illustrated April Shower's column had depicted Ali at her desk, the door shut and a sign saying '*Out to lunch*'. Ali was depicted as a vampire, her trademark widow's peak exaggerated, fangs protruding, slurping a straw from a bottle marked, '*Staff blood donations*'.

'They're not kind. Perhaps Showers will rain on someone else's parade soon. I mean, they must be scratching around for material.' Larissa lifted a questioning eyebrow.

'People like that make up dirt when they can't find any.' Ali turned away thinking how this scurrilous campaign could damage her quest to win John O'Donnell's interest.

'The reason April Showers' column is so popular is because it doesn't appear to dish dirt. It's clever and witty, and obviously people feed stuff to the column. It's always timely with inside stuff. If the names weren't powerful and it wasn't smart, it would be just another gossip page. At least you're not in there with soapie stars and models. You're mentioned in the same breath as a media chairman, a politician and a new American CEO.'

'That CEO isn't going to last,' said Ali curtly.

Larissa blinked. 'How do you know that? The Australian company is paying him several million dollars a year plus share bonus.'

For the first time this morning Ali looked faintly cheerful. 'I have my sources too. Besides, Australians don't like Americans coming in and telling them how to run things. No offence to you, Larissa.'

'I don't run things, you do, and you're as American as I am,' said Larissa tartly.

'I think I might need to remind everyone I was born and raised here. I have the advantages of American know-how but I still qualify as an Australian.'

'It might be an idea to do that.' Larissa was annoyed. 'Why not get one of the friendly TV people to do a profile on you. Go back to your roots, all that. I mean, where is your family?'

Larissa hit a nerve and was unprepared for Ali's vehement reaction.

'Don't you DARE ever suggest that. My personal history, my private life, is totally private. I will not agree, under ANY circumstances to talk about it. Which is another reason this white-anting by April Showers angers me.' She hurled the paper, neatly refolded by Belinda, into the wastepaper basket.

'Did you ask me in here to yell at me or for constructive advice?' asked Larissa icily.

Ali's anger dissipated and she slumped back in her chair sounding tired. 'What possible strategy could we make? See what we can dig up on April Showers and attack back? I'm sick of taking the high moral ground.'

'If you can't beat 'em, join 'em. Isn't that the rule in publishing? Hire April Showers,' said Larissa calmly.

'What?' Ali jerked upright in her chair.

'Whoever he, she or it is, they're good at what they do. People read that column. So buy it.'

'Larissa, when you do have a good idea, it's a great one. How much is this going to cost us?'

'Do you care?'

Ali was reaching for the phone. 'Of course not.'

Larissa walked thoughtfully past Belinda who looked up. 'Manage to fix anything?'

'Time will tell. I might have just invited the lion into our field of lambs,' sighed Larissa, adding as an after-thought, 'Put it on record that Ali thought this was a good idea. Not that I apparently have them often. But there you go. Write that down and date it. See you, Bee.'

TAKE ELEVEN . . .

Miche realised she'd overslept. It was past 7 a.m. She opened the door to go down the hall to the bathroom and brave a plunge in the wonderful tub . . . and tripped over her cleaned shoes. Jeremy. What a thoughtful person he was.

Arriving downstairs she couldn't hear anyone stirring. She checked the dining hall – it had been cleaned and tidied with the drapes drawn, blotting out the misty morning that threatened rain. No hint of the madness of last night.

She opened doors to a library, a small sitting room and a formal drawing room, until she found the airy conservatory. Several small tables by bay windows were laid for breakfast. The morning papers were spread on a small wicker table and cut fruit, croissants and preserves were set along a sideboard. She helped herself to a few pieces of fruit and sat at a table. The maid instantly appeared holding a pot of steaming coffee.

'*Bonjour mademoiselle. Voulez vous un café?*'

'*Mais oui. Merci. Où sont les autres visiteurs? Les hommes?*'

'*Ils ont fini le petit déjeuner.*'

Already. She had slept in if the men had finished breakfast and were out setting up the shoot.

'*Et les jeune filles? Sally? Et Sophie?*'

The maid shrugged. '*Elles dorment.*' She tapped her head. '*Une mauvaise nuit.*'

Miche nodded, wondering how late and how bad a night it had been. She didn't expect they would be photographing Sally this morning. Just as well. This was Donald's territory, deciding where and how to photograph the series of pictures to illustrate her article about Sally.

Miche began to feel nervous as she finished her fruit. There was a lot of effort and money behind the story she was putting together. But what was she going to write about? Should she tell everything that had happened – and was still happening – to Sally? While parts of it were funny, parts were awesome with the powerful ambience of moving at the top of the fashion world. There was a dark underside to the modelling business that scared Miche. She would be glad to leave this scene for Australia. At least she knew Larissa and Ali out there. And now Jeremy. Donald rarely went back home. He moved in the heady world of international cities and famous faces. And Sally wouldn't be returning to Australia in a hurry.

As Miche finished her breakfast, the maid began clearing her place then asked, '*Vos chaussures, sont-elles assez propres? Ça, c'ést la fange de la vigne.*'

That was too much fast French for Miche's basic vocabulary.

The maid pointed to her shoes.

'Oh yes. My shoes. Thank you very much. They're fine.'

Miche wandered outside, taking an umbrella from the entrance.

The air was warm, a drifting rain mist beginning to lift, the light hazy and mysterious. The vineyards marched up the terraces on either side of the narrow valley. She headed down the driveway with no plan in mind and within minutes, as she went around the stables, she came across Donald and Pete. Each lifted an arm in greeting and, although they looked seedy, Donald was all business.

'This is great. Check if this weather is going to hold. I love this light. Be bloody marvellous for what we have in mind.'

'And what's that?'

'Fantasy, you said. What could be more dreamlike than this?' He waved a hand at the landscape. 'Plus our props and extras.'

Miche gave him a questioning look.

'Chateau and cast. Trust me.' He crossed himself, throwing his eyes heavenward. 'You do the words, babe. I'll do the pictures.'

Miche wasn't in a mood to debate. Donald was one of the world's top photographers – stars would kill to be profiled by him, especially for a quality magazine. Miche changed the subject. 'So how long did you guys bat on for last night?' she asked cautiously. 'I'm surprised you're even awake.'

'Been in training for years.'

'Those girls are wild,' added Pete. Donald gave him a glance and returned to the theme of the pictures.

'Sally is prepared to do a Lady Godiva – jump on Poirot bareback, naked, with hair covering her tits, and ride through the dawn mist with the dwarf leading the horse. The guy still has a few of his circus outfits.'

Miche saw the image he described. 'Hmmm. Could look effective. What else?'

'The musician as the Black Knight. He's a good-looking guy with fantastic skin and with oil on him he'll look ebony. Might do a "rescuing the damsel in distress" scene, use the lake and the moat around the old mill by the orchard.'

'What about something contemporary?'

'Back in the studio for that. Turn her into a holograph as a space chick.'

'Or spaced chick,' laughed Pete.

'Listen, I don't think she should be doing drugs. She's too young to handle all this so soon,' began Miche. Donald held up a hand to cut her off.

'Don't preach to me. If that's how you feel, you speak to her.'

Miche looked at Pete who gave a half-smile. 'It's the way, this modelling is a crazy world. All the girls do it. The pressure . . . or something.' Miche was no puritan, but she couldn't help feeling protective towards Sally. She tried to think back to what she was like at sixteen. Not like Sally, who was so small, so light, so fragile, so innocent.

As if reading her thoughts, Donald grinned. 'Listen, she's a great little Aussie kid from a country town. She's not as impressionable as you think.'

'I'm a New Yorker and I don't know how I'd deal with all this sudden fame and attention,' said Miche.

'Enjoy it – and sock the money into a Swiss bank account like all the girls. I need coffee. Let's go.' Donald headed for the car.

They spent the rest of the day lining up locations, choosing two inside the chateau. The first was the formal eighteenth-century sitting room with its high, domed ceiling painted in blue and gold, valuable Louis XV furniture, Greek vases and classical marble figurines from mythology. French doors led onto a small terrace and formal garden.

'Blue filter,' said Donald to Pete, who nodded. The second choice was the library and Indian room, which was darkly lit, the floor covered in fine Persian carpets and skins of endangered rare animals. Indian tapestries hung on the walls beside trophy heads shot on safari. Stepladders leaned against tiers of tomes. In one corner centuries-old books were sealed behind locked glass doors. The air smelled of moth-eaten animals, a place where the breath of infrequent visitors did little to disperse the dust or dispel its mustiness. 'Red filter,' said Donald. 'Now we need to talk to Sophie about wardrobe, styling and so on.'

'Who's doing hair and make-up?' Pete asked Donald.

'Some chick sent by Piste is arriving this afternoon.'

At sunset Miche went for a walk. At the end of the driveway she stopped as a car swung through the gates. Jeremy leaned out.

'Hello there, just the person I was looking for. How are you?'

'A bit tired. Having an early night, we have a dawn start.'

'Oh. Well, if it's not too early, Monsieur Soulvier was hoping to reciprocate for last night. Thought you and your friends might like to come over to the winery for dinner. There's a small dining room in the cellars. How about it?'

'Sounds fun. Don't think I could cope with another weird meal at the chateau. Or the after-dinner entertainment.'

Jeremy nodded. 'Know how you feel. Fellow who was here before me ended up in a drug rehab unit. The old Count has the money to indulge his passions. All kinds of them.'

'So where, what time?'

'I'll pick you up. Say, two hours? Maybe the others

had better come in their car, it's a bit too far to walk. I'll bring you back anytime you want, just give me the word.'

'Thanks. Oh, and thanks for having my shoes cleaned.' She looked down at her grey kid ballet flats. 'I'll wear my boots next time we go climbing around vineyards.'

'Come and visit the vineyard when you reach Australia. No boots required.'

The supper in the cellars was more festive than the previous formal dinner. Without the Count in attendance, everyone felt more relaxed, the mood informal and jolly. They related anecdotes, trivial details that gave glimpses of their lives, and the protocol of wine appreciation was put to one side as the team drank as much of the wine on offer as fast as they could. Madame Soulvier kept putting out dishes that were passed up and down the long wooden table . . . asparagus, mushroom tart, green beans and veal in a hollandaise sauce, garden salad, fresh figs and local cheeses. The black musician and dwarf clown joined them halfway through the meal.

'We 'ave been readying the 'orses,' said the little clown.

As the joke-telling and singing began in earnest, Miche glanced at Jeremy who gave a nod of acknowledgement. 'I'm going to bed. I want to be up at dawn to see the photo shoot.' Miche gave her thanks and said goodnight.

Yvette, the hair and make-up girl who'd arrived in the late afternoon, looked at Sophie. 'Perhaps I should also leave. I should start working on Sally at 3 a.m. Those hair extensions and make-up will take ages.'

'Oh, God, that's the worst part of this job,' cried Sally.

'Can't I just lie on my bed in the morning and you do it all? In the meantime, guys, I need another drink to cheer me up. I must have had an awfully heavy night last night. I can't remember anything and I still feel dreadful.'

'You'll be able to grab some sleep in the make-up chair in the morning, Sal. We've improvised a room for make-up et cetera in the milking shed,' said Pete. 'And now here's your champers. This party's about to get serious. The Count is coming down for a nightcap with some stuff.'

'Then I'm outta here. Do you want me to get you guys up?' asked Miche pointedly.

'Who's going to bed?' asked Donald. 'But sure, you can get me up any time!'

Miche ignored the innuendo. 'See you at sunrise. Jeremy is going to drive me back up the hill.'

Miche and Jeremy sat in his car talking for half an hour, finding a lot to share, until she yawned and apologised. He opened the car door as the Count suddenly appeared around the east wing of the chateau driving a small sulky pulled by two Shetland ponies.

'Tally-ho, as *les Anglais* say. *À bientôt!*' He cracked a small whip.

'He lives in a perpetual world of make-believe. Don't think he's ever thought of putting in a day's work. The estate managers, accountants, banks seem to run everything,' said Jeremy.

'Must be nice, I suppose,' said Miche. 'On second thoughts, I don't think so. This trip has shown me how old-fashioned I am. When I was a rebellious teenager, I messed around in the club scene with the wrong kind of guys, made my mother nervous that I was in with wild, rich girls. Now here I am fussing about a teenager trying a few drugs.'

'Just as well someone is . . . some pretty kinky things

267

are whispered about the Count and his strange pals. Sleep well. I might come and watch part of the circus – though from what I've seen of other photography sessions around here, there's more standing around than action.'

'Goodnight, Jem. And thanks.'

Sally was naked, tied to a four-poster bed. The Count, wearing a ludicrous nightcap, was beside her. The musician was holding a strange farm implement and bending over her as the dwarf danced and sang, trailing with him the saxophone that was almost the same size as the little man. Sally appeared drugged, drunk, struggling slightly, unaware of her situation.

'NO!' Miche sat bolt upright, shedding the horrific vision. She wiped her forehead. Her head was thick with sleep and wine. But she was alert enough to realise that it was after midnight and something had awakened her. She stumbled out of bed and looked out of the windows into the cool clear night. Nothing stirred and she couldn't hear anything. But her nerve ends tingled and she felt fearful. Wrapping her robe around her, she opened her door and went to the top of the stairs. All was silent.

On impulse, she hurried down the hallway to Sally's room and tapped lightly at the door. There was no answer. Not wishing to wake her, she cautiously opened the door and peered into the room. Immediately she knew Sally wasn't there. She stepped into the room. Clothes were flung on the bed, and she could tell it was as Sally had left it before dinner. Miche began to panic. It was 2 a.m. While Sally was sure to be still partying with the others at the winery, an instinct was telling Miche to check it out, to ignore the rationale that it wasn't her problem. She hurried to her room, threw on clothes that were to hand and rushed into the night.

In the shock of the fresh air, Miche took stock, finding her bearings. The winery was at least a twenty-minute fast walk away. She set off at a jog.

She saw the lights and heard the music and started to relax. They were still at it, partying or who knew what. She relaxed slightly, feeling somewhat embarrassed at bursting in on the party.

Further on she saw the cottages where the winery staff lived. Jeremy had pointed out his place. A light was burning. Miche felt silly now, having fled the chateau, imagining wild scenes of bacchanalia. She hesitated, then walked closer and tapped at the door. To her relief Jeremy stood blinking in the light wearing shorts and a T-shirt, holding a book.

'Miche! What's up? Come in.'

'Sorry, Jeremy. I feel so stupid.'

He took in her appearance and asked softly 'What's happened?'

'Nothing. I woke up. I had this awful dream and I checked Sally's room, she wasn't there and . . . I panicked.'

He reached out and took her arm. 'Sit down. I was in bed reading. Do you want something to drink? Tea, coffee, brandy?'

'No thanks. I'm sorry. I saw the lights on in the winery and heard the music. I guess they're all still at it. God knows what is happening with the dawn shoot.'

'Come on. I'll take you back to the chateau. Unless you want to stick your head into the winery and remind them they have an early start?'

'I don't think so. I'm resigning from being mother superior.'

He chuckled as he pulled on a sweatshirt and gym shoes. 'Let's go. I left the car outside the cellars.'

They walked in silence and he took her hand. It seemed a natural thing to do.

But as they sat down in the car Miche suddenly said, 'Could you peek in, see if she's there? How she is.'

Jeremy gave a resigned shrug. 'Sure.'

Miche felt she had overreacted, but wished she could shake the feeling of gloom that hung over from her dream. Jeremy slid in beside her but didn't speak.

'So what are they doing?' probed Miche.

'She isn't there.'

'Oh God, I knew it. Hell, where would she have gone? What did they say?'

'Not much. They're all stoked. Bombed out of their brains.'

'What do you think?'

'Not sure. Could've started walking back to the chateau and become lost.'

'Let's go then.'

Miche leapt from the car and started up the laneway leading from the cellars. 'Where does this go?'

'To the storage tanks. Where the wine matures before bottling.' Jeremy became concerned and quickened his step.

Miche was about to rush ahead when something made her pause and put herself in Sally's head. She is walking along here, and what does she see? A small path in the moonlight. It looks inviting. She follows it. Miche turned down the path. Jeremy was about to say something, but silently followed.

Miche walked without reason and seeing a dim, intriguing doorway went through it. She was in a cavernous cellar. A small light burned and moonlight sliced through the narrow windows high in the walls, shining on the rows of old oak storage vats that held the vintage wines. As soon as she stepped inside she felt she hit an invisible wall. The heady, rich smell of wine almost overpowered her. Then her instinct drew her forward. With one hand attempting to shield her nose, she looked around.

The closest vat was open and empty, ready for cleaning. A small door at the base was latched open, like the entrance into the White Rabbit's warren. It looked mysterious and inviting. Miche knew, just knew . . . that Sally, stoned, might curl up in such a comforting dark nest. It was an opening only a small adult could crawl through. She leaned down, imagining a girl, confused and in a dream state, unable to resist the invitation. Intuitively, Miche poked her head through the doorway that came to her shoulders.

'Miche, don't go in there, it's dangerous . . .'

Miche's head spun and she straightened up. 'Wow, what an incredible smell – it's kind of nice, but, whew . . . Why is it dangerous? It's empty.'

'Those vats are only used periodically, they've been cleaned and are drying out, but the fumes are very strong. They can asphyxiate you.'

'What if Sally is in there?'

'Why would she be in there? She'd better not be . . .' Jeremy moved closer to the vat entry and stared into the massive oak barrel. But Miche elbowed him aside. 'I have to check, I just feel she's gone in there.'

'Mad, bloody madness,' muttered Jeremy as he rushed to where he knew a torch was hanging.

Miche was on her hands and knees crawling into the dark, seemingly airless, space. It was womb-like, protecting. The wine-soaked wood smelled sickly sweet and blood came to her mind. Her head started to reel. God, what would the sensation be to come in here high on drugs? She felt dizzy, but then the beam from the flash-light shone on her, fixing a link between herself and Jeremy. He reached her.

'Let's leave. Now.'

'Sally . . .' mumbled Miche.

'Forget it, turn around, the door is behind you.'

Miche felt disoriented. She grabbed Jeremy's wrist, insisting he wave the torch around the chamber. And in that swift arc of light they saw a crumpled flash of white. Jeremy caught his breath and focused the light as Miche stumbled forward.

'Sally!' Her voice boomed in the vat, but there was no answer. Jeremy thrust the torch into her hands and shakily Miche aimed it at where Sally lay only feet away from them. Jeremy scooped Sally up and pushed Miche towards the tiny doorway. She scrambled through and held the torch as Jeremy pushed Sally's head and shoulders through the opening. They laid her on the cold stone floor.

'CPR. Start CPR,' directed Jeremy.

Together they began pumping and breathing into Sally's still form.

'There's a pulse. She's alive . . . Just . . .' said Jeremy.

'Call a doctor, ambulance, somebody to help us,' gasped Miche.

Jeremy was counting aloud. 'Take over.'

Miche put her hands over his and continued pushing on her chest as Jeremy dashed for the phone.

Miche had her mouth pressed over Sally's, gently breathing into her, when the young girl suddenly gulped and coughed slightly. Miche sat back on her heels as Sally regained consciousness. She opened her eyes and looked blankly at Miche, then turned her head and vomited.

*

The screen credits rolled in a blur. With a shock Nina saw the logo beside the name of Lucien's film company – a dragonfly. She had chosen the same emblem for *Blaze*. They had each chosen the symbol of the moment they'd met as their identifying sign.

Nina sat motionless as the audience around her began to applaud. The noise brought her back to the present after being lost in the sweeping drama of visual richness of medieval Scandinavia. She had been right there, riding the sturdy horse partially covered by her flowing hooded cape as they picked their way through the crusted snow of the bridle path, above which steep dark mountains rose beyond the rushing icy stream. Behind them in the woods, the handsome shepherd stayed alone in his croft. The lover she'd left behind to marry her betrothed – a rich merchant chosen by her father. Would she go through with the marriage, or defy her family and bring shame on the village? It was a question left dangling as the film ended. Or would there be a sequel from the master film-maker, Lucien Artiem?

On cue, as the lights went up, the director, writer, cinematographer, walked onstage.

Nina's eyes filled with tears and her heart was squeezed by bittersweet memories.

Lucien gave a slight bow and held out his arms as he stood before the microphone without introduction. The curtain behind him swung across the screen. 'Thank you. Thank you for your kind attention. As you know, this is a special film for me, many years in coming to fruition. It was not easy to shoot in the high mountains of Norway in winter, but I hope you agree the splendid light on the ice and snow, and the camera's capturing of nature have made it worthwhile.'

The questions began, the first of which brought a

murmur of agreement from the audience, 'Will there be a sequel?'

Nina listened keenly as Lucien answered with charm, wit and his still familiar intensity. He looked so much the same to her. A deepening of lines on his strong lean face, his now silver hair suiting his tanned skin.

The theatre manager eventually gave a short speech of thanks and Lucien stepped down into the auditorium where a group from the audience clustered around him, asking questions or seeking autographs on the leaflets advertising the film.

Nina watched for a while as the theatre emptied, then walked down the aisle and stood on the fringe of a tiny group of friends. A key light from the wings shone into the corner near where Lucien was and Nina, although unaware, was caught in its spotlight. Lucien glanced up, saw her, their eyes met and he froze. Her face was a vision from his past, as lovely as he'd always remembered her. He was stunned for a moment, then hurriedly thanked his fans and moved through them to Nina. They stood facing each other, silent, smiling. Then Lucien spoke.

'It is you. Nina, my Nina. Look at you.' He spread his arms, words failing him.

'Yes Lucien. It's me. Nina.'

He opened his arms and embraced her. They clung together, speechless, then drew apart, both shocked at how the years melted away and they were as familiar and as dear to each other as when they were young. 'You haven't changed. You look utterly wonderful.' He shook his head in disbelief. 'Let's leave here and go to somewhere we can talk.' He took her arm and Nina finally found her voice.

'Don't you have work to do, people to see? I can wait . . .'

'Everything has changed as of this moment. Come

on.' He led her out of the cinema. 'Supper. A drink. God, I'm shaking. How could you spring this on me?'

'Would you have met me if I'd called and said I was here?' she asked gently.

He didn't answer as they walked along the street. 'I don't know. It's been a long time since you broke my heart. What, thirty-something years?'

'Lucien. It was not a one-sided decision. I suffered too. But please let's not go over all that,' she chided softly.

'After so many years, it's hard to come face to face suddenly with someone who meant everything to you. I see you again and I hurt like hell.'

Nina stopped and withdrew her arm. 'I'm sorry. Perhaps this is a mistake. It was an impulse. I just saw the notice a few hours ago . . .'

'You didn't plan this?' He stared at her, then took her hand again. 'In that case, we can't fight the gods. Are you alone? On business? Where are you staying?'

Nina smiled. 'Le Chapeau Rouge.'

'They have a superb restaurant. *Très bon*. Where will we start?'

'A glass of champagne sounds an excellent place to start.'

His bantering manner faltered for a moment. 'I meant, all the catching up.'

'I know you did. And you mean other than what we've read about each other over the years.'

He nodded and tightened his hand on hers, unable to speak as a rush of memories flooded over him.

Nina had made a big impression on Lucien from the moment she'd asked him to free the dragonfly he'd been filming so long ago. They had met again at the premiere of Franco's film and naturally gravitated to each other. From there a friendship had developed based on their mutual interest in film and writing. But Nina's focus was always towards print, while he wanted to write a film and bring it to fruition.

They had explored Sydney, spent hours in dark coffee clubs around Kings Cross listening to jazz and folk singers. They'd found a wine bar frequented by Europeans that had flamenco guitar music and dancing. They stayed out late, talking endlessly of their past and plans for the future. Lucien was fascinated with Nina's memories of her early childhood in Yugoslavia.

'It would make a wonderful film. Though obviously filming at present sounds dangerous. Tito's heavies would think we were making a propaganda film,' he told her. 'But your Clara sounds a fabulous character.'

'Would you like to meet her?'

'Ah, I'm being taken home to meet mother. Is this becoming serious between us?' he laughed.

'Of course not,' she'd quickly retorted, then seeing a flash of hurt in his eyes, added lightly, 'only serious fun.'

Clara and Lucien had adored each other from the minute they met. Clara practised her poor French and flirted outlandishly, to Nina's amusement. Clara cooked Lucien sarma, rich and heavy with finely minced beef, pork and veal wrapped in pickled cabbage leaves and boiled, and told him stories of Nina's beautiful grandmother, whose own mother had been a medicine woman who'd lived in the forest and cooked up herbs and plants to cure everything from stomach ulcers to a broken heart.

'Tell me how you and Nina escaped from Zagreb,' said Lucien, feeling enough a part of the family to venture into the territory of sensitive memories.

'You've heard that story,' sighed Nina in exasperation.

'But from your mother, there will be more detail. I want to soak it all in. Clara, one day I'll make a film about you and Nina.'

Nina smiled quietly as Clara rose to sing for Lucien. She had a glorious voice and from that moment on Lucien never tired of listening to Clara's Croatian love songs.

As the friendship between Lucien and Nina grew, their passion intensified. Lucien, learning Nina was a virgin, was gentle, loving and not insistent. But the fifties postwar puritanism was behind them and a new decade loomed as a time of freedom, a time to experiment, a time of hope.

Nina was promoted from cadet to D-grade journalist. And so, on the threshold of seeing her dreams become possible, Nina and Lucien swore that no two people had ever felt so committed in heart and soul, understood each other so well, or loved so hard. It had been Nina who shyly suggested they should make love. And when they did, it was not Nina giving herself to him, but a mutual expression of all that they felt for each other.

The very next time she spoke to her mother, Nina sensed Clara knew. She found Clara and Lucien talking quietly together as they looked at the small vegetable patch Clara nurtured in the tiny back garden.

Clara never said anything to Nina – their mother and daughter talk about sex and reproduction had been years before. It had been a frank exchange based on the old medicine woman's mystic as well as pragmatic practices that had been handed down through the family. Nina had been quick to realise she had a better grasp of sex and contraception than her Australian girlfriends at school. They seemed to find it hard to talk about sex to their mothers. Only with her best friend, Claudia, could she share whispered secrets and information.

Claudia was from Belgium and as the only two European girls in the class they had gravitated to each other.

They discovered they had similar backgrounds – Claudia came from a well-to-do family from Brussels and they shared tastes, humour and thinking. It was to Claudia, now working as a doctor's receptionist in Macquarie Street, that Nina confessed she and Lucien were 'now one'.

'Did it hurt? What if you have a baby?' Claudia, despite her exterior sophistication, was suddenly a wide-eyed schoolgirl again.

There had indeed come a brief scare when Nina thought she might be pregnant and Claudia arranged a discreet appointment with the doctor she worked for. However, when Nina arrived for her appointment a flustered Claudia greeted her.

'The doctor was called away to deliver a baby. His locum is here – Doctor Jansous.'

'Well, that's all right. I'll probably never see him again.'

But Nina felt awkward and embarrassed when she saw the handsome doctor sitting at the desk. He was in his early thirties and looked coolly professional, even distinguished, in his crisp white shirt and navy tie with a private school emblem on it. Nina had stammered and blushed and looked down at her hands. He had helped her by asking softly, 'Is the reason you're here something to do with a boyfriend?'

She'd nodded and he'd questioned her further, then taken a urine sample and asked her if she'd rather have the examination when she came back to find out the results. Both seemed relieved at the notion of postponing an internal intrusion.

'My next question is . . . Are you going to continue to see this fellow? If so, he'd better take precautions. But, remember, you sit in the driver's seat. It will end up as your responsibility.'

'Thank you, doctor. I'll remember that.'

'Good luck, Nina.' He'd looked a trifle wistful as she left the office.

The urine test was negative and when she told Lucien, he'd hit his head with his hand. 'God, I could kick myself for putting you through that. I promise to take care of things next time. That is . . .' he'd given her a worried, questioning look.

Nina kissed him softly. 'Good. But my life is my responsibility, Lucien.' And she made a pact with herself that from then on she, and she alone, would decide her destiny.

Their love affair absorbed them deeply, and it stimulated rather than interfered with their work. Each was pleased to see how the other was progressing. Lucien had written a script and sent it to a producer in France in the hope of having it financed through an independent studio that supported new work. More and more of Nina's articles were being accepted and she had been promoted to a C-grade before her year as a D-grade journalist was up.

Six months passed and Nina's life was full, happy, busy. She was given her first out-of-town assignment and Lucien drove her to the airport. She was gone for a week and adored the pressure and madness of chasing and digging around for a story in the wild underground town of Coober Pedy. The quest for opals – the 'fire in the stone' – drew a colourfully diverse group of dangerous misfits and adventurers. The magazine wanted the story behind the exquisite opal jewellery now in demand around the world. The rare black opals, the cream stones that flashed a red fire, the glittering rainbow colours of boulder opals fascinated Nina. What her editor didn't know was that the place harboured a hotbed of radical and energetic Yugoslavs, who continued their centuries-old conflict of racial antagonism – Serb versus Croat – even in remote Australia.

Nina, speaking Croatian, began to uncover a different story. One of heartbreak, loneliness, theft, sudden riches and sudden death. She wrote an article as searing as the sun in this desert place and as sensitive as the quiet outpourings from bitter, despairing, funny, optimistic and wildly eccentric characters who inhabited the cool limestone tunnels and caverns they called home.

She submitted this story to the *Weekly*'s sister daily newspaper, which ran it as a big feature with her own photographs. Lucien had lent her an old Leica camera and taught her how to use it.

She was overflowing with ideas when she came back to Sydney. 'Lucien, I don't want to stay in women's magazines. I want to travel and write about other places, other people.'

'Be a photojournalist?' he asked quietly.

'Yes, I know it's not considered a woman's job. But why not?' She caught a whiff of reticence. His enthusiasm was watery. 'Don't tell me you think I should stay here writing about roses, knitting and legendary old ladies?'

'No. I think it's a fine idea. It would be fantastic in fact. Seeing as how I'm going to be in . . . those places.' He looked away from her.

'What do you mean?' She felt cold, a small shiver starting at the bottom of her heart.

'Good news and bad news. I've been offered an assistant director of photography job. With Truffaut. In Paris. I have to leave in a week for pre-production. Franco helped me land the job. He re-edited my reel and sent it to them with a personal letter.'

'It's what you've always dreamed of doing.'

'Yes,' he said miserably.

There was a silence as the realisation of what this meant sunk in.

'How long?' asked Nina finally.

'Now there's the rub.'

Nina couldn't help smiling at this expression coming out in a French accent.

'So?'

'Indefinite. The shoot is eight weeks, but there is an offer to stay over there. My time here was only meant as a training period. I've graduated, I suppose.'

Nina fidgeted with the bracelet he'd given her. 'I suppose I'd better look into finding work overseas.'

He grabbed her and hugged her to him. 'I really adore you, Nina *mon bijou*. But I am not a whole person if I am not making my pictures, my little movies.'

'And one day big pictures, eh?' She knew only too well how he felt. When a career was more than a vocation, when it was a passion, as important as breathing, when you woke every morning thinking of how and what you would create that day, then it was more than just a job. The childhood dreams and ambitions, suddenly in reach, could not be ignored. Nina felt it, breathed it, thought and dreamed of this too. 'I know. I do understand, Lucien. We will find a way. We're soul mates. We will work this out.' But in her heart she knew, she was saying – I will find a way to fit my life to yours. And her heart ached with pain, anger and fear of losing this, her first love. A love that could never be matched.

They met again a few months later in Paris. Phone calls had been unsatisfactory due to the time changes and the pressures of their work. She was covering her first couture collections and it was a frantic, heady, fabulous time. She visited Lucien on his movie set and he swapped accreditation with a photographer friend and stood in for him at one of the showings. He managed to go backstage, and the photos he handed over to Nina were a scoop that once again marked her for promotion.

They stole several wondrous days together in a small hotel in Provence. But once they were rested, were satiated sexually and had eaten their way through the village menus, they were both anxious to pick up the threads of their careers. They parted, clinging and crying together at the train station at Marseilles, Lucien running along the platform, blowing kisses to her face pressed to the window, until the train slid from his reach.

And so they had gone their separate ways. There was no cut, no decision to do so. It just became harder to find time to be together. Lucien begged her to come to France and find work and, as she wavered, Nina was offered the position of features editor. Her flair and story sense were highly prized.

Then came a day when she picked up a rival magazine to see a picture of Lucien at his film premiere with his arm around his leading lady, described in the caption as his lady partner.

Nina telephoned him, but was told he was in Turkey making a film. With his lady love starring. She put down the phone with a heavy heart and waited for him to return the call.

If he ever did, she never knew. She was sent to work in London for several months on a sister publication, to learn the nuts and bolts of magazine production. And it was at a dinner party in London given by Australian friends that she again met the charming and sophisticated Paul Jansous. Their hostess quietly told her he'd been recently widowed, his wife, at only thirty-five, had died swiftly from a brain tumour.

Paul and Nina were drawn together, and he took a delight in showing her London. He'd been working for a year in Harley Street and planned to open a gynaecology clinic in Sydney.

Arriving back in the harbour city at about the same time, they settled into a comfortable, warm and loving relationship. Nina decided one last time to try to talk to Lucien, and was told he had recently married and was on his honeymoon, so she agreed to marry Paul Jansous.

It had been an uncomplicated and happy marriage, if pedestrian. Both had consuming careers. Paul – to Clara's joy and relief – was immensely wealthy, his Hungarian parents bequeathing him the fortune they had made in property development after their arrival in Australia. Paul's medical clinics were acclaimed for their attention to women's health.

The only sadness that clouded their marriage was that Nina discovered she could not have children. And this led Paul to finance a research group seeking ways to combat infertility in women.

Then, in his late forties, Paul had collapsed while playing tennis. He'd died of an unsuspected heart ailment. Nina received the large inheritance.

As her life gradually came back to normal, and she immersed her grief in work, Nina wondered again if she should contact Lucien. If only for the comfort, she yearned to feel his arms around her. She'd read a while ago of his divorce. But her staff researcher came back to her with the news that he was in Hollywood, had already remarried and was fighting with a big studio over the film he was making. She decided not to intrude into his life.

Nina and Lucien had finished an exquisite meal, but neither had appreciated the cuisine as much as each other's company. There had been so much to tell each other. Nina was not married, nor was she in love with Baron Triton, she told Lucien, no matter what he'd read in the press.

He was divorced – '*Alors, encore!*' He threw up his hands. 'Too many wives, too many children, too much expense. No wonder I have to keep working.'

'You'd wilt on the vine if you weren't making films,' smiled Nina.

'Sadly, that is true.' He touched her hand. 'And it has cost me dearly.'

'We were both selfish,' said Nina. 'I have had a wonderful career, an interesting, enriched life. But I have no children. And never had again the love we knew.'

He twirled his glass of wine. 'Do you think . . . if we had stayed together then . . . would it have worked? Would we still be together now, like this, with forty years under our belts?'

'Probably not. We were both ambitious. When you're young and achieving you never stop and think that everything won't work out the way you want,' said Nina softly.

'Does it ever?' sighed Lucien. 'I have friends, they seem to have everything, and yet suddenly their lives fall apart or you discover they are quietly miserable, but they stoically deny the unfathomable sense of loss in their life.'

'Nothing is ever as it seems, eh? But you can't have regrets,' she sighed.

'I have regrets. Heaps of them. But long ago I put them behind me. Go forward. You once told me you control your own destiny.'

'I always have,' she said sitting straighter, but avoiding his direct gaze.

'Was it worth it, Nina?'

'No comment.' Her voice trembled as she tried to smile.

'I'm in my sixties and I feel like a lovesick schoolboy. I

feel like I did the first time I really saw you. With a dragon-fly quivering on your shoulder. Oh Nina, what have we done . . . ?' his voice broke and his eyes filled with tears.

'Stop, Lucien. We can't look backwards. We did what we did . . . and that's the end of it.' Nina spoke as if to an errant child.

'And now? This so-called accidental meeting . . . it has happened for a reason. Nina, to me you haven't changed. You are so beautiful, I just see you as you were then . . . you have changed so little . . .'

Nina gave a small laugh. 'Lucien, don't be ridiculous. I'm ages older . . .' but as she said the words she felt flushed and joyous that he thought so. She too felt young again. But with all her adult wisdom and experience, there was a voice warning her to take care. The angel – or was it the devil – on her other shoulder spoke the hope that was ricocheting around her heart. What have you to lose, Nina? He was the great love of your past. Remember that.

Lucien had paid the bill. 'Let me escort you to the elevator. And if I may, I shall ring you in the morning. We are on different trajectories, but while we are here, in this place, at this time, I believe the gods are smiling on us being together.'

Nina suddenly felt extraordinarily tired. 'À bientôt, Lucien.'

As the old doors of the elevator clunked apart, he leaned over and kissed her on the cheek. 'Sleep well, my Nina.' It was a brief kiss, a gentle brushing of lips permitted from an old love to another, perfectly acceptable, a gentlemanly gesture, one that mere acquaintances might exchange. But for both of them, it brought back an overwhelming memory of sensation – of how strong their bond had been. How instantly it was recognised, by each of them, that the bond had never been totally severed.

TAKE TWELVE ...

It was a perfect Sydney summer Sunday, made to celebrate Larissa's birthday on the harbour in Kevin's boat.

Everyone was meeting at Rose Bay marina at ten o'clock.

As Larissa walked to her car in front of the small cottage, she barely noticed the taxi across the street.

She slipped into her car, put her basket on the back seat, her handbag and cotton jacket beside it, and was snapping the seat belt into its buckle, when there was a knock on the rear of the car.

'What the devil . . .!'

Someone was standing by the car. Larissa fumbled with the seat belt and was half out of the car when the man reached the door and held it open.

Larissa found herself looking up into Gerard's grinning face.

Her jaw dropped, then she gave a cry of surprise and delight as he pulled her out of the seat into his arms, kissing her. 'Happy birthday, sweets. Surprise, surprise.'

'Oh my God, Gerry! Why, how . . . why didn't you tell me you were coming! You mad, crazy man!'

'Telling you would have spoiled the surprise. It was a kinda last-minute thing. The plane just landed an hour ago. I miss you, babe.' He kissed her hard then drew back taking in her shorts, yellow canvas deck shoes, yellow gingham shirt, a daisy pinned in her hair.

'You look wonderful. What are you doing? You're off somewhere, and it's not church.'

Larissa looked down, suddenly uncomfortable. 'Friends from work, they're giving me a little birthday party. On a boat.'

He stood back and gave her a shrewd look. 'Would I be in the way? I'm a bit jet-lagged. I'll take a nap.'

'Don't be silly. Of course you're invited. Grab your bag and put it inside.'

She headed for the front door, trying to think of someone she could call about the new arrival. As Gerard followed her inside, she wondered why she felt so guilty about Kevin, since there was nothing between them other than a nice friendship. But in her heart she knew Kevin was hinting they could be more than friends.

'Where's the bathroom?'

'Left off the hall. I'll just phone and let them know I have a surprise guest. A wonderful present,' she added, searching for the portable so she could move out of earshot.

She caught Belinda just as she was about to leave home and explained quickly that Gerard had arrived out of the blue and she was bringing him along and to let the others know as they'd be the last to arrive.

'You sound nervous, what's the problem? Kevin?' asked Belinda.

'I feel uncomfortable. He's gone to so much trouble.

And I think he has hopes . . . about me. You know,' began Larissa.

'Stop worrying. There's nothing you can do – just enjoy your birthday. Hey, you have two really nice guys wanting to make it a special day. Relax and enjoy it. Someone will take one of them off your hands,' she laughed helpfully.

Kevin was charming, welcoming Gerard on board and, as they cruised around Sydney Harbour, he pointed out the various bays, famous homes and restaurants. Gerard seemed quite stunned at finding himself in brilliant sunshine in such a fabulous setting.

'Raid the Richard, Gerard looks like he needs a bubble or two,' cried Tiki. And Laurie quickly obliged, pulling champagne from the ice in the Esky.

Being the skipper, Kevin made the toast. 'To Larissa, may this be a birthday to remember. And welcome, Gerard. We're glad you're here to help us celebrate!'

Gerard lifted his glass. 'I thought I was doing a white knight and coming to rescue a woman flung into miserable solitary confinement, with regular lashes from the dragon editor. Instead I find . . . she's living a fairytale! Thank you all very much for taking Riss under your collective wing and for making me so welcome.'

Larissa watched Gerard turning on the charm despite his jet lag. He could be reticent and silent at parties, sometimes passionately argumentative, or like this, utterly poised and smooth.

As everybody went into the main cabin where a luscious buffet was spread, Belinda pulled Larissa aside. 'We've done the birthday cake bit. So you have to blow out the candles. And Larissa, you have a really nice guy there in Gerard. But he seems adamant about you moving back to New York, says he couldn't move out here. A word of advice from a friend – don't make any rash decisions. You could have a terrific life here. You have your career too. I've seen a lot of girls come through the ranks then throw it away.'

'I know what you're saying, Belinda. Thanks for being a friend.'

But Belinda's words unsettled her. And she realised it was because Belinda had voiced the thoughts Larissa had been trying to ignore. In the general chatter and laughter of the confined space, Larissa looked as if she were paying attention to what was going on around her. Instead she felt like an island in a choppy sea and, in the quiet centre of the swirling conversation and laughter, she reflected on her relationship with Gerard. When they'd been busy with their separate careers and overlapping lives in New York it was easy to keep on going on as they were. Now, with each of them on opposite sides of the globe, it had come down to two choices – staying here to further her career and possibly lose Gerard, or going back to him in New York. While she could continue to work at *Blaze USA*, a big opportunity may have been missed. But working its way to the surface was a slow fury that she was the one who had to make the choice.

That night Gerard clung to Larissa, both of them too tired to talk, both lost in the lapsed familiarity of their entwined bodies, awash with too many feelings to talk more than mumbled words of love and longing. Tomorrow could wait, Larissa decided.

Ali arranged to meet April Showers on neutral ground. She chose a quiet, little-known Lebanese restaurant at the edge of the city and arrived early, curious as to what the controversial gossip columnist April Showers looked like. April didn't put her photo atop her column and made an effort to remain as low key as possible. She'd been in Aspen when *Blaze* was launched so hadn't met the hottest new editor in town. Ali imagined a tall, feisty, dark-haired girl, no doubt unattractive – her column was so often snide about pretty women – with a chip on her shoulder. Who'd want to make a career as a bitchy gossip writer? If you had talent you'd be doing something else or regarding it as an interim step, not flaunting yourself as if you ruled the media from an imperious pedestal. The power of the old-style gossip columnist had waned in New York and Ali was hoping to talk April Showers into writing a different type of column, more like 'The Talk of the Town' had been in the *New Yorker* magazine. She also didn't want a writer like April Showers to promote herself the way she'd been doing. Ali was the person at *Blaze* to be talked about. She was running *Blaze* as a committee of one.

She arrived early, settled herself and watched the door. When an attractive, short blonde wearing huge dark glasses walked in, Ali was taken aback.

April came straight to Ali's table, offering her hand. 'I'm April Showers, it's great to meet you at last.' Her voice was husky and April settled herself at the table with poise and ease. She didn't appear intimidated by Ali.

Ali instantly recognised a strong personality. This woman would not be a walkover. She mentally began re-figuring her offer.

Ali waved the menus aside, asking the waiter to bring them a selection of dishes and both ordered mineral water. 'Well,' said April in a relaxed but direct tone, 'shall we dispense with the small talk and get to the reason we're here?'

'I'd like you to write for *Blaze*, but not the same type of stories you've been doing.'

'You don't like my current column?' April sounded faintly mocking. 'A lot of people read it.'

'I'm aware of that. Needless to add, I haven't been too amused at your references to me.' Ali spoke lightly, to mask her real feelings about April's digs at her.

'Many people aren't amused, but just as many become terribly distressed if they don't rate a mention.'

'You have excellent sources.'

'Of course, but I never reveal them. There'd be no more column if I did.' April paused, then jumped in. 'If you're asking me to write for *Blaze*, I assume part of the deal is no mentions of *Blaze* employees, eh?'

Ali was slightly annoyed the girl had seen her ploy and was one step ahead of her. 'I wasn't thinking of a gossip-type column. Sure, cover people, events, places, but from a personal perspective. I was thinking of something more along the lines of "The Talk of the Town" . . .'

April wrinkled her nose. 'Bit olde-worlde. Bitch, bite, and blitheness is more my style. It's human nature to gossip. People love to read a bit of inside dirt – especially about the rich and famous. It makes plain, everyday folk feel a bit superior.'

'Plain, everyday folk aren't *Blaze* readers,' said Ali stiffly.

'Who says? Nina Jansous? You have to toe the party line, do you? I could bring a breath of down-home realism to what seems to be an elite magazine.'

The girl's cockiness was annoying Ali. Or was it the fact she felt she was on the back foot? They must be the same age, yet this hard-faced blonde was making Ali feel like she was pushing forty. Over the hill and out of touch. Ali struggled to take control of the situation. 'Our advertisers want readers with money in their pocket. People with taste and style who buy classy products. We're not into the meat pie-and-chips market. Unless you work for that kind of money,' she added with an attempt at humour.

'Can *Blaze* afford me?' asked April quick as a flash.

Ali was tempted to tell the bitch to forget the whole thing and get stuffed, but she knew that would be inviting trouble. This whole scenario would be embellished and turn up in her column. She was saved from answering as their food was spread before them.

'Hey, this looks delicious. What's this again?' April asked the Lebanese owner who served the food himself. He leaned close to the buxom blonde who openly flirted with him.

'Kibbi balls in yoghurt. And next time you come, you call me and I make something really special for you. I will need a day to prepare it. You call me, eh?' He took a card from his top pocket and dropped it by her plate. 'Bring your friend. Bring lots of your friends. We look after you real good.'

'Righto. Tell me, you ever see any famous people in here?' asked April.

Ali glanced around at the unprepossessing establishment she'd chosen because she'd been told the food was good and authentic, the ambience different, and yet it was stuck in an industrial suburb on the way to the airport.

'You betcha sweet life. I can't say too much but . . .' he leaned forward and mentioned several well-known business leaders and the chairman of a TV network. 'They have secret business lunches here, they come for my food. Lot of big deals been done in that back room. Lot of romances too,' he winked.

'Really? Gee, you must let me in on a couple of your secrets sometime, eh?' April pouted at him and gave a lewd smile.

Ali couldn't help suppressing a grin as the old man appeared to salivate and went back to the kitchen beaming. April was a smooth operator – that was for sure.

'Well, the food looks good, don't know about the

quality of his goss. Could be okay,' said April as she started to serve herself.

'Do you ever have any qualms about how and what you do?' asked Ali mildly.

'No. Should I? Just doing my job.'

'You sleep well then?'

'Yes. I don't believe I've ever caused people to suffer. A twinge, a prick to the ego, but I'm no Heather Race.'

The mention of the TV current affairs journalist with a reputation for her foot-in-the-door, inaccurate, confrontational stories, made Ali shudder. 'I'm glad she doesn't work for me. One day someone is going to sue her and win.'

'Yeah. Or kill themselves for being unjustly accused. It's happened before.'

'Television will do anything to rate,' said Ali.

April gave her a hard look. 'And you wouldn't in order to sell magazines? Where's your line in the sand?'

'You'll know when you've crossed it,' said Ali tartly. 'I'm more concerned with legal issues. People sue newspapers and win, it's harder to win against a TV conglomerate.'

'I'm very aware of that.'

On this note of mutual agreement Ali nibbled a small savoury meatball then put down her fork. 'So April – I assume that's a pseudonym – what do you want?'

'I'm tempted. I rather like the idea of personal, in-depth pieces in the future, but for now, the gossip stuff is what I do best. It's taken me a lot of work to build up the network I have and it seems silly to throw that away, especially when it draws a lot of readers. Where am I if I lose that? I try something new and it doesn't work? It reduces my marketability.'

'And money? How big a factor is that?' asked Ali affably.

'Oh, huge,' said April cheerfully. 'I have expensive tastes. I'm not into meat pies and chips either.'

'Would this be more to your taste?' Ali pulled a letter of appointment from her Prada bag. 'Points and figures and the bottom line summarised on the cover sheet.'

April grinned. 'Then I'll start from the bottom up.' Her face gave nothing away as she looked at the package Ali was offering to lure her to *Blaze*.

Ali toyed with her food as April sipped water and read. After Larissa's initial suggestion, Ali had become ambivalent to the idea of hiring April. Nina's philosophy had always been not to poach rival talent but develop and nurture her own. And if they in turn were poached or moved on, Nina regarded this as a compliment and advised her editors to continue the process of discovery. 'It means we're setting the benchmarks.' Ali knew Nina would regard hiring April as breaking a Triton understanding but Ali decided that, as long as April was out there sniping at her, the more damage she was doing. Not just to Ali, who was personally wounded, but to the magazine. And while Ali was editor, she wanted *Blaze* to be above the daggers of a jumped-up blonde with boobs taking pot-shots at her. The bigger the success of *Blaze*, the more kudos went to Ali.

April felt her eyes start to cross as she worked out the full value of the money and perks Ali was offering. It was above what she'd hoped. It meant Ali wanted her badly. April wasn't fazed by the tough young editor's stance. She knew now how her barbs at Ali must have penetrated the steely exterior. She was vulnerable – somewhere she had an Achilles heel and a secret. Ali looked like a whippet, but April had noticed she only played with her food and there was a high-strung tension beneath the slick laid-back facade. Ali no doubt terrified her staff, but April knew she would need ammunition against Ali that would give her security and protection if she went to work for her. It would only take a little time to uncover what that might be. She put down the paper. 'I assume there is room to move here.'

'I didn't come to haggle or negotiate. That's the deal. And, as we agreed, this meeting and offer is to remain confidential. I'm not into game playing. I think I have been more than generous in order to prevent a ping-pong match.'

'I won't say yes or no on the spot. I'm interested or I wouldn't be here. Give me twenty-four hours and then I'll respond.' April tucked the papers into her bag and Ali hoped the details wouldn't be the lead item in April's column.

April resumed eating. 'So tell me about New York. How well do you know it? You've been with Triton for a long time, right?'

'I love New York. Grew up there. Do you go there much?' Ali quickly deflected questions about herself and instead lured April into talking about her travels and various dabbles in show business. Quite a number of her stories were outrageously defamatory and Ali found herself laughing frequently.

'See, you like scurrilous gossip the same as the rest of us,' said April.

'But I'm not publishing such trashy material, or repeating it,' added Ali. She quoted Nina's cautionary saying, 'Believe half of what you see and none of what you hear.'

Back in Paris, Miche and Donald watched the finale of the collections with Sally as the star of the show. The young model had made no reference to the night Miche had found her in the winery. Sally had appeared late for make-up the next morning. And when they'd gathered for a lunchbreak during the day's photo shoot, she'd made a light-hearted remark about 'losing it last night' – at which point the Count quickly leapt in and swept her off for a horse ride.

Sophie, the stylist, had panicked. 'If she falls and breaks a leg and can't work, Piste will sue me. She's not insured yet.'

However Donald's assistant had seen them along the road when he returned from the village looking for newspapers and tobacco. 'They're in a carriage contraption, like an old sleigh and horses with bells.'

'Sally had better watch out,' said Sophie. 'She could be another of the old Count's conquests. Lures them here then, when he and his circus pals are finished with them, they're sent by train back to Paris. I've seen it before. By then she could be heavily hooked. Last model I knew who went through that scenario ended up a prostitute. She could have worked for any of the top fashion houses, but she died of a drug overdose. Her body was fished out of the Seine. Tragic.'

As Miche watched Sally on the catwalk, the photographer caught her downcast expression and read her thoughts. 'London, Paris, Milan, New York – it's the same scene, Miche. Girls too young, too much, too soon. When all they have to sell are their looks . . . it's a dangerous gift,' added Donald.

Miche took the details of the model-prostitute who'd died and, with Claudia's help, checked out the story with the Paris police department's anti-drug unit. Donald gave her the names and numbers of several top models – some whose fame had been in the seventies and eighties – as well as a few current cover girls who were prepared to talk about their own experiences and what one described as 'the black hole in the underbelly of modelling'.

The rumour Claudia's husband had heard in the diplomatic fraternity came to light when Miche learned how poor, pretty, very young girls were lured to Paris from Eastern Europe, Russia, South America, with promises of money and glory on the catwalks of the fashion world. Instead, they were taken advantage of by older men, who soon turned them over for fresh, young meat and they generally ended up in brothels, hooked on drugs.

While it was not a new story, it gave Miche a different slant on what had started out as a 'sweetheart story'. How Sally, the girl from small town Australia, was a potential victim of the big bad world of money, muscle and marketing.

Miche'd been knocked out by Donald's photographs. 'They look like stills from a Fellini or Ridley Scott movie. Wow! High fashion marries the forces of good and evil. The child bride of Frankenstein meets Dior couture. I love them, Donald!'

'Any time, kid. I think you have it in you to discover the meat of a story. You're not just a pretty face.' He tweaked her nose. 'Look me up in New York if you wanna good time. If not, keep in touch. I reckon we'll work together again.'

Claudia read Miche's finished article. 'This is not a pretty picture you paint behind the scenes of the catwalk and the covers. But it is fascinating. I hope you weren't planning on a modelling career after all this,' she laughed. 'You will not be a favourite person with the agencies when this comes out.'

'You think it's good enough?' worried Miche. 'It's

become a bigger, heavier story than I ever imagined at the beginning. It's not what Nina was thinking of, I'm sure.'

'Send it to Australia. I think it will make quite an impact,' said Claudia reassuringly.

Miche sent the package off to Larissa with a note . . .

Hi, Larissa!

Here it is. It's taken ages to trawl through a lot of interviews, research and just 'hanging out' in the fashion scene. What a crazy world! Could you read this and see if it's okay before you show it to Ali. I'm so nervous about it. Claudia and Bernard are taking me with them to their holiday place in Nice for a week. Then I'll head Down Under. I plan to sightsee in Asia on the way. I'd like to take the break before hitting Sydney and starting work at *Blaze*. Thanks for the offer to stay with you. I accept. Can't wait to see you.

Lots of love, Miche.

Larissa opened the package that had been sent in the diplomatic bag from Paris to Canberra and forwarded to her home. She was thrilled with the photographs. As she read Miche's story, her heart started to flutter and she felt a growing sense of excitement. She went into the small courtyard where Gerard was working on a huge canvas propped against the jasmine-laden fence. Gerry had been captivated by the clear Australian light and was furiously painting bright, bold water scenes, sketched as he rambled around the harbour foreshores. 'Gerry, Miche has sent in her story from Paris. It's fantastic!'

'The one she did with Nina . . . the fashions or something?' He was squinting at his work, half listening.

'Nina made the introduction, but Miche was on her own. It was to be a simple story about local girl makes good in the top fashion echelon. Miche has turned in a shocking exposé of the other side of the lights. Oh, I'm so proud of her. Ali is going to be staggered.'

'The bitchiness behind the glamour smiles as they strut their stuff? Nothing so new in that angle.'

'Wait till you read this. She describes the wildest dinner party in a French chateau . . . Oh boy! I can't wait to see her. She'll be here in a week or two.'

'Ah, too bad. I might miss her.' Gerard took a step back to study his painting, not looking at Larissa who stood still, feeling suddenly cold in the late morning sunshine.

'You're leaving?' she managed after a pause.

'Riss . . . I have a job to go back to . . . I came for your birthday because I missed you.' He turned to face her, his arm holding the paintbrush limp at his side. 'Come home with me, Riss. Let's get married.'

Riss closed her eyes. 'Oh Gerry. I don't know . . . I can't . . . I want to . . .' She burst into tears.

Gerard put down the paintbrush, ran his fingers through his hair, smearing yellow paint in it, and opened his arms. Larissa threw herself against him, crying like a young girl.

Gerard buried his face in her hair. 'Riss, why? This isn't your home. You say you're not happy working with Ali. Or is there another reason . . . someone else? I haven't probed, but I can't help feeling, wondering about Kevin for example . . .'

'Oh, Gerry, he's just a friend. One of a fun group. I was lonely, it's nothing.'

'You could have a nice life here – boats, big houses on the harbour, be a big fish in a small pond. But it's still a small pond. God, Riss, America is where you belong. With me.'

Larissa's voice was muffled. 'Why can't you stay here and work . . . just for six months . . . ?'

'And be a kept, bored man? Darling girl, we have to come to terms with our careers. I love my art, but I can't support us on it. My savings wouldn't keep us for more than two years.'

Larissa jerked away. 'But I earn enough to keep us. Why can't we trade off for a year? You could see where your art takes you, maybe sell a few paintings, make a name for yourself. You won't know if you don't try it. This is a perfect opportunity for both of us to take time out.'

'A year. It was six months a moment ago,' he said wryly. 'Larissa, I don't understand why you can't just come home. The party's over. Nina isn't here – she's taken off – Ali is a dragon, you do half the work, she takes all the credit, our lives are on hold. I'm forty, you're thirty-six. What about babies and holidays in the Hamptons, lunch with our folks on Sundays, all the stuff we laughed at and said we'd put off for another day? Now, for me, it's important. I want it. You choose . . . because that's what I'm going back to.' There was a catch in his voice, no anger, just a worried sadness.

'With or without me, that's what you want?'

'Yes. And it's what you want, Larissa. Why do you hang onto this damn magazine world? Why does it have such a hold on you? It's not your life. I am. And if you can't see that . . . then . . . I give up.' This time frustration and anger surfaced and he picked up the brush and flung it at his canvas leaving a dribbling splotch of paint. Gerard turned on his heel and walked around the tiny cottage and marched blindly down the suburban street.

Larissa fled inside, fell on the sofa and sobbed. Tumbling thoughts and emotions flooded through her. Anger at Gerard for creating the problem, bitterness that the whole situation was so unfair, confusion over where her priorities were and what she really wanted. Yes, she wanted to be successful, to achieve, to have that substantial salary package and bonus goodies. That was tangible evidence of where and who she was in the world. And then, sweeping through her body, came the urgent desire to have a baby, to share her life with Gerard. But where? How? And at what cost?

It was after 5 p.m. Ali walked into John O'Donnell's office as his two assistants were leaving for the day. They gave her a knowing smile and told her he was waiting to see her.

He greeted her warmly. 'Ali, my sweet. How did it go?' he gave her an embrace and kissed her cheek.

'I don't know. She's thinking it over for twenty-four hours.'

'That's not unreasonable. She didn't say no. Did you offer what I suggested?'

'Yes, after a hassle with the board. I told her it was pretty well set in cement. No haggling.'

He gestured to her to sit down and went to the drinks bar to make them each a Scotch. 'April will still feel it necessary to make a stand, ask for something extra. I assume you left a little negotiating leeway.'

'Yes. I hope she's not going to be unreasonable.'

He handed her the drink and sat beside her, dropping his arm over her shoulders. The intimacy in their relationship had developed considerably each time they saw each other. Both had taken an interest in the other's work and he trusted her enough to share company machinations before they became public. It gave Ali a sense of power to read about deals in the business pages that she had known about long before they came to fruition. He had kissed her gently several times and both were aware they were moving towards going to bed together. He was hesitant. Ali had learned that sex with the late wife had not been much of an event. They'd married as virgins, made infrequent love – always in the dark – and when she'd become ill, it was with relief his wife had announced their sexual life had come to a close. Ali didn't know whether to believe him when he said he'd never slept with anyone other than his wife. No wonder he was cautious.

'I have to confess the damn girl unnerved me. April is very assured, very self-confident. She knows the power of bitchy gossip and exposing foibles, true or not. She had no qualms in hinting I was offering her the job to stop her writing about *Blaze*. Me in particular.'

'Well, that's precisely what you're doing. If she knows the score, then that's the deal. Leave yourself an out if she breaks the understanding.'

Ali drained her drink. 'We'll see what happens. I could do with another one of those.' She handed him the glass and he wrapped his hand around hers.

'I thought we might have a quiet dinner. I want to run something past you.' He looked at her and Ali read the signs and smiled to herself. The lovemaking time had arrived. He was attractive, gentle-natured, and had been treading carefully with Ali. The arrangements for the establishment of a centre in his wife's name, with funds going to ovarian cancer research and education, were under way. By now they were seeing each other socially on a regular basis and chatting on the phone several evenings a week. He was walking into deeper and deeper waters and Ali knew sex would clinch the relationship. He was rich, influential and committed to her. He had become her mentor, though their managerial styles were at different ends of the spectrum.

'Why not run it past me now?' She snuggled into his shoulder.

He put the glass on the coffee table and spoke softly. 'I don't want to offend you, but it seems we've been travelling in a certain direction and . . .' he drew a small breath, 'I thought it might be nice if we had a weekend away together. Somewhere relaxing like the Hunter Valley, the Blue Mountains, further if you like. I have the plane . . . but of course, it's on your terms.'

Ali gazed at him, her toffee eyes slanted into a cat-like smile. 'Ever the gentleman, eh, O'Donnell? It sounds lovely. But why wait? If you want to take me to bed, let's do it. Then we can go off and enjoy ourselves and not be waiting for The Big Moment in a strange bedroom.'

He laughed. 'God, you're a bold girl. You're not serious?'

'Why not? I bet you've never done this.' Ali leapt up, clicked the lock on his office door, pulled off her top, kicked off her shoes and stood in front of him continuing to peel off her clothes. 'Come on, O'Donnell, race you. Take that tie off.' She bent down and yanked off his Bally slip-on shoes and silk socks, kissing a toe in the process.

His face went from amusement, to disbelief, to shock and then a mental, 'What the hell,' as it registered with Ali that this elegant and cultured man had never indulged in the business executives' fantasy of sex on his office couch, or floor, or desk.

As he pulled off his shirt and tie and reached for his belt he mumbled, 'The windows. I'll pull the blinds.'

Ali, naked, pushed him back and helped strip off his pants. 'Leave it, O'Donnell. No more sex in dark corners. I can see I have to teach you a thing or two.' She pushed him onto his back and he surrendered as she showed him how to experience and enjoy sex as he'd never known it before.

*

The following morning, Tony Cox wandered down the hallway with a sheaf of papers to present to Ali. They were the plans for a series of travel stories supported by a huge advertising spread from a major travel company. It was a deal pulled together by Reg Craven and it had such massive advertising support, Ali wouldn't be able to knock it back.

But as he passed an office that was not permanently occupied, and was only used for occasional interviews or private meetings, he smelled paint and noticed it was newly decorated. He glanced in and was surprised to see, perched by the desk, a large papier-mâché parrot. The colourful bird looked familiar. Then, as he turned, a figure rounded the corridor and came towards him, a large grin breaking out at his dropping jaw.

'Tallulah! What are you doing here?'

She held out a hand. 'Sorry I haven't returned your friend Jacques' messages. I figured we'd meet eventually. I'm the latest *Blaze* recruit.'

'As what!'

'The name is April Showers. I'm the new columnist.'

'Well, bugger me. I'm gob-smacked, to use my mum's favourite expression. Boy, you really had me going. What was with the Tallulah cover?'

'My girlfriend Patti's dad, who you met in the bar, is a fan of the old movie legend Tallulah Bankhead. He likes to call me that. He knows I prefer not to be introduced to strangers as April Showers. No one will tell me anything.'

'My God, what did I say?' He clapped his hand to his head. 'You'd better not tell Ali I told you she was the Yank Tank. Did I say anything else?'

'Nothing I didn't already know. Don't worry about it. It's our little secret. Besides, now I'm one of the team I can't write about you guys any more.'

304

Tony followed April into her office thinking, 'Shrewd move, Ali.'

April pointed at Jacques' gift. 'See – I brought the bird. I thought his crooning might soothe me. You free for lunch? Fill me in on everyone – off the record.'

Tony quickly dumped his lunch plans with Reg. 'Yeah. I have a meeting with Ali in a minute, I'll probably need a decent lunch afterwards.'

Ali was tight-lipped as Tony outlined plans for a revamped travel section.

'Reg has sold a lot of pages, he has a few ideas for a competition – all very up-market.'

'Has he indeed. Well, I have a few ideas myself,' snapped Ali. 'And I might remind you all that Reg is not running this magazine, I am. In fact, I'm introducing a new system for ideas and you can be the first to try it out.'

Tony glanced at his watch. 'Will it take long? I have a lunch appointment. Business, of course.'

'This will take ten minutes, which will leave you fifty for lunch. Ample,' said Ali, striding onto the covered terrace outside her office.

Tony trailed behind her, then stopped in shock as he saw a large wooden box containing a sandpit the size of a child's wading pool on the terrace. Chairs were grouped around it and in its centre was a Lego village. A sort of castle surrounded by small huts and tiny plastic people.

'What's this? A crèche for a kid's playgroup?' He was having trouble stifling his laughter.

'No, it's the ideas pit. When anyone on the staff has a brilliant new idea, like a big paid-for travel section, the relevant staff will sit in the jury seats. Now what you have to do is present your idea, not to me, but to the towns-people here. And then we'll all vote. I have the deciding vote as I live there.' She pointed to the castle. 'So, off you

305

go, explain the concept and rationale of the travel section to the people.'

'What, now? Here?' Tony's amusement was turning to annoyance. Ali sat in a chair and crossed her legs.

Tony stared at her across the pit. 'I told you all about it a minute ago.'

'They didn't hear it. Tell the chief.'

Tony decided to humour her. Slowly, he began running through his spiel. Each time he lifted his eyes to Ali's face, she nodded at him to direct himself to the tiny toy in the centre of the village. He finished lamely, 'And advertising has sold a six-month ad campaign for full-colour pages which will bring in enough revenue to pay for a colour lift-out on a major destination each month.' He found himself staring at the tiny figure waiting for a response. He shook himself and looked at Ali. 'What now?'

'The chief will call a meeting. And everyone will vote. Regard this as a dry run – I'll ask the appropriate staff to attend and vote.'

'Can I go now?' Tony felt stupid. Like a kid at school. This was madness.

Ali had talked about implementing some new idea that was being trialled by 'out there' Japanese and US companies. But no one, least of all Tony, paid much attention to her enthusiastic embracing of what she called 'new-century methods'. As they were discovering, if Ali talked about something, it generally eventuated.

April was standing by her desk gathering up her handbag and sunglasses.

Tony marched in grim-faced, took her by the arm and propelled her towards the elevators. 'You're not going to believe this.'

TAKE THIRTEEN ...

Nina lay awake under the settling goose feathers, lightly touching her cheek, dreamily recalling the tingle of Lucien's lips kissing her goodnight at the elevator.

It had been an overwhelming evening. From the shock of the reunion with Lucien, to the reaffirming warmth of familiarity and intimacy, to the creeping questions about where to go from here. She was now reeling from the emotional roller-coaster ride. Her defences were down in this dark, anonymous bedroom in a strange city. Suddenly the flashbacks started again, increasingly vivid, spooling through her mind like a movie on fast forward.

And linking them together were recurring images of Clara. 'Quite natural,' she'd been told by the psychiatrist friend she'd visited in Sydney. She was grieving for her mother. It was, in part, the reason for this journey and now, how glad she was that she'd followed her instincts. She smiled in the darkness and squeezed her eyes shut. 'I've found him again, Mama. Our darling Lucien.' Perhaps it had been Clara in heaven pulling strings and nudging fate to bring them together again. Clara had always adored Lucien, as he had delighted in her.

Clara had been such a constant in Nina's life. Not a day had gone by without Clara murmuring a word in Croatian, repeating a few of her mother's aphorisms, singing one of the old songs. At other times, she related stories and happy anecdotes about the family. And so, by osmosis, Nina had absorbed threads of her culture. She had a rudimentary grasp of Croatian, enough to speak and understand the language.

Since Clara's death, Nina realised that she still had a lot of unresolved questions about her childhood. But there had never been time to think of visiting a place, a country no one around her even knew how to find on a map.

Nina looked at her watch on the bedside table. It would be just after 9 a.m. in Sydney. She lifted the phone and rang Ali's direct line. Belinda answered.

'It's Nina. I'm calling Ali. How are things, Belinda?'

'Where are you, Nina? Are you having a wonderful time? Everything is fine here.'

The smile in Nina's voice carried to Belinda. 'Everything certainly is wonderful. I'm in France, in a tiny, wonderful town. I met an old friend. Miche and I had great fun in Paris, has she arrived there yet?'

'She's still in Bali. Larissa is expecting her in a couple of days.'

'I have an idea I want to discuss with Ali. When will she be in?'

'I can put you through, Nina.'

'I thought this was her direct line.'

'Ali doesn't have one. She prefers I screen all her calls.' Belinda sounded uncomfortable. Ali had gone out of her way not to make herself easily accessible. She was distancing herself from her staff, putting all communication on a more formal basis.

'Take care, Nina, enjoy your break. You sound very relaxed. I'll put you through now.'

Ali came on the line. 'Hello, Nina. Checking up on us? Everything is in hand. No problems.' Ali made a stand straight off, thinking, 'Why can't Nina let the reins go?'

'Pleased to hear it. I didn't anticipate any,' countered Nina. 'As a matter of fact, I wanted to talk to you about a story idea.'

'We don't have any contributors or staff in France at present,' said Ali quickly.

'It's something I want to write. And not about France. I've been thinking I'd like to write about my own journey. Back to my childhood in Croatia.'

Ali dropped her head in her hand as she listened. Oh God, she hadn't seen this coming. Nina hadn't written a feature for years. Who knew where Croatia was? Who cared? It was an area torn by sectarian, racial, political strife that Australian readers didn't buy *Blaze* to learn about. And they would care even less about an older dame's family saga or whatever she was doing. 'Write? You mean your memoirs?' said Ali brightly.

'Heavens no! A piece for *Blaze*. Croatia is regaining its tourism appeal and a personal perspective might be intriguing. Depending on what I find. I wouldn't inflict an unusable article on you.'

Ali was thinking quickly. Unusable was exactly the word that came to mind. But then another thought crossed her mind. Researching and writing an article would keep Nina occupied and out of her hair for an extended time. 'Nina, it could be interesting. Listen, take as long as you want, do the research, travel around, don't rush back. You might end up with a book,' suggested Ali.

'It's just an idea at this stage. I'll let you know what I decide. I just thought I'd run it past you.'

'Terrific. Whatever you want, Nina. Take as long as

you want. If you do decide to write something, let me know so I can wave it at the editorial meeting.' Ali wasn't going to take responsibility for lumbering the magazine with a deadly article. Nor was she going to be accused of stroking Nina's ego.

'I'll be in touch, Ali. Glad the magazine is going well.' Nina hung up and turned out the light.

As Nina lay in the dark, it was as if the conversation turned on a movie projector in her mind. Clara's family stories continued on in fast-forward mode. Mentally, Nina clicked the Play button when she wanted to savour certain incidents. Now she had a reason to let the memories flow. She'd start making notes in the morning.

She picked up the thread of her thoughts. After Nina's grandmother died, Clara had become agitated and fixated on her parents' homes in Croatia 'that must be worth a fortune today'.

Nina had spoken gently. 'Mama, there were no records kept, and if they were, where are they? You can't go back now and expect to find things as they were in 1948. Besides, your name could still be on a wanted list. We fled the country illegally.'

'Some things never change,' Clara had sighed. 'The old hatreds never die. Even here, in this lovely country, they bring the same stupid ideas of hating each other. Serbs, Croats, Muslims, Christians . . . why can't we just live together? We all want the same things in life really.' Another sigh. 'When I think back to how it was, the Dalmatian coast, so beautiful. You should go, Nina. See your country once more. Can't you ask your friends in high places to help? To find out what happened to our family home?' Tears had welled in Clara's eyes.

'Mama. Australia is our home, even though I have a good life in America too. When we left Yugoslavia, you told me how Opa and Grandmama said you had to start a new life. With me. For me. And look what we've achieved. They knew and were happy for us. They made the choice to stay.' Nina had spoken gently.

'There was too much to leave, they couldn't just go. The house, the art, the furniture, so many beautiful belongings . . . where have they gone? When my papa died, your grandmama wrote and told me they were taking the house away from her. Because Papa was a doctor, they left him alone, but after the war the state took it over. My poor mother, she cried in her letters to me. What could I do?'

Clara had begun to weep. 'There's so much you don't know. You were just a little girl, you barely remember the old home in the country. You don't even remember your own father. You were three when he was killed. That was when I moved back home. It was safer in Zagreb with my parents. There was the country estate and a town house in Zagreb – now all gone.'

Nina had vague childhood memories of long hallways leading to huge rooms, a walled garden with a fountain and a maid who played with her. After her bath, she'd be taken to a room with a fire to kiss her grandparents goodnight. Grandfather, whom they called Opa, smelled of tobacco and Grandmama was soft with silken clothes and a sweet flowery smell.

Clara had continued her story. 'When I left with you for Australia, my father took me into the garden of our town house and showed me something. He said I must come back there when it was safe. You and I were smuggled out. After Papa died, my mother was sent away. The state took the houses, everything, they told a foolish story – taxes owed or something. That my father had borrowed money and never paid it back. My mother lived with friends. And I never went back again. Australia was our home.'

'But why didn't she come out to Australia? We could have brought her,' wondered Nina.

'You were twenty, working your way up at the magazine, we didn't have a lot of money. I tried to persuade my mother – we could have found the money somehow, I know – but she was ill. To come so far to a strange country where she knew no one, much as she loved us . . . she was too old. She stayed with her friends. They were good people she had known all her life. She did write to me about some family belongings she desperately wanted us to have. But now it's too late.' Clara wrung her hands and rocked to and fro.

It had always upset Clara that she'd never been able to return to Croatia for fear of being arrested. And Clara's mother had been too fearful to visit them in Australia in case she was not allowed back in.

Nina had comforted Clara. 'Yes, Mama dearest. We'll talk again about all of this.' The story seemed too fantastic. It was typical of Clara to fling something at her out of the blue and expect Nina to fix it. The trouble was that Nina had always risen to the occasion and, being a widow, she was used to sorting out problems and managing her own and Clara's life.

Now Clara's dying words of a few months before came back to Nina. 'Seven paces from the old tree . . . to the left, looking at the house.'

Was that what Clara's father had told her before she'd left with Nina for Australia? Nina knew there was only one way to settle the myriad questions bursting into flower in her field of dreams.

Nina had made discreet inquiries. She'd been granted a private visit with the Yugoslavian Ambassador to the United States. 'Is it safe to visit?' asked Nina.

The ambassador hesitated, then gave a small smile. 'Mrs Jansous, I am aware of the position of influence you hold in this country, and your adopted country, Australia. I am also aware of the circumstances of your family. While I sympathise, there remains the fact your mother left at a time when emigration was not permitted.' He'd spoken in the language of the diplomat, an oblique reference to Clara's escape, engineered by her wealthy parents. 'It could be difficult if you went back as a private citizen.'

'Meaning?'

'Unless . . . if you were to visit as Madame Jansous, famous magazine publisher, with a view to undertaking a philanthropic exercise, or perhaps promoting tourism . . .' he left the suggestion dangling.

Nina had seized it quickly. 'Such as writing about Croatia today, helping a school, or hospital, or orphanage perhaps.'

The ambassador beamed at Nina as if she had just come up with the idea out of the blue. 'A promising notion indeed.'

And so Nina had begun to plan her trip to France and then on to Croatia. It was part sentimental journey, part a much-needed break and in part a desire to find her roots, to put to rest the questions raised in her subconscious by the flashbacks she'd been experiencing. And armed with Clara's dying words and shreds of memories, Nina had a second secret, if hazy, plan.

The next day, Nina and Lucien walked through Dijon in a happy daze.

Later, over lunch, Lucien reached for her hand. 'Is this to be another interlude in our lives, Nina? Is this our destiny – paths that briefly cross too many years apart?'

Nina returned the pressure of his hand. 'It's not how I imagined things would be. One's dreams in life seldom work out as we'd like them to. But I don't believe in having regrets. It's too painful considering what might have been.' There was a catch in her voice.

With the prescience she remembered, he asked, 'Why are you really here in France? I believe it's more than just a little holiday. You've cleared the decks for a reason.'

'You always saw things coming before I did.' Nina smiled fondly at him and then continued. 'Family has become something of an issue for me. Since my mother died, it has hit me that I know so little of my own parents' background . . . even more, perhaps, because I have no family of my own to concentrate on. Except for my god-daughter, Miche, and she has, because of sad circumstances, become even more precious to me. I know she will make a life of her own, but for the moment we are very important to each other.'

'Why isn't she here with you?' asked Lucien.

'We spent time together in Paris. She's going to Sydney to spread her wings. With my help, but from a distance initially. I want her to find her way for a bit without my shadow swallowing her, to let her feel she's doing it on her own. Which she is.'

'And you?'

'Clara told me a few stories before she died and they have been haunting me. I feel the need to go back to my homeland and assuage old ghosts. As much for Clara as for me.'

Lucien poured her another glass of chardonnay. 'We have all the time in the world. Tell me Clara's stories. I always loved them.'

The wine was finished and Nina realised she'd been talking for over half an hour about what Clara had told her, what she remembered as a child, and what she hoped to find and how she had set her plan in action.

Lucien listened attentively, nodding his head in agreement now and again. Nina stopped speaking and took a long deep breath.

As if discussing whether to order coffee or dessert, Lucien merely commented, 'I'd be interested in going to Croatia with you. I'm between films and have the luxury of choosing what I do next. I've often thought of making a film there, ever since Clara told me stories of her childhood, the setting of the Dalmatian coast, her escape with you. Your family saga is intriguing . . .' He glanced at her. 'I even thought of weaving in the story of Einstein's abandoned daughter who was sent to a home in Croatia. What are the chances of finding, or making a claim on your family heritage?'

Nina couldn't help laughing. 'Lucien, you just keep going forward don't you? You were always impetuous.' But she couldn't subdue the tingle of excitement at the prospect of spending more time with him. 'The area has been through so many wars and such political and economic upheaval. So many people displaced, homeless, killed, families splintered. I wish I could help in some way. I've been so fortunate.'

'You're a very powerful woman, you just have to find the right avenue for practical, effective assistance,' he advised. 'Surely as a media mogul you could drum up attention in the press.'

Nina chewed her lip as she thought for a moment – a habit Lucien remembered with a pang from their early years together. 'I've been thinking I could write something. I'd like to do that. I started out as a journalist. I suggested it to Ali, my Australian editor, last night. I am, after all, going on something of an intriguing journey,' she said. 'There must be a way of entwining my personal

315

odyssey with raising awareness of how Croatia is today and what has happened there.'

Lucien was immediately enthusiastic. 'It would be much safer and easier for you if I came along. I could take stills for your story.'

'Lucien, wait. I have to think this through. Of course I'd love you to come with me. But I want to be sure . . . that you really want this.' She looked down.

He read the subtext of what she was really saying. 'Nina, there are no strings, no pressures, no obligations. Yes, we have both changed – how could we not after living our lives these many years?' He paused and reached out to lightly touch her cheek. 'Nina, could we try again? To spend a little time together? I will accept whatever terms you impose. It just seems to me that this accidental meeting wasn't an accident . . . what do you think?'

He looked almost shy, his voice was hesitant, but his sincerity and passion made it impossible for Nina to refuse. She shivered, a tremor of nerves and anticipation, as a long-built wall around the core of her heart dissolved into nothingness.

With their bags in Lucien's car, they drove south to Nuit St Georges, a famous winemaking village. It could have been the moon. But they would never forget what they ate, the name of the little restaurant, the name of the small pensione they checked into.

They strolled around the village shops and, finally, after a romantic dinner – where they tried to make sensible conversation but kept breaking into smiles – reaching for each other's hands, they slipped between crisp cotton sheets, two naked bodies, too many years apart, that melded together as the one they should have always been.

In the dawn light they woke and stared, smiling into each other's eyes.

'Happy?' Nina nodded and stretched and then studied

Lucien who looked, felt and smelled of the same sweet musky odour she'd always remembered. Looking at his silver hair, the softening jawline, she saw only the virile handsome young man of her youth – her first lover, the man she had once imagined she'd spend her life beside.

'My Nina.' He kissed the tip of her nose and reached for her body, drawing its still slim yet rounded shape into his. 'I was so worried about this . . .' He began kissing her throat, moving down to her breasts.

She tangled her fingers in his hair, smiling like a contented cat. 'Lucien, how could you . . .'

'I confess to you, my darling. It's been years and years since I made love. I thought it was over, I just was never able . . .' He clutched her to him. 'You've made me a man again, a young man. I can't let you go, Nina. All my life, it's only ever been you.'

'You're a more wonderful lover than I remember, the best, my darling. Don't fret – we have a lot of catching up to do.'

He nuzzled her belly. 'It might take a while . . . like years.'

Nina refused to think about those lost years, or what might be ahead. For now, there was the utter joy of feeling a whole and luscious woman, worshipped by a man she'd always adored who saw her as she'd been, and would always be, the utter love of his life. He accepted her as she was now, remembered her as she'd been when a girl, and cherished her as a precious gift that could be snatched away at any time.

But for now, there was now.

Nina called Ali once more. Ali listened to Nina's excited voice as she outlined her proposal for an article on her journey to Croatia, weaving in historical background details, the effects of the wars and how it was now becoming a burgeoning tourist destination once again. 'All told from a personal perspective as I go back to my childhood,' enthused Nina.

Ali yawned, glad they were on different continents. 'Sounds great, Nina. I'll be interested in what you come up with. Sounds quite a challenge . . . making that part of the world and your personal experience relevant to our readers. But it needs pictures. Finding top professional shots could be tricky,' said Ali, already looking for reasons not to use Nina's piece at the end of the day. Ali thought the whole idea sounded old hat and boring. But she feigned enthusiasm. The longer Nina stayed away, the better it suited her.

'By an incredible stroke of fate I've run into an old friend – a movie man who knew my mother. He's going to join me. He'll take photos.'

'Bummer,' thought Ali, beginning to back-pedal. She had no intention of running Nina's story – she doubted Nina would actually do it. 'Don't make any promises, and bear in mind our budget,' Ali cautioned.

Nina chuckled. 'Glad to see you're keeping an eye on the bottom line, Ali. By the way, have you seen Miche's story yet?'

Ali groaned inwardly. God, was Nina trying to turn *Blaze* into a family effort – 'How I Spent My Summer Vacation' by our editor-in-chief, 'My First Time in Paris Seeing A Fashion Show' by the editor-in-chief's god-daughter. Just as well Nina had no other family. 'No, I haven't seen it yet. Larissa mumbled something. I'll check on it. Now you go off and have a fantastic time, I don't imagine we'll hear from you in the depths of Yugoslavia.' Ali tried to keep the hopeful note out of her voice.

*

In the bright light of their last minutes together, Lucien was matter-of-fact. 'I will join you in a few days. I have to finish this film tour and tidy up loose business ends. I'll join you in Zagreb.'

They parted with long hugs. Nina glanced over her shoulder as she went through the airport departure gate at Metz. Her breath was short, her chest tight. Would she really see him again?

The hotel clerk insisted on holding Nina's passport and airline tickets in the hotel's safe as was 'customary', which made Nina nervous, but she didn't want to make a fuss. For her own reasons, she'd decided not to take the ambassador's advice and draw attention to herself. While Zagreb seemed cosmopolitan, clean and catering to tourists, she still shivered as past memories crowded in on her.

From the first day, Nina set a pattern of behaviour of walking and travelling alone at night, eating at restaurants outside the hotel. For a while she had a feeling she was being followed, but dismissed it as paranoia. But she knew she was being studied, openly and surreptitiously, wherever she went because of the way she looked – her grooming, her clothes, even though she had brought simple, unostentatious outfits. She was obviously a woman from the West and she elicited envy and curiosity. When she spoke in halting Croatian, it became evident she was one of the lucky ones who'd been fortunate enough to leave and enjoy a comfortable life, and was simply revisiting her homeland. The people she met had no idea she was successful, famous or influential in her own right.

Nina merely told people she had grown up in Australia as a young girl. When asked about her family, she had given her father's name, Trivitza. Clara had used her parents' name, Bubacic, after she was widowed. Nina still had a niggling worry about Clara Bubacic escaping illegally from Croatia with her toddler.

She fretted there could be repercussions given the fact their homes had been taken over by the state and Clara had escaped at a time when permission to leave the country was rarely given.

Nina tucked a new notebook in her handbag and set out late one afternoon to find the street where she had been born and where she had lived with her mother and grandparents after her father's death. She had the address and recalled the grand and elegant building from Clara's treasured photo album.

The area was heavily built up, not the quiet residential street Clara had described. There was an industrial plant, a few shops and a café.

Nina walked to the end of the block looking in vain for the street number – 78. She retraced her steps. She double-checked and finally saw a number high above a set of doors in a four-storey building.

It resembled a concrete box, with small windows. Absolutely no sense of style infused this functional building, either for those who inhabited its depressing flats or for those who paused to look at it. There was no grace, no beauty, no personality to this postwar piece of communist architecture. If buildings reflected their time and era, then how matter-of-fact, how unadorned, how intellectually impoverished this time had been. Many buildings in Zagreb were grand, with a fading, peeling glory, where they had once been elegant and admired. Many had been restored and sophisticated new buildings attested to the fact that Croatia was reclaiming its past glory and moving on in the new millennium as a tourist destination once again. But this dreadful block of boring flats would only ever display a lack of colour and imagination until, in decay, it would one day disappear.

Nina was aghast. The Bubacics' beautiful town residence had been replaced by an architectural monstrosity of public housing. The stylish heritage house, which had graced the avenue for more than two centuries, had been destroyed. Why? Because, she told herself, in the postwar era of communist revolution, housing the underprivileged was more important than the preservation of a wealthy family's conservatory, formal lounge and huge dining room, maids' quarters, reception foyer and five luxurious bedrooms. But attempting to understand the possible reason for demolition did nothing to ease the pain of loss, a pain of such intensity that it almost had her in tears.

A man emerged from the entrance and she glimpsed a small, gloomy lobby. She pushed open the door and stepped inside to find an old man sitting behind a desk with mail slots set to one side. Behind him on the wall hung a large print showing heroic workers rallying behind a red flag carried by a man with a raised fist and a rifle slung across his back.

'You want something? Looking for someone?' asked the man at the desk rather gruffly, after giving Nina a swift assessment from shoes to hairdo.

'Good morning,' replied Nina politely in her best Croatian. 'I am a visitor. I once lived in a house at this address. A long time ago.'

He briefly raised an eyebrow, the only acknowledgement that the encounter was of uncommon interest. She was obviously a foreigner of Croatian background. No doubt American. Her grasp of the language was, he decided, only very basic, so he spoke slowly. 'Your house went years ago from what I remember. I grew up in this area after the war. Probably all that's left of those days is the garden out the back.'

Nina tried to control her excitement. 'I vaguely remember playing in the garden. It was a magic place for me as a child. Could I have a look?'

The old man took time to light a cigarette before answering. 'Yes, I suppose you can. But there's nothing much to see now. Down the hall there, and through the big door at the end.'

'Thank you so much.' Nina turned and walked down the corridor, momentarily closing her eyes as her steps echoed on the bare wooden floor. Wishing she could have been walking down the hallway of the family home, an image that had gone through her mind over the years.

At the door she paused, took a deep breath, then opened it and let out a light gasp. The past came flooding back as reality, not an image of memory. The courtyard style garden was real. Despite the changes, there was something familiar and welcoming and she quickly recognised what it was – the tree.

She walked slowly over to it, reached out and stroked the bark, then stepped closer, wrapped her arms around it, pressed her lips to it and cried.

From the doorway the old caretaker watched and scratched his head in puzzlement, then went back to his desk and the morning paper's analysis of Sunday's big soccer match.

The tree was a solid link into her childhood and Nina closed her eyes, smelling once again the beautiful garden flowers her grandmother had lovingly tended, seeing her dolls set out for a picnic, hearing Opa's favourite music drifting from the upper floor, Clara singing. Despite the tragedy that had unfolded around them daily, music gave normalcy to their lives. How loved and treasured Nina had been. How glad she was that she had given love, care and security to Clara in return. How sad she was that she had no children of her own to cherish.

Nina sighed and looked around the untidy, neglected garden with its few stunted shrubs and plants, patchy grass. The glorious garden of her grandparents had vanished. She glanced back at the building, which had only a few small windows overlooking the garden. She studied the ground around the tree. Was it possible that whatever grandfather had buried was still there? After all these years the garden didn't appear to have been disturbed since the flats were built. How could she bring a shovel here and start digging? Should she even bother? This brief pilgrimage had given her fodder to write about. But curiosity and the memory of the intensity of Clara's last words convinced her to continue.

Nina began working out a possible scenario. She went back to the old man.

'Are there any empty apartments in this building that I could rent for a short time?'

Within a day Nina had possession of the key to the vacant rear ground-floor apartment. Before checking out of the hotel, she rang and left a message for Belinda asking her to notify the Baron, Ali and Larissa, who would pass the news onto Miche, that she was staying longer than planned. She rang Lucien and told him what had happened and that she'd be staying in the flat, but only for a few days. 'Not that they know that – I've paid two weeks rent in advance.'

'I'll meet you at the hotel on the seventh, Nina darling. We can go back and take whatever photos you need and then play ordinary tourists,' said Lucien. 'Perhaps the tourism people could help us. Have you contacted anyone yet?'

'No. I want to keep my personal inquiries private. If my grandparents kept something so secret for so long, it could be sensitive.'

'Perhaps, but it's more likely monetary and material

objects that were hidden during the war. It's a shame they were never able to go back to retrieve whatever it is.'

'A government official probably lived there without knowing what was in the garden. And now that beautiful old house is gone. At least Clara kept a photo of it. Oh Lucien, I feel so odd. It's like going back in time and re-entering my grandparents' life.'

'I'm worried about you creeping around. Be careful, Nina my love, I'll be there soon.'

Sitting in the very basic and sparsely furnished flat, Nina began making notes about what she remembered of her childhood in this place. While she had centred on her own desires in life – helping the cook in the kitchen, dressing up in her grandmother's hats and shoes, playing under her magic tree – other images began to have meaning. Worried visitors who came to the house and hurried into Opa's study and closed the door. Peeping out of the window at night with Clara who was frightened of a big, dark car across the street. Finding her grandmother and Clara weeping and being comforted by Opa. Rushing into Opa's study to tell him something and finding him opening a safe in the wall behind a picture – which made him shout at her to go outside. Opa never shouted. Had that really been a gun she'd seen?

Nina worked out her plan. Hers was the only flat that had immediate access to the garden and she quickly befriended the old concierge with gifts of cigarettes and a few American dollars for his help in small ways. She asked him if it would be all right to plant a tree in memory of her grandparents. With summer on the way, she wanted to make the garden pretty. The concierge thought it a waste of money and energy and put it down to rich Western behaviour.

Nina made a show of appearing to settle into the tiny apartment, keeping her distance from the neighbours and trying to avoid prying questions from the local shops and café.

Late on her second afternoon at the apartment, she marked a spot to plant her tree. It was seven paces to the left of the old tree as she faced the house. The concierge wandered into the garden with a cigarette and watched her for a while and then strolled back inside.

Nina turned over the hard soil until the light was fading and then made a show of stopping work, sticking the shovel into the soil and returned indoors in case she was being watched. She was shaking. Not from the exertion, but because the shovel had hit something hard. Something metallic.

After dinner Nina packed her bag and sat in the dark waiting.

The hours passed slowly. Then, at 1 a.m., she tied her hair under a scarf, pulled on black pants and a dark shirt and crept out to the old tree. She began prodding and digging. Finding the boundaries of the hard object, which seemed to be the size of a large suitcase, she crouched and dug around it with a heavy trowel, throwing aside the loose dirt until she felt metal. Her heart pounded as she realised it was a metal handle. She scraped around it, snapping through narrow root tentacles from the old tree and, finally, she was able to lift out the rusting box.

She quickly half filled the hole so it looked roughly like it had been that afternoon when she had finished digging. She hurried back into the flat and locked the door. She was shivering with cold, excitement and apprehension. Then, after her racing heart had settled down, she brought knives and a tin opener from the kitchen and managed to break the lock. The lid creaked open.

The first object she pulled out was a rolled oilskin cloth that contained documents. Beneath that were several soft leather pouches containing jewellery. She turned the pieces over in her hands, utterly charmed at their art deco and classic styles. She struggled to recall her grandmother or mother wearing them, but the only jewellery she had loved when she was a little girl had been her grandmother's dragonfly brooch. The pin that now nestled in Nina's safe in her apartment in Sydney.

Hastily she put the jewellery in her bag, then changed her clothes. She made a coffee and took a longer look at the papers, which were in surprisingly good condition. There was a journal and a file packed with papers, letters, photographs, birth and death certificates. But a number of the formal documents puzzled her, as did the crest imprinted at the top of each. She put them to one side and opened the journal that had obviously been kept by her grandfather. She struggled with the language, slowly translating as she went. But soon enough, it became disturbingly clear what it was. Nina sipped her coffee and wondered whether to burn the journal.

No wonder Clara had been so concerned. The journal contained lists of names, code names, locations, completed, aborted and failed missions, names of people listed as missing, others as killed. And contained in a sealed section at the back of the journal were the names of Nazi collaborators, local people who had betrayed their own for what advantage it gave them. It was appalling evidence of the war crimes of World War II. And just as surprising to Nina was the realisation that her beloved Opa, a gentle, scholarly and caring doctor had been a central figure in a dedicated network of Croat citizens who'd worked to resist the Nazis.

Several names appeared frequently among the collaborators' list, each time marked as Nazi sympathisers believed responsible for the torture or disappearance of people whose names were listed below them. Nina recognised one collaborator's surname and middle initial – it was the name of a popular, internationally known senior minister in the current government. Was it possible this minister's grandfather could be outed as a hated *domobran* – a Croatian who supported the Nazis? This journal could embarrass and incriminate a lot of people. Even if they were dead, it would bring pain and shame to families. This could be a powerful piece of information for the Nazi hunters, who were still tracking down anyone who'd helped enforce Hitler's holocaust against the Jewish people, even though those few remaining men were now in their eighties.

Looking through the diary, Nina found compelling, emotional stories of individuals. She could see how this would be valuable material for Lucien. In this journal was the core of a film about bravery and inspiration. Her grandfather had kept this record. She could not burn it.

But Nina also knew these papers would place her in danger if she were caught with them in her possession. Where could she hide them in her luggage? Nina wanted to leave the flat as soon as possible. She had brought with her half-a-dozen copies of *Blaze* in a promotional kit. Quickly she ripped out every second page of the magazines and replaced them with the personal papers. Then she returned them to their presentation folders.

She wrapped the journal in her underwear and stuffed it in a bag with her shoes. She put on a few pieces of the jewellery, leaving the others in a pouch pushed into a shoe. It all seemed a bit melodramatic, but Clara's stories and the turmoil and tragedy of past years could not be ignored. Here the hatreds ran deep, suspicion was still an ingrained instinct. Silence could mean survival.

She turned out the kitchen light and walked through to the bedroom to nap on the lumpy bed that had come with the flat. She glanced out at the garden, shadowed in the pale night light. A movement caught her eye. And, as her night sight adjusted, she saw a man hurry across the grass and crouch at the freshly made hole. Nina strained to see who it might be. Why was he there? She must have been watched. Maybe she had been watched and followed since she'd arrived in Zagreb. Or maybe it was just the concierge, who was simply curious about her insistence on digging the hole herself. But then why would he be out there at three o'clock in the morning? Nina decided to leave the flat at once.

TAKE FOURTEEN ...

Ali put down the last page of Miche's story on Sally. The photo of Sally wearing a diaphanous dress that showed her thin body looking so pubescent, hair threaded with flowers and trailing below her hips, barefoot and leading Poirot, the big white stallion, through a misty field, was highly evocative. She looked all of twelve years of age. It was timely because an argument was currently raging over the use of child models as young as twelve made up to look eighteen and older.

It was a terrific piece with stunning photographs. It needed tightening a little, but Ali knew she had a hot article that deserved a big splashy spread. Ali had little time for a girl well connected to Nina and a reminder of her late, one-time rival, Lorraine. But if she could turn in a feature like this, she'd have to be nurtured.

'It's bloody good. When does she arrive?' asked Bob Monroe.

'I haven't offered her a job. This was a spec piece. Do you suppose she did it on her own?'

The features editor bit his tongue. 'Nina has a professional eye, and she wouldn't push someone on board who couldn't do the job. This girl will go places. If this came in from a potential contributor, I'd give them another story.'

'Hmmm. Let's see if she can do it again. I'll use her on a freelance basis.'

Bob thought it odd that Ali wasn't hiring Nina's god-daughter full time. He wondered what Nina would make of this, then reminded himself that Ali was running the show now. He made one more try. 'If she comes up trumps again, you'd better sign her before someone else does.'

'I'll think about it,' conceded Ali. 'Remember, she was writing on her peer scene to a degree. I don't intend *Blaze* to be for teenoids. If the Baron wanted a magazine for fifteen-year-olds he'd launch one, not hijack *Blaze*.'

'It's just one article, Ali, not an entire magazine. The photos are pretty erotic and the issues raised about who controls the strings in the modelling business are quite frightening. Scarcely lightweight reading for teenyboppers.'

'Unless they want to be models. The mother of every wannabe model should read this.' She started rifling through Donald's photographs. Bob was dismissed and he left Ali's office shaking his head – she always had to have the last word.

Larissa and Gerard walked hand in hand through Centennial Park, the green oasis in the centre of Sydney. They'd been jogging and had slowed to a walk as the light began to fade from the day.

Gerry lifted his arm and dropped it around her shoulders. 'When are we going to have our talk, Riss?'

'Oh. You sound like I'm avoiding the issue.'

'Aren't you? Every time I start to talk about going back to New York, what I want to do when you finish up here, you change the subject or don't hear me.'

'I suppose I don't want you to go.'

'Or do you mean you don't want to go?' There was a chiding tone to Gerard's voice.

'I'm on a contract for a year remember.'

'You can walk out any time. And go back to New York. Nina would never let you leave the company.'

'I so hate the idea of leaving Ali to run roughshod over everyone. Her ego is totally out of control. The sandpit deal started as a joke, but the staff members hate it and are nervous wrecks when they have to confront it.'

Gerry shook his head. 'I can't believe she seriously wants her executives to address their ideas and explanations to a bunch of toy people in a sandpit. Sounds like a touch of Mussolini with his toy trains. What about her affair with the big shot CEO? Maybe he'll take her off to a life of luxury and travel.'

'Ali would go for the luxury but not the travel. She won't leave her chair for more than a few days at a time. Even her annual vacations are token holidays.'

'Why are we talking about Ali? See, again, you've changed the subject.'

Larissa twisted out from under Gerard's arm and plopped on the grass. He crouched before her as she idly plucked pieces of clover and studied them. 'You have to decide about us, Larissa!'

'Of course I like Australia – and my job. And I just don't want to go back to the way we were. I don't understand why.' She sounded teary and confused. 'I don't know what I want.' How could she be in her mid-thirties and feel like an angst-ridden teenager? She used to think she had her goals and priorities worked out. Now her aspirations and Gerry's weren't meshing, the timing was all off. She felt like an old-fashioned watch about to burst a spring.

'It's time for us to make a new life,' said Gerry reassuringly and continued speaking without waiting for her reaction. 'Let's get married. There's something I haven't told you yet because I didn't want to spoil our time together . . . But it has to come out. I've been offered a job in New Hampshire running a start-up investment company. For me, it's a great chance. It means I will be half out of the rat race. I'd have time to paint . . .'

'And what would I do?'

Gerry nuzzled her ear. 'Have babies . . . ?'

'Oh Gerry. I just don't know. I feel so . . . torn. Like I'm at a crossroads and I don't know which way to go.'

He looked forlorn. 'There's nothing more I can say. It's up to you. But I'm not going to keep my life on hold. I'm moving to New Hampshire in four months. Let me know what you want to do. If you want to keep the apartment, it's yours.'

Larissa could only stare at him. She was in shock at the suddenness of his announcement, that she'd known nothing about his plans. A niggling anger nipped inside her. She held her hands as if warding off a physical attack.

'Whoa! Let me take this all on board. In one mouthful you propose . . . then tell me we . . . you . . . are moving, you're taking up a new job, I'm to leave my job and career, have babies, settle in a place I've never been to . . . I mean. I may want to *think* about this!'

His enthusiasm wavered as he sat back on his heels. 'Oh. I thought you'd love my plan. It's what we always talked about wanting and doing.' He looked hurt, bewildered.

Larissa saw he was perplexed and really didn't understand why she just hadn't fallen in his arms, saying '*yes,*

yes'. She took a deep breath. 'Gerry. I do love you. I don't understand why I feel so confused. But I just can't imagine not working for *Blaze*, not travelling, not having the challenges, the stimulation, the friends. It's been my life.'

'Maybe it's time you started a new life, Riss. Or you can stay in your comfort zone. Talk to someone for God's sake. Can't you find Nina and talk to her about it?' As Larissa shook her head, he gave her a quick hug – he could see she was in no state of mind to make decisions. She had to become accustomed to the idea. 'Come on, let's go and eat. I'm not saying any more. The ball is in your court.'

'Don't make it hard for me, Gerry.'

'It's not hard, Riss. And I won't bring it up again. I don't want an emotional farewell at the airport tomorrow. In fact, I'd rather you didn't come out. I'll grab a cab and drop you off at the office. It'll be easier that way. Quick and painless.'

Quick it might have been, but painless it wasn't. Gerard sat back in his airline window seat and buckled his seat belt in an agony of hurt, anger and frustration. As the plane soared over Sydney, he glanced down at the beautiful harbour and foreshores he'd seen from Kevin's boat and his heart ached with love for Larissa. He felt fearful about their future, but what else could he do? He'd meant what he'd said – he wasn't going to put his life on hold. He was ready to move into the next phase of his life. With or without Larissa.

The women noted Larissa's red eyes and left her alone until Belinda, Barbara and Fran invited her to lunch.

'I think we need a decent bottle of red,' said Belinda firmly as they settled themselves. She rarely went to lunch, let alone drank alcohol, on a working day. Today was an exception.

The other women quickly agreed. 'One of the best

from the Margaret River,' declared Fran. 'You'll have to go over to see the west, Larissa.'

'I don't know where I'm going,' she sighed. 'I thought I'd like to see more of Australia while I'm here, now it seems I'll be tooling around New Hampshire.'

'It's a hard one, all right,' said Belinda. It was a vague remark as none of the women wanted to advise Larissa too strongly. They could all see what a hard choice it was. For any of them. Belinda was glad of the diversion of the wine being poured. She sipped the shiraz with appreciation. 'God, this is more like the good old days. Leisurely lunch with friends, toss around ideas, share gossip.'

'Some damned hot stories came out of those weekly lunches,' sighed Fran.

'Days of the long lunch on expenses are over,' agreed Belinda. 'It used to be something of a badge of honour for the blokes to get really sozzled, insult the boss, grope a poor young woman, throw up in a cab, end up at the old Journo's Club and lose a fortune on the pokies. Then pass out on someone's floor, not able to remember a thing since lunch started.'

'It's not politically correct any more. These young birds go to the gym after work and drink water laced with chlorophyll,' sighed Barbara.

'That was a fad in New York for a while,' said Larissa. 'Everyone wanted lean green bodies. Well, alkaline in their system.'

'Ali must have an acid system,' said Barbara tersely. Belinda and Fran stared at her briefly, then broke out laughing. It was so unlike the always ladylike Barbara. She was still smarting from her sidelining by Ali and she missed her colleague, Tiki. Apart from Fran and Belinda, there was no one else on the staff of Barbara's generation.

Belinda raised her glass. 'Here's to you, Larissa. No

matter what you decide, we'll always be your friends, and we all want you to be happy.'

They lifted their glasses and Larissa shocked herself by bursting into tears. 'I don't know what to do . . . And I don't know *why*. I don't know what to do . . .'

It was a welcome diversion for Larissa when she met Miche at Sydney Airport. They hugged warmly, both deeply glad to see the other. For Miche it was a familiar friend in a strange place, for Larissa it brought back memories of New York, of *Blaze*, of Gerry, of Lorraine – a world that seemed now so far away, so long ago.

Miche loved Larissa's cottage and, after she'd struggled to stay awake through the day, they walked up to Oxford Street for dinner.

'This is hip. Very Greenwich Village,' said Miche approvingly. She lifted her glass. 'Here's to you, darling Riss. I'm sooo glad you're here.' They clinked glasses and Miche braved the subject of Gerard. 'You must miss him. I'm sorry I didn't see him. He adores you so, why doesn't he move here?'

Larissa clutched her chest in mock alarm. 'Ah, the directness of youth. An arrow straight into my heart. I'm grappling with one of those life decisions.'

Miche merely raised an eyebrow and Larissa looked crestfallen. 'Oh, Miche, it's so hard. I'm really confused. I like it here, except Ali is . . . difficult, as you'll discover.' Larissa paused at the cloud that passed over Miche's face as they both thought of Lorraine. 'I adore Gerry, but I feel I've moved on in some way and I can't put my finger on it. I just know I can't go back to my old life. Having him here was so wonderful – and I know he enjoyed it too. He loves Sydney, but he felt like it was a holiday being here. Gerry wants to move to New Hampshire and on to a new life, but I don't know that I want to give up my career and be . . . mother, wife, whatever.'

'That's not a lot of comfort to me, Riss. I thought life became clearer with age and wisdom,' said Miche gently. Then, seeing Larissa's sad expression, she sighed. 'Why is it women always have to give up something in order to do something else? I always wondered what my mother was going on about, raving on that I was the inheritor of the breakthroughs by the baby boomers. But Nina and Mom had to fight to achieve what they wanted. They talked about saving the world, making it a better place, easier for us. Yet look at you . . . me . . . even Ali . . . our lives aren't exactly perfectly laid out on a platter. The world still seems to be run by and for men.'

'I sort of agree,' said Larissa. 'Until men have the responsibility of looking after the kids, the old folk or the sick, nothing will change. We still have to fight over pay, lack of child and home-care services, violence against women, the glass ceiling.'

Miche threw up her hands. 'I'm not going to fight that one. Be like Ali. If you hit a glass ceiling, put a boot through it and to hell with anyone else. Mom always told me not to be modest, to believe I can do anything. That's how men think.' Miche sipped her wine and briefly stared into the glass as if looking for an answer to the question she had often asked. 'When does it become simple?' she asked softly.

'Maybe never. That's the whole female trip,' replied Larissa slowly. 'Fundamentally, we still want a career, to be acknowledged as thoughtful intelligent beings, to be a mother, to love someone and be loved in return and live in a healthy, clean, safe environment. Why should that be so hard?'

'Well, to a lot of men that's a big shopping list,' said

Miche. 'And another thing, any time a problem comes up in our lives – like finding legal or financial guidance, signing a contract, just putting your life in order, we think we have to find someone else's advice,' she continued. 'And women like my mother seemed to think that using outside help was a failure on her part. I'm just starting to realise that I am talented at some things, but there are things I can't do – hey, why not spread the load?'

'I suppose as long as women feel their status is unequal, there will be the need for organised feminist action,' said Larissa. 'But you and Ali's age group seem to operate more as individuals, even competitors. What happened to the sisterhood that your mom and Nina were part of? I'm in my mid-thirties, have a promising career, a lovely guy. But the days of being superwoman and doing it all are gone with the power suits. It's back to the olden days – I'm supposed to choose.'

Miche spread her arms, warding off Larissa's intensity. 'Hey, gimme a break. I'm just a kid. What do I know?' At twenty-three, Miche was excited about the future, but it worried her when all the women around her seemed to find life so difficult.

Her mother hadn't been able to cope with ageing. She'd been left with a baby and a husband who didn't want to settle down, so Lorraine had made her life working for *Blaze*, clawing her way up the ladder and raising a child as a single parent in New York City. But it had killed her.

Nina had also dedicated her life to her work. She had looked after her elderly mother, been widowed young without children and probably now had secret regrets. Ali was an aggressive ambitious bitch and, uncharitable as it might be, in her heart of hearts – despite her mother's problems – Miche blamed Ali for pushing her mother over the edge, emotionally and physically.

And here was Larissa, not much more than ten years older than Miche, unsure of how to deal with the crossroads she faced. Where did the men fit in, wondered Miche. Once again she cursed her absent father. She was beginning to realise she harboured a deep anger towards her unknown parent. Where was he when she'd needed him to give her a cuddle, read her stories, attend school functions? To teach her to dance, and what to say to boys? Fathers contributed so much to a girl's self-confidence, self-esteem. She'd always resented him for not being there when she needed him.

Larissa broke her train of thought and reached over and squeezed Miche's arm. 'Don't take any notice of me. I'm just having a bit of a freak-out. I think you'll love it here and do brilliantly. Your story on Sally Shaw was quite excellent. Knocked us out.'

Miche looked pleased. 'Well, I had a lot of good material to work with. It was quite an experience. And spending so much time with her was a luxury. I hope Sally doesn't feel I betrayed her confidence. I can't imagine having that sort of access to other subjects.'

'It's likely you won't. But if you are thorough and careful and balanced, you can build up a reputation so that people want to be interviewed by you.'

'I don't want to do puff jobs to please the subject like so many journos seem to do!' exclaimed Miche. 'Nor do I want to be an utter bitch and rip into people just to be sensationalist. I've noticed that many writers who take that kind of tack spend half of the article talking about themselves.'

'Good point. So what are you going to do next?'

'Depends on Ali. I'm going in to see her on Monday.'

'Make an appointment with Belinda,' advised Larissa. 'Ali doesn't subscribe to an open-door policy.'

*

Miche sat before Ali's desk trying to reposition the shadowy figure that had so haunted her mother. Miche always thought of dinnertime with her late mother as 'Time for Tales of Ali'. Lorraine always came home and bitched about the young woman she was so threatened by. Now Miche faced this same woman who was boldly wearing the mantle of the sleek, slick editor.

Ali was inscrutable behind the dark Chanel sunglasses, yet it seemed to Miche she was uncomfortable. 'You're staying with Larissa?' asked Ali.

'Yes. Until I find my own place. I'll share, I guess.' Miche paused, waiting for details of the job she was here to take up.

'In Sydney?'

Miche stared at Ali. 'Of course. Unless you plan to send me somewhere else?'

'It's up to you. Your piece on the model Sally Shaw is excellent. I'm glad I organised for Donald to do the photographs,' said Ali, making it sound as though Donald's photographs had saved Miche's article. 'However, I don't know that you'll find a story so suited to your, er, talents every month. We are happy to consider any suggestions or submissions.'

Miche flinched. 'Excuse me? Ali, I understood from Nina I was to take a full-time position here. I have come all the way across the world on that assumption.'

'Assume nothing,' said Ali cryptically. 'Nina mentioned your talents and I am buying your Sally Shaw piece. Finding subjects so suited to your . . . interests might not be always so easy.'

Miche was close to tears, but too angry to cry. 'I feel confident I can write well about any subject I might be given. I realise I'm not that experienced but . . . I do have to support myself,' she added pointedly.

'We pay the going rate for articles. It's quite generous.

I suggest you go and talk to Bob Monroe, our features ed, about story ideas. As far as being on staff, that's out of the question. You'll be a regular contributor depending on editorial space and content.'

'I see.' Miche rose, furious at Ali and scared about her prospects. 'I'll make an appointment to see Mr Monroe.'

'Ask Belinda now. He may be free. And Miche, in your own best interests, downplay your association with Nina. You don't want murmurs about nepotism. Surviving on your own merits is always best.'

'You bet. It's what my mother taught me.' Miche headed for the door. 'Thanks for the time.' She didn't look back at the figure behind the desk.

Ali groped for a parting pleasantry. 'Your article is the lead feature next issue, by the way.'

But Miche was quietly shutting the door and in minutes had been directed to Larissa's office where she burst into tears.

Larissa gave her a hug. 'God, she's a bitch. Of course you should have a full-time job. She doesn't want you on the staff payroll so she doesn't have to pay all the loadings. You'll make more money freelancing anyway. And, you're a free agent, Miche. You can sell your articles anywhere. She may have done you a favour.'

Miche wiped her nose with a tissue. 'I guess so. It's not what I expected. I guess I was remembering how comforting *Blaze* used to be in New York, when Nina was there. God, no wonder everyone here seems so scared of Ali.'

'What do you mean? You've just come into the building.'

'I watched a few of the younger girls in the hall outside Ali's office. They scurried with their heads down like frightened mice. Albeit rather elegant mice.'

Larissa laughed. 'Yes. Ali sent out an edict that she was

not to be publicly addressed by the juniors. She doesn't pass the time of the day with minions. If they walk in the elevator with her, they stand at the back looking at their shoes and wait till she leaves before moving, even riding past their floor.'

'Well, I'm glad I have to pitch ideas to Bob Monroe and not Ali,' sighed Miche.

'Yes. Be glad you're not an executive or senior staffer having to pitch their ideas to the playpen.' Miche looked at her quizzically. 'I'll explain later. Come on, I'll treat you to lunch.'

It was just before daylight when Nina arrived back at the city hotel she'd left two days before. The lone concierge, who'd not been at the desk on her last visit, seemed suspicious of a foreign lady turning up at 5 a.m. He explained she could wait in the early-opening café until the day manager came on duty at six.

The dark-walled Dalmatian Café had carpet the shade of dried blood, musty brocade curtains and solid chairs and tables with functional settings. She imagined the food was as heavy and stodgy as the surroundings. It was a room designed to brood in over the thick coffee that Nina sipped as she waited, trying not to fume.

She did not see the old concierge from the apartment block where she'd been staying, hurry from the hotel manager's office.

The duty manager appeared half an hour later and explained a room would be ready as soon as possible.

'I don't need a room for very long. I'm leaving for the airport as soon as I shower and make a phone call and collect my papers from your safe,' said Nina.

He shuffled and clasped his hands together. 'Madame,

I am not authorised to open the safe. I am only the duty manager. The hotel manager and the receptionist will be here very soon.' He gave her a pained, somewhat puzzled look. 'Madame, you checked out of our hotel. Why did you not take your passport? It is an important document.'

'I am aware of that. Which is why I preferred to leave it here in your safe while I was travelling and . . . sight-seeing. I told the receptionist I would be checking back into the hotel.'

'There is no booking here, Madame.'

'I know, I didn't know when I'd be returning. Your hotel doesn't seem very busy,' commented Nina, who had rarely seen more than a handful of guests in the hotel. 'I felt confident you would have a room for me.' She tried a smile in the hope of thawing the frostiness of the little man who wore his official position like a giant, fur-lined cloak. Was he naked like a plucked bird beneath the enormous coat of officialdom? Nina's smile became genuine and she inwardly giggled at the concept of her metaphor. The duty manager saw no humour in the occasion.

So she sat, waiting for the hotel manager to arrive, sipping another lukewarm coffee, convinced there was a room ready. The duty manager seemed to be one of those officious types who bustled and bossed, appearing to be very busy, yet rarely making a decision.

Nina finished her coffee and decided she would wait no longer. As she headed back into the lobby, a man in a dark suit politely greeted her. 'Mrs Jansous, I am Mr Zarvic, the manager. Your suite is ready. Please, forgive the delay.' He spoke in English.

'Where is my luggage?'

'It has been sent to the room. I understand you wish to retrieve items from the safe?' He went back behind the dark-wood reception desk. He leaned across the oak divide and spoke in a low voice. 'Madame, would it not be best to leave your documents in safe-keeping? Until you leave?'

Nina hesitated. Yes, it would, but instinct told her to retrieve her passport and extra travellers' cheques. 'I have other documents I wish to put away and I'd like to take out some money.'

The manager paused a fraction then quickly waved a hand. 'Please, Madame, you can obtain money from our cashier and add it to your bill.'

Nina was gently insistent. 'I'd like my documents, please.'

'Of course. Would you mind signing this form so we may match the signature on the deposit slip? Then it will be sent to your room. Which I hope is to your liking.' He gave a slight bow. 'I will escort you to the lift, Madame.'

'Could you please arrange for a taxi to take me to the airport in an hour or so.' Nina was going to jump on the first plane that took her closer to Lucien.

The manager reacted with instant concern. 'But Madame, there are no planes. There is a bomb scare. The airport is closed. I suggest you stay here for a day. The planes will be flying again in twenty-four hours,' he explained cheerfully.

'What do you mean a bomb scare? Why? Who?'

'Madame, such things happen at any time all over the world. The actions of one desperate person or group cannot reflect on whatever unfortunate city or country or airline they choose. Please, we have a beautiful suite for you. Enjoy our hospitality and our city.' He gave a slight inclination of his head and smiled.

Nina sighed. She had little choice, it seemed. He handed her a key. 'We will be happy to take you to the airport in our hotel limousine. If you want to leave your rental car here we can arrange for it to be collected and the account added to your bill. As soon as the airport is open, we will let you know.'

'Thank you. That would be helpful. I don't suppose I can make a reservation now?'

'To where, Madame?'

'The first plane out that can take me to . . . France or Italy.'

He gave her a flash of a raised eyebrow look, but remained obsequious. 'We will do our very best.' He led her gently towards the lifts.

Nina felt she was being bulldozed, that they were avoiding producing her passport. But she was more concerned about her luggage, so she followed the manager to the elevator as he handed her a key.

The room was large and lavish in an overstuffed, ornate, antique European style. A maid was opening the heavy drapes in the sitting room, a vase of fresh flowers sat on a coffee table. Nina walked through to the bedroom to find her suitcases open, spread on the bed. Her coat was hanging in the open closet.

The maid bustled in, apologising for not having unpacked. She lifted the top outfit from the bag, but Nina politely stopped her, speaking in Croatian. 'That is not necessary. I will manage. Thank you very much.'

As the door closed behind the maid, Nina hurriedly checked her bag. The journal and jewellery were intact. She breathed a sigh. Why did she feel that these documents were looming as a liability? Why did she feel she had to hide them in her luggage? It was doubtful customs officers would search her bags and they were, after all, her family possessions. She longed to show them to Lucien.

She rang his home, but there was no answer. She then dialled his office. The answering machine came on. 'This is a message for Lucien from Nina. Don't come to Zagreb,

I'm taking the first plane out, hopefully to France . . . or Italy. I've found more than I expected. There's no trouble, but I want to come back. I'd like you with me . . . for lots of reasons. Not just because I love you. If you return in time, call me at the hotel. I'm in room twenty-six. Otherwise I'll call you from the airport and give you my destination and you can meet me there. Bye, darling.'

She began to dream about returning to Zagreb with Lucien and discovering the city and surrounding areas. How wonderful to explore it all with him. It hit her hard how much she had missed this – travelling for pleasure with a loved companion. All the trips she'd made around the world had been dedicated to business. The few times she'd taken true holiday breaks had been with Clara or on her own. Even after her marriage to Paul Jansous, she and her new husband had postponed their honeymoon, but had never taken their planned world tour due to work pressures. They'd thought there'd be time for that later. Instead she'd become a young widow who'd taken on an enormous responsibility with her own business.

Nina took a leisurely bath, ordered coffee and cake then began to make notes of events over the past few days.

After a while she paused, twiddling with her pen as she reread what she'd written.

Nina then called Belinda who put her through to Ali.

'Hello, Nina . . . this is a surprise. I'm just about to go into a meeting. I thought you were travelling, exploring, researching and so on.' Ali pre-empted a long conversation.

'I've been researching my grandparents' old home and I think I've stumbled onto something interesting. A kind of buried treasure. From what I can make out with my basic language and a dictionary, I think my grandfather led something of a secret life.'

345

'Really? Well, I'll look forward to reading it . . . in due course. Was there anything I can do . . . ?' Ali didn't sound the least bit interested.

Nina hesitated. 'I wanted to discuss it with you, or perhaps with Larissa if you're busy. I may need assistance from someone with historical and political knowledge of this part of the world.'

Ali groaned inwardly. This was sounding more boring than she'd imagined. 'I'm sure this is all fascinating to you. But are you sure it's going to interest *Blaze* readers?' Ali didn't want to put Nina off the idea as long as it kept her away. 'I mean, maybe you should do a bit more digging while you're over there. What sort of treasure, by the way?'

'Family artefacts and old papers. Buried in my grandfather's garden. Can you believe it? The house has long gone, a dreadful block of flats is there, but part of the garden is still intact. I found a journal he kept during the war . . . I think it could embarrass or even incriminate a few powerful figures here.'

'Hmmm. You sure you haven't stumbled onto a Hitler's diaries type of hoax?'

'This stuff hasn't been touched since around 1946. The political issues aside, it's a pretty interesting personal story, don't you think? It's turning out to be a bit more than a visit to the old homeland and looking for family roots,' Nina pointed out.

'You know what we want in the magazine, Nina. You just keep delving. Maybe there's a lot more to find. Take your time – all is well here. Now I really have to . . .'

'Can you transfer me to Larissa or Bob Monroe please, Ali?'

'Editorial meeting,' said Ali quickly. 'I'll have someone call you. Nice talking to you, Nina.'

Nina stared at the handset as the disconnected phone

line began humming. She put the bedside phone back in its cradle.

The doorbell buzzed. The hotel concierge, who had made her wait earlier that morning, stood smiling politely. He handed her a manila envelope. 'Your papers from the safe, Madame.'

'Thank you.' Nina took the package then, on a sudden impulse, asked, 'I have something else to leave in the safe. Could you wait a moment?' She went into the bedroom and retrieved the old journal. She shook out her passport and traveller's cheques and put the journal in the strong manila envelope, resealed it and twisted the cord around the two tabs and signed her name across the flap.

She handed it to the manager. 'Would you return that to the safe for me, please. I'll sign whatever you need when I check out.'

'Of course, Madame.'

As he opened the door, Nina added as an afterthought, 'It's not valuable. Just sentimental.'

He nodded and closed the door quietly behind him. It was only much later that Nina wondered why he was in casual clothes and not the formal suit he'd worn on duty.

Nina spread the jewellery on the bed, carefully studying each piece. These had belonged to her grandmother and Nina had faint memories of Clara carrying her in to say goodnight to her grandparents. Her grandfather's smile reserved just for her, Grandmama stooping to kiss her on the cheek or smooth her hair in place. She liked to think she could remember her wearing these pieces of jewellery, but was more likely recalling photographs of her elegant and wealthy grandmother. All Nina really remembered was the dragonfly pin. Its glittering ruby eyes and diamond wings had always fascinated her. These pieces needed cleaning, so she put the necklaces and ornate chokers, the elaborate bracelets, the pearls rolled in a silk bag, and the rings in their boxes back into the leather pouch. She kept out one piece – a gold signet ring that had what looked to be a family crest on it – and slipped it onto her finger. She didn't want to go through the drama of having the safe opened again, and something told her not to let anyone see her putting away what appeared to be a fat stash of jewellery. So she looked around for somewhere to hide the pouch, finally settling on an ornamental vase high on the shelves above the bureau.

Nina then went for a walk, hoping the situation at the airport would soon be resolved and planes could start moving.

Sun washed over the beautiful old stone buildings, but they still looked cold and impersonal, like black and white photographs in an album compared to colour prints. She came to a row of cafés that looked more cheerful than the mournful coffee shop at the hotel. Nestled alongside the cafés were a few boutiques selling luxury items – leather shops, a furrier, an expensive food store with imported goods including liquor, liqueurs and chocolates. Nina was in the up-market section of the city where tourists or the very wealthy local residents shopped. An antiquarian bookstore and a jeweller were across the street and Nina crossed the wide avenue, heading for the bookshop, but on impulse swerved into the jewellers. Antique estate jewellery and a replica Fabergé egg were displayed on dusty black velvet. The signage was in English as well as Croatian. The door tinkled as she pushed it open.

A balding, bespectacled gentleman lifted his head from the jewellers' eyepiece that he'd been using to study a ring. He pushed his glasses on top of his head and rose to greet her.

'Good morning, Madame. How may I assist you?' He spoke Croatian with a German accent.

Nina answered in English. 'I was wondering if you can tell me anything about this.' She pulled the ring from her finger. 'It has been in storage a rather long time, I'm afraid.'

The jeweller squinted at it through his eyepiece. 'Dear me. Yes, it needs cleaning badly.' He spoke passable English with a thick accent. 'There is an engraving here.' Nina was silent as he turned the ring, gave it a rub with a soft cloth and looked at it closely, hunching his shoulders. He laid the ring on a square of black velvet on the counter. 'This is a family ring? Your family, Madame?'

Nina hesitated. 'I believe so. My grandparents came from here. It belonged to them. I'm not sure how they acquired it. It could be a piece they bought which came from another family. It's a family crest, I take it?'

'In a manner. If it is your family, I would be discreet about showing it around. I have a log of family crests and insignia that could prove helpful.' He turned to the small, cluttered cubicle behind the counter, shuffled a few delicate-looking instruments, papers, boxes and an electric engraving tool to one side and reached for several books and folders on a shelf. He began thumbing through the pages, checking the ring frequently through his eyepiece.

Nina waited for a moment or two, then said, 'I might just go into the bookshop next door. I'll only browse for a bit.'

'Take your time, Madame. I'm sure I can identify this seal.' He didn't lift his eyes from where he was scanning lists of what looked like small etchings.

Nina smiled to herself. Everyone was telling her to take her time when inside she felt a constant sense of pressure to keep moving. Maybe the old jeweller could tell her something that would add another fragment to her family story.

She almost lost track of time among the leaning

towers of old books. When she returned to the shop, the jeweller was busily drawing an enlargement of the crest on the ring, which he'd polished and now shone on the black cloth.

'Oh, that looks wonderful. Thank you so much,' exclaimed Nina, picking up the ring and slipping it back on her finger. 'And what have you found?' She reached in her handbag for her notebook and pen.

'Indeed, I have found something, Madame,' he answered in a low voice. He put down his pencil and motioned for Nina to sit on the chair drawn up at the counter. He leaned across it to speak to her, his face serious, his voice still very low, almost conspiratorial.

'Madame, it is as I thought. So I would advise you to be very careful about identifying your family. I presume you are a visitor here?' Nina nodded curiously. He continued, 'My family are German Jews, my wife is Croatian. We escaped from Germany and settled here. I lost many of my family.' He seemed to shake himself and return to the present. 'Family is important, yes?'

'Very. That's why I'm here. To try to find out more about my grandparents.'

'You know a little . . . yes?'

Nina read into the simple question his real question. Did she know about her grandfather's secret life? It seemed this man had some answers. She decided to confide in him. 'Yes. I think my grandfather led something of a double life. He was a physician doctoring the rich and the high-ranking officials while working for the resistance movement. After the war, he was forced to move from his home here. I have just visited . . . where their house used to be.'

The old man nodded, pleased she had told him about her grandfather. 'The name attached to this crest is Bubacic. One of the old, elite families. After the war,

Dr Bubacic was hailed as a hero by the people. But not by the communist government. He was one of those who wanted democracy for our country and so his name was featured on The List.'

'What list is that?'

'A list, circulated by the old government, of names of people Tito saw as having the potential to undermine the order of things – to him, they were possible traitors and spies.'

'My grandfather was none of those! He *was* a hero for helping the partisans to fight the Nazis, and I'm not surprised he wanted democratic rule for his country.'

'It's different now that Tito is gone,' said the old jeweller. 'But I warn you, this period in our history is still a very sensitive one. Croatia today has the chance to rebuild and open itself to the world again as a major tourist destination in Europe. Some people do not like interference with things they think are better forgotten.'

'I just want to find out more about my family, but do you think this could be dangerous? Surely after all this time and with Tito's communists no longer in power, times are very different.'

'Times have changed indeed. But for some whose families suffered, the need to see atonement made or perpetrators brought to justice, is very strong. If it became known that your grandfather's personal records were still in the family, for example, it could be dangerous for you.' The jeweller sighed. 'Be discreet, Madame, and be very careful. Do not bring attention to yourself. Have an intermediary do the research you need,' he advised.

Nina thought instantly of Lucien. Her plan to leave as soon as possible and return with him made even more sense. She reached for the sketch of the crest on the ring.

'May I keep this?' She was thinking of using it as an illustration for her article. Already her mind was skirting over the surface of topics to write about. The courage of people like her grandfather and what they had fought. How deep and lasting were these wounds and prejudices that kept flaring up like summer bushfires. No wonder so many migrants to Australia carried such passions and hatreds with them.

The jeweller rolled up his sketch and slipped a rubber band over it. 'Good luck with your search. One should honour the past and the family. Shalom.'

It had been an intriguing, if disquieting, encounter. Nina hurried back to the hotel and rang the airline office at the airport.

'I want to know when any aircraft will be able to leave Zagreb Airport. Any airline,' she stressed in Croatian.

'I do not understand you. Please repeat the question.'

Nina switched to English. 'The bomb scare. When will it be safe to come out to the airport? I want to be on any flight. I have an emergency.'

'I am sorry, Madame. What bomb scare? There are no problems here at Zagreb. Where do you wish to go?'

Nina felt suddenly very cold. Slowly she asked, 'Are all flights departing on schedule?'

'Certainly, Madame. Which airline are you travelling on?'

'Never mind. I'll come to the airport and make a booking. Thank you.' Nina hung up, staring at the phone that suddenly seemed an enemy. Who else was listening? And how long had they been listening?

TAKE FIFTEEN ...

Larissa caught Ali in the corridor. 'Hi. Belinda tells me Nina rang. How is she? What's she doing?'

'My, how quickly people spread no news,' said Ali dryly. 'She's planning on being away longer. Writing a story. For herself. Family archive stuff, I think.'

'Oh. I wanted to tell her Miche is here and settling in well. Perhaps we'll call her.'

Ali waved a hand. 'Don't bother. She has no mobile link and is setting out on the road. Said she'd check in when she had news.' She moved quickly away. Ali didn't encourage chatting in the hallways. And she certainly didn't want to encourage Nina to keep tabs on the staff while she was away. 'God, I hope someone shoots me if I can't let go when my time comes,' thought Ali.

Larissa watched her walk away with quiet fury. She knew very well Ali was trying to keep Nina at a distance. Ali didn't want any of the staff passing on information about her antics. Not that there was anything major that would warrant complaining to Nina on the other side of the world. But it was clear to Larissa that Ali was intent on making a grab for power, profile and prestige. If only she didn't try so hard and alienate those around her in the process, thought Larissa as she headed back to her office. Ali was clever at her job – and in how she achieved her objectives. But if only she could be softer, show a touch of vulnerability, show interest in those she worked with – or, in Ali's mind, those who worked *for* her – and smile with real warmth occasionally, then relationships and the mood around the office would be more bearable. Ali concentrated too much on schmoozing with the outside heavyweights, the corporate world ('potential advertisers'), media chairmen ('networking'), even Ian Marcello, Nina's lawyer ('defamation advice'), who Ali had charmed over lunch. These meetings were always casually mentioned to Dane at the Yellow Brick Road beauty salon and were then inevitably repeated in a social or business news column. And the impression given was that these senior gentlemen were always suitably impressed by Ali.

Over dinner in Victoria Street that night, Larissa told Miche how Nina was deep on the trail of a personal story.

'That's terrific. Claudia told me Nina was a good writer in her day, that she pushed it to one side to be an editor.' Miche took a bite of her pasta. 'Which reminds me that I should be starting on another story. Seeing as I'm working as a contributor. No stories sold, no money,' she grinned ruefully.

'You know you can stay with me as long as you want, Miche. It's a company house, thanks to Nina,' said Larissa. 'I like having company . . . I miss Gerry.'

'No chance he'll come back?'

'No chance. Lovely place to visit . . . but . . .'

'He might come back and surprise you again. But in the meantime, thanks for the offer to stay,' said Miche.

'So . . . any ideas about a story?' asked Larissa, keen to avoid the painful subject.

'Hmmm, the Sally Shaw saga isn't over. Did you see the report that she collapsed on the catwalk in Milan?'

'Yes, it looked tragic. Are the stories that she's on drugs true?' asked Larissa.

'Sadly, I'm sure they are. That started me thinking.'

'About . . . ?'

'About vulnerable young people, such as Sally, who come from a sensible, stable background and can still be taken advantage of. What about young people who come from alcoholic, homeless, addicted parents? What chance do they have of breaking the cycle? Making good? And further along the path . . . heading into dark woods here . . . what about kids who are victims of violence? The ones who have either been assaulted, abused, tortured or witnessed such things. What about them?'

Larissa sipped her wine. 'That path could take you into frightening territory, Miche. But from what I've read, it seems those victims of violence cover it up best. Many do overcome childhood traumas, many don't. Many don't admit it. Consciously or subconsciously.'

'Repressed Memory Syndrome? That's been vilified as well as proven. Quite a few people have falsely claimed ghastly events happened to them, just to get themselves a bit of notoriety, fifteen minutes of fame, sympathy, whatever. Which is pretty sick in itself,' said Miche. 'In fact . . .' she delved into her handbag for a notebook and flipped pages. 'Listen to what a trauma specialist told me.' Miche scanned her notes and then began to read.

Many people do hide their trauma. Some even forget that it has happened and the memories flood back many years later when they are exposed to something that has an association that triggers the memory. When the memories flood back, they are sometimes overwhelming and extremely difficult to cope with and it is possible that a person, who has managed reasonably well with his/her life up until that point, can break down with Post-Traumatic Stress Disorder, although it is unlikely to be diagnosed as that because many will not trust their memory. In fact, there is a huge debate right now based on the denial of adults who have been accused of child abuse, including sexual abuse. Some years ago they formed themselves into an organisation called the False Memory Syndrome Association. It has caused the genuine therapists great distress and some therapists have been implicated in uncovering false memories, and sometimes rightly so. It is extremely disturbing for those who have suffered to have their memories and traumatic experiences questioned and doubted. It is as bad for them as the perpetrators making them keep secrets and so on.

Miche closed her notebook. 'So you see there is a lot to explore in this story.'

Larissa put her glass back onto the table. 'It may be dangerously revealing for someone like you to explore this subject. Rather than an academic or a therapist,' she said gently, wondering if Miche was aware she could fall into the victim category herself – a father who abandoned her, a mother who committed suicide.

'It could be an interesting in-depth piece. Something to prove I can write about more than lightweight generation X and Y stuff, which is what Ali seems to think I should do,' said Miche, pursing her mouth in distaste.

'It could bring up a few uncomfortable personal issues for you, Miche,' warned Larissa.

Miche didn't answer for a moment. Then she gave Larissa a frank look, but the slight lift of her chin and set of her body gave an added determination to the lightly tossed remark. 'It's what I came here for. Confront the demons. Settle my soul. Something like that.'

'You're sure?'

'No.' A grin flickered.

'But you're going to try to find your dad?'

'I guess that's part of this whole issue, isn't it?'

Larissa reached over to touch Miche's hand that was gripping her glass. 'Be sure. Ask yourself if it's going to change your life for the better. Do it if it feels right. Whatever you decide, I'm here as surrogate aunty, big sister, Nina fill-in, whatever.'

'Thanks, Riss. You're so kind.' Miche gave an awkward laugh to release the tension. 'And you're not even a relative.'

'That's why it's easier,' smiled Larissa.

Miche thought more about her story idea. She rang a psychologist and the trauma therapist again and realised she had tapped into a deep well of behaviour patterns, an emotional landscape of quicksand with cause and effect that went from the hidden events of childhood, which remained unacknowledged, into adulthood. It intrigued her. The more she thought about Sally, the more research she did, the more she found that even in an apparently well-adjusted, easygoing, happy-go-lucky country like Australia there were dark threads of suffering children. There was the issue of the stolen generation of Aboriginal children. These youngsters, mainly of mixed blood, were for decades until the seventies, forcibly removed from their families to be 'assimilated' into the white community. There were also stories of sexual abuse in church schools and institutions – individual stories now being talked about that had been hidden for years. There was childhood trauma of all kinds from violent parents, sexual abuse and sheer neglect.

What interested Miche was the idea of how these children had coped, or were able to ignore traumatic childhoods and, in many cases, become high achievers or lead normal lives. But then, what was perceived to be normal? We all keep secrets. But the pain of children who had been victims of violent crime, who felt shame, who worried they too could exhibit the same tendencies, who felt damaged and different to their friends . . . what had it done to them? Or did they live in such denial it changed their whole personality?

As the specialist told her, 'Their need to keep secrets and not to tell the truth sometimes affects their way of being in the world, in the way they live their lives. They can be notoriously difficult to work with as they are unpredictable, have trouble with interpersonal boundaries, can be tragically unhappy and are frequently economical with the truth. They are often those who make multiple attempts at suicide – largely unsuccessfully – and when they go into therapy, they are extremely hard work for therapists.'

What led them to therapy? Who were they? How can society help them? Or was ignorance bliss? How many would repeat the cycle?

Miche put together an outline of these thoughts, the types of people she'd like to interview, where the story might lead and how she saw the relevance of the story. She had the feeling she was dipping her toe in deep waters and that once she disturbed the apparently calm surface, other people might find the courage or strength to come forward, to drag their dark secrets into the sunlight and let them go. Once one person stands up and shares an experience they'd been too ashamed to admit, it eases their burden and others tend to follow suit, relieved to know they are not alone.

She rang Belinda to make an appointment to see Ali, confident this would be a story that would suit *Blaze*.

Belinda came back to her. 'Ali says she is a bit swamped. Talk to Bob Monroe, he's features editor.' Belinda was pleased to see Ali delegating work. 'He's very attuned to ideas, Miche, and he loved your piece on Sally. We all did.'

Bob listened, made a few notes and asked questions. 'Where are you doing the research? Which specialists do you have who are willing to talk and quote case histories on the record? What's going to make a reader want to read, and keep reading, this story? Who are you going to use to tell their personal story?'

Miche was prepared for most of Bob's questions and rattled off her answers. But the last two weren't so easy. 'How do you ever know what interests people at any given point in time? I can only go on instinct.'

'Hmmm.' Bob tapped his pencil against his teeth. 'It needs a more personal angle. Shame we've done Sally. You'll need to find someone, probably someone in therapy, who's willing to share what they're dealing with.'

'That could be hard if it's something horrific and violent,' said Miche.

'The personal story doesn't have to be along the lines of "My Father Was an Axe Murderer". Maybe something readers could identify with more easily. Someone unravelling the tangles in their life.'

Miche was thoughtful, then said slowly. 'What about me?'

Bob reacted openly, his surprise unconcealed. 'You? You fit into this category? In what way . . . if I may ask?'

'Well, it's not as traumatic as the theme of the story, but it could be a springboard to those deeper waters,' said Miche. 'I'm thinking of looking for my father. It might turn out he's not alive, not in Australia, he could be in jail, could be a boring suburbanite or a university professor.'

'How long since you've seen him?'

'I don't remember him at all. I just feel I need some kind of closure before I can go on with my life. After losing my mom and all . . .' she shrugged, unwilling to elaborate as the emotion built up inside her.

Bob nodded. 'It would certainly give the story an additional angle. But what if you find your old man and he's a shit? You ready to reveal that too?'

Miche raised her hands in a gesture of acceptance. 'No point in hiding it. I can walk away from him if I so decide and if I can't be honest, there's not much point in asking others to do the same.'

'I'll talk to Ali. Sounds compelling. Where are you going to begin your search?'

'Not sure. But I'll make a start . . . now I've made up my mind.'

At the next editorial meeting, Bob ran through the list of story suggestions including the details of Miche's idea. As he outlined Miche's theme, there was a murmuring of interest.

'Sounds intriguing.'

'She started digging with the Sally Shaw piece.'

'Seems like a sensitive writer.'

Ali looked down at her agenda pad, fiddling with her pen, her face immobile. No one knew what she was thinking until Larissa asked, 'What's your opinion, Ali?

It's a touchy area for Miche, but I think she could come up with something.'

'It sounds like something one of those TV current affair shows would do . . .' butted in Reg Craven.

Bob Monroe glared at the advertising director. 'Give us a break. She's not that kind of tabloid journalist . . . that's not our kind of story. What do you think, Ali?'

Attention at the table focused on Ali. She had been silent abnormally long.

'I think it stinks.'

'What?' There was an intake of breath.

Bob spoke up defensively. 'What's your objection, Ali?'

The table fell silent, everyone looking at Ali.

Ali was struggling. For the first time the staff could recall, a glib, swift, sharp answer didn't spring from her lips. But her body language, her expression, made it clear she didn't like the idea. Finally Ali gave a brusque shrug. 'What is this? Old home week? Nina looking for her old rellies and now her god-daughter churning through her family blankety-blanks. Everyone has a broken branch or two in their family tree, why should we inflict it on *Blaze* readers?'

A row of bland faces struggling to hide their feelings stared at Ali, alone on the other side of the table.

Larissa broke the silence. 'I don't know if that's the case, Ali. I think everyone can identify with family and personal insecurities in one way or another. Okay, not all of us are dealing with the same specific issues, but if we follow one person's journey to wherever it takes them, it shows us all the value of the exercise.'

'Whether it has a so-called happy ending or not,' added Bob. 'I think the girl has potential as a serious journalist.'

Ali refocused on the discussion. 'Oh, for chrissake.

Let's not make this a new-age, inner-search deal. I've told Nina to see what develops from her trip. Tell Miche the same, Bob.'

'If it passes that litmus test, it's in?' grinned Bob.

'Not if I don't like it,' snapped Ali. 'I'll wait and read what they deliver first.'

'Can we move on?' interjected Larissa. She sensed the mood of discomfort in the room. She knew the decision was a touchy issue with the staff writers and contributors, who did a lot of work only to have it tossed away by Ali. Larissa knew Ali was good at making some judgements, especially when the finished article was put before her. But she seemed less sure about hypothetical, philosophical and speculative thoughts on story ideas. Ali was not a polished writer, yet she picked over articles making the writer redo whole chunks for obscure or pedantic reasons.

For the first time, Ali was unwittingly sharing a sense of disquiet with the rest of the staff. They too were thinking of family hiccups, family secrets, family upheavals. It was universal. Just never shared. Miche and Nina were tapping into a nerve that jangled in all their systems.

Ali moved on, turning her attention to Reg Craven. 'What the hell is this?' She waved a mock-up of an ad showing an older woman rocking with laughter. The headline read, 'Have you pissed yourself lately?'

There was an intake of breath around the table.

'It's an ad for a new health company. For incontinence pads,' he said as matter-of-factly as he could.

Several people burst into laughter. A few were appalled.

'I don't understand,' said Larissa.

'It's an Aussie expression . . . when you laugh so much you wet your pants,' explained Reg.

'Reg, that's so tacky,' interjected Fran Hirshcombe.

'It's not exactly the kind of classy ad that appears in *Blaze*,' added Larissa.

'What's with this old people stuff?' raged Ali. 'Dump it, Reg.'

'Listen, I know it ain't a glamorous product, but at least it's different and funny . . .'

'That's debatable,' muttered Bob.

'There's another reason. The mob behind it is a huge health care company. They're ready to advertise all their products and services with us. That's a motza moola.'

'Reg, the advertising dollar isn't everything. There's such a thing as quality control and image,' broke in Fran. 'The media will make hay about us over an ad like that.'

'Any publicity . . .' began Reg, but Ali cut him off.

'Ask them to start out advertising other products with us first. And I don't mean a retirement village.'

'Even if it costs close to a million bucks to move in?' persisted Reg.

'Leave it, Reg,' advised Larissa, seeing Ali's anger mounting. It wasn't the issue of the product itself, but Reg's manner that irritated Ali. Larissa would step in and find a compromise later. Striving for a positive note, she commented, 'Great reaction to Miche's story on Sally Shaw. Talkback radio shows have already picked it up.'

'That reminds me,' said Ali casually. 'You might like to know an American studio is interested in making a film, inspired by Sally Shaw, about the modelling world. Based on the story we ran.'

'Miche's story! That's fantastic,' said Larissa.

'It's *Blaze*'s story, you mean,' Ali corrected her. 'We own the film rights.'

'We do? Since when?' said Bob Monroe. 'First I've heard of us buying film rights as well for a feature article. And I'm the features editor,' he added half-jokingly, seeing Ali's displeasure at being queried.

'It's now in all the contributors' contracts. Remember that's how *Saturday Night Fever* started. It grew out of an article in, I think, *Vanity Fair* or the *LA Magazine*. I don't want *Blaze* to lose a potential small fortune from a cut of the profits if the film is a hit.'

'I can just see Sally's story as a film. Hot young stars, the latest music, fashion, drugs, rock and roll – way to go!' exclaimed Fiona.

'Did we pay Miche an extra amount for the film rights?' persisted Bob.

'She signed away all the rights to *Blaze*,' said Ali.

'Did she know she was doing that? I had no idea,' said Larissa, alarmed.

'That doesn't seem fair to Miche, she's a nice kid,' muttered Bob. 'I wonder what the MEAA would say about this.'

'If you're worried about the union, it's too late now. No one cares what they think, anyway. The contract is signed and sealed,' said Fiona. 'I think it's a fabulous idea. Make sure *Blaze* has a screen credit, Ali.'

Fran, Barbara and Bob, who trained as journalists at a time when joining the union was mandatory, and who believed the journalists' union had done its best to push up salaries to where they were today, exchanged glances at the comment by the new young fashion editor.

'How did an American studio find the article?' wondered Fran. 'They'd been reading *Blaze USA*.'

'I sent it to them,' said Ali quickly.

Larissa bit her tongue at Ali's takeover of Miche's story, knowing it wouldn't do Miche any good if she tried to defend her rights. Ali would dance on their graves if she was making something out of it. Belinda had told Larissa about the gifts arriving from expensive perfume and jewellery stores for Ali. April had also been receiving lavish flower arrangements, expensive bottles of wine. Belinda said April had contacted the mailroom and asked for her mail to be forwarded to her home. Ali hadn't thought of that one. Larissa was sick of the payola, the scheming, the bitchiness and rivalry. Her work was ceasing to be fun.

As they left the editorial meeting, Bob walked beside Larissa. 'What do you make of the film deal?' she asked.

'Shocking rip-off. You'd better alert Miche, see if she can have a credit. I bet Ali received some sort of kickback, excuse me, "commission", for setting it up.' Bob was angry. 'That Ali is a predator. And dangerous. I wish I didn't like Nina and this magazine so much or I'd be walking.'

Larissa was still depressed. 'I'm too soft. I should stand up to Ali more. The trouble is she goes behind your back and does stuff and it's a fait accompli when you find out.'

'You won't make it very far trying to second-guess Ali. I like Miche's story idea. I'm surprised Ali didn't go for it.'

'Maybe it's not movie material,' said Larissa with a trace of bitterness.

'Can I raise something else?' asked Bob. 'Jonathan Gibb is becoming fidgety. He is our senior writer. He feels a bit sidelined.'

'Does he have a story he's itching to do by any chance?' asked Larissa.

'He certainly does. It's a bit sensitive, which is why I didn't bring it up in the meeting. He wants to do a story on Heather Race, the bitch tabloid TV journo.'

'Why?'

'He's not telling all, but says it's the right timing. Whatever that means.'

'What do you think of Jonathan?'

'A top journo, an excellent writer and a good bloke. He's still young, but he's going to go places.'

'Do you trust his judgement?'

'When it's *his* judgement. There was an incident where he came back from a long interview with an attractive lady novelist. Told me she was different from the blonde romance writer image and was an intelligent and deeply thoughtful woman. I assumed it was going to be a flattering article after his rave.'

'And?' asked Larissa, though she sensed what was coming.

'He turned in a rather cutting piece. More than a few snide comments which didn't sit well with what he'd told me after the interview.'

'Why the change? What happened?'

'His wife was in his ear. Passed on comments supposedly from her woman friends and told him he'd been schmoozed and hoodwinked by a blonde witch. He'd look a fool if he wrote a drooling article. So he sharpened his pen.'

'With the jealous wife looking over his shoulder? What did you say?'

'I expressed surprise, but he was defensive. I didn't discover till later that his wife is known to be somewhat poisonous. And a frustrated author.'

Larissa shook her head in resignation. 'I hope you've made the point to him that in future he should stick with his instincts and be objective.'

'And not to take his work home.' Bob changed the subject, feeling that the incident showed his judgement was also flawed. 'Speaking of taking work home, is there any news on the leaker?'

'No. Ali says she has a plan that will catch whoever it is leaking our stuff to rival magazines. I'm not privy to what that plan is,' said Larissa.

'You're her deputy!' burst out Bob. 'But then, Ali does keep things close to her chest, doesn't she? Not exactly a team player.'

Larissa lowered her voice as they passed an open work area where employees were concentrating at their computers. 'When you're trying to catch a member of the team, you have to hold your own counsel.'

Bob glanced around at their colleagues. 'Not a nice feeling to know there's a viper in the nest. Ali does seem to take it personally, though.' He was tempted to add, 'And who can blame her,' but held his tongue. He figured Larissa was well enough aware that Ali was not exactly adored by her staff.

'The buck stops at the editor's desk,' said Larissa.

'While the editor-in-chief is away, anyway. See you, Larissa. Let me know what crumbs I can toss to Jonathan.'

In the offices of *Reality*, the tabloid current affairs show of the top-rating commercial television network, the producers and story editors were kicking around ideas.

'We still need a juicy brawl or someone spilling their guts. Too much poison in our foods causing two-headed babies and medical stuff,' sighed the executive producer.

'A cream that will supposedly freeze osteoarthritis and a drug to cure kleptomania isn't *really* medical,' suggested one of the segment producers.

'Who's hot, who's not, who wants t'be?' asked another of the four producers.

'Did you see the piece a couple of months ago by April Showers about the Baron's son, Jacques Triton? He's shunning the company of our own media mogul sons to hobnob with the staff. Very poor form on his part.'

'Tony Cox may be staff, but his mummy and daddy build rather large shopping malls and even whole suburbs.'

'Rumour has it Tony and Jacques frequent a few less than salubrious bars, call up their dealers for backdoor deliveries of coke – and I don't mean the fizzy stuff – while wannabe models strut in the front door.'

'Now how do you know that for sure?' The executive producer had an interrogator's edge to her voice.

The young segment producer gave a grin. 'Because I went lap dancing – in the course of research – and became very friendly with one of the bar girls.'

'Would she talk on camera?'

'For a price.'

'So what's the story here? Rich European playboy, whose daddy owns newspapers and magazines, can play up out here knowing that nothing will appear about him in print. Even rival mags won't badmouth him. People in glass houses . . .'

The executive producer raised a hand to still the chatter. 'Hold on. We're missing the real story angle . . . listen to what April Showers says.' She rifled through a stack of papers in front of her, pulling out the clipping.

Scene . . . a certain bar that moved from the film milieu to the bizoid's fave, which put a whole new meaning on aiming for bums on seats and, seen at the scene, none other than Jacques Triton, leader of the European my-daddy's-richer-than-your-daddy-set, spurning minor royal chums and local media sons, to hang out with one of the local staff and get down and dirty without having to travel far. Did they swap goss on the next move of the Yank Tank? She'd better watch her rear – the son-of is talking about making a permanent move here. And there's only room for one in the blazing editor's chair. Or she could turn her hand to novel writing. It seems to be the trend for former *Blaze* staff. Will the mag's former fashion hackette kiss and tell about conflict with the Yank Tank in her new novel? If she does, it could make a move by Jacques to stay on these shores a sure bet.

The editor looked around expectantly until one of the producers slapped his head. 'Of course. The Yank Tank. Ali Gruber. She wields a big broom. Swept out an old biddy who'd been there for yonks and the biddy turns around and writes a book about the magazine world, warts and all. I mean, how'd you feel?'

'The ole biddy better have a top lawyer if she's going to spill the beans on Gruber. Besides, nothing new in that, loads of ex-journos reaching their use-by date try to reinvent themselves as novelists.'

One of the segment producers spoke up. 'If Jacques Triton is hanging out with a hip young travel guy on Gruber's staff, then that guy might be worth talking to.'

The exec producer turned over a page in her notebook. 'Okay, so how do we stick it to Gruber? What's the drum on her?'

'New York. Aussie background, but unknown. She's around thirty. Must have a connection with Nina Jansous for her to give Ali the plum job,' said one of the researchers off the top of her head.

'Did she train here? How come we don't know anything about her? Did she go to the Big Apple as a kid, a journo, a what?'

The question was met with blank stares.

'So who do we go after? Ali, the Yank Tank? Set up Tony the travel ed, or go for the charming Jacques?'

There was unanimous agreement. 'Ali. Let's storm the Yank Tank.'

'And who wins the guernsey?'

Again it was unanimous. 'Heather Race.' She was their star reporter and she was the biggest bitch in television.

She always nailed her man . . . or woman. And brought home the story.

Heather was an anonymous-looking young woman who passed for pretty, until you noticed the gimlet-eyed stare and pointed teeth that gave her smile the look of a sly weasel. Her body had the lean lines of a girl who sweated hard at the gym and those at *Reality* knew her skin had been tanned to an impervious hide. An irate producer or a target of her brash interrogation could scream, yell, abuse or threaten her, and she merely paused and continued as if nothing had happened. Most attacks on her fizzled out in the face of Heather's obstinate implacability.

Heather listened as the segment producer assigned to the Ali story outlined the concept.

'Hmmm. That story needs a lot of digging and time,' she said unenthusiastically. Heather wasn't known for her patience – or thoroughness – in doing research. 'I'll make a few inquiries. See if it's worth pursuing.' She moved away. The subject was closed. The young producer knew better than to challenge her if she decided a story wasn't worth her talents. It irked the researchers, who did the grunt work, to have Heather tell the executive producer she didn't feel a story was up her alley. While none of the staff knew the details, Heather had let it be known she had signed a lucrative new contract and was one of the 'gems of the network'. She hinted her next move would be fronting her own show. While Heather was acknowledged as tops at what she did, even if often by devious means, most of the *Reality* staff didn't give a damn where she moved on to from here. Filling tonight's show was their immediate concern. And tomorrow? There was another empty timeslot. Television was a hungry monster.

*

370

Nina called the reception desk. 'I will be leaving the hotel shortly. Please have my account ready.'

In a moment, the duty manager called back. 'Mrs Jansous, our car is at your disposal to take you to the airport. We will return your rental car.' He made no reference to the supposed bomb scare.

Nina hesitated for a moment, then accepted. 'Thank you. I'll call the car company and arrange to settle the bill.' It would save her time. She wanted to make it to the airport as soon as possible to finalise a flight out of the country. She planned to be on the first plane available, no matter where it was going. The hoax about the bomb scare had unnerved her. Lucien would just have to change his plans and meet her. He would help her rethink their return to Croatia and work out how to follow up on what she had found. Perhaps he could say he was researching a film. In fact, maybe this could become a documentary based on the story taking form in her mind. Croatia intrigued her. On the surface it was growing as a thriving tourist destination again, recovering from the wars better than the rest of the Balkans, but from her personal viewpoint, she saw the remaining sinister shadows of an unsavoury past.

Nina dressed and had almost finished packing when the doorbell rang and the door was instantly opened by the duty manager who was elbowed aside as two men in dark suits stepped into the room.

Nina glared at the intrusion. 'Excuse me, I haven't checked out yet.' Their expressions were unfriendly. The heavier-set man stepped forward holding out his hand.

'Mrs Jansous, we must ask you to please come with us.' He spoke in heavily accented English. In his outstretched hand was a badge. He was obviously a police officer of some kind.

Nina looked at them and at the duty manager hovering nervously in the doorway. 'Who are these people?'

she demanded. 'You have no right allowing them into my suite like this.'

The other man spoke up. 'We are from a special investigation unit for the Department of Security. We have reason to believe you intend to smuggle items out of the country. Items that could be of concern for national security.' He noted Nina's shocked face.

'What on earth are you talking about?' She was tempted to instantly pull rank and point out she was Nina Jansous, the international publisher, but instinct told her to say as little as possible. 'What sort of items?' she asked as calmly as she could, but her heart was starting to pound as she thought of her grandfather's journal in the safe at Reception.

'We do not have to answer your questions, Madame,' said the other man. 'We are asking the questions, and so you will please come with us.'

They motioned her towards the door, but Nina recoiled, glaring at the duty manager. 'Ask Mr Zarvic, the manager to come up here at once, this is outrageous.'

'I'm sorry, I am on duty. The senior manager is . . . unavailable.' He looked decidedly uncomfortable, avoiding her eye as he mumbled, 'It is best you go with them, Mrs Jansous.'

'Go where?' asked Nina, thinking the whole incident was like a charade. She was in a plush suite in an international hotel, in a sophisticated city.

'To headquarters. We wish to obtain information.'

His stilted English sounded threatening, but Nina decided she wouldn't let them know she spoke Croatian, even poorly. She shrugged, feigning nonchalance. 'All right, let's be done with this. I have a plane to catch.'

One of the men glanced at the duty manager, who quickly said in Croatian, 'We told her there are no planes going out.' He sounded defensive.

It occurred to Nina now that it was the hotel manager who had told her of the supposed bomb scare. They must have been trying to keep her here. The heavy-set man produced a paper from his jacket. 'Before we leave, Madame, we have a warrant authorising us to search your luggage.'

Nina glanced back at the neatly packed, open suitcase on her bed. She lifted her arms. 'I don't believe you have authority to do this, but go ahead.'

The second man swiftly raked through the clothes, checking inside her shoes and then the lid and outside of the bag as if looking for a secret compartment. She kept her eyes on the man, avoiding the temptation to glance at the vase on the shelves in the sitting room. He then checked Nina's handbag, glancing in her wallet.

When he was finished he shook his head. The heavy man courteously took Nina's elbow. 'Please, this way, Madame.'

Nina picked up her handbag and jacket and followed the two men. She gave the duty manager a firm stare. 'Lock my suite please, and do not allow anyone to go in there. I will be back for my belongings shortly.'

The manager nodded, clicking the door shut behind them. The maid, standing by her trolley of fresh towels, soaps and cleaning items, watched them go. 'Leave that suite,' the manager barked at her and she nodded quickly, busying herself with the next room.

Nina walked through the lobby, uncomfortably sandwiched between the two men. She was grateful the receptionist kept her head down and made no reference to Nina's documents in the safe.

The men sat on either side of her in the back of a large black car as they sped with undue haste through back streets rather than the main boulevards. They pulled up before an anonymous stone building and Nina was escorted through a doorway into an anteroom with a small desk and several filing cabinets. A woman in a drab suit sat writing at a desk piled with folders. She glanced briefly at them and looked back down. There was a door leading off this room and one of the men opened it, stepping aside for Nina to go in first.

Nina froze, glancing around the room. Surely this was a joke. A farce. It looked like a movie set. Old black and white movie scenes of Gestapo interrogation sessions flashed into her mind. The two chairs facing each other beneath the stark light bulb, the rest of the room in darkness, a window of dark glass on a wall. She swung back to the two men. 'You must be joking.'

'Joke? No. I do not think so.' He motioned her to one of the chairs. 'Please, take a seat.' He sat opposite her, neatly adjusting the crease in his trousers. The other man leaned against a wall, folding his arms across his chest, a faintly pleased expression on his face. The woman from the anteroom bustled in and handed the seated man a folder. From the darker recess, she pulled out a chair, sat and opened a notebook, pen poised.

Nina frowned. 'I don't believe you have introduced yourselves.'

The man opposite nodded. 'Excuse me. I am Mr Puskar and that is Mr Molnar.' He didn't bother to introduce the woman. 'We are interested in your activities. Why did you come here?'

Nina was uncomfortable, but more angry than afraid. 'Let me say for a start, I do not have to answer your questions at all. I should have embassy and legal representation here.'

'Yes. But that would take considerable time. A lot of unnecessary delays, which I don't think you want to wait here for.'

'I have no intention of waiting here, as you put it,

under any circumstances,' replied Nina. 'You could have asked me questions in my hotel room. I am not hiding anything, doing anything other than being here on a personal vacation.'

'Is it usual to rent an apartment and then disappear in the night? Or dig in the garden when one is on holiday?' he retorted.

Nina's nerves tightened and her stomach twisted. She swung on the defensive. 'If you have been following me, or checking up on me, I demand I have a representative here.'

Puskar pointed to the lady making notes. 'Mrs Vartec is making a copy of our conversation for you.'

Nina rolled her eyes. 'Don't be ridiculous. This is a nonsense. I demand to return to my hotel and if you want any information, you should contact either the US Embassy or the Australian Embassy.'

'We will do that in time, Mrs Jansous,' said Molnar, leaning casually against the wall.

She turned to glare at him. He nodded at the man opposite him, who pulled out a sheet of paper and handed it to Nina. It was a photocopy of her passport.

'We have traced your background. We were most interested to learn of your grandparents' names,' he continued.

'How did you come across this? This is my private property. Kept in the hotel safe.' Suddenly she realised the hotel staff had been a part of this whole scenario. The hoax bomb-scare story that held her in the hotel, the evasive dance about not being able to take her documents out of the safe, how she had been hurried to her suite. Her passport probably hadn't been there at all. It was being photocopied for these goons. She recalled the duty manager, dressed in casual clothes when he'd brought the documents to her room. He'd been off duty, yet he had her papers! How had they known about her? Who had tipped them off? Had they been back to the safe since she put the journal in it? These thoughts rushed through her head in an instant but, before she could recover, Puskar was opening the folder on his lap again. With a shock she saw her grandfather's journal. She bit her lip and said nothing.

His fingers drummed idly on the journal. 'Mrs Jansous, may I acquaint you with a few facts about your former country?' He paused, drawing out his advantage. 'There are a lot of unresolved matters relating to past, shall we say . . . misguided . . . nationals who abandoned their country at a time of need, of crisis. Others who stayed chose to be traitors in their own land. A shame, don't you agree?'

Nina sat stoically, staring straight at him, ignoring the drumming fingertips. That was not how Clara had explained things to her. There'd been few opportunities for young people in postwar communist Yugoslavia. Exit visas and passports were rarely issued, the border closed. Helping them escape to travel to Australia had been the parents' great gift to Clara and her young daughter.

'Now, while Croatia today is very progressive and friendly to visitors, there are a number of visitors that our people feel are not welcome here. Visitors with links to a disturbing chapter in our history.'

Nina jumped in. 'Times have moved on. I do not have to answer to some postwar, out-dated, vengeful mob of troublemakers who only create ill will and disruption by manipulating people,' she said as firmly as she could.

'Accountability for spying and propaganda, the actions of war criminals and theft during war, do not change,' he answered smoothly. 'If such people and actions are unmasked today, it can be very political. Very embarrassing. Very unfortunate. For example,' he paused, fingering and lifting the cover of the journal. 'The documentation of the activities of certain families, *by* certain families in the past, could today be considered sensitive. And dangerous.'

'Just what are you trying to say?' snapped Nina, losing her patience. 'If you have a complaint to make against me, then say so and I will take appropriate measures to deal with it. I have done nothing but visit my homeland where my grandparents and parents lived.'

Puskar recrossed his legs. 'Let us be frank.' He held up the journal. 'You intended to remove this document from our country. You have retrieved this by fraudulent means. It has been taken from private property. And, as we have learned, the incriminating, subversive and secret information in here comes from your family. The Bubacic family.'

To Nina, these men seemed to be still living in the forties. The stamp of the Slavic personality Clara had often criticised – dour, gloomy, depressed – was evident. She wondered if they knew who Nina Jansous was in the world away from here. She soon had her answer. Molnar walked to stand behind the seated Puskar.

'Mrs Jansous. We are disappointed you did not announce yourself when visiting our country. A famous publisher like yourself carries enormous influence in the world. We hope your intentions did not include giving a poor impression of our country.'

'I had no poor impressions . . . until now,' said Nina tartly. 'I request you return me to my hotel and return the personal papers that you have taken from my possession.'

'I'm afraid that is not possible. This document can be used against our country. You are aware of its contents – or you wouldn't have gone to such trouble to obtain and hide it.'

'Who told you about this?' Puskar held up the journal, his manner suddenly more aggressive.

'If you are going to continue to treat me like a criminal, I demand you bring an embassy representative here.' Nina spoke firmly but she was feeling sick inside. The farce was becoming a frightening nightmare.

'Very well, Mrs Jansous. It may take a while. We have told the Australian Embassy we have caught one of their nationals attempting to steal items of national heritage and significance out of the country as well as spying.'

'Which country are you working for, Mrs Jansous? Australia or the USA?' Now Molnar was on the attack.

'This is laughable. What do you mean . . . spying?' Nina was exasperated. 'I'm not a spy. Look, I came back merely to try to find out where I came from. I wanted to know about my family. It is natural for older emigrants to want to know about their roots and homeland. I was a little girl when I left here for Australia.'

'Escaped you mean. You and your mother are still listed as leaving the country without a permit.'

'That doesn't apply any more! You're dragging up an event that happened governments ago! Besides, my mother is dead. Now, I am not saying another word until I have representation here. And I want to use the telephone.' She was feeling panicky. She had to reach Lucien. As soon as she could contact the embassy, she'd ask them to call Baron Triton to help sort this out. These power-mongers were living in the past. Then she recalled the name in the journal that was the same family name as one of the high-profile ministers in the current government. No wonder they were concerned. If it was shown one of his relatives had been a Nazi sympathiser, it would no doubt do terrible damage to his current image.

She looked at both men. The woman was also looking at Nina, waiting for her to speak. Nina recrossed her legs and folded her arms, her body language saying clearly that she would not speak until they had done as she demanded.

'Very well, Mrs Jansous. We will all have to wait until your embassy can send an official. It might be a number of hours, or days. Please make yourself comfortable.'

They rose and the room was flooded with a harsh neon light and Nina saw a narrow bed and a partition beside it where, she assumed, she'd find a toilet. She swung back to them. 'I'm not staying here. This is like a jail cell!'

'We are aware you are used to more comfort, Madame. But until this matter is clarified to our satisfaction, we have the right to detain you.' Molnar turned away.

The three of them left the room. Nina stood up and found she was shaking. She went to the door. It was locked. She looked around the brown-walled room, which looked worse in the bright cold light. She went and sat on the bed, glancing up at the tinted glass high on the wall. Were they watching her?

TAKE SIXTEEN...

Ali pinned up the minis – the reduced images of pages – of the next issue of *Blaze* on her wall and thoughtfully walked along them, looking at the ebb and flow of the material, judging the rhythm and pace of the entire magazine.

This was the time she liked best, when she felt most in control. This was the real thrill of being editor, when she could cut or kill a picture or a story. Throw convention out the window into Sydney Harbour and blow a picture to full page, or angle a single line of copy to be more effective than all the text fought for by the creative director.

She looked at the advertising layouts and mentally patted herself on the back for the two new heavyweight clients she'd brought in – thanks to John O'Donnell making a phone call to the chairman of the board at his bank and a large firm of innovative commercial architects who were branching into home and apartment design.

While Ali had aimed for a more cutting-edge look and approach to attract younger readers, she had readdressed the issue of mature readers (anyone over forty in her mind) by pushing Bob, the features editor, to introduce a slightly sharper edge to the writing style and the subject matter. While Larissa had described the change as beneficial – going more highbrow and interesting – Ali declared it was just lateral thinking.

'People are still interested in their own homes, lifestyles and pursuits as well as the esoteric,' said Larissa.

'So, instead of interior decor,' responded Ali, 'I've commissioned a piece about comparative religious designs reflected in architecture. Instead of boring recipes disguised in lavish layouts, we want a series on the culture of cuisine.'

Larissa ran down the list of upcoming articles – male menopause, men's search for spirituality, family health including sexual abuse, violence and Chi Gong healing. 'I think we're covering all the bases,' she commented, 'including the fashion scene with Fiona.'

Fiona had proved herself to be innovative and creative. Her appointment had raised a few eyebrows in the incestuous fashion world as she was only twenty-five – and untested. Ali seemed impressed by Fiona's creative flash-and-dash style, which complemented the new fashion editor's clear ambition to be at the top one day soon. Fiona had a master's degree in the history of textile design and was a smart, sharp writer. She saw clothing trends as a reflection of the psychological mood of where society was heading. She saw the representation of fashion as art, which in turn reflected the wider world. Her approach to fashion was that of a museum curator – it may not be something you wanted to own, but you could still appreciate its design and beauty. Or argue that it wasn't beautiful – grunge, heroin chic, sweats and trackies may not be your taste, but they made a statement. As lace, beads and couture did for others.

Ali's war with the printers continued. She had a passion for being up-to-the-minute in a news sense, which was hard for a monthly publication where unfolding events could change dramatically overnight. Ali would hold back pages so she could make last-minute changes. It drove the printers and staff crazy when Ali decided to revamp a story an instant before publication. She felt it gave *Blaze* a fresh and current feel and to hell with what it cost – economically, or in the emotional toll on those expected to make it happen.

Her bugbear, her nemesis, her sparring partner at every turn, was Reg Craven. He wielded the power of the advertising dollar, which he used as a big stick to threaten Ali at every editorial turn. He was like the school bully, knowing he had the backing of the senior management who'd been to the same school of executive training and shared a disdain for women executives. Especially young women with opinions, talent and arrogance like Ali.

At this moment, Reg felt he held the aces. After many lunches, he had a big new client in his pocket. The client – a French importer of leather, fashion accessories and crystal – wanted a big spread in the current issue to tie in with their upcoming promotional campaign.

'Reg, the mag has gone to bed. The ad pages are done,' said Ali firmly.

'So dump a story,' he said authoritatively.

'There's nothing I can drop. The balance is right, the timing and value of the stories are what I want. To change it now will upset the whole scale of the magazine. Do you want it to look like a catalogue?'

'I don't give a shit. These clients pay the bills – without their money there ain't no magazine.'

'Without the look and style of *Blaze* no one would want to advertise in it. You're jeopardising that.'

'Bullshit.'

Ali gritted her teeth, longing to grab his bow tie and twist it around his short, bulbous neck, so short it seemed to Ali his earlobes rested near his shoulders. She wondered if this asshole would use such standover tactics on Nina. She gave a nonchalant shrug. 'If you want to take it up with Baron Triton, go ahead.'

'I don't need to go that far. Jacques will do, and he's just down the hall.' Reg stomped from her office leaving Ali fuming.

Jacques was becoming a problem Ali didn't need. He had divided the staff and was eroding her power and authority. Most of the male executives were in the Reg and Jacques camp while most of the editorial staff knew their existence rested in Ali's good graces. Tony Cox, the travel editor, was the exception, having become a permanent fixture in the circle that swirled in Jacques' wake. Ali knew a showdown was coming.

She began to think of strategies to put Reg on the back foot. An effective advertising manager was a main artery in the magazine, pumping through the advertising dollars to keep it alive. But there must be someone else out there who could deliver the goods, yet be prepared to accept Ali's rule that she was top dog. She buzzed Belinda. 'Come in and shut the door.'

Belinda was always nervous when summoned like a servant. She stood before Ali's desk, notebook at the ready.

'This is confidential.'

Belinda nodded emphatically.

'Who is the best headhunter in town?'

Belinda's knees quivered. Oh dear, who was being replaced or brought in now? 'I'll check, but I believe Critchlow Burns is the one I've heard mentioned.'

Ali nodded. It was a company that was often in the business news when CEO's appointments were announced.

'Find out how good they are. I'll give Mr O'Donnell a call to see what he knows about any others.'

'Can I ask what kind of person you're looking for?' asked Belinda, trying not to appear too curious.

'No,' said Ali shortly.

John O'Donnell had no compunction about delving into her motives. Now they were sexual partners and a whole new world had opened up to him, he regarded Ali as the love of his life. He had invited her to join him at several business dinners and agreed to accompany her to high-profile receptions, parties and shows, revelling in having the famed Ali Gruber on his arm. He gently advised her, 'Darling, is it wise to start hunting for a new ad manager before you talk to Nina? Live with him a little longer – it's a pretty drastic move. Think it through.'

'I feel I have to strike some kind of blow. And I think I know how. If I make a stand and rattle him, that might be all that's needed.'

'Ali, wild Ali, I'm glad I don't work for you,' chuckled John O'Donnell. 'Now, to more interesting matters. Us. I wanted to ask if you'd help me host a dinner at my home. A gold watch event, low key and discreet. My general manager is retiring. What do you say?'

Ali's heart sank. While she enjoyed being seen with the high-profile CEO in public, playing hostess to a retiring old fart from his company didn't appeal at all. She knew she had won John O'Donnell over by being fun, energetic, youthful and professional, but she didn't kid herself that introducing him to exciting sex had been the key. He confessed he'd been a virgin when he'd married, that his wife thought sex was for making babies and it had to be done in the dark with the blinds drawn. He'd never experienced lovemaking in a variety of positions and places. Not to mention the mind-blowing experience, for him, of making love in the open air. He often replayed the event in his mind as he dawdled over budget projections.

Ali had persuaded him to take an afternoon off work – a major undertaking for he was always in the office at 7.30 a.m. and rarely left before 7 p.m.

She told him to dismiss the driver – she was taking him for a surprise. She'd driven him up to the northern beaches, parked on a small headland and they caught a water taxi across to a tiny beach below West Head.

'We're having a picnic. Take the shoes and tie off, O'Donnell.'

He'd refused to leave his bulky briefcase even in a locked car at Palm Beach because it contained important company papers. So Ali carried it, while he took the picnic basket as they clambered ashore.

On a midweek afternoon, the little-known beach was deserted. Ali produced chilled wine, poured it into two iced silver goblets, then unwound her sarong to sit naked on the sand. Gradually she'd peeled O'Donnell out of the grey business suit and persuaded him to go skinny-dipping in the surf. It was the first time he'd swum naked in the sea and he revelled in the sense of utter freedom. Bobbing in the water with Ali like a wet naked seal entwined around him, he sighed wistfully, 'I suppose other people do this lots of times.'

They had made love on a beach towel between the rocks when the tide was out, and on the way home he couldn't stop exclaiming about how wonderful it had been, how wonderful she was. She was giving him a life he thought he'd never experience. 'You make me feel young and spunky,' he whispered shyly.

Once the barriers were down, he became putty and she knew it. He liked her being independent, self-sufficient, and yet always prepared to meet him, even on short notice. His trust in her grew and he confided business details and quietly opened doors by an introduction or a phone call. He had taken her to casual and formal parties hosted by his friends, delighting in showing off his young, attractive and successful new girlfriend to his men friends. The wives loathed Ali, though they were interested in knowing more about *Blaze*.

The biggest move he made in showing Ali how much he cared for her was introducing her to his children at a sailing club luncheon. It had been a stilted and uncomfortable occasion for all concerned and was not repeated.

'So, what do you say to being hostess for the night?' he prompted her.

'Oh, I was thinking,' Ali came back to the moment. 'I'm sorry, but I have to work late, that's the night the magazine goes to bed. I especially have to oversee the final pages. Just in case there are any last-minute changes.'

He sounded disappointed. 'You have to delegate sometimes, Ali. You can keep in touch by phone.'

She laughed. 'I'm sure! There I am playing charming hostess to the retiring gentleman on my right when my mobile goes off and I have to argue with the printers! We'll do it another time.'

His voice sounded strangely choked up. 'Yes, we will. Lots. I hope. Are you coming over tonight?'

'Can't, a meeting or three. Lunch tomorrow? A long lunch?' She made it a sexy-sounding invitation.

'Board meeting at the bank. I'm on too many boards, I'm going to start easing out. No time to play, eh?'

'You said it was an excellent way to keep in touch with what was happening round town.'

'True. But I'm losing interest. Spending time with you – travelling round Europe, skiing in Aspen, maybe shopping in New York – sounds a lot more appealing.'

Ali changed the subject. 'Darling, I have someone waiting, Belinda is waving at me. Talk to you later.'

She leaned back in her chair. The novelty of having won over the very private head of a massive company was wearing thin. While he presided in his chair of influence, he was highly desirable. Talk of him easing back and letting go of the reins to toddle around the five-star hotels of the world with her in tow was not what she wanted in the least. Ali, while ambitious and manipulative, had bigger plans than a retired CEO, even if he was the head of a powerful corporation in Australia. This country Down Under was, to her mind, still a small pond.

Ali decided it was time she checked into the New York scene again. The Baron had been urging her to visit. His emails were always warm and encouraging.

She hit the intercom between her desk and Belinda's. 'Call Baron Triton and put him through, then bring me my diary and a coffee.'

Sally Shaw, Australia's new modelling sensation, flew into Sydney Airport. Without make-up and her hair in plaits, she slipped through the new international terminal dressed like just another tired, teenage backpacker coming home. At the taxi rank, she caught a cab to a boutique hotel at Elizabeth Bay. There she rang Larissa's number, which Miche had given her in Paris.

'No one knows I'm here, Miche. I'm supposed to go home for a short holiday, but the country is the last place I want to go. Come over and we'll have a blast.'

Miche was shocked when she saw how sickly Sally looked. She tried to persuade her to venture outside into the sun, to go to the beach for a walk or to meet her for a snack by the sea.

'I'm too scared a news photographer will spot me. I feel like I'm made of glass . . . everyone looks at me, sees right inside me and out the other side. And if I trip, I'll fall over and break into a zillion pieces. I'll just hang out here. Don't you know a few fun people you can bring over to party a bit? I'm trying to talk Donald into coming back for a visit. And I rang Jeremy – remember him from the chateau vineyards? He's back this week too.'

'Sal, I've only been here a short time myself. I'd like to catch up with Donald and Jeremy. In the meantime, you need to get out. I wouldn't worry too much about being photographed in the street . . .' Miche didn't know how to say to Sally that if they went out together no one would give her a second look, other than perhaps to notice her thinness. She looked gaunt, pubescent, almost plain. There was no colour or vibrancy to her and she would never be picked as a top model. Compared to the healthy, cheerful Australian girls Miche saw around her, Sally was a pale, scrawny, lank-haired compatriot.

Miche stopped by Larissa's office. 'Hi, just passing. Guess who is holed up in a hotel at Elizabeth Bay? Sally Shaw. I think she needs help. Her family lives in Queensland, her agent is in Paris and I would say she was on the edge of slipping badly off the rails. She needs friends.'

Larissa saw the pain in Miche's eyes and realised she was thinking of her mother. No one had seen how she had needed help.

'I'll speak to Ali. See if *Blaze* can help find her some kind of a health farm,' said Larissa. 'Now, what are you up to?'

'I had a meeting with Bob and he's told me how I might be able to track down my father through the electoral rolls. Or contact the Salvation Army, who will do a search for a fee. I have copies of my father's birth certificate and his and Mom's marriage certificate and that's about it. Mom had a bunch of photos of people, but I've no idea who they are, could be her parents or something.'

'How do you feel about this whole thing? About your dad?' asked Larissa carefully.

Miche shrugged. 'Ambivalent, I guess. He's a total stranger. If I find him, I'm not going to throw myself in his arms crying "Daddy". In fact, I'm trying not to hate him. Mom was pretty bitter about him leaving us.'

'Did she never tell you why?'

'No. Only what a struggle it was. Thank God she had a well-paid job. And, anyway, we were better off in the long run.'

'Do you think so?' asked Larissa curiously, thinking of her own loving father.

Miche's casual stance fell away. 'Not really, I guess. Every girl wants a doting dad and even though my best friend's father was really sweet to me, it wasn't the same,' she sighed.

'Listen, Miche, be careful. What if you find him and he's a bum, or worse? I don't think you should become involved. Or write about it. Because you'll be trapped. If you turn your back on him, he can talk to the media and they'll both accuse you of being heartless.'

'Calm down, Larissa. I don't even know if he's in Australia, dead or alive!'

'Okay. But I just don't want you to get hurt,' said Larissa. 'I'll see you tonight.'

Miche was walking back down the hallway and stopped in to say hello to Belinda. While she was there, Jacques came out of Ali's office, stopped and gave Miche an appraising look.

'Hey! Are you a new recruit?'

Belinda quickly stepped in to make the introductions.

'Miche's mother, Lorraine Bannister, was editor of *Blaze* in New York. Miche is Nina Jansous' god-daughter.'

'And I know who you are. How are you enjoying Sydney?' Miche shook his hand.

There was a flicker on Jacques' face as he considered whether he should offer Miche the appropriate words of sympathy. He decided the subject was better avoided.

'This is an exciting place. How long have you been here? I haven't seen you around. You working for us?'

'Just arrived really.'

Belinda saw an opportunity for Miche. 'She did the story on Sally Shaw, the model. Miche is looking for work.'

'Have you seen Ali?' Jacques assumed, with the connection to Nina, Miche would be on the staff. 'I'd like to hear more about the model scene. I bet there was a lot you didn't write about, eh?'

'You read my story?' Miche was flattered.

'Of course. It was sensational. Are you working on anything else? I hope not for anyone else. Would you like to go for a latte?'

Miche hesitated. She knew Jacques' New York reputation as a playboy who only dabbled in publishing, but maybe here in Australia he had a more serious influence. 'Sure, I'm still discovering the city.'

Belinda watched them go with a satisfied smile.

Lucien waved away the elderly porter, dropped an old leather bag at his feet and pressed the bell on the reception desk.

'Can I help you, sir?' The manager looked as though he'd just woken from a nap in his office behind reception.

'I'm here to join Mrs Jansous. Please let her know Monsieur Artiem is here.'

The manager twitched slightly, as if coming awake. He shook his head. 'There is no Mrs Jansous here.'

'You didn't look,' said Lucien with a slight smile, indicating the large registration file beside the dark computer.

'She checked out, Monsieur.'

'That can't be right. She is waiting here for me. Is there another hotel with the same name as this, a sister hotel or something?'

The manager's head moved from side to side. 'No sir.'

'But Mrs Jansous was registered here?'

The manager appeared to be thinking and didn't reply.

Lucien was becoming angry, an anger that sprang from a sense of dread. 'When did she check out?'

The manager pointed to his computer. 'It's down. I'm afraid I cannot give you that information.'

'What about that?' Lucien pointed at the old-fashioned registration book. 'See if Mrs Jansous has checked out.'

The manager continued to shake his head. 'That is not up to date, I'm afraid.'

Exasperated, Lucien snapped, 'She rang me from this hotel soon after she arrived in Zagreb. She was expecting me. She can't have left.' He began to wonder whether Nina was still at the flat she'd told him she'd rented. Perhaps she was there and would return to the hotel tomorrow. He hadn't heard from Nina since they'd spoken on the phone. She'd told him her plans about going to the apartment at her grandfather's old house. He wondered what had happened and if she were all right. He'd just have to wait until she came back to the hotel. 'Check me into a room then, please.'

Again the manager hesitated as if debating whether to oblige.

'No wonder Nina might have left here,' thought Lucien as he impatiently watched the manager finally pull a registration card out of the file and push it towards him. The service was abysmal. He quickly filled in the details, writing his passport number from memory, pushed the card back to the manager. He pulled his passport from his jacket pocket, opening it and showing it to the manager.

The manager reached for the passport, but Lucien held it firmly. 'You can read the details. I never let go of my passport. Sorry, but I've had a few unfortunate incidents.'

'It is our custom to hold guests' passports until departure, sir.'

Lucien shoved his hand in his pants pocket and pulled out a roll of money. He peeled off one hundred US dollars and put them on the counter, returning his passport to his pocket. 'Will that secure me a room?'

The manager's hand swept up the bills as he turned around and lifted a key from the boxes behind him. 'Twenty-one, sir.'

Lucien paced about the room. He didn't unpack, but ordered coffee and a light meal. He'd avoided eating on the flight, hoping to share a celebratory meal with Nina. While waiting for room service, he picked up the phone and rang his Paris office to check his messages on his private number.

His heart leapt as he heard Nina's voice. 'This is a message for Lucien from Nina. Don't come to Zagreb, I'm taking the first plane out, probably to France . . . or Italy. I've found more than I expected. There's no trouble, but I want to come back. I'd like you with me . . . for lots of reasons. Not just because I love you. If you return in time, call me at the hotel. I'm in room twenty-six. Otherwise,

I'll try calling you from the airport and give you my destination and you can meet me there. Bye, darling.'

But, wondered Lucien, why had she never called him from the airport . . . Had she just not been able to contact him? Then she would have left another message on his machine. Had she flown back to France? There was something wrong with that phone call, thought Lucien. Why would she want to come back later with him, when he was meant to be joining her now? And what was it she had found?

Number twenty-six would be down the hall. Excitedly, Lucien opened his door and couldn't help looking up and down the hallway. A maid's trolley stood at one end, no one was around. He found the room marked Suite 26 and tapped on the door. There was no answer. He knocked more firmly, trying the door handle. 'Nina?' he called softly as he rattled the locked door. Disappointed he turned away and found the maid holding a set of folded towels and watching him curiously.

He gave an embarrassed smile, then asked, 'Are you going inside?' He spoke in English, and when she shook her head he pointed at the door making opening gestures. Again she shook her head. There was something in her expression that made Lucien persist and he pointed to his wedding finger saying 'ring' and 'husband' and crossed his hands over his heart indicating love and pointed at the door. 'Mrs Jansous.'

The maid looked frightened and glanced around and then nodded her head.

'You do know the lady in there? Where is she? Please let me in.' He spoke in French.

'*Deutsch?*'

'German? You understand German?' He repeated his question, adding, 'She is my wife.' The words tasted wonderful.

The maid swiftly opened the door with her master key and Lucien strode through the suite. 'My God.' Instantly he saw Nina's suitcase on the bed. He swung back to the maid. 'What happened? Where has she gone? They told me she had checked out.'

The maid answered in fluent German. 'They took her away. Two men came with the manager and she left with them.'

'What sort of men? When?' Lucien's head and heart began to pound.

'I don't know . . . they looked like official men. She said she would be back when she'd sorted out a problem. But that was yesterday. She told the manager not to touch anything in her room.'

Lucien checked the suite again. Nina's message said she was leaving, so she must have been preparing to leave when she was detained. But by whom?

'I'll speak to the manager. Thank you.' He thrust twenty dollars in her hand. 'What is your name?'

'Greta. Please, don't mention I told you this. That I opened the door . . .'

'Of course not. Thank you.' Glancing over his shoulder, he hurried back to his room, poured a drink, then carefully began to examine the situation from every angle.

Something had gone badly wrong, he concluded, and it involved the hotel management. He let in the room-service waiter and then ate his meal, trying to think how to tackle the manager without putting Greta's job at risk.

Lucien returned to the lobby and waited until the manager had finished with a guest. There were few people about.

'Sir, can I ask you about Mrs Jansous? I have telephoned my office and there is a message from her telling me she had two visitors here at the hotel. They were brought to her suite by the manager. Perhaps you can tell me who they were, it might help me work out where she . . .'

The manager's head waggled again. 'Not me, sir. Not me, sir. I am just the duty manager. The hotel manager, he knows these sorts of details. He is not here.'

'Then find him for me. This is rather urgent.'

'That is not possible, sir. Tonight. He will be here tonight. Possibly tomorrow.' The man's face started to flush. Lucien didn't believe him.

'Phone him. Or I'm calling the police.'

'Sir, he may be out. It is his day off.'

'Then try,' said Lucien fiercely.

The duty manager dialled, spoke rapidly, listened for a moment and hung up. 'His wife says he is not at home. He will be here at 9 a.m. tomorrow. I am sorry sir, that is all I can do.'

Lucien turned away. He was loathe to call the police, Nina may not want to draw attention to herself. Slowly he returned to his room.

Nina was dozing as best she could under the relentless harsh light. Basic meals were delivered by a young man who nodded, then retreated quickly, never speaking a word. Molnar and Puskar came and continued questioning her, promising that an embassy representative was on the way. Nina lost track of time, not knowing if it was day or night. The constant light was a form of torture that drained her of energy and a will to argue.

She kept repeating, 'I can't tell you any more. I had

395

no knowledge of what my grandfather did. My mother merely wanted her family possessions for sentimental reasons. What harm is it now?'

She never received an answer. They rattled off names mentioned in the journal.

Nina could only shake her head. 'I know nothing of these people.'

And then came the question that for Nina illuminated this whole interrogation.

'But what do you intend to *do* with this document, Mrs Jansous?'

'Nothing. I have no children to pass on this heirloom to. Perhaps donate it to a library. But that is my choice.'

'I don't believe it is.' Molnar leaned closer to where Nina was sitting on the hard, narrow bed. 'We believe you have been used to obtain this material in order to embarrass our country.'

'Nonsense. I didn't know it existed.'

'What were you looking for then?'

'Family mementoes. I was simply following up a vague comment by my dying mother.'

Puskar peered closer, speaking in a tone that suggested the playing and innuendo had stopped. 'Mrs Jansous, we are aware of your position in America. It now seems to us you were planning to make propaganda of this document in your publications.'

So they had figured out who she was, but she controlled her reaction and said quite firmly, 'Don't be absurd.'

They were not put off by the denial. Puskar poked a finger at her. 'Well, we say that a very prominent lady with powerful media connections intended to do certain people in our government today a lot of harm with this information.' He slapped the old journal on his thigh.

Nina was tired. She could see this whole long interrogation was heading nowhere. She changed tack. 'I could also do you a lot of good. Seeing as you are so concerned about public perceptions, propaganda, whatever you want to call it.'

Puskar hesitated, cocking his head and narrowing his eyes. 'And how is that?'

Nina rallied, seeing a chink in their manner. 'This is a fascinating country. My mother always told me how beautiful it is. Croatia has suffered, but surely what is important now is continuing the progress by encouraging more tourists to come here and spend money. They will also learn to understand something of the history of this part of the world. All we ever see on TV or in print is fighting and hate. I could write about the positive side of Croatia.' She paused. The two men were silent. 'I have a friend coming to meet me.' Silently, Nina prayed that Lucien had missed her message to put off his trip. 'He is a film-maker who will take pictures. I can write as someone who was born here. That's why I came, to find out about my past, my family. Where I was born, where my mother played as a little girl, the places she took me as a baby. Where she went on a honeymoon with my father – the Dalmatian coast, which she loved.' Nina paused for breath. 'You might call it propaganda. I call it public relations . . . a good news story.'

'How do we know you will not write negative stories?'

'Why should I? Unless I write about this . . .' Nina was about to shout interrogation, enforced, illegal, damned imprisonment, but she held her temper and forced a smile saying instead, '. . . this little misunderstanding. We both have a choice.'

Molnar rose. 'We will consider this suggestion.'

'We will discuss matters with your embassy. There will have to be agreements,' added Puskar.

They left her alone. Nina reached for her handbag,

which, after checking, they had allowed her to keep. She took out her notebook and began writing. Her story for *Blaze* was taking on an extra dimension.

Lucien couldn't sleep. He worried that hours were ticking by. He hated not being able to take any action. He lifted the phone and rang *Blaze Australia*, asking for the editor.

'Hello, Ms Gruber, this is Lucien Artiem, I'm a close friend of Nina Jansous. We were travelling together and we arranged to meet in Zagreb. Now she seems to have disappeared.'

'What makes you say that?' asked Ali, somewhat taken aback.

'She has left the hotel with a couple of men and left no message. It seems she may have been detained, although the hotel management say that's not true. The hotel tried to tell me she had checked out, yet her bags are still in her room.'

Ali was at a loss to offer any help. 'Look, she could have hooked up with relatives, old friends, just gone to visit someone for a day or so . . . don't you think?'

There was worry in Lucien's voice. 'No, I don't think so. We were looking forward to meeting. She would have left a message.'

Ali wondered if this Lucien guy was a panic merchant. 'So what do you want me to do? Rather hard from this side of the world.'

'I was hoping she might have contacted you as she's writing a story for *Blaze*.'

'No, but I'm not expecting to hear from her. I told her to take as much time as possible, really dig into it.'

'She left me a recorded message that she was leaving

Zagreb as soon as she could. And she said that she'd found something.'

'Really?' Ali suddenly sounded interested. 'If her bags are still there, then she must have changed her mind and taken a quick trip somewhere, and she's planning to return to the hotel. Don't worry too much about her. Nina's sensible and she doesn't like to cause a fuss. I'm sure she'd do nothing illegal.'

'God, I hope not. But that's why I'm worried. I intend to speak to the hotel manager in the morning. If he can't help me, I'll contact the Australian Consul here for advice. In the meantime, I'd appreciate it if you just kept this between us. I agree Nina wouldn't want a fuss, if there isn't any problem.'

Ali closed the conversation. 'If there's anything we can do, Monsieur Artiem . . . well, keep me posted. I'll ask my secretary to take your contact details.'

Ali spoke briefly to Belinda about a later appointment, then glanced at her watch. Bob Monroe wanted to see her. She called and asked him to come around to her office.

Heather Race and Jonathan Gibb were at a pavement café on the strip at Bondi. The laid-back surf set, backpackers, youthful e-commerce millionaires and dot-com high-flyers, strolling in casual gear along the seafront, took little notice of the tabloid TV celebrity.

'I want to do a story on your chief. You owe me a favour or three for all those contact numbers I've been giving you lately,' she said cheerfully to Jonathan. 'Does Ali live up to her Yank Tank title?'

'I guess so. She's tough, but she's smart. Ruthless – if you're on the wrong side of her – but ambitious. Most of the staff hang on for the wild ride as it's taking us all upwards.'

'Yeah, *Blaze*'s circulation figures have jumped. Very impressive.'

Jonathan sipped his latte. 'They are up and they're accurate. Normally we don't take too much notice of the numbers magazines print with their mastheads. They artificially bump them up. Take into account the freebies they airdrop over the New Guinea Highlands, multiplied by the number of people in an average household who might pick it up and read it . . . or some such rubbish.'

'Sounds like TV ratings. Now, who do I talk to for an interview with Ali Gruber? She's a dark horse. No one knows anything about her.'

'Her PA, Belinda, would be the best bet. But Ali will knock you back if you go in the front door. You're better off sliding in the back door. You're good at that,' he added with a sly grin. Heather had been outed in the rival print media several times for devious means of obtaining an interview or information. She was regarded with shocked awe by many press people. The worst cases of her unethical behaviour had been hushed up by the network. 'Anyway, Ali's off to New York any minute. Better find yourself another story.'

'Do me a favour. Let me know when she's going. What other suggestions do you have? I'd love an exposé like that Sally Shaw piece.'

'I heard she's back in town,' said Jonathan casually.

'Really? I could do a follow-up. What's Sally doing?'

'No idea. I heard Jacques Triton was chasing her.'

Heather lowered her voice. 'There are stories and stories about that clique . . . there's a club somewhere in the city where he's set up a private room for his new mates . . . sex, drugs and you name it.'

'I wouldn't know. I'm not invited to those kinds of scenes. I'm pretty dull,' said Jonathan blandly. Heather had hit a nerve with him as he had also heard whispers around town. He knew Tony Cox was part of the Jacques clique. Jonathan felt excluded, curious and slightly peeved. 'That'd be a story. But it would never see the light of day, of course.'

'Not when the mogul's son and high-flying friends are involved, that's for sure,' agreed Heather. 'Okay, tell me where Sally Shaw is and we're square.'

'I'll do my best. Be careful with Ali. I can't help you there.'

'More than your job is worth, eh?' grinned Heather. 'You gotta take risks in this business, Jon. Only way to score points.'

'I'm more interested in just hanging in there,' he answered. Life under Ali always seemed precarious.

Jonathan dropped by Bob Monroe's office and leaned against the doorway. 'Can I run a couple of ideas past you? Unless you have a hot story for me to chase?'

'Nothing cooking at the moment. Let's hear your ideas.' Bob knew Jonathan was feeling aggrieved. April Showers was constantly in the news, her column widely read and now he was probably seeing Miche as a threat, despite the fact she was younger and less experienced.

'I hear Sally Shaw is back in town.'

'Yeah. Don't even think of trying to follow that one up. End of story.'

'Possibly. What I was thinking was doing that deep-throat piece on Heather Race I mentioned to you a while back.'

'That bitch. You'd never make it past first base. No

offence, mate, but she'd eat you alive.' 'Unless you take your poisonous wife along to protect you,' thought Bob, who liked Jonathan but considered him weak. 'Besides, the TV PR machine manufactures every word written about her. They'd never let you near her.'

'I just had coffee with her. If we give her Sally Shaw's number, I think she'd be grateful.'

Bob thought for a moment. 'I take your point. Telly people always follow up on our stories. I'll have to run it past Ali.'

'I'd appreciate it if you'd try to do it before she leaves for New York. I'd like something to get my teeth into.'

Bob drifted around to see Larissa. 'How's it going? Shall we break out the booze and dance band while Ali is away? Tell Reg he has another six pages to sell?'

Larissa laughed. 'You guys wish. No, everything seems to be staggering along as usual. She won't be away more than a week . . .' she looked out the window. 'Wish I was zipping back for a week. Even a couple of days.'

'A dirty weekend with the boyfriend? You miss him, eh? Must be tough. Do you take the time to see people outside the office, Larissa? I mean, you're always welcome to come over to our place – we generally have a barby on Sundays, friends drop in, nothing fancy.'

'Thanks. Sweet of you to offer, Bob. Belinda and her Laurie are always fantastic. I think I have a nice group of friends here . . . it's just hard to maintain a close relationship with my man over a long distance.'

'Yeah, I imagine.' He remembered the good-looking and charming Gerard and wondered if he was being as true and loyal as Larissa. They had no formal partnership as he recalled. 'Gerard seemed a nice bloke,' he said, not knowing what else to say. 'Now, what I wanted to ask you concerns Jonathan. He's looking for a meaty story and he's still talking about doing that in-depth piece on

Heather Race, the tabloid TV journo from *Reality*. Looking at media ethics, that kind of thing.'

'Seems unlikely that she'd agree.'

'There's a trade-off.'

'Uh oh,' said Larissa.

'*Reality* wants to do a follow-up on Sally Shaw. Where is she?'

'I see. Miche has been in touch with her. I'm reluctant to tell you where she is without consulting Miche. It was a personal contact, not professional.'

'Come on, Larissa, we don't have any obligation to that girl. Miche did the right thing by Sally. I suspect she could have made the scenario sound much worse.'

'So the deal is Heather will bare her inner soul if we hand her Sally?'

'An interview without the station's PR people sitting in monitoring is a big step. Go, Larissa, give Jon a break.'

Larissa caved in. 'Okay. But I'll run it past Ali before she leaves. And Sally is in a hotel near Kings Cross. There can't be too many. Make sure you talk to Miche first and we do this only if Sally agrees to a TV story.'

Bob gave her a thumbs up and left her office. Larissa wondered if she had done the right thing – he might be a member of the *Blaze* staff, but should she have trusted him?

TAKE SEVENTEEN ...

Ali had capitulated and agreed to host the private retirement dinner for John O'Donnell's general manager – provided John added several names to the invitation list, even though it was short notice.

'I only planned on including company people,' he protested mildly.

'How boring. Let the office do that at their official farewell party. It will be helpful for the guy to meet people outside the company. He might latch onto a bit of consultancy work or something. It's a bigger compliment to gather a few heavies together for him than toasts from people he probably loathes by now. The gold watch is an add-on,' said Ali emphatically.

John O'Donnell caved in and marshalled an impressive guest list that made even Ali catch her breath. She'd insisted on doing the invitations for him. 'Handwritten is far more personal.' She'd cleverly worded them so it sounded like the Friday night dinner was a business function that didn't include spouses. They'd been couriered to the men's offices.

Ali had Belinda call on the morning of the dinner to confirm each was coming. 'And if they mutter about a companion, sound hesitant, a little surprised but polite, and utter something like, "Well, of course, if you want to bring so and so, we'll make a place for her. Leave it with me." And hopefully they'll back down, understanding it to be a men-only affair.'

Ali didn't want to state this outright in case it found its way back to John, who was quite happy for wives to come along. Ali was not.

She'd pre-planned the evening, especially the seating arrangement, putting her choices on either side of her. The head of a big international cosmetic company on her right, the CEO of an international airline on her left, the biggest luxury car importer opposite. These were potential advertisers she wanted to target for *Blaze*. She had worked out a strategic plan to wrest the power from Reg Craven and undermine his credibility within the company and out in the marketplace.

Two weeks previously, Ali had approached a young gay man, Eddie Kurtz, recommended by the headhunter agency. She had read about him in trade magazines as being one of the new breed of advertising IT whiz-kids working for small niche agencies that were challenging the top-heavy established organisations. People like Eddie Kurtz were dubbed the hot new contenders of creative advertising. Ali called him, offering him the job as director of promotions for advertising, answering directly to her. It was a vague title she'd deliberately coined for someone she wanted to push her barrow and keep Reg in his place.

Eddie had thought about it for a day, then accepted. Ali explained he would work with her in attracting big new advertising clients and then book their ads directly through her. With Eddie designing and managing the account, doing the blueprints and passing it onto the advertising department as a fait accompli, Ali would earn kudos for bringing in clients with money, and totally ride over Reg Craven, hopefully putting him in an intolerable situation. Ali and Reg shared equal status in the power hierarchy, but Ali intended to tip the scales in her favour. She had wanted a gay man who would stay loyal to her camp and not be lured over to the male management network.

It added to Ali's workload, but through John O'Donnell she had an impressive calling card and access to the men who controlled big budget advertising accounts.

The dinner had been a success, though the guest of honour and the occasion of his retirement was somewhat overlooked, apart from a heart-warming toast from John O'Donnell. The GM made a small vote of thanks especially to Ali for organising the evening. Ali was not expected to reply, just smile graciously, but she was on her feet in an instant, fully prepared for this.

She thanked John for making her so welcome and for the support he'd shown her and *Blaze* and she hoped they had enjoyed the evening, which was her way of returning John's kindness.

She carried it off impressively, on one hand a bright, charming and gracious hostess, while references to her professional life made it clear she was an independent, successful woman in her own right and not attempting to merely replace the late Mrs O'Donnell. It was a speech that cleverly trod a fine line between not usurping the retiring guest of honour, nor taking the limelight from John as host, but, as she candidly admitted with a broad grin, 'I can't let this opportunity pass when confronted with such a prestigious and charming group without mentioning I do have under my wing an eminent publication . . .' There was an acknowledging response that they would all do the same, indeed subtle networking had been active during the evening. Ali continued, 'I believe I can provide more than simply competitive and creative thinking – a platform which would be highly suitable to presenting your corporations to the public. I would be honoured and delighted to go into further detail at an appropriate time, so I look forward to continuing the friendships begun here this evening.'

She'd stayed the night and the next morning. Despite John preferring to stay home with the Saturday newspapers, swim in his pool and potter in the garden, Ali had dragged him into cosmopolitan Double Bay. They were soon mixing with an international crowd of wealthy socialites. This was a crowd who wore name-dropping designer weekend wear, a uniform they all recognised, accessorised with heavy gold and carefully casual hair. John felt uncomfortable, he was a private man who – unlike this company – hated seeing his name in the paper or mixing with people who wanted to impress people who considered they had gone one better than their neighbour and never let you forget they had overcome incredible odds . . . real or imagined. They all read *Blaze*.

John's family was 'old money' and he was culturally a world removed from the weekend cafélatte set. For Ali's sake, he tried to appear as if he were enjoying the scene.

Ali's boldness in speaking up at the dinner had brought in her first client, Small World, a new international travel corporation recommended by the airline company CEO seated near her at the table. The head of the company, a charming Italian, Signor Sergio Bristini, was visiting the Australian office and had asked Ali about advertising the company's launch.

Ali ran through suggestions of advertising and promotional tie-ins, special rates and dedicated attention from her team headed by the newly appointed Eddie Kurtz.

She sparkled with professional enthusiasm, making rapid notes about the clientele he wanted to attract, persuading him *Blaze* was exactly the right venue to use to reach the target market. She won over the courtly Italian who'd hoped he'd be meeting Nina Jansous. But when it came to smart business opportunities, Signor Bristini recognised the opportunist in Ali and, after a short sparring round, where he wanted a cover-line thrown in as well, he clinched the deal by asking Ali a subtle question, 'And will you be travelling in the near future, Signorina? Perhaps my company can look after you. I would say you are a lady who only travels first class.'

'When someone else is paying,' she laughed. 'And, as a matter of fact, I'm about to fly to New York.'

'Let me handle the details,' he said pointedly.

'Thank you, Signor Bristini. I'll arrange for Eddie to bring a presentation to your office before you leave Sydney. I'm sure you'll be pleased with his ideas.'

Eddie understood he was not to talk about what he was doing. Reg had regarded his appointment as another Ali indulgence in raising her profile, that Eddie would be promoting Ali more than *Blaze*, looking for the loan of couture clothes and booking her the best tables in restaurants. Reg dismissed Eddie as an Ali accessory that Nina would sort out on her return. Meanwhile, he went on with the important business of being an executive. His staff were cowered by him, he made a habit of reducing women to tears and had once made an account executive who'd displeased him carry a client's briefcase and mobile phone to the car like a trainee porter. It hadn't endeared Reg to his young executive or the client. But Reg saw it as a display of his power and position.

Ali briefed Eddie, who wolfed up the idea of a major travel corporation with delight and said he'd have a packaged campaign with creative concept and costs ready in a few days.

Ali felt more than pleased with herself as she packed for her trip. The next issue would carry a double-page spread for Small World Travel which would bring in big dollars, but what pleased her most of all was the fact Reg wouldn't know about it until the last possible moment. He was going to run a seminar in Melbourne and Ali hoped he wouldn't hear about their new client until the ads were at chromaline stage. That would cheer up Reg's staff to see him so undermined and bring her a lot of credit.

She called Belinda. 'No more dates in the diary, I'm going to New York.'

'Oh. Which airline and hotel do I book?'

'It's being taken care of, Belinda. It's business. I'm meeting with Baron Triton.'

Lucien's encounter with the hotel manager had proved another dead end. The man claimed to know nothing of Nina's whereabouts and said the hotel was happy to hold the room for madame while monsieur was staying.

Lucien made his next move. The Australian Consul had been sympathetic and concerned, and he'd recommended that they consult the American Consul as well, because of Nina's long-standing business interests in that country. The more help, the better, he told Lucien. They rang and were told the consul was at a trade presentation in a country town. An appointment was arranged at the US consulate the next morning. Time, Lucien realised, ran very slowly in Zagreb, even where Westerners were concerned.

After they were ushered into his office next day, the

young American listened to Lucien's story and shook his head. 'It's a bit vague. If it were anyone else, I would say wait and see. But Nina Jansous . . . I had no idea she was visiting here. I would have organised a welcome for her, a cocktail party . . . We would have rolled out the proverbial red carpet for her.'

'She wanted her visit to be low key. Just a family affair. She was hoping to find some link to her grandparents . . . property, personal belongings . . . But after all these years . . .'

The consul held up his pen. 'No, wait. That could be very dangerous. If she was discovered with family documents that were . . . sensitive . . . and that's very possible with Croatia's recent history, she could well have been detained by security officials for questioning about espionage activities. The authorities would not want such documents to leave Croatia.'

'Nina Jansous hardly falls into that category,' said Lucien.

'Maybe . . .' mused the consul. 'If she has been detained, it could also cause internal troubles here and these things usually take ages to resolve. The more progressive leaders have done a couple of very big deals with the US recently. A powerplant, telecommunications set-up, a highway between here and Dubrovnik, the Sports Recreation Centre, which is a big up-market tourist complex of hotels, a marina, sports facilities, that kind of thing. A lot of US money is backing the rejuvenation of tourism here. I doubt some in the government would want to upset a top US publisher, especially someone as well known as Nina Jansous. But, as in all countries, authorities don't always communicate, you know.'

'They should be claiming her as a wonderful expatriate. These security people, if they have her for questioning, they won't harm her, will they?' worried Lucien, thinking of how the nearby Serbs had treated a number of international aid workers during the recent Kosovo conflict.

The consul shrugged. 'I doubt it. I can't imagine she'd have serious information they'd want. Unless you know anything else about her family?' He raised his eyebrows, inviting Lucien to reveal anything else he might not have mentioned.

'I really can't say. She told me she was planning to visit her grandparents' old home. Then she left me a message that she'd found something, but didn't say what. And she said she was leaving the country . . . and she wanted to come back here again, with me.'

'Why leave the country then come back?' asked the consul.

Lucien had no answer and the question alarmed him. Nina must have found something important for her to want to leave the country so fast. 'What do we do now?'

'I'll brief our embassy on what you've told me, you'll no doubt be briefing yours,' he said to the Australian Consul. 'We'll work together on this since Mrs Jansous is a resident of both our countries. But I'll have to warn you, Monsieur Artiem, these things take time, sometimes weeks, sometimes months. We will talk again as soon as I have news.'

The American Consul's casual attitude had changed to a serious and slightly concerned manner when Lucien and the Australian returned.

'I've spoken with the ambassador who has just been informed of Mrs Jansous' whereabouts. The people holding Mrs Jansous have made contact with the US Embassy . . .' he held up a restraining hand as Lucien almost leapt from his chair. 'She is, unfortunately, being held by the special investigation unit of the Security Department, who stopped her leaving for the airport with potentially incriminating wartime documents. Those documents, I'm told unofficially, could also be very embarrassing to a certain local official today.'

'What! That sounds like a trumped-up charge,' exclaimed Lucien.

'It seemed the same to us. However, our embassy and the Australian Embassy have just recently been made aware of Mrs Jansous' detention and the contents of the documents. Mrs Jansous could be facing very serious charges. Both embassies have advised that no information about this very delicate matter should be released publicly. It would seem that we must make some agreement with these people. It is therefore my task to act as intermediary and negotiate the compromise.'

'Can I see her?' asked Lucien. 'Where is she?'

'That we're not sure about. We have asked that she be released into our custody. They now realise they have a rather valuable person on their hands, so I'm sure they'll milk it for all it's worth. They can delay her release while the everlasting paperwork is being prepared – a form of blackmail over us, and over Mrs Jansous.'

'Money? Can we pay them money to release her earlier?' Lucien figured if he couldn't supply enough, Oscar Triton would contribute to whatever the price on Nina's head. But he wouldn't contact him yet. Better to play it quiet, Lucien decided. It would give him more control in the negotiations for Nina's release.

'In these cases a payment of some kind is generally extracted,' commented the American with a wry grimace.

Lucien studied the classic Ivy League young man opposite. Button-down Brooks Brothers shirt, plaid jacket, navy tie, an air of having grown up on the East Coast among political and intellectual heavyweights. He'd do things by the book. It was his job.

'Listen, these people are outsiders, rebels, people with a cause – they're not going to play by the rules,' said Lucien. 'Why don't I step in as negotiator? Then we could be a little more, er, flexible. Then the embassy is saved any embarrassment.'

'I'd have to speak to the ambassador . . .' the consul looked unsure.

Lucien pressed the point. 'I am sure I could at least sound matters out, before it all became too official. Please, let me step in. It can't hurt at this early stage. This woman is the love of my life, I will do anything to help her.'

'A cool head, not emotional involvement, is called for in these circumstances . . .' began the consul, but Lucien cut him off.

'I'm here, I have access to all Mrs Jansous' friends, she will do as I advise. Please, tell me where she is. Help me to see her. Tell these people holding her that I'm your representative.'

The consul rose, speaking in a brisk voice. 'I'll contact you at your hotel when I've spoken to the embassy.'

Lucien paced his hotel room, tried to sleep, picked at room-service food and counted the hours until the consul called the next day.

'Very well. One meeting initially. You are an independent negotiator familiar with the situation. Do not make any promises on behalf of the Australian or American governments, try to ascertain what the detaining officers want in return for releasing Mrs Jansous immediately, and find out anything she has on them. Okay?'

Nina was tense but hopeful. Molnar and Puskar had finally allowed her to make one phone call – and only to the US Embassy. Her conversation with the American official was at least a big step forward. They'd told her someone would visit her at the security headquarters as quickly as it could be arranged.

Nina wished someone would turn off the overhead light. She'd lost track of the time she'd been trapped in this awful room. The clean but utility-type clothing she'd been offered, when her clothes needed changing, did nothing to raise her spirits. She'd been taken once a day for a shower by a surly woman who spoke no English and wouldn't make eye contact. She'd come to dread the rattle of the door handle, whether it was Molnar and Puskar, the woman or the silent man with her tray of plain food.

The door rattled again, but she didn't bother to lift her head, and sat on the edge of her bed with eyes closed, resting for a minute from the bright light.

'Mrs Jansous, I am from the American Embassy.'

The voice! She must be dreaming. Her eyes flew open and there was Lucien standing in the doorway looking . . . subdued.

She jumped up, but he quickly stepped through the door, putting himself between her and the guard behind him. Lucien was frowning and sending signals to her. She caught his message and said nothing.

Lucien continued, 'I'm here to advise you on behalf of the embassy.'

Nina sat back down, letting Lucien lead. He glanced back at the man.

'Leave us, please.'

Nina repeated the request in Croatian and the man withdrew, closing the door. 'They can watch us, be careful.' She pointed up at the tinted mirror on the wall.

Lucien sat and put his briefcase on the table. Nina rose and sat opposite him.

'I want to kiss and hold you,' said Lucien in a low voice while opening his briefcase, not looking at her.

'Me too. How on earth did you find me?'

'Through the embassy. Be careful. What the hell did you find?'

Nina quickly filled him in.

'Do you want to keep this journal, do anything with it?'

'Only to find out about my grandfather . . . they've taken it, anyway.'

'They might want more to release you quickly, rather than drag out the paperwork, which they can do. A bribe. If I can't raise enough, would the Baron help us?'

'I'm sure he would. But hopefully that won't be necessary. I have . . . saleable pieces in my room . . . I told them I'd write something positive. Trade off in a PR sense.'

'Good thinking. *Où sont-ils, ces objets?*'

She answered quickly in rapid French in a low voice. 'In my hotel room. In the ornamental vase. Pieces of fine old jewellery. And there's a jeweller who I met that could help us, I'm sure. His shop is opposite an antiquarian bookshop. Just a few blocks from my hotel.'

'You're willing to part with the pieces and the journal? Then no more hassle, no bad news, just tell the good news?'

'I suppose there is some,' she said ruefully.

'We'll find it. Let me strike a deal. Sit tight.'

'Tell Ali and the Baron what's going on.'

'I certainly will. Don't worry, darling. Everything will be fine.'

'I don't want any publicity. We'll decide what is released publicly. I might have more of a story than I thought.' She was feeling better and managed a stab at humour.

'Leave it with me. I love you.'

'Bless you, darling Lucien.'

He asked her a few more questions and made notes in case they were being observed, squeezed her hand, both resisting the yearning to cling to each other, and banged on the door, which was immediately opened. He struggled not to turn and look back at his beloved Nina as he left her.

Nina sat on her bed, relief rushing through her. She was about to wake up from this unreal dream. Poor Opa, did he ever imagine what problems his journal might cause? He must have, to be so meticulous in the notations and to bury it so secretly. What good had he hoped the revelations might bring? Now the war seemed so futile, it was all so long ago. But for many people, the pain and anguish and fear persisted, overshadowing the present, restraining the future. Learn from the past by all means, but some things, no matter how painful, had to be cast aside. While she was curious about the full contents of her grandfather's journal and wanted to keep this precious document that he'd felt obliged to record, at risk to his own safety, she had little choice but to leave it behind. She hoped it wouldn't be destroyed. She would never know. Now all that mattered was leaving this awful place. Seeing sunlight, being with Lucien, enjoying life. She realised her priorities had shifted. Loving, living life fully, appreciating the freedom of every day, that's what mattered.

Miche and Larissa were lingering over their dinner at the long pine table in the country kitchen of the small terrace house.

'I'm so concerned about Sally. She's taken up with Jacques' crowd and I know she's doing heavy drugs.'

'It's difficult to know how to help her,' agreed Larissa. 'You seem to have avoided that crowd. I heard a whisper that Jacques and Tony were courting you.'

Miche shrugged. 'Sort of. They're not my type. I can hear sirens going off all over the place. I liked seeing Jacques on his own a couple of times, but he's not comfortable unless he's surrounded by sycophants like Tony. I was hoping I'd catch up with Jeremy, a nice guy I met in France, but I think he's a bit afraid of Sally's crowd. He's never showed up to parties she's asked him to,' said Miche.

'So why don't you ring him yourself?' said Larissa. 'You have a connection outside of Sally, it seems.'

Miche thought back to her moonlight walk in the vineyard with Jeremy, their long talks, and their discovery and subsequent rescue of Sally in the old wine vat. 'Yeah, we have a lot in common, including Sally. Maybe I will. I doubt he even knows where I am. If Sally mentioned me, he's never called.'

'Men never make the first move. Call him,' advised Larissa. 'And speaking of men . . . how's the father hunt going?' she asked lightly, not sure if she was straying into forbidden territory.

Miche toyed with her fork. 'I've put it on the back burner. I took my father's birth certificate and my parents' marriage certificate into the Registry of Births, Deaths and Marriages in Haymarket. They wouldn't tell me anything because of the *Privacy Act*. They told me to go to the Salvation Army, the same thing Bob told me.'

Larissa leaned back in her chair. 'So what are you going to do?'

'I don't know. What if they find an address or phone number for him? That's a hard conversation to start. What do I say? Hi, Dad? This is your daughter that you walked out on twenty years ago?'

'What do you have to lose by talking to him?'

'He might hang up,' confessed Miche.

'He rejected you once and you're afraid he'll do it again,' said Larissa softly.

'I guess so.' Miche bit her lip. 'I'm thinking what to do. I'll let you know what happens.'

Larissa took the hint and backed off. 'Right. Now, to business. How's the research for the trauma story going? Children of violence?'

Miche stretched. 'Okay, it's a huge story. Bob thought it was a good idea to weave in my search for my dad, but I'm not so sure.' She moved on. 'I'll have to buy a laptop. Know any IT people?'

'As a matter of fact I do,' said Larissa, suddenly remembering young Dan who worked in Kevin's agency. 'We'll ask Kevin to bring him over for dinner.'

Kevin insisted they come to his place for a meal and Dan and Miche hit it off immediately. Kevin and Larissa gave each other conspiratorial smiles. Kevin had been relaxed about Larissa and hadn't called her since Gerard left, although they had seen each other at several functions and had enjoyed a warm exchange of news.

While Miche and Dan talked, Larissa and Kevin moved to his sitting room and settled cosily on the sofa.

'You all right?' he asked.

She nodded. Then shook her head. 'Sort of.'

'Meaning?'

She shrugged. 'I don't know. And that's the problem. I'm a bit confused about my life.'

'You need time out. A little holiday,' suggested Kevin.

'It seems like I just arrived!'

'It's a big change. And working for Ali can't be easy,' he said gently.

Larissa started to choke up at his caring tone. He

moved close to her and put an affectionate arm around her. 'Listen, I have a holiday cottage down the south coast at Batemans Bay. Go and stay there for a couple of days. You can leave on Friday and come back Monday. It's only a three-hour drive. It will feel like you've been away for a month. It's nestled on the beach, very private, just a simple place, but fully fitted out. Buy a bit of fresh stuff at the local store and move in.'

'Could I?'

'Why do you think I suggested it? I'll give you directions tonight.'

Miche edged into the room. 'Er, Larissa, Dan has tremendous ideas and samples of some fabulous new technology I think you should know about.'

'You check it out, it's bound to be beyond me.'

Dan followed Miche into the sitting room. Kevin gave him a grin. 'Is this the new generation version of come and see my etchings? I have this great new computer program?'

'Better than that,' Dan retorted. 'Frankly, the only girls who interest me are those interested in IT. Miche has suddenly identified another use for my hand/eyeglass unit.'

'Your what?' asked Kevin.

Miche laughed. 'Seriously, we're onto something. You'll thank me when you can show this number to Ali.' She moved closer and squeezed Larissa's hand. 'Is it okay if I make my own way home? Leave the side door unlocked.'

'See you at breakfast, kiddo,' whispered Larissa and gave a wicked smile. 'Or at lunch.'

Left alone, Larissa helped Kevin clear up the kitchen. 'I'd better leave too. Miche will be okay with Dan, I assume.'

'He seems a nice guy. Been through a string of

girlfriends and he's apparently some sort of IT whiz-kid. Another glass of wine?'

Larissa didn't want to leave and was tempted, but she was concerned he might take it as an overture or invitation.

He saw her hesitate. 'Just a pal suggesting you still need to unwind. If you want to dump some of your confusion . . . troubles . . . I'm a willing ear.'

'You are sweet. Seeing as I came in a cab, I will have that last glass.'

It turned into a last bottle of fine Bordeaux and Larissa suddenly found she was pouring out her heart and shedding a few tears. She talked to Kevin of Lorraine's death, of her friendship with Nina, the constant pressure from Ali, and she articulated what had been deeply bothering her but which she hadn't liked to admit to herself before – that she was doing so much of the work while Ali was taking the credit and leading a high-profile life.

'Not that I want to be photographed and made a fuss of, but a bit of recognition for what I do would be nice,' she sniffed, looking for a tissue.

Kevin dropped his arm around her shoulders and drew her to him. 'Of course you should have recognition. Everyone deserves that when they do a terrific job, and it's especially galling when someone else takes the credit. And by devious means at that.'

Larissa nodded emphatically. 'It's worse than devious. She's sneaky, with the morals and ethics of a rattlesnake.'

Kevin laughed.

Larissa smiled. 'Thanks for letting me get that off my chest. Poor Ali, it's not just me that feels like this about her. I'm her deputy and I do try to back her up. I'm just tired of being the ham in the sandwich.'

'You're tired. I don't just mean physically, you're

ready to wake up, start something fresh. Burnt out. How many years have you been doing this?'

'Too many. But I can't imagine not working in this world, even with the pressure. The alternative of going to live a conservative East Coast existence and being a wife and mother doesn't appeal at all. I'd miss that adrenaline hit. Yet . . . deep down it's what I thought I was always working towards. I've seen too many spinsters and divorcees in the magazine world.'

'I think you're afraid. Afraid to move away from what's familiar. I suspect you kind of like the angst.'

'I'm not a drama queen. I've worked with enough of them. I'm always the one trying to calm them down.'

Larissa fell silent, thinking about what Kevin had said. Gerard had often accused her of being hooked on hassles, that if everything was going smoothly then she would feel something was wrong, and that she always hung about until she found a problem. She'd never thought of Kevin and Gerard as being similar – Kevin was polished, rich, highly gregarious and somewhat self-centred. He'd created the life he wanted and filled it with the people and possessions that suited his lifestyle.

Gerard was retiring, sensitive and could be whimsically funny, a side of him only those who knew him well ever saw. He was forgiven for his reserve and disinterest in what involved others around him. He was regarded as complex. A man who dealt in money matters by day and threw paint at a canvas at night was not easy to define. Larissa knew he wasn't an easy man, but they had a comfortable understanding and had long ago come to terms with each other's personalities and idiosyncrasies. 'Comfortable,' she mused aloud, startling herself, then she was aware her head was leaning on Kevin's shoulder and he was stroking her hair. It felt comfortable, caring, affectionate, sexy.

She turned her head to look at this new friend and instinctively their faces swam towards each other, seeing through half-closed eyelids as their lips met.

It was Larissa who responded first to the rush of desire. Blindly she reached for him, wanting the fulfilment of sex to alleviate the pain, make her feel whole, desirable and in control again.

If Kevin was taken aback, he didn't show it. If he hesitated, it was momentary – he too clutched at Larissa and they fell back onto the large deep sofa, grasping for each other's bodies.

The sex was over before they spoke, looked at each other, or acknowledged what had so swiftly happened. Larissa turned her face and began to sob. Kevin wrapped his arms about her.

'Don't be upset, Larissa. We needed this. It doesn't have to mean anything.' He caught himself. 'I mean, I don't want you to think this is any kind of uncaring act . . . or a big deal. No emotional hang-ups. Just two friends sharing a special moment.' He cursed himself for his clumsy words. For once his self-confident poise deserted him. The brief sexual release had been enjoyable and unexpected and he hoped she didn't feel he had taken advantage of her vulnerable state and the wine they'd consumed. He was ruffled because Larissa was starting to grow on him. For a man who kept to pretty, uncomplicated women who knew better than to try to trap him, Larissa had stumbled into dangerous terrain – the paddocks of his true feelings.

Now he felt disconcerted, confused and unsure of himself. As they both fumbled for clothes and a common ground to deal with what had happened, the phone rang. Kevin debated, then picked it up. It was Dan.

'Hey, hope I didn't disturb you . . .' he paused diplomatically.

Kevin gave an exaggerated yawn. 'No, I'm veging out on the sofa. What's up? Miche with you?'

'No. She took a cab home. I'd had too much wine to drive. Nice evening by the way. But listen, I'm really turned on by Miche . . .'

'Wow, you just met her . . .'

'Oh, I don't mean that. Sure, she's cute and nice, but man, is she bright. Tonight we came up with a plan, an idea for *Blaze*. I think we should talk, you could become involved in this.'

'Danny boy, I'm a bit groggy for this if you're talking technical stuff. Can it wait?'

'Yeah, yeah, sure. Sorry to disturb you. But hell, we figured out tonight a whole new way of delivering, accessing and selling a magazine like *Blaze*.'

'Hmmm. Okay. Let's join up tomorrow for lunch. It's Saturday, so we can have a leisurely one. Miche, you, me and Larissa, okay?'

Larissa was glad of the diversion. But nervous at seeing Kevin again so soon. 'Lunch tomorrow . . . I'm not sure. Look, if I can't make it, I'll ask Miche to brief me on what the story is.'

Kevin smiled at her, seeing through her excuse, but understanding her feelings.

As the taxi pulled up outside his house, he kissed her tenderly, saying softly, 'Don't leave it too long before we see each other. It's all right, really.'

She mumbled goodnight. He really did understand. He was nice. She leaned back in the cab and thought of Gerard and was overcome with pangs of guilt and tears rolled down her cheeks. By the time she arrived home, the remorse had turned to unfathomable anger at Gerard.

She hoped Miche hadn't waited up. Indeed, she fervently hoped Miche hadn't realised she was the one who wasn't tucked up in bed. Larissa tiptoed to her bedroom feeling like a teenager breaking curfew. And she cursed Gerry once again.

Ali was stepping into her limousine outside the Yellow Brick Road when an attractive young woman stopped her. 'Ali? Ali Gruber?'

'Excuse me, I don't believe we've met.' Ali was annoyed at being accosted, though the girl looked vaguely familiar.

She extended her hand. 'Heather Race. I work for *Reality*. I've left you several messages . . .'

Ali recalled Belinda relaying the messages that someone from *Reality* had called. She'd assumed they were following up on one of their stories – undoubtedly the one Miche had done on the model, Sally Shaw. It was an explosive piece that had caused a lot of media comment. TV shows like *Reality* hung on the coat-tails of the print media and picked their stories up from newspapers and magazines, giving them a sensational twist.

'Is this about Michelle Bannister's story on Sally Shaw? Look, now our story has come out, feel free . . .' It suddenly occurred to Ali this was odd, being stopped on the street like in a TV-doorstop story.

'Actually, it's about you. We'd love to talk to you. We're not *This Is Your Life* by any means, but we feel you have a story, your success with *Blaze* . . .'

Ali brushed past the girl, so close she could smell her musk perfume. 'Absolutely not. If you want to talk about *Blaze*, contact Tracey Ford. She handles PR.'

'We've done that. It's about your own story, about you, and your family . . .'

Ali suddenly saw the TV camera looming over the

girl's shoulder. She reached to slam the car door shut, but found the girl's body wedging it open.

'Tom, get me out of here! Go to the airport.'

'The door's still open, Ms Gruber!'

'Drive forward!' screeched Ali and, in shocked response, Tom's foot hit the accelerator. Lightly, but enough to throw Heather Race off balance. She stumbled backwards and Ali wrenched the door shut as the car slid away, pushing Heather down on the pavement.

The cameraman, still rolling, stepped into the road to film the car speeding away before swinging back to Heather Race sitting on the ground.

She began speaking to camera without rising from the pavement. 'So what is the secret that Ali Gruber fears so much that she almost ran me down? Stay tuned.'

The cameraman put down the camera and helped Heather to her feet. 'You okay? She sure was in a rush. So what is this secret of hers?'

'Who knows if she even has one. What else was I going to say?' Heather brushed herself down. 'Bitch! She would have run me over if she'd been behind the wheel. Here, take this radio mike off me.' She began pulling the cable linked to the small microphone taped to her bra.

Ali settled into the first-class club lounge at Sydney Airport and ordered a vodka tonic. The wretched TV journalist, stopping her outside the beauty salon, had rattled her. Why would she be interested in doing a story on her now? *Blaze* was well established, there was nothing new to talk about. The fact the reporter had mentioned her family was what had upset her the most. Ali reached for the phone and called her personal publicist, Tracey Ford.

She didn't waste time with niceties. 'Tracey, what's this about the *Reality* TV show wanting to interview me?'

'Ali! I thought you were on your way to New York.'

'I'm at the airport. That god-awful Heather Race person accosted me, literally, outside the salon as I was getting in the car. Why did she lie in wait for me, why didn't she speak to you?'

'She did, Ali, and I told her most emphatically you wouldn't be interested in doing a personal interview. I'm sorry, I had no idea she'd bail you up.' Tracey was holding her head, she could lose her job over this. Damn that TV bitch.

'What sort of story? Why me?'

'You fascinate people, Ali. She said you were a super dynamo that no one knew anything about. You know how they do those probing personal profiles on successful people.'

'You bet I know. They come on like you're the hero of the month and then they pull out enemies and long-forgotten relatives to bag you. Programs like that only dish dirt. She even said it was no *This Is Your Life* ego stroker.'

'That's why I refused, Ali. I'll ring her producer. It's outrageous she door-stopped you . . .'

'Never mind. Let it rest. Less said the better. But pull out everything you can on her. Email it to me. Now put me through to Larissa.'

And have a good trip, thanks very much, Tracey muttered to herself. Ali was a difficult client for a publicist. On one hand she wanted maximum exposure – seen at the A-list functions, wearing borrowed designer clothes – yet she shunned any serious publicity that could reveal anything about her. Ali was an enigma.

Larissa listened calmly as Ali shouted over her mobile about the incident with Heather Race. 'It's odd this has happened,' said Larissa when Ali paused to take a breath. 'Jonathan Gibb wants to do a profile on her.'

'Hmmm. That's an interesting thought. We reverse the tables,' said Ali slowly. 'I gather no one has ever been able to take her on. Being a face on a top-rating show with a powerful network gives a lot of protection. What sort of angle will he follow? Apart from showing what a bitch she really is.'

'Pretty faces who push themselves in front of a camera and never have any formal training, no ethics, no scruples, no care or responsibility.'

'Take Jonathan off the story.'

Larissa was surprised – it seemed the kind of story Ali would go for. 'Defamation problems?'

'Not if we're careful. No, put April onto it. She's been pushing to do something more than her column. She'd be perfect.'

'Controversial. Putting April and Heather in the same ring could result in a field day for lawyers. And what about Jonathan – it was his idea? He has the in with Heather Race.'

'Then he won't reach paydirt. Tell April to do it and ask Bob to find something else for Jonathan.'

Larissa gave it one more try for the senior writer's sake. 'Jonathan's been looking for something meaty to do for a while.'

'Tell him to keep looking. They're calling my plane. G'bye.'

TAKE EIGHTEEN ...

Bob called April to his office. 'You've made noises about wanting to do more than your column,' he said without any preamble.

April did a double take, glancing over her shoulder, from side to side, then asked, 'Me? You *are* speaking to me, I take it?' She gave him a disdainful look, thinking to herself, what a wimp. 'That's right. I can write more than two paragraphs at a stretch. I have a lot of ideas. Naturally personality-focused. Call me Set 'em Up Joe. I can make people tell me stuff they've never told a soul.' Bob winced imperceptibly. He was scared she'd write something too controversial. April flung out her arms. 'Sure, I know where you're coming from and, hell, we all have to answer to Ali, right? What say I do a sample piece. On a big name.'

He fiddled with a pencil sharpener in a model steam engine to cover the discomfort he experienced whenever he had to deal with this unpredictable woman. She was so self-confident, so sure of herself. Why was he intimidated by a short, stocky blonde broad, a fraction of his weight? Because he felt she could bowl him over with a small fist or a sharp tongue, that's why. 'Well, it's an interesting idea. If you can land the big names – social, business, political, not just showbiz and sports – to open up, then we could build you as the ultimate interviewer. The surgeon of zing. We certainly don't need the same chewed-over popular stuff from old files and PR people.'

April looked unconcerned. 'I'll hit the big names like you've never seen or heard them before. Trust me, Bob.'

The last thing Bob would ever do was to trust April Showers. But he was still a newsman with a nose for the sensational. 'Let me give you a name – Heather Race.'

April caught her breath. This was too good to be true. She gave a nonchalant shrug. 'She may not agree.'

'I've fixed it,' said Bob pleased to one-up her. 'Call her personal publicist at the station.'

Ali felt a different person being back in New York. On one hand there was anonymity, on the other a sense of being where the power and action was. And she was back with a raised sense of her own power. Australia might be on the periphery of New Yorkers' sensibilities, but her position as editor of *Blaze Australia* gave her entrée to the top levels of New York publishing, media and society. Thanks especially to Baron Triton.

She felt at home here and cruised Fifth Avenue, delighted by the second looks she received and shop assistants in Bendel's and Saks asking where she'd bought her 'darling shoes and such a fabulous outfit'. Ali was travelling with complimentary clothes from her favourite Australian designers, Brave, Saba, Scanlan & Theodore. Tracey Ford had set up a permanent personal shopper for

Ali and she delivered a selection of clothes, accessories and jewellery to Ali each month. They were borrowed from the designers only too happy to have their clothes seen on a top editor and photographed at smart functions. Now Ali was looking forward to shopping in Manhattan's NoLIta district, to trawl through treasures in the funky and gorgeous one-off shops. These outfits, and especially the shoes and bags, would stand out in Sydney.

Ali had already had her first meeting with the Baron at Triton headquarters. Nina's name had not come up, so Ali didn't raise it. She'd also joined the Baron at a board meeting to report on what was happening with *Blaze* in Australia. This evening she had been invited to dine with him at a small private party at his penthouse.

When Ali arrived, no other guests were present, though the table was set for ten. The Baron kissed Ali on both cheeks and ushered her into his study. The butler brought them champagne.

'So, Ali, are you enjoying being back in New York? Or has your old country claimed your heart?'

'I am doing time in Sydney purely for professional reasons. I think of New York as home.'

The Baron gave her a slight smile. 'No gentleman in your life, here or there?'

'Not in a romantic sense. I find men in my age group a bit boring. I have enough men in my life at *Blaze*. One in particular.' She wrinkled her nose and gave a mock wince of pain.

'Ah, let me guess. Would it be someone senior on your staff?' The Baron could imagine Ali locking horns with male management. 'I hope it's not my son,' he added as an afterthought.

'Jacques and I have our differences on occasion,' said Ali frankly. 'But he leaves the running of the magazine to me. No, I have more of a problem with the advertising manager. I have been bringing in clients with large accounts myself, which he seems to resent. A power and ego trip, I guess. My concern is the bottom line. The more dollars we rake in, the more I can do with, and for, *Blaze*.'

'That's very enterprising of you to attract clients.' The Baron gently steered the conversation away from business to the current theatre scene in New York.

Ali expressed her own enthusiasm and how she had missed the Broadway and off-Broadway plays. She had made her point about Reg Craven. Small pebbles in a pond would cause a bigger ripple to hit its banks eventually.

The Baron took up her hint about the theatre. 'Perhaps you would like to join me for the opening night of *Ambrosia* tomorrow evening?'

Ali accepted graciously, in the same friendly manner the invitation was extended by the courtly Baron.

Over dinner Ali was the centre of attention. She was the youngest by far at the table and was surprised there was no one else there from Triton. The sophisticated group of the Baron's friends asked questions about Australia, which was considered the hot new destination for tourists and corporate investors. Ali was informed and entertaining. She'd had Tracey email her each morning an updated digest of each day's Australian news – financial, political, sport and entertainment, latest polls and comment – to keep her abreast of events for occasions such as this. She knew she was impressing the businessmen at the table, while the wives wondered about the relationship between Ali and the Baron. It had always been Nina seated at the Baron's right.

To Ali's right was one of New York's favourite sons, Winston Hauser, an author of several controversial books – one on an undercover agent who'd worked with the Mafia and had turned state's evidence at a drug-boss trial and, despite sinking into the witness protection program, had been outed and murdered. Many believed Winston's book had been the man's death warrant. Another of his works was about a gay longshoreman leader. It had made startling revelations about the water-front workers and had provoked a mayoral inquiry. Winston had moved to the West Coast at the suggestion of the police commissioner, but he didn't soak up the sun and keep silent as advised. Instead, he cast his caustic eye on Hollywood and wrote a searing, satirical novel where thinly disguised celebrities were pilloried on the tip of his lethal pen.

Ali found the older man supercilious, cynical, rapier-tongued and arrogant. She liked him instantly. 'I don't suppose a visit to Australia has ever loomed on your horizon?' she asked.

'God, what for?' He raised a quizzical eyebrow. 'Mind you, dear heart, I'll do anything for money. What are you offering?'

Ali thought swiftly. 'Come over, give us your eye on Oz.'

He chuckled. 'Oz . . . is that what you call Australia? Hmmm, Winston, The Wizard of Oz . . . that could be me. But what would I write about? I'm tired and bored with serious stories. Hollywood was a buzz, but I've done that. Who are your celebs, darling?'

'The nouveau riche,' said Ali quickly. 'Money – newly acquired by fair and foul means. The old money hates to be in the press, which always makes them more desirable.'

Winston clapped his hands to his head. 'None of them are desirable. I am SOOO bored with that scene. I want to run away and live in an igloo for a while. But, a social scribe would add a cachet to your magazine, darling. A society scribe, not a gossip-monger.'

Ali jumped in. 'The whole world loves gossip. We have a gossip columnist. I believe you could easily outdo Suzy's column in W . . . being outrageous and quite vile in your witty indomitable style.'

'Wouldn't the socialites in Sydney hate to be portrayed that way?' asked a woman at the far end of the table. 'That's not Suzy's style.'

'You have to find a vile bitch,' said Winston cheerfully. 'The ruder she is about them, the more they'll want to read the magazine, despite their professed indignation.'

'Could boost sales,' mused Ali. 'Everybody will be talking about who's been savaged . . . and whose party's hailed . . . or failed!' She glanced at the Baron. 'What do you think, Oscar?' It was the first time she'd used his Christian name and he didn't appear to notice. Everyone at the table noted the familiarity.

'It's your call.' Then, as if not to appear unsupportive, he asked, 'What is the social scene in Australia these days?'

'Parochial,' answered Ali. 'It took itself very seriously in the old days, Lady this and Sir that. All very toffy and British. Then Australia brought in refugees from Europe and suddenly there was a new breed of self-made wealthy. Money bought status but not necessarily class. Unlike the US, there isn't much philanthropy.' She turned to Winston. 'A society writer wouldn't cover as many museum and art collections as here – more football and TV big-time events, like LA. Imagine a full-back from the leading league, switching teams and posing nude for a calendar then marrying a soapie star who admits to a boob job and a mental breakdown and you have the best known couple in town. As I said, the true socialites are rarely seen at public functions.'

Winston rubbed his hands together in glee. 'Sounds like rich pickings for someone with a cruel sense of humour. I'm tempted, but I'm sure you'll find the right nasty bitch.'

April Showers' face flashed into Ali's mind and she suddenly knew that's what she'd do. Ask April to write a second column that was a society page with photos – a cross between the pages in *W* and *Hello!* magazine, with added spice. Ali could see the line in the sand between the gossip and the society writer with a penchant for clever and sophisticated wit. It may stop April wanting to do feature pieces and upsetting the other writers. She'd see what April turned in on Heather Race. If she gave her a second column there'd be a skirmish or three with April over money and assistants that would cause headaches with the staff, but no doubt the double column would attract more readers. She'd talk to Oscar about an increase in the budget. She had only a few full-time staff writers and occasionally guest contributors who wrote for free in return for the exposure to plug their new book or show. She still had a well to dip into, but if Oscar could see the value in attracting more up-market readers who'd follow society's doings, she'd push for extra money.

Ali was the last to leave. The Baron was tired, or maybe it was an over-indulgence in his fine wines. Ali decided to casually raise the idea of the extra column as they shared a last nightcap.

'I'm glad I met Winston. I think the society column will work brilliantly. I found Winston fascinating. Of course, I was glad it wasn't me he was ripping into.'

'Hmmm. He's far too old for you to find attractive.' The Baron eyed Ali.

'I like older men. I told you I've outgrown my peers. I'm ready for someone more worldly. Not that I'd see Winston as a potential lover,' she laughed. 'I suspect he might be gay.'

'I trust you keep your personal and professional

434

relationships apart. Never become involved with your staff, dear girl.'

Ali stood and gathered her wrap. 'I never would.' She leaned over and kissed him lightly on the mouth. 'Nor, I suppose, would you.'

He couldn't help smiling at her cheek that was part repartee and part dare. There was something dangerous and risky about this smart young woman. 'I have been known to break the rules on occasion.'

Ali patted his arm. 'That's okay, when *you* make the rules. Goodnight. I'm looking forward to our night at the theatre.'

She saw him for a budget meeting the day of the play, followed by a leisurely lunch which developed into something more intimate. Oscar Triton found himself telling an attentive Ali about his childhood, how his grandfather had started their empire and how he'd expanded it into a media conglomerate. The mention of his wealth didn't appear to impress her and she asked personal questions about how he must have felt and what had been his dreams and aspirations as a young man, as well as pertinent business questions. Ali had done thorough research on Baron Triton and knew his family background and had read every quote he'd ever made in the press.

At one point the Baron leaned back and studied her. 'You know, Ali, you and I are very similar. We tend to think along the same lines. I am looking forward to finding out more about you. If I may.'

'Personally or professionally?' asked Ali lightly.

'I believe that in your case there isn't a great ocean between the two,' said the Baron sagely.

During intermission at the theatre, Ali linked her arm through the Baron's. As the play came to an end, he took her hand and together they left the theatre in his limousine. Nothing was said, but an understanding had been reached. In the private elevator sliding towards his pent-house, Ali leaned over and kissed him recklessly, plunging her tongue into his mouth and pressing her body against his.

John O'Donnell had been a challenge, the Baron turned out to be a pushover. They both understood it was power sex. Her youthful, taut body in return for his position and influence. No strings attached. But favours to be returned.

It didn't take long for the gossip to filter back to Sydney. Tony Cox broke the news to Reg Craven with nefarious pleasure. 'Ali is screwing the Baron. By the time she returns, she might be the new Baroness. Been known to happen.'

Reg seethed, but brushed it aside. 'Old man Triton has more class than that. What's a quick lay with an ambitious bitch? He probably hasn't had any since Nina moved out.'

'Ali wouldn't stack up against Nina Jansous – even with a thirty-year age gap. But I believe the grass roots talk – that the Baron and Nina really are just good friends. Ali may not win a ring on her finger, but she'll have his ear and that's more dangerous for us.'

'Yeah,' agreed Reg gloomily. 'Does Jacques know what's going on? If not, you'll no doubt tell him. I thought the old boy belonged to Nina. I didn't figure Ali would make a play for him.'

'Come on, Reg, you know Ali. She goes for the top . . . and for the jugular . . . every time.'

Ali called Belinda from New York. 'I'm leaving here tomorrow. Any contact from Nina?'

'No. Were you expecting a call?' asked Belinda.

436

'Hmmm. Possibly.' She sounded vague. 'So are there any major problems?'

'Nothing that can't wait till you return.' Belinda didn't want to say how calm the office had been with Ali away.

Ali hung up and doodled on the Peninsula Hotel stationery on the desk in her suite. She was due to meet the Baron in the office before leaving. She'd said nothing about Lucien Artiem's strange phone call about Nina. Before she'd left Sydney, she'd had one try at ringing the hotel number Lucien had given her, but she'd never got past the switchboard, the language difference proving impossible. Nina must have turned up, she told herself. Otherwise she'd have heard from Lucien Artiem again.

The longer Nina was away, the better it suited Ali. But, then again, if Nina had been in trouble – and God knows how it could be with these Eastern European countries – she would have a hot media story on her hands that would put *Blaze* in the news. Ali's instinct for publicity and promotion – never mind Nina's safety – overrode her initial inclination to do nothing.

Ali thought for a moment or two, then decided she had better cover herself, just in case. If something had gone wrong with Nina, and she hadn't made a move, it could look bad for her.

She arrived early for her appointment and the Baron's long-time assistant, Irene, looked up in surprise. 'Sorry about this, Irene, I need to talk to the Baron about Nina.'

'My goodness, is there a problem?' Irene heard the slightly worried tone in Ali's voice. Irene had known Nina as long as she'd known the Baron and was devoted to her. It had always saddened her the two had never married. If she couldn't marry him, then Nina had been her only choice. Irene, the loyal spinster, had dedicated her quiet passion for the Baron to smoothing the wrinkles from his daily life. She exercised her own form of power. If Irene didn't think you should talk to the Baron, you were not put through. She was privy to every aspect of his life, even making bedside visits to his ailing wife. It was Irene who made the discreet and elegant funeral arrangements, composed thank-you notes, suggested he move from the old brownstone into the penthouse in the Triton building. She'd arranged for the sale of the Baron's home and hired the decorator for the penthouse. Now Irene's infallible antennae were sending out warning signals in Ali's direction.

'This is a pleasant surprise.' Baron Triton was his ever-charming self, despite the intrusion.

'Sorry to barge in. Have you heard from Nina?'

'Not for some time. I think she is deep in her old country.'

'I haven't heard from her for some time either. I've tried to contact her a few times without success. And recently I had the strangest phone call . . . from Lucien Artiem, an old friend of hers. He asked me to keep our conversation confidential, which is why I haven't brought it up until now . . . but I would rather hear what you think about it.' Ali relayed the message from Lucien.

The Baron was instantly concerned. 'Dear God, we must contact the US Embassy in Yugoslavia immediately, to see if they've heard of any problem with Nina. And Australian Foreign Affairs.' He buzzed Irene to check the time difference between New York and Zagreb. 'What on earth is Nina up to? We must make contact with her.'

Ali heard the loving worry in his voice and it brought home to her how much he felt for Nina. She was now convinced they'd never been lovers, but there was a deep, strong bond between Oscar and Nina. A bond Ali could never break or usurp. 'I hope I'm not jumping to conclusions. Maybe this Lucien was fretting unnecessarily.

But I didn't want to leave anything to chance,' said Ali smoothly.

'You've done absolutely the right thing to confide in me, my dear. A few phone calls and I'm sure this will be sorted out. It is worrying. It isn't like Nina at all. I had my doubts about this expedition all along. What purpose does it serve?'

Ali shrugged. 'The past is the past, I say. She says she wants to write about it. Maybe for *Blaze*. Possibly a book.'

The Baron looked pleased. 'Really? Nina never had the chance to spread her wings as a writer. She was a natural-born editor. This could be a new interest for her.' His face clouded again. 'I just hope her research hasn't put her in some sort of diplomatic trouble. Eastern Europe is very volatile.'

Ali didn't raise the issue of publicity for fear of seeming crass, but she saw the potential media interest if the news hit that a famed and influential woman had 'disappeared' in a former communist bloc country while researching a personal story for *Blaze* magazine.

The Baron gave her a quick embrace. 'I'll start the inquiries. Don't be late for the plane, my dear. Take my car. Irene will arrange it. I'll call you if I have any news.' He lightly kissed her cheek and pushed a button on his desk. The door swung open and Irene appeared.

'Irene, call Dixon to take Miss Gruber to JFK and put me through to Charles Brace, the Australian Ambassador in Washington. Also, find out who is representing the US in Yugoslavia.' After a brief smile at Ali he turned back to his desk, all business. Ali had the feeling that before she was out of the building she'd be out of his mind.

In the limousine, Ali put through a call to an executive she knew on the *Australian* newspaper in Sydney, rapidly filling him in on the possible disappearance of Nina Jansous.

'Christ, that would be a story. What was she doing over there?'

'She was born in Yugoslavia. She'd taken long-service leave to delve into her family history,' improvised Ali. 'If it's confirmed she has disappeared, the details will appear in *Blaze*. And you and I can do a cross-promotional deal to give you an extract in return for promoting Nina's story in the magazine.'

'So what's the embassy or Foreign Affairs have to say? She's a pretty valuable personage to muck around with. Or could she have been in an accident. What's the spin on it?'

'I'm just leaving New York. Baron Triton is tackling it from his end. Maybe you could try Foreign Affairs in Canberra and see if they have heard anything. Do you have any people on the ground in Yugoslavia? If there is a story in this, be sure to mention she is there on assignment for *Blaze*.'

The executive rolled his eyes. Typical of all he'd heard about the Yank Tank. She rings the press for coverage before finding out about her missing editor-in-chief. The authorities wouldn't want publicity, but he wasn't going to wait with this story. 'Yeah, we do have a bloke over there. I'll put him onto it. When can you confirm whether she's been detained? In the meantime, can you give a statement that she is missing?'

Tracey Ford wrote the press statement as Ali dictated it over the phone:

Concern has been raised over the whereabouts of Nina Jansous, publisher and editor-in-chief of *Blaze* magazine, who was visiting Croatia on an assignment for the Australian edition. The Australian magazine's editor, Alisson Gruber, is concerned at her apparent disappearance and has asked authorities to investigate. 'When I last spoke to Nina she hinted at a problem regarding research for an article,' Ms Gruber said. 'I am deeply concerned as her personal effects have been left in her hotel and no one has heard from her.' No threats or hints of a kidnapping have been reported.

Ali then called Belinda. 'This is confidential for the moment. Don't panic. I'm about to arrive at JFK and leave, but there is a bit of a problem. No one has heard from Nina. Her friend is concerned as she hasn't met him as arranged.'

Belinda gasped. 'Oh my God. Nina! What's happened? What can we do?'

'The Baron is on the case. Probably nothing has happened – she's off on a wild-goose chase. Her friend is there, she'll be fine. But we don't want to miss a chance of coverage for *Blaze*. It may help her.'

Belinda was shocked. How could Ali be thinking of promotion and publicity when Nina could be in trouble? 'What happened? How do you know there's a problem?'

'The story she is after . . . it appears she found more than she bargained for. I'm having Tracey put out a statement to the media, but nobody is to speak to the media about this. The Baron and I are handling this.'

Belinda was upset and frightened. Ali was treating this as if Nina were an investigative journalist she'd sent out to uncover a mystery. When all Nina was doing was looking for time out, a lovely break to revisit her mother's homeland. And by a stroke of luck she had met up with a friend from her past. How had Nina's personal odyssey become what Ali saw as a dangerous mission for *Blaze*? Belinda didn't like the idea of Nina's welfare being in the hands of Ali. She rang Larissa.

'It's a nightmare. Dear God, I'll call the Foreign Affairs Department in Canberra. And the US Embassy.' Despite her fears, Larissa was trying to think what to do.

Within an hour, Larissa had feedback from a Foreign Affairs contact who said they'd already heard from Zagreb. They'd been advised to keep the matter under wraps. But now the press had it, they were releasing some of the information. She rushed into Belinda. 'About Nina. I have news.'

There was a small knot of people hovering by Belinda's desk, as she repeated the same non-committal words in phone call after phone call. Word had quickly leaked from the *Australian* to the press world.

Walking in, Larissa took Belinda's phone off the hook and faced the others. 'Nina has been detained for allegedly breaching security. Apparently the people who are holding her will probably want to negotiate a trade-off.'

'What people? What kind of trade-off?' asked Belinda.

'Why is she being held, for God's sake?' asked Bob.

Larissa lifted her shoulders. 'It's strange. They say Nina is being detained because she was holding sensitive documents.'

'I can't imagine what,' said Belinda.

'Who is detaining her? asked Fran with a worried frown.

Tracey Ford hurried into Belinda's outer office. 'Ali has given me a press statement to release, but now she's on the plane and doesn't know this latest news.'

Larissa thought this was a positive step. 'Don't release anything about Nina until I see it first.'

'Do they want a ransom, or what? I mean, is she being detained, held up in a bureaucratic queue at the airport, or is she being detained – as in held by the authorities for questioning?' asked Bob, who'd covered a few hot spots in the world in his time.

'We don't know. Belinda, please call Baron Triton for me and let's see what he knows. In the meantime, everyone go back to work and don't talk about this outside the office. We don't want to say the wrong thing. Foreign Affairs will be in touch as soon as they know more.'

As the others straggled back to their desks, Larissa waited for Belinda to reach the Baron. 'Nina must be terrified. God, I hope she's all right,' said Belinda as she waited for the call to connect at the other end.

Larissa dispensed with small talk. 'Baron, we've heard news from our Foreign Affairs people here. Any news your end?' asked Larissa quickly.

'It appears the documents she retrieved from her grandparents' old home reveal details of Nazi collaborators during the war and implicate the family of a current minister in the government. A lot could be made of this politically in the country and cause embarrassment abroad. There is a negotiator with her working out a deal.'

'What kind of deal? Are they asking for money?'

'That is not their main concern, but it will probably help.'

'But she hasn't done anything wrong,' said Larissa.

'The security investigators insist on keeping the journal from the documents Nina had in her possession,' said the Baron. 'We are working to find a way to salvage this unfortunate incident before either side makes propaganda from it.'

'How is Nina taking all this?'

'I'm told she is in good health. That's all. I'll keep you informed, and you me.'

'Of course.' Larissa handed the phone back to Belinda in mild shock. 'Well, if the diplomatic people and the

Baron are handling it, our role seems to be managing the media. We don't want Nina portrayed in a bad light. Or *Blaze*. As far as I can ascertain, I don't think Nina has broken any laws.'

'She wouldn't. Her safety is the most important thing. You hear such stories about these countries. And someone of her calibre . . . It's like holding Bill Gates or Rupert Murdoch to ransom.'

Tracey Ford was still hovering. 'We can get positive mileage out of this, no matter what the outcome,' she said, ignoring the bristling stance of Belinda and Larissa.

'Let's hold off until we're properly advised,' said Larissa, thinking to herself, dear heavens above, where was Nina and what was happening to her?

Nina had almost filled her small notebook. She was writing down everything – events, feelings, sensations and memories. The timeless neon light seemed to illuminate episodes in her life she hadn't thought about for years. These were all connected to Clara, her grandparents and Croatia. Through the prism of a child's eyes she now saw how her mother and grandparents had lived. How privileged her upbringing had been, how wide the divide between them and others. No wonder there had been resentment and conflict. Yet she still felt that her grandfather, a doctor, had been motivated by humanitarian rather than political reasons. How she wished she could sit down and talk to them. How much had been lost by the geographical gap between them. Distance splintered families, especially when one side was assimilating into a different culture. Had she gone back to Croatia as a teenager to visit her grandparents, how hard might it have been? She was an all-Australian beach girl, with only a token appreciation from Clara of her heritage. She would have had little in common with them. But now her interest was intense. Is this why, as people aged, they sought to trace family histories? To reconnect with their past, to find a continuation, a cyclical sense of the ongoing family line, as mortality loomed?

These thoughts kept her mind occupied as she waited to hear what Lucien had achieved.

After leaving Nina, Lucien had held a brief conversation with Molnar and Puskar and returned to the hotel. He looked for Greta on his floor, but the maid was nowhere to be seen. He rang housekeeping and asked for fresh towels on the off-chance she might be on duty. Then he'd rung the American Consul to fill him in on the meeting.

'You have done well. I believe they will return Mrs Jansous to the hotel soon. Our ambassador has had discussions with Washington and Canberra. A few final details to be ironed out, I gather. Unfortunately the press are asking questions.'

'We can try to control that,' said Lucien, thinking Nina could make a few phone calls and stop any stories from being printed if they moved quickly. 'You mean an agreement over the PR side of things?' said Lucien. 'Nina has already agreed to give up the journal and never reveal its contents.'

'She will have to attend a debriefing with embassy officials before she leaves the country. The US Information Office will help with any public statements needed. I believe Mr Molnar and Mr Puskar are to be thanked for agreeing to speed this up. They could have been far more recalcitrant. Naturally the embassy is unable to assist in this matter.'

'I understand. Perhaps I can handle that aspect on behalf of Mrs Jansous.'

'Don't be overgenerous. While they realise she is a wealthy woman with influential contacts, Molnar and Puskar are members of a government investigative unit, officially they shouldn't take bribes. This is off the record, of course.'

Lucien made murmuring noises, thinking how pathetic the diplomat was to pussyfoot along the fence. If he, Lucien, hadn't stepped in, they would still be quibbling. As if sensing his antipathy, the consul added, 'When this is concluded satisfactorily, we will make sure it is known you were not part of the embassy but acting on your own as a friend of Mrs Jansous. That way the embassy is not implicated.'

'Very well.' There was a tap at the door. Lucien opened it to find Greta there with the towels.

'I need to go back into suite twenty-six,' he said in German.

Greta nodded and started looking for the master key on her belt. 'Do you know anything about your wife?'

'Yes, she has been held for questioning. Over a silly matter. She will be coming back, but I need to take something from her room.'

Greta hovered in the doorway looking down the hall as Lucien hurried to the vase on the shelf in the living room. He caught his breath as he felt the wad of jewellery stuffed in the leather pouch in the vase. Nina's bag was still open on the bed. No one appeared to have been in the suite. He thanked Greta, giving her another tip.

Lucien left the hotel after asking the concierge where he could find a bookshop that dealt in second-hand books. He was directed to one only a few blocks away. Lucien spotted the small jewellery shop opposite the bookstore and knew it must be the right one.

The old jeweller looked up as the bell over the door tinkled. He put down his eyepiece.

446

'Good afternoon. I hope you can help me.' Lucien smiled.

'If I can sir,' replied the jeweller in English.

'A friend of mine, a beautiful elegant lady, was in here last week, I believe. She had a family ring you identified.' Lucien paused, noting the old man's face seemed to close up. He didn't answer.

'Her family is Bubacic and she is in a spot of trouble. She thought you could help us.'

'How could I do that?' The jeweller remained non-committal.

'By selling these for us. She is being held by security investigators because she had family documents that they don't wish be made public.'

'Ah, The List. I warned her about these people.'

'We have negotiated a deal, but we need money. You understand.'

The jeweller glanced down as Lucien unrolled the pouch with the necklaces, bracelets, brooches and rings. 'This will bring a substantial amount of money.' He glanced through the pieces, lifting a gold chain with a medallion on it and squinting at the engraving. 'Ah, the same family crest. This all belonged to Mrs Bubacic, I take it?'

'My friend's grandmother. It is not stolen.'

The jeweller nodded. 'I will need a little time. The pieces have to be cleaned, recorded and a buyer found.'

'Could you give me a small portion now?' asked Lucien. 'I am happy to use my money, but it will take time to transfer it from my bank in France. I need the lady released as soon as possible.'

The jeweller twisted his eyepiece in place, picked up several items and examined them. He then reached for a small book and wrote down a brief description of the pieces, then went to his safe and put the jewellery in it, taking out a wad of banknotes. He peeled off an amount, which he handed to Lucien. 'I trust this will suffice for the time being. Be careful and bargain well. These people are greedy!'

It was all over. Nina signed a form relinquishing her grandfather's papers and journal. Lucien handed an envelope to Puskar, who glanced inside and put it in his pocket. Molnar escorted them from the building. A pool photographer, organised by the embassies to share the shot with his colleagues, took a picture of Nina and Lucien as they got into the same dark car. A silent driver took them back to Nina's hotel.

Nina strode to the reception desk where a young woman greeted her with a smile. 'May I help you?'

'The key to room twenty-six please . . . Jansous.'

The girl paused, hit the computer keyboard, then turned and took down the key, handing it to Nina. 'There you are, Mrs Jansous.'

Nina felt like laughing, but was too tired. 'Is the manager here, Mr Z . . . Zarvic?' she suddenly remembered.

'I'm sorry, Madame. He has gone on holiday. Can someone else help you?'

Lucien nudged her, 'Leave it, Nina.' He followed her across the lobby. 'Anyone that had anything to do with informing on you will be conveniently on leave, I'd say.'

Nina pushed the elevator button. Yes. I suppose that goes for the old concierge at the apartment. I'll never know who reported me. And now, it's too late.'

He took her arm as the elevator doors slid open. 'It's over, darling.'

Once inside the suite and seeing her suitcase still on the bed, Nina slumped in a chair and dropped her face in her hands. For the first time she began to crack and tears rolled down her face. Lucien knelt before her, trying to comfort her. She hadn't given in to her emotions through this whole ordeal. Now everything overwhelmed her.

'Darling, do you want to leave? In an hour we have the press conference we promised the reporters, for staying away from the security headquarters. Then we can leave the country. Do you want to go back to Sydney? New York? Home to Paris with me?'

Nina lifted her head and gave him a tearful smile. 'My darling, thank you. No. Now, more than ever, I want to continue what I started. Except I have a different slant to my story – looking for the positive.'

'So, they're going to look after us. We'll just fool around and play tourists.'

'I know I said I'd try to portray the good things about this country, but I don't want to do just a bit of paid-for puffery,' sighed Nina.

Lucien leaned over and kissed her. 'You'll find something special, I know it. Now we'd better call the Baron, who's been in contact with me, to let everyone know you're safe. This little nightmare is over, my Nina, let's order a wonderful dinner and tomorrow . . . is another day.'

The door buzzed and Lucien went to answer it. Greta was at the door. 'Is everything all right? Your wife?'

Lucien drew her inside. 'Everything is just fine. Nina, this is Greta, she helped me enormously.'

'*Guten Abend.*' She turned to Lucien, 'Can I help your wife?'

'Tell us somewhere wonderful to have dinner. Is the hotel food good?'

Greta shook her head. 'The hotel is . . . adequate. But my brother has a small restaurant not far away. It is excellent. He will look after you. I shall call him.'

Nina, not understanding German, asked Lucien. 'What are you two concocting?'

'Dinner, my darling. With Greta's brother. Write down the name please, Greta, and while we're away, would you move my bags from twenty-one.'

Greta smiled. 'Enjoy your dinner. I'm so glad you are together again.'

The Haven Clinic was in the Blue Mountains outside Sydney. Perched on a cliff edge with commanding views of the Megalong Valley, its misty landscape and classic English gardens were reminiscent of parts of Europe. But Sally paid no attention to the view or the gardens. Her world was encased by the walls and enclosed terrace of her suite. A clinic, passing as a hotel for the self-flagellated, it was as much a jail to her as if she were chained to a hospital bed. Staff were constantly close by, monitoring her mood swings, bowel movements, eating habits and how she passed each day. There was tai chi, yoga, water therapy, meditation, health checks and counselling sessions.

All Sally wanted was to curl up in her bed and be left alone, in silence. This was not allowed.

Sally was finding the whole health clinic scene claustrophobic. After sneaking out with Jacques and Tony for a blast, she was now being watched. She'd only agreed to come here because her agency had gone into a tailspin about how she was looking and her parents were nagging her to come back to the country. She thought it would be a kind of resort or retreat, not a sort of prison. She managed to grab a phone and leave a message at her Sydney hotel, leaving the name and phone number of the clinic in case friends wondered where she was. She'd been about to ring Miche when a nurse came into view and ordered her away from the phone.

Sally was bored, so when the receptionist rang her room to tell her that a clinical psychologist and assessment team had arrived, Sally didn't know whether to be interested or tell them to go away. 'I don't want any tests and stuff.'

'They're here for an assessment interview that's necessary before you can leave,' said the girl at the desk. 'They have a letter from Dr Brennan.'

'No. Let me talk to whoever is running this operation.' Sally had no recollection of any such plan, but if it meant leaving this place, then she'd see them.

'Hello.'

'Miss Shaw, we have been advised that this morning was booked for our little session,' the woman's voice was bright and firm. 'You may recall speaking with our medical superintendent, Dr Michelle Bannister?'

'Miche? Is that you,' giggled Sally.

The girl lowered her voice and sounded conspiratorial. 'I'm a close friend, she told us where you were. Said you might like company. Unfortunately she can't be here. Can we have a talk? My name is Heather. Don't let on about this. I'm pretending to be a therapist.'

'Wild. Sure, come on down,' shrilled Sally. 'I'm in a room in Frangipani House on the left of the curve in the driveway.'

Heather hung up the phone and spoke quietly to the receptionist. 'The doctor briefed me that Sally is a little paranoid about her privacy. We'll just make our own way over there so as not to make any fuss.'

'They all like to keep to themselves,' agreed the receptionist. 'Oh, do you know where to go?'

'Yes, we do. Come along, gentlemen.'

The sound recordist and cameraman, dressed in sober

suits, followed Heather, who was wearing a white dress and navy jacket that hinted of a crisp, professional uniform. They slipped into the station wagon that had a sticker over the TV station logo on the door that read, 'North Shore Medical and Therapeutic Assessment Services'.

Heather Race was all concern and caring charm. 'Sorry about the subterfuge,' she said. 'I work for a TV show and we want to do a story about how fabulously well you've done overseas. Miche told us the clinic is a bit thingy about the media. We only want what's best for you. I guess Miche explained how great it would be for you to tell a bit of your story.'

'Sort of,' said Sally slowly, having no recollection of such a conversation. But there were a lot of blanks in her mind over the past few weeks. She eyed the two men carrying in lights and a tripod and several long metal boxes. Her mind was still fuzzy from the pills they gave her three times a day. She clung to the anchor of Miche. She trusted Miche. She was her friend. If Miche has sent these people, then it was all right. 'Where is Miche?' asked Sally.

'She's out of town, sends her best, said she'll come round and see you in a day or so. I gather you'll be out of here then,' said Heather cheerfully, hoping this was what Sally wanted to hear.

'I will? Cool. This hasn't been the fun trip I expected. What a hoot you're here. So what are we going to talk about?' She curled up on her bed.

'You've had a lot of experiences in the modelling world in a short time and maybe you can pass on a few pieces of advice to other young girls who want to do what you've done.'

'I wouldn't do *all* of it again,' said Sally wryly. 'I mean, I haven't done anything really bad . . . I'm just in here for a rest. My life was a bit out of control. The whole scene was fun at first, but it becomes a bit of a treadmill. I don't want to look like a flake or a druggie airhead, you know?'

Her voice was pleading. They knew and she knew they knew, that she had a serious drug problem.

Heather flattered, she listened, she nodded understandingly and promised to present Sally in a story that would make everyone appreciate what she'd achieved, how tough it was out there in the so-called glamour world of fashion, and how easy it was to slip off the rails.

Heather thought back to Miche's article that, reading between the lines, hinted at a few dangerous escapades.

'Listen, Miche told us some . . . stuff. What really happened?'

Sally took the bait. 'Look, I didn't do anything seriously wrong. I just had a fun time. I'm young – and look where I was at? It all happened so quickly, so unexpectedly. Any girl would have grabbed it as I did. The trouble is that people take advantage, you're led astray. It's hard to say no to all this stuff. I'm not stupid. I don't want to look like a total victim. I made a few crummy choices and didn't pay attention when I should have. I think any other girl in my position would have done the same.'

'So what did you do, Sally?' asked Heather softly. The two men were still setting up the gear. 'Let's just talk for a minute, relax, before we do the real interview, okay.'

'God, what didn't I do? Don't put this on air, but I mean, hell, those photographers and agency people rape you. I mean, your mind, your soul, and financially. Though there have been lots of cases of physical rape. Those old guys in the modelling business in Europe feed on new young blood like vampires. Anyway, what are we going to talk about on camera?'

'How you were discovered, why you were successful, what you thought of the designers, stuff like that,' said

Heather breezily. 'Hey, we thought you might like a little present. Now's the time to give it to you – hey, Jonesy?'

'You betcha.' Out of the metal box that held cables and spare lights, the cameraman pulled two cold bottles of champagne.

'Wow! Groovy. That's banned in here. Pop the cork quickly.' Sally laughed, 'I only have a toothpaste glass.'

'We brought glasses, only plastic, but there you go.' Alan, the soundman, opened the first bottle and poured drinks as Jonesy set up the camera, peered through the Betacam eyepiece and adjusted a light. He leaned on the camera and took a glass of champagne. 'Cheers, Sally.' At the same time, he switched on the camera, but Sally was unaware it was rolling. Or that Heather was wearing a hidden radio microphone.

Sally, sitting cross-legged on her bed, lifted the glass of champagne. 'Up all their arses. When I'm out of here, I'm starting a new life. Don't know what as though,' she giggled as she gulped down the champagne.

Heather leaned forward, 'Just between us, what was the deal at that chateau in France . . . ?'

Sally loved being the centre of attention again, so she began to enjoy regaling Heather with tales of the naked black jazz saxophonist and the dwarf and the horses razzing round the dining room, although she left out the part about the old Count. Heather and the guys hooted and topped up her champagne. Soon Sally was telling one outrageous story after another.

She paused and asked, 'Gee, when are we going to do the interview? They'll be coming around on patrol soon.'

'Right. Let's start.' Heather pulled her chair out to face Sally and the soundman fiddled with a large boom microphone covered with fuzzy fur fabric. Heather's manner changed from the intimate friend to the professional interviewer. Skilfully, she ran through standard questions that Sally had been asked many times before.

Sally struggled to say the things she felt were appropriate to go on air. 'Modelling isn't the glamorous world you read about. You're put under a lot of pressure. You work up to eighteen hours a day. There're a lot of temptations out there. Unless you have someone who really cares about you, watching out for you, you can be led astray.'

Heather cut her off, switched tack and asked about her parents. 'So, they aren't into this glamour world?'

'God, no. Country people. Nice and sweet, but it's not my scene any more.'

'What do they think about you being in here?'

'I'm having a holiday at a resort for a bit. They think I'm too thin. I'm at a health farm.' She raised her glass and giggled. 'Good health!'

The cameraman made a surreptitious gesture of scratching his head and Heather wound up the interview. 'So listen, Sally, maybe we can take a few sneaky shots of you in the gardens. We need a few extra pretty shots to overlay the interview. Where aren't we liable to run into people?'

Sally rose unsteadily, the champagne had hit her hard after enforced abstinence and it was starting to mix with the strong medication she was taking. 'Oops. We can walk around a little pond. It's hardly a foot deep, someone threw themselves in the other day.'

'Deep enough to drown if you're stoned.'

'No such luck here. They check visitors' bags. How'd you manage to bring all that stuff in?' asked Sally suddenly.

'When you're a journalist, you can do anything,' smiled Heather.

Heather took Sally's arm and they strolled beneath

the trees. To an observer, a child was being walked by a thoughtful, if youthful, protector. Using a long lens, Jonesy took shots from the trees.

Heather and Sally returned to her suite. 'What's next?' asked Sally. 'Have we finished the bubbles?'

'I have to do my reversals and noddies.' Heather and the cameraman exchanged a look. They needed to film Heather asking questions in the same setting where the interview had taken place.

Alan had linked his sound gear to the camera. 'Wanna come for a bit of fresh air with me? They can do it without me.' He grasped Sally's elbow and led her outside.

Sally was confused and tired, the champagne had gone to her head. 'Sure. Whatever.' Obediently, she allowed Alan to take the lead.

Heather and Jonesy worked swiftly. He angled the camera around to face Heather as she scribbled notes, rewriting a few of her questions to suit Sally's answers. She would cut the questions and answers together in her own way, taking some of the replies out of context, if necessary, for maximum impact, even down to splicing widely spaced phrases together, making them quite different from what Sally had actually said. Pulling out her compact, Heather powdered down her face. 'Set the camera up, Jonesy. Don't shoot low, it'll give me double chins.'

'You gotta be on the same angle as her. She was low, on the bed,' he muttered. 'You have some top stuff here.' He had an inkling of what Heather might do with all the secretly filmed and recorded pre-interview material that unaware young Sally had burbled on about.

'Yeah, it'll rate well. Let me just run through a few questions and do a few nodding cutaways of me looking sympathetic, shocked, compassionate, caring, worried. That should cover it.'

'You want a shot of you pouring champagne into the kid's glass?'

'Get knotted. You do your job, I'll do mine. Here we go.' Heather composed her face and ran through a series of expressions, moving her head from side to side, looking up, pen to lips thoughtfully, hand up under her chin. Jonesy grinned to himself. Christ she was a pro. A bitch. But, good at being a bitch.

When Alan returned with Sally, Heather explained they were ready to leave.

Sally was upset. 'But we've hardly talked. Can't you stay longer? I'm so miserable and lonely in here. It's like jail.'

'Why stay then? You seem okay. Check yourself out,' said Heather.

'Can I do that?'

'How old are you?'

'I just turned seventeen.'

'Sounds adult enough to me. Listen, if you have enough up-front arrogance and balls, no one challenges you. Just tell 'em and do it.'

Sally was about to ask where she should go. Home to her parents wasn't an option. She'd consider the hideaway hotel in Elizabeth Bay as a first step. Then call Tony and Jacques, the good-time boys to organise something for her. 'Yeah. I'll do that.'

Heather pulled out her business card and handed it to Sally. 'I'll call you. Don't worry about anything. You're going to come out looking and sounding like an angel. Say hi to Miche for me.'

Heather sat in the car with the crew. 'Drive around the corner. We'll wait while you take a couple more shots, Jonesy. Do you have the little digital?'

'Yeah, the hand-held will do the trick in case someone walks in on me. Do I look like a specialist or someone supposed to be there?'

Heather reached into the back seat and handed him a starched white jacket. 'Here, put this on.'

'A doctor's jacket. What, no dog collar?' he grinned. He was referring to the fact that Heather used to have her crew carry around different religious collars and insignia to suit any occasion. It had allowed cameramen with hidden cameras into many homes and institutions uninvited. 'So what do you want inside?'

'Hospital stuff, rooms that look like treatment rooms, cupboards filled with drugs and medications, medical gear, whatever you can find that says rehab.'

'You watch too much television.'

'Shoot what you can. Alan, help me take this radio mike off.' Heather took off her jacket and unzipped the back of her dress revealing an elastic waistband holding the cables of the radio microphone in place. She unclipped the small mike from her bra. 'How's it sound?'

'Haven't checked it, should be okay. Boy, she sure was smashed quick. You're not going to take the boss's advice about talking to the hospital staff later, are you?'

'Hell no, it could spoil the story,' Heather assured him. 'Anyway there's not time for it. Two hours of her raving is going to end up a twelve-minute story. Maybe a little longer. I reckon it's a lead piece.'

TAKE NINETEEN ...

Miche had set out a work area on an old table in Larissa's sunroom that faced the small walled courtyard.
Her laptop, borrowed from Dan, notebooks and tapes
were spread around her. She slowly flipped the pages of
her notebook, re-reading the interview with Dr Friedman,
the trauma specialist. On the next page she found the
details of the hotel in Elizabeth Bay where Sally was staying. Underneath it was the number for Jeremy that Sally
had given her. Miche felt badly that she hadn't returned
Sally's calls, but the Jacques and Tony party scene was not
for her. From what Sally had intimated, it was pretty wild.
She drew a little box around Jeremy's phone number, then
doodled loops and squiggles for a minute, deep in thought.
Finally she put down the pen and reached for the phone.

A woman answered and Miche was surprised when
she called Jeremy to the phone. 'Hi. This is Michelle Bannister, remember me, we met in . . .'

'Miche! Of course I remember you. Where are you?'

'In Sydney. Sally gave me your number. I just rang

on the off-chance. I didn't think you'd be around, I was going to leave a message. It's super to talk to you.'

'Yeah, it sure is. I'm having a smoko. How're things with you, where are you, what're you doing?'

'Smoko?' she queried with a chuckle.

'Morning tea, Oz-speak. I'm at the vineyard. Working out among the vines. So, fill me in on you.'

'I was hoping to be working full-time on *Blaze*, but at the moment I'm freelancing. Staying with a friend of my godmother's.'

'Hey, you shouldn't have any trouble finding work. I saw the story you did on Sally. It was . . . very fair. I mean, you didn't hide anything, but you could have ripped into her and made her look stupid. I felt so sorry for her. I bet it was a real eye-opener for a lot of people. And Donald's photos were fantastic. I didn't want to hook up with her . . . I was surprised she even rang me.'

'She's lonely. A bit lost, I think. And mixing with a fast crowd, as my mom used to say.'

The reference to her mother reminded him of her loss. His voice became softer as he asked, 'How are you coping?'

'I'm doing okay. Thanks for asking.' Then she changed tack slightly and forced her voice to sound upbeat. 'I'm thinking of searching out my lost father.'

'I remember we talked about that. Where are you going to start? Can I help? I mean, I don't know how, but if you want to bend my ear or something, I'm a good listener.'

'I remember.' She was smiling. Larissa was right. Picking up the phone and calling him now seemed the most natural thing in the world.

'So how are you going to start?' prompted Jeremy.

'I have a copy of his birth certificate and my parents' marriage certificate. I can go through the Salvation Army, or the electoral rolls.'

'Yipes, that'd be a job. You have time to do all this?'

'I want to do it in conjunction with a story I'm writing.'

Jeremy thought publicly plunging into uncharted personal waters a risky idea, but more personal feelings pushed this view to one side. 'So when are we going to see each other? Seems to me I promised you a tour of an Aussie vineyard.'

'I'd like that. I haven't seen anything outside Sydney. Where are you?'

'The Hunter Valley . . . it's a terrific area. Two hours drive north, lots of vineyards, places to stay, eat . . . I'll send you a list of places. Or I can find someone to put you up, if you like?'

'Thanks. I'd love a few days break to be out of the city. We can do lunch?'

'We'll do that. Give me your number, we'll plan this properly, okay?'

Miche gave him her number. It was like finding an old close friend and the pleasure was enhanced as she remembered how attractive he was.

That night she told Larissa. 'I guess I'm going to take a little trip. Mull over my story idea.' She gave a grin. 'Gives me an excuse to hang around with a very cool guy up in the Hunter Valley.'

'The Hunter! I've heard that's very stylish,' enthused Larissa. 'I'm happy for you, honey. You need to build up a circle of friends here. As for your proposed mulling, are you having trouble with your story? Is your conscience telling you to drop the finding the father angle?'

'Reduces the strength of my story somewhat if I drop it,' said Miche, reflecting on Bob's encouragement to write the story of her search.

'What's most important in all of this?' asked Larissa. 'Think about it. Selling family soul-searching for the sake

461

of a magazine article? Digging up painful memories for a possibly even more painful present? Listen, put it on hold for a few days. Go visit this guy up in the Hunter, have fun, then come back and make up your mind. I'd be off in a flash to check out this hunk of a man if I were in your shoes,' said Larissa a little wistfully.

Miche knew Larissa was thinking of Gerard. She was enjoying the idea of Miche teaming up with Jeremy. 'You missing Gerry, hey?'

'Sure am, damn it. It's the old story, somewhere along the line it always does come down to a choice,' she said bitterly. 'All the women I know who have careers have had to compromise in one way or another.'

'You have regrets? What have you had to give up?' asked Miche. 'Gerry is waiting for you back in New York, you're having a terrific time out here . . . I mean, I know you miss him, but . . . this has to be a great experience, right?'

'If I were your age . . . maybe.' Larissa's shoulders slumped. 'I'm miserable, Miche. Gerry served me an ultimatum when he left – I didn't really believe him. But he's sticking to it and that means I either leave here or lose him.'

'That's so unfair of him,' exploded Miche. 'If he loves you, he should wait. Let you do your own thing. Anyway, when you go back, you'll be in line for an editor's job!'

'He doesn't want me to be a New York editor. He wants a wife in New Hampshire. With babies.' She rubbed her eyes. 'God, I've been through all this with him. He's moving whether I stay or go.'

'But that's unfair,' repeated Miche with greater anger. 'I can't think of any other way to describe it, Riss. But then, maybe it's a good thing. Maybe you should stay here. There must be heaps of men who'd grab you in a shot. Tell him to go to New Hampshire, you're staying here.'

Larissa gave a rueful smile. 'Easier said. And the problem is, I do love him, Miche. And I really believe he loves me. He just wants to move on with his life. There's a clock ticking in him too.'

'He doesn't love you enough then.'

Larissa suddenly felt a hundred years older than Miche. What did Miche know about the agony of finally finding someone who you could spend all your life with? What did she know about the scary years of thinking you'd never find anyone, that you would age alone? And then the scramble to zoom ahead in your career while younger, energetic, fearless young women surged in your wake, nipping at your heels. In order to stay in front, targets like marriage, a settled life and babies could easily drop off your radar. Then one morning you'd wake up, treading water, to find you'd been overtaken in the night. And that person by your side was looking at other women. A younger and attentive woman, prepared to throw up her career to meld her life with his. Miche was right. It was unfair. Damned unfair. So what was she to do? Choose to go to him or take a punt and go it alone?

'Why do I feel it's over when I'm facing my late thirties?' she wondered aloud.

Miche didn't have an answer. But some survival instinct kicked in – she had a decade and a half to go. She'd make sure she wasn't in the position Larissa was in now. No way. She reached out to give Larissa a hug. 'Stop fretting. You look fantastic, you're doing a terrific job, everybody loves you. And you have a suitor or two out there if you want them. Your call, Riss. Go home to Gerry and do what he wants. Or stay here and do what you want.'

'Ah, sweet bird of youth,' smiled Larissa. 'You make it sound so simple.' She stood up and closed the discussion. 'Let's go out. My treat. Italian, Greek or Vietnamese?'

*

463

Since Ali's return to Sydney, the women on staff had been trying to work out what was different about her.

'There's an aura about her that's new,' said Fran. 'As confident and self-assured as always, but more . . .'

'Relaxed,' suggested Barbara. 'Like she knows something we don't.'

'But we do know, don't we?' said Fiona, who'd been told by Tony about the rumour Ali was sleeping with the Baron.

'No. We don't know anything,' said Belinda with a warning note in her voice. Whatever she thought privately, her duty was to protect her boss. Then they all packed up files and notebooks and headed to Ali's office from the cafeteria where they'd been having lunch together.

The editorial group was gathered around the sandpit on Ali's terrace.

Ali stood to introduce a slim young man with soft features, doughy skin, a wide Cupid's bow mouth and small, even teeth. On closer inspection, his eyes were possibly outlined with dark pencil, mascara on his lashes. To offset his prettiness, he had a closely shaved head and wore one gold earring that he thought gave him a rakish, dangerous air.

'This is Eddie Kurtz. He is our new director of promotions for advertising.' As all eyes swung to the crimson-faced Reg, she continued, 'This is a parallel position with Reg, our director of advertising. Eddie has been working with me to create new account campaigns, seeking out new, non-traditional clients where possible.' She glanced at Reg. 'In addition to the work of the existing advertising and sales team.'

'So why do we need him?' Jonathan muttered out of the side of his mouth to Bob.

'Eddie, would you like to present your first effort to the village please.' Ali sat down.

Eddie Kurtz was on his feet, ready to address the little plastic men. Unlike the rest of the staff, Eddie appeared unfazed at facing the pit, as Ali's ritual was known. He immediately became a performer, playing up to the moment with a campy, theatrical air.

Larissa was quick to realise he was using this as a shield to hide a smart, shrewd mind.

He bowed to the toy villagers. 'Darling hearts, I'm here to report that the ad spread for Small World Travel has been a HUGE success, not only for the financial buy, but in creating a buzz in advertising and marketing circles. Because of the favourable response to the travel company campaign, there's interest from other companies to buy Big Space in *Blaze*. No hints now, but I have a killer I'm working on – you'll die when I tell you who it is. Just waiting for the ink on the dotted line.' He fluttered his fingers and several staff smiled as he did a little twirl and sat down.

Reg leaned forward and spoke in a furious low voice. 'Listen you little . . .' He bit back the word and settled on . . . 'dickhead. I'm head of advertising. If there's any advertising to sell, I'll do it.' Reg turned to Ali. 'What the fuck is he here for anyway? What kind of a title is director of promotions for advertising? You have a promotions lady and I'm advertising. What's he do?' He jabbed a finger at Eddie without looking at him.

'Dear village people,' chirped Eddie, leaning forward towards the sandpit figures. 'I DO, darling hearts. I don't talk, I don't wank, I don't promise and bullshit. I go out and DO,' finished Eddie, quite enjoying the stoush.

'Eddie has one of the most creative minds in advertising sales,' explained Ali. 'You're a top salesman, Reg, but Eddie conceptualises, works out a campaign style and

465

strategy to persuade a client to advertise with us because they see results beyond just buying space on the page and letting their agency whip up an ad. Eddie delivers the whole box and dice to them. It's the difference between selling and packaging.' Ali leaned towards the sandpit. 'What do you guys think?' She waited, then straightened up. 'The tribe says let Eddie have his head. What he brings in benefits the whole magazine, Reg,' said Ali affably.

The other staff all stared into the sandpit village with growing discomfort, avoiding looking at Reg, Eddie or Ali. While Reg wasn't popular, he was devoted to his job and was always the swaggering braggadocio. To see him sweating, bordering on humiliation, was unnerving.

Reg went a deeper scarlet, seeing the rise of Eddie as a threat to his power. He jumped to his feet. 'This is a load of bullshit.' He kicked the sandbox, scuffing his expensive Bally shoe and stormed indoors.

Ali took no notice and continued around the circle. Bob Monroe, the features editor, was next.

He'd learned not to look at Ali and fixed his gaze at a point near the middle of the pit. He was buggered if he was going to actually speak to a two-inch plastic figure. 'Jonathan has done a terrific story on Australian radio's formidable queen.'

'Ooh, do I know him?' joked Eddie.

Bob took no notice. 'Dottie Heath. She's reigned the airwaves for three decades, the first woman broadcaster to win a breakfast slot, take drive time through the roof, broadcast from outside the studio at wild locations. She's notched up a lot of firsts, still has millions of fans. But she's been given the heave-ho since hitting the big five-0.'

'Why? You can't see wrinkles on radio. TV has never accepted older women in this country, but Dottie still looks fabulous anyway,' remarked Barbara, who had once done a beauty spread with the remarkably glamorous and honey-toned radio journalist.

'They can't use her in promotions though,' pointed out Fiona, who thought it disgusting such an old woman had been hanging onto a job someone young and trendy should have. 'She looks old. And boring.'

'They say she's taking on new challenges. I think her ratings had slipped, the station just fudged. She says she was syndicated all over the country and had over two million listeners – The Queen Rules. But if you break down the figures and analyse them, another story emerges,' said Bob. 'It seems she's getting some very sharp younger competition. And her station has decided it's time to down-age.'

'What's the angle of the story, Bob, and why has Jonathan written it himself rather than one of his contributing writers or our own Kaye?' asked Larissa.

'She wouldn't be interviewed by a woman. They've been so bitchy in the past – envy, of course. And Jonathan says he's gradually won her confidence and so she agreed to a revealing interview. He's done a soft piece, woman turning fifty, at a crossroads, what's next, given her life to the job. Now feeling vulnerable . . . talks about losing her only child. First time she's opened up. She's never given personal interviews, always the consummate professional.'

'You mean it's all mushy, nice stuff?' asked Ali grimly. 'Surely there's something less than perfect. It can't all be good.'

'It's a very candid, let's say a very positive, piece,' said Bob carefully.

'Sounds terrific,' said Larissa.

Bob glanced at his notes. 'There's another thing. A request came in to me from outside. A researcher at *Reality*. Asking questions about you, Ali. Personal questions, they seem to be researching a piece ... the guy was vague,' finished Bob, anticipating Ali's reaction.

'I presume you said nothing,' snapped Ali.

'More than his life is worth,' hissed Eddie in an undertone.

'I've already dealt with that,' snapped Ali.

'Just thought you'd like to know there's something afoot.'

'I had Tracey call *Reality*'s executive producer. That bitch Heather Race hit on me on the way to the airport.'

'Do you think that was wise, Ali? Asking them to pull the plug could be a red rag to a bull,' suggested Larissa.

'I only speak about *Blaze*. My personal opinions or history are off limits to the media. And that goes for everyone on the staff.' Ali glared around the circle.

'If you don't talk to them at all, Ali, they don't have a story,' said Bob quietly. 'You give them one quote and that's a licence to run with anything they have on you.'

'I'm not doing anything. April is out gunning for Heather.'

'The story I wanted to do?' said Jonathan with a pinched look. 'I didn't realise it was to be a massacre. Whatever happened to the code of ethics?'

'Cool it, Jon,' chided Bob. 'Your talents are in other directions.'

'I can see I'll have to ask my wife to show me how women sharpen knives.' Jonathan made a brave effort at humour, but his hurt anger was plain to see.

Ali stood looking rattled. 'The tribespeople say it's time to go.'

They all filed solemnly past the sandpit, bobbing heads at the unmoving plastic people.

'They don't look like happy campers, do they?' hissed Eddie to Fran.

'Us, you mean?'

'No. The mob in the pit. I think a head might roll in telly land if they start taking pot shots at Ali.'

'Well, they'd have a lot of ammunition,' whispered back Fran, and Eddie dug her in the ribs in delight.

'Ooh, naughty girl! I wouldn't worry, I think Ali has her rear covered.'

Ali sat in her office with the door closed, which signalled to anyone who might approach, Do Not Disturb. She made a phone call, spoke for a few minutes and waited.

The woman on the other end of the phone returned and spoke to Ali. 'I'm sorry dear, the information we have on Ali Gruber only goes back a few months, since she was appointed to edit *Blaze*. It says she's Australian, but there's no reference to what she did here or about her background. All our old files are on microfiche in archives and can only be accessed by staff people. Unless there's anything that can be found under the *Freedom of Information Act*. I'm sorry I can't be more help. You're the second person to ask about her in a week.'

'Fine. Thanks anyway.' Ali hung up, satisfied but concerned about that second person.

'I don't give a shit if the Pope is in there, I'm going in.' Reg stormed through the door, past the protesting Belinda and marched up to Ali, shaking his fist across her desk. 'I don't know what you're up to, but you mess with me and you'll be in deep shit. If you think that little poofter is going to take over my territory, you'd better think again.'

Ali smiled. 'C'mon Reg, you're not scared of a little competition? The more the merrier. The bigger accounts we land, the bigger impact we make, the more money we build up for the magazine.' Ali knew very well that Reg received a bonus pegged to the amount of advertising he sold each year. By Eddie eating into the market, he was hitting Reg in the hip pocket.

'You might think you can call the shots while Nina is away, but the boys upstairs aren't going to stand for this. You don't hold the purse strings, baby doll, they do,' snarled Reg. He was a member of the informal club of senior male management and they all loathed Ali. She was tolerated because circulation was rising. The minute she put a foot wrong, she'd be gone. He made no attempt to disguise his feelings. The gloves were off.

Ali didn't blink. 'I'm not worried about the sixth-floor boys, Reg. If I have a problem, I'll talk to Oscar about it. Was there anything else?'

Reg reeled from her desk, but turned at the doorway. 'Don't expect me to play along with your stupid games any more. I have as much power here as you do. You want to see me, come to my office.' He slammed the door so hard a picture fell off the wall.

Belinda tapped at Ali's door and was relieved when she answered as if nothing had happened. 'I just wondered if . . . you needed me.'

'Thank you, Belinda. If you can fix Reg's temper it would be nice.'

'I guess he's not happy with all the . . . er, changes.'

'Life moves on, Belinda. Keep up or ship out,' said Ali blithely.

By the time the *Reality* story was ready to air, Sally had disappeared from the Haven Clinic and moved back into her favourite hotel, the Vanguard in Elizabeth Bay, under her usual pseudonym. She telephoned Tony. He was interstate, but back that evening. Then she called Jacques. He was away too. Miche was uncontactable at *Blaze* and Sally couldn't find where she'd put Miche's home number. Sally hunkered down and ordered room service. Then she rang Heather Race at *Reality*. Heather was out and when she came back she found Sally's strung-out message on her voice mail. She didn't bother returning the call.

Miche was thinking hard about looking for her father. She had the number of the Salvation Army but couldn't bring herself to make the call. She hadn't slept properly for several nights, and was haunted by nightmares. Shadowy figures pulled at her body, out-of-focus faces swam before her, and then she was in her mother's arms as Lorraine jumped from the terrace of *Blaze* into the New York night. Miche woke with a start each time, just before they hit the ground.

Miche confided in Larissa over breakfast. Larissa looked pale and drawn. She wasn't sleeping either.

Miche sighed. 'I'm having nightmares. I feel like a jilted lover one minute, a lost little girl the next. I can't go off on a trip to see Jeremy feeling like this.'

'It's just what you need to do,' advised Larissa, adding, 'Jilted is the right word. While your father didn't exactly leave your mother at the altar, he ditched you both and hasn't gone out of his way to make amends. No wonder you feel like that. But Miche, to be fair, there are always two sides to every story. You need to hear his side of it before you can pass judgement. I'm not making excuses for what he did, but you need to know why. Until you sort this out – find out whether he's good, bad or indifferent – and let it go, you can't settle down and move on with your life.'

Miche nodded, but didn't answer for a minute. Then she looked at the sad-faced Larissa, 'And what are you doing about your life?'

'I'm not sure.' She headed for the shower.

Three nights later, a *Reality* promo went to air screaming of 'the folly of beauty and the beasts'. It showed Sally waving a glass of champagne saying, 'Up their arses.'

Jeremy rang Miche. 'Jesus, what have they done with Sally? That Heather killer-bitch Race has done her over. Where is she?'

'It hasn't gone to air yet, maybe it's not as bad as the promo makes out.'

'Sally struck me as being pretty easy to manipulate. Surely she'd be putty in the hands of a pro like Heather Race?'

'That's why I'm afraid,' confessed Miche. 'This sort of thing makes me ashamed to be part of the media.'

'Oh, that's a bit tough. Surely they're not all like Heather Race? Wait and see what it's like. Anyway, what else would you do for a career?' Jeremy suddenly asked.

'You know, Jem, I've been thinking about that. Listen, let's talk after the show goes to air. I'd better speak with Larissa.'

'Riss, how on earth did they find her?' Miche said, furious at Heather Race's sensationalist story on Sally and at the same time fearful for the vulnerable young girl. 'I thought she'd gone to a clinic. What happened? I feel somehow responsible for her.'

Larissa felt sick and mumbled that she'd check it out.

The nauseating feeling was caused by the knowledge she'd been instrumental in setting up the story by trading off the whereabouts of Sally to make Heather agree to an interview with April. And, more worryingly, no one knew where Sally was. There'd already been a call from one of the papers asking if *Blaze* had a contact. Apparently Sally had stormed out of the clinic with her overnight bag, jumped in a cab and dropped out of sight. Her parents hadn't heard from her, nor her agency, nor *Reality*.

'Where she shacks up is nothing to do with us. She agreed to be interviewed, we're not her keeper,' the *Reality* producer commented when Miche rang.

When the *Reality* program had gone to air, the publicity in that day's papers ensured a big audience. Heather Race's story opened with Sally sitting on her bed, waving the glass of champagne. 'I haven't done anything really bad . . . it's hard to say no.'

Next came a close-up of Heather wearing a concerned face and asking gently, 'What did you do, Sally, while you were living the wild life in Europe?'

'God, what didn't I do. Those photographers and agency people rape you. Those old guys in the modelling business in Europe feed on new young blood . . .'

They cut back to Heather looking slightly shocked. 'How wild is the feeding frenzy? What kind of situations did you fall into?'

There followed an edited version of Sally laughingly describing the chateau party with the horses, dwarf clown and naked black sax player. It was edited to leave out the subtle, funny comments, leaving in all the ribald and raunchy bits from the anecdotes Sally had told Heather, believing it was an off-the-record chat before the actual interview started.

The reporter's voice-over managed to mention that particular shoot had been for the recent *Blaze* story on

473

Sally. Then followed more interview with a cutaway showing Heather looking suitably horrified. 'What do your parents think?'

Sally sounded flippant as she was shown saying, 'Not my scene any more. They think I'm having a holiday at a health farm.' Then, lifting her glass she'd added, 'Good health.'

The next sequence had Heather talking over pictures of the clinic gates, the grounds, inside the clinic, showing cold, bare rooms with hospital beds, a pharmaceutical dispensing room, doors labelled 'Private. Therapy Session in Progress' and 'Detox Unit'.

Her commentary was delivered in a hushed voice-over. 'In this place, down these quiet halls, behind closed doors, a number of the rich and famous we know so well, are being treated. They're here because they have dangerous and severe disorders, from bulimia and depression to drug addiction and anorexia, to name a few. Patients – they call them clients – are often rebellious, their behaviour unpredictable, and one only can hope that the treatment they receive here, at this resort retreat, will help vulnerable and tragic cases like young Sally Shaw. Sally is a girl still in her teens who has lived so hard, achieved so much. She had a meteoric rise, now she could crash and burn out. I'm Heather Race and this is *Reality*.'

In her hotel room, Sally threw her glass at the TV set screaming, 'You tricked me! I didn't say that like that . . . you've cut bits out!' Sobbing, she flung herself around the room feeling violated and devastated. What would her mum and dad say? Oh God, she looked so awful. To see herself so harshly filmed without the benefit of careful make-up and flattering lighting, she looked haggard, gaunt and sick. It was frightening. 'Please, I'm not like that,' she sobbed. Grimly she picked up the phone and made a brief urgent call.

Miche was alone in the house and, as the *Reality* segment on Sally ended and they went to a commercial break, she felt like rushing to the bathroom and throwing up.

Her phone rang and a horrified Belinda was on the line. 'That dreadful woman . . . poor Sally . . . they made her out to be such a bimbo!'

'Well, she has been led astray and been in that flighty world,' said Miche, also close to tears. 'It's so frustrating. She was so keen to tell her story in a sober way to help other girls.'

'This'll stop a lot of parents sending their kids out to be models,' said Belinda firmly.

'Sally and I talked it through. She trusted me. Someone should have warned her not to trust that TV reporter.'

'Ha! Remember this is *Reality*. They don't know the meaning of the word trust,' snapped Belinda. 'Anyone is at the mercy of super-bitch Heather Race.'

'Sally is very impressionable, very easy to manipulate. I've heard about how unscrupulous and unethical TV people can be, but these people have gone even further. I just know how they work – they brought in the booze to give her and they cut up all her words like a jigsaw and pieced them together the way they wanted.' Miche sighed. 'The worrying part is, I don't know where Sally is. If she saw that show she'll be . . . I don't know what she'll do.' Miche could hear other calls coming in. 'I'd better go, Belinda, in case it's Sally.'

But the other calls were from staff at *Blaze*, expressing their dismay. Several were working late and they'd watched it on the office monitor.

Miche decided to again try the hotel in Elizabeth Bay where Sally had stayed. She'd rung already and they had no one registered under Sally Shaw. Wildly, Miche tried to think of the fake name Sally had used in Paris. Donald the photographer might remember, but he could be anywhere in the world. Miche closed her eyes and tried to think . . . world, planet, moon . . . an image sprang into her mind. A pink moon. That was it, that singer from the seventies – Nick Drake. Sally had played his music when they drove from Paris to the chateau, *Pink Moon*. She'd called herself Miss P. Moon.

She dialled the hotel and asked for Miss P. Moon. There was a silence as the receptionist clicked on the computer keys. Miche held her breath.

'Ah, yes, Miss Moon . . . I'll try her room. Oh, I'm sorry she has put a stop on calls.'

'Is she there, in the hotel?'

'I'm sorry, I'm not allowed to give you that information.'

'Look, this is important. I think she could be really upset . . . can you send someone up to her room? Just to check on her, please, she had a bit of a shock this evening . . .'

There was an awkward pause and then, 'I'll do what I can, Miss. Do you want to leave a message?'

'Yes. Tell her Miche rang and . . . loves her. And I'll give you my mobile number. Could you please ask her to ring me and let me know she's all right.'

Miche hung up the phone feeling hollow and fearful. She called Belinda back to get the number of Jacques Triton.

He sounded surprised, yet pleased to hear from her. Miche cut off his small talk. 'I was wondering if you've heard from Sally Shaw, there was a piece on her tonight on . . .'

'I saw it. Very cutting and spiteful. Unfortunately that's how she is, eh?' His rolling French 'Rs' sounded bored.

'No, that's not how she is,' said Miche firmly, stopping herself from adding, 'With decent people who don't offer her drugs.'

'Come on, Michelle. Don't be stuffy. She's a good-time girl. She knows what she's doing. We saw her a week ago. She was pretty wild and wired.'

'With your help, I suppose. She's only just seventeen and is very vulnerable. I feel a bit responsible for that nightmare on TV tonight. She's gone to ground and I'm worried about her. Do you know where she might have gone?'

The friendly tone evaporated. 'I 'ave no idea, and why should I care? I have no association with this girl any more. Ask Tony Cox what he knows. Goodnight.' Jacques hung up the phone, leaving Miche seething. Bastards, while the girls are around to party and rave and sleep with, they count for something. Out the door and they mean nothing. She hunted down Tony Cox, who at least sounded slightly concerned.

'Well, hell yes, Jacques and I did spring her from that clinic one night for a bit of a buzzy outing with a couple of other models.'

'Have you heard from her since?'

There was a pause and Miche pressed her point. 'Tony, this is important. I really think she's going over the edge.'

'Christ. Maybe I've done the wrong thing here . . .'

'What, please tell me, Tony. I'll keep you out of this.'

'You'd better. Promise me. This conversation hasn't taken place,' said Tony with an edge to his voice.

'Okay, okay. Now what do you know? Time is important.'

'She rang me a little while ago. An hour maybe. Babbling about a TV story. She wanted some stuff. I wasn't going to go near her. But I gave her a dealer's number.'

'Oh, God. Who, where?'

'I can't tell you that.'

Miche's voice was rising. 'Would she go to him or he to her?'

'I would think he'd go to her. She didn't sound like

she was up to going anywhere. She was pissed as well as stoned.'

'Oh, my God. Okay, thanks Tony.' Miche dropped the phone in its cradle, grabbed her wallet, rushed to her car and drove as fast as she dared to Elizabeth Bay.

She left her car at the front and raced into the lobby to the reception desk. 'Please, can you help me? I think a friend of mine is in the hotel and could be in trouble.'

It was just after ten-thirty. The hotel restaurant and bar were full, people were chatting in the lobby, everyone looked so prosperous, fashionably dressed and comfortably carefree. Miche felt like shouting at them as they insisted she wait downstairs while the hotel security and the duty manager went to check on Miss P. Moon.

Karen Charles was the resident manager on duty at the Vanguard Hotel that night. It was a classy hotel that dealt discreetly with its share of guest dramas. This was Karen's first potential crisis. She was only twenty-seven and since doing a hospitality course at college, had worked hard to climb the management ladder.

'So who's the guest?' asked the security man as they stepped out of the elevator on the eleventh floor.

'A model. Young girl who made it big overseas.'

'What, she eat a piece of meat and fall over in shock?'

Karen didn't answer as she followed the striding security man to Suite 1101. He rang the buzzer then rapped on the door. There was no answer, so he used his pass key and opened the door calling out, 'Miss Moon? You in here? It's security.'

Karen followed him into the suite, flinching at the mess in the living room. Clothes and magazines were scattered about, glasses and empty champagne bottles were everywhere and a couple of unfinished bottles had tipped over and spilled red wine on tabletops and the carpet. Chocolate and peanut wrappers from the mini-bar were tossed on the floor. 'Heavens, did one person make all this mess?' wondered Karen aloud.

The security man headed for the bedroom, which was even more of a shambles – the sheets hanging off the bed, a pillow on the floor, empty bottles and several barely touched room-service trays of hamburgers, chips and cake.

'She's not here,' remarked Karen, relieved she didn't have to confront the occupant about the mess.

But the security manager pushed open the bathroom door and gave a short exclamation, 'Oh, shit.' He turned back to Karen. 'Call Triple 0. We need help up here.'

Karen glimpsed the figure of a young girl, or was it a child, lying on the floor. She didn't need to see the pills, the needle or the coke spoon to know something was badly wrong. She grabbed the phone by the bed and punched reception. 'Quick, call an ambulance. Tell them the back door. Suite 1101. Hurry, oh God, tell them to hurry.'

The security man stepped back into the bedroom. 'Tell 'em not to hurry. She's checked out.'

'What? You mean she's . . . dead?'

'Very.'

Karen's hands flew to her face. She'd only been appointed a duty manager three months ago and this was a first for her. 'What will I do?'

'I'll call the cops. We have to keep this quiet. Phone the girl on reception and tell her to keep her mouth shut. No publicity. Who is this bird again?'

'Her real name is Sally Shaw, a model. She was using a pseudonym. Didn't want any publicity.'

'Yeah, well, neither do we. The police will move her to the morgue and go through her stuff. They'll want to talk to that girl downstairs. We'll move all this, and them, out as fast as possible.'

Karen nodded, glad the older security man knew what

to do. She glanced back towards the bathroom. 'Drugs, I suppose. Did she have too much?'

'Of everything I'd say,' sighed the security man as they went back into the living room. 'Too much, too soon and too young to handle it.'

He sat down and flicked on the TV as he waited for the police to arrive from the Kings Cross station up the road.

Ali switched off the light in her office and looked in on Larissa and the art staff working on the layout. 'I'm off. I have an appointment.'

Larissa decided not to ask her if she'd seen the *Reality* piece on Sally earlier in the evening. Ali was unlikely to be sympathetic. And she'd probably complain about them watching TV in the office, though everyone had been glued to the set during their dinner break.

Ali was distracted. She could put this off no longer. She had agreed to see John O'Donnell at his home later this evening.

As Tom dropped her outside the Vaucluse mansion she told him to be on call. 'Pick me up at 11 p.m. unless I call for you earlier.'

'Yes, Ms Gruber.' Tom made no comment. But he was surprised – she normally spent the night. It was already after 9.30 p.m. Tom had been pleased about Ali's growing friendship with the influential CEO. It put him up there with the other limo drivers when they hung around the airport together boasting of the prestige of their passengers.

Dinner for two was set up on the terrace by the pool. Candles burned and a single red rose lay on her napkin tied with a silver ribbon.

John O'Donnell kissed her, and after opening and pouring the champagne, the butler quietly left them alone.

They chatted about *Blaze*, but Ali kept turning the conversation back to him. 'So what else? With you? What's happening in your neck of the woods? You've been quiet lately. Brewing up a mega deal?'

'Actually I was going to talk to you about that.' Ali leaned forward expectantly – she loved to know what he was planning. Sometimes there was an opportunity for her or for *Blaze*, though she never told him that she had bought shares on several occasions, based on what he'd told her. He'd be accused of insider trading and everything would be blown out of the water. But he continued slowly, looking into glass. 'I'm taking a bit of a sideways step. I'm removing myself as executive chairman and CEO and the board has agreed I take the position of non-executive chairman.'

'Which means . . . ?' Ali didn't like the sound of this.

He looked up and gave her a loving smile. 'It means I'll have a lot more time to myself. I won't be so hands-on every day. I'll have a life. After Carol died, I went on every board that asked and carried a far too heavy workload. It was a means of distracting myself. But now . . .' he was still smiling at her.

Ali thought he looked soppy and ridiculous. 'For God's sake why? You're still young enough to run the company for another ten years! What are you going to do? Start another business?' she asked hopefully.

He laughed and shook his head. 'Ali dearest. Surely I don't have to spell it out. I want to spend more time with you!'

'No, John. We've been through this. I never thought you were serious about it, or I would have put my foot down. You can't opt out, especially because of me. Look, I'm really devoted to my career. I can't travel with you, do things you want to do like cruise the Greek islands for three weeks . . . lovely as it sounds.'

He stood and took the rose from the small table and handed it to her. 'Would this make a difference?'

Ali looked at the rose and back to him in growing frustration. 'What's with the roses all of a sudden? Am I supposed to clench it between my teeth and dance the flamenco for you?'

He chuckled, not hearing the anger in her tone. 'Hey, now that's an idea. No, here, look at the ribbon.' He pointed at the fine silver ribbon and she saw the end was tied in a delicate bow, threaded through a beautiful sapphire ring. He pulled the ribbon and slipped off the ring, lifting her left hand and wiggling it onto her third finger. 'I want to marry you, Ali. You're fun, you make me happy, let's enjoy time together. I can give you a luxurious life.'

Ali stared wildly at the ring. She hated blue. Where was the pink Argyle diamond set in platinum? God, what was she thinking? She didn't want to marry this man.

Thinking she was too overcome with surprise and joy to speak, he rushed on, saying all the words she didn't want to hear. 'You can quit your job, you won't need the money, we have this house, we'll buy a holiday home, travel, buy a dog, buy a boat, whatever you want.'

Ali found her voice. 'That's not what I want, John.' She pulled the ring from her finger and thrust it back at him. 'I like my job. I still have mountains to climb. I want to be bigger and more powerful than Nina Jansous. I want to choose my own life. This has been fun and wonderful knowing you, but I can't go through with this. I'm sorry if you didn't see it coming, but . . .'

He blinked and sat back in shock, the diamonds around the sapphire shining in the candlelight on the table between them. 'What do you mean, Ali . . . once you slipped through my defences, you knew I was falling in love with you. I thought you loved me back . . .' He paused as her words sunk in. 'See what coming?'

'I thought you realised . . . that our relationship was changing . . . me being away . . . seeing less of each other. My time in New York . . .'

'I thought you were busy, the pressure . . .' he began slowly, all the delight fading from his face.

Ali continued to sit and stare at him, struggling to find the words. 'It's been special, really lovely. I always want you as a friend . . .'

John O'Donnell sat back, his face hardening, feeling very, very foolish. 'I don't think so. Is there someone else? Some young man? You told me you didn't want babies . . .'

'And I don't.' She tried to lighten the atmosphere. 'I'd never fit all my clothes in here.' It was a joke, but she meant it. Ali's extensive designer wardrobe would never fit into the late Mrs O'Donnell's modest dressing room. But John O'Donnell was unamused. 'Look, John, I'm a career girl. And no, there isn't anyone else.' Ali began to worry that she'd lose this valuable contact. 'Please, try to understand. I'm not ready to settle down. I'm about to turn thirty, I have a lot to do. Please, stay friends with me. I need you. I value our friendship. I really do, John.'

His face was set. 'Only while I'm in the chair, right? While I'm O'Donnell with influence, you want to see me. When I'm O'Donnell, retired CEO, you don't want to know me. You just loved my seat, the position I held, Ali. No matter who was in the seat, it would have been the same.'

'That's not true!'

'I hoped by asking you to marry me, you would realise I wasn't playing with you. I never wanted you to feel cheap. It seems I'm the one that now feels cheap. And used.' He turned away. 'I think you'd better go. If Tom isn't available, I'll have Roger drive you home.' He hurried from the room.

'John, please, let's not leave it like this . . .' Ali felt panicky. Had she totally burned this bridge?

483

She pulled herself together. She could always win John O'Donnell around again. Maybe she had only imagined that Baron Triton had any interest in her. She was alone in the room. She fumbled for her mobile phone to summon the driver.

As she heard her car arrive outside the mansion and the butler open the door, she stood and looked down at the twinkling ring. For a moment she wanted to grab it, but turned away. She hated blue.

Ali didn't feel like going home. She told Tom to take her back to work. Lights burned in several offices as people worked late to meet deadlines and prepared for tomorrow's editorial meeting. Larissa and the art department had left.

Belinda's desk was neatly cleared. Ali could see past it that the lights were on in her office. She'd speak to Belinda about that. And there was a strange and ugly smell about the place.

When she stepped inside the door she stopped, sniffed and gagged. Glancing quickly around, she couldn't see what was causing the vile smell. The lights were also shining out on the terrace. Holding her hand to her nose she rushed outside. No one was there. But the smell was overwhelming. Then she saw it.

There was a large red stain on the terrace, running from the sandpit. And as she edged closer, she saw the source of the smell – a bucket lay on its side spilling blood and rotten animal excrement over the model village as if a putrid volcano had erupted, smothering them all.

Ali wanted to vomit, but anger overcame her heaving stomach and she rushed inside, grabbed her bag and picked up the phone, yelling at the startled operator, 'Get fucking Reg Craven on the line. I don't care where he goddamn is!'

TAKE TWENTY...

Lucien and Nina returned to the jeweller's shop hand in hand. The old man threw out his arms in delight, reaching across the counter top to pump their hands.

'I am so happy to see you, Madame. I was worried something bad had happened.' He reached out to touch Nina's cheek before turning to Lucien. 'Your little gift worked, it seems.'

'Yes. That and a rather agreeable arrangement to travel around the country and write about the good things.'

The jeweller nodded at Nina. 'And there are good things in this country. We have a fascinating history. And so many beautiful places.'

'We wanted to thank you for coming up with cash so speedily for us,' said Nina. 'My grandmother told my mother that the jewellery would always help her out of trouble. She gave me a dragonfly pin, which I've never had to sell, but knowing it was there helped me to take a risk years ago.'

'Not as big as the risk you just took,' observed Lucien and grinned as she dug him in the ribs.

'Beautiful gems shine even more brightly on beautiful women,' said the jeweller with a slight bow to Nina. 'Now, speaking of beautiful pieces. I did as you asked and have arranged their sale.' He looked suddenly concerned and said to Nina, 'That is, if you still wish to sell them. Perhaps they are sentimental and now you do not wish to part with them?'

'I am keeping this little ring, that's all,' said Nina, touching the small gold ring with her family seal on it.

'You mean, you've sold the jewellery already?' asked Lucien.

The jeweller nodded. 'I have a buyer lined up.' Lowering his voice he added, 'It is worth a substantial amount. Fine stones and beautiful old workmanship. An international dealer will put them to auction. I believe I have found you a worthwhile price. Unless you wish to wait for the auction in London?'

'No. And you must take a commission,' said Nina.

'There is a slight problem. You might have trouble taking this money out of the country. Especially after your little, er, predicament.'

Nina looked at Lucien. 'What do you think?'

'We can talk to the embassy. May we leave it in your safe while we're travelling?'

'Of course. Enjoy your little holiday.' He gave a courtly bow once again.

Larissa sat at her desk with her hands over her ears. While she couldn't actually *hear* Ali's voice, she could *feel* it in her marrow. All hell was breaking loose over the desecration of the sandpit village. And while Ali was not blatantly accusing Reg – or anyone else – it was the philosophical, moral and ethical outrage that Ali ranted had been violated. Her space. Whoever had done the vile deed might as well have thrown the excrement over Ali herself, she took it so personally.

While the staff kept po-faced about the incident, outside the office there was much giggling and comments like 'I wish I'd done it'. Eddie adored the scenario and dared April to write about it in her gossip column.

'And keep my job?' she snapped. 'I'm keeping my mouth shut on this one.'

But it was too good to keep under wraps. Two days later, the episode was gleefully written up in a Sunday newspaper column with a photo of Ali taken at a cocktail party. It was pulled from the files and showed her wiping her mouth with a paper napkin. The caption read, '*Gung-ho flung dung leaves tacky taste*'. And went on to describe the 'foul deed'.

Ali summoned Larissa. 'Find out who leaked this story. It's an outrage. And how dare the editor of that rag run a piece about another editor like that?'

'Ali, you know how superior newspapers think they are to magazines. I mean, wouldn't you run it if you were the newspaper's editor? And April does take more than her share of digs at people. It's payback time,' said Larissa feebly. She knew every media outlet in the country would pounce on the titbit. Whoever had leaked it had chosen the column that rated next to April's in popularity. 'And I wouldn't begin to know where to start to find out. You'll never know. Let it go,' advised Larissa.

'If it wasn't Reg who leaked it, it could have been April. These bitch columnists can't help themselves.' Ali slammed her fist on the table. 'I will not be made to look a fool.'

Larissa realised what was also bothering Ali about

487

the leaked incident was the fact that she hadn't been able to control it. Ali was fanatical about running her life precisely the way she wanted it. The unforeseen rarely ruffled her existence. With no children, no live-in lover, no hobbies or interests outside her work, Ali kept a tight rein on her lifestyle. And suddenly Larissa saw how shallow and self-centred that life was and how frighteningly similar it was to her own.

Larissa stood up, surprising Ali, who hadn't terminated the meeting yet. 'Get a life, Ali. What's it matter in the big scheme of things? Maybe it's made you seem more human.'

Ali was so shocked that Larissa was out of the office before she could think of an answer.

Larissa stopped by April's office. Leaning in the doorway she asked casually, 'You don't have to answer, but do you have any inkling about who leaked the flungdung bit?'

'It wasn't me, goddamn it! How stupid would I be?' April's voice was gruff with annoyance.

'I agree it would have been foolish. Tempting though.' She gave a grin and April thawed a bit.

'Yeah. But if there's a hot piece I can't use, I'm certainly not going to give it to a rival.'

'Makes sense. What about the culprit of the deed, any thoughts there?' asked Larissa. 'Not that I'm doing Ali's dirty work for her, even though she asked.'

'She would. Well, she should know she has more enemies than friends around here. But, put it this way, in my book the finger points to the dreaded Reggie. He was ropeable after that last meeting, but frankly I never thought he'd have the guts. He could have hired a hit man to do the flinging.' April paused. 'Come to that, he could have done the telling too. It's really made her mad.' April looked pleased. 'Well, I don't envy you your job. Good luck.'

'What do you mean?'

'Fronting the staff and reporting back to Ali.'

Larissa frowned. 'I'm not being her lackey. I was hoping to shake the culprit's hand.' She moved down the hallway deep in thought and went back to her office. Glancing at her watch, Larissa wondered if Gerard was in bed. It was late in New York. They hadn't spoken in two weeks, other than by email. There was a distance more than physical between them since he'd gone back.

She dialled his number, but the phone rang in their New York apartment without being answered. Depressed, she picked up her bag, left the office and went home. Once again the indecision about her life rattled her. If Gerry still wanted to marry her, why wasn't he there? Where was he?

There were dozens of reasons for him to not be by the phone – Gerard was working hard and organising the move to New Hampshire – but his absence reinforced Larissa's insecurity. He was moving on with his life. She was treading water. And a nagging resentment chewed at her because of it. And there was some jealousy in there as well. She began to visualise Gerry with another woman. Sleeping with her. Murmuring into her hair in the night as they cuddled. Holding hands as they wandered through the city looking for a café for breakfast. Larissa's blood began to boil. This was too painful to contemplate. She shook herself and admonished herself for being so stupid. Served her right for such silly fantasising. But the devil on her shoulder whispered, 'Ask yourself why you care so much.'

Eddie Kurtz sat in Ali's office nodding sympathetically. 'It's a bitch. Who would do such a thing? I mean, we all have an idea of whoooooo might have done the vile deed . . .' He drew out the word and rubbed the edge of his nose and mimicked straightening a bow tie.

'You think so too?' Ali looked thoughtful.

'Chuck him out. He's so behind the times,' said Eddie airily. 'You can do better than him.'

'It's not that easy,' sighed Ali. 'Reg is part of that upstairs boys' club.' She didn't elaborate on the fact that she and Reg Craven held equal positions of power or that she was in no position to push Reg out the door. He was in charge of making the magazine financially viable.

'Well, darling heart, you and I can show him up. I have a hot prospect lined up to buy space – only the biggest hair product company in the universe! I told them a few ideas I had and they're hot to trot. You don't need to work with some redneck who throws shit then tells the world about it.'

'You think he talked to that Sunday rag columnist?' Ali began to seethe again.

Eddie shrugged. 'Who am I to say? Just know who your friends are, Ali heart. I'm off. Anyone divine you want in the way of ad clients lined up, just say the word.'

'Tiffany, Sotheby's, Bollinger, Chanel. We're missing some international names. Too many local people.'

'For you, anything.' Eddie skipped from Ali's office and gave Belinda a wave. 'Toodle-loo, Bee.'

Belinda gritted her teeth. This so-called promotions cum ad manager was too familiar for her taste. She didn't like him and she didn't trust him. He seemed an unlikely choice to be Ali's confidant. But then he was an outsider, and he was certainly clever – and Ali had found him, so no wonder he kept on her good side.

Twenty minutes later, Eddie was sitting in the Yellow Brick Road salon. He was regaling Dane, Miles and Rex with the story of the sandpit saga. 'God, it was hysterical. She's been ranting up and down the hallways. The shit smell is still there on the terrace, it soaked into the cement. But what really pissed her off was the whole she-bang going public on Sunday.'

'You're a wicked, bad boy,' said Max, shaking his finger at the unabashed Eddie. 'Doesn't she suspect you leaked it?'

'No, she loves me. Okay, girls, what other gossip do you have that you haven't given to that April bitch?'

'April comes in here for the goss on the social set, we don't mind passing on titty bits. We just have to be so careful our clients don't discover how she finds out. I mean, why do you hate April Showers?' asked Dane.

'Let's just say we had a run-in one time. We go back a long way,' said Eddie somewhat ominously. 'I'm an ele-phant, I never forget.'

'So you're nice to everyone's face and knife them in the back at the first opportunity,' laughed Rex.

'It's called survival, sweetie, keeping your options open,' sniffed Eddie. 'You'll never know who you'll need to call on in the future.'

April's society page, written under the pseudonym of Beau Monde, was proving a big hit. Not-so-gentle digs at the cognoscente had only increased its appeal. She wrote about top names, whether they liked it or not, in the worlds of big business, politics, arts, diplomacy and old money with a sprinkling of academia and genuine philanthropists. Wannabe do-gooders trying to big note themselves by pro-moting A Cause, celebrities from movies, TV and sports, the normal fodder for tabloid press, rarely rated a men-tion. Beau Monde annoyed socialites when their parties and inside moves were written about in not-so-flattering detail. When the old money set entertained, extra precau-tions were taken with staff and outsiders to make sure no whisper of the details were leaked to Beau Monde.

Ali had grudgingly complimented April on her work,

adding, 'If you get us sued, you're out of here. It's in your contract if you recall.'

Larissa was sitting at her desk, staring morosely at Sydney Harbour, which today gave her no joy. Like Miche, she was still in shock over the death of Sally Shaw. She felt so guilty about it and had confessed her role in the *Reality* segment to Miche.

'Don't blame yourself, Riss. *Reality* would have found her one way or another. And there's no way we could have stopped them doing what they did. I blame myself too, for not realising how depressed, how flaky, she was. I just didn't want to involve myself in that world. I should have warned her about the Jacques and Tony scene.' Miche bit her lip and Larissa knew she was thinking of her mother again. No one had realised how depressed and lost Lorraine had been feeling.

'Let's not beat ourselves up,' sighed Larissa. 'We can look out for one another as best we can, but we still have our private lives to lead. Even you and me and Nina, close as we are.'

'But I think of you as family,' cried Miche. 'I don't have any family any more.' Tears had washed down her face. Larissa quickly wrapped her arms around her. 'Of course we're family. You know that. You're the closest family Nina has too.'

Miche had shaken her head. 'No, she has Lucien now.'

'You'll find a lovely guy soon enough Miche,' murmured Larissa, searching for the right words to say. 'Who knows, it might even be Dan or Jeremy.' She decided it would be prudent not to mention Miche's mystery father.

'Will I, Riss? It seems so hard for so many women to find the right man. Belinda is the only woman I know at

492

Blaze who's happily married.' Miche raised her tear-stained face to give Larissa a penetrating look. Larissa had turned away, changing the subject. Miche had hit a nerve.

Larissa caught herself thinking more and more of Gerard, who was probably sorting out his belongings in their loft, getting ready for the move to New Hampshire. He'd emailed to see if she wanted to keep up the apartment for her return, or should he pack her things and put them in storage? She didn't know the answer. She thought back to their shared bed with the night view of the Hudson, the noises of New York, his familiar shape beside her, his deep regular breathing, the faint smell of oil paint wafting from his studio. The ringing phone jarred her to the present and she grabbed at it, wanting it to be Gerry.

'Riss . . . it's me, Kevin. I have Dan over here for a working boardroom lunch. We want you and Miche to see what Dan and his IT team have come up with. Can you make it?'

Larissa tried to clear her head. 'I'm sorry, what's this about?'

'You know . . . Dan and Miche cooked up an idea for *Blaze* using the new technology they're messing about with.'

Larissa was tired. 'I'm not the right person to look at this stuff. I'm not up with basic new technology.'

'If you and I can grasp it, then it's a step forward. Let Dan talk to the boffins and Ali. Come on, Larissa, it's been ages since we've seen each other.'

Miche and Larissa stared at the rolled silver cylinder in front of them on Kevin's boardroom table.

'It doesn't look like anything I've ever seen,' said Miche, giving it a tentative poke.

'Feels like fabric. What is it?' asked Larissa.

'Where *Blaze* could go,' answered Dan unrolling the cloth-like material. It was the same size as the magazine with the word *Blaze* and a shimmering dragonfly on it. Dan pressed a corner and the picture rippled making the dragonfly flutter its wings, then like a movie, images and words unrolled on the flexible cloth.

'It's a movie, a living magazine. Good grief!' exclaimed Larissa. 'How's it do that?'

'A tiny transistor is embedded in it which can receive information from a satellite broadcaster.'

'The idea is that this new type of reusable fabric is the screen, which can be rolled up and shoved in your pocket and, depending on who you subscribe to, you can download what you want. *Blaze*, the *New York Times*, sharemarket updates . . .'

'I can't believe you've developed this just from that conversation we had. How far off is this?' asked Miche excitedly.

'Who knows? This prototype came from one of the hot IT companies. Here, what about these . . .' he handed Miche and Larissa a pair of clunky glasses.

'I love these,' said Kevin.

He helped Larissa on with the virtual reality glasses and explained how it worked. 'Dan had it programmed for *Blaze*.'

Suddenly Larissa was looking at the last issue of *Blaze* in colour on a screen before her eyes.

'Just give a verbal command if you want to turn the page, go in closer, or blow a picture up,' said Dan. 'These have the latest high resolution, so the quality is excellent. This is why books on computer screens haven't been so popular, the quality hasn't been as good as the printed page. This will change all that.'

'Do you see what this could mean for *Blaze*?' said

Miche excitedly. 'You subscribe to *Blaze* and you receive the magazine in this format, or the traditional print version or both. This way you can look and listen to it like a movie.'

'Speaking of which, you can watch a movie with these. Leaves 3D days for dead,' said Kevin. 'But you know it's a bit frightening. I went down the coast, beautiful drive, three hours, with a client. Took his kids. They wanted to go in the company limousine with tinted windows so they could watch a movie on the video in the back. Didn't want to look out the window at the scenery. I can't help wondering if this generation is going to view the world through a screen and even live half their lives on the Internet?'

Larissa lifted the glasses off her head. 'Is this the new advance you guys wanted to show Ali?'

'It could be adapted for the market quite soon,' said Dan. '*Blaze* readers could be the first to use it.'

'Cool idea, huh? Everyone would buy this *Blaze*, don't you think?' said Miche.

'I think it should be approached with a cool head,' said Larissa slowly. 'Frankly, I'd wait till Nina is back. Ali could blow a heap of money on this if she took the bit between her teeth. Board or no board.'

'Yeah, I take your point. She could make Jacques or the Baron enthused and jump the gun. You're right. Nina is creative and innovative, but pragmatic too. What do you think, Kevin?' Miche turned to him.

'I can see why you and Dan are excited. It is a buzz to be jumping into this kind of stuff, but I think you're wise to let things advance a little further. Technology is changing day by day.'

'This company has a lot more toys. When you want to leapfrog over the competition, I'm your man,' said Dan, not at all put out that Larissa had been so cautious. From what he'd heard, Ali Gruber was a bit of a loose cannon.

Kevin glanced at Larissa and felt a rush of sympathy. She looked drawn and depressed. She needed to take that break at his holiday cottage as he'd suggested weeks back. But this time, he wished they could go away together. He gave her arm an affectionate squeeze. 'Let's eat. Only sandwiches. But gourmet ones!'

Heather Race took the hairbrush from the hairdresser's hand and stroked it firmly through her hair. 'I prefer it to go that way.'

The make-up and hairdresser assigned to the *Reality* team bit her tongue. She had learned to let Heather do things her way. If Heather wanted that shade of lipstick instead of the softer, more flattering tone the make-up girl suggested, let her look like she'd been sucking a mulberry. If Heather wanted her hair that way, fine. 'What are you shooting? I haven't seen any of the crew around,' she commented conversationally.

'I'm doing a big interview for *Blaze*. They're doing a profile on me. Could be a cover story, so that's why I want to try to look halfway decent. You know how critical those bitches can be,' she said, peering at her reflection in the mirror surrounded by soft lights in the studio's make-up room. 'All those magazine girls want to be in TV.'

The make-up girl refrained from smirking. Hell, if anyone knew how to be a critical bitch, it was Heather. 'That's super. Fabulous magazine.' She couldn't help wondering why such a classy magazine would want to write about the biggest bitch in television. 'Who's the journalist?'

'You're not going to believe this, but April Showers is doing it.'

'I thought she wrote gossip?'

'She's branching out, upgrading to feature profiles. And she's written a novel, you know,' said Heather suddenly defensive.

'Has it been published?' asked the make-up girl innocently. How many people had sat in this make-up chair and talked about 'their novel'. One big-time, American 'trash and glitz' writer, who'd sold millions, had told her about how so many people thought they could write novels. The glamorous author confided she would smile sweetly at those who made such remarks and simply say, 'Go right ahead babe – write.' Then she'd added with a dismissive flick of the wrist, 'They find out soon enough it ain't as easy as it looks.'

'April is talking to publishers,' said Heather as she stood up from the make-up chair. She didn't add that rumour had it that April Showers' book had been knocked back by Tiki Henderson's publisher and that's why she'd taken pot shots at Tiki in her old newspaper column. Heather also didn't mention that she had struck a deal with April – in return for the feature in *Blaze* on her – that she would do a TV story on April and her manuscript for *Reality* in the hope the publicity might generate keener interest from publishers. Both women were relaxed about this scratching of each other's backs.

April was pacing in the green room where guests waited before their TV appearances until a young girl guided her to Heather's dressing room.

It was a cosy refuge with a sofa, easychair and coffee table with flowers arranged on one side, a lighted mirror and bench with a stool along the opposite wall. There was a walk-in wardrobe and en suite with a shower. April glanced around, there was nothing personal in the room except for the framed official glamour photo with Heather's signature printed under the channel logo.

'Welcome to my home away from home,' said Heather brightly.

'Does anyone else use this room?'

'Hell no,' declared Heather with some emphasis. 'They're only my clothes in the closet.' She gave a short laugh, 'Well, whatever the wardrobe mistress has collected for me this week.'

'Your on-camera clothes are on loan? Do you pick the designers?'

'Sure, you know how it works. Same as in magazines. If you look at the show's credits, the freebies flash by at the speed of light. I think the fashion people are mad actually. I mean, who sees my shoes?' Heather kicked out a foot. 'And the clothes are always so mucked up with make-up and sweat, there's not much they can do with them . . . except sell 'em to the wardrobe department for a bargain price. And guess where they end up?' she chortled.

April grinned. 'In your closet.' She wouldn't want to buy an outfit worn by Heather Race, even immaculately dry-cleaned. She reached into her shoulder bag and pulled out a clipboard of notes.

'Ah ha, the ubiquitous clipboard. The accessory of every self-respecting journo,' said Heather inaccurately, but she liked the line.

'Shall we make a start? The photographer will be along later.' April uncapped her pen, suddenly businesslike. She was more accustomed to uncovering information under the guise of social banter over a glass of wine where unsuspecting companions fed her information about people that seemed innocuous, until coloured and enhanced by April's dipped-in-bile designer ballpoint. But now her journalism was on a new course and this interview was an important opportunity for April, who desperately wanted to move away from lightweight columns.

Bob, sanctioned by Ali, was giving her a shot at this

as a trial run so she wanted to make it a winner. A big winner. She felt very confident. In doing her research, snooping, as she privately called it, April had discovered Heather was keen to lift her image and standing at the network. An insider had told her how Heather had stormed out of a recent production meeting when it was hinted some other young chick was being groomed in the wings. That information gave April the power. While they both needed each other, April figured Heather needed this publicity more than April needed her as a subject, despite the book deal.

April sat in the armchair facing Heather, who was curled up on the sofa, legs tucked beneath her, posing prettily in black pants and a loose tailored blue shirt with embroidered cuffs. Her jewellery, borrowed from a boutique in the city, was heavy gold trying to appear low key. She wasn't a stunning beauty, but she had been groomed by the station to look credible and attractive, toning down her taste for too much gold and bright colours.

April looked down at her notes. 'Have you ever been sexually abused? Any history of incest or bulimia in the family?'

'What! Why ask that?' Heather exploded as the block-buster question hit like a punch in the solar plexus. 'I'm not going to answer that.'

'Because it's true? Does that account for your aggressive interviewing of helpless subjects?'

'Aggressive? That's rich. You're doing pretty well.' She uncurled and sat up. 'Just where the hell are you coming from?'

'Was your father domineering?'

'Jesus,' exclaimed Heather in desperation and defeat. 'No, the opposite . . .'

'So he was a weak man,' cut in April. 'Does that mean you are only attracted to young men you can dominate?'

This hit home. Heather had been photographed at a party with a young pop singer and there had been snide comments about her out-of-tune toy boy.

'I don't dominate anyone . . .'

'So it was your mother who was domineering?'

'Listen, April, don't try your amateur therapy experiences out on me,' snapped Heather, who had also done her homework on April and been told she had tried various therapists and counsellors, psychics and healers.

But the verbal war continued until suddenly April changed course. 'Now, how vulnerable is your position at the network, Heather? You've had a few legal problems with some of your stories and they're grooming some young bird as a hot reporter, I hear.' It was the beginning of another extended duel.

April was relentless, cutting in on Heather's answers when they didn't match the answer she wanted. It was a technique Heather employed as a matter of course, but she didn't handle it well when she was on the receiving end. Professional pride stopped Heather from walking out of the room in anger, but a deal was a deal and several days earlier she and April had been friendly enough.

Heather had agreed to April's suggestion that she follow her around for several days, 'observing' her at work, including attending a film premiere as a commentator for a small segment on *Reality*. They'd both gone to the after-premiere party and become more than a little tipsy. April was in her own milieu and seemed to know everyone, so once Heather had done her piece to camera she had relaxed, drunk and gossiped more than she should have and kept turning to April slurring, 'This is off the record, right?'

April had sat in on a *Reality* production meeting with her little tape recorder on the table for all to see. Heather and the network publicity chief had met beforehand with the producer and key staff to make sure that this meeting would 'favour' Heather – showing how workmates respected and liked her, how Heather's ideas for stories would be pounced upon. Heather was given advance details of several stories to put up at the meeting. She felt she'd made a good impression. By the time they'd settled in for the interview in the dressing room, Heather had been lulled by April into what was obviously a false sense of security.

Now she couldn't believe this 'chat' session in the dressing room. It was like being cross-examined.

She tried to be disarming. 'April, this is not the friendly chat I imagined. I feel like I'm on trial.'

'A lot of your interview subjects might say the same. What do you say when they ring up to complain about how they've been treated by you and your show?'

'I don't receive such calls,' said Heather stiffly.

'You mean they're vetted by some poor producer?'

'I wouldn't know. I'm just doing my job.' Heather frowned and fussed with the flowers in the vase on the dressing table. 'I don't think this line of questioning is taking us very far. If you just want to be confrontational and not listen to me . . .'

April gave a relaxed laugh. 'How many times has someone said that to you?'

Heather rose, turned and went to the mirror to fiddle with her hair, but April could see her furious face in the mirror and knew Heather had heard that phrase many times.

'Okay, if you want to stop at this point.' April switched off her tape. 'Would you like to give me the names of some friends – and enemies, if you have any – who can give me a quote or an anecdote about you?'

Heather handed over the list she had prepared. April

clipped it to her papers. She had her own list of names to follow up and she doubted they'd be on Heather's list.

'I want to see what you write before it goes to the editor,' said Heather in an authoritative tone.

'Aw, come on, Heather,' smiled April calmly, 'Good try. You know better than that. There's no way we'd do that. Maybe in the US the celebs demand copy and photo approval and a cover story, but not here. Even the biggest names don't see the copy before it's published,' she added pointedly, hinting Heather was yet to become a big name. 'Once one magazine caves in here, we're all gone. No way.'

Heather snarled at her without any pretence of civility. 'Listen, April, we had a deal to help each other . . .'

'Did we?' said April archly as she prepared to leave.

'You've just overstepped the mark. If you write anything that will damage me, or my career, the station will sue the arse off you and I'll make it my personal job to even the score.'

'Tut-tut. It would take a lot more than I could do to puncture your hide, Heather. But it's nice to see I've at least ruffled a feather or two. Toodle-loo.'

April shut the door to the dressing room behind her, feeling well pleased with the way it had all gone. She could write a killer article. She nodded at the photographer lounging in the hallway. 'She's all yours. You may have to quieten her down a bit.' He would take the obligatory posed shot, which may appear in the article. But April had seen a terrific photo of Heather taken by one of the freelance society photographers who passed as pseudo paparazzi in Sydney. It was after the film premiere at a karaoke nightclub and Heather, very drunk, had been on stage clutching a microphone. Heather fancied she had a voice and it had amused people to see the hard-nosed journo attempting to be club torch singer. April could see her headline over that picture – 'Heather Race – off the record'. April had every intention of writing about all she had seen and heard while partying around with Heather . . . all the ugly and embarrassing details. And she'd write it all – with such a moral tone. Ali would love it.

Miche and Jeremy were talking on the phone every other day. Their shared experience with Sally had given them a lot to talk about.

'Larissa is going to the memorial service in Sally's home town,' said Miche. 'I just couldn't bring myself to go with her. I should have, I suppose. But I couldn't face it. Though I would have liked the break. The city seems a bit claustrophobic.'

'That's rich, coming from a New Yorker,' said Jeremy. 'There are lots of gorgeous, uncluttered areas around Sydney.'

'I know. Larissa's friend, Kevin, has a boat and takes us around the harbour or up the Hawkesbury River.'

'Sounds great. But, listen, you promised to come to the Hunter Valley. Take a long weekend. You might find a story up here. There's a comfy B&B near us. Not flash. But comfy and not too expensive.'

'I'm tempted.'

'I reckon it's time we saw each other again. Save on the phone bills,' he kidded.

Miche wasn't deceived by his light tone of voice. They were both curious about each other. They'd shared a lot of personal detail that bordered on the intimate. It had seemed safe and uncomplicated to do so at a distance. He'd told her he'd broken up with a girlfriend when he went to France and, while he saw her occasionally, it wasn't the same. A year in Europe had changed him.

'Okay. I'll come. And seriously, it would be fantastic

if you can think of any stories I could do in your neck of the woods. I can write the trip off to tax then.'

'Terrific! I'll fax you a little map. And dinner Saturday night is on me. Sunday lunchtime my boss always has a bit of an open house, wine tasting and so on. You'd be welcome to come along. It's always kind of fun. I have a few chores Saturday morning, but you'll find plenty to do.'

To Miche's foreign eyes, the Lower Hunter was lovely – the scrubby native bushland, farms and paddocks neatly ploughed and planted. No billboards, no drive-through roadhouses. In the misty distance, the Brokenback Ranges cut into the blue canvas of sky.

Soon she was driving past trellised rows of low nubby vines, and near the entrance to the first winery she passed, she saw a sign announcing she was in the Home of the Hunter Wines.

Several of the wineries looked quite large and sprawling, but there was no sense of age as there had been in France. Even so, it was picturesque. Seeing a small restaurant with a courtyard shaded by grapevines, Miche pulled in for lunch.

There were several tourists wandering about, the cellar shop was crowded and the restaurant half full. The waitress was busy but pleasant. She gave Miche a menu and the wine list that featured mostly local wines. She was trying to decide what to try when an older man stopped to ask if he could help her select a wine.

'I'm new to the country, first time in this area, so the names mean very little I'm afraid,' smiled Miche. 'I was using the same method I do to pick horses – whatever name appeals.'

'Could have merit,' he agreed with a big smile. 'You really can't go wrong in this area with the local vintages.'

'Well, a glass of something local, light, crisp and dry,' said Miche closing the wine list. 'Surprise me.'

'Wonderful. I'll do that. Are you staying here for a while or just passing through?'

'I'm visiting a friend. He works in a vineyard.' Miche had to think for a moment. 'It's Palmerston Wines.'

'Ah, Steve and Helen. Know them well, great people. Excellent wines. Who's your friend?'

'Jeremy Foster. We met in France.'

'Young Jem. Good lad, he's coming on well. One of the local flying winemakers. That's what we call them. They go overseas to have a bit of European training. But, frankly, I think we can teach the Europeans a thing or two these days. You interested in the wine business?'

'Not really. Though I'd like to learn more. I'm a journalist. Looking for a story,' said Miche.

He saw the waitress trying to catch his eye. 'I'll choose a wine for you. And think about a story. This area has a very colourful history.'

Her meal was delicious and the wine exactly what she wanted. She made a note of it so she could order it with Jeremy and not seem the wine neophyte she was. Miche lingered over her lunch, enjoying her own company, the pleasant surroundings and being away from the city. She realised she'd been pretty strung out since arriving in Australia; still mourning her mother, the concern over work, the death of Sally. This time out was exactly what she needed. And there was the anticipation of seeing Jeremy.

The restaurant was less busy, the tourists didn't linger. Her host, as she assumed, returned to refill her glass.

'Compliments of the establishment. Maybe you'll write about us.'

'I'm not a foodie writer,' confessed Miche. Though

505

it seemed a good idea. She'd heard that food and travel writing was the best meal ticket in journalism.

'So who do you write for? I'm John Sandgate, by the way. This is my place. Started as a hobby and has become the love of my life.'

'I'm Michelle Bannister. Please, join me, seeing as I'm enjoying your wine,' said Miche. 'I'm a freelance writer, but work mostly for *Blaze*.'

'I'm impressed. So what do you write about?'

'Well, I suppose what interests me,' said Miche slowly.

'My wife subscribes to *Blaze*. I usually browse through it. Would I have seen anything of yours lately?'

'Maybe. I did a story about a young Australian model in France. Sally Shaw, sadly she . . .'

'Oh God, yes, she died. Suicide or overdose or something. I saw it on the news.'

'I had already been thinking of writing about tragedy and violence in the lives of young people when it happened,' said Miche sipping her wine.

'Can spring out of nowhere,' said the vintner, who found the subject rather disconcerting. Vineyard visitors were usually more upbeat, enjoying a day or so away from the rat race.

'Road rage, hostage crises, plane hijackings, can happen anywhere.' Miche looked around the gracious vineyard setting. 'Though not in a place like this, I guess.'

'Oh, we've had our share of dramas in this neck of the woods.'

'Like?'

'Well, let's see. Fires – suspected arson. Drought and floods. Industrial espionage where someone turned a tap and we lost a whole sublime vintage. A murder and a couple of spectacular divorces.' He gave a chuckle. 'All good material for a soap opera, eh?'

'It could be interesting.' Miche decided to ask Jeremy

more about the area. Maybe there was a story here.

She paid her bill and John Sandgate handed her a bottle of the verdelho she'd enjoyed at lunch. 'Share it with young Jeremy. And tell him if he ever wants to move over from Palmerston's I'll give him a job here in a flash.'

After settling into her Bed and Breakfast – in a quaint old farmhouse – she drove to meet Jeremy at Palmerston Wines.

A wall of slim poplars bordered the road, sandstone pillars held gracious wrought-iron gates that stood open, a white gravel driveway edging smooth green lawns that curved out of sight. It looked luxurious.

She drove past several utilitarian-looking buildings, noting the vineyards and what appeared to be the main house in the distance. A small stone building with several cars out the front was signposted 'Office'. Next to it was the cellar shop. She walked into the office and asked for Jeremy, but someone had followed her indoors and a cheerful voice behind her called her name.

'Miche! I saw you drive up.' He pulled a stained and battered broad-brimmed hat off his head and in a blur she was instantly reminded of her first vision of him coming into the dim dining room of the French chateau – fresh air and sunshine.

'You look just the same!' She felt it a silly thing to say, but Jeremy was giving her a warm hug that set off a confusion of feelings.

He stepped back to look at her. 'You don't look the same. You look even better than I remember.' He took her arm, 'Come on, hop in the wagon and we'll do the tour. I have to check on a few things as well.'

He helped her up into the four-wheel drive and threw his hat onto the back seat. 'Settled into the B&B all right? Did you have lunch?'

'It's perfect. I treated myself to lunch at one of the

vineyards. I met John Sandgate . . . who said he'd hire you in a flash if you're interested.'

'John's a top bloke. I'm well settled here with Helen and Steve, they've invested a lot in me. John'll probably come over to lunch on Sunday. Now, let me fill you in. It's going to be a boom year, I reckon. We're experimenting with different blends of grapes with our merlot. The shiraz is going to be great this year and the semillon looks good too. We're having a big wine tasting in a week or so.'

'For tourists?'

'No, chefs and waiters from Sydney's best restaurants and hotels. You'll have to come along. There'll be a few of the prominent interstate vignerons as well. They'll also be checking out the food. There are a couple of terrific eating places around here. Regional cuisine is being teamed with the wines and it's turning out to be a winning combination.'

'It's very pretty . . . I was winding around little back roads that seemed in the middle of nowhere, then you spin around a corner and there's a vineyard. They all look rather new and very neat.'

'It's becoming a bit too trendy, if you ask me. Little country clubs, and golf courses, lodge retreats and hobby places – and weekenders are popping up everywhere. Too close to Sydney in one way. But the tourist trade is a big part of the marketing scene now. Mind you, back in the 1850s there were over thirty vineyards in the area. It dropped off until the sixties when the boutique wineries started. They compete with the old, established boys.'

'Do you want to start your own place one day?'

Jeremy thought for a moment. 'Well, if I win Lotto I may think about it. I'd need big investors. I'm happy just learning all I can, and experimenting with varieties at the moment. It's a fast-changing industry.'

They drove to cellars, the crushing plant, fields, dams,

pumps and high points of land simply for the view.

She was enchanted by his enthusiasm and knowledge as he talked about the varieties of grapes, the climate, the differences between French and Australian winemakers. 'You know that's something I'd like to do – spend a season in the Napa Valley in California. They know a thing or two that may work here. Similar environments. You been there?'

'I'm an easterner I'm afraid.'

'You miss New York?' he asked gently.

'I miss my mom. And it's been a bit hard settling in here with my godmother away in Croatia. But I'm liking it. There's just the little matter of work and money.' In their phone talks, Miche had discovered how easily she could open up to Jeremy. It was comforting to share what was going on in her life. She hadn't yet found a circle of friends her own age. She missed chattering with her two college girlfriends and emails just weren't the same.

'You'll find your niche, Miche,' said Jeremy. 'Go with the flow as they say. Come on, let's go back and I'll introduce you to everyone. Sixish, I'll take you back to the B&B and wait for you to change or whatever and then we'll go out somewhere nice for dinner. I have to show off our little valley to you.'

'Sounds fabulous. Thanks for going to so much trouble.'

Jeremy laughed. 'Taking a friend to dinner – that's no trouble.' Then he added shyly, 'I've been looking forward to this all week.'

'Me too,' smiled Miche and felt herself relax. A small bridge had been crossed.

Miche rang Larissa on Sunday morning as she sipped her tea. 'I'm sitting in the sun outside my room with a home-cooked breakfast – and still in my PJs. Couldn't wait to tell you how fantastic this is. Dinner was divine – you have to come up here, glorious vineyards, terrific people.'

'Sure, sounds great. What about your guy?'

'Jeremy?' she laughed. 'He's gorgeous. Just lovely. I don't know why it didn't register with me so heavily when we were in France. I guess I thought we stuck together then because we were the only normal people in that mad group.'

'Normal is lovely. Hang on to him, Miche. Well, see how it works out. Just enjoy the company and the break,' cautioned Larissa. With a pang she remembered how she'd fallen in love with Gerry. How shy he'd been. They'd met at an art gallery opening and it was his reticence, his refusal to try hard to be entertaining and clever that had appealed to her. Her gradual discovery of his warmth, charm and humour had been such a joy. She did love him. She really did.

'I am just enjoying it all, Riss. But I can't wait to see him again. I think he'd like to see me too. He's talking of coming to Sydney.'

The Palmerstons' Sunday lunch turned into quite an event. Twenty people spread around the garden where a buffet table was set up under a vine-covered terrace. One table held a variety of wines for tasting and around it a knot of serious wine buffs knowledgeably discussed the merits of each bottle.

Miche popped into the big kitchen and asked Helen Palmerston if she could help in some way.

'It's under control, thanks Miche. Plenty of spare hands in here. Go and decorate the terrace, everyone is keen to meet you. A new face.'

'I feel like I'm being scrutinised . . . in a nice way,' she laughed.

'Oh you are, dear girl. Been a long time since Jeremy

has brought a girl to lunch. We're like family, so you must be special.'

'Oh, we're just friends from France, you know how travellers all connect up.' But she couldn't help feeling pleased.

John Sandgate, from the winery where she'd had lunch, singled her out. 'You know, Miche, I've been thinking about our talk. Why don't you write up the history of this area for *Blaze*? Be interesting to see it through your eyes – a well-travelled young person, new to Australia. As I mentioned yesterday, its history is quite colourful. And so are the characters.'

Miche thought for a minute. It was an idea worth considering.

'It does sound appealing,' said Miche. 'I'd have to do a lot of research, I don't know a thing . . .'

'That's what you journalists are best at. You'd have all the help you need. There's a lot of archival stuff, historical photos and most of the old vignerons kept diaries. Not just about their wineries, but about life in the district. Like I said, it's as good as any soap opera.'

Miche saw Jeremy wending his way towards her. She'd talk it over with him. 'I'll have to run it past my editor, but thanks for the suggestion.'

Jeremy was all for the idea. 'But then, I'm biased,' he added.

'Because you work in the wine business and you love this area?'

'Partly. But it would mean I'd see a lot more of you.' He kissed her long and hard as she stood by her car, ready to drive back to Sydney.

Miche returned his kiss, then grinned at him. 'I'll think about it as I drive back to Sydney.' She waved to him as she drove away. She could only think of positives. How she longed to talk to Nina. But in her heart she already knew what Nina's answer would be.

TAKE TWENTY-ONE ...

Was it the sense of freedom after being incarcerated, living with an ever-gnawing fear, that suddenly made Nina feel so free, so light-hearted? That made the unfolding scenery as they climbed into the hills so breathtaking? Or was it sitting beside Lucien, her hand resting on his leg?

Lucien suggested they stop for lunch. He sensed Nina was running on euphoric overdrive. So much had happened to them in such a short time, he wanted her spirit to settle. They pulled into a township inn and ordered a lavish spread.

'This is a huge meal, but so wonderful. I never used to eat lunch in New York or Australia – unless it was business. This meal is utter pleasure.'

Lucien poured her another glass of wine. 'I'm glad, my sweet. So, as we're setting off on this little adventure, tell me what you know about Grandfather Bubacic.'

Nina felt a warm glow rush through her. Maybe it was the wine, but seeing Lucien's attentive and loving face across the table, sharing this companionship and knowing neither of them had to hurry away to another life, sent her head spinning. 'I feel like telling you anything and everything, Lucien my darling. I can't believe we're here, that you're part of my life again . . .' She was about to add, '. . . for the moment, anyway,' but bit her tongue. How did they know what was ahead for them? She took a deep breath, telling herself to be calm and take life day by day.

Nina had such an expressive face, he knew what she was feeling so reached for her hand and squeezed it. He didn't speak, because he too felt suddenly emotional.

Nina sipped her wine and began, 'The part of the journal I managed to understand made sense. My grandfather led a double life. One was as an eminent physician, who treated some very rich and influential people during the war years, in the other he was a hero who worked against the Nazis for the resistance movement. It's also clear that my grandparents ran a safety house for resistance agents betrayed by Nazi collaborators. It was those collaborators' names that Puskar and Molnar wanted suppressed.'

'Clara and her mother must have known about it then.'

'Yes, but my mother didn't like to talk to me about these matters. Croatia seemed a long way away from the life she made for us in Sydney's Double Bay. Now that I know about this, I think it's rather fine that my grandparents helped people escape the Nazis.'

'I wonder how he did that,' mused Lucien.

'In the journal I read about one case where he'd offered to treat a very important prisoner of the Nazis who'd become ill. He'd drugged the prisoner into such a comatose state that he was able to pronounce him dead. Then he'd ordered the guard to take the man to the morgue.'

'Then what happened?' Lucien was intrigued.

'The mortician was a friend. He quickly administered a shot to restimulate the man's heart, which had been beating very slowly, and within two hours friends were able to put him in a car to be smuggled out of the country. Apparently a lot of supposedly dead men were taken away in the middle of the night in a hearse that stopped somewhere to let the bodies run away. They buried the empty coffins.'

'Your grandfather recorded all this detail in his journal?'

'There were a stack of stories. That's why I was so sorry to lose it.'

'What happened to your grandparents? When was the house taken over and turned into those ugly flats?'

'My mother told me that once the war was over, the new communist regime plundered what they could in the name of the state.'

'So where did your grandparents go?'

'Grandfather died soon after and Grandmama went to live with the housekeeper at their country house.'

'Where?' asked Lucien with sudden interest.

'The estate is called Miljovec. Grandfather's family built the house in the sixteenth century. His family was descended from the local Ban, or governor, who had built the original palace, which I believe is now in ruins. The village of Miljovec grew up around it.'

Lucien excused himself to pay the bill at the counter and sat back down as Nina finished her coffee. 'As we have no formal itinerary . . . I just asked the owner and he says Miljovec is not far out of our way.'

Nina carefully put her cup back in its saucer, peering at the sticky sludge of coffee grounds patterning the bottom of the bowl. 'Yesterday I would have said, no way – I'm just going to write a lovely scenic piece.'

'And now?'

'How far is Miljovec?'

They drove until they passed through tiny picturesque Sestne, a twelfth-century hamlet steeped in folklore. Nina looked at her map and pointed out the car window. 'The trails to Sljeme start here and go up to the ski fields of Zagreb.'

They nosed into the shadows cast by the fortress Medvedgrad, the 750-year-old symbol of Croatian struggle for freedom, and within half an hour Lucien drove down a narrow street between crumbling walls and turned into a village. 'Welcome to Miljovec.'

They stopped at a café and Lucien asked a man sweeping the sidewalk whether he knew any of the old families who used to live here before the war. The man looked at him blankly. Nina leaned from the car and repeated the question in Croatian. Still he shook his head, as he spoke a local dialect.

'Bubacic . . . ?'

At this the man nodded knowingly and spoke with passion. Nina leaned back in her seat and rubbed her eyes. Lucien sat back in the car.

'What did he say?'

'I can't believe it – I understood most of what he said. There are plans to turn Miljovec House, the old home of the Bubacic family, into a resort, a casino. For the tourists. It's only an hour and a bit from Zagreb.'

Lucien let out a surprised whistle. 'Well, that's one scenario we didn't consider.'

For the first time, Nina's attitude changed from sanguine wait-and-see to a quiet fury. 'How dare they! It was my family home. Stolen from my family. And now to be a damned casino! It's outrageous.'

'Sounds like something that would happen in the West,' said Lucien dryly.

'Why couldn't they do something constructive with

515

the place for the local people? A museum, an institute – anything but a place for international high-rollers.'

'Stop gnashing your teeth, Nina darling. Let's go to see it. Maybe there is a way you can prove family ownership and seek compensation. After all, they have acknowledged your family connection.'

Nina's vehemence subsided. 'You're right. It's not the money but the principle. My grandparents would be heartbroken.'

They drove through lush, neat fields where tiny stone cottages perched beside ancient rock terraces. In the distance, steep hills dense with majestic pines rose from the landscape. Soon there was a slash in the green blanket – a broad swathe was shaved into the hillside. A magnificent pastoral building was set in its centre. With turrets and wings surrounding a courtyard and lush grounds, it looked melancholy. Its upper storey of shuttered windows shunned the distant lake. Even at a distance it did not look inviting.

They reached the stone gates where the driveway swept between trees, bowing to each in greeting, as if dancing in line to a minuet, their leafy fingertips close to clasping. There was a bare patch on one stone pillar where a plaque had recently been removed.

Lucien stopped the car and Nina silently pointed at the rusting iron gates that hung open and Lucien saw a wrought-iron crest.

Nina showed him the small gold ring she wore. It had exactly the same crest. He smiled, patted her hand, then drove slowly towards the house.

'I assume there'll be someone around,' said Lucien as the main entrance came into view.

Nina leaned forward with a sharp intake of breath, suddenly recognising the building she'd seen so often, years ago, in family photographs.

'It looks terribly neglected,' said Lucien, thinking shabby would be a better word. But his cameraman's eye was alert and soaking up the setting, seeing it as a perfect movie location, almost as incredible as the true story of a family's fall from fortune.

They parked and walked to the solid wooden front doors and tugged at the rusting bell chain. It tolled through the innards of the mansion but failed to stir a response.

'Let's try the back door,' said Nina and set off briskly.

The rear of the old mansion was more welcoming. A vegetable garden was flourishing and fresh washing hung on a line by one of the courtyard wings. Smelling smoke, Lucien looked up to see a wisp rising from a big chimney close to one of the back doors. The kitchen, he guessed. Then he noticed beside the door a row of boots, several coats and jackets, pails for drawing water, bundles of twigs and firewood.

'Looks like a barn and stables down there,' said Nina, pointing to a few old stone buildings surrounded by a weathered fence. Nearby, several cows grazed contentedly.

Then they heard it. Sweet singing. They headed past the stables and came across a group of children scrubbing milking pails in the small river. An old woman was leading the singing. Younger children played on the grass. Lucien wished he had his camera.

At the sudden appearance of Nina and Lucien, the singing instantly stopped. Visitors were unusual – visitors like these surprised them. The smaller children gathered close to the old woman, who straightened and stared at them with a measure of hostility.

Nina lifted her arm and gave a friendly wave, calling out in Croatian. The woman eyed them curiously and the older children hurried forward. They looked to be aged between three and twelve years.

The oldest, a boy, came up to Nina and Lucien and pulled a woollen cap from his head. 'Who are you? Who are you looking for please?'

'We are just visiting,' said Nina quickly in Croatian. 'Tourists.'

The boy relayed this back to the others, who now ran to cluster around them. Nina waited for the woman to reach her as Lucien tried to find words in any language to make himself understood. Laughingly the children imitated him.

Nina greeted the woman and took her hand. It was the hand of a woman who did a man's work in the fields as well her woman's work in the kitchen, yet it had a tenderness for touching a child's cheek or hair. In the moment of that clasp Nina looked into the kindly eyes of a woman who appeared to be so many years older than her, yet was possibly the same age. She saw shadows of sorrow and pain, yet strength and laughter too. They each felt they had much in common – instinctively they recognised something about the other in the softness of the eye, the honesty of the face, the unflinching gaze, the firmness of the grip. Their life circumstances had been very different, but their hearts matched.

Nina introduced herself simply as Nina. 'And this is Lucien. He would like to take a few photographs of the old house. Are you living there?'

'We live in the house. We all do. We manage. My name is Mara. So you are not here about the casino business?'

'Indeed not. What a dreadful fate for the house. The café owner in the village told us.'

'In that case, would you like something to drink? You can see inside the house if you want.' The woman directed the older children to bring the young ones indoors and taking a silent little girl's hand, she directed the boy to sprint ahead and perk up the fire. As they began walking to the house she confided in Nina, who in turn translated the words for Lucien.

'Where are they from? Who are these children?' he asked.

Mara gave Nina another penetrating look and, as she walked, she told the story of how she had been caring for orphan children, victims of the recent conflicts around Croatia's borders.

'How do they come to be here?' asked Nina. 'I realise there is a huge crisis in Bosnia, but you are far from all that.'

'There is a network of people – priests, international aid workers mainly. It is all done very quietly. I was living and working on the estate and when the last people moved out of the house it seemed, well, sensible, to shelter children here. A few who have come here have been reunited with relatives, but there are always others needing a home. For the moment they go to the school in the village and we live on charity and what little government assistance we can scrape together.'

'Who was living in the house these past years? How long have you been there, and what's going to happen to you?' asked Nina as she watched the children take off their boots and shoes before going into the house in their thick hand-knitted socks.

'Ah, so many questions. Come, let us have a warm drink first.'

Inside the rear of the house, as Lucien had guessed, was a huge kitchen, pantry and storeroom. A table set for twelve ran almost the length of the kitchen.

Soon hot milk flavoured with vanilla, pieces of home-made cheese and slabs of bread were set before them and, slowly, Lucien was fed chunks of information digested by Nina from all the eager faces around the table.

Mara picked up her story again. 'Some time after the

widow who was living here died, this place was taken from the family. Over the years it was used as a country retreat for government officials. I was one of the cooks. Then it was closed up and there were many plans for it. But nothing happened. With the new government and a change in the old system, this place was forgotten.' She gave a broad smile. 'Fortunately. And, as I have lived here a long time, no one asked who I was, or if I had a right to be here.' She winked at Nina. 'I did rather give the idea I belonged here. I like to think the old family wouldn't mind.'

Nina had difficulty in speaking. 'I think you are quite right.' She passed all this on to Lucien.

'Are you going to tell her who you are?'

Nina gave him a conspiratorial wink. 'In good time.'

'So how long have you lived here?' Nina's head was reeling. This was almost too much to take in. Now she was under the roof of her grandparents' home and it all seemed very close and personal. But she was unprepared for Mara's reply.

'I was born here. My mother was very close to the Bubacic family. She looked after Mrs Bubacic until she died.'

Nina's hand flew to her mouth and Lucien looked at her in alarm.

'What's wrong?' he asked.

'Mara . . . is . . . like family.' She reached out to her across the table, tears filling her eyes. The chatter amongst the children stilled. Slowly she said, 'Mara. I must tell you who I am. I am Clara Bubacic's daughter, Nina.'

Mara clutched at the front of her dress, but her shock was quickly replaced with a huge smile. 'Clara went to Australia. With the little one. Little Nina. Once I was taken with my mother to Zagreb, to the big house, and I saw you before you left.' She rolled her eyes. 'We must be about the same age. I thought you were so brave going to the other side of the world with just your mama. I came back here and married a man from the village and we lived here in one of the cottages. He helped run the farm. My husband died a few years ago. Now young men in the village help us when they can.'

'You have no family?' asked Nina.

Mara waved an arm around the table. 'These are my children!' She explained to the children in more detail about who Nina was and Nina did the same for Lucien.

'Now, you must see the house,' exclaimed Mara. But added, 'Please don't feel sad. It is nothing like it was in your grandparents' day. So elegant. So many beautiful pieces of furniture, ornaments, paintings. My mother sometimes let me help in the house. To me this was so wonderful – until I saw the town house in Zagreb. That was a palace. But I missed the gardens and the fields.'

They all rose from the table and Mara took Nina's arm and linked it through hers.

Lucien stood back and let Nina walk through the doorway into a house of unknown family ghosts.

It was a house of grand proportions, expensive detail and expansive windows that were still partially framed in once costly brocade. Views from every window were picture postcard. Adapted now to house a family of ten children, it had the air of a happy, homely dormitory. Much of the furniture they had for the children was either homemade or second-hand and battered. But in each room Mara described to Nina how it had once looked, colouring the description with comments about her grandparents, bringing them to life for her. In the future, when she looked at Clara's photo albums, these words would mean so much more to her.

They went into a study and Mara sighed, 'There were so many books in this room, all along that wall. Your grandmother let me borrow them. She had a collection of nature books and art books. She painted too – did lovely watercolours. And up there on the wall was a stag's head with antlers. It used to frighten me. Until one day I saw it with your grandfather's walking hat hanging off one antler, his walking stick on the other and his pipe stuck in its mouth. I think he did it to make me laugh.'

In the last room they entered, Nina found a definite connection to her family. It was a small room, a sewing room perhaps. The window was in three sections, clear glass on either side of a brilliant work of stained glass. The leadlight design surrounded a central panel of pale blue background on which glittered an exquisite painted dragonfly. Nina was mesmerised. The sunlight, shining through the delicately inset picture made the translucent wings shimmer so that the dragonfly appeared to dance. The picture caught and captured the moment as the delicate insect alighted on a lily pad, its sheer rainbow-hued wings glistening in a sunray. Nina bit her lip and sat on a chair, staring at the wonderful glass picture.

Sensing her mood, Mara shooed the children away. 'I'll let you look around on your own for a bit.'

Lucien hovered in the doorway. 'If I believed in ghosts, I'd say your grandfolks were still enjoying this house.'

'I think they are too. They must be happy to hear children's laughter and singing.' She went to the window and gently touched the glass. 'It's exquisite. Clara told me how my grandmother loved dragonflies. She gave me that diamond pin . . . it's why I chose it as the emblem for *Blaze*.'

Nina was close to tears. Lucien put an arm around her shoulders. 'It's meaningful for me too. Remember when I first met you, how you made me free the dragonfly . . . Nina, stay with me. Let's you and me . . . dance through this last part of our lives. Be as free and light-hearted.'

Nina turned back to face him. They were alone. 'Be your dancing partner? What does that mean?'

He wrapped his arms around her. 'Marry me, Nina. We should have done it forty years ago.'

She buried her face in his shoulder, her response muffled. 'I'm so tempted.'

'But?' He held her at arms-length.

'I haven't quite finished this little trip. And I worry about *Blaze* in Sydney. And now there's . . . this.' She waved her arms around the room. 'First things first, my love.'

Lucien let her go and snapped his fingers in a show of sudden understanding.

'I think I know what you're contemplating,' he grinned. 'Just what you need – another project.'

'I want to fix this place up for them. Make it secure, a permanent tribute to my family.'

'The Bubacic Children's Home?' mused Lucien.

'Something like that. I need to find out how to do all this legally. Let's stay a couple of days.' She hugged Lucien. 'I've really found my family.'

'You should still write about all this for your magazine article. I'll take the photos. It's a lovely, positive story of family found and triumph over war that will fascinate *Blaze* readers around the world. And that will please the local authorities, I'm sure,' said Lucien as he followed Nina downstairs.

'But they won't be so pleased when they learn I intend to stop my family home being turned into a casino,' said Nina firmly.

They checked into an inn in the village and the next morning went back to the house to explain Nina's plan to Mara and the children.

Lucien roamed the house and grounds with his camera as Nina and Mara discussed renovations and necessities.

523

'The children need a proper classroom and many more facilities,' said Nina. 'Perhaps I can help the village school improve its amenities as well.'

'Everywhere is a classroom,' said Mara. 'We teach the children about the world around them,' but she added, 'It would be lovely to bring the big gardens back to their former glory, not just for food but to help the children understand nature. When you have nurtured a plant, you appreciate all living things.'

Nina gazed at Mara thinking how wise she was. 'That is true. How about we add a gentle old horse or two, and more cows?'

Mara laughed at Nina's enthusiasm. 'The dairy still has everything we need to make butter, cheese and yoghurt for ourselves. We could even sell some. We once had very strong and healthy goats – and pigs too.'

Nina added goats and pigs to her list. 'Now, Mara, we need other people here to work. This is too much for you and the children to care for. There must be people in the village who would like to help – and be paid for their services.'

Mara fiddled with the folds of her long skirt. 'And how long will this be for, Nina?'

'It's forever, Mara. My lawyer will make sure of that. And I think I can stop this place being turned into anything other than what I want . . . it is my family home that was taken over illegally. I intend to write about this place and your wonderful work. I don't think the authorities will fight too hard.'

Tears flooded Mara's eyes. 'I'm so relieved. I was becoming so worried about what would happen to these children, and the many others out there who need love and care.'

'And you have to be looked after too, Mara. Call it what you will – God, the angels, fate, but I knew there was a reason I had to make this trip and, now I've found it, I can move on with my life. The way ahead is quite clear.'

Mara shook her head in a gesture of astonishment and acceptance. It was all so complex and it was happening too fast for her to completely comprehend the sudden change in fortune for her and the children. 'We'll have to talk to the priest and the people who've been helping us, Nina. They need to know.'

'Of course,' laughed Nina. 'I'll talk to them with you, and I'll come here as often as I can.'

Lucien had quietly entered the room and taken photos of the two women as they talked. He lowered his camera. 'And what about *Blaze*?' he asked in a casual aside. 'This is going to put a big hole in your time and pocket.'

'Perhaps it's simply a matter of putting my priorities right, eh? What else do I have to spend my money on? I don't have children of my own, but now . . . I have this huge family!' Nina rushed at him to give him a kiss, 'And that includes you!'

Days later, after long discussions with Mara, Nina had a notebook full of detail about her new family. Somehow she would weave it all together for an article that could grow into something much bigger. Lucien was continuing to talk of putting money towards the orphanage to use part of the old house and the grounds to make a film.

Their goodbyes were tearful but happy. The youngest girl was chosen to present Nina with a circlet of flowers the children had made. Nina bent down to kiss her as the child placed the garland on Nina's head. Lucien snapped the moment and knew he had a photograph that said it all.

'Is there anything you want to take away with you?' asked Lucien softly.

'I have everything in here.' Nina touched her heart.

'Working to have this place running properly will be the best tribute I could make to my grandparents for all the good work they did.'

Lucien wondered if Nina's lack of children was driving her to seek a sort of monument that was more meaningful and lasting than any magazine. They had just found each other again after such a huge chunk of their lives had passed. They had so little time left. Please, God, let them spend it together. But he wasn't going to dampen her joy. He kept his voice light as he raised an eyebrow. 'Where do your old friends fit into this exciting new vision and living?'

'Life is like a big delicious pie, my darling. We have a wonderful kids' book in Australia called *The Magic Pudding*. It's about a pudding you keep on eating forever. No matter how many slices you take, there's more for the eating. We can all share the magic pudding of life with the right attitude.'

Lucien looked at the happiness – and determination – on Nina's face. 'Okay. Count me in.'

It was late, Ali was tired as she flipped casually through the final proofs of the magazine that were due at the printers the next morning. April's story on Heather Race had been pushed through and it was a dazzler . . . though Heather wasn't going to think so. The piece had been thoroughly checked for legal problems, but Ali was still worried Heather would sue for defamation. How April had convinced so many people to confide their horrific experiences with the TV woman, was beyond her. Ali was the ultimate mistress of the tight lip, but how to keep others from talking about you was hard to control.

For a brief moment, a series of nightmare images

from the past flashed across her consciousness and a tension replace her tired casualness, but she forced herself to resume control. She told herself she was more secure than she had been in years. She had position, she had power – and both meant a lot to her. No one would dare speak out against a powerful media personality, as she was now. Yes, she was safe and secure. She focused more intently on the material on her desk, flipping through the pages to make sure *Blaze* advertisers were receiving the right level of subtle editorial support. She was pleased the beauty section had given their cosmetic advertisers a favourable splash for their new products. She made a note to replace the circulation figures with the readership figures on the cover of the next issue. You could always fudge the numbers upwards by estimating more than one reader for each household, rather than the actual magazines sold.

As she continued flipping pages, something caught her eye. She stopped and went back to a page where an ad ran down a right-hand column. She had placed a story there. She realised, to her fury, it had been replaced by this advertisement.

In the ad, an arrangement of wineglasses and wine bottles spilled from a package tied with red ribbon. What shocked her was the name '*Blaze* Connoisseur' stamped on the box. 'What the hell . . . ?' She read the ad, which offered membership in an exclusive club that gave members preferential options to buy exclusive boutique wines from a winery in the Margaret River district of Western Australia. Normally the ad wouldn't attract her attention, but for the fact it carried the word *Blaze*. There was a mail coupon and a website address. She flipped open her laptop, logged onto the Internet and found the site. It was impressive, listing the financial and social advantages of the club, 'established in conjunction with *Blaze* magazine', and the details of the attractive winery, showing photos of the vineyard and the resident vigneron. It looked like a quality product, but who the hell had given permission for them to link up with *Blaze*? Nina would never allow such crass commercialisation. Ali didn't care about that, so long as she'd known and been involved. Bloody Reg. She grabbed the phone, went to her directory in her laptop and punched in Reg Craven's home number. It was just before midnight.

Reg's wife sleepily answered the phone.

'Put Reg on,' snapped Ali without preamble.

'What is it?' mumbled Reg, knowing it was Ali.

'What the hell is *Blaze* Connoisseur? Who authorised it?'

'It's a wine club. They bought an ad. Big deal.'

'Reg, stop bullshitting. Who gave them permission to use our name? And, what's more, how dare you replace a story with this ad.'

'You're not the only person authorised to do deals on behalf of *Blaze*, Ali.' There was now a smug tone to Reg's voice. 'They're bloody good wines. Don't worry about it.'

'I suppose you have a cellar full,' retorted Ali. 'And so do the rest of the men upstairs.' She was furious that this had slid past her and it was far too late and costly to pull it. 'I'll let it go through for this edition, but I want a full accounting of the deal tomorrow.'

'Jump in the lake, Ali.' Reg hung up the phone.

It was to become the biggest-selling edition of *Blaze* so far . . . but not for reasons Nina would have liked. Thank God she couldn't be reached in Croatia. All hell was breaking over Ali's head.

Everyone was talking about April's story on Heather Race. April was decried as a viper, while privately virtually everyone in the media – including a number of network heavies – was glad someone had given the dreaded Heather a rich serve of what she so often dished out.

The TV network Heather worked for went into damage control and issued a statement that Miss Race was speaking to her lawyer and further action would be taken. Heather was forced to go to ground and did not appear on that evening's edition of *Reality*.

April patrolled the hallways of *Blaze*, revelling in her moment of fame.

But behind doors there was endless discussion. 'How could Bob let that through?' asked Barbara. 'It's just so unclassy. Nina will loathe it.'

'Come on, Barbara. It's an absolute ripper of a story. The issue has almost sold out and another run is likely. No matter what people think about the subject matter or how she's written it, everyone is reading it with relish,' said Tony Cox. 'The ad people have clients queueing up to reach the obviously growing readership.'

'You guys just like to see two women in a cat fight,' said Kaye, one of the staff writers. 'I think it's disgusting. I would never write a piece like that . . . even if the girl is a bitch, you can write it more subtly and still make it a good read.'

'Watching someone shrivel up from slow poisoning isn't as dramatic as seeing them hit over the head with a big shovel,' grinned Tony.

'Well, some of that dirt on the shovel might well fly back in April's face,' said Kaye.

'Times have certainly changed,' sighed Barbara, who wondered why she was now embarrassed to admit she worked for *Blaze*. Even in her now minor capacity. She answered her own question – Ali. This tribe of young women were all utterly alien to her. There was no place for her any more in this free-wheeling, back-stabbing, no-holds-barred journalistic bunfight. How right – and principled – Tiki had been in walking out from the start.

Barbara wasn't so brave. She was looking at her mid-fifties and a downhill slope. What would she do with the rest of her life? Her glamorous days as a woman's magazine beauty editor were gone. Women's magazines, as she knew them, were gone. She thought back to how she'd been trained by the editors to dress and speak with style, to write honestly and politely, and to ignore rude or vulgar comments dropped by those you interviewed. Only pleasant pictures appeared in word and print. The editorial ethos was safe, predictable and superficial. Now she was trapped in a fast-changing scene that could destroy her. Barbara felt a tiny tremor – suddenly it was quite clear to her that she had to leave. Leave before Ali booted her out with no ceremony or acknowledgement. There one day, gone the next. The decision suddenly gave her a small sense of self-esteem and power. God knows what she would do with herself. But anything had to be better than being trampled down or ignored. She became aware Eddie was saying something to her with his curled lip.

'Don't become a dinosaur, Babsy. Change with the times. You have to keep up, darling. Kaye is miffed because April is claiming the star writer banner. I think April's story is sensational, but you watch, Heather will bring the network heavies into the fray. Nothing surer.'

Belinda had been listening and made note of the comment. Maybe she should alert Ali. Eddie knew something. As for poor Barbara . . . well it was a pity – they now treated her so dismissively – but old values, old loyalties counted for little these days.

An impromptu lunch was arranged at a trendy

brasserie to celebrate the biggest-selling issue of *Blaze* since its launch. April and Eddie were star turns, each trying to outdo the other with viciously witty verbal ping-pong. No cow was sacred and between the two of them they seemed to know everyone and what went on – and came off.

Turning away from the noisy table, Larissa leaned close to Miche. 'So, have you decided what you're going to write about? Childhood trauma, searching for father or the delights of the Hunter?'

Miche grinned. 'I think the Hunter might win this round. It means I'll be in the area for some time so Jem and I can see a lot more of each other.'

'How do you feel about that?'

Miche smiled. 'Good. Really good.' She paused and broke into laughter. 'I mean *very* good! I really like him. But I don't want to rush anything. This is a terrific way to keep seeing him without making it a . . . big deal.'

Looking at Miche's flushed, happy face, Larissa felt suddenly old. How well she remembered those first rushes of excitement, attraction and passion when you wondered, was this the one? How she'd felt when she first met Gerry. Nearly a decade of her life with one man. A man she adored, who made her laugh, loved her, cared for her, wanted to marry her. But on his terms. Miche was talking to someone else and, in the swirl of the group, Larissa sat arguing with herself as if the sound around her had been switched off. She knew there were other men out there who were attracted to her – Kevin, for one. But would they last as long? To be brutally hon-est, she suspected Kevin was the type to want a younger, updated version of Larissa on his arm in a few years time. He was sweet and attentive, rich, available, successful. But that all came as baggage. He'd call the shots. So, she reasoned, how bad, how stifling, was Gerry's plan?

Marry, move to New Hampshire, settle down, have kids. It's what she'd always wanted. She'd always have that. How secure, how important was *Blaze* to the rest of her life? That was the problem. She was swept up in the short term. The day-to-day competitiveness, the treadmill of daily goals and deadlines. The minutiae of a small world. The world of *Blaze*.

There should be more to life than helping edit a magazine, which entertained and informed people for a while until they dropped it into a bin. Larissa lifted her head. The sound returned around her. Colours seemed brighter. She tugged at Miche, who was talking to Dan on her left, interrupting her mid-sentence.

'Miche, you know something? I've just decided.'

Miche still had half her attention on what Dan was saying. 'Excuse me Dan, sorry, what were you saying, Riss?'

Larissa looked at Miche and said slowly and distinctly, 'I'm leaving. I'm going back.'

Miche blinked as the simple sentence, spoken in a steady voice, suddenly sounded like a shout. 'Leaving? Here? You mean, you're going back to the US? To Gerry?'

Larissa nodded, a huge smile breaking out as the tightness in her chest eased.

'To get married?' cried Miche. And as Larissa nodded, she flung her arms about her.

But no one else in the group heard or paid any attention, each anxious to capture centre stage with their anecdotes and witticisms.

The next afternoon, Miche went to see Larissa in her office with flowers and a sweet card wishing her joy.

'How sweet of you, Miche. I needed a boost like this, really needed it.' While Larissa's intent hadn't wavered, she felt a little wobbly at dealing with the logistics.

'Have you done the deed yet?' asked Miche.

'Ali has been unavailable most of the day, but I have been granted an audience in fifteen minutes.'

Miche went to make coffee while Larissa rang New York again to try to reach Gerard. When Miche returned with the coffee, Larissa looked glum. 'Haven't found him yet. God, I hope I'm not too late. I've been trying since yesterday afternoon to reach him. He said he was moving on with his life. It was up to me.'

'So pack up, take a plane and walk in the door. Do what he did, arrive on the doorstep.' Miche spoke confidently, but in her heart she fretted for her friend and mentor. What if Gerry had moved in with a new girlfriend? You just never knew with guys, the ones like Gerry were lousy at being on their own.

'You're right, it's one way to sort things out,' agreed Larissa. 'He hasn't actually taken back his proposal.' She tried to make it a joke. 'Okay, step one – I'm off to see Ali.'

'Go girl, go,' called Miche.

Miche continued to clear out Larissa's office and was busily packing books and folders and the personal photos and knick-knacks off the desk. She was kneeling on the floor, securely taping up a carton, and didn't notice the soft step behind her until a heavy hand slapped her on the bottom.

'Howdy! Need a hand? Ha ha.'

Miche recoiled and turned to see Reg Craven standing over her. She began to scramble to her feet when he leaned down and 'helped' her by grabbing her upper arm, his fingers pushing against her breast.

'Oops-a-daisy,' he leered, his boozy breath radiating into her face.

Miche slapped his hand away. 'Do you mind!'

'Nope. Do you?'

He was still smirking and was obviously drunk. Miche took a step backwards and glared at him. 'Did you want to speak to Larissa?'

He glanced around the disordered office. 'What's going on? She moving? Are you moving in, babe? Be great to have a bit of young blood in the place. Too many uptight chooks around here.' He took a step towards her and Miche pushed an arm in front of her.

'Stop right there and keep your hands to yourself.'

He froze and lifted his arms above his head in mock surrender. 'Hey, girlie, don't be paranoid. Ole Reggie is only trying to be a gent.'

'You'll have to try a lot harder,' snapped Miche. 'I suggest you come back later.'

He looked at her furious face and backed down. Without a word, he wandered out of the office.

Miche expelled her breath – the encounter had shaken her. The thought of having to deal with office politics and men like Reg Craven depressed her.

Reg was not concerned about the incident with Miche. Can't blame a bloke for trying, right? After returning to his office, his attention wandered, so he sauntered down the hall and stopped at an office and leered again. 'Hey babe, what's up?'

It was April's office and she didn't look amused. 'Don't call me babe, Reg. I'm not one of your lunchtime bimbos. Why are you strolling the halls? Looking for a quick grope?'

'Tacky, my dear. I've heard you've been seen in a few less than salubrious hang-outs.' His voice slurred on the last words. He ventured into the office.

April, who'd been standing next to her desk, perched on its corner crossing her legs and giving him a challenging look. 'What's that mean? I doubt you and I frequent the same places.'

'A little dicky bird told me they saw you coming out of a strip joint in the back of Oxford Street in the wee hours. Don't tell me that was a party you were covering for *Blaze*.'

'Did they tell you I was with Jacques and Tony? There's a lot that goes on around here that you don't know about, Reg. You're a little old for the fun.'

The zinger stung him more than April knew. The anger Reg harboured towards Ali hadn't been assuaged by his late-night strike on the sandpit. He was feeling alienated and he knew the ground was shifting beneath him. April's arrogant, impudent amusement suddenly annoyed him and, in an unplanned move, he lunged at her, ramming his hand up her skirt, 'I'll show you, bitch . . .'

April was knocked off balance and stumbled to her knees on the floor and Reg lurched backwards as if burned, his staring face drained of colour, his mouth trying to make words that wouldn't form. Then, as he turned to the door, he found it blocked by his nemesis.

Ali raised her eyebrows. 'Do I dare ask what the hell is going on?'

As April and Reg struggled to regain their composure, each waited for the other to decry or shout abuse. Strangely both were silent.

April was first to recover. She straightened her shoulders in a shrug and smoothed her micro skirt. 'I slipped off the desk.'

'We were having . . . a disagreement. Nothing to do with you, Ali.' Reg gave April a hard look, but she didn't respond.

Ali folded her arms. 'Any harassment of my staff is my business, Reg, thank you very much.'

Reg pushed past her. 'Ah, get fucked, Ali.'

Ali glared, but let him go. She turned back to April. 'Want to tell me about it?'

'No.'

'The man's a pig. Don't worry about it.'

Ali left and went to her office where Larissa was waiting.

TAKE TWENTY-TWO …

Morris Brown, the general manager of Network Five had agreed to see Heather Race privately. He'd considered including the station's lawyers, but they were currently busy on a case before the Broadcasting Tribunal for breaches of the advertising code.

For a wild moment he'd hoped she was coming to see him to resign, she was such a headache. There'd been more threatened lawsuits and complaints over her stories than the rest of the reporters put together. However, this last contretemps over the *Blaze* magazine article had boosted the ratings of *Reality*. People loved to watch people they hated. The next morning, after a Heather Race interview, people would gather around the water coolers to trash what she'd done. 'Did you hear what that bitch said?' they'd say. 'She's outrageous. That show is the pits.' But they all watched it.

As Heather was shown into his lavish office, Morris Brown rose from his executive chair and crossed the room to shake her hand. She spoke first with a bright, 'I haven't come to resign.'

'I should hope not,' smiled her boss, waving her to the smaller of the two sofas. 'The show is rating well.'

'Yeah, thanks to that bitch, April Showers. Where are we at with the defamation case, by the way?'

'They're still weighing it up. While we want to redress the issue of a quite unnecessarily vicious article, we have to make sure we're on firm legal ground before taking action. Or it could be very costly.' He paused, wondering how he might broach his next point and this seemed a good opportunity. 'The legal team were wondering if the publicity about the case and your feelings of outrage, which have been expressed in the media, might have already put your side of the story in balance without pressing any further. They would prefer a settlement or an apology, but *Blaze* is only going to agree to that if they feel they're in the wrong. And I understand from the *Blaze* lawyers that Miss Showers thinks she is very much in the right.' When Heather didn't answer he continued, 'How do you feel about it all? And what specifically did you want to see me about?'

Heather gave a small smile that was more of a smirk. 'About April Showers, actually. I have a way of settling this whole thing for far less money and in a way that will be to the station's advantage. And it will keep me happy too.'

'I'm all ears, my dear.'

Heather recrossed her legs, flashing an expanse of thigh at the general manager who was trying to remain aloof and businesslike and forget the drunken Christmas lunch in the boardroom the previous year.

Heather leaned forward, lowering her voice. 'I want revenge on Showers for that bitchy story. So I have a promise of a story about April Showers that would blow her to bits. The source is excellent, but there is, of course, a price.'

'How reliable is the information, how true is it, and how much?' he sighed.

Heather ticked the points off on her fingers. 'One. The source is an old friend of April's who says he knows every detail of this part of her life intimately. Two. I believe him because he wouldn't be so keen to make it public and ask for what he wants and not have the goods. Three. The asking price is a job. In television. Here. On camera.'

'Oh Christ, no way. We can't throw amateurs in front of a camera.'

Heather raised a sceptical eyebrow and Morris Brown knew he'd made a silly remark. Half of their shows were stacked with first-time presenters. Some were talented, others were made to look good, some were pretty awful, but they hung on for various reasons. 'This guy could work out. He's gay, he's funny, he has a sharp wit and an even sharper tongue and he's a bit of a performer.'

'And he wants to be on TV so badly he'd ruin a friendship with an old pal?'

'You bet.'

'So what's the story on April Showers?'

'He won't tell me till he has an assurance of a job here.'

'We can say the same to him.' Then, seeing Heather's face set, he capitulated. 'Let's make it a provisional agreement that if what he has is strong enough to blow April Showers out of the water and drop the case against us, we'll give him a three-month contract.'

'Six.'

'Okay, six months.' If the guy didn't cut it on camera, they could pay him out the six months and see him off the station. 'So tell me who I've just hired, for God's sake.'

'Eddie Kurtz. He's a creative advertising–marketing whiz-kid.'

'Who wants to do what? Sing? Tap dance?' Morris was weary. He wanted Heather out of his office.

'Talk. Do a bitch April Showers gossip segment. She has been angling to find a spot on TV and it would kill her to have Eddie achieve it. It could actually work well on *Reality* as an end segment. People would hang out through the whole show for it. I think he has what it takes.'

'That's up to your executive producer. Firstly, how are you going to release this bombshell about April? Leak it to what paper? Whoever wins it will owe us a favour after this. Unless April Showers sues them.'

'We're not. Going to release it, I mean,' said Heather mildly. 'Apparently it's so hot, as soon as I threaten April with what I know she'll run for cover. You watch.'

'I'm not so sure. She was pretty ballsy writing what she did about you.'

'If she doesn't give me an apology, we go public with it. What I really want is to knock her off her arrogant perch. As long as she knows I have the goods on her, I'm in a very strong position of win–win–win,' said Heather smoothly.

Morris Brown stood up. 'I'll await the good news from our lawyers that you're saving us the trouble of a lawsuit against April Showers and *Blaze*. And this conversation hasn't taken place.' He went back to his desk.

Heather stood. At the door, she turned back to him. 'You won't regret this Morris.'

'I regret a lot of things,' he said in a tired voice. 'Sometimes, hiring you was one of them.'

'I still have eighteen months on my contract to go,' smiled Heather. 'We'll talk then.' She closed the door behind her with a confident yank.

*

Although Larissa was determined and sure about her decision to leave, the short walk to Ali's office felt like a marathon. With every step came a flood of images and sounds. A high-speed replay of moments in her career at *Blaze*. Not all were positive, but even the down moments were memorable. The pressures, the creative disagreements, the occasional disappointments had drawn them together, learning from mistakes and failures, testing imagination and wits for the next issue. Australia had been a highlight and while there was still disappointment that she hadn't made it to editor, she knew she had done her best at all times.

She was brought back to the moment by Belinda who put her finger to her lips and nodded over her shoulder to show that Ali was on the phone.

Ali's rapid-fire conversation ricocheted towards Larissa as Ali waved her to come in and sit down. 'Sure, it's a departure from what readers expect to find in *Blaze*. But the day we become predictable and safe, we're doomed.' Ali paused and rolled her eyes towards the ceiling indicating it was someone from the male management above them. 'You're entitled to make the point, but I'm the editor and I make editorial decisions. And I've decided to shunt April into this new tack. If you've got a problem, take it up with Nina when she returns. I've already run it past Baron Triton,' she added pointedly. 'End of story.' She hung up.

'Upstairs giving you a hard time?' asked Larissa.

'Yeah, trying to justify their existence. I think the TV network boys, who are part of the same club, have told our boys to give April a hard time. Want her to back off or give her the boot. At least they tell me the network has dropped the case against us. Now . . .' she began rifling on her desk as Larissa wondered how to start the conversation. Before she could open her mouth, Ali pushed a

541

sheet towards her. 'Here. April sent in some more profile ideas. See what you think of them.'

'I don't think so, Ali.'

Ali lifted her head. 'Excuse me? What are you saying?'

'I'm quitting.'

'You're quitting?' Ali didn't believe what she was hearing.

'Yes, Ali. As of now. It's a personal thing. I've been struggling with a deep personal issue for some time and at last I realise I have to confront it right now. Make a hard decision. So I've decided to go back to the States. To Gerard.'

'The boyfriend? You're walking out on your contract, giving up a job for your boyfriend?' Ali sounded incredulous. 'Surely you're not going back to *Blaze USA*?' For a fearful moment Ali hoped Larissa hadn't been offered a job back in New York that might do her out of an opportunity. No, Oscar would have mentioned it.

Larissa shook her head. 'Another reason. It's complicated. Gerry is moving interstate from New York. I'm going to marry him.' She gave a small smile. 'It's come down to the female's dilemma – marriage or career.'

A dozen scenarios began to buzz through Ali's brain. Already she was thinking who she could hire to replace Larissa – someone who would do her bidding. She groped for something to say to Larissa. But all she could think of was that she would never allow herself to be put in such a position. After all the years Larissa had spent working her way up to deputy editor and being in line for an editorship . . . and she was tossing it away for some guy just because he was moving. 'It can't have been an easy choice,' said Ali.

'That's an understatement. I wrestled with it for a long time, and now I've suddenly decided and it seems

542

the right thing to do. I won't have regrets. I'm only sorry I'm getting out ahead of my contract.'

Ali cut in, holding up her hand. 'Hey, no worries. Your life comes first, Larissa.' She didn't want to say she'd get someone in to replace her as quickly as she could. It struck Ali that finding someone to do her bidding and yet take on the responsibility and unstinting workload of Larissa may not be so easy.

Larissa guessed Ali's first reaction would be to plan her replacement. Well that was her problem. She wasn't going to make any recommendations. She wouldn't wish Ali on her enemies. And Ali really had no idea how much of a burden Larissa carried in the office. Especially her role as mediator, soothing the ruffled feathers and hurt feelings that Ali constantly engendered.

'What triggered this decision?' asked Ali, genuinely curious.

'I was giving Miche some advice about relationships and their importance when I realised I should be listening to my own counsel.'

'You know something, this could make a story,' mused Ali. 'A lot of women face this kind of crisis, right?'

Larissa wasn't sure if Ali was serious, but firmly dismissed her involvement. 'Unfortunately it's the case, but not my story thank you.' She gazed at Ali and, to her surprise, found herself asking, 'Do you face this sort of crisis, Ali? What keeps you awake at night?'

Ali tensed slightly and for a moment Larissa thought her remark had pierced a chink in Ali's famed armour-plate. Just as quickly it closed and Ali was flippant. 'Not a lot. I take pills if I have to.' She turned her attention to the papers on her desk. 'Okay, let's do some housekeeping. I'll make the announcement at the editorial meeting on Wednesday. We'd better run through what you've been working on.'

For the next fifteen minutes they talked amiably and professionally about the changeover. Then Ali rose, obviously intending to walk Larissa out the door where Belinda sat, unaware of the bombshell Larissa had just dropped. She shook Larissa's hand, a gesture that surprised her. 'I hope you'll be happy. Good luck, Larissa. In a way I envy you.'

'You do?' Larissa was shocked to hear Ali say it.

'That you have the choice.' Ali hesitated. 'Yeah, but I can live with that. See you.'

Larissa turned away wondering what else Ali had learned to live with. Somewhere in her past was something that had the power to disturb her cool and collected demeanour. Something that stopped her deviating from the path she'd chosen. And just then she'd come close to letting her guard drop.

The following day Nina rang Ali. Once Ali had been told of Nina's safe release she had put her to one side of her mind. But Nina's voice had a new vibrancy to it. Even down the phone line her enthusiasm was catching. Ali sat up straighter in her chair and began making notes as Nina relayed the gist of her experiences.

'Nina, back off from the children's home. Repeat the stuff about being held. What you're saying to me is you were held as a suspected spy?'

'That's what they thought. I mean, it wasn't me – it was the old journal. It could have caused a political embarrassment . . .'

Ali felt the excitement growing. She knew Nina herself, the most famous magazine publisher in the world, was the story – not what she might have found out about her family. There'd been a brief burst of publicity over Nina's detention and release. Now it was time to run the real story. Ali could see the shout line on *Blaze*'s cover – '*Exclusive! Blaze's Nina Jansous writes – My ordeal as a captured "spy" in Croatia*'.

'Did they mistreat you?' Ali was looking for grisly details.

'Emotionally and mentally it took a toll, yes.'

'I can't wait to read your story. How soon can you send? We could drop a spread and start on a TV campaign for the issue. Can your friend email his photos to us?'

Nina saw where Ali was going with her story. 'Ali, I don't want to play up that part of my trip any more. It was really just a misunderstanding, if a lengthy one. The authorities and I came to an agreement. The deal is that I write about all the positive things here. And it's a beautiful country. Combined with my personal discovery, I think there's a lot more richness to this story than the one about me being detained.'

'Nina, come on. This is a fantastic scoop. We can really run with this. Do you have good pix? Any from inside the place you were being held? The guys who interrogated you? The story has politics, intrigue, sleuthing and family drama, you know. Top stuff. We'll sell heaps.'

Nina's enthusiasm cooled. 'Ali, I don't want to be pressured. And I don't want my copy changed without discussion, and I want to know every detail of what you're doing with publicity.'

Ali was soothing. 'Sure, Nina. This is such an opportunity for us to cross-promote your story and achieve coverage everywhere. When are you leaving there? We can arrange for a film crew to interview you when you return to Paris, New York, wherever.' She avoided mentioning Sydney.

'I don't think I want to do that, Ali. Wait until you read my story. I'm glad you sound so keen,' added Nina wryly.

Ali changed tack. 'Nina, if you can see your way clear to giving us the story so we can get it in the issue we're compiling now, that would be so great. That is, if you can do it. I know you haven't written for a long time . . .'

The dig hit home. 'I'll see what I can do, Ali. We've just had a wonderful couple of days on the Dalmatian coast. I'm leaving for Paris in the morning. How is everything there?'

'No probs. Going gangbusters,' said Ali cheerfully.

'I'll be in touch. Can you transfer me to Larissa please.'

Ali hesitated for a moment then said, 'Nina, Larissa has just resigned.'

'What! Why?' The shock reverberated from Dubrovnik.

Ali was matter of fact. 'No surprise, really. Couldn't stand the separation from her guy. I think she's going to marry him. From a career point of view, she's been there and done that.' Ali's voice had a faintly disparaging tone as if Larissa had reached her use-by date and choosing marriage and kids was a last option. It would never be an option for Ali. She had decided many years ago never to have children. Marriage would only be when it suited her and would bring her what she wanted most – security, extreme wealth, position and power. Realising the effect her news must have had on Nina, she added insincerely, 'Larissa's been fantastic of course. But that old biological clock is ticking. It's no big deal. I have a few very able people in mind as deputy.'

Nina bit her tongue. Losing Larissa was a very big deal. Certainly she was happy for her if marriage and babies was what she wanted, but she sensed there was more to Larissa's decision. 'Why now, though? While I'm away?'

'Her man is moving to a new job interstate, so it's

a now-or-never kinda thing.' Typical of Nina, thought Ali, to think Larissa would wait until Nina was back to ask permission. Too controlling. Who cared about other people's personal lives? They were there to do a job. She had made it a rule never to become remotely involved in the private lives of her staff.

'Any other news I should know about?' asked Nina with a touch of irony.

'Circulation is up. Thanks to one of the new writers I hired.'

'That's good to hear. Please transfer me to Larissa so I can give her my congratulations.'

'I look forward to reading your story, Nina. Let me know about the pictures.' Ali switched the call to Belinda. 'Nina for Larissa.'

'Nina! I'm so relieved you're okay. I really want to talk to you. I have so much to tell you.' Larissa was surprised at the surge of emotion she felt at hearing Nina's voice. More than she'd felt when she'd broken the news to her family that she was coming back home and planning to marry Gerard. They had been happy for her, but terribly surprised. Nina and Miche had been closest to her turmoil over Gerard. They understood the choice was not easy for her. They knew the lure of the magazine world, the stimulation of creating an issue from scratch each month, the adrenaline hit of creative and pressured energy. The people, the travel, the inside news. It was a heady world to exchange for suburban life.

'I know. Ali just told me. Are you sure, Larissa?' she asked gently. 'I know Gerard is wonderful, but it seems . . . well . . . sudden.'

'I'm sorry to leave before my contract is up out here . . .' began Larissa.

'That's not my concern. I just want you to be sure the trade-off is what you want.'

The brightness disappeared from Larissa's voice. 'You know me too well, Nina. No, I'm not totally sure that I want to be wife, mother, whatever and move to New Hampshire, give up my career. But I am sure about Gerry. It's been coming for a while and I guess . . . a lot of other things helped me to decide. I don't think I'm meant to be a top editor.'

'Nonsense. You're next in line when an opening comes up. But Larissa, I want you to be happy. Your career will always be there waiting for you.'

'Will it, Nina? You and I both know it's changing. Even Ali had better watch her back. You never think it's going to happen to you. That one day you're not ahead of the race, but trying to catch up with new young sprinters.'

'Larissa, you sound tired. I bet you've been doing more than your share of work. Has Ali been difficult?' asked Nina bluntly.

'Not so much with me. But I'm tired of being a buffer all the time. She is a hard taskmaster. Clever, I admit. But too clever sometimes.'

'Meaning something I should know about?'

Larissa hesitated. She didn't want to dump on Ali and worry Nina, and there was nothing reprehensible, immoral or illegal that Ali had done. 'She always has *Blaze* – and therefore her own – best interests at heart. It's her style, I guess. And there is a constant war between her and Reg. Look, don't worry about it, Nina. Are you happy? Tell me your news. Where are you? We were so worried when you dropped out of sight for so long, what happened?'

'You'll read all about it in *Blaze*,' said Nina dryly. 'But I am blissfully happy with Lucien. Hard to believe we've come together after all these years. I don't know how we're going to juggle our lives together. He has a rather mobile career too. I confess the more I'm away

548

from *Blaze*, travelling and just being with him, I find I'm enjoying this totally new experience. But I'm not taking my hand off the tiller by any means. I'm about to leave for Paris with Lucien then I'm going to New York for a Triton board meeting. Lucien will meet me there.'

'And then back here?'

'Not necessarily. Unless you think I should?'

'I think you should.' The words were out before Larissa thought. It was an instinctive reaction, so she didn't try to diminish what she'd said.

Nina was thoughtful. 'In that case, I think the sooner I return to Sydney and see for myself what's going on the better.' The news of Larissa's abrupt departure had shaken Nina and she realised she had taken her hands off the wheel for too long. While she didn't resent Larissa suddenly choosing to put her personal life first she knew that, for Larissa to leave while still under contract, things must have been very difficult. 'It sounds like Ali's ambitions have gone to her head. At least the circulation figures have stayed high.'

'I'm sorry, Nina, I feel I've let you down. Maybe I should have tried to contact you sooner, but Ali wasn't about to listen to me . . . and I assume you know she's been in contact with Baron Triton.' Larissa didn't want to repeat the gossip that Ali had bedded the Baron.

'That's an editor's job. When the editor-in-chief and publisher is out of the picture, the editor should talk to the proprietor over important, substantive issues,' said Nina calmly. Larissa couldn't help thinking she slightly stressed the words, 'important and substantive'. 'Larissa, I know you did as much as you could. If anything seriously dangerous had been undertaken I know I would have heard from you. Did you share any of your concerns with Jacques?'

'He is very much aware of Ali's machinations. I'm

549

frankly surprised they went head-to-head over some things. I figured Ali would use her feminine wiles with the handsome proprietor's son. Jacques has divided the camp somewhat, but Ali, to her credit, has fought for her position and views. She cares about the magazine because it's helping her power base. Jacques dabbles at being an executive but he's more into being a serious playboy.'

'Yes, it must be hard to be taken as credible and responsible with the stigma of nepotism hanging over your head,' said Nina, who knew very well of the concerns Baron Triton had about his son and heir. 'I'll make plans. I'd appreciate it if you don't mention I'm coming. When are you leaving?'

'As soon as I can – if that's okay with you? Perhaps we can overlap in New York? I'd love to see everyone. And there is one small detail to finalise.'

'If you have any problems with your contract . . .'

'No, it's not that. It's Gerry. He doesn't know I'm coming back to marry him. He gave me an ultimatum and sort of dropped out. I rang his mother and he's shuttling between New York and finding a place in New Hampshire. I figured I'd better grab him before he changes his mind.'

'Just walk in the door and surprise him?' laughed Nina.

'Yes. I hope he'll think it a nice surprise,' said Larissa, her heart twisting as frightening images of walking in and finding him in bed with another woman sprang to mind.

'I'm thrilled for you. Things will work out for you, I just know it,' said Nina firmly. 'Let's meet in New York. Belinda has the schedule. Is Miche staying on in Paddington? Is Miche okay . . . is she selling stories?' Nina had decided to tackle Ali's refusal to hire Miche later when she got to Sydney. As long as her god-daughter was happy, it could wait.

'I've offered her the house. She's fine. She's met a nice young man she's keen on, so she's travelling up to see him for a bit. He works for a vineyard, she met him in France.'

'That's wonderful news. Well, what do you know? See how the dominoes fall? Now we all have a love in our lives. It changes how you see the world, doesn't it?'

'Sure does,' said Larissa, and a feeling of calmness settled on her. Nina always seemed to have that effect. 'See you soon.'

Miche watched Larissa as a small group from *Blaze*, including Tiki, took Larissa to a farewell lunch. Larissa looked happy on the one hand, if nervously excited, yet genuinely sad to be leaving beautiful Sydney and her friends. Belinda's husband Laurie was there along with Kevin and Dan. Kevin had been gracious and warmly hugged Larissa as he arrived with a huge bouquet of roses and a small opal pendant.

'Can't leave without a keepsake – the national gem of Australia,' he said putting the jewellery box in her hands.

'Kevin, this is so sweet of you.' Larissa was captivated by the blue and green stone which shone with fiery-red lights.

'Are you sure, Riss? 'Cause if you change your mind, I'm here, you know. And I'll always be your friend.' He kissed her cheek. 'Drinks all round. I've ordered champagne. Here's to you Larissa – much happiness and come back and see us soon.'

It was a long and jovial lunch. Larissa was leaving in two days. One more editorial meeting and she would be on her way back to New York. Miche would stay on in the Paddington house.

'You going to be all right on your own in that place?' asked Dan. 'I know people looking to share.'

'I'm fine. It belongs to *Blaze* – I'm just sitting out Larissa's lease. But honestly I think I'll be spending a lot of time up in the Hunter. You must come up and see where Jeremy works. It's a great place.'

'Any excuse will do to go to wine-tasting country. I'll bring some pals up for a weekend. How's work going? Onto any more hot stories?'

Miche grimaced and put down her wine. 'I'd better go easy. I have a meeting with Ali. Putting up a series of articles to her.' She excused herself and Larissa gave her a thumbs-up.

'Don't be intimidated, Miche. They're good stories you're doing. I'll see you at home.'

Miche again felt like she had been called to the principal's office as she sat opposite Ali. She waited as Ali finished making notes and fiddling with papers on her desk before she looked up and gave Miche a cursory smile.

'So, you wanted to see me?'

'Yes, Ali. As you know I've been researching a story on children of violence, how innocent victims of childhood trauma cope with their lives . . .'

'Yes, yes. How's that going?' Ali frowned.

'Slowly, to be frank. Not that I'm giving up on it. I have some great material so far. But it will be a while before it's ready. And as I'm living on what I sell,' Miche gave a rueful smile which Ali ignored, 'I thought I'd put it to one side and follow up a story I've just come across.'

Ali brightened immediately. 'Like what?'

Miche had rehearsed her spiel and rattled on about the Hunter Valley, the comparison between it and France and the Napa Valley, the tourism opportunities, its history, the statistics Jeremy and John Sandgate had given her.

'What do you know about wine?' asked Ali.

'Not much. And that's the idea. Rather than write for the elite connoisseur, I tell the story from my perspective. My peers have become major wine consumers.'

Ali spun her chair and stared out the window. Miche found her expression hard to read. In fact she was surprised at Ali's furrowed brow.

Finally Ali spoke. 'Dump the trauma piece. Don't go too heavily into the Hunter region, instead look into the wine side of it. Make it something people in their twenties and thirties can relate to. How you do that is your problem. I don't want a snooty wine piece, you don't know enough anyway, nor do I want a grand tour of the vineyards. Make it personal, quirky. Lots of fab pictures, sexy stuff, funny stuff.'

Miche blinked at her. 'That's a tall order. Though it's what I was kind of thinking . . .'

'I'll talk with Reg. We have a *Blaze* wine club deal, maybe it can tie in with that.' She glanced down at her desk as if Miche was dismissed, then asked, 'Oh, by the way, weren't you doing a personal bit with the trauma piece? Something about your father?' Ali lifted an eyebrow as if she were asking Miche about the sore throat she had last week.

Miche shifted in her seat. 'I mentioned that to Bob. He wanted a personal angle to the trauma story. He thought a section about looking for my father was a good . . . hook.'

'Forget it. Dump the whole thing. Too dark. Go with the wine and food gig. Who wants to know about other people's problems? Just don't make it sound like a foodie or travel mag piece.' She paused. 'A piece of personal advice – forget about looking for your father. Move on with your life.'

Miche left Ali's office feeling confused – half pleased, but also a little daunted. Maybe the trauma piece on children of violence, would work for another publication. She'd write it up after this next project. In a way she was relieved as it gave her a reason to put the issue about her father on the backburner again. She was surprised at her eagerness to do the Hunter Valley story. Of course, one reason was that it would give her the chance to spend time with Jeremy and to find out about his world. But there was another reason Miche was drawn to the idea. The tenacity and richness of the sturdy vines that clung to the hillsides were like the people who worked the vineyards. The old vines bursting into delicate greenness from the soil and the sun, producing the luscious full-bodied grapes that ended up in bottles that travelled the country and the world. The mystique and mythology, the blends, the guesswork and sheer art that combine to create the wines. It fascinated her. If she could marry it all together, this harvest of dreams, she'd have something that was more than just a standard article. She'd have to do a lot of research. It seemed to her it was like the goldfields – this area drew men and women who hoped to find and create something wonderful, something they could draw from the land, water with their sweat and market with élan. The Australian wine industry was like a glorious hot-air balloon soaring aloft in a clear, sunny dawn, silently stealing across the sky so that everyone would soon notice it and want a ride.

Fanciful? Maybe. Miche was surprised Ali had pushed her other idea to one side. Bob had been so keen. Well, if this was the one Ali wanted her to do, that was fine by her. Ali's cautionary remark rang in her mind, 'Just make sure it's not fuddy-duddy or elitist. Make it the kind of article I'd stop and read.' Now that was a challenge.

Miche couldn't wait to ring Jem. First off, she planned to dig through the old newspapers in the State Library. Her mother had always told her to go backwards into a story. 'You never know what you'll dig up that could apply to the current story.'

Eddie was surprised to find that Heather's apartment in Wollstonecraft was so suburban. It was a large apartment with leafy views over the northern suburb, but it was in an extremely ordinary block of red-brick units. Eddie lived in Bondi in a small, trendy apartment with glimpses of the famed surfing beach. It was smartly furnished and he lived far beyond his means – another reason for wanting to increase his profile. The higher the public profile, the more opportunities he could muster to make money. He already had a bunch of ideas for a radio show, and a website and he had enough worldwide contacts to do segments about the Australian show biz and celebrity scene. His creative mind had devised a stunning promotional campaign that would skyrocket him to prominence once he started his TV appearances.

He hoped this meeting with Heather would bring him what he wanted.

Heather opened a bottle of wine.

'So, we're celebrating?' he asked.

'Looks like it. I've cut a deal, now it's up to you to produce the goods.' She handed him a glass and poured the wine.

'So I go on trust? What happens if I tell you what I know and then Morris Brown or whoever at the network says they don't know a thing about hiring me?'

'And how do I know that what you're going to tell me is of any value as far as discrediting the Showers bitch?' countered Heather.

'Okay, let's bite the bullet.' Eddie took a sip of his wine. 'April Showers is a man. Well, half a man shall we say.'

'What!' Heather burst out laughing, then looked sceptical. 'Bullshit. How do you know? If I may ask.'

'Well may you ask, indeed.' Eddie paused, a master of timing as he delivered his line. 'We were lovers when he was a boy. An adult male, that is.'

'So April has had the whole sex change thing?' said Heather thoughtfully. 'That's not exactly taboo these days.'

'It is when your current lover is a politician into cross-dressing. And she hasn't done the full op, she's still kept her boy bits if you get my drift.'

Heather was elated. 'That's too rich. But she looks so . . . girlie. A bit stocky, but a petite blonde with boobs . . . is she on hormones?'

'She's on everything, darling. She had an op, but left the little dangly bit. I had already parted company with her by then. I prefer my boys to be all boys, thanks very much.'

'Who knows? For sure? I'm going on your say-so here.'

Eddie emptied his glass. 'Enough of us know. There are others willing to spill the beans. She's not the sort to want it made public. She's gone to a lot of trouble to hide her real identity. You threaten her with an exposé . . . I know the doctor who did it. She couldn't afford to go overseas, so had it done here.'

'What about her family . . . who else knew her as a bloke? I mean, how long ago was this done?'

'Five years ago. I have lots of photos of us when she was Adrian Rein.'

Heather clinked wineglasses. 'Thank you very much, Eddie. You just got yourself a starring spot on Channel Five.'

Ali paced along the terrace outside her office, passing the sandpit, which had been cleaned up and was looking as new.

Eddie matched her stride for stride. 'Listen, Ali, you would do the same in my place.'

Ali did a sharp about-face and paced in the other direction, her move mirrored by Eddie. 'No I wouldn't. I have no desire to be on TV.'

'You're so good at what you do. But you need people like me. I can feed you stuff.'

'Rubbish. I pay people like April Showers to do that. What could you give me that I'd want? Once you're over there, being a little TV squirt, how do you know you're going to become a so-called star? If you fail, don't come to me looking for work. I gave you a big break to come here, and you've used me.'

'Ali, come on, sweetheart, it's called networking. Believe me, I'm really grateful for you springing me from the ad world. I'll pay you back in more ways than you can imagine. You and I need each other. We understand what we want and how to get it, eh?' He looked at her scowling face and lifted an eyebrow, then, seeing no reaction, cheekily nudged her in the ribs. 'I have gossip . . . hot off the press.'

Ali's lips twitched. Only audacious, outrageous Eddie could get away with calling her sweetheart and cajoling her into listening to his snippy bitchy prattle. But they both knew that she couldn't risk not hearing him out. 'So, make my day, babe.'

'Oh I will, dear heart. Believe me, I will.' Eddie glanced around in an exaggerated and absurd gesture to be sure they weren't overhead. They were totally alone on Ali's private terrace.

'I'm listening.' Ali turned and retraced her steps. 'So what's your parting present then? Is it about April? I think she has the makings of a good muckraking, in-depth profile writer. Gossip was just scratching the surface. She's found her milieu with these interviews.'

Eddie digested this. 'You want her to do more pieces like the Heather Race article? Isn't that the same as saying to your lawyers, I'll make you millionaires, we're going to be sued every month?'

'Not everyone is as vile as that vicious Race broad. Why you want to move into that TV world is beyond me. No, April will ruffle a lot of feathers, push a lot of noses in the dirt, but she has style and everyone will read her. If you loved the column, you'll die for the four-page spread,' chuckled Ali. 'As a feature writer, Kaye doesn't have the killer instinct. She can do the soft stuff. April will be one of the big pulling cards for *Blaze* in the future. Believe me, I was prepared to wear a bloody legal suit from Heather Race against April if it happened, but I knew the TV station wouldn't launch it for her.'

'Well, that's a measure of faith. You hired April, you stick by her. I'm impressed. However, I wouldn't fret – the boys upstairs were right when they said *Reality* had dropped the suit. Do you know why Heather agreed, Ali? Because Heather and April have come to a deal.'

Ali looked at Eddie. 'I won't ask what. Somehow I think it best I don't know.' She was thoughtful for a minute. 'I'm pleased it's not going to cost us money. What's really strange is where the allegiances suddenly come to light. You know who has come to April's defence since the Heather Race case flared up?' mused Ali. And when Eddie shrugged, she answered, 'Reg. Bloody Reg Craven. I think he's siding with her to piss me off.'

'Now that's interesting,' sniggered Eddie. 'I wonder if he ever made a pass at April.'

Ali turned back to her office. 'Oh, that clown has made a pass at everyone. I'm lucky we haven't had a dozen sexual harassment suits. The boys' club upstairs keep smoothing the girls over by paying them to drop the charges and shut up.'

Eddie gave a knowing smirk. 'Hmmm, that could explain why Reg doesn't want the world to know he made a pass at April.'

But Ali didn't hear him. Or if she did, she took no notice. Ali's mind was on other matters. She had to find a replacement for Larissa before Nina did. And now she'd have to replace Eddie too.

TAKE TWENTY-THREE...

In one respect Larissa felt she'd never been away. Leaning back in the dim cab it was as if Sydney had never happened. She felt like she was trundling home, late in the evening, after a long day at *Blaze USA*. In a few minutes she'd walk into the loft apartment and there would be Gerry with a glass of wine and dinner ready.

The reality shook her.

The loft was cold and almost bare. One light was left burning and most of their furniture had gone. Some of her favourite personal items were piled in a corner – rugs, photos, books, vases. She assumed her clothes were still in the closet in the bedroom loft above. The TV, sofa, kitchen table and chairs and the microwave remained. What chilled her the most was the absence of Gerry's paintings. His huge, bold and vibrant canvases, which had hung everywhere and been stacked in his studio area, were gone.

Larissa dropped her bags and, still in her coat, walked around the near-empty apartment, suddenly remembering the stack of his paintings left behind in the house in Paddington. In the couple of weeks he'd been in Sydney, he had tried to capture the clear, bright light that glittered over the harbour and city.

Had Gerard already settled in New Hampshire? She had no idea where he was, who he was going to work for. He could have just dropped out of her life, swearing his mother to secrecy. Silly, perhaps, but looking around the shell of their former life, it didn't seem impossible. She sank onto the sofa and huddled in her coat. The apartment was chilly. There were no familiar smells. 'Oh, what have I come back to?' she wondered.

Larissa began to berate herself. She should have waited till she had spoken to him, found out what he really thought, what he really wanted. Had he meant what he'd said? Had she read more into his remarks than was there? Had it just been a flippant remark with no serious intent? She felt like he was the boy who cried wolf . . . good old Gerard, always there for her, making idle ultimatums which she didn't take to heart. Until this moment. Alarm bells were ringing in her head, her body was tense and fearful. The way forward was uncertain and she knew she could not, did not want to, go back to Sydney – or to *Blaze USA*.

And there was no one who could advise her. A face-to-face, heart-to-heart with Gerard was the only solution. She recalled their parting in this apartment. Nothing much had been said, so much left unsaid. Neither of them was adept at really saying what they felt. Sure, he'd said toss up Sydney, come back and marry me. But the way he'd said it had irritated her. She didn't like the idea she had to choose, or his attitude that she was being a silly woman . . . 'Now pull your act together and come back here. Be sensible.' As if her career hadn't meant as much as his life. She'd so wanted to make it to editor by the time she was thirty-eight. Well, by forty. It had been a goal that once achieved could then have been put to one side. Forty wasn't too late to do the marriage and motherhood trip. And she did want kids. She knew many of her peers didn't, and Gerard was right about her being basically old-fashioned. All the arguments over nuclear and extended families, over the selfish choices of baby boomers, the issue of care and support in declining years; *Blaze* had discussed these issues. Now it was a reality in her life and she was very sure this was what she wanted. But had she put Gerard on hold too long? She didn't care who else was out there to answer her needs – Gerard was the one she wanted.

Larissa's chin slumped on her chest, her eyes filled with tears. She was jet-lagged and weary. It had been a non-stop flight from Sydney to San Francisco, then a change of planes to JFK.

Her departure had been quick and low key. She didn't want a big party or even the small gathering Belinda had arranged, preferring instead to say her goodbyes informally one by one.

At the last editorial meeting Ali had made the announcement of Larissa's departure, saying it was personal, that she was leaving 'to marry and we all wish her well'.

By then most of the staff knew Larissa's plans, so they hadn't reacted with the shock and sadness they'd felt when first hearing the news. Ali hadn't dwelt on it and moved on to the next point on her agenda.

Bob had walked beside Larissa as they left the meeting. 'Have you been in touch with Nina? Won't she shit a brick –'scuse the expression – when she finds out you're gone? We all figured she had you in here to keep an eye on Ali and the magazine for her.'

'That was the general idea. But I'm capitulating. I

can't fight the Ali syndrome any more. I'm tired of being the ham in the sandwich. And frankly, I want a life of my own, Bob. I've given all I can to *Blaze*. I adore Nina and I'm proud of what I've done. I had dreams once of running the magazine, being editor of *Blaze* is the icing on the career cake. But I've discovered I don't have what it takes.'

'You're too nice, Larissa. Talented, without a doubt. I wish you well. I wish I could walk away.'

She gave him a grin. 'And write the great Australian novel?'

'You mean fall in line behind all the other ex-journos writing out their fantasies?'

'You're turning cynical on me, Bob.'

'Hell, you gotta laugh or you go mad. Just in case we don't catch up for last drinks . . . It's been a real pleasure knowing and working with you.' He held out his hand and kissed her cheek.

Tears had sprung to Larissa's eyes. How she liked the down-to-earth Aussies. The reality that she was leaving Australia hit her. As if to confirm it, when she reached her former office she found two painters in there, rolling yellow paint over the walls.

Was she asleep, or sunk in a tired stupor? Was she dreaming?

Gerard crouched before her, concern in his eyes as he took her hands and rubbed them between his own. Larissa stared at him, slowly taking in his unshaven face, the jacket with an upturned collar, the tousled hair and a strong smell of . . . Chinese food.

'Is it really you?' she whispered.

'I was about to say the same thing. What on earth are

you doing here? Oh, Riss . . .' he swept her in his arms and she tumbled from the sofa and they fell to a tangled heap on the floor, laughing, kissing, crying.

'Where have you been? The place is deserted. I thought you'd gone . . .'

Gerry sat up, smoothing her hair, studying every feature of the face he had etched on his heart. 'I've found us a place . . . nothing permanent – I want us to find our more permanent home together . . . if you ever came back. I was so worried you wouldn't come back. I've just driven from New Hampshire. I just had this feeling . . . it's been crazy lately what with moving . . . my work . . .'

'Why didn't you call me?'

'I had this big struggle with myself and, inevitably, decided on putting it off for another day, convinced that you would call in the meantime, or convinced that if I called I'd find you with someone else . . . and that was too hard to live with. But yesterday I actually tried your house and Miche's voice was on the answering machine. That almost destroyed me. I was worried that you really had moved in with another guy.' He paused to kiss her tenderly on the forehead, then the lips. 'God, it's wonderful to see you here,' he said softly.

'Oh, Gerry. How stupid we are.' They kissed again, long and hard, until Larissa pulled apart. 'Gerry, what's that smell?'

He leaned over and waved a paper bag. 'Chinese takeout. A late supper. Come on, we'll heat it up. There's a bottle of champagne in the fridge. Not much else, I'm afraid. But our bed is still here. Let's light the candles and picnic in bed.'

'Sounds terrific.' Larissa dropped her coat and kicked off her shoes. 'Tell me all about my new life.'

*

Miche missed Larissa, but not as much as she would have without Jeremy. They spoke for an hour at least several nights a week. Jeremy confessed he'd never had such long – or intimate – conversations with anyone before. They shared dreams, hopes, fears, family anecdotes and the events of the day. It was different from the closeness Miche had shared with girlfriends, but she had come to regard Jeremy as somebody very special. She hoped the friendship would continue when she moved to the Hunter.

'Where are you starting these stories?' asked Jeremy.

'Well, it's going to be a personal account of my discovery of the place and the wines and the people, so I may start at the beginning and relate my impressions of that first day I drove into the valley, the weekend I met you again. Then pick a town to focus on. John Sandgate suggested Cessnock.'

Jeremy tried to be helpful. 'It doesn't matter which town you start with – Newcastle, Morpeth, Pokolbin – they all have a connection with wine in one way or another, and no doubt more stories than you can handle. It really is an exciting idea.'

'Yeah, it is. But it's also challenging in so far as I have to develop a style of story-telling that is a long way from the publicity handouts and well-rehearsed trade blurbs. It has to be more than a travel-guide drive around the old wineries in the Hunter. Fortunately, I already have a list of a few old guys to interview. It's a very macho industry, isn't it?'

'Sure, the men dominate, as almost everywhere, but there are a few women forcing open the cellar doors. Hearing from them should be worth a column or two.'

'Working on this made me think about the Napa Valley in California. I went there when I was a little girl with my mother. I don't know why, maybe she was writing something. She was very down on Californian wines – Americans drank sodas, not coarse rough reds in bottles with handles and straw wrapped around them and made by families whose names ended in vowels,' laughed Miche.

'How times have changed. Didn't she move out of the sixties?'

'She drank French wines. She would never have considered Australia a fine wine producer.'

'An odd prejudice to hold onto for so long,' observed Jeremy.

'Yeah. Anything to do with Australia was *verboten* in our lives,' said Miche, a sudden bitter ring to her words.

'Your old man?' said Jeremy softly.

'Obviously. It's one of the reasons I'm so interested in learning about this country. It's part of me. The part I don't know,' sighed Miche.

'What are you doing to find out about him? You mentioned in France that was a reason for coming here.'

'Sometimes it seems less important, other times I feel really sad and angry. That makes me feel mad at my mom and I don't like that. I'm torn between feelings of disloyalty to her because she was determined to shut him out of our lives, and yet he's an important part of my being. But all that's there is a gaping hole.'

'Miche, I hope you don't think me out of line, but I don't believe one parent has the right to deprive a child of knowledge of an unknown, absent mother or father. Knowing one's total identity gives you a full sense of who you are. God, look at all the trauma caused by our stolen generation of Aborigines.'

'At least it's now recognised. I was thinking of working that into my piece on children of violence.'

'I thought you'd put that article to one side?'

'Only while I do this Hunter Valley story. I'm still working on it in my mind.'

'Miche, if you want me to help, hold your hand as you ask the questions, I'll be happy to do it. I have such a big, happy family, I think it sad you're so . . . estranged.'

Miche could just imagine the jolly, easygoing, loving family that surrounded Jeremy. He couldn't begin to know the depth of her sense of loss the absence of a father meant. Or know the bitter anger she harboured towards him and, sad to say, that she also felt towards her late adored mother. She'd always felt it unfair that she, the only child, had to suffer because of the rift between the parents.

'What do you know about him, Miche?' Jeremy suddenly asked as if reading her mind.

She rattled off basic facts. His name, place of birth, age. A few anecdotes from her mother. 'They met in the States, married, separated then divorced. She was a New Yorker, he wanted to move to California. My mother always said he made her choose between her career and him. To her mind it was unfair. To quote her, "You can't transplant a career Manhattanite to somewhere in the southern Californian boonies." She always said he was probably lazing on a Pacific atoll. I was given the feeling he was never as driven as my mom.'

Jeremy was silent.

'You still there?' asked Miche.

'Yep. So . . . and who do you take after? Are you the driven career girl or the casual Californian?' asked Jeremy lightly.

But the question made Miche pause. 'I thought I was ambitious. Look at my mother and Nina Jansous, my godmother. I grew up surrounded by achieving women. Now I look at women like Larissa and Ali and I don't know any more.'

'Listen, stop worrying about all that stuff. Just enjoy each day. Too much wallowing makes you stuck in mud, or some such saying to quote my mum.'

Miche laughed, but couldn't help thinking that was how men dealt with heavy-duty issues – by avoiding them. They changed tack. They waded out into clear, fast-flowing water that took them away from the muddy foreshores.

'When are you coming to see us? Steve and Helen have a spare cabin you can stay in. They're keen you write about our neck of the woods.'

'That's so sweet. As an unbiased *Blaze* journalist, I'm not supposed to accept free hospitality.'

'You're coming to see me. That's different. Pay for your own motel in Cessnock or wherever,' countered Jeremy. 'Say, I've just had a thought. I have a mate who lives in Cessnock. His wife, Jane, works for the local newspaper, the *Advertiser*. She might be a help to you. How soon before you're coming? I'm starting to forget what you look like,' he teased.

'Maybe next weekend. Tell Helen I'll call her. And, Jem, thanks for being a pal.'

'Any time. You can count on me, Miche. I mean, if you do decide to try to find your dad, I'm here. A shoulder to cry on, bit of hand-holding, anything like that.'

It choked her up to hear him say this. And suddenly the idea that she would have emotional support should she find and have to confront her father gave her added strength. 'Oh Jem, that's so terrific of you. I think one of the reasons I've been stalling is because I'm doing it alone. Sure, it's very personal and private. But if it didn't work out or if he didn't want to see me . . . It would be hard to handle on my own. Without Nina and Larissa here, I guess I was shelving the whole idea.'

'And now?'

'I want to do it. I don't know if he's even here. I suppose finding him isn't going to change my life that much,' said Miche, trying to lighten the conversation.

'It could settle the questions you have. You resolve one part of your life and then you can deal with the next stage.'

There was an unspoken understanding that whatever the next stage of Miche's life might hold, Jeremy would play a part.

'Thanks for being a friend, Jem,' said Miche.

'I'll see you soon, Miche.'

After he'd hung up the phone, Jeremy paced around the room, then came to a decision. He raised his eyes to the ceiling and murmured, 'Lordy, I hope I'm doing the right thing.'

Ali was preoccupied as she dealt with Larissa's news. While not unhappy with the turn of events, she knew it would upset Nina that Larissa had left so suddenly. Ali didn't want to know about the details of Larissa's personal life, but she hoped Nina understood Larissa was opting out of the race and choosing the soft and easy option of settling down rather than trying to compete with Ali. She'd better make sure Nina knew Larissa had to run and grab her fellow or lose him and that working with Ali had not had anything to do with Larissa's decision. She'd ask Belinda to draft a personal note to that effect and assure Nina that while Larissa was a loss to the company her private life and happiness must come first, blah, blah, blah. Ali could now pull in a replacement of her choice to present as a fait accompli to the board. Someone who would toe the line, someone who'd do Ali's bidding, but also be able to carry on the nitty-gritty workload that she realised Larissa had unobtrusively achieved each month for the magazine. Ali decided she'd also discuss it with Oscar in their now daily phone calls.

Another problem niggled at her, which she would not raise with the Baron. It was one she didn't know quite how to handle. Jacques had become a serious problem, socially and professionally. And his connections with the magazine could do serious damage to *Blaze*.

While he had now virtually removed himself from anything to do with running *Blaze*, rumours about his private life were becoming more insistent. It seemed to Ali it would only be a matter of time before something blew up publicly.

It was at times like this that she really missed her once close relationship with John O'Donnell. Now she wished she could discuss with him her worry about Jacques and his boys' club – the sycophantic followers who hung around him – led by Tony Cox.

The *Blaze* Connoisseur Wine Club was, she suspected, the tip of a very murky iceberg that involved Reg, Jacques and Tony. She hadn't spoken to, or heard from, John O'Donnell since the night she'd walked out on his proposal with the sapphire ring. Now she needed him, she regretted losing the contact. He'd been a useful ally on the local scene.

She had probably hurt him deeply. It had been a big step for him to let her into his life. He once admitted that if he hadn't been so vulnerable after the death of his wife, she'd have never found her way under his defences.

As Ali lifted the phone, she knew he'd undoubtedly be missing the sex. But he would not have replaced her. Above all, he was a gentleman. He'd take her call.

John O'Donnell's voice was cool, cautious. But he had accepted the call. Ali was up-front and disarmingly frank.

'I wouldn't blame you for not talking to me. I really miss talking to you. I miss a lot of things, but most of all I miss our friendship. I have a problem and I don't know how to deal with it. Now, I could offer to root you silly on your desk or office floor, or I can ask you outright. And I'll understand perfectly if you tell me to rack off,' she said affably, using the familiar Australianism.

His voice was soft and courteous and she knew he was smiling. He couldn't help himself. 'That's not in my vocabulary. I'm sorry to hear you have a problem. How can I help?'

'God, what a good man,' she thought. Quickly she filled him in on Jacques' nefarious activities and then told him about the wine club. 'On the surface it doesn't seem any big deal. Except, I knew nothing about it. Reg Craven is in on it and he sneaked the ads in.'

'Nothing too unusual in a magazine pushing spin-off merchandise. Is the wine any good? Which vineyard is supplying it?'

'That's what's off. It's mostly coming in from overseas, with a few bottles of Margaret River wine thrown in to give it an Australian touch. It seems to be run by an international group. Furthermore, there's no proper paperwork going through our accounts department. I think it's a front for something heavier.'

'Don't be alarmist until you know more, Ali. I take it you haven't raised it with Nina or the Baron?'

'No. It's my responsibility and if Jacques and his pals are pushing through something dodgy, the buck still stops with me.'

John O'Donnell spoke in a steady, calm voice. 'Ali, you can pursue this personally, but it will take time and energy. You can ask someone, perhaps outside the magazine, to check it out. You can pass it on to the Baron, though I understand the sensitivity of doing that when it's his son who's involved. Or you can remove any future reference to the wine club. Perhaps run a small box stating the wine club has been disbanded.'

'That would make *Blaze* look bad. As if we hadn't received enough interest or the product was second-rate.'

'Then simply erase it. If it is a scam of some sort, you'll know by how Jacques et al. react. Tell them to take it up with Nina or the Baron and see what they do.'

'You're a wise owl, O'Donnell. Thank you.' Before she could say anything else he cut in. 'Ali, I think it best we don't have any further conversations in the future. It saves opening up old . . . feelings. But I wish you well, my dear. You are doing a fine job. But don't become complacent, there will be someone at your heels soon enough. Don't burn any bridges,' he counselled, knowing how impetuous – and imperious – she could be.

She winced slightly at his remark that others could be biting at her heels, but dismissed the comment. He was the one taking backward steps towards retirement, she was still ascending.

Nina flew into Sydney unannounced. She'd met Larissa in New York, but learned little from her about what had been happening at *Blaze Australia*, preferring to discuss her future plans with Gerard. Larissa's careful avoidance of talking at length about Ali concerned Nina. It clearly had been an unhappy partnership between the two top editorial staffers in Sydney.

Lucien had joined her in New York, but only for a short stay, then he'd moved on to Los Angeles to talk film financing. After a board meeting and lunch with the Baron, Nina caught her plane to Sydney, slightly puzzled with the Baron's clearly expressed pleasure with the performance of the Australian publication. It contrasted so starkly with the impression she had received from the little Larrisa had given away.

At Sydney Airport, Nina picked up an issue of *Blaze Australia*, which had been published the day before and had not yet reached the Baron's office. She looked through it in the limousine, mentally giving ticks, and noting queries about some stories and several ads. What was this *Blaze* Connoisseur Wine Club, for instance?

She walked into her apartment, which had been cleaned and filled with flowers, food and fresh linen by her housekeeper who was expecting her. It was early in the morning, so she stood under the shower trying to wash away the fatigue of the long flight. She then made herself strong coffee, dished up yoghurt and her favourite pieces of Australian tropical fruit and flicked through the morning newspapers left on her doorstep. There were so many local stories that she had to catch up with. They were big stories for Australian readers, but they travelled poorly overseas. Nina had been aware, while in France, of how little space was given to Australian news, except for major sporting events and disasters. And, she reflected, her time in Croatia had been a time of being completely out of touch with what was happening in the rest of the world. Including her world of *Blaze*.

At 9 a.m., Nina's driver collected her and dropped her at the office. She walked down the hallway, startling several juniors who gave delighted smiles and chorused, 'Good morning, Mrs Jansous.'

The news of her return was flashing around the floor by the time Nina had settled into her red cedar chair. She picked up the phone and called Belinda.

'Nina! How super to talk to you. We've been wondering what was happening. Are you still in New York?'

'No, I'm right down the hall in my office. Can you pop along and see me? Is Ali there?'

'Oh, my goodness! Yes, she's here early every morning,'

reported Belinda, pleased to be able to say something positive about Ali.

'I'll make my presence known to Ali shortly. I have a few small jobs I'd like you to arrange first, if you wouldn't mind.'

Belinda grabbed her notebook and hurried the two doors down to the editor-in-chief's office, a smile of relief breaking out as she ignored the buzz of Ali's intercom.

They exchanged warm greetings and Belinda sat down and flipped opened her notebook. 'What can I do?'

'Belinda, first off I want you to schedule a private meeting with Ali as soon as possible, then with Jacques Triton – he's still here, I gather?'

'Er, yes. He doesn't come into the office every day, he's kind of involved with . . . other aspects of the company,' improvised Belinda.

Nina didn't react and continued, 'Then stagger meetings with Reg Craven from advertising, the financial controller and the head of human resources. Then call a general staff meeting for 3 p.m. Set up an afternoon tea, keep it informal, but make it clear I want everyone present.'

'I'm sorry, I didn't know you were coming back today or I would have arranged flowers for your office,' said Belinda. 'Do you want one of the secretaries to assist you? I can do anything you want, of course. I mean . . .' she paused and gave an embarrassed small laugh. 'Am I to remain with Ali? I mean, are you back full-time or what?'

'What would you suggest, eh Belinda?' Nina smiled.

'Oh goodness, I hope you're here to stay . . . for a while, anyway,' answered Belinda with enthusiasm. 'Things have been a bit . . . hectic. Well, maybe more than that. Emotional, I guess. How long are you back for, if I can ask?'

'As long as I need to be, Belinda,' said Nina quietly. 'How is Miche? How is she settling into Sydney? What stories has she done since the Sally Shaw piece?'

'Um, I'm not sure. You know she's not working here full-time. She's a contributor. Which is just as well, as it means she can spend time with her boyfriend. He sounds lovely.'

'Yes, Larissa filled me in. Did Miche turn down the job? What does Bob Monroe think of her? If you prefer, I'll talk to him.'

'Oh, he says she's great. Bob wanted to hire her, but Ali wanted her to work as a freelancer. Last I heard, Miche was researching a piece about looking for her father, linked to the Sally Shaw tragedy . . .'

'Tragedy?' responded Nina with surprise, and Belinda hastily sketched in the details of the *Reality* story on Sally with its tragic outcome. Nina made notes. Her only comment was a quiet, 'Hmmm. Very tragic indeed.' After a moment's reflection, she asked Belinda if she knew where she could reach Miche at that moment.

'Miche is still staying at Larissa's place, but she goes to the Hunter a lot. We so miss Larissa. Her leaving took us by surprise, though it was . . . understandable.' Belinda looked down and twiddled with her pen. 'I mean, wanting to be with Gerard and everything.'

'Yes. Now, could you tell Ali I'm here and ask her when it would be convenient for me to see her please, Belinda.'

Dear loyal Belinda, thought Nina. Trying to be circumspect.

Nina was concerned that Miche was persisting with the search for her father. She'd seemed so happy-go-lucky in Paris, Nina had hoped she would find a fun and fulfilling life in Sydney and let the father issue go.

Belinda walked back to her office, glad to have Nina

back with her old-world courtesy and an executive manner that was totally the opposite of Ali's abrasive style. Nina's politeness and calm was now a soothing balm. Nonetheless, Belinda had the feeling an eruption was not far below the surface.

Ali was caught off-guard and didn't like it. She rose and mustered a tight smile as Nina walked into the editor's office. 'If I'd have known I would have . . .' she held out her hands.

'Baked a cake? You don't seem like a cake-maker, Ali,' quipped Nina lightly. 'I'm sorry about not announcing my arrival. I have been juggling a pretty amazing itinerary. Zagreb, Paris, London, New York.'

'If it's Thursday, it must be Sydney, eh? So how are things in your world, Nina?'

'*Blaze* is my world, Ali. And I would like to hear from you how things are.' Nina sat down and waited.

Ali was unprepared for this. 'Well, the circulation is up. I'm looking for a deputy, though I have two promising people in the wings,' she quickly added, in case Nina decided to foist one of her people into the position.

'Good. I look forward to hearing about them. I hope you don't mind, I have asked Belinda to arrange a staff meeting at three this afternoon.'

Ali was miffed Nina had sidled in ahead of her. 'Any special reason?'

'I think it's important to keep the staff informed about how things are going along. They will know I'm in the building, I'd like to catch up with everyone.'

'Oh, it's social, not an addressing of the troops,' said Ali.

'Depends,' said Nina easily.

'On what?' Ali was defensive.

'On what transpires between now and then. I smell smoke. I have an excellent nose.' When Ali didn't respond,

Nina continued, 'You know the old saying, where there's smoke, there's fire. I think I smell a few barely snuffed-out grass fires. Is there anything in particular you'd like to fill me in on?'

'Okay, Nina. There have been a few problems, but I've handled them. Reg Craven has been especially obstructive. I hired a very creative advertising promotions manager, Eddie Kurtz, who brought in a lot of business, which upset Reg. Eddie was good. So good, he's been grabbed by a TV network. April Showers joined us as a columnist and last month we published her first feature. It was sensational.'

'On what?'

'A profile on the biggest bitch in television, Heather Race. She's from one of those so-called current affairs, foot-in-the-door and mouth, shows.'

'And why? What was the reason for the profile?'

'April can fill you in on that. Race kicked up a bit of a stink, but I gather matters are in hand.'

Nina made a mental note, but didn't pursue this news for the moment. 'What's the *Blaze* Connoisseur Wine Club?'

Ali hid her annoyance. Nina was onto things quickly, but she did sound genuinely puzzled. 'Reg has yet to come back to me on that. The bastard dropped a story I'd placed to put that in after the book had been made up. It slipped by me till I checked the final proofs.' Ali pre-empted the expected retort from Nina that nothing should 'slip past' an editor. 'As you well know, editors are fallible, but not much finds its way past me. It's one of my major headaches – Reg simply doesn't communicate. He refuses to come to editorial meetings, he thinks he's running his own ship. I guess he's a bit resentful that I've brought in quite a few big accounts,' she said pointedly.

Nina merely nodded. 'It's not helpful when the two

key elements of a magazine – editorial and advertising – aren't on speaking terms. One can't exist without the other. It should be a close collaboration.'

'Collaboration isn't in Reg's vocabulary. But I'm sure he'll give you his version of events. Do let me know what you find out about the wine club. I have knocked it on the head for the moment. I haven't any knowledge of anyone asking permission to use the *Blaze* name for commercial purposes. I suspect there's something shady going on, it's not going through our books. I'm afraid Jacques is involved.'

'I'm certain all will be revealed soon enough.' Nina stood up then paused as she saw over Ali's shoulder the terrace with the sandpit. 'And what is that? A children's area?' She looked bemused and lifted a questioning eyebrow.

'It's the latest in social and managerial experiments. It forces the staff to confront not only the issues at hand, but how they deal with analysing their true motives, and it enables them to assess the worth of their ideas within the big picture.'

Nina decided not to venture further into this territory for fear she'd laugh, lose her cool or tell Ali what she thought of her managerial skills. She'd find out about it soon enough. She merely gave a low, 'Hmmm. Interesting.' And left Ali's office.

On the way back to her office, Nina found herself comparing the different editorial and managerial styles of people she had employed over the years.

Lorraine, Miche's mother, had been such an effective editor, utterly devoted to the firm and her craft, and totally professional until booze, pills and emotional insecurities started to destroy her.

Ali was so different. A hard worker, but she was out for herself, loyalty beyond self-interest counted for nothing. Typical of so many of her generation of hard-nosed, ambitious women precariously balancing on the executive tightrope. Proving they could be as tough and as ruthless as the men. And then there was Larissa. Fifteen years younger than Lorraine, but a similar character with similar skills, but choosing a different path. Who could blame her for deciding to be with the man she loved?

Through informal meetings with staff, Nina found many of them cautiously defensive about the level of morale and the quality of their teamwork. Everywhere she detected antagonism towards Ali. Nina began to unravel a picture of a ruthlessly ambitious young editor who wanted the magazine to be successful at all costs. This meant breaking the long-established Triton ban on doing editorial deals in return for contra arrangements, accepting free inducements to promote or favour an advertiser's interests. It also meant forcing staff to limit their initiatives and follow her ideas so that the content of *Blaze* reflected Ali's views and vested interests.

When Nina pushed Reg about the wine club, he was vague and fobbed it off. 'They're top-quality wines, it's not schlock stuff with our name on it,' he ventured, and then blushed as he saw Nina mentally registering the idea that cases of wine had most likely landed on his door-step. 'If they want to offer wine at a bargain price to our readers – and by having our name attached to it, readers know it's a good product – what's wrong with that? They've bought six months worth of ads.'

'And who is behind this club?' asked Nina. 'I'm sure you've checked it out if *Blaze* is endorsing it.'

Reg shifted uncomfortably in his seat. 'It's been Jacques Triton's baby. It's a special deal through a European group that's running the club internationally. The wines come from all over the world and include a few Australian ones. So long as our readers receive a good deal, the structure of an offshore company doesn't concern me.'

'It should. Ali thinks it's a shady operation. Maybe a front for God knows what. So, who is the client or agency placing the ads and on whose behalf?' pressed Nina. 'It seems odd the editor wasn't informed and the ads were placed at the last minute.'

At the mention of Ali, Reg's eyes narrowed and his mouth tightened. 'When Jacques presented me with the deal, he said they wanted to be in this issue, so something had to go. Can't help a last-minute change when it's a potentially big, long-term client.'

Nina was quiet. It sounded reasonable, but she was not convinced. 'So tell me about Ali. I understand there is a bit of conflict. I know she isn't the easiest person to work with, what are your concerns?'

'Can I speak openly, off the record?'

'That's why I'm here.' Nina leaned back.

Reg suddenly unleashed a torrent of anger against Ali. 'She's a predator, a conniving bitch. She has set everyone against each other, not just me. She brings in April, she brings in Eddie, she flicks off Miche, she stops the perks and still sets up her own deals.'

'What do you mean?'

Reg had exposed his feelings and they poured forth. 'Hell, everyone used to be swamped with freebies. Ali says it's a no-go area, that's the Triton way, and then she turns around and expects to be handed everything that isn't tied down.'

'But Reg, you know Triton's policy is we pay for everything. *Blaze* is not like those women's magazines where contra rules the content of every page.' Nina reminded Reg they had gone over this thoroughly before the magazine was launched.

'We pay for everything in order to maintain our

objectivity and credibility. In the rare instance that we do accept a deal, we say in print the travel or accommodation or whatever was paid for. That doesn't mean we are under any obligation to write about it – or favourably if we do.'

'Tell that to Ali. There's been more stuff sent to her than you can poke a stick at. And you can double that for what has been sent to April's home. And we're not talking free perfume and night cream here – we're talking serious gifts from all manner of first-class shops. April puts out the line that it's no one's business if some company sends their products to her.'

'Hmmm. They receive favourable mentions, I assume,' said Nina tightly.

'You bet,' boomed Reg. 'But I'll give April her due, she's clever and that story on Heather Race was a ripper. Anyway, my problem is Ali undermining me. Sure, she brought in a few clients – with help. But I draw the line at that goddamn, stupid sandpit. Her power trip is out of control if you ask me. I think she has lost the plot, and if you hadn't come back the workers would have mutinied against Captain Ali Bligh.' He was breathless from pouring out his angst.

'Thanks for your opinion, Reg.' Nina's tone betrayed no reaction. 'If you find out more on the wine club, please let me know.'

Reg left Nina's office wondering if he'd said too much – or not enough.

Nina wandered casually around the offices, popping in to say hello and pass a few minutes in relaxed chat. Kaye, Fiona, Bob, Barbara showed huge relief that she was back – 'to take over' – as they put it. Barbara decided she'd rethink leaving if Nina was back to stay.

Nina merely commented, '*Blaze* is selling well, thanks to all your hard work. I gather it hasn't been easy for you guys.' This unlocked a series of complaints, whinges and cynical anecdotes – and the underlying common theme was, 'Ali is a bitch and she's going to run the magazine into the ground in her personal drive to surge ahead.'

Nina merely nodded, smiled and moved around the building, listening to her staff. And they all told the same story. Ali was a dragon. But, grudgingly, they'd also had to admit she was very, very clever.

The painting in the office high in a tower block overlooking Sydney Harbour and its spectacular opera house was a mysterious creation of dots and a rough geometric network of intersecting lines. It defied easy interpretation, but had something about it that never ceased to capture the attention of even the most casual viewer, and then almost hypnotise them. It was created by an artist who was represented in many of the world's major galleries, an artist who lived in a tin shed with a dirt floor in a remote part of Northern Australia. An Aboriginal artist. Nina swivelled in her chair and gazed at the painting on her office wall in an effort to lose herself in the maze of images formed by the tiny daubs of ochre. She felt herself drawn into the vortex of the picture, travelling through the surface layers into the heart of the story. The secret country of the artist's spirit. It stilled her mind, steadied and calmed her. She sat in thought for some time then came to a decision.

She called Belinda. 'When Ali is available, I'd like a private meeting with her in my office.'

Ali had been waiting for the call. She mentally encased herself in protective armour and walked purposefully down the hall. Belinda watched her go. Ali radiated confidence that bordered on the defiant.

When neither had emerged after half an hour from behind Nina's uncommonly closed door, half the staff had stopped working and were waiting to see from Ali's face whether she'd won or lost.

Barbara dropped by Kaye's office. She gave a shrug. 'No news from the lioness's den. An Olympic-standard event almost, don't you think?'

'They should have sold tickets,' said Kaye with a chuckle. 'I bet there's a bit of fancy footwork and sparring going on. By Ali. Nina will be asking a few hard questions.'

'I wonder if Nina knows someone in this office leaked a cover story to a rival mag.'

'Ali lucked in with her replacement cover, but it must feel nasty knowing you're being undermined by your own staff.'

'Yeah, it could only have come out of here. Who do you think could be talking to the gossip columns and giving out content secrets?'

Barbara shrugged. 'Could be one of the junior staff before Ali cracked down on security. Could be anyone Ali has upset.'

'Well, that covers all of us.'

'Reg hates her, but he's still loyal to *Blaze*.'

'Unless he's leaving and has had a better offer,' mused Kaye.

'Everyone has a reason for revenge on Ali, but most of us are loyal because the magazine is Nina's.' Barbara sighed, 'Poor Nina, I bet she's wishing she never started this now that she has a love and the chance of a different life.'

'I would be out of here like a shot,' agreed Kaye. 'I've seen Lucien interviewed on TV talking about his films. A really charming and talented man. She deserves him.'

A sudden thought struck Barbara. 'You don't think

583

she'd close the magazine? I mean, she doesn't need it now if she's going off to live with Lucien.'

'We don't know that. I think the Tritons would have a say in that. But it is a worry.'

Both women were silent, trying to imagine this worst-case scenario.

Kaye voiced what Barbara was thinking. 'We shouldn't have too much trouble finding a job with another magazine now that *Blaze* has been such a success. And there's always radio. They're looking for more women.'

'I'd never be able to do that!'

'I might find an editor who's more in line with my interviewing style than Ali seems to be lately,' said Kaye with bitterness. 'April has landed the next two big features after that profile on Race. I could never have written a cynical, tough piece like that. I wouldn't want to. Couldn't live with myself.'

'You're too nice, you mean. I'm amazed Heather Race hasn't gone ahead with the defamation suit against us.'

'Hard to prove, I imagine. I mean, April didn't print any actual untruths, just made the facts as she saw them look pretty ugly. It was a damned clever article. I have to say she's made a big leap from bitchy gossip to surgically removing a subject's public face. I'd like to see her tackle a few of our politicians,' said Kaye thoughtfully.

Barbara gave the star feature writer a strange look. 'You're sounding like her mentor rather than her competitor.'

'I'm tired, Barb. I'm forty. That's over the hill in magazines these days. I'm fed up with Ali. But I can't afford to quit. I suppose I'll find a job with a PR firm writing press releases. Thank God I've always made it a policy to be nice to everyone. You never know who's doing the hiring.'

Barbara touched her immaculate hair with a perfectly

manicured hand. 'I'm already half out the door. I wish I had Tiki's guts to tackle something new. She's not that much younger than me. I pass my time doing stuff I did when I first started out as a cadet.'

'The beauty biz here ain't what it used to be, that's for sure. So you had the high-roller times – perfume launches in Monte Carlo, trips to Grasse and dinner with Karl Lagerfeld. They were the days, eh?'

Barbara smiled, remembering when she was one of the top beauty editors that advertisers fawned over and her cupboards overflowed with free products. 'Yes, you're right.' Then, aware of where she was now, and recalling Ali's uncharitable shoving of her to the background and her plan to resign, Barbara seemed to deflate. The present was a pale life indeed.

'And how do you see your future panning out here Kaye?'

'Let's say I'm looking at options, and over my shoulder.' She gave a laugh. 'For once I'm glad I'm not the editor. It's a job for the young lionesses these days.'

Ali and Nina had reached a stalemate. Neither was prepared to concede any ground.

Ali again listed the advances the magazine had made under her leadership. 'That's the bottom line and that's what counts, Nina.'

'How gains are achieved is just as important. If we abuse our advertisers, they won't come back. Trust in *Blaze* is paramount. We trade on our name and reputation. I won't have that jeopardised,' said Nina angrily.

'I have no knowledge of, or have ever condoned, anything that wasn't totally above board,' rejoined Ali.

'But it is your responsibility to know exactly what

is going on in the organisation and if anyone is taking advantage of their position, to put a stop to it.

'This feud between you and our advertising manager hurts the magazine. No matter what personality clashes you might have, it's essential you work as a team.'

'I'm well aware of that. I don't need lessons in personnel and corporate relations,' snapped Ali. 'Why don't you attack the boys upstairs, the finance guy that Manny put in is a closed shop. He and the management men protect Reg. They operate on the divide-and-conquer principle, like the way they kept digging at Eddie about his expenses. We lost a terrific talent. And someone in here is leaking stuff to rivals, undermining me and the magazine. Tony Cox has lost the plot and he and Jacques are running riot through *Blaze* – and this town, from what I hear. If it hadn't been for Eddie tipping me off, the situation could be a lot worse. If I don't know about problems, I can't fix them.'

'Ali, this is not a war,' said Nina quietly. 'While I appreciate you have *Blaze*'s best interests at heart, you can't achieve the right solutions with animosity.'

Ali leapt in well prepared, knowing the ground was shaking under her feet. 'Nina, let's talk about solutions. I have drawn up the business strategy for the next six months – promotion possibilities, potential advertisers to tackle, better package deals for existing big advertisers. I also have ideas for a series of articles that could be sensational. April is turning into one hot writer. I think she should be the major features writer and Kaye should be moved into something more administrative.' Ali tried to soften her voice, 'She just doesn't fire on all cylinders when it comes to going in hard, fast and deep. Like a shark,' said Ali helpfully. 'Kaye is more from the softly, softly school.'

She paused, feeling quite pleased with her enthusiastic

ideas, backed up with a slick, point by point presentation.

Nina folded her hands and leaned forward, not reacting at all to what Ali had said. Her voice was low and gentle, her eyes sympathetic as if telling a child there was no Santa Claus. 'Before plunging too far ahead, I have to deal with the immediate, and that means finding solutions to our internal personnel problems.'

'You have a solution to these internal problems? Other than moving Reg?' asked Ali somewhat superciliously.

'I do. I've thought long and hard since I have been presented with the rather unpleasant facts of the manoeuvrings within the company. And moving Reg on isn't part of the solution.'

Ali frowned. 'If I'm stuck with having to deal with a recalcitrant advertising manager, it could be difficult.'

'You won't be in that situation,' said Nina smoothly. 'I won't move Reg. It's better that I move you.'

Ali jerked as if smacked. She blinked, trying to clear her vision that had momentarily lost focus. 'To where? Why?' Her voice was raised, shocked. She attacked instantly. 'Why should I be the one to be forced to wear the mantle of blame? I figured the buck stops with the editor-in-chief. That's you, Nina. I have been incredibly vigilant. I came down hard whenever I found a problem. Moving me isn't going to fix the situation.'

Nina was soothing. 'It's an upward move, Ali. A promotion. You've had almost six months here, more than enough time to have launched and established *Blaze Australia* and move on to the next challenge.'

Ali couldn't believe this nightmare was happening. What was killing her was that suddenly she was in the same position as Lorraine had been in. There was no promotion above editor, except editor-in-chief and Nina wouldn't be giving that up. It was a gentle sideways push. Well, she was damned if she was going to give them the satisfaction of jumping off a terrace, or jumping ship. Ali's body language signalled fight not flight. 'And what is my next challenge?' she asked, knowing she had no call and wouldn't like whatever Nina said – unless it was editor of *Blaze USA*.

Nina knew what Ali was thinking. 'I can't offer you New York. Irene da Costa is doing a fine job and so is her deputy. I am proposing that you become publishing director of *Blaze* in Australasia. That includes Australia and New Zealand, where we may open a local edition in time. We'll talk later about where you'll be based. I'd like to hear your suggestions.'

Ali didn't answer until she was able to spit out the words, 'Publishing director?'

Nina nodded and Ali shook her shoulders, a movement like a wet dog shaking itself. Nina had a sudden bizarre image of the letters that spelled out *Publishing Director* being fragmented and sprayed around the room like splashes of water from a dog's coat.

'Nina, publishing director is the same as saying special projects manager . . . it means nothing. It wouldn't matter where I was based, you're consigning me to nowheresville.' Ali didn't add it was a slap in the face and would be considered a demotion among those who knew the print media. 'And who do you have in mind to replace me?' Her voice was hard.

'I have given this a lot of consideration, Ali. I think it best for the magazine and in view of the staff problems and the abuses, which I realise you did not condone. It is not a reflection on your abilities. Having Jacques override you on occasion was . . . unhelpful. I intend to stay on and run the shop with you until I appoint a new editor.' Seeing Ali's furious face, she softened. 'Ali, I will make sure this is seen as an important career appointment – which it is. You've been with the company a long time, you're very valuable to Triton Communications, how you are treated will send a significant message to those inside as well as outside the company.'

Ali rose. 'I see there's not much point in discussing this further. I would like to take a short break before basing myself in an apartment back in New York.' She gave a cynical half-smile. 'As I'll be travelling a great deal, I assume it's immaterial where I call home.'

'You can stay on here in the company apartment as long as you wish,' said Nina, underscoring the point that *Blaze* would not be paying for a place for Ali in New York.

'I'll make my own arrangements. And, please, no jolly goodbye drinks.'

'Ali, I hope you will rethink that. I believe a prestigious function to congratulate you on your promotion and for the brilliant job you've done in establishing *Blaze* here in the marketplace would be more appropriate than you quietly leaving town as if there were a problem. Which there isn't.' Nina smiled. 'I thought you were enjoying being back in your homeland again?'

Ali picked up her things. 'Nina, this place has never been home. I just happened to be born here. I might say the same to you. Why not go and settle back in Yugoslavia?'

Nina acknowledged the touché. 'Quite. However, I am intending to go back to Croatia quite frequently. I am very keen on upgrading the existing children's home and I plan to establish more such homes. There are so many homeless children after the Balkan conflicts.'

Ali wasn't interested. 'Let me know when I'm leaving. I would like to go as soon as possible.' She left the office without another word.

Nina felt her body slump and release the tension she'd been holding inside herself. Still, she was surprised that Ali had taken it reasonably well. She knew Ali would be fighting hard to save her career. Her people skills were lamentable, but she was clever and bright. A bit too ambitious and ruthless. A short cooling-off period where she had no real power would be good for her.

That night, Nina poured it all out to Lucien on the phone. Not knowing Ali, he only half listened, making sympathetic noises. But he had one nagging fear.

'Nina, darling, I am concerned about you staying on to run the magazine in Sydney. For how long? This isn't what we planned at all. I thought you were easing out, not taking on more.'

'Lucien, I want to ease off and be with you more than anything in the world. But it's not something I can just drop. I'm in partnership with Triton. I have an obligation to myself as well. It won't be for long, I hope.'

'Do you have anyone in mind? There can't be too many top people floating around that can be an editor in Sydney at a moment's notice.'

'When it's *Blaze* calling you'd be surprised how many people would walk out of high positions. Please, be patient, my darling.'

Lucien felt helpless. He had no control over what Nina did and no right to tell her to walk away from what had been her life. But he couldn't shake the awful knowledge that when it came to a choice between him and *Blaze*, the magazine would always win. 'Nina, after so many years apart I truly believe we've found each other for a reason. I'll plough on with my film idea. Perhaps I'll come and write the script in Sydney.'

'It's only for a little time, my darling. If everything works out the way I hope, we'll have the rest of our lives together.'

'I love you, Nina.'

'And I you. As I always have.' She hung up and found the tension in her body had gone. Sleep came easily and quickly.

TAKE TWENTY-FOUR . . .

The picturesque Mulbring Valley, with its new homes and holiday retreats for Sydneysiders, gave way to the edge of Cessnock where a few of the original mining cottages had yet to be renovated. Following directions, Miche parked in the *Advertiser's* parking lot. As she stepped out, she saw the modern, large city centre and plaza. She walked through an alley to Vincent Street, where the older style shops and offices sat next to newer neighbours selling discount electrical goods and music.

She turned into the small, single-storey building plastered with signs for the *Advertiser*. Jane Parsons met her with an exuberant smile.

'You're Jeremy's friend. How can I help you?'

'I'm researching a story on the Hunter area. A pretty broad canvas, but essentially linked to the wine industry.'

'That's a lot to write about. Come and have a coffee and tell me more. Is this going to be for *Blaze*?'

Miche followed Jane to her office. It was a typical

small-town newspaper with a staff of ten. Some permanent, some part time. 'How long have you worked here?'

Jane laughed. 'Fifteen years! I started as a youngster with dreams of going to the big city. I did my time and travelled and here I am, back in my home town, married with two little kids. That's the nice part of journalism. It's portable and you don't lose the skills. I work flexible hours, now the kids are in primary school. And I'm still planning to write a murder mystery. I'll get around to it one day.'

Miche looked at Jane, who she guessed was in her thirties. She looked and sounded so different from the writers and editors on big-city magazines. Yet Miche envied her, she was so obviously content with her life, enthusiastic and friendly.

Jane began making them instant coffee.

'Milk and one, thanks,' said Miche before she was asked. 'I've read a few terrific books about characters in the Aussie bush, but most of them were written ages ago. Is the countryside still producing and harbouring such offbeat guys?'

'Sure, they're around in odd places, and they still make stories for us from time to time. But the new breed of bush characters are a bit of a surprise. Many of them are high-tech, well-educated drop-outs from the city, chasing a lifestyle rather than material wealth. And the boom in a few of our rural industries has brought a lot of new management and marketing skills. So, in a way, it's more interesting for a journo than ever before. And then there's tourism. Big time now,' said Jane as she handed over the coffee and a plate of biscuits. 'Anzac biscuits from the CWA stall at the weekend.'

'Traditional fare?' queried Miche.

'Very. Now, what are you looking for? How far back are you starting your research?'

'Round the seventies, with the expansion of commercial and hobby vineyards. I want to weave in local colour, the old families, the immigrant influence, the lifestyle, tourism taking over from coalmining to become the huge, trendy business it is today.'

'That is a big picture! I'll introduce you to our editor, Bruce Wilson. Bit of a history buff as well as a goldmine of gossip about who has made news and who may in the future.'

'Do you keep the back issues here?' asked Miche, looking around the cluttered, cramped offices.

'Not any more. They're at the town library, as are the microfilm versions.'

Bruce Wilson, Miche learned, was a mine of information. A local boy, at twenty he'd started writing the cricket reports for the local paper, had been hired as a cadet and from there worked his way to the top. He'd been editor for the past thirty years. He was a stickler for correct grammar – no split infinitives, and no clichés. He wore a tie to work every day, except for public holidays, and on special occasions wore his Journalists' Club version with pride.

'Ah, we've been discovered at last,' he said with a grin. 'A big spread in the international editions?'

'Would be nice,' responded Miche. 'I'm trying to write it from my perspective, a young person from abroad discovering the place, the region. But not just a puff, touristy piece.'

'A personal slant on a story like that works best I'd say,' said Bruce and for the next fifteen minutes talked non-stop about people, places and past events that would help her recognise the diversity of angles available for her story.

Miche made notes and thanked him for being so generous with his time and knowledge. 'A pleasure, but there's a price.'

'Oh!'

'A story for the *Advertiser*. About you, your assignment. And a picture. At the right time, of course. Don't want to have you scooped by the opposition. Just stay in touch with Jane. The locals will love the attention.'

'Fair enough. Thanks for your help. Now, could you point me towards the town's library?'

'It's just up the road. Any help you need Miche, give a yell.'

Miche was soon scrolling through microfilm pages of the *Advertiser* from the sixties, seventies and eighties. Occasionally she stopped to read a story under a headline that caught her eye. In the steady parade of pages, she caught a taste of life in the district and what made local news. While often covering parochial issues, the stories reflected national and international events. Farm and food prices, French wine subsidies, a suspected horse infection at a prominent stud, brought in from overseas.

After about twenty minutes of pleasurable scrolling and taking notes on stories that may provide background for something up to date, the steady flow of work came to an abrupt halt as one headline shattered the routine research.

Her hand froze on the scroll control and her eyes locked onto the story. She read the first few paragraphs of the front page story quickly, then stared at a blurry photograph, a head and shoulders shot of a woman.

'My God,' she said softly. 'Surely not.' She was shaking slightly as she stood up and found a librarian. 'Can I see the original back copy of the *Advertiser* dated June 17 1982, please?'

'No worries. We'll dig it out for you. We hold them here for safekeeping.'

The librarian eventually handed over the dusty leather-bound binder labelled the *Advertiser, 1982*.

It didn't take long to find the story she was looking for and, with mounting tension, she read and re-read it and looked at the photograph. 'Has to be,' she murmured to herself, astonished that she was staying so calm. She was making notes when the librarian passed by, paused and asked quite casually, 'Having any luck?'

Miche almost bit her tongue, but it was too late. 'Sure am. Astonishing,' and then seized up.

'Oh, really,' said the librarian leaning forward to look over Miche's shoulder and clicked her tongue. 'Terrible story. I remember when that happened. Shocked us all. I wonder what happened to her?'

Miche closed the large file. 'I wonder indeed.' She left the library and walked slowly to her car, deep in thought.

Reg Craven lowered his voice as he spoke into the phone, even though he was alone in his office. 'We have to talk. Meet you at the bonk hole. When can you get there?' He listened for a minute fiddling with his bow tie.

'Christ, is that all you do, lunch? Okay, I'll see you at four this afternoon.'

It was an old Sydney landmark. The building stood at the edge of the city – a stone edifice with views across Elizabeth Street to Hyde Park. Musty offices of father and son accountants, solicitors and city agents for country organisations were clustered on the quiet lower floors behind frosted glass doors with gold lettering. The building's owners were on the top floors, which used to belong to a fusty publishing company that printed comic books and niche market magazines featuring photographs of muscled men and girls wearing bikinis. In recent years the company, struggling from dying circulations, had been sold to one of the biggest advertising and media buying outlets in the country. The magazines were closed down and the offices had been redesigned in modern, high-tech style. Part of the basement was now a recreation centre, gym and squash courts.

The building was overshadowed by taller, gleaming structures, offices and hotels filled with glittering shops, salons and restaurants. So the little 'burger building', as it was called because of its squat, bun-shaped dome, was easily overlooked and little notice was taken of the figures who slipped in and out of its arched stone doorway.

Even so, Reg Craven still looked over his shoulder as he entered the building at 4 p.m. He need not have been nervous about being seen, as many well-known media people had business at the ad agencies at the top of the building and this was adequate cover. Reg, however, walked past the restored iron-cage lifts, turned left and went through an unmarked door to a flight of steps that went to the basement.

He walked beyond the gym and used a pass-key card to access a tiny, softly lit and sparsely furnished sitting room with two more doors. Both were closed. He lowered his bulk onto the small chaise longue, glancing at his watch. After a few minutes, one door opened and an older man dressed in a dark suit, white shirt and dark tie appeared. His face was expressionless. He spoke in reserved, polite tones that seemed subservient, but to a listener who paid attention, his voice resonated with a thinly veiled disdain.

'Mr Cox is in the green room, sir. He asked that you join him.'

Reg winced. 'I'm here for a business meeting, I was hoping we could go somewhere else.'

'It may be best if you discussed that with him, sir.'

Reg knew it would be pointless sending the valet back upstairs. He stood, thinking that Tony was becoming more flaky and difficult the more time he spent with Jacques. At first, Reg had found it titillating to be included in the powerful young brat pack of Jacques, the media mogul's son, and Tony, the heir to an Australian fortune thanks to his developer father. But Reg was canny enough to know he would always be an outsider. He may be the office sleaze after a few drinks, but he was still a married man with young kids. He was an old man by the standards of Jacques and Tony, and they included him in deals like the wine club only to do their bidding when it suited them. Reg had played along with the blokes when it was mainly about booze and girls, but now Jacques was sailing into more treacherous deals involving drugs and prostitutes. While Tony was an eager crew member, Reg could see only storms ahead.

Very few people knew of this private club's existence, and Reg assumed the licensing authorities were being paid off. It gave him a certain satisfaction to know he held a key card to a very, very exclusive, if scary, world.

At the top of the narrow flight of stairs, Reg tapped at the door and heard Tony's voice. 'Come in, sport.'

Tony was lying in his underpants on the large bed beside a girl with huge breasts spilling out of a lacy corset with suspenders and black stockings. She wore red, spike stilettos and a long strand of fake pearls. She was glamorous and looked like what she was – this month's men's mag pin-up.

'Hey, man, what's up? Wanna join us?' Tony's voice was slurred, whether from cocaine or vodka he couldn't tell. Tony reached for the bottle of Russian fire and waved it at Reg. 'Have a drink, mate. Take the tie off, for God's sake.'

Reg absently fiddled with the knot of his tie, but left

it in place. 'Tony, we have to talk.' He looked at the girl. 'Business stuff, about Connoisseur.'

'Can't it wait?'

'No. Where's Jacques?'

Tony grinned and inclined his head towards a small curtain on the wall. Reg stepped over to it and drew the short drapes aside, revealing a two-way mirror. It showed the bedroom on the other side in which a naked Jacques was in bed with two women wearing black leather. Reg turned away. What had once excited him now made him feel ill.

'Listen, mate, there's a big problem. Nina is asking questions about the wine club. She's sharp.' Reg hadn't been officially told what Jacques and Tony were doing with the wine club except that it was a lucrative cover for an international deal. Reg had made a few guesses, then stopped asking questions, deciding ignorance was safer.

'It's Jacques' magazine, too. He can advertise his own business in it.'

'There are a few other problems. Ali is not going to carry the can on this one 'cause she didn't know about it.'

'Told ya we should've cut her in,' grinned Tony.

'Nina is back in the saddle. Jacques can't keep stirring things up in town. Nina will close the magazine before allowing her name to be rubbed in dirt. There are rumblings about shady operations,' said Reg pointedly. While Reg had helped set up a few deals with advertisers for holidays at a luxury resort, kickbacks of products and a car deal for a contest winner related to clients, he had not been included in the far bigger deal being engineered by Jacques and Tony. While he hadn't wanted to know the details, he suspected Jacques was using the wine club as a money-laundering exercise to cover the retailing of drugs and prostitution, a far more profitable operation than selling wine. Even the best wines.

'I don't want any part in your deals,' said Reg, opening the door to leave. 'I'm writing off my interest in the wine club.'

'You mean you're handing me your shares in Connoisseur,' said Tony with a smirk. 'If you want out, there's a penalty, mate.'

Reg knew he was going to lose what they'd talked him into investing. It might be a small amount to Tony, but it was the cost of taking the wife and kids on a family skiing holiday on his budget. In a normal commercial deal, he would have sold his interest, the lack of option to do that was another indication there was nothing normal about this little operation. 'Okay, on the understanding my name is wiped off the record. When the shit hits the fan, I know nothing.' Reg glanced at the girl who was finishing a champagne and looking bored.

'You're a wimp. Take your eyes off your arse, Reggie. Hey, speaking of arses.' Tony reached for the girl, grabbing her backside and pulling her onto the bed.

Reg turned to leave. 'Take it easy, Tony. Your days are numbered if you get caught in sleazy deals. Watch the company you keep,' advised Reg.

'I am. Believe me I am, and I like it very much.' He laughed as he rolled the girl over onto her stomach. 'I'm riding high with the new young guns of Sydney town. The old guard is on the way out, Reggie. Check your super fund, old fellow, you may be dipping into it sooner than you think.' Tony turned his full attention to the girl.

Reg turned and strode out, ignoring the little squeals coming from the bed . . . He wouldn't be back in here again.

*

'You're very quiet,' said Jeremy as Miche settled into the room set aside for her at the Palmerstons' vineyard.

'I'm tired after the drive from Sydney. And I stopped in Cessnock to talk to your friend at the paper. Jane was very helpful.'

'How is the research going? Found any interesting angles, ideas?' he asked watching her unpack her bag.

'I think I have a long way to go,' said Miche in a weary voice and she made no attempt to explain the enigmatic statement.

Jeremy gave her a questioning look, clearly puzzled by her attitude, then tried to change the atmosphere. 'There's a nice bottle of wine chilling,' he announced brightly. 'When you're ready, come and have a drink.'

'Sounds inviting. You finished your work? How are plans coming along for the big wine conference?' said Miche in an effort to respond to Jeremy's good intentions.

'Pretty well together. Steve and Helen have hosted this before. A lot of important winemakers are coming from all over the country and a few from overseas. A few members of the foreign media too.'

'I may find something for my story then.'

'I'll be surprised if you don't. This sort of event doesn't happen every day around here. I'll see you by the fire.'

Miche touched up her hair and changed her top and splashed on a little of her favourite Jonquil perfume before joining Jeremy in the family room where a log fire burned. Usually there were lots of people about the large and gracious home, but this evening Jeremy and Miche had the place to themselves.

'Lots of conference planning meetings on at the moment,' he explained. Jeremy rose and poured her a glass of wine. 'Here's to you, Miche.'

She sank into the deep, soft cushions of the big lounge,

'Lovely, just what I need.' She smiled at him and sipped her wine, then leaned her head back and closed her eyes. 'This is bliss.'

The fire crackled, the crisp wine tasted cool and refreshing. Jeremy's warm body was close to her. She felt herself begin to unwind and for a moment had to fight not to share the shocking discovery she'd made earlier in the day at the library.

'Miche,' said Jeremy softly.

She opened an eye. 'Hmmm?'

'Can we talk?'

'Sure.' She sat up, wondering at the tone of his voice. He seemed to be having difficulty in framing his words. 'What is it, Jem?'

He put his glass down on the coffee table, clasped his hands between his knees and looked at the floor.

'I've done something and I'm not sure how you're going to take it. It seemed a good idea at the time, but now I think I might have overstepped the mark. Been a bit too presumptuous about our friendship.'

Miche touched his arm. 'I don't think so. I mean, unless you tell me, I can't say.' She had a tingly feeling in the pit of her stomach. Was he going to suggest they go away together? The growing sexual tension between them had not been acknowledged, they had spent time becoming friends first. And she was glad about that. She really liked Jeremy. But she couldn't deny there was an intense attraction between them that could certainly become something more serious.

He took a deep breath. 'Miche, it's about your father. How do you feel about him? At the moment, I mean. Forgetting all that past stuff, what if he walked in that door?'

Miche threw a frantic look at the door for an instant. 'I can't "forget all that past stuff" as you put it. How do you think I feel? What are you getting at?'

'I thought you wanted to find him so you could hear his side of the story, balance the picture a bit.'

Miche was tense and hesitant. 'I guess so.' She sipped her wine and Jeremy watched, resisting the temptation to keep talking. She took a deep breath. 'So tell me, Jeremy, what would you know about my father for God's sake?'

'I've found him.'

Miche was stunned into speechlessness, her jaw dropped, their eyes met, each momentarily trying to penetrate deep inside the other in an effort to see some instant enlightenment, some immediate rapport. An instant sympathy. But Miche felt like she'd been hit with a hammer. A terrible pain, followed by anger, swept over her. 'What do you mean? You've contacted him? Why didn't you come to me first?' she demanded furiously, her fists clenching as she struggled to control the anger.

'Miche, I had to know if I had the right bloke,' said Jeremy defensively – and as gently as he could to help her cope with the shock. 'It seemed such a long shot. Would you have agreed if I'd asked first?'

She stared at him, swirling emotions making her dizzy. 'What have you found out? Have you talked to him?' she asked incredulously.

Jeremy nodded. 'When you told me his name was Gordon Birchmont and that he was born in Adelaide, it just seemed too much of a coincidence. You mentioned his birth date and it all checked out. I've had dealings with Gordon, but it wasn't an easy subject to raise,' he added.

'No. It's very personal. Between him and me,' snapped Miche. 'So he's still in the same area? I was told I'd have to go through the electoral rolls.'

'He lives in the Barossa Valley in South Australia. He's a winemaker. That's how I know of him.'

Miche stared at Jeremy, finally managing to whisper, 'You're joking.'

'No. He spent years in the US. In California in the Napa Valley. He came out to the Barossa after that.'

Miche was silent, a sudden flash hitting her. Her mother had taken her to California when she was about five. She remembered going to Disneyland, with a man sitting beside her in a little boat as they went through a tunnel full of dolls with 'It's a small, small world' blaring from speakers.

And she remembered her mother sitting next to her on a plane and crying.

'What's he like?' She could hardly breathe, barely manage to speak. 'Does he know about me?'

Jeremy reached for her hand. 'I told him you were here. He wants to meet you. But only if you want to. He's emphatic that he doesn't want to intrude.'

'Intrude! That takes the cake! When I was a little girl he walked out of my life! Left Mom. Left me.' Hot, angry tears burned on Miche's cheeks. 'Now he wonders about intruding!'

'I understand the confusion of emotions that this must unleash. But that is something you two have to thrash out. There are two sides to every story, Miche,' said Jeremy lamely.

The idea of suddenly coming face to face with her unknown father shook her. What did he look like, what was he like? It was as if you'd lived with one leg all your life and suddenly there was the opportunity to have an artificial leg grafted onto your body. She remembered a friend who'd lost half a leg and he had said the phantom nerves still screamed in pain and remembrance of the missing limb. Miche had only a sense of severance, she couldn't remember what it had been like to be whole. She'd always had a part of her missing. 'I can't, I can't,' she whispered, dropping her face in her hands.

'Yes you can, Miche. He isn't asking for anything

other than to meet you. If you don't do this, it will never be resolved. You'll wonder all your life.' Jeremy touched her hair and lifted her face to look at him. 'Miche, you can't move forward, and make your own life, until you do this. I think there is a special reason I found him. I'd like to think that you . . . and me . . . that we might sort of stick together . . . down the track.' He broke off, worried he was putting too much emotional pressure on her.

Jeremy handed her the glass of wine and Miche took a sip and leaned back, wiping her hand across her eyes. 'I don't believe this.' A tremulous smile crept around her lips. 'You cared enough for me to do this, huh?'

'I guess it shows how much I feel for you. So, I said I'd let him know what you want to do. A phone call, a letter. Or just meet face to face. Or you can leave it and do nothing.'

'I think first I'll talk to Nina. And maybe Larissa,' said Miche slowly.

'Do that, Miche.' He shifted on the sofa. 'Er, Gordon is on the invite list for the conference. He's quite respected in the wine business.'

Miche didn't know whether to laugh or scream. 'You mean he's coming here? In the next day or so?'

'I didn't plan it this way. His name was on the list and when you told me about your father's details, it rang a bell. So I asked him when his birthday was and sort of crept the subject of you into the conversation. He was a bit stunned at first. Then very excited. But he doesn't want to push you.' When Miche didn't answer, he continued, 'Listen, no one else need know anything. You can see him somewhere else, you can stay at my place rather than here. The visitors all stay in the guesthouse and here in the main house. I'll bunk with a mate.'

Miche wrapped her arms around her head. 'Oh, my God! What will we talk about, what do I say?' She lifted her head in sudden distress, 'Does he know what happened to my mom?'

Jeremy nodded. 'He knew. I didn't ask how. He seems to have a lot of pain too, Miche.'

She flung open her arms and settled back in the lounge, signalling an acceptance of the situation and that a degree of emotional control had been reached. 'So? What now? You're stage-managing this scenario.'

'Darling Miche, I'm just trying to be a friend. It need go no further than this moment. He understands that. If you don't want to see him, he won't blame you at all.' Jeremy touched her arm. 'Surely there has to be a reason this has dropped into our lap? I find it bizarre he's in the same business as me.'

'Is he an alcoholic?' asked Miche.

Jeremy burst out laughing. 'What a mad thing to ask. People who work in the wine business are quite circumspect in their drinking. Did your mother hint at such a problem?'

Miche felt suddenly traumatised remembering how heavy drinking had been a big problem for Lorraine.

She said nothing, so Jeremy continued. 'This is how it is . . . your father is well respected and, frankly, quite well to do. He'll be here on Friday. He was coming anyway. The fact that I have told him you are here . . . that you came out here trying to find him . . . he interprets as a series of fateful circumstances. He says all he wants is a chance to talk to you and to try to explain his feelings. He didn't go into personal stuff with me, but I sense he feels an obligation to you and also a deep sense of loss. He is thrilled to know how well you are doing.'

Involuntarily there was a flash of pride, an inkling of what she had missed all her life. Recognition by her dad for what she was doing. 'A bit late to be interested,' she countered.

'Come on. Stop judging him on the past. At some point you have to let go and move on with your life.' Jeremy felt his heart twist as he looked at her pinched, tight face. She was holding in so much pain. He put his arm around her, 'Miche, I think things are going to change, and be really wonderful. For both of us.' He stroked her hair and, as she leaned into him, he kissed her softly and slowly and felt the rigidity melt from her shoulders as she returned the kiss that held so much promise.

It was only later, alone in her bed, that the tears flowed. Years of pent-up anger, hurt and loneliness were released. Finally she left the bed, splashed cold water on her face and, as she stood at the window staring into the moonlight and at the distant serried rows of vines, it came to her that there must be a bigger plan for her life being orchestrated by fate, the gods, whatever mysterious power was out there. It could not be a coincidence that on the day she rediscovered her father, she had also discovered another young woman's painful, pitiful secret.

Now that knowledge was showing her the path to take with her father – forgive, forget, go forward. Hard as it may prove to be.

Nina was finding it difficult to settle back into her routine, something that normally didn't take more than a day after returning from a big trip. Now she was struggling to stay involved and focus on the minutiae of the day-to-day running of *Blaze*. While not wanting to overrule Ali who was, after all, still editor until she flew out, Nina wanted to be on top of what was planned and what had happened. She was still judging April Showers. She'd read her work and, while she didn't like the article on Heather Race and the subsequent legal bunfight, she could see April had talent.

It just needed more intelligent targeting. Her style of attacking writing was not one that Nina personally liked, but she was astute enough to recognise that it stirred up readers and critics and this translated into sales.

Reg was not a problem. He had pulled in his horns once Nina returned, and with the announcement of Ali's promotion and the promise of a new editor, he felt secure once again. He tried very hard to smarten up his act. Life without Ali could be absolute bliss, he decided. He knew he'd made mistakes, but in the changed corporate environment he'd recover soon enough.

Nina began to make plans for Ali's public farewell and the more pressing issue of replacing her as editor. But the corporate issues, no matter how urgent and complex, failed to diminish her obsession with the totally enchanting prospect of a whole new way of life, a sample of which she had discovered while being with Lucien – travelling, setting up more children's homes in Croatia and, hopefully, neighbouring countries still suffering from displacement due to the continuing conflicts and crises. She wanted the freedom to explore the challenges and joys of these new paths into the future, freedom from the constraints and spiritually barren environment of the bottom line, the next edition, the next lot of circulation figures.

She stopped by Belinda's desk. 'I have to make a quick trip to New York, just a few days. A meeting with the Baron and, hopefully, the new editor. I want to leave in a few days. Can you arrange the booking?'

Belinda nodded and didn't ask questions. Nina would confide information when she was ready. 'Nina, there's personal mail here for Larissa that Miche dropped off. Do you have her new address?'

'I'll take it with me – it will be quicker. She's still between New York and New Hampshire. Making wedding plans.'

'I'm so happy for her. Tell her we miss her very much.'

Nina took the letters from Belinda. 'I'll tell her. Let me know the flight details.'

'Will you be here for Ali's farewell?' asked Belinda anxiously. It wouldn't look good for Ali if Nina wasn't there to make a speech.

'Of course. We'll make it as big an exit as the launching of *Blaze*. It's very much a promotion, not a sideways move,' she said firmly.

Belinda nodded. Nina must have seen the sniping in the press. Already there were rumours that the ground was rumbling beneath the Yank Tank.

Ali paced around her sleekly sterile apartment. It looked no different from the week she moved in. She hadn't acquired anything personal in the way of mementoes of life in a new city, and the continent that sprawled around it. The apartment had the professional, temporary, ordered air of an expensive hotel suite.

She walked around the suite restlessly, deeply perturbed. Despite the magnificent harbour panorama outside the tinted windows and the sense of spaciousness it conveyed, she felt the world was closing in on her.

A conversation with Nina and Belinda earlier in the day had affected her more than either of them suspected.

Nina had told them both about a phone call from Miche pouring out the story of the discovery of her father and that she had agreed to meet him at the end of the week. She had explained how Jeremy had made the connection and contacted Gordon Birchmont, the vigneron from the Barossa. Nina and Belinda had been slightly taken aback at Ali's vehement reaction, 'I think that what that young man did is absolutely shocking. He had no right to talk about Miche with her father. What if she hadn't wanted to know about him? What right has anyone to meddle in her very private business?'

'Well, Miche did come out here with the intention of looking for him. She made that public knowledge,' said Nina gently.

'She was even going to write about it,' Belinda interjected. 'Do you suppose she still will? It's an amazing personal story.'

'And what if she hates him? I think it's a gross invasion of privacy.' Ali had stomped away, leaving them open-mouthed.

Now, in the seclusion of her white space, she prowled, wrestling for hours with long-buried emotions that insisted on surfacing.

After a long and very emotional night, Ali had made her decision. She called the Yellow Brick Road and Belinda and told them both she would be late. At 9 a.m. she made another phone call from her apartment, not trusting even the privacy of her office for the security the call demanded. She made an appointment for later in the morning.

Two hours later she arrived for the secret engagement, struggling to act her new persona. The Chanel dark glasses were firmly in place. Dressed entirely in black, she looked funereal. To the woman behind the desk, the tag of black widow spider sprang to mind.

'I am Alisson Vidal. Here are the appropriate papers you require,' announced the spider curtly, handing several folded certificates across the desk.

The assistant commissioner at Corrective Services leaned forward. 'Thank you very much. I have the file here, Miss Vidal. Sorry to ask you to produce documentation of your identity – the rules, you understand.' She scanned the documents, folded them carefully and slid Ali's birth certificate and those of her parents back across the desk. Ali didn't answer, pushing the papers into her handbag. The assistant commissioner continued, 'Your inquiry will remain confidential, as you requested. It is entirely up to you whether or not to pursue contact.'

Ali nodded sharply, wanting this meeting to be over as quickly as possible. 'Is he still at Bathurst?'

'No, Miss Vidal. Your father has been released.'

Ali jerked in her seat. 'He's free? You mean he's . . . outside? Where?'

'I really couldn't say. He was released in 1989. I can give you his last known address, but that was 1992. You could try it.'

Ali lifted her hand to stop the flow of words. 'I have no intention of doing that.' She did not elaborate further.

The Corrective Services officer glanced back down at the file and record sheet before her. Among the mass of detail, only two words mattered – 'Convicted' and 'Manslaughter'. Radiating pain and anger, she glanced at the young woman across from her. 'These problems are not easy to deal with. You may consider seeing a counsellor. If you are thinking of making contact, it helps to have an objective professional involved.'

Once again Ali cut her off, rising to her feet. 'Thank you for your time and assistance.' She left the office without a backward glance.

The older woman watched her leave, wondering how many years it would be before the hurt that young woman was holding inside herself blew up.

And whether it would it be too late.

*

It had been a long time since Nina had felt a romantic excitement on being processed by Customs and Immigration at an international airport, but her arrival at Los Angeles this time had put her feelings in such an unaccustomed state. With her heart rate slightly higher and feeling flushed, which generated a readily dismissed embarrassment, she emerged and was swept into the welcoming arms of Lucien. They clung together, making heads turn at the passionate embrace between the handsome man and the elegant woman. Nina was overcome at the strength of her feelings. How she had missed him, and how she was already dreading returning to Sydney and being apart from him. Her old life now seemed totally inadequate, much less fulfilling than being with Lucien.

'An easy trip, I hope?' he asked as they parted slightly and looked into each other's eyes.

'Fabulous, and you can guess why,' she grinned.

He gave her a quick kiss in reply and took her arm as they headed to the luggage carousel. 'Now, Nina, my darling, how soon will you have the editor in place in Sydney and we can swap these passionate airport reunions for a less public acknowledgement of our new-found happiness?'

'I'm not sure. No matter what, my sweet, I'll have to stay on in Sydney during the changeover. It's a tricky time for any publication and I have too much of myself invested in *Blaze* to leave it to chance. But I know how you feel, believe me.'

'That settles it then. I'm returning with you. I can't stand these separations. Could you put up with me hanging around for a couple of months? I can work on finalising the script for my next film. The money is looking good so it could be off the ground and go into pre-production in the next financial year.'

Nina linked her arm through his as he lifted her bag

onto the trolley and headed for the car. It felt cosy and domestic after the years of chauffeurs and impersonal limousines.

Two days later she was in New York in the conference room at Triton headquarters meeting with Oscar Triton. To her surprise, the Baron, though outwardly warm and welcoming, had little time for talking. He announced that due to a complicated schedule he only had time for a review of possible candidates for the editor's job in Sydney.

Nina sensed, despite his warmth and courtesy, he was holding something back. It puzzled her immensely because her past association with him had been so open, so mutually trusting.

However, all such concerns were pushed from her mind as Larissa hurried into Nina's temporary office to greet her.

'Nina, what a lovely surprise! I'm so glad we can catch up on all the news. But first things first. Is there a chance you and Lucien and Miche can come to the wedding?'

Nina laughed. 'Where and when? Tell me all. Over coffee.'

'Well, we're planning something small and intimate for very close friends and family only. In Santa Barbara. We're trying to decide where to splurge for the honeymoon.'

'What about New Hampshire – have you found a place to live?'

'It's been hard. Gerry has a few problems.'

Nina poured the coffee. 'What sort of problems?'

Larissa's cheerful demeanour dropped for a moment. 'The position he was promised has had a hiccup. A contractual mix-up over detail of duties and responsibilities, but it will be solved in a few months. A bit of staff shuffling is needed as well. A good thing in a way, as it gives us time to find a place, settle in, you know. How's everyone in Sydney? Miche rang me to tell me about finding her dad. Have you met Miche's young man?'

'Not yet. She's staying with Jeremy's boss at the vineyard, doing research for a week or so. Your little Paddo house is empty. I think Miche may want to move closer to the Hunter,' smiled Nina. 'By the way, Belinda gave me a few pieces of mail for you.'

Larrisa quickly thumbed through the envelopes. 'Nothing that suggests I ought to instantly reach for the letter opener,' she said smiling. 'Thanks for doing courier duty.'

'No worries,' Nina replied, and they both laughed. It was an expression used constantly in the Sydney office, even when editorial hell was breaking out.

Then Nina switched into a serious mode. 'Larissa, I asked you to come in and see me for more than a catch-up. I'd like to run something past you.'

Larissa recognised the tone in her voice. It was the Nina executive voice and it came as a surprise. Nina still looked a little weary, jet-lagged, she supposed. But her usual energetic verve was missing. In a flash it seemed to Larissa that Nina was losing her passion for *Blaze*. It must be the deepening relationship with Lucien. She could understand that. 'Shoot, Nina.'

'I've moved Ali. It's considered a promotion, "Publisher at Large" for Asia and the Pacific as well as Australia. She'll be on the move with a lot less opportunity to create a power base. She didn't seem at all happy being in Sydney. That disappointed me, as I had hoped that being in the more casual Aussie work environment and different culture would soften her approach to life a little, perhaps enable her to see there was more to life than just being an imaginative and tough editor.'

'Find a little bit more yin to go with the yang, you mean?' queried Larissa.

'Quite,' said Nina. 'It didn't work out, though she certainly made sure the magazine was started professionally and running in front of the field.'

Larissa was impressed with the way in which Nina had quickly diagnosed what was going well and what was going wrong at *Blaze*. 'But who is coming in to replace Ali as editor in Australia?'

'I was thinking you would be perfect.'

Larissa put her cup down with a clatter and laughed. 'Nina! We've just been through all this. I didn't leave because of Ali. I chose Gerard.'

'Seems to me, Gerard's career is treading water for a bit. Why not have a honeymoon on the Barrier Reef and take the reins at *Blaze* for six months? There is a sweetener to this. Stay for twelve months and you're in line to come back here and replace Irene. She wants to move to Europe.'

Larissa was stunned and it took a few seconds for her to respond. 'Why didn't this arise when I was still there?'

'Would you have changed your mind about marrying Gerard?'

Larissa rubbed her forehead. 'Nina, this is so cruel. You know I always wanted to be editor, I figured the opportunity had passed me by. I love Gerard. But I'd adore to go back to Sydney.'

'I'll talk to Gerard if you like.'

'No, I'll tell him what you've offered. Let him decide. I'm not going back on my promise to be with him.'

Nina touched her hand. 'Come and have lunch with me tomorrow. Let me know then. I'm back to Sydney. Lucien is moving down for a couple of months to write his script, then we'll return to Croatia. I'm working with several agencies to help set up two more children's homes. Lucien is setting his film there.'

'I'm really happy for you, Nina.'

'Follow your heart, Riss. I'd love you to run *Blaze*, but I want you to be happy most of all,' said Nina softly.

They arranged to meet at Giovanni's, Nina's favourite Italian restaurant on West Fifty-fifth. Nina was pleased to see Larissa come in accompanied by Gerard. He kissed her on both cheeks with a rueful smile.

'Are you cross with me, Gerard? Can't blame me for wanting to keep her, but she's made it clear to me that you come first,' said Nina trying to instantly reduce the tension she could sense.

Giovanni escorted them to their table and fussed around Nina making suggestions for their meal. Once they'd settled on Giovanni's menu and the wine was opened, Nina lifted her glass. 'Here's to you both. Much, much happiness. How are the preparations coming along?'

'Our mothers are still in a tizz over the final details.' She gave Gerard a fond look.

'We're sorry you and Lucien can't be there, and Miche won't be able to make it either,' said Gerard. 'However, we'll see everyone on the way to our honeymoon. We've decided on the Great Barrier Reef. Heron Island.'

Nina smiled and raised her glass in acknowledgement. 'I'll drink to that decision.'

'Thought you might,' said Larissa and raised her glass to Nina's. Her face broke into a huge smile. 'We've decided to take up your offer. Gerry is coming out while I edit *Blaze*. He's going to paint!'

Nina was elated. 'That's wonderful! Oh, Gerard, I'm so pleased. Larissa will be brilliant, the staff will be thrilled. What changed your mind?'

'Quite a few things,' answered Gerard. 'The fact Riss was prepared to give up her career for me, the frustration of my job appointment being delayed, and well . . . that letter you brought clinched it for me.'

'Letter?' asked Nina in a puzzled voice.

Larissa's eyes were shining. 'It was from a prestigious art gallery in Woollahra. Miche and Belinda had the owner look at Gerry's paintings that he left behind in the house and she's asked him if she can represent him. She wants him to do an exhibition. That'll keep him busy for six months.'

'It'll be a test of whether or not I can sell, that's for sure,' said Gerard.

'Our parents weren't too thrilled at first, but now they're planning trips Down Under,' laughed Larissa. 'So when do I start, Nina?'

'As soon as the honeymoon is over . . . I mean the one on Heron Island. I hope the magic never wears off,' she said, raising her glass for another toast. 'To our futures, joyous, one and all!'

TAKE TWENTY-FIVE ...

After talking to Nina, Miche tried to settle her mind and her heart to the forthcoming meeting with her father. She fluctuated between being scared, nervous, sad and angry. She ran through the scenario in her mind a dozen times, each time with a different script, a different ending. She finally decided she was driving herself crazy and the best thing to do was to distract herself. She decided to refocus on her Hunter Valley story.

The Palmerstons had given her a large room and the run of the house, for which she was grateful. Jeremy lived across the vineyard in a modern cottage with two other winemakers. As everyone was busy, Miche had the house and its gracious walled courtyard to herself most of the day. She set up her laptop on a big hardwood table and spread out her notes. But her concentration span was short. Thoughts of her father kept breaking through.

And now she couldn't help relating the turn in her life with the uncanny parallel, that she alone knew, with Ali.

Once more she looked at the photocopies of the newspaper cuttings from the *Advertiser*.

The article that had caught her attention was headlined, 'MINEFIELDS MURDER. JEALOUS RAGE SHATTERS THREE LIVES'.

The feature photograph was of a wild-eyed young girl being led away by a policewoman. The caption read, '*Alisson Vidal, 10, is taken into protective care while a search for relatives continues.*' The story went on to elaborate on the events of the fateful night when Alex Vidal had driven home inebriated after being sacked from the Barn Darset Mine. In what was believed to be a domestic dispute, he'd argued with his wife, had struck her and driven away leaving her and his sleeping daughter. It is not known how badly injured the mother was, except when a fire broke out – from the open fireplace – the daughter had tried to drag the mother to safety, but was overcome by smoke. The daughter fled the burning building by jumping from a window and had run to a neighbour's house for help. By the time the fire trucks arrived, the home had been destroyed. The mother was pronounced dead at the scene.

There was the poignant follow-up story dated a few weeks later of the young girl who'd lost her mother – the late Katherine Anne Gruber. Her father, Alex Vidal, was now on remand in jail awaiting trial. The ten-year-old girl was pictured standing at Sydney Airport with a large tag pinned to her chest, staring defiantly at the camera like a frightened doe. The caption explained she was on her way to a new life with a distant cousin of her mother's in America.

It was Ali. Who now looked uncannily like the picture of her mother taken at the time of her death. They were approximately the same age. In the story, neighbours described the father as European. The family had no relatives in Australia.

Miche was overwhelmed by sadness for Ali. No wonder she had kept her past life a secret. Her father had been charged with manslaughter when it was found Ali's mother had died, before the fire engulfed the house, as a result of being struck by her husband. No wonder Ali hadn't been keen to come back to Australia. It was a terrible wound to re-open, thought Miche. But along with the sympathy she felt for Ali, came the disturbing knowledge that in her hands was a story that many journos and, no doubt, every city editor, would grab with relish. She could imagine how this would be played in the hands of a few of the less scrupulous journalists like Heather Race. She didn't imagine Nina or anyone else in the *Blaze* corporate scene knew about Ali's background. Miche shook her head in another spasm of shock at the horror revealed by the articles and the implications if the story was ever uncovered. It would ruin Ali's life. Everything she'd achieved as a successful editor, everything that meant so much to Ali would be washed away in the sensationalist discovery of her innocent part in this tragedy. As Miche folded the cuttings slowly, she reflected on how the lives of Ali and her own mother had come together from such remote and different pasts. Ali had been Lorraine's nemesis, and now Miche realised that she had the power to undo Ali by releasing what she knew.

The next question confronting Miche was what, if anything, she should do with this stunning knowledge? Ali had shut down her past and constructed a new history, burying the terrible secret that her father had killed her mother.

At least Miche's father was successful, respected and liked, from what Jeremy had said. How lucky she was. Whatever had happened between her mother and father, whatever pain she had suffered as the child of divorced parents, was nothing compared with the anguish Ali must feel.

Dozens of questions ran through her mind. Was Ali's father still in jail? Had Ali kept in touch with her father, how had she dealt with it, had she forgiven him? Ali had taken her mother's maiden name, and stayed in America. It didn't sound like the American aunt had worked out. Miche knew from what Nina and her mother had told her that Ali had turned up in New York at sixteen, another runaway, who worked at odd jobs, including cleaning Nina's house, before landing the job at *Blaze* as a gofer.

But the more she pondered over Ali, thinking back on small incidents, comments and her obsession with privacy, the more she realised what a shell Ali had built around herself.

Miche now understood Ali's reaction to her suggestion of doing the story on children who were the innocent victims of violent crime.

How close that must have hit Ali – no wonder she had tried to steer Miche away from the story. And yet the substitute story she agreed Miche could do was also risky. The Hunter Valley . . . the area where Ali had lived, the scene of her tragic secret. Miche thought back to how Ali had briefed her on the story to concentrate on the vineyards and to look for an upbeat angle that would appeal to the twenty and thirtysomethings who were investing in wines. It was a long way from one sad story in the fabric of a whole district. Ali had gambled that in researching such a story it would be most unlikely her secret past would be discovered. It was a calculated move to steer Miche away from writing about a subject that was so painful and so close to Ali's own story.

Miche was staggered when she looked at the overlapping connections between herself and Ali. Miche's mother, Lorraine, tormented by the ambitious, younger Ali. Nina throwing Miche and Ali together in a place where they both had to confront the memory of lost fathers. Then Miche ploughing into an emotional minefield of children who were victims of childhood abuse. Miche saw their similarities as well as their differences. How each had handled the situation so differently. They'd both lost their mothers and needed a father during their crucial growing years. Both were known by their mothers' maiden names. Ali was not the sort of person who liked people feeling sorry for her. Strangely, Miche felt suddenly protective of Ali. Then came a blinding realisation that this knowledge about Ali was a test. A powerful one.

The issue of ethics, the use and abuse of power and knowledge. Blackmail and persuasion, power and position. Talent, ability, creativity, integrity. On the big media merry-go-round these days, so many people believed everything could and should be manipulated for personal advantage. Loyalty counted for nothing. It was a matter of debate whether newspapers or magazines took the crown for bastardry. Since coming to Australia, Miche had heard all the arguments, all the opinions, again and again at dinner after dinner with journalists, over many a latte or bottle of red.

She thought back to the life her mother had lived in New York. The constant pressure and obsession with work. How her mother would never take time out to sit and watch a video, just veg out, or even go for a walk in the park. There was always something to do for the magazine. Her argument was that if she didn't put her work first there'd be no treats, no luxuries, no staying in their smart apartment. Lorraine had brushed aside Miche's childish pleas that all she wanted was her mother's full and constant attention for an hour or so.

Even when they went somewhere special it was generally connected to *Blaze*. The magazine world followed them home as Lorraine had vented her frustrated anger over the male hierarchy who treated her so badly. The constant refrain of her mother had been the fear of age, losing her beauty, and her job. Miche hadn't understood, she'd seen her mother as beautiful and talented and clever.

In this reflective state, Miche thought about the staff at *Blaze* in Sydney. The same problems her mother had faced years before in New York were still alive and well Down Under. Men ruled. Girls had to flirt or be devious and stab each other as well as their male competitors. The pretty, soft, new girls landed the best jobs over the experienced, better writers. She remembered one time in New York her mother and Nina becoming angry over a strong suggestion from a male executive that they find a woman psychologist to write a column – 'Someone who is young and pretty.'

Lorraine had slammed her hand down on the table as she'd related the episode to a less than interested Miche – 'And not a flicker of embarrassment when he said it! They still haven't learned!'

When Miche told her mother she wanted to write, Lorraine had urged her to keep away from the newsrooms of the metropolitan dailies. 'It's usually a cesspit of piranhas,' she had warned. 'Survival depends on the men's club. A mistake by a woman means a blotted copybook for years. The same mistake by a man is simply a learning experience that can be smoothed over with a beer or two.' Miche had found it difficult to believe until she started her career in print. Still, she hoped the new and fast-changing world of magazines, into which she was trying to make her way, would somehow find a solution to many of these issues and provide a more satisfying and fulfilling opportunity for women who wanted to write, to communicate in the mass media. At this stage, she wasn't quite sure how it was all going to work out. But she was glad she was freelancing, rather than being tied to one office and its internal politics. Miche was determined not to touch the nest egg her mother had left, and while it was a struggle to find the rent, she had flexibility and freedom.

It was with an effort that she forced her mind back to the necessity of focusing on the Hunter Valley research and, after a concentrated effort, was able to nut out a concept of how she could structure a fairly interesting yarn. But then, as she packed up her notes and laptop, once again into the forefront of her mind came the knowledge that in a day or two she would be meeting her long-lost father.

Ironically there was only one person in the world Miche felt she could share her fears with who would truly understand how she felt – and that was Ali.

This time when Nina and Lucien embraced at the airport departure lounge, it was not tinged with overwhelming sadness, but with joy knowing they would soon be settled together in Sydney. They had been back in touch with Mara in Croatia to confirm that the local authorities had suspended the casino proposal pending Nina's application for restoration of her family's home. Nina had no doubt she would win. Now Nina's energy and enthusiasm was directed at setting up a village school. A teacher had returned to her family home in the village and was willing to run it. Nina and Lucien agreed to help. Nina had already begun to make notes about the logistics of establishing schools at the two new children's homes. 'We'll be out in the spring, Mara, laden like pack mules,' promised Lucien. He was writing a character into his film based on the indomitable Mara.

*

Back at *Blaze*, Belinda, who was privy to Nina's plans, was having trouble keeping her mouth zipped. Instead, she kept smiling and looking, Barbara declared, like the cat who'd swallowed the cream. Plans were under way for Ali's farewell bash and a favoured newspaper journalist had been given the exclusive about Ali's promotion to splash in a positive spread. News about Ali's replacement was being down-played, though columnists speculated the new editor of *Blaze* was unlikely to be a major high-profile appointment.

Nina, publisher and editor-in-chief, was back at the helm, and the trade assumption was that the magazine would hum along quite smoothly and competently.

Jeremy tried to be as attentive and caring as he could towards Miche in an effort to make the coming meeting of father and daughter as amicable as possible. Without elaborating to Miche, he had many long conversations with Gordon Birchmont, telling him what he knew about Miche, how they'd met, what she was like and, without breaking personal confidences, what he thought Miche's fears and dreams may be.

'Look, Gordon, I have to confess I'm rather smitten with Miche. She's very special to me. It's early days in our relationship, but I've never felt like this about a girl before.'

'I appreciate your sharing that with me. I have to confess, Jeremy, that I haven't had anyone with whom I could talk about the sudden appearance in my life of the daughter I last held in my arms when she was five.'

Jeremy was glad he had a professional friendship with Gordon that had allowed him to step into this sensitive area. His role of bringing Miche and her father together was now weighing on him. It brought a huge sense of responsibility and the fear he might lose her. What if there were animosity, pain, guilt and anger between Miche and Gordon that could then be directed at him? Meddling in people's private lives, crashing through barriers in place for years, made him feel like the proverbial bull in a china shop. The fact that Miche stubbornly rejected the idea that she speak on the telephone to her father before the meeting worried him. The stand suggested a tension that Miche was not able to explain to herself, let alone Jeremy.

It was arranged that Gordon would arrive ahead of the other delegates at the mini wine convention and stay at a motel nearby. Jeremy had told Helen and Steve about the circumstances – with permission – of Miche and Gordon. Once over the initial shock and delight, they were supportive and offered whatever help they could. They refrained from making any judgements, even though they knew and liked Gordon Birchmont, were fond of Miche and privately thrilled about the obviously growing attraction between Miche and Jeremy, who had become more of a surrogate son than employee.

Feeling the need to unburden himself about the situation, Jeremy had talked it over with his parents in Melbourne. And, while they didn't know Miche and were a little concerned he might be interfering too much, they believed he had done the right thing.

Miche changed clothes four times, trying to decide what to wear. She was shocked at how nervous she felt. 'This is worse than going to the dentist, a job interview and to court all rolled into one,' she told Jeremy.

He stood back and threw out his arms. 'Miche, you're

gorgeous. You look lovely. Just right.' She'd chosen a simple dark wool skirt, a soft pale blue cashmere sweater and the unusual blue bead and gold earrings designed by Kevin Friedman she'd bought in Paris. Her blonde hair fell smoothly to her shoulders and she'd taken pains with her make-up – a subtle look that was artfully achieved. Jeremy took her hand, 'Anyway, he's bound to be more nervous than you are.' While he had no idea what had happened between Gordon and Miche's mother, he imagined Gordon was the one on the defensive.

With Jeremy acting as go-between, they agreed to meet in a small restaurant near Gordon's motel. Gordon had suggested eleven-thirty for an aperitif rather than lunch, leaving Miche the opportunity to escape early depending on how their meeting went. Jeremy knew the owner of the restaurant and he reserved a table on the terrace that was secluded and promised not to book other tables close by to give them privacy.

It turned out to be a magnificent sunny day and Jeremy was in high spirits as he drove Miche to the restaurant.

'Fantastic day, isn't it,' he enthused. 'This is when the Hunter is at its best. And I think it augurs well.'

'I hope you're right,' replied Miche softly.

'Nervous?'

'A little.'

'I'd be surprised if you weren't. Remember, I'll be right alongside you in spirit.'

'You're a sweetie,' said Miche affectionately and leaned over and gave him a quick kiss on the cheek.

'Careful now, you may make me lose control.'

Miche could not help laughing out loud at his response. 'One day I may. One day!'

Jeremy joined in the laughter, and when he dropped her off at the restaurant she was a lot more relaxed.

He took her hand and walked her to the door. 'Good

luck, kid,' he said with feeling. He didn't know what else to say, so he kissed her and walked quickly to his car.

The hostess smiled at Miche. 'Are you meeting someone?'

Miche nearly crumpled as her assumed calm disintegrated and she felt like bursting into tears. 'Yes, I'm meeting my . . . er, Mr Birchmont.' She managed to say before words deserted her.

'Oh yes. On the terrace.'

For Miche it felt like the longest walk she had ever made, but it was over in less than thirty seconds as the hostess led her out to the terrace. Miche had gone through this moment in her mind a score of times, trying to visualise the man she was about to meet, rehearsing many introductory remarks, and now she was desperately hoping the girl would leave them and let them meet alone.

Once outside, the hostess indicated the furthest table, where a gentleman was seated. 'Over there. Best table on the terrace.'

At that moment the man looked up from the wine list that he had been studying and saw her.

Everything went into slow motion for Miche – she'd heard that often happened in accidents. The background hum of voices around the terrace and birds in the garden seemed to be suddenly switched off.

She was aware she was walking forward, but it felt like she was stepping through glue. And for a moment she thought her eyes were failing her too, for she couldn't make out his features. She had a blurry impression of someone tall, a navy jacket and blue shirt, silver hair. Suddenly he was no longer an imagined being but a real person, right there slowly rising to his feet. The distance between them closed, sounds of low talk, clinking of glasses and plates, background music slowly returned.

He was standing, smiling, slightly tremulous, a little awkward.

The hostess pulled out Miche's chair and suddenly glanced at them. There was not the easy normalcy of two people greeting each other. The tension between the man and the young woman communicated to her and she too felt suddenly awkward.

She leaned forward to take Miche's napkin, which was twirled in her wineglass, at the same moment that Gordon stuck out his hand towards Miche. The momentary confusion when Gordon's hand collided with the hostess was the trigger for a small release of tension and father and daughter were both smiling when their hands first touched. The hostess laughed and excused herself, retreating to fetch the menus.

'Hello,' Miche managed in a small voice.

'Hello to you too. And thanks so much for letting this happen.' He gave her hand a little squeeze then withdrew it. 'Sit down, sit down.'

Miche sat and found herself desperately needing to do something, so she reached out and took the stiff white linen napkin and began fiddling with it, then quickly put it down again. Her rehearsed lines just wouldn't come out.

Gordon knew he had to say something and all his practised opening lines were forgotten. 'I thought long and hard about what I'd say at this moment, but I'm damned if I can remember,' he said in a low voice.

Miche couldn't yet look at him, she straightened the fork by her bread plate. His voice was softly modulated, a pleasant Australian accent. A voice she didn't know, yet every syllable rang through her head in an echo.

She surprised herself by suddenly finding her voice. Found herself able to respond. 'I'm having the same problem.' She managed a weak smile and was able to look him in the eye to see the relief he obviously felt.

'Would you like to choose a wine? Or something else, perhaps?' He looked at the wine list rather than at his daughter.

'I think you know more about wine than I do,' she said.

He nodded in acceptance and gave her a quick smile.

With a shock, Miche now saw that his eyes were the same colour as her own. His face was weathered, slightly rugged and attractive. Pleasant was the adjective that came to mind.

'Does a light dry white sound appealing?' Miche nodded in agreement and he indicated the selection to the hostess. 'A local vintage Jeremy recommended,' he added. 'I have to say, I'm very grateful to Jeremy for arranging this.' When she didn't answer, he steered away from the subject. 'Jem says you met in France?'

'Yes, I was writing a story on a young model. We did the photographs at the chateau where Jeremy was working. Very different from the vineyards around here.'

'Australian winemakers have a different ethos in many respects. A lot of blokes in the business now learn the European techniques and then adapt them to our conditions. Jeremy is good at that. He will go far if he sticks at it.'

'I don't know much about winemaking and vineyards. What are your prospects when you work for someone else? Sounds a bit like being a hand on a ranch. It's not like you own the property,' said Miche.

'Depends on your abilities. Vignerons, or those who have the nose and specialist knowledge, are far more valuable than the guy who owns the dirt,' said Gordon. 'It's more intricate than farming. You don't just plant the vines and a vintage wine ends up in a bottle.'

'So everyone keeps telling me,' she said a little defensively. And suddenly the easy flow of words between them

629

seemed to run into a dry patch. There was brief silence that was instantly awkward.

He sipped his glass of water. 'Michelle, I know this is hard. Where do you want to start?'

She took a deep breath, 'Well, for a start I'm called Miche. Michelle seems so formal. Why don't you tell me a bit about yourself? All I know is where you were born.'

'Fair enough. I was born in Adelaide, but grew up in the hills behind the city. On the edge of the grape country. I loved the area, so always hankered to go back there. But as a young man I wanted to see what was on the other side of the world. Did a bit of travelling, then came home and was conscripted. I was caught up with the war in Vietnam. When that was over, I took off for the States. I particularly wanted to see my best buddy's sister. I had made friends with an American helicopter pilot who spent time at Nui Dat, the Aussie base camp. He was killed and I went over to the States to look up his sister. He'd talked about her, showed me her picture. They were very close. She was a budding big shot in journalism. Guess who?' He gave a wry smile.

'Yes, Mom talked a little about her brother,' said Miche.

'So that was how we met. New York was a buzz to a country bumpkin like me. I landed a job with a pretty far-sighted Aussie fellow who decided to export Australian wines to England and the States and I was hired as a salesman trying to persuade liquor outlets to stock Australian wine. Quite a challenge at the time. However, thanks to my mates in the New York Rugby Club, who did a lot of serious drinking at the Mad Hatter's Bar, we started to spread the word.' He chuckled at the memory, then paused as the girl brought the wine, showed him the bottle and asked if he'd like to try it. 'The lady can be the judge,' he said gesturing to Miche.

She took a sip and nodded. It was a lovely wine. 'So how come you're back here?' It was an oblique question that, translated, meant, 'Why did you leave my mother and me?'

He didn't pick up on the subtext and continued chattily, 'Big cities didn't suit me. And when some friends back in Adelaide told me about an opportunity to buy a few acres in the Barossa I was dead keen. I'd always had it in the back of my mind to be a winemaker. I was working my way around the Napa Valley in California by that time. Spent time in a handful of the wineries there. I figured the Barossa property that came up was about as cheap as it was ever going to be, so I went out on a limb financially and had a go. It was hard for a while, but we seem to have come good.'

'Wine all over Australia seems to be doing okay. But everyone I talk to here says the best years are yet to come,' said Miche.

'Yeah. Could be. No argument that the product is top quality, and we have a lot of land that's every bit as good as the best in France and California when it comes to wine production.'

There was a brief pause as they both searched for a neutral topic.

Gordon plunged ahead. 'Can I finish telling you my story?'

She nodded, glad he was doing the talking.

'Look, Miche, what happened between your mother and me was sad, but it wasn't any horrendous event or mystery . . . I always assumed you knew what happened, which was simply, that our worlds didn't mesh. We were young, in love, having fun and suddenly there was all this responsibility of finding work, supporting a wife and a baby in a culture completely alien to a boy from the Adelaide Hills.'

Miche was silent for a moment. Her mother had said something similar about the country boy not fitting into New York as if it were a fault on his part.

Miche had sometimes found it hard to settle into Australia with its idiosyncrasies and so many little things that were different from America, so she could imagine how it must have been for her father. 'So why did you leave us, if you loved us?' she blurted out, terrified she was going to cry.

At the sight of her hurt and bewildered face, Gordon longed to reach out and hug the daughter he hadn't held for so long. But he kept his fingers tightly interlocked – he hadn't earned that right yet. He spoke quietly. 'I didn't think of it as leaving in any permanent sense. It was difficult when the New York job didn't work out, so I went out to California with the idea of seeing what I could find out there and my plan was that you and Lorraine would come over. Well, as you probably know, your mother was working in newspapers and then she moved onto Nina Jansous' magazine – they were good friends. She told me in one of the last letters she wrote to me that she'd asked Nina to be your godmother, your protector, even though she didn't believe in religious ceremonies. Anyway, Nina's magazine became her life. She loved it. She didn't want to move to southern California. All the action she wanted was in New York.'

Miche certainly couldn't imagine her mother being comfortable anywhere other than in New York. The countryside was, in her mind, adequately represented in Central Park. A casual coffee in Greenwich Village was Lorraine's idea of dropping out of the high-rise, big city milieu. Vacations had meant visiting friends with homes in the Hamptons or Long Island, or a trip to a five-star hotel with her mother on assignment. Once Miche had stayed with a girlfriend whose grandmother had a big

632

country home and there had been horse riding, canoeing and picnics. It was an unforgettable holiday for her. Lorraine had shuddered at the idea and been glad Miche enjoyed it and she hadn't had to go along.

Miche spoke slowly, 'I remember a vacation one year when we went out to California. All I remember was Disneyland. I was about five. Was that to see you?'

He nodded. 'I kept trying. I wanted her to see the kind of life we could have as a family. But she was totally wrapped up in her career. There was no question she would allow me custody. Sharing you when we lived on opposite sides of the country was impossible in those days. When your mother wouldn't move to California, I came back here. A couple of years later I went back to California and managed to scratch together a bit of backing from the winegrower I'd worked for over there. I went armed with a pretty fair plan, so he flew out for a look at the vines I'd planted, and gave me the ground stake to set up my own winery. His investment eventually paid off handsomely,' he added. 'Sadly, your mother couldn't see the potential as he could.' He shrugged, 'By then she was working for *Blaze* and totally wrapped up in that world. I called her in New York one last time to see if she'd let you come and stay for school holidays, anything. She said it was too late, so I asked for a divorce. You were ten years old. I'd never been very flush with money. I sent what I could, but everything was returned to me. The lawyer who handled the divorce over there has been my only point of communication.' He swallowed a mouthful of wine. 'I did what she wanted and kept out of the picture.'

'Mom said you never tried to keep in touch, you never helped her financially . . .'

'I don't want to criticise her, especially now, God knows . . . but she had her reasons. I remarried and I don't know if she ever did . . .' Seeing Miche shake her head, he sighed. 'Her career was everything. Yet it doesn't sound like it made her happy.' He paused and studied her then went on gently, 'You must have been her life.'

Suddenly Miche found that tears were spilling from her eyes.

Gordon couldn't bear it. He reached across the table offering a hand in support and Miche, while wiping her eyes with the napkin, reached out and let him take her free hand. It was a move she hadn't thought about. It just happened, as if she needed to do it and there was no alternative. In a moment she was back in control and their hands parted.

For Gordon the contact, albeit so brief, had been far more significant than their initial touch. He looked into her face, wishing the years could roll back to the day he'd first held his newborn daughter in his arms. 'Miche, I would give anything to turn back the clock, but I can't.' They stared at each other for a moment, registering every detail of the face opposite, seeing the surface similarities, trying to see beneath the skin, to somehow reach inside each other and pull out the tangled feelings that bound them both.

'Miche, let's talk about us, the present, and let the future take care of itself. But first there's something I have to give you.' He reached down by his feet and lifted a cardboard carton onto the seat beside him. Miche leaned over and looked at it curiously. 'I had this put away safely, I pulled it out to give to you.' He gave a shy, embarrassed smile.

The hostess returned and asked if they wanted to order lunch. Gordon gestured to Miche, letting her make the decision to stay or go.

'Just something light. A salad. Quiche perhaps.' She was feeling light-headed and her stomach was churning.

Food might help. Painful as all this was, she wanted, she needed, to hear it. She might never see him again, so this was the moment to have her unanswered questions dealt with. They quickly gave their orders then Gordon pushed the box towards Miche who slowly lifted the lid.

There were letters tied in bundles, a slim photo album and a small cardboard box about the size of a shoebox. She lifted out a packet of letters. They were addressed to Mrs Lorraine Birchmont, the string around them neatly tagged with a date. Slowly Miche went through the piles, not undoing them, but aware all had been returned to the sender. A few were addressed to Miss Michelle Birchmont, one pile of fatter envelopes was tagged, 'Birthday and Christmas cards'. These too had been returned unopened.

A small claw began to scratch at Miche's heart. 'Why did these come back?' She recognised the old addresses.

Gordon sipped his wine. 'Your mother preferred it that way. She was possibly afraid of losing you. I had a family out here, she really only had you. She was worried I might take you away, so she severed all contact. It was very hard for me.'

'Me too!' The words sprang from Miche. She was in shock, this was a scenario she hadn't anticipated. She closed the lid on the box, as if trying to lock back in the memories and the issues that it held, then she didn't know what to do with it.

Gordon understood and he gave the box a little shove. 'I think it would be a good idea to take all that away with you. Lift the lid again when you're ready. Sorry about the late delivery.'

She smiled weakly and mumbled a thanks, then put it beside her chair.

'Now, tell me how you're doing out here. Coping with the eccentricities of Oz?' he asked brightly, instantly changing the mood. 'What are your plans?'

She was relieved to be back on neutral ground. She told him about her research for a series of articles about the Hunter for *Blaze*.

'Terrific idea. Why not extend it and come to the Barossa? I'd love you to see my vineyard. The Barossa is interesting, old German connections. I've been trying to lure Jeremy over. Why don't you both come?'

'Maybe. I don't know what Jem's plans and time are like,' she said cautiously.

'I'm sorry. I don't want to pressure you. I just thought you might find it . . . interesting. There's a little bit of the vineyard dedicated to you, by the way.'

She stared at him. 'What do you mean?' It suddenly occurred to her she hadn't asked about his present life. He said he'd remarried. 'Do you have family there?' she asked tentatively.

'No. Sadly my wife died a number of years ago. She had two sons from her previous marriage. They're both married – one is an investment banker in Perth, the other an accountant in Adelaide. Not interested in the actual producing of wine, but they like to visit when they can. And take away a couple of cartons of our best,' he laughed. Then added, 'They know about you. That I lost touch with you. And there's something else I want you to know. There is a small rose arbour at the house with a little fountain and a seat. There's a small plaque that simply says Michelle's Place.'

'I don't know whether to believe you.' It seemed too convenient, too unreal.

'It's true, Miche. And it has been there a long time.' He leaned across the table. 'Miche, please look through that box. Contrary to what you may have believed, I have never stopped thinking about you. You are my only child. The older I become, the more regrets I have about losing you . . . and your mother. Please, give me a chance

636

to make it up to you. I was so sorry to hear about what happened to Lorraine. She devoted herself to you, yet that career of hers didn't give her the peace and happiness she deserved. I want more than anything else to make sure you are happy. Please, give me that chance.'

Miche bit her lip, and couldn't speak as tears again rolled down her cheeks. And she could see tears shining in her father's eyes.

Silently the hostess put the food on the table and asked gently, 'Bread? More wine?' Gordon shook his head and she quickly left, aware that this was no time to intrude with service niceties. He took a deep breath and pulled himself together as Miche took a tissue from her bag. Somehow they both managed to concentrate on the food. It had come at the right time. Gordon made polite comments about the quality of the cuisine, and Miche responded with the information that she was a fresh food fanatic, hated takeaway fast foods, and was opposed to genetically modified food ingredients. It was an over-reaction, but it worked for her. She was back in control.

As they ate, Miche reflected that Nina Jansous was right. There was always another side to every story. While Miche had always loved and understood her mother very well, she now saw a small bright light shining into the dark corner that represented her absent father. And, in its beam, she saw a man who'd tried as best as he could, and had suffered too.

Gordon lifted his glass of wine. 'Here's to the future, Miche. Let's just take it as it comes, okay?'

She raised her glass to his and managed a little smile.

By the time Jeremy arrived to collect her, Miche was feeling light-headed from the wine and emotional over-load. They met in the bar and all that Jeremy needed to know was written large in the smile of welcome that she gave the moment she saw him.

She went to him and kissed him lightly. 'Thanks for taking the gamble, Jeremy. It's been a memorable lunch.'

'Well, that's made my day,' he said with relief and pumped Gordon's hand.

'Made mine too, mate,' said Gordon, happily thumping Jeremy on the shoulder with his free hand.

They chatted for a while about the wine business and the forthcoming convention, then Jeremy took Miche's hand and smoothed the parting. 'We'll see you tomorrow then. Miche is coming to the cocktail party.'

Gordon leaned forward and kissed Miche on the cheek. She hesitated for a second, then put her arms around him and gave him a hug.

'Thank you for that, Miche,' he whispered and turned away so the two young people wouldn't see a dam that was bursting inside his chest, threatening his shaky composure.

Jeremy put the box on the back seat and gave her a questioning look, but she closed her eyes. 'Later, Jem. I'll tell you later. But, thanks, it was easier than I thought in lots of ways. Harder in others. It wasn't as black and white as I always believed it was.'

Jeremy squeezed her hand. 'Tell me when you're ready.'

That afternoon Miche lay on the bed, the pale lemon curtains fluttering in a slight breeze. Faint sounds of machinery, far-off voices, the closer hum of insects in the garden, birds singing in trees next to the house, combined in an hypnotic and harmonious symphony that enhanced the dreamlike state in which she drifted. She felt as if she were walking along a high and narrow ridge, a great divide between two worlds, the what-was or the what-might-have-been and the here-and-now on the other side. With her eyes closed, she tried to fit together the jigsaw of her life from a fresh perspective.

Her mother, Lorraine, had been outwardly strong, self-disciplined, ambitious and talented, yet she'd always clung to her young daughter who'd often felt the protector of the vulnerable and insecure side of her mother. They had needed each other and together had coped. But now the second half of her being – her father – had emerged from the depths, from the unknown. She had always imagined him to be a cold, heartless, uncaring loser. Instead she'd found a man of charm and success who had loved her mother and her, but hadn't been strong enough to fight for a failing marriage. A man who hadn't been strong enough to fight a wilful wife who'd wanted her career and her child above all else. It was a war they'd all lost.

As Miche lay there, she tried to imagine what her mother would say about today's reunion. It was impossible to answer that with any certainty. More importantly, what did she, Miche, think about the new family picture that was becoming a reality that required a fresh attitude and offered so many unexpected opportunities? She still had to come to terms with value judgements on his sincerity and his proclaimed enduring love. Was he being totally honest about all this? It was one of many nagging questions that she worked through ever so slowly.

Cynical, testing questions. But that was what her mother had taught her. Be strong, be in control, before you are walked over. It was an uncomfortable exercise, but it had to be done.

Nina's words about taking life day by day, came back to her. Today had been a massive step. And it was still to be completed.

Miche sat up cross-legged on the bed and drew her father's cardboard box to her.

She went through the piles of letters, registering the dates that went back to when she was eighteen months old. She put them aside and turned to the pile of cards, which she opened for the first time since they'd been sealed by her father. They brought tears to her eyes. There were birthday cards and Christmas cards from him, wondering how the year had been for her, was she happy, what was she doing at school . . . questions that had gone unread and unanswered for so many years. But what made her cry the hardest were the contents of the shoebox. It was marked, '*Souvenirs for Michelle*' and contained a collection of small objects a father might pick up on a walk with his daughter on the beach or in the bush . . . each sealed in little jars or plastic tubs, labelled with a place and a date. On so many occasions, when she had been in his mind he marked it by something he had picked up – a shell, a bird's feather, a dried flower, a teddy bear badge, a bird's nest. As the years went on, he'd added more grown-up items – a pearl on a chain with a '*sweet sixteen*' gift tag, a small pair of gold earrings marked '*18*'. And then, in a small plastic folder, was a collection of special wine labels and an explanatory note, '*Put down for Michelle for her twenty-first birthday. The best of every vintage of Birchmont wines. Stored in cellar CV12.*'

The thought that had gone into these tokens touched her more than she could bear. To realise he had saved the mundane, sweet things like a pretty bird's feather, and had thought of her, that he had indeed remembered every birthday and special occasions – and she'd never known – almost broke her heart.

She cried and she cried, face down on the bed, the mementoes so lovingly collected by her father crushed to her heart.

*

Miche awoke from a deep, dreamless sleep. It was after five o'clock. And she felt wonderfully refreshed, cleansed somehow. She stood luxuriating under the shower and then took pains doing her hair and make-up. Her eyes were still a little red, but she hoped no one would notice. She then added the gold earrings, the small pearl on a chain and pinned the whimsical teddy bear badge to her shirt. By the time she walked out of the room, she could hear voices on the verandah and felt happy about joining them. The crisis was over.

Jeremy rose as she appeared and held out his hand. 'You okay?'

Miche nodded. 'Thank you, Jem. Everything is okay. Really okay.'

Helen Palmerston passed a plate of scones. 'We're all so happy for you, Miche. You and Gordon are going to be the star turn at the party tomorrow. That is, if you want to break the news,' she hurriedly added.

'Very much so,' smiled Miche. 'I want everyone to meet my dad.' But for an instant her joy dimmed as the pinched face of Ali flashed into her mind. Could there ever be such a reunion for Ali and her father?

Gordon extended his stay after the conference and spent time with Miche and Jeremy. Reluctantly Miche was the one to leave first, explaining that she had to go back to Sydney for the big farewell bash for Ali. It was a case of doing the right thing. Also, Nina had told her about Larissa coming back out with Gerard, a secret she had shared with Jeremy. 'Her return hasn't been announced yet, but it means I'll have to give up the Paddo house and find a place of my own. And Nina asked if you and Dad want to come with me to Ali's party. They're taking over Catalina's for the evening. It's a Friday, so why not stay for the weekend?'

'Sounds fun. What about your dad? Is he going?'

'I haven't asked him yet, but I'll bet anything that he'll come.'

Nina invited Miche to dinner to hear all about her reunion. 'It's wonderful, Miche. It's like a fairytale. And I'd like to meet your father, and Jeremy too. Will you write about this do you think?'

'I don't think so. It's too personal. And not everyone's story has such a happy outcome as mine.'

Nina insisted on hearing every detail about the contents of the box of memorabilia from her father and it was some time before Miche had the opportunity to ask, 'How does Ali feel about leaving?'

'She's adjusting now her move is seen as a step up rather than sideways. She is anxious to return to New York and get an apartment, but it's not practical that she bases herself there. Still, we'll deal with that problem as it arises.'

'What's happening to the apartment she had here?'

'I'm moving Larissa and Gerard into it. Gerry will have to find a studio to paint in.' She gave Miche a grin, 'Unless you let him use the space at the Paddington house. You'll stay on there, won't you?'

'Wow! Nina, like a shot. Thanks so much. If Gerry could put something towards the rent he can have the whole back area and family room as a studio.'

'I'm sure we can work something out. Miche, has your father said anything about . . . helping you out either financially or in other ways?' asked Nina quietly.

'He made the right noises. But I said I didn't want to talk about that. The main priority for me is getting to know him and enjoying his company. I'll miss him when he goes back. We had a terrific time roving round the Hunter vineyards together. I learned a lot. He's very famous in his world you know,' she added with pride. 'He did offer to bring Jem and me over for a holiday any time we want.'

'And?'

'Jem is keen to visit his connections in the Barossa vineyards, but I don't want to force our relationship. It's a bit cosy having your father arrange a holiday together. I mean, much as we like each other,' Miche blushed slightly, 'I mean, we haven't slept together or anything.' She gave a grin. 'Not yet, anyway. Jem is special, I don't feel the need to rush our relationship. I think we might be together a long time.'

Miche had an appointment to see Ali on her last full day in Australia. Ali had told Belinda she could spare only ten minutes.

Ali was tidying the last of the papers on her desk and the office looked more sterile than usual.

'I just wanted to wish you good luck, Ali, and thank you for the opportunity to be published. I think it was a fine way to launch my career and I will always remember it.'

Ali look slightly startled for an instant. 'That's very nice of you, Miche. Your wishes are appreciated. I trust the latest assignment is progressing satisfactorily?'

'Yes, the story on the Hunter is shaping up nicely. A couple of super angles.'

'Well, that's fine. I look forward to seeing the finished product.'

'I'd still like to work up that story of trauma we discussed a while back,' said Miche.

Ali was brusque and dismissive. 'See Bob about that, but you know my attitude. It's probably not a goer.'

Miche was not deterred. 'I had an extraordinary experience while up in the Hunter. I found my long-lost father.

I just thought you might be a bit more . . . sensitive to the themes of my trauma story concept.' It was a carefully planned and carefully aimed shot.

'Why do you say that?' Ali resumed casually sorting papers from a drawer, not looking at Miche, forcing herself to stay calm.

'I came out here with an idea to find my father and find out why he abandoned my mother and me when I was a toddler. I was angry and hurt and figured he was a bit of a bastard or a loser. It turns out that he's a handsome, nice, successful man.'

'That must have been very nice for you, Miche, but it is hardly relevant to a story about violence, is it?' Ali paused in her fussing about the desk, and Miche sensed a rise in tension between them.

'I thought my story might inspire others to do the same. To face up to the past. It's proved to be a cathartic and very valuable experience. No matter what the lost parent turns out to be like, confronting it and coming to terms with it, is cleansing. Well, that's how I'm finding it. Wouldn't you agree it's an angle worth exploring?'

'We're not running a lonely hearts' club or a clinic for reconciliation therapy,' she snapped. 'This is a magazine.'

Miche could practically see the solid wall Ali had constructed around herself. It was like a fortress to repel invaders. Her reply was glib and hastily contrived. But Miche was dubious about how much further she could go down this emotionally dangerous path. 'True,' she said disarmingly. 'We have to keep the big picture in mind. Will you be coming back to look around Oz in a more personal way, other than for *Blaze*, I mean?'

Ali's eyes narrowed. 'Why? Should I? And do what?'

'Well, you haven't had much of a chance to move around since you took over the editorial desk. I can recommend a trip around the Hunter,' said Miche brightly.

'I'll read about it in *Blaze* when you finish your piece. Once again, thanks for the wishes. Was there anything else?'

'No, Ali. But congratulations on your appointment.' Miche held out her hand and Ali shook it loosely and briefly, then Miche walked from her office and quietly closed the door. Ali flopped into her chair, and spun it around to face the Darling Harbour view but she failed to notice the sunlight playing on the white buildings opposite. Instead, behind the defensive dark glasses she was seeing a young girl, huddled in her seat on a plane, leaving Sydney and sadness behind. But the haunted memories had followed her and never left. Now Ali was about to board another plane and leave this city and her past behind her again.

No one knew her secret. But somewhere out there was the man that had caused her unhappiness. Unlike Miche, she would not be making her father a part of her future life.

THE WRAP...

Eddie propped up the portable mirror on the roof of the car and dabbed at his face with powder. The boys at the Yellow Brick Road had done a terrific job – the new haircut, the very subtle make-up – just for on-camera, of course. He licked his lips to make them shine and took up his place outside the entrance to Catalina's Restaurant. 'Ready when you are, Ms de Mille.'

Christine, his producer, stepped forward with her clipboard. 'This is just a brief intro to set up the party segments for later. Be excited, this is an exclusive. *Reality* is taking you into the A-one of A-list parties.'

Eddie waited until the soundman nodded and the cameraman lifted a finger. 'Rolling.'

Eddie waited a couple of seconds, then began. 'Darlings, here we are outside the most fabulous restaurant in this most gorgeous setting . . . you'll see all that when we go inside. You are coming to the A-plus party of the minute as our guests. Remember the launch party for *Blaze* magazine? Well, that went down in history as one of the best ever . . . so let's see what they've whipped up to outshine that event tonight as the city says farewell to its star editor, Ali Gruber.' He started to turn, then swung back to stare straight down the camera. 'Stick with me, sweeties, and you won't fall in the harbour!' Then he pranced out of shot up the steps.

'Cut. God, he's sickening. A total natural,' sighed the producer, aware that so many people were lousy performers in front of a TV camera.

'He just loves what he's doing, so it comes across,' said the cameraman hoisting the tripod onto his shoulder and picking up the camera. 'I'll set up overlooking the water, put up a light or two and you bring the talent out there as Eddie snares them.'

'A lot of people won't do that, there will have to be grabs on the run, taps on the shoulder jobs. Eddie's good at it, charms them no end. He asks frivolous stuff and people don't seem to notice he's actually making them drop their facade and reveal more than they should.'

'True,' acknowledged the veteran cameraman. 'Not exactly mastercraft journalism, but great for a giggle, and that's all a lot of the customers want.'

Ali's farewell party had finally come together quite impressively, thanks to Nina's team at the office marshalling a heavyweight guest list from the media, show biz, the arts and high society. It had been fanfared with a huge, flattering spread in a Saturday paper and they'd finally agreed to allow *Reality*'s new star talent, Eddie Kurtz, and his camera crew in to capture the atmosphere. There was something about TV lights that gave any party a higher rating, particularly among the guests, most of whom would kill for a few seconds on camera.

Ali was first, pausing to stare into the bright lights. Her sleek figure was draped in a pashmina shawl, sparkling sequins sprinkled on the soft cashmere worn sari-style over her head and wound around her throat. Her long black dress was strapless and outlined every inch of her pencil body. Her shoes – 'Manolo, eat your heart out,' was Eddie's line to camera – had jewels across the toes and, in the high, sculptured heels of clear acrylic, tiny plastic fish were suspended. Her make-up was dramatic – the Yellow Brick Road team had gone to town with gold eyelids and heavy kohl eyeliner that swept upwards to give the effect of large, topaz cat's eyes. Her lipstick was blindingly red. Ali had decided that if she had to make a public exit it would be a grand exit with impact.

After Ali had made her entrance in the glare of flash-bulbs and camera lights, Nina appeared in a simple white pants suit, her dramatic dragonfly pin sparkling in her upswept hair. Around her throat was a strand of pearls and diamonds, a gift Lucien had ordered from a jewel-ler in Broome. She was followed by Jacques, who was adorned in tight black pants, a white T-shirt and black and white plaid silk jacket, with Tony Cox in tow wearing a red vest over a full white pirate shirt and black pants.

Most of the senior management executives of *Blaze Australia* waited inside the entrance, an informal recep-tion committee.

'I wonder if they'd all be here if it weren't for Nina,' mused one of the lower-rung *Blaze* staffers watching on the sidelines.

'It's a lot more informal than I expected, no string of heavy speeches planned. I'm surprised Nina allowed a film crew in though.'

'Ali's idea,' said her companion staffer. 'She and Eddie were pretty close. She wasn't thrilled when he left, now she's acting like she pushed him in front of the camera.'

'If he'd flopped on TV, she wouldn't have wanted to know him.'

Nina was stopped briefly by John O'Donnell, who

kissed her cheek. The two corporate contacts had been friends for years. 'It's lovely to see you back in town, Nina. I heard you were staying in Europe.'

'I will be spending more time there. As well as in London with Lucien. We're very happy. And you, John?' She gave him a certain look that told him she knew, or had guessed, how involved he'd been with Ali.

'I'm all right. I still miss Carol. I guess one does a few silly things while grieving. But I'm on track now. I'm retiring, may stay on a board or two, but I plan to travel. Sailing round Greece this Christmas. Stuff like that.' He gave a half smile and a shrug.

'Keep in touch, I have a project going on back in the old country you may be interested in having a look at. Come and stay with us in France. I mean it. And take care, John dear, you'll be a vulnerable target for a bit.' She squeezed his arm.

'I've learned my lesson. I'm trying to age gracefully,' he smiled.

Miche hugged Nina. 'You look sensational, Nina. Now, here he is . . . my father.'

Gordon shook Nina's hand. 'It's so lovely to meet you. Thank you for all you've done for Miche . . . and for Lorraine,' he added softly.

'And this is Jeremy,' said Miche.

Nina took his hand. 'So you're the young man who made it all happen. Well done. You've brought a lot of happiness to all of us.' Nina turned back to Gordon. 'It's wonderful the way events have worked out. It's a delightful reunion and I know it will bring both of you a lot of pleasure. Being godmother to Miche has been a joy for me, I do hope you'll come with her to Europe to visit us.'

Gordon smiled. 'Lovely idea, but young Jeremy might have something to say about that.'

'Ah,' said Nina with a wink, 'I imagine he will.'

Eddie, with camera in tow, was moving fluidly among the guests enjoying pre-dinner drinks. He'd been told to be out by the time everyone was seated. 'Monsieur Triton, are you going to give me a teensy hint about the new editor of *Blaze Australia*?'

'Of course not,' said Jacques, who had no more idea than Eddie who Nina was planning for the job. Nor did he much care.

'Oh, boring. Give me your news then,' chirped Eddie.

'Now Nina Jansous is back from leave, I'm returning to New York and then possibly Europe,' drawled Jacques, as though he was telling Eddie about a ferry trip across the harbour.

Tony was not so laid-back. 'I'm leaving too. I'm off to New York, going to work for the Tritons there . . . well, for Jacques . . . in a new secret enterprise,' said Tony, preening before the young women attracted by the camera crew.

'Secret!' screeched Eddie. 'You've tickled my curiosity! That's a word I love . . . tell me all about the secret.'

And if Jacques hadn't given Tony a hard look, he would have told Eddie all about it – even on camera.

Eddie took the cue, 'Oh,' he cooed after a pregnant pause, 'one of those sorts of secrets, is it? Thank you, darlings,' and scanned the room for his next target.

Tony was still very swept up in the heady world of Jacques Triton. With Nina back in the driver's seat looking very closely at all aspects of the magazine, Jacques was making a quick exit from town. He liked having smart, fun, agreeable – never say sycophantic – pals around him. So Jacques had invited Tony, his new best mate, to move to the US and work for a vague e-commerce company Jacques and his New York friends had been creating. Tony saw glamour, the jet set, the life of an international playboy looming. Had anyone pointed out to him that he was no more than a groupie doing Jacques' bidding, Tony would have instantly dismissed the idea. By the time he realised he'd sacrificed his individuality, career and well-being to Jacques' hedonistic lifestyle, it would be a long way home to Australia.

April Showers was in a corner talking to John O'Donnell when Eddie sashayed up. 'Well, if it isn't one of my oldest and dearest . . .' Eddie angled himself for the camera and kissed the air either side of April, who gave him a forced smile and a look that said, watch what you say.

'Hi, Eddie, congratulations on making it in show biz. Telly suits you – quick, slick, knock you off at a flick,' said April.

'You're the megastar, darling. You've blossomed from the columnist bitch to the feature witch. Who are you ripping into next month?'

She wagged a finger at him. 'Be careful, Eddie, could be you next. I'm the new senior feature writer at *Blaze*,' said April whose smile hadn't moved.

'Congratulations to you too then. I'm not worried about you doing a Heather Race on me, sweetie.' Eddie made an exaggerated aside to the camera. 'I have all the goods on this lady, darlings. Ooooh, believe me.'

'Fine,' said April a little uneasily. 'You read me and I'll watch you.'

'You do that, sweetie. Millions do, tra-la,' he wiggled his fingers at her in a limp wave and sauntered off. The cameraman and his assistant glanced at each other know-ingly. That little exchange would be edited out.

The evening ran smoothly. Nina made a short, elegant speech praising Ali and attributing the landmark arrival and success of *Blaze Australia* to Ali's flair and acumen. She then called upon the head of the biggest consortium of companies that advertised heavily in *Blaze* to propose the farewell toast.

The corporate heavyweight made a short, silky speech, and everyone raised their champagne glasses – 'To Ali' – and the formalities were concluded. The noisy par-tying continued.

John O'Donnell sought Ali out and kissed her cheek. 'I hope this is what you want, Ali dear.'

'Not exactly. But I'm afraid you can't offer me what I want either,' she said with sudden candour, and added, with warmth in her voice for the first time that evening, 'You really helped me. I'm grateful for that. Thanks.'

'You also helped me through a difficult time. I appre-ciate your discretion and I think I understand what drives you. Good luck to you, Ali,' he answered gallantly.

Before anyone noticed, Ali had left. Nina suddenly looked around and sent Tracey to check with Tom the limo driver, who reported he'd taken Ali back to the *Blaze* offices an hour or so earlier.

Nina glanced at her watch. 'It's nearly eleven. There isn't really anything for her to do back at the office . . .' her voice trailed off and she looked worried. She didn't want to say anything, especially in front of Miche. For suddenly, Nina couldn't help thinking about Lorraine. She glanced around the room, wondering who to confide in.

Her eyes fell on Reg Craven and she asked the waiter to bring him to her table.

Reg was feeling very pleased with himself and had

strictly limited his drinking on this evening so that he could gain maximum enjoyment out of observing every nuance of the farewell to the woman he hated most – Ali. Also, he knew he needed to re-establish his standing with Nina. He didn't care who Nina appointed editor next, no one could challenge or upset him the way Ali had.

Jacques, with Tony permanently attached to his side, was leaving the country and taking his shady dealings with them. So Reg was ready to reoccupy his territory and standing in the company. He'd spent a part of the evening schmoozing with Miche and her father. It occurred to him Birchmont Wines should be advertising in *Blaze*, no special deals because of Miche being Nina's god-daughter, but perhaps there could be a crossover promotion deal. Maybe *Blaze* could hold a classical music evening or something posh at the Birchmont Estate, which he'd heard was pretty swish. Yes, that could be a beneficial connection. When the waiter approached, he was elated that Nina had asked him to join her.

As he approached the table, Reg was struck by Nina's serious face, and for a moment his heart sank. No, Nina would never say anything critical in public. He smoothed his moustache. 'A delightful party, Nina. Very impressive round-up of guests. But then, *Blaze* on top of an invitation helps, doesn't it?' he said, making the point the guests had come because of *Blaze* and not Ali.

Nina picked up her tiny Hermès handbag. 'Reg, I want to go back to the office, I wonder if you'd accompany me?'

Reg did a double take. 'Now? I mean, of course, Nina. Is there a problem?' Reg couldn't imagine what could have gone wrong on a Friday evening with still plenty of lead time before the next edition's print schedule.

Nina spoke quietly. 'It's Ali. She's such a dark horse, you never really know what she's thinking. I'm a bit concerned because she slipped out of here without letting anyone know. Tom says he took her back to the office.'

Nina began to walk slowly through the dwindling crowd, nodding and smiling to people as she went. 'I don't want to upset Miche, I'll just tell her I'm going home – I needn't mention via the office. The car's out the front, Reg.'

Reg patted his pockets making sure he had everything – phone, glasses . . . He nodded and headed for the door.

The limousine stopped outside the building, which had a few lights scattered throughout various floors. They caught the lift to the *Blaze* editorial offices and stepped out into the softly lit reception area. Without saying anything, Nina turned towards Ali's office, her heart tightening as she saw the light under the door.

She called out, 'Ali! Are you there? It's Nina.'

There was a muffled noise. Nina opened the door that led into Belinda's office and saw the light and heard movement in Ali's office. The door was locked. She rattled the handle and raised her voice. 'Ali? It's Nina.'

'Why are you here, Nina?'

'I was worried about you when you slipped away and came here. Can we talk for a minute?'

There was a pause, then, 'Are you alone?'

Nina hesitated.

'For God's sake, I'm not going to jump,' snapped Ali.

Nina threw a relieved glance at Reg. 'Why the locked door, Ali? What are you doing? I just called in on my way home with Reg.' Nina tried to sound conversational.

'Reg! Is that bastard out there?'

Reg grimaced and gave a shrug indicating, 'See what I've had to put up with?'

'Ali, this seems silly, please come out,' said Nina, sounding a little exasperated now.

'Nina, send that prick home. And I don't need to see you. I'm tidying up my office. Clearing out, if you must know. I'm on a plane to New York tomorrow.'

Nina looked at Reg.

'I'll be off then. See you round, Ali. Good luck with the new job,' said Reg trying to keep the smirk out of his voice.

There was no answer but a thump that sounded like something going into the rubbish bin. 'I'll take a cab home, Nina. Thanks for a nice evening.' Reg strode away. He went to his office to call a cab. He was tired now. He was sick of working with women – bloody neurotic hysterics most of the time. Why couldn't Nina just go home and leave Ali to whatever she was doing? Ali was smart enough to know when not to hang around. Nina was such a mother hen.

He pushed open his office door and gagged.

His office was a shambles, everything was upturned, everything on his desk had been swept to the floor, including his computer. Files hung open, books and papers were thrown around, then his heart raced as he saw a huge overflowing pile of shredded paper. A quick glance at his files and drawers and he knew that Ali had run all the paper in his office through the shredder. It lay like spaghetti confetti all over the carpet. 'Bitch!' he screamed, falling on his knees, picking up a strand of paper. On it he could make out only a few letters, but he knew it was bound to be something important.

He started dragging the snowflakes of paper into a pile, cursing Ali, knowing it was a payback for his dumping on her sandpit.

His mobile phone rang and he scrambled to his feet, pulling it from his pocket. It was his wife. 'Reg, you have to come home at once . . .'

'I'm on my way, I was delayed. Nina asked me to come

back to the office. I'm still here. Christ, what a mess . . .'

'Reg, don't give me that,' her voice was weary, strained. She'd heard similar excuses over these past months when he'd come home smelling of Scotch and cloying perfume. 'Tina isn't well. I'm worried, it's that appendix playing up again.'

'I'm on my way. I'll call a cab. Jesus, Lori, you can't believe what that bitch, Ali, has done to . . .'

'I don't give a damn! I'm fed up with you ranting about that woman. She's leaving *Blaze*. You're not. Your kid is sick. Come home, for God's sake. We need you,' shrieked his wife.

Despite the hysteria and anger in her voice, it was music to Reg's ears. 'I'm coming, honey. I'll be there soon. Don't worry. Tell Tina Dad's on his way. If she has to go to the hospital, I'll take her. I love you, Lori. Look after our girl. I'm on my way.' Reg poured out the breathless words as his anger at Ali slipped away and he surrendered to the warm feeling of concern for his family. He hoped it wasn't too late to reunite with them. He'd been an arsehole. He'd make up for it. He punched in the cab number, gave them the address and, without looking back, left his office and caught the elevator downstairs.

Nina's limousine still waited at the kerb. Reg stood in the shadows till the regular taxi slowed and, seeing him waiting, pulled up. Reg sat in the front and gave his address. He didn't give Ali another thought.

Nina came outside alone a few minutes later. Tom opened the door for her and wearily she slid into the back seat, leaning her head on the soft leather.

'Long day and evening, eh, Ms Jansous?'

'Too long, Tom. Has Mr Craven left the building?'

'Yes. Caught a taxi a few minutes ago. You working back late?'

'Not really. Just a last goodbye to Ali. She's packing up. Leaving tomorrow instead of next week. She'll call you in the morning.'

Tom didn't answer. Driving Ali Gruber to the airport tomorrow would be no different from when he drove her to her first day of work at *Blaze* in Sydney. After six months of driving her almost every day, he knew her no better.

Nina slipped between the white damask sheets, too drained to pick up the phone and talk to Lucien. This evening had been a strain and the final confrontation with Ali had put a cap on it. Ali had not packed up her office, but had stripped it by flinging everything in a giant rubbish bin she'd wheeled in. She'd said she'd been tidying up loose ends, ready to start afresh. Nina chided her gently for disappearing from the party and causing her concern, but Ali was adamant no one would have cared even if they'd noticed.

'I'm sick of being in your shadow, Nina. I think it's time I made a move.'

Nina had tried to reason with Ali. 'This is not the moment to make such decisions, Ali. Give your new position six months and you'll be able to think more clearly about where in the world of the *Blaze* network you want to go. An editorship could come up.'

'I'm not prepared to wait thanks, Nina. I'm resigning from *Blaze*. The letter is on your desk, with a copy to Baron Triton.'

'I see. Then there's no point us discussing it at this time of night. I'll deal with it and be in touch through the appropriate channels. This seems an emotional decision, so I will allow every opportunity for you to change your mind.' Nina was not about to argue with Ali who nonetheless seemed sober, calm and determined.

'I'm not changing my mind, Nina. I'll send you my contact details when I have them.'

Nina fretted a while longer, becoming cross at herself for losing sleep over someone as selfish and ambitious as Ali. But she couldn't help feeling disappointed. She remembered the scared yet tough and eager teenager who had pestered her for work, any kind of work, at *Blaze* in New York. How she had watched Ali slash and burn her way to the top. Ali had never allowed anyone to grow close to her. Now Nina wondered if there'd been a point when the girl was crying out for love and attention, but it was so deeply buried beneath the aggression, no one had noticed. She couldn't help thinking of the parallels with Lorraine. Ali was still young, she would continue to fight for what she wanted. But, wondered Nina, how long would it be before Ali would be pushed aside by a new-generation Young Turk, and would she end up like Lorraine, bitter and lonely?

Ali dialled New York, the Baron's direct line memorised long ago. 'Oscar dear, it's me.'

'It must be late. How was the party?'

'As one would expect. I told Nina I was resigning from *Blaze*.'

'How did she take it?'

'She is giving me every opportunity to change my mind.'

Baron Oscar Von Triton gave a low chuckle. 'Always so thoughtful. Dear Nina. And did you tell her your future plans?'

'She didn't ask. And I'm not sure myself,' added Ali lightly, but with an edge to her voice.

'*Chérie*, I told you – no promises. Career-wise you will have many choices. Let us spend a little time on the yacht and in Europe first.' Anticipating Ali's interjection, he said, 'I know, I know, you still want to carve out a career, go where no bright young woman has gone before, or something like that?'

'I want you to be proud of my achievements, Oscar. And I want to do it on my merits.'

'But being with me may help a little, perhaps?'

Ali laughed with him, but her eyes were icy dots. He was indulging her, sure she would find the lavish lifestyle more enjoyable than writing or perhaps, publishing. Ali had big plans, but she knew she had to go slowly and carefully with the Baron. There was no promise of a ring or formal commitment either, but give her time. Once she was established and had eclipsed even Nina Jansous, anything could happen.

'My driver will meet you at JFK. Sleep well, my dear Ali.'

'I certainly will.'

Ali stepped into the rear of the limousine without a word. Tom handed her a manila envelope from Belinda as he went to put her luggage in the boot.

Ali glanced inside at several letters and papers from the accounts department. She put them in her handbag and settled back to watch the city slide past the tinted windows. It meant no more to her than the day she'd first arrived.

It wasn't till they were well over the Pacific and she had eaten the specially ordered and cooked gourmet meal that Ali went through the mail Belinda had left for her. A few personal notes from corporate clients wishing her well, tax papers, and one sealed letter addressed in handwriting she didn't recognise. Inside was a folded press clipping that turned out to be the recent weekend newspaper article about her and a handwritten letter. The steward arrived with coffee just as she was unfolding the letter and she didn't notice a smaller piece of paper drop to the floor.

Ali took a sip of coffee then started reading the letter before she realised who it was from. But having begun, she couldn't tear her eyes away. In the dim privacy of the first-class cabin she felt stripped naked without even the protection of her dark glasses.

Dear Alisson,

I read this article with a mixture of pride and sadness. How well you have done. Despite the terrible handicap I inflicted on you all those years ago.

I can't blame you for never wanting to speak or write to me. But I want you to know – and maybe when you are ready – to understand how it came to be.

It should never have happened. It was a dreadful, horrible accident. I had a drinking problem long before, but the mine closing and no hope held out to me was too much to bear and I broke. And in doing so, I lashed out at your mother. I didn't know how hard I'd hit her or that the fire would break out. They told me at the trial you tried to save her. God, I wish that it had been me who was taken. But Ali, the time behind bars, hard as it was, set me straight. I will never come to terms with what happened, but I have been dry for some years now, and have put my faith in the Lord for many years. I live quietly with an old cat

660

by a pretty bay on the north coast. I couldn't go back to the Hunter area. I make a modest living as a wood-turner, selling my work at markets. I learned the craft in the nick. I read a lot, another good habit I picked up in prison, and find some poetry quite moving. I've included a verse from one poet I particularly admire. The work sprang to mind when I read the newspaper article about you and decided to write this letter. The poem says it all. It may help you understand me.

You are leaving Australia again and going on to bigger things, I read. Well done. If at some stage you feel moved to at least acknowledge this letter, it would give me great joy. Even a postcard perhaps.

God bless you, daughter.

Your father,

Alex Vidal

Ali looked in the envelope for the poem he said he had included, but it was empty. She studied the address at the beginning of the letter, then very deliberately tore the pages into small neat squares and pushed them far down into the seat pocket. She leaned back and turned on the headset to listen to Maria Callas and shut her eyes.

The jet streaked into fast gathering night. To the east, a distant streak of lightning for an instant ripped across the night sky. Then all was darkness once more.

The next day, in Los Angeles, a matronly woman cleaner methodically worked through the first-class cabin. She removed the torn letter and a few foil chocolate wrappers from the seat pocket where Ali had been sitting, and tossed them into a plastic rubbish bag, then reached under the seat for another piece of paper. The only thing that stopped her immediately consigning it to the rubbish bag was the handwritten poem that took up most of the page. She leaned against the seat and read . . .

A Dead Past

Spare her at least: look, you have taken from me
The Present, and I murmur not, nor moan;
The Future too, with all her glorious promise;
But do not leave me utterly alone.

Spare me the Past – for, see, she cannot harm you,
She lies so white and cold, wrapped in her shroud;
All, all my own! and, trust me, I will hide her
Within my soul, nor speak to her aloud.

Cruel indeed it were to take her from me;
She sleeps, she will not wake – no fear – again:
And so I laid her, such a gentle burden,
Quietly on my heart to still its pain.

Leave her at least – while my tears fall upon her,
I dream she smiles, just as she did of yore;
As dear as ever to me – nay, it may be,
Even dearer still – since I have nothing more.

By Adelaide Anne Procter (circa 1858)

The cleaner folded the poem carefully and put it in her pocket. 'So beautiful, so sad,' she murmured. Then resumed collecting rubbish.

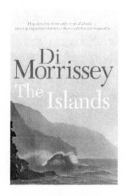

CPSIA information can be obtained
at www.ICGtesting.com
Printed in the USA
LVOW11s1114041017
551154LV00005B/286/P